TWISTED IN
OBSESSION

DESTRUCTIVE DEVASTATION SERIES BOOK ONE

I0635286

ALY BECK

Cover Design: Pretty in Ink Creations

Dev Editing: Steph Rawlins

Editing: Jenni Gauntt

Formatting: Jenni Gauntt

INTRODUCTION

Welcome to Twisted in Obsession.

This is a book on the darker side of things with several Red Flags that may tick your yays or nays. Please see the next page and visit my website www.authoralybeck.com to view the full list to ensure you know what you're jumping into.

And if you happen to come across something that needs to be added, please email me at alybeck1129@gmail.com

Thank you so much for once again reading my work! I appreciate you all so much and I hope you like Journey's thiccccc story! Ha.

RED FLAG SHOPPING LIST
AKA TRIGGERS TO BE AWARE OF

Please note that Twisted in Obsession does dabble in darker themes and have situations that might be uncomfortable.

- BC removal without FMC's consent—AKA—she's heavily drugged and not conscious when this scene happens.
- Knife Play
- Blood Play
- Orgasm denial.
- And much more...

Check out www.authoralybeck.com for the full list.

DEDICATION

This is for all the readers who love the phrase:

"Can't waste a drop of this cum." As it's pushed back inside.
This one's for you.
Enjoy.

CHAPTER ONE
Jericho

SILENCE RESTS BETWEEN US—SHEPPARD, Arrow, and myself—the Devils of Briar Cove.

We're the three youngest members of the Viotto Crime Family. Not yet to our full potential, but so close we can taste it with our initiation happening in three weeks—just after our twenty-first birthdays.

Since we were sixteen, we've proven how reliable we are, time and time again—how dangerous we've become wielding our weapons in the face of our enemies.

No one will ever forget our names or the blood on our hands.

Three years ago, my boys and I were solely responsible for taking down our greatest foe. We were only eighteen and tasked to eradicate the biggest threat Briar Cove had ever seen. They were threatening to bring dangerous weaponry, human trafficking, and drugs to sell to our people.

Not in our town. Or on our watch.

The amount of bloodshed that night left our names in the history books. People feared our very existence. Cowered when we waltzed into rooms.

Fifty-five.

That's how many men chose the wrong side and lost their lives as we eliminated them and their warehouse. In the end, we lit it up, watching the empire they invested in blown to smithereens with the name of their leader on their dying lips—Shadow.

That night we earned our name. The Devils. The three of us together are unstoppable and deadly. Bound by our duty to our family, but more so to each other.

Tonight, we stand outside a large brick mansion, filled to the brim with people from all over town partying their lives away. Their loud voices and thumping music carry through the empty private lane we're currently occupying.

'We shouldn't be here. We shouldn't do this.' Shepp signs with agitation. 'Your father is going to murder us all.'

Maybe he will. Maybe he won't. Honestly, my father is probably too busy with the raging party he's throwing at his infamous tower in the middle of town to notice we've slipped away. Mafia families under the Viotto umbrella, from all over California, are drinking the night away in celebration of life.

In fact, he was too busy to notice my arrival earlier this evening before the festivities at his precious tower, overlooking the expansive city he thinks he owns. His arrogance will get the best of him one day, and I'll make sure it's me who delivers the karma.

"When the funds are in my hands, yes. Then the exchange will be made. My collateral, for what he's keeping of mine," my father chuckles, leaning back in his chair with his phone plastered to his ear. "My collateral will continue to do what I ask until the big event. Once that's out of the picture, Chloe Satin is on the line. Her father and I had a nice long talk about the future."

My jaw tics at the sound of her name. Chloe Satin. Annoying. Clingy. Bratty to the extreme. She's the daughter of a known mafia family, straight from Italy. Her father owns Satin Firearms, producing the deadliest shotguns on the market.

What exactly does he mean on the line for? Marriage? And for who? Arrow? Sheppard? Someone else in the family? Doubtful. He doesn't fucking care about anyone other than me and the boys when *it comes to marriage. It's all about who benefits him more or who can provide the most money.*

So, no. That's not happening. Not under my fucking watch. Besides, I'm promised to Journey West and have been for years. That woman is my past, present, and future. Chloe was never on our radar. In fact, she has been lurking around for years, eager to sink her claws into someone powerful. But that won't be Arrow, Shepp, or I.

My fingers twitch at my side as desperation clings tightly around my throat, slowly closing it. My father's words from earlier this evening settle heavily on my chest, repeating in my head. He can't take this away from us. He can't take Journey from under my nose and replace her with Chloe.

Fuck!

He can't do this to me—to us. I'll never allow him to make connections behind my back and take Journey from my greedy fingers.

That familiar feeling gnaws at my insides again, aching for me to get a move on.

We need to go to her—to Journey.

I need a plan. I need someone to look into this for me and examine the marriage contract he has with whoever. If there really is one. There's always something in writing.

I just haven't found it yet.

"We're going out," I state when I make my rounds through the overly-rich crowd gathering on the top floor of my father's tower in the ballroom, standing before Arrow and Shepp.

'Where?' Shepp signs.

"We're going on a hunt."

If one of us is getting married off to someone other than Journey, then we need to make our moves. Make Journey ours now. Our time is slowly running out, and we need to put a claim on her before my father tries to take her away from us.

In this game of chess, I'm the goddamn winner. Not Gabriel Viotto.

'Why?' Shepp signs with confusion, furrowing his brows.

"Because my father was just discussing marrying us off to Chloe Satin." I cringe when I say her name, getting the same reaction from the other two. "So, shall we?" I ask, gesturing toward the door.

"My kitten is at a nice little party in Millionaires Row." Arrow turns his phone, displaying a picture of our girl dressed in a sexy kitten outfit with a mask secured over her face.

Her head is tipped back, and her curls dangle past her shoulders in a frizzy mess. Euphoria takes over her expression. Lips popped open. Eyes squeezed shut. Hands in the air.

She looks too good to be all alone in the midst of a high school party. Especially with all the fools around her, staring her down with desire in their blown eyes.

It's time to leave our mark.

"Then it's settled. We'll sneak away."

I blow out a breath, getting out my frustrations. In three weeks, that will be our celebration. Our initiation. Where we will fall to our knees and bleed for our family in front of the commissioner, my father, who is the head of it all, and his four underbosses.

I inspect my second-in-command's stoic face for a moment. Worry lines crease his brows, pulling at the large scar slicing through the right side of his face. A deep battle wound. Just one of the many wounds and traumas courtesy of his father, Thomas Mondelli, who once served mine. He was his second-in-command, ruling over Briar Cove, but now lies six feet deep.

Good riddance, asshole.

I mull over his words. He's my voice of reason, after all. Ironic? Yes. Shepp hasn't uttered a word since that fateful night when he was ten—only using his hands to communicate through sign language. Something Arrow and I have learned for his sake and ours.

He's the man pulling me back from the edge when I want to do something rash or stupid.

But this isn't one of those moments.

"Only a few more weeks now," my father, Gabriel, teases, stepping up to me with pride as the party begins.

He thinks I'm his prodigy—his only son. The next great ruler of the mafia, he has so carefully constructed before I was born and through my childhood. Boy, does he have a rude awakening for what my friends have in store for his long-running business.

"This will be you. And then, this will be your playground." He gestures to the people around us, dressed to the nines, sipping their fancy wine. Their laughs and murmurs fill the room over the orchestra that plays softly on the raised stage.

My father needlessly messes around with his wealth, throwing it here and there. Showing it off with fancy cars, jewels, and clothing.

Maybe that's why he's bleeding money through every one of his operations.

Rave, the club he owns. The Four Raven's bar that sits downtown is nearly bankrupt. The list goes on and on. But he keeps spending as if he has it.

Slowly but surely, Shepp, Arrow, and I are cleaning them up under the guise of helping my father, of course. Right now, we've got our claws in deep at Rave, his nightclub. Gambling machines. High stakes, elite poker games. They're all played and maintained in our VIP room. One day, it will be ours. People respect us despite our age. They've seen what we can do to our enemies—a bloodbath. They also witness the good we do for this community through our charity work. We help the people of Briar Cove get back on their feet after hard times through our loans.

"And then, we can throw you the wedding of the century." His grin widens even further, borderline predatory when he claps my shoulder. *"You'll make your stepmother and I so proud when you say I do."*

My eyes cast toward Shepp's mother, Aurora—my stepmother. The woman barely standing on her own two feet. Her eyes glazed over even more than they were ten years ago. She's just a passenger in this life. My father says jump, and she asks, how high? But I guess *that's what he thinks makes the perfect mafia wife—subservient, obedient, and pliable.*

It's not how I like them. Give me a fight—someone to slap me. Challenge me, for God's sake. I don't want a useless sack of skin hanging off my every word. I want a fighter.

I smile at the prospect because my future holds just that.

"Wonderful," I say as he squeezes my shoulder again.

"Work the room, Son."

But what I heard was—leave the room, Son. So, I did. Even better, I left the property after learning what my future wife was up to and took my two best friends with me. We were miserable anyhow.

"Fuck my father," I hiss, pulling out of his grip. "I want her." My runner. My challenge. The girl who will slap me until I come.

Journey West.

My eyes set on the masked girl shining through the opened window, swaying her hips to the loud music. Dressed in a tight, black, leather corset, one-piece that shows off her lean legs and hips. Paired with fishnet tights and high heels. Fuck. I want to fucking burn it off her body and put a sack over her. No man should see what I will see every morning when I wake up.

Only, she hasn't a clue.

Boys around her ogle what's mine. Ours. The Devil's property. Like she's their next meal. Greedy douchebags. I want to pluck their eyeballs from their sockets. I take a deep breath, settling the anger festering beneath my skin. That's why I'm here, to sort them out and show them their place in Journey's life. Nowhere.

They're all sporting masks to celebrate the holiday—the annual Briar Cove Masked-Up Celebration for all outgoing seniors of Briar Cove Public.

Come one. Come all. Hide your identities and party like you've never partied before behind an anonymous mask as one last hurrah.

It's the one night everyone is allowed to put a mask over their faces and lose themselves to debauchery without consequence. My eyes narrow when their attention is on her, the lonely dancer in the middle of the dance floor, pushing everyone else away.

She swivels seductively again, surveying the room. Her hands roam through her wild, brown curls as she turns circles. She is a lost sailor at sea, drowning in the ocean of people.

We're the lifeboats, ready to save her. And then keep her.

"I'm with him! We can all share." Arrow steps forward, his eyes lasering in on our girl through the window. "Sharing is caring, Sheppy boy. And I need her more than I need orange juice." He grins widely, showing off his pearly whites.

Orange juice? I sigh. It's his favorite drink after a night of work when blood spills and hearts stop. No clue why. Or how the tradition got started.

Most men our age—twenty-one—would have a glass of bourbon, reminiscing about the night's activities. But not Arrow. Not with how he got his start at fifteen, curbing his bloodlust with my father, murdering traitors, and taking out the trash. That's when the tradition started. He'd come home to the mansion covered in blood and sit at the kitchen island with his favorite snack as my father praised his efforts.

Gabriel Viotto knew how to mold psychopaths. We're living proof of it.

Especially Arrow, who was born in the shadows. The bastard child of a Catholic Priest, who loved Arrow but knew he could never provide for him and stay in his position at the church. He had no wife, only a mistress who fled the moment Arrow was born, leaving him on the doorstep of Briar Cove Catholic Church. The Priest tried to keep him concealed, raising him secretly, but failed miserably with all the trouble Arrow got into. Finally, at six, he handed Arrow over to my father; the rest is history.

But I digress.

Our girl has no idea we've been watching for so long.

We, the three Devils, see everything and everyone. We're in the damn wind, watching and waiting with patience. Especially for her. Our future. The woman we hunt in the dark, following her whenever possible. She's ours. And no one can take her away from us.

Not even herself.

She can run and hide if she wants to, but we'll always find her.

'So, you're really giving up your promise?' Shepp signs again with worry on his silent face.

"Would you keep a promise to the family? The same family that silenced you? The same family that didn't protect you or me!" I shout, pushing my finger into Shepp's hard chest so forcefully, that he stumbles back a step.

Anger rushes through me, thinking back to what our parents put us through. They've put us through hell and back without remorse, claiming to build our characters. Shepp more than me. His father took his voice. He took everything from him without even blinking. But my father has done the same in other ways, locking me in the dark and throwing away the key. His paranoia will eat away at him until he's pacing the floors and pulling at his hair. Everyone in the Viotto Crime Family has seen the turn of events and the senseless torture he's put his victims through. Even six years ago, they were starting to question his motives.

"This will be your kingdom someday, Nephew," my uncle says, squeezing my shoulder as we stand back from the crowd, gathering in the ballroom.

I look up at him. "I'm only fifteen," I murmur, shaking my head. "My father will rule until he dies." And knowing him, he'll live forever just to prove a point.

"Watch him, Jericho. Watch your father as he spirals. This will be yours soon. Start building your army before your father turns his rage on you." His dark eyes stare me down when I swallow hard.

He's already made my life a living hell. What more could he do?

That was the stupidest question I ever asked myself. What more could he do? Everything.

Shepp's features harden—all six-foot-six of him hovers above me with a menacing glare.

'You're acting like a two-year-old brat,' he signs, clenching his jaw.

I run a hand down my face. Determination takes hold, drawing me forward, toward the girl I've been obsessing over since I was eight and she was six when she punched a bully in the nose, made him bleed, and then kicked him square in the nuts.

"You're ours now," I say, touching her shoulder. We may be eight, but I know what I want. "We'll take care of him." A grin stretches across my lips when Leighton, the boy she pummeled, shivers in place.

Her face twists when she shrugs off my hand. "I don't need you to protect me," she huffs. "And I don't need you to take care of him. I punched and kicked him in the nuts."

But she did need us—even when we couldn't directly keep an eye on her.

Thanks to my father and his asinine rules we had to cut off contact after an attempt on my father's life and mine. From then on out, he insisted on bodyguards to protect us. So, we were cut off from the world around us. Only keeping her safe from afar and in secret.

Although there was a top-rated private school with the city's wealthiest children wandering the halls, my father sent us to public schools, giving us access to potential threats and future customers. This worked out incredibly well for protecting Journey. Throughout school, we fought off her bullies in the shadows until they didn't exist anymore. Everyone knew she was off limits—untouchable. Ours. Only, she wasn't in on the secret.

That was, until she turned sixteen. That's when everything seemed to change. She changed... walking the halls like the haunted version of herself after being missing for six months. According to her records, she rotted at a military school for a crime I'm not sure she committed. Little Journey West got busted for robbing a convenience store. Or did she?

Conveniently, every file on Journey West went missing at the same time she disappeared. Every day in the halls, we searched for her high and low. After school, we asked around. Yet, nothing was found except a single record pointing to her punishment.

Nothing more. Nothing less.

Every day that she was missing drove us insane. She was no longer at our fingertips. We could no longer protect her from where we were. We were in the goddamn mafia and yet, no one had answers for us. Not our PI or lawyer. Nothing we did brought her back. Then she walked through the school doors with a blank expression and silent wounds. Our bodyguards still lurked around us, protecting us from unseen enemies, so we still couldn't speak to her and figure out what happened. Not that she would have told us. She talked to no one.

That day, everything changed for us, too.

I take a deep breath, trying to keep the words at bay. How can I explain to them how I'm feeling? The mere thought of leaving her vulnerable again has my stomach twisting into knots. We're so close to the end of training, still unable to watch her 24/7, and she's finishing her last few weeks of school until she graduates and leaves for good.

Only three more weeks.

She's ours.

Now, it's time to take our place with my father and join his ranks for good.

We'll wait for her.

We have to.

Because she's our future wife.

"I'm acting like a man desperate enough to march in there and take what I want for once in my damn life. Don't you understand?" My chest heaves as I rein my anger back in again. Shepp deflates beside me, nodding in understanding. A look of resignation takes him over. "Together?"

Something flickers in him. Maybe memories of that fateful night. Maybe it's the realization that our allegiance is to each other and the allies we're building together. Our brotherhood is more important than the promise to keep our virtue intact until our initiation night.

Our soldiers. Our kingdom. Not my father's. Not his rules. He's taken enough from me. From Shepp. Arrow couldn't give a shit about my father. He may have trained him from the moment he landed in his lap, guiding him through the incessant call for blood and helping to shape Arrow into who he is now. But Arrow's loyalties lie with Shepp and I. We are his brothers. A family together.

"You in?" I ask, looking at Shepp and Arrow, who both gaze at our girl continuing to dance.

Arrow whoops, tossing me a manic grin. "I've always told you, your dad's barbaric ass rules were dumb. If I want to stick my dick in our woman, then I will. It'll only aid in my murder sprees." He rubs his hands together like he's planning something.

Maybe getting laid would chill his bloodlust out.

Shepp growls when a guy approaches Journey, putting his hands on her ass. His bulky muscles tighten, and his jaw tics until she pushes the man away and flips him off.

Don't worry, baby. I'll take care of him later. Draven Croathers. Eighteen. High society member and son to two fuck wits. Comes to my club, Rave, often. Drinks. Dances. Yeah. I'll remember those nuggets for later.

'*Yes. Fuck the family,*' Shepp signs with renewed venom. '*Fuck our promise.*' He runs his finger across his throat, signaling their death.

That seals it. Screw the pledge we made on our knees when we began training for our roles in the Viotto Family. Like every man before us, we promised ourselves wholly and truly to the Viotto name, dedicating every second to the family. No distractions. No women. Nothing in our way. How'd he know? Well, he has his spies. That we're sure of. He seems to have eyes on every surface of this city, especially on his new recruits training beneath his men.

But right now? I don't fucking care. Chloe Satin's name rings in the back of my head. As does my father's conversation from earlier. I've waited years to claim Journey as my own. I intended to wait until my father gave me the green light, like the dutiful son I pretended to be. But I won't anymore. I can't. She's mine and was always meant to be. So, tonight, we're taking what we want, when we want it. Fuck the consequences.

"You're to keep your dicks in your pants. No parties. No girls." My father shakes his head, pacing in front of us. *"Your focus is on this family. And when the time comes, you'll marry."* He stops short, looking us over as we kneel on the cement floor of the church he's dragged us to. *"Your full cooperation goes to the family!"* he shouts, holding his arms wide, gesturing to the men in suits around us, watching as we swear ourselves in. *"Do not disobey the simple rules given to you. Or your place with us will be cut short. We have our ways. We'll know if you step out. Step out and you forfeit your lives."*

"Yes, Sir," Arrow and I say in unison, while Shepp nods in agreement.

"Then let the training begin. For the next few years, you'll be the family's property. You'll shadow our every move, strengthening yourselves. Gun training, endurance, gathering information and answers. You're ours." His grin intensifies. *"In five years, you'll return to this room on your knees and pledge yourselves to the Viotto Family. You'll seal your fates with a slash across the chest. Blood spilled. Blood pact."*

Hearing my father say those words nearly five years ago made my blood boil. He planned my whole life for me from the moment I took my first breath outside the womb. Then, he expected me to marry some girl just to further our connections and allies?

Hell no.

Little did he know that I've had my eyes set on Journey since I was eight. He thinks we are obedient little fledglings, but he doesn't know that he is a bird in a nest of vipers.

Being the Devils that we are, we started weaving our web of

destruction that night and are nearly done putting the final pieces into place.

What my father doesn't know, won't kill him.

But we might.

Times will change in the future. You can't overthrow an empire overnight. It takes carefully laid plans and ass-kissing. *It began long ago.*

Arrow grins, throwing his arms over our shoulders. "When you're the leader of this city, we'll rule this place with iron fists!" he hoots; his decision is made.

'*You're willing to risk this?*' Shepp asks, ever the worrier and over-thinker.

Two seconds ago, he was ready to rock the boat, and now, he's taking a step back. But I get it. We have three measly weeks until our training under my father is over. We've worked hard over the years, beating his enemies and taking notes on the roles he expected us to play. We've completely obliterated the ones seeking revenge on my father. Blood has been spilled and rests on our hands. All in the name of learning how to become men.

Soon, we'll be fully inducted. A few more weeks until we can truly claim her as ours, as it was always intended. Only, she doesn't know what's in store for her. But I do. They do.

"She's worth every risk," I say with certainty, clapping him on the shoulder. "We've done the training. We've proven ourselves time and time again. Now, I want to take a vow for you, him, and me."

"What vow?" Arrow asks, rubbing his hands together.

"We vow that Journey West will be ours tonight in every way." I want to feast on her damn pussy and fuck her until the sun goes up. Only then will I be satisfied until she graduates in a few weeks.

Then, we'll be reunited.

"Damn straight! Now, let's go catch a kitten." Arrow's grin disappears beneath the Halloween mask, locked forever in a scary, skeleton face with blood dripping down it.

"Time to reign in my little Chaos." I grin, bringing my mask down over my face, hiding my identity from the world.

No one will suspect the three Devils to be at this raging mask party. We're above parties with our peers. Or so they think. We've sipped champagne since we were sixteen and meandered through alliance dinners with other gangs and mafia families, making a good impression and solid connections for business.

"You're an extension of me, Jericho. You three will act accordingly. You're the heir, ready to inherit this kingdom when the time comes. And they're your seconds-in-command." My father's voice rings through my mind. Possibly at the worst time.

Because the moment I walk into this party, I'm defying all his orders. The moment I touch her, I'm disobeying his direct command.

"You're not allowed to talk or touch Journey until she graduates. Then the deal begins, and she is all yours." His cruel smile reminds me of the terror he causes daily. To his soldiers and second-in-command, Thomas Mondelli, Shepp's father, but primarily to me, his son. I'm the one who gets the worst of it.

If only he knew.

So, I adjust my bloody skeleton mask one last time before walking through the massive mansion door. If we entered this party as ourselves, filled to the brim with people from our area. We'd be mauled to death by our fangirls, wanting a sweet taste of the mafia life. They see the expensive cars, the mansion on the hill, and the money in our accounts. They see the potential for power and ruling.

But they don't see the carnage we've left behind—the blood on our hands or the bodies in the dirt.

We're the goddamn Devils of Briar Cove.

Fear us.

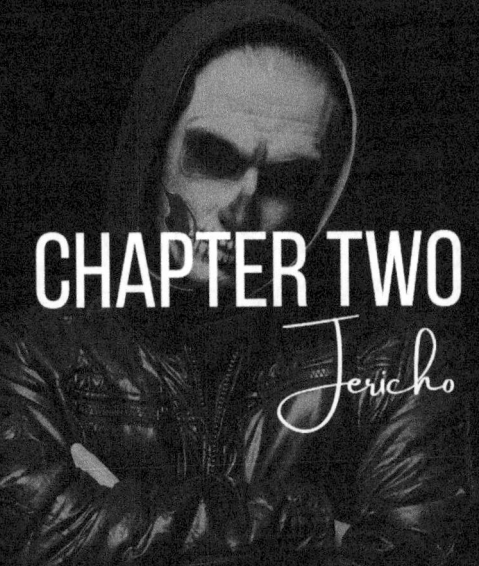

CHAPTER TWO

Jericho

HUMID AIR SURROUNDS us the moment we walk through the front door. The music bears down on our chests with every beat of the bass, vibrating me to the core.

Shepp and Arrow flank me on each side, instinctively protecting me from the bouncing shoulders. It's the same dynamic we've had since we became inseparable as kids. They protect me in public from harm, and I do the same for them when necessary. We're in this brotherhood together. We're family. But their roles are my seconds-in-command.

People get lost in the melodies. Losing themselves in each other. We get lost in her.

Silently, we circle our little prey with hunger in our eyes, and possession tingling our fingertips. And she doesn't have a clue. Finally, we're within touching distance, soaking up her presence.

The only things visible through her black cat mask, covering her just under her eyes and forehead... are her moss-green eyes, plump red-stained lips, and cheeks. Those beautiful eyes pop open when my hands brush against her hips, and I pull her forward and into me.

God, this feels right.

After being denied access from her for so long, first for our safety as kids and then because of my father's rules, it feels surreal standing in the same room without a barrier preventing us access.

This is our moment. I can't wait to slide my hands over every inch of her. She's my dangerous temptation that has been withheld from me. I'm taking what was always meant to be mine. For so long, we've held back and watched her from afar. A reach away, but never allowed. Now, being so close to her has the hairs on the back of my neck standing on end and my stomach fluttering from excitement.

Finally.

A visible gulp slides down her delicate throat, just begging for my hand to wrap around it and squeeze.

One day, my Little Chaos. One day, she'll be the queen of it all by my side. But for now, I'll enjoy what I've been forbidden to touch for so long. For God knows why.

"Care for a dance?" I ask in a low voice, disguising myself.

Not that she'd know. We had been in school together for years but only passed each other in the halls. Never knowing each other. Not really. I wasn't allowed to befriend my peers. Only Shepp and Arrow. They were father-approved and a part of the family. The rest of the school was potential enemies or clients.

"Sure," she says hesitantly, searching my mask for any sort of recognition.

Fire bursts to life in her eyes as they stay focused on me, narrowing with interest when I bring her body flush against mine with force. She gasps, fitting to my front like a glove. Arrow wastes no time, plastering himself to her backside.

"What the—" She attempts to turn, but I force her gaze back to mine by gripping her chin, instantly silencing her.

"Move your hips. Surrender yourself to us for the night," I demand pleadingly.

She blinks several times, and her brows furrow. "You're awfully fucking bossy," she grunts but complies after a second. "Who are you?"

Her body moves with mine so fluidly we're in perfect sync as the beat drags on. She loses herself in me, loosening her limbs and melting into my front.

"You dance so well," I rasp in her ear, giving into the effect she has on me.

She snorts, not bothering to answer when her head lolls back. Her hips continue to sway with Arrow, working faster. Quicker. A small moan slips from her lips when she feels my want for her grinding against her front. Dancing like this shouldn't be so damn euphoric. But it is with her. Always with her.

I take in her flushed face, not blocked by the mask. Her fingers dig into my shoulder, nails piercing my flesh.

Another gulp slides down her throat, and this time, I don't hold the desperate feeling back. My fingers wrap around the delicate flesh, gently squeezing until her blood-red lips pop open and a gasp escapes. Her brows furrow. Defiance flares in her eyes. She attempts to step back but fails due to the large body still behind her. I pull my prey into me. Not letting her go. Ever. No more. Our hips continue to move, our bodies melting further into each other.

Her question from before: *Who are you?* Comes back to mind, the perfect answer on the tip of my tongue.

"I'm yours for tonight," I boldly whisper directly in her ear.

She has no say in this decision.

Her eyes widen, the determination sizzling out. Something must occur to her when a deep flush tints her flesh, and her body loosens again. Whatever retort she had fizzled out, and her neck elongates, allowing my fingers to squeeze again gently. Her body shudders, her breaths pick up, and a small moan falls from her plush lips.

Good girl.

Lifting my gaze, I connect with Shepp, dancing an inch away. I subtly nod, pulling him closer, until we all surround her.

"My friends and I are going to dance with you. The three of us," I whisper, wishing I could plant my lips on hers and show her how much I need this—need her. "Lose yourself in the feel of our bodies." It's a demand—one she can't refuse. I won't let her.

Her breath hitches as Arrow moves against one-half of her

back side and Shepp does the same with the other half. Somehow, they move together with her, until we're in a circle and she's in the middle. Snapping out of her lust-induced trance, she turns and narrows her eyes at the men behind her. I see the defiance there. She wants to push them away. Her teeth grind together, and I can tell she's two seconds away from telling us off and storming away. Why would she stay between us? She kicked everyone else to the curb. Why not us?

"Relax," I whisper directly in her ear.

"Who the fuck are you?" she hisses, slamming her hands into my chest. "You think you can just fucking waltz in and start demanding things from the first girl you see? You can't just surround a girl like this. It's rude." I almost stumble back from the force of her blow, and I grin, although she can't see it.

"Dance with us, and we'll keep the wolves at bay. Maybe later I can reward you for giving into us."

Indecision rests in her eyes as she visibly weighs her options. Her hips continue to sway, her body molding to ours like it was meant to be here. It was. And it's only a matter of time before she realizes it.

"One dance," she concedes without more fight, moving her body more and staying with the heavy beat.

"Good girl," I whisper, earning a glare.

"Watch it, fucker," she growls, clenching her teeth.

I grin again. She's going to be so much fun.

Arrow slides his hands over her hip and down her thigh, grabbing whatever he can get ahold of. Keeping himself close, he grinds against her, working with the heavy music pouring through the speakers.

The lights dim more.

The music grows louder, filling the space.

People cheer at the midnight hour.

And we lose ourselves in each other.

No more words are exchanged between us. Not even a protest

when I lift her chin, revealing her flushed face. Her eyes widen as she stares deeply into mine, forging the rest of our connection.

Something clicks into place, like my soul has finally found its perfect match. Electricity sparks through my body. My hair stands on end.

There's something there, between the group of us. We're meant to be. No questions asked.

My eyes flash to Arrow, who enthusiastically gives me the thumbs up—no doubt, grinning beneath his bloodied, skeleton mask. Shepp nods, closing in on her and completing our circle around her.

Ours.

Forever.

The people around us continue dancing with one another. They don't pay us any attention. Despite the oddity of three men with one girl, they don't seem to care and give us space.

Perhaps it's the booze running through their veins and distracting them from what's right before their eyes.

My hands roam her body when she sways with me, feeling everything she has hidden beneath her kitten suit. Her breath picks up. Fuck. Her chest heaves, barely contained in her outfit, begging me to peel it off her skin and splatter her tits with my cum.

"Fuck," she rasps, turning in my grip and facing Arrow. I can practically see the smile through his mask when he takes advantage and grabs her ass, pulling her closer. She grinds against him, gripping his black shirt hard.

"That's it, Little Kitten. Take what you need from me," he says, barely above the music.

But I hear it—the need in his voice. We've watched for so long. Now, we finally get to touch. Everything.

She shudders against him, enjoying their short-lived dance, but turns toward Shepp, pulling him into her body. Whatever reluctance she had before about dancing with the three of us, she's lost it now. She's too engrossed in the music thumping through the speakers and our bodies to fucking care.

Shepp tentatively moves his hands to her hips, helping her move against him. If he could, he'd whisper sweet nothings into her ears as encouragement.

I lick my lips. This is it. This is our moment to take what we've wanted for so long. We have her in the palms of our hands. Without a single thought, I let my momentary stint of jealousy grab hold, and I take her from Shepp's tight embrace, pulling her against me.

Now, I have two options. I could walk away now and follow the rules put in place for us by the very family I look to defy. Or, I could continue with my plan, raise my middle finger to my father, and fuck her.

"Come with us." It's all I demand when I grab her hand, leading her away from the party.

Or attempt to.

Her reasoning must kick in when she halts us near the stairs leading to the second floor.

"You can't just expect me to follow you," she says with a stubborn glint. "I can't..." She shakes her head, tension forming in her brows.

"What's stopping you?" I ask.

I watch in fascination as the array of emotions takes her over. Something runs through her mind, displaying on her face as she runs through what we've said. Her muscles loosen, and her brows raise like she's relaxing into the thought of going with us.

Her body shudders when two people push past us, hand in hand, heading toward the front door. Their presence takes her gaze away from ours as she watches them retreat with interest.

My eyes stray to the back of the man's head where tattoos line his neck, but I don't get a good look at his face. The redhead catches my attention, but I quickly look away. People exiting the party don't matter to me. What matters is the woman before me.

My brows furrow when I turn back to Journey, whose eyes

restlessly scan the area uneasily. Her lips roll together in a tight line as stress stiffens her shoulders. She's overthinking this entire thing, wanting to pull back and not go through with it.

She just needs a little more encouragement from me—anything I can do to make her want to do this. I won't take her up there if she doesn't want to. I'd never take a woman against her will, especially not my obsession.

"I'm going to kiss you now and show you what you're missing if you walk away," I growl possessively, wanting to own every inch of her now that I have her in my grasp.

Her moss-green eyes widen at my words and her body sags. Almost in relief.

She doesn't say another word when I shove part of my mask up and go in for the kill. My lips slam down on hers, rendering her speechless. My tongue begs for entrance, poking at the seam of her lips.

"Let me in," I growl, palming the back of her head, aching to feel her tongue against mine.

"Let him in, Little Kitten," Arrow eggs her on, quietly whispering in her ear. "Let us in."

Shepp watches from the side, with lust brewing in his eyes. He can't whisper dirty words in her ear or beg her to open up like he wants. But he does what he can, exploring her body with his hands.

Finally, the encouragement works, and she lets me in, relaxing more into our passion. Our tongues dance in a frantic mess, begging for more. My cock grows rigid, poking against her stomach, and I nearly cum when she moans into my mouth. Her fingers clutch at my shirt, pulling me tighter against her.

I never want to let her leave my arms.

Pulling back, I secure my mask once again, not wanting to give her my identity just yet. Not tonight.

"What will it be?" My voice comes out huskier than normal.

She looks between the three of us, furrowing her brows. But

slowly, I see the confidence filling her. Her chin raises and her chest puffs out.

"No names. No taking off our masks," she says, lifting her chin. "No numbers. I can't be me tonight..." She blows out a breath, red tinting her cheeks. "I've never..."

My heart thumps, nearly exploding out of my chest.

Never? She's never fucked another man. Well, good. We'll all experience this together.

I grin behind my mask. "No names," I confirm with a nod. "And you've never?" I point between the two of us.

She shakes her head. More deep red creeps over her cheeks until she lifts her chin higher. Determination clenches her jaw and her fists.

"To my fucking freedom," she mumbles more to herself than anyone.

The guys and I exchange looks when she squeezes her eyes shut and nods.

"Are you going to change that?" Her brow raises. As does my damn cock. Her confidence fuels me. "So, here's the deal. No names. No numbers. Nothing. We walk away from this as strangers." There's no room for negotiations with her as she sets a hand on her hip.

"Strangers who've seen each other naked," Arrow quips, earning a deadly stare from the temptress laying down the law.

Shepp huffs his annoyance. *'Say yes before she changes her mind. She looks like a runner,'* he signs, eyeing her up and down.

She shifts her weight from foot to foot. Definitely a runner when things get tough. We'll have to keep that in mind and store that away for later.

"No names. No numbers. Just strangers. And we'll leave these on," I say, grinning behind my mask when she raises her brows. "Truly anonymous."

But not entirely.

Journey doesn't need to know that her name is constantly on the tip of my tongue. Sounding in the back of my mind on a constant loop since the moment my father slid her picture in front of me.

My future.

"What's this?" I ask rigidly, sitting in the leather seat across from my father in confusion.

"Oh," Arrow hums, looking over my shoulder at the picture of a girl I recognize immediately—Journey West—staring back at me with wide eyes and a smile. I tilt my head, taking in her beautiful features.

Red cheeks, dotted with freckles, and a dim smile, lighting up the frame. I know who she is immediately. My fascination with her has done nothing but grow over the years. From afar, of course. I've never allowed myself to get to know her or anyone else. Why would I? All I've been brought up to need is the family, and I've been brainwashed for far too long into believing in the future of an arranged marriage. It's something my father has always droned on about.

I've been out of his grip for a few months now, after witnessing him completely lose his mind to paranoia, convinced I was turning on him and so were the boys. We're only eighteen. There's no way we could be trying to turn everyone against him, but everyone in his eye is the damn enemy, including his son and his friends. No matter how hard I proved myself to him and the loyalty he instilled in me, it was never enough.

"Journey West?" I ask, blinking rapidly.

"Journey West," my father smugly confirms without adding any context to his decision. "Her mother and I have formed an alliance of sorts, and in return for her loyalty, she gave you her daughter's hand in marriage."

Something shines through his eyes, and a slight smirk pulls at his lips. Funny, he never shows any sort of emotion. Not to us. Not to his men. Nada.

An alliance with a random woman? My brain turns over these weird little details, fumbling over them repeatedly. Usually, the family only does business with people within our network. Other mafia families looking to create stronger bonds over marriage and business transactions. Hence the rise in arranged marriages. Barbaric to some, but lovely for others. And in this instance, I'm stoked to see Journey West by our side.

We share everything. It's how we were taught.

But Journey? Unless she has a long-lost dad who is in our line of work, which she doesn't, then why does my father want to make a deal involving her? Her father was a famous musician, Corbin West, who was worth billions of dollars but died and was never a part of her life. And he was never associated with our family. That much I know about him. But other than that, it's crickets.

My father has something up his sleeve, and I can't figure out his angle—time to research.

"Why her?" I ask, running my finger over her picture, enamored by the innocent look in her eyes. "And why are you telling me now?" *This kind of announcement usually comes later at our initiation ball, held after we've pledged ourselves to the family. It's a celebration of our future.*

Only then is the arrangement revealed. The wedding date will be set. So, why is my father bringing this to us years too early?

Between the three of us, we've seen enormous amounts of bloodshed while helping my father and other members of the family deal with the city's trash. We've always been in the thick of it, getting our hands dirty even at the ripe old age of ten. My father wanted Shepp, Arrow, and I, elbows deep in everything he did. Torture sessions? Tracking men through the city? Yeah, we've been there. Held the guns in our hands, and the knives when need be.

All for the family—always. We rarely question our orders. But today, we have to know.

My father cuts his steel eyes to me, gritting his teeth. "Isn't my word enough, Son?"

I hide the anger bubbling inside and stiffen my shoulders. "Of course it is."

"There are rules, though. Considering I'm breaking protocol. This union won't happen until her schooling is done. She will *graduate after you. And you can't touch her, talk to her, or even inform her of this." His voice rings out with such authority, that my spine stiffens. Reaching across his desk, he takes back the papers he handed me and shoves them into his desk. "I want you to focus on your initiation tasks and prove yourself. She and your marriage are your reward for a job well done."*

"Wait. She doesn't know?" Arrow asks, bouncing on his toes.

I continue to eye my father when his jaw tics with irritation. He hates being questioned. But this? This is something we deserve to know about. Especially her. How can someone not know they've been entered into an arranged marriage?

"No." My father raises a brow, eyeing the three of us like we'll be a problem. "And she won't know until after your training is complete. Journey West is your reward the moment her diploma is in her hand."

In that moment, my eyes find Shepp and Arrow as my father paces before us.

'She doesn't know? Is he for real?' Arrow discreetly signs to me with a blank expression, trying not to give our secret conversation away.

'Later,' I quickly sign back, hoping my father doesn't catch on.

My eyes roam back to my father. "Thank you, Father. Are we done?"

He stops mid-pace and nods. "Go on. But keep what I've said in mind. No touching her. No talking to her or trying to tip her off. Her mother would be pissed..." he trails off, shaking his head. "And this is just between us. The family is not to know about this just yet."

'He's serious?' Shepp signs when we walk out of my father's office with determination, heading straight out of the tower my father calls home and into our SUV, waiting for us on the curb.

Shepp settles into the driver's seat as Arrow and I take the back.

"He can't be fucking serious?" I sputter. "She doesn't know and can't know until she's graduated? And why tell us now? Why didn't he wait like everyone else does?." I stroke my chin, recalling my uncle's words from years ago. "I think he's finally lost his shit."

"*Yeah, well, we can't exactly jump her bones without him finding out,*" *Arrow grumbles, crossing his arms.*

"*No. What we need to do is follow his orders for now and leave Journey in the dark for her safety. Who knows what that unstable prick is capable of if he gets wind, we've stolen her away for safety reasons.*"

'*I agree,*' *Shepp signs with a nod, directing us into traffic.*

"*I don't really want to wait,*" *Arrow pouts until I shoot him a look.* "*But I will. God. I want her so damn bad.*"

You and me both.

"So, shall we?" Arrow asks, gesturing up the stairs with an edge to his voice. His patience is dwindling. He's liable to throw her over his shoulder. Willing or not.

"Your choice," I say in a low voice, stepping back.

She can either run away or up the stairs.

CHAPTER THREE
Journey

ON A SCALE of one to ten, this is the stupidest thing I've eve
considered. Three masked men I don't know from Adam, who
cornered me on the dance floor in the middle of my stakeout
wanting to take me upstairs and...

Fuck.

I look around the circle they've created around me. I should
be shaking in the high heels I was ordered to wear by him. The
man who thinks he owns me. Maybe he does right now. But afte
the shit he pulled earlier, my thoughts are in other places.

"But my sister?" I plead, trying not to show my desperation. It'
been three years since I saw her in person, ever since he took her awa
from me—my monster. The man pulling my strings like I'm hi
little puppet.

"Can I talk to her? Make sure she's okay?" I beg.

His eyes look me over in the corner of the burned-dow
warehouse where we always meet. When he sent me our secret cod
via text, indicating he needed to speak to me, I came running as fas
as I could. He's my only connection to her—the only person wh
knows where she's at.

"Have you earned that?"

"But you promised, Sir. You promised me if I completed th
strip club task, that I could talk to my sister. It's her fourteent

birthday today. I want to talk to her," I sputter, showing my desperation.

It happens so quickly that I don't even see it coming. He strikes my cheek with his open palm, forcing my face to the side. I'm used to this abuse and his smug attitude. I've been subjected to it for three years, since I was sixteen.

The stinging lasts hours. Even after he sent me on my way, with no phone call to Sunshine to sing her happy birthday—he did this. He took my goddamn sister from me after I... After I did the one thing that I shouldn't have. Something overcame me when I saw those hands on my sister, and I...

I shake it off. His parting words sit with me as I walk back to the trailer my mother and I have lived in for years. If only I could go to the damn cops and tell them everything that happened to me at the hands of my depraved monster. The basement he threw me into. The torture he forced me to endure. The people he made me watch die at his hands. For six months, he broke me down and rebuilt me into the little snake he needed me to be—his perfect spy.

But he owns the law. He is the goddamn law. And If I went to the cops with my sob story, they'd throw me in prison for the crime that forced me into my monster's hands.

"Find Jenni Thomas. Find Elias White. They'll be at this address. This is your mission for tonight. Prove to me you can handle it again. Then maybe I'll reconsider letting Sunshine speak with you. Be a good little snake."

Fuck him. He wants me to be good and go to this party? Yeah, I'll do that. I'll go. But I'll enjoy my goddamn freedom along the way. I'll cover my bruises with a mask and lift my middle finger.

My monster doesn't control me tonight. Freedom does. And what does my freedom want? To pull the ultimate wool over my monster's eyes.

I'm going to lose my virginity. But not just to anyone. No. I'll know when the time is right and with who.

And these three are the right ones. I feel it in my damn bones.

Three bulky men fit with identical skeleton masks dripping

with fake blood, devouring me with their stares. They each have a black t-shirt on, clinging to their hard chests and tight jeans. There's nothing particularly special about them.

But they call to something inside me, begging me to break all my promises.

Promising me a sliver of the freedom I crave.

Something inside me aches, throbbing at their touch. My panties fill with wetness when I stare at them. This is my moment. Even though I'm supposed to... I shake my head. I'm so tired of him—my monster—delegating everything in my life.

Do this job, Journey.

Don't fuck up, or your sister's life is in danger, Journey.

Don't you dare lose your virginity.

Follow all my rules or else.

Well, fuck his rules.

Fuck him, the sick bastard. This is my body, and I'll do whatever I want to do with it. I'm nineteen, and in a few weeks, I'll graduate from high school and hopefully be on my way to finding where he hid my sister. The girl he took from me so I'd comply with his stupid rules, hiding her in a health facility I've yet to find. I know she's taken care of by the pictures he's shown me and the few video calls he's allowed. She's no longer the sick little girl barely making it in the trailer, unable to get the medical help she needs. Now, she's better. Or seems better. I can only hope for the best. And it's all my mom's damn fault. She's the one who sold her out. She's the one who won't help, but gladly takes the drugs my monster gives her.

My monster runs my entire life.

The moment my sister is back by my side, our identities are changing, and we're hitting the road to an isolated cabin away from everyone. Away from our mom, who doesn't give a fuck about us. Away from this stupid town fueled by the ruling mafia. All I need to do is find someone capable of making false identities for me and my sister. In this town, it shouldn't be too difficult. I just need the right connections; then we'll be all set.

I'm living for myself right now.

I'm abiding by his rules, but I'm sick and tired of it. I'm ready to get out from under his thumb and take back some semblance of my fucking life. So, why not let three handsome strangers fuck me into oblivion for the first time in my life? I need something to make me feel alive instead of the nightmares that plague my every move.

A spark. An ignition. Anything to warm me.

I need to find myself again.

It'll be my greatest rebellion yet.

Without another word, I go up the stairs, ensuring my mask is back in place. My lips tingle where the first one kissed the hell out of me, and I ache to run my fingers over them.

God, this is so stupid. My monster could have a spy following me, ensuring I'm doing my job. But I always do. I have the best motivation—my sister's life hangs in the balance.

"What did you do, Journey? What did you do?" her wails echo through my skull.

"I did what I had to do," I say through a breath. "For Sunshine."

"It was her! It was her!" my mother's voice rings in my mind no matter how hard I fight it.

Tonight, I'm free.

For some stupid, selfish reason, I need to do this for me.

I hear her voice. Something she's written in a letter to me before. *"Have fun, Sis. You know I'm safe."* My little sister's voice runs through my mind. Hell, I can even see her bright smile of encouragement. *"Don't worry about me. Worry about you, Journey."*

Fine.

Looking around, I see no one up here, much to my relief. I can't hear if they followed me over the music thumping from the speakers on the first floor. Or over my rapid heartbeat. Once on the second floor, I finally look over my shoulder. Right on my tail are the three strangers who seem vaguely familiar.

From where? Who knows? I don't put that much thought

into it. We're strangers. That's it. In a city of fifty-thousand people, I'll never see them again.

I turn to face them, staring into each of their expressive eyes. Dark brown. Light gray. Ocean blue. Reflect back at me—each holding secrets within their depths and desires on the surface.

"One night," I whisper, holding up a finger.

That's all I can spare. I got what I needed when I showed up at this pre-graduation party. I followed the man I was instructed to follow and took note of my classmate following him into the basement. I took the pictures I was instructed to take. Then, I watched as he made his way out and attached himself to a girl with red hair—Jenni from school, taking her upstairs to rock her world.

My job is over. The evidence was sent.

Now, I deserve a reward.

"Okay," the one who has done all the talking says, stepping forward.

His bloody skeleton mask gleams in the moonlight, faintly shimmering through the cathedral-style windows.

I crane my neck when his fingers brush against my exposed throat again. I shiver, a thrill running through me. My life hangs in his enormous hand, wrapping around my flesh with the intention of stealing my air.

Steal it all. Take it until I turn blue.

"One night of us," throat-squeezer gestures to the other two behind him.

If I'm going to break the rules, I might as well do it three times over. They're probably going to break me in half. But bring it on. I need this. Deserve this after all the shit I've been through in my stupid life. Give me pleasure or give me death—it should be my new motto. I swallow hard. The pain will be worth it. Even if they obliterate me through the night.

But more importantly? It'll be absolutely fucking worth it to stick it to the stupid monster who is my puppet master.

I'm no puppet of his for the next few hours.

I'm theirs.

Whoever they are.

"As long as you understand the rules. You'll never see me again."

"Then, you'll understand that we're in charge tonight." There's no room for argument in his tone. Shivers fall down my spine, and goosebumps erupt with every word and touch. "Say you understand," he demands, stepping up to me more. All I see are the color of his eyes behind the mask—deep brown with specks of gold dotting through like a darkened galaxy staring back at me.

"Tell us, Little Kitten. Tell us you understand our rules, too. I'm hard as a rock just staring at you," the grabby one says, roaming his light gray eyes up and down my body with interest.

They say eyes are the windows to our souls, revealing more than we realize. And tonight for me, that's true. There's a darkness present within each of their gazes, promising me unspoken words of pleasure and pain.

Just like me, there's a black hole inside filled with nothing. Maybe that's what drew me to these strangers and why I let their hands roam over my body on the dance floor when I had pushed every other perv away. Not them, though. The moment I heard Brown Eyes speak, his voice caught me in his web.

The four of us are similar. Yet, so fucking different.

Especially the one with light gray eyes. There's almost nothing behind them. Just darkness staring back.

Ocean Eyes steps forward with a slight hesitation trembling through his hands. Unlike the other two, he hasn't said anything, opting for silence in the midst of chaos. My eyes drift south, over the enormous bulge straining against his jeans. Jesus. It looks huge. Will it even fit inside me?

Their identities are all hidden. Mine is, too. Their eyes track me like I'm a precious gem they want to steal away. But it's a risk I'm willing to take. Maybe it's the excitement. The rush of going against my puppeteer. Or maybe it's me taking back my life, one little defiant act at a time.

"You're in charge," I say, letting Brown Eyes constrict my air.

My lips pop open, begging for oxygen when he squeezes his fingers over my throat. Thrills soar through me. I tremble in his grasp. A white haze takes over my vision when soft lips press against my neck, sucking and marking me with his sharp teeth. More shivers erupt when his hot breaths blow against my ear.

"You won't regret this," is all he says with a slight rasp, filled with the desire I feel brewing in my lower abdomen.

Maybe I will. Maybe I won't.

But it's something I've longed for, for so long. Sex has been on my mind for years, curiosity killing me to explore. But I've always been the dutiful little snake following my monster's rules for fear of my sister's life. Is this a gamble? Yes. Could I lose it all in a matter of seconds? Also, yes.

But I need this.

I need them to choke me and fucking use me until I'm boneless.

So, for tonight, I'm falling into the arms of strangers, aching to feel alive again after being surrounded by darkness for so long.

These strangers will bring me solace.

CHAPTER FOUR

Journey

M Y BREATHING PICKS up when I blindly follow them down the hall. It's a blur making it through the door.

The lock clicks into place. And then... I'm alone with three masked strangers in a dark bedroom that doesn't belong to any of us.

I'm really living on the wild side tonight. Insane. Out of my mind. What the hell was I thinking? I swallow hard, staring at the three men standing before me. Strangers. About to wreck my life. And my vagina—the one who got us in this situation in the first place.

Butterflies burst to life in my stomach when they stand side by side like a brick wall, not uttering a word. I shift from foot to foot. The aching need to run away pushes heavily on me.

Run. Get out of here!

But it doesn't outweigh the pulsing between my legs, which I instantly recognize as my arousal. Wetness pools in my panties, begging for them to make me feel the desire I've held in for so long and want to set free. I've felt it plenty of times before when staring at handsome strangers or before using my trusted vibrator. That's all I've had for a year, and now, I'm about to feel the real thing. And it's only amplified by their intense stares, eating me alive like they want to devour every inch of me.

I'm doomed.

The hairs on the back of my neck stand on end when they move as one entity. Marching toward me like they're the wolves and I'm the rabbit on the run.

"When we're done here, you're going to wish you knew our names..." Brown Eyes says with promise in his words.

Feelings of instant regret claw in my mind, urging me to flee from their stares and to run home with my tail tucked between my legs. Visions of my lonely bed come to mind with my half-read book on the nightstand. *Go there,* my mind says. *Don't do this tonight.*

I shiver when my monster's face pops into my mind with his controlling smile and vicious fists. But I push it away.

Screw him and his control. He can't take this moment away from me, like he's taken so many other things.

"We're going to ruin you for everyone else, Little Kitten," Light Gray Eyes says, touching the cat ears on my head with a chuckle. "You'll feel us deep in your cunt for weeks to come. Every step you take, you're going to remember us." I can practically feel the grin beneath his mask as his eyes light up for the first time. There's the sign of life I was waiting for.

The third one remains silent and stoic. Stepping up, he wraps my hair around his fist, forcing my head back. My lips part, and a gasp falls out. In a flash, his deep blue eyes track all over my masked face, taking in as much as possible.

"This is coming off," Brown Eyes says, pulling at my black leather corset snugly resting against my body and forcing my tits up.

Seriously. Who invented corsets? They're death contraptions. But when the man who rules your life hands you a skimpy costume at your meeting place with instructions on what to do, you do it without question.

"First, I'll bite these off." I hold my breath when Light Gray Eyes drops to the floor, kneeling before me like I'm his damn queen and takes my hand in his, lifting his mask just far enough to reveal his mouth. I shiver when his hot breath works through the black satin gloves, and he slowly pulls them off with his teeth. Finger by finger, he works them off with only his mouth doing the job.

Despite my rules, I'm aching to see their faces and know their identities. Maybe they're princes from another land and are here to whisk me away to safety. A girl can dream.

But that's the thrill of it, right? Strangers doing strangers and never looking back. No names. No faces. Just the pleasure we're about to receive from one another and the memory we cling to in the future after we've separated. I know they'll be on my mind for weeks to come.

Pale skin reflects off the moonlight shining in from the open windows, giving me a little glimpse at the man on his knees for me. Soft blond facial hair is the only feature I see besides a dimple hiding beneath as his lips curve into a smile.

"How about these?" he asks in a deep, husky voice, making my toes curl in my heels when his fingers run down my thighs, still covered by my fishnet tights.

"The heels stay," Brown Eyes demands in a low voice, catching my chin in his grasp. He pulls my face in his direction, forcing me to look into his eyes. "We're going to blindfold you now."

My heart pounds, beating out of my chest. Panic claws at me when he lifts my mask without my permission, exposing my face. He holds me still, taking in my flushed features and nods his approval.

"Fucking perfection," Brown Eyes confirms in his deep voice.

My teeth set on edge, knocking me out of my stupor. How dare he deviate from the plan we put in place and fucking expose me like that.

"No! That wasn't a part of the agreement," I say through clenched teeth, shaking my head, attempting to run from his grasp.

But he clings to me. Hard. Practically pushing his nails into my cheeks to hold me still.

The spider has officially caught his prey in his web, and now, I'm never getting out.

Run, run as fast as you can—my brain screams the second he runs off course.

"Because we're in charge," he says before my vision disappears under a dark blindfold that materializes out of nowhere. "And you're our good girl, aren't you? You want us to fuck you until you can't speak a full sentence?"

Well, that does sound promising.

I heave in a breath, trying to gather my senses through the darkness I'm bound to. I swallow hard, wanting to fight tooth and nail for my sight. And my damn plan. But I let it go, leaving myself in the hands of the three men promising a night I'll never forget.

So fuck it.

I nod in compliance, willing my fight away.

"That's a good girl," Brown Eyes whispers, kissing my cheek as shivers roar through me.

My senses come alive under the veil of darkness. Light fingertips creep over my skin, touching everything. My hair stands on end. Anticipation pours through my nerves, and I'm trembling with need before they've done anything. My eyes dart around, searching for any sliver of light I can find. But there is none. Without the use of my vision, I let the darkness take hold for once. It'll be the only darkness I allow right now.

"Wait," I breathe, reaching out for him, grasping his shirt, and holding him hostage within my grip.

"We may be strangers, but I promise we won't do anything you don't want to. But I'd really like to have my tongue in places my mask won't let me reach. You want the blindfold off? Say the word. I'll comply with any request you have. Although we are in charge, I like to think we are fair," Brown Eyes says, running his fingers over my arm and holding him to me.

"I'm going to suck your cum out of your pussy," the one

kneeling in front of me rasps, as the sound of ripping material hits my ears.

"I..." My words get lost in the air when my lips pop open from shock. My arm drops from Brown Eyes, losing him from in front of me. Warm fingertips glide over my bare thighs. My nipples harden. My breaths pick up.

"Fuck." I shudder when fingers work around my panties and thrust into my pussy.

"So tight, Kitten," he grunts, working a finger in and then another slowly.

Light Gray Eyes—I mentally chant through the heavy pants heaving my chest. My head falls back and finds a shoulder to land on. Their hands work up my ribs, tearing into the top of my corset until it's gone and off my body.

"Holy shit," Brown Eyes mutters from beside me, running his fingers over my exposed nipples, hardening them more.

So, that puts Ocean Eyes behind me, holding me upright as Light Gray takes his tongue to places I never thought imaginable, and Brown Eyes plays with my tits.

Need rushes through me when someone tweaks each nipple, sending liquid heat straight to my pussy which is currently being ravished by the man kneeling in front of me.

"What's this?" one of them asks, running his fingers over my nipple and straight to the underbust corset I had beneath, enabling my tits to look ten times bigger and perkier. It also hides my greatest sin—the burden I carry. The scar marking me. The entire reason I wear it under revealing clothing and only when I need it.

"It makes your tits look amazing," Brown Eyes murmurs until his tongue encases my nipple, sending electric bolts through my fucking body. Allowing me to forgo my explanation of why I'm wearing such a device in a low-cut corset.

"Oh, God!" I cry out, digging my fingers into Light Gray Eye's hair, crushing him against my clit as his tongue swirls and laps at me.

"She's close," he grunts, taking in a deep breath before plunging in again using his fingers and tongue to make stars burst behind my eyes and my legs turn to Jell-O.

"That's right, come on his fingers," Brown Eyes murmurs against my breast, lapping away at my nipple, even biting down as hard as he can, sending me over the damn edge.

My body stiffens from the overload of pleasure. Black dots take over my vision, nearly sending me to the damn ground. A cry gets stuck in my throat when my lips pop open, and my pussy convulses around Light Gray's fingers, locking them in place. Pure pleasure pulsates through me like fire licking at the walls and consuming everything in its path.

I suck in air when it finally subsides. Holy orgasm. It was the best of the best I've ever had. Not even doing it myself could garner these types of results. And that's what I've been missing out on my entire life.

"Oh, we're not finished yet," Brown Eyes rumbles, taking my sore nipple between his teeth and nibbling on it. "Far from fucking finished," he grunts.

"Let's lay you down, Kitten," Light Gray says with the sound of his lips smacking together. "Then we can fuck you until the sun comes up." A sharp shiver runs through me at his promise. "Oh yeah. I think she likes that idea. You want us to spread your legs apart and fuck you until you're numb?"

"Please," I gasp out when hands guide me to a soft bed, and my head hits the pillow.

The thought of being fucked until I'm completely numb has my limbs tingling in anticipation.

Fuck me to freedom. Fuck me so I don't have to think of the consequences of my actions.

"Then be a good fucking girl and stay there. We're going to take what's ours now," Brown Eyes says as fingertips crawl up my bare legs, sending a shiver down my spine. "You're so responsive to me," he murmurs when his fingers brush through my wet folds and dive straight into my pussy.

My back arches off the damn bed as desperate moans fall from my lips. My fingers curve into the sheets, clutching them tightly in my grip. My body bounces as his fingers curl inside me, and my walls spasm around him, throwing me into another blessed orgasm sent straight from heaven.

I'm breathless by the time his fingers slip out of me. "I'm going to use your cum as lube," he says softly. "I'm stroking myself right now. Your cunt was made for me."

Shivers roll through me when he slowly climbs on top, pressing his defined chest to mine, pressing his nude body to me. At some point in the process of them bringing me to the bed, he stripped down. And I'm assuming the other two did, too. I'm practically salivating to see them with my own eyes, but I let my fingertips do the exploring down his muscular back and over his asscheeks that are defined, too.

Holy hell. He's like a devil sent straight to tempt me.

"You say that like we were fated to be together," I murmur when his lips brush against mine several times, softly kissing me until his tongue rolls into my mouth.

Fuck.

Kissing this stranger from beneath my blindfold has every nerve in my body on high alert. Anything could happen to me. And I don't fucking care. As long as his lips stay on mine and his body presses against me, I'm fine. Kidnap me. Fuck me. Do whatever you please, but just don't stop touching me and giving me this pleasure.

His forehead presses against mine when he finally pulls back from the heated kiss. "I'll be as gentle as I can, okay?" he whispers. "As much as I want to pound into you until my dick is completely inside, I'm a gentleman."

Someone snorts in the background. But he pays him no mind, solely focusing on me.

"Okay," I say, swallowing hard.

The head of his dick pushes into my entrance with slow, measured thrusts. Over and over. In and out. Shallow thrust after shallow thrust. Only allowing a tiny amount of himself inside me.

A part of me is overjoyed that he's taking it slow and letting me get used to the feel of him and his massive girth invading my pussy. But fuck. My breaths pick up when he rips through me, almost slicing me in two with one thrust.

I always heard sex hurt the first time. But I didn't imagine that it would be like this. Fuck. I'm panting by the time he's completely inside me and still.

I groan, trying to clamp my legs shut and soothe the ache inside me. It burns. It hurts. It's fucking miserable, but that's what I wanted, right?

Freedom. Pain. The feeling of being alive. It's exhilarating, setting my nerves on fire. And then his fingers dig into my thigh, holding me wide open.

"Keep them wide open," he whispers in a demand, straight into my ear. "You're doing so fucking amazing for me. Do you like that? Does it hurt so fucking good?"

His partial moans set me on the edge of an orgasm. Just hearing his pleasure has me on a completely different plane. Like the entire room has disappeared, and it's just the two of us. Despite the other two guys watching us fuck.

His breath brushes over my skin when he works his hips again, bringing his cock almost completely out. Through ragged breaths, he stills again, keeping his tip at my entrance.

"It's beautiful torture," he moans. "I'm savoring every second until I cum in your cunt," he groans again, thrusting forward a little harder than before to the hilt.

"Yes!" I gasp out, arching my back when he bottoms out. "Fuck, it hurts. But so, so good," I whisper, sinking my teeth into my bottom lip, practically whimpering when he shifts, his dick grinding inside me.

"The pain is temporary," he whispers. "It'll hurt for now. I bet your blood is soaking my cock."

Heat takes over my cheeks, and I'm thankful I have a

blindfold on so I can't look into his eyes. I'm sure they're blown with lust, like mine. But the thought of my blood soaking anything has my fingers digging into his back, grounding me.

"Blood is hot. You better save some for me, Kitten," Light Gray says as the bed dips beside me.

Warmth encases my side as rogue fingers brush over my nipples, tweaking them between his fingertips.

I gasp at the sensation, my pussy tightening around the cock inside me.

"Fuck, yeah. She likes that. She's tightening around me," Brown Eyes grunts, pushing forward again. "Keep that up and I'll embarrass myself."

I moan when Light Gray takes my nipple completely into his mouth, rolling his hot tongue over it repeatedly. I swear it's like a passageway right to my pussy. It flutters around the cock buried deep inside it.

"Fuck," I quiver as I teeter on the edge of another orgasm.

So close. Getting closer and closer. My toes curl. I babble inside my head, unable to make any sense of my thoughts as he works himself in and out of me.

I cry out when the man beside me bites down on my boob over and over, taking every inch of it into his mouth and leaving teeth marks behind.

But that does it. The pain of his bites sends me over the edge. More black dots litter my vision, and my scream erupts into the air as my pussy clamps on his dick.

"Jesus!" Brown Eyes sputters, losing his words just as he loses his load inside me. Marking the walls of my insides with his cum. He stills. Nothing but his breaths and the moans from his throat filling the room. "Oh, you're heaven," he murmurs, burying his face into the crook of my neck. "And I'm keeping you forever."

My lips pop open at his confessions. Forever? This is supposed to be one night. We have no idea who each other is. So, how can he make such bold promises that he'll never get to keep?

"Live for tonight," I rasp, slumping into the comfortable bedding beneath me.

After three orgasms, I'm sure I could just sleep the night away. But where's the fun in that? Or the freedom? Despite feeling sore and used, I need them all.

"For tonight," he murmurs, sinking his teeth into my damn neck and sucking my skin into his mouth. "But we'll mark you so you remember us for the next few weeks."

"And any man who lays his eyes on you will know you belong to someone else," Light Gray quips in a playful tone. "Then, I can cut off their toes as presents."

Toes for presents? Holy shit. I got into bed with someone who likes to cut off body parts. Go figure, that's how my first time turns out. Memorable? Absolutely. Frightening? Just a little. So, I push his odd comment to the back of my mind, silently hoping I'm not a victim in his crusade against toes, and I breathe.

My eyes widen behind the blindfold. "Only for tonight. This can't happen again. This..." I swallow hard, whimpering when he pulls out of me slowly.

A slight pain rests between my legs, throbbing with every frantic beat of my heart. Proving to me, I'm alive and in the present. The feelings of dread and emptiness I had before when I was merely existing evaporate in the stranger's presence.

And it feels liberating as hell to be normal.

"Look at that," Brown Eyes rasps. "Your blood is soaking my cock. You marked me, too," he whispers in awe. A gentle kiss presses against my cheek, lingering there for longer than necessary. When he pulls back, hovering just above my face, I feel his finger brush over my cheek, softly tracing every freckle and line like the boys in romance books. "Keep thinking this is just a one-time thing. I'll track you to the ends of the universe before I truly let you go."

Well, okay then. So, not like the boys in romance books. Unless they're a little unhinged and threatening to stalk you everywhere. Or threaten to chop off toes for you. That's where I categorize Brown Eyes and Light Gray—slightly obsessed with the need to follow me everywhere. Is their silent friend this way, too? I can only hope he's just a tad bit more normal. I should definitely be looking over my shoulder when our night comes to an end.

Because they're never going to stop by the sound of it.

Am I naive enough to think this will be a one-time thing? Probably. But I can only hope these men don't attempt this again. It'll only bring me more danger, especially if my monster finds out what I did tonight.

He'll murder me.

And them, too.

"Just fuck me." My voice quivers slightly when he smiles against my cheek.

That's all I need. More dick. More pain. More time to feel alive under their touches and to drown out the morbid thoughts running through my brain on repeat. Just give me what I need to make it through the night and then, set me free.

"You don't have to ask me twice. Move over! It's my turn to play!" Light Gray proclaims loudly with a laugh.

A few grunts happen, and then the man who was on top of me falls to the wayside, replaced by the man I've come to call Light Gray. His deep voice rumbles, vibrating against my chest when he plops down on me. Every inch of his naked flesh lays against mine. He chuckles, leaning down to run his nose along my neck, over my jaw, and finally stops near my chin.

"You're an exquisite woman," he murmurs just for me to hear in a slightly higher-pitched voice. Like the deepness he's been using hasn't been his true voice.

I want to say something back, but his lips press into mine. His tongue tangles with mine inside my mouth as he groans over and over, rocking his hips against mine. My fingernails dig into his back, collecting the details of his defined muscles. Although Light Gray seems leaner than Brown Eyes, he's still very muscular. The scent of cinnamon and spices fills my nose when he pulls back, leaving me breathless in his wake.

"I'm absolutely going to fuck you silly, Kitten. Once my dick enters your pussy, it's over for me." I can hear the grin in his voice when he thrusts forward without warning, filling me up.

"God!" I shout into the void with my back arching off the damn bed.

My fingernails pierce through his flesh, ripping through as I drag them down. It's the only thing grounding me there with him as he fucks me silly.

"That's right, Kitten. Mark me with your claws and show the world who this cock belongs to. Oh, I gotta see," he moans, breathlessly above me.

Without warning, he pulls out, leaving me empty as I scramble for more. I moan, trying to grasp him, but he's too far away from me.

"Fuck," he chokes out in that deep voice again. "I'm covered in your blood, Kitten. I'm going to come." He grunts several times, thrusting back into me. "Going to come with your delicious blood on my dick, and I'm never going to wash it again."

Gross. Absolutely disgusting. He better wash himself after this, or he'll die of an infection. Fuck. Why am I thinking about that when he's essentially fucking my name from my memory. Who am I? No clue. Just some hopeless hussy getting her brains knocked from her head by a man obsessed with blood and cutting toes.

My lips pop open when a hand wraps around my throat. Not too gently, either. It squeezes hard until white dots form behind my eyelids, and I'm gasping for air. They don't stop. And I don't beg them to.

Light Gray pounds and pounds, thrusting his hips roughly against mine. Over and over again as he mumbles incoherent words under his breath, sounding suspiciously like my name on his lips—Journey.

"Journey!" he shouts into the room on a long, drawn out moan, stilling on top of me as he comes deep inside me.

Unlike Brown Eyes, I physically feel his dick jerk, and the hot spray of his cum lines my convulsing pussy walls.

Great. So, the toe cutter knows my actual name. I'm definitely going to have to move somewhere else and change everything about my personal information. Time to invest in that false identity I've always wanted for myself. No more Journey West here.

I cough when he lets go of my throat and leans down, pressing his forehead into mine. Our noses squish together, and his lips softly rest against mine, letting me feel every word he's about to speak.

"You're as perfect as perfect can get. An angel in the flesh," he murmurs sleepily. "And now, it's our silent friend's turn." With a loud yawn and what sounds like his fingers scratching across his flesh, he removes himself and flops on the other side of me. Leaving me squished between the two men who have already screwed me beyond words.

"He can't speak," Brown Eyes says from beside me on the bed. His fingers run across my throat, tracing the spot I was choked at. "But he'll take good care of you. We can speak for him."

Shuffling happens around me, and my anticipation spikes.

"Spread your legs again, Kitten." Hands grip my thighs forcefully, spreading me completely wide. "Look at all that cum dripping out of your spent cunt." I gasp when fingers run through my sore folds and then push inside. "We can't have any of that dripping out. You have to keep every damn drop." He chuckles when my hips rock into the fingers, and he curls them inside me. Despite the pain spearing through my insides, I go with it, moving with him and enjoying the feeling of his fingers inside me.

"Oh," I moan, squeezing my eyes shut.

My nipples harden all over again. Shivers fall down my spine, and I swear a fire brews in my lower abdomen, preparing me for another orgasm. How? I have no fucking clue. I've gotten extremely lucky so far without them finding my clit.

Maybe I'm one of the rarities that can cum from penetration alone.

A gasp falls from my lips when Light Gray's fingers abruptly fall from my pussy, leaving me hanging on the edge of another orgasm. Bastard.

"Good fucking girl," Brown Eyes growls in his deep voice, lazily tracing my nipples. "He's going to fuck you now. Take it like a good girl," he murmurs, sucking my nipple into his mouth again.

Large hands rub up my thighs, gently working my muscles with care. There's something different about this man's touch. Soothing. Respectful. Hell, it's borderline loving. He rubs me like he's known me my whole life and wants to take away the pain inflicted by the other two.

For a split second, his fingers leave me, and someone sighs.

"He wants to make sure you're okay. That you're not in too much pain."

"I'm okay. I really want this," I whisper.

"He says thank you," one of them says.

"And that his dick is going to completely obliterate you. Ouch! Asshole!" More commotion happens. "He's mean, Kitten. He hit me."

"He said none of that. Now, lie back and enjoy." Hands hold my shoulders down when the last man's body presses onto mine, completely encasing me.

The silent one with ocean eyes.

He's huge, broad, and completely swallows me whole when he lies on top of me. Gently, he moves my hair from my face, placing a kiss on my cheek.

"Please," I softly moan, letting him know I'm so fucking ready for him.

"You want him?" one of them asks, but I can't tell who. Their voices are beginning to swirl together, sounding like the same damn person. Maybe they're identical twins. Or maybe my imagination is going haywire.

"Yes," I moan. "Please."

"You heard our lady. Don't leave her hanging, bro. Fuck her good." That sounded closer to Light Gray's voice, egging Ocean Eyes on.

And with that, the third man slowly slips inside my well-used pussy.

A low, raspy groan vibrates against my chest.

"Oh, yeah. The big lug loves it! How about we go a few more rounds, Kitten?"

Fucking Light Gray—my mind screams at him to shut up and let me enjoy this moment.

"Fuck," I breathe when he thrusts a few times, filling me completely.

He's so damn big compared to the other two that more pain flares to life. But so does my arousal. Someone's fingers rub over my clit in fast circles, bringing my orgasm closer and closer, until I'm exploding in a silent cry of pleasure.

Within a few silent thrusts, his entire body stiffens, and he groans. Not lasting as long as the other two, which doesn't hurt my feelings one bit. After tonight, I'll need to soak in a bathtub of warm water. His large hands cover my cheeks, and he pulls me in for a simple kiss on the lips. His weight gently lifts off me, and I feel the bed shift to my other side.

"He says your pussy is magical, and there's rainbows coming from it." One of them chuckles, but my brain is too mushy to tell them apart again.

"I'm sure that's what he said," I rasp.

I slump into the bed with them surrounding me. Despite being blindfolded, I'm relying on them to continue to keep me safe. Hopefully, Mr. Toe Cutter doesn't get any bright ideas and wants a souvenir before he leaves.

I like my toes, thank you very much.

Exhaustion pulls at my weary limbs. My pussy aches, but the pain is beyond delicious. I'll feel my defiant act for days to come, remembering the way their dicks felt deep inside me, using me to achieve their pleasure. Thank God I have birth control in place, because I don't even think these assholes used condoms.

My brows furrow. They most definitely didn't. What if they have diseases or something? Then, I'm screwed if I have to go to the doctor. How do I explain to my monster that I'm a dumbass who defied his rules and fucked without a rubber for the first time?

Fuck.

Stupid. Stupid, me.

Whatever. I push those insane feelings to the deepest, darkest part of my brain and mentally wash them from my mind. For now, at least. For the time being, I want to embrace the freedom humming through my soul.

I've never felt more alive than in their arms. And I don't even know their names. Tonight will live in my mind for years to come as I dig myself out of the grave I've thrown myself into these past two years.

I'm ready to live...

I'm ready to...

"Sorry, Little Kitten."

I feel the sting in my neck before I can even react. My body grows numb. My head swims in a fog of darkness, and then...

My world shuts off.

And darkness takes me again.

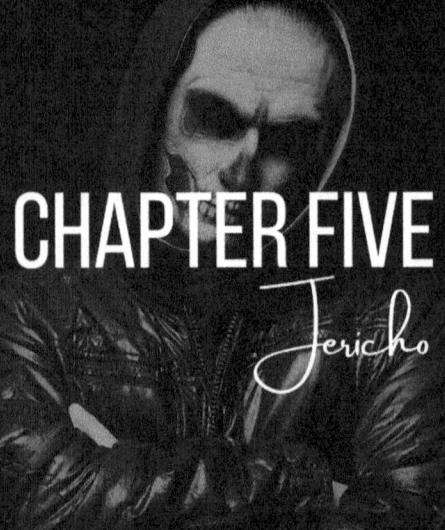

CHAPTER FIVE
Jericho

"You..."

"Drugged her. Yeah," Arrow remarks with a grin, running his fingers through her curly hair and then pulling her partially nude body into his lap, where he lovingly rocks her back and forth. "She's so beautiful when she sleeps, isn't she?" Pure obsession shines in his eyes when he leans down and kisses her lips.

"Stop," I grunt, whacking the back of his head until he shoots up from the kiss and glares at me.

Shepp clicks the rings on his fingers in aggravation, alerting us he wants our attention. I sigh, turning my gaze to his tall form. Shepp frowns with his hands curling into fists at his sides.

Many years ago, my father gifted Shepp two metal rings that sit on his thumb and pointer finger. To the naked eye, they don't look special. Simple rings on his fingers like a decoration. But to Shepp, they were a game changer. Imagine walking into a loud room, and you needed to get someone's attention urgently. Instead of running to them and silently tapping them on the shoulder, you can simply tap your rings together, bringing their attention to you.

Perhaps it was a guilt-induced measure to help Shepp in communicating with us. Maybe it was selfish on my father's part. Considering he's never done a positive thing for the people around him. Ever. He's purely out for himself. So, why were these rings pertinent for Shepp? No clue. Besides, it's not like my father has kept up with the replacements Shepp's had to get over the years as he's grown into the massive man he is now. Shepp has done that on his own, picking out his own designs, fitting for the man Shepp has become.

After the incident happened, Shepp, Arrow, and I learned sign language together. It was many months of grueling tutoring, along with our regular schooling. But we knew it was important for Shepp to have a language he could speak, considering his father took his voice from him.

'You didn't have to do that! Why did you have that in your fucking pocket, anyway?' Shepp signs with agitation.

"Um, who doesn't carry around a plunger full of knock-out meds?" Arrow looks between us like we're the crazy ones for not having it in our pockets. "It comes in handy." He waves his hand down at the naked girl passed out in his arms.

'We could have helped her get dressed and walked her home. Now...' Shepp signs, dropping his hands when he shakes his head. *'Idiot.'*

I purse my lips. "Now, we have to find her some clothes and sneak her out without anyone noticing we were here." My eyes fall to the torn fishnets and discarded leather corset lying on the ground. "Or that we have a drugged woman in our possession. Discretion is our finest attribute, Arrow," I huff, picking up the pieces of clothing, refusing to leave them behind for the owner of the home to find later.

Shepp rolls his eyes, waving to the window. *'Well, the sun is starting to rise, so I don't think many people will still be here,'* he signs.

"Or... and hear me out. Why can't we just keep her? I'll feed her, clothe her, and..."

"You know we can't. She needs to graduate," I cut in sharply. "Besides, she's not a pet."

And we cannot have her yet. Per my father's asinine rules that we so clearly broke last night. But I'm tired of waiting in the wind while he dictates my life. Every step of the way he's been there, looking over my shoulder, and telling me which way to piss. Never again. I've never rebelled so hard against him, and it feels *oh so fucking good* to step over the line he created. Now, I just have to keep up the illusion that we're under his ruling thumb.

So, for now, Journey will return home and continue living her life until she graduates. Or until my father gives me the go-ahead to take what I want.

"Boo! You're no fun! Ours!" Arrow grunts, burying his face into the crook of her neck. Breathing deeply, he savors the smell of our girl before he has to let her go.

"Yes. She's ours," I confirm, rubbing my chin. "She's ours, most definitely. But we have to appear like we're following the rules my father put in place."

My eyes dart to Shepp. *'Keep your friends close...'* he signs.

"But your enemies closer," I confirm with a nod.

"Can't I hide her in my closet or something? I've had a taste, Jer. A big, long drink, and it was delicious. I need more. I'm addicted to Journey West." Arrow gives us his best puppy dog eyes while holding her close.

"Arrow," I sigh, feeling the agitation boiling under the surface. "You know we can't. If we could keep her, we would. You knew going into this that this was a sliver of the pie of our future. We wait..."

"We wait," he sighs, kissing her temple and stroking his hands over her bitten up breasts. "I know. These next few weeks will be torture..."

'We need to focus on continuing to build our empire for her,' Shepp signs, as his light eyes focus on our obsession with renewed vigor and determination.

"Yes. We've had a taste, and now, we need to prove ourselves worthy of her. When she steps in as our wife, she will never have to worry about anything again. Especially my father." I pace naked in front of them, my thoughts going wild about our future with Journey by our side. With talks of a new wife coming into the picture, my brain turns over our options. Something has to happen. Something drastic, and I have just the idea. "We'll start tripling our efforts and building our own army of faithful soldiers. We have a few men right now, but we need to go bigger and find more allies within the family who believe in us. Journey will be ours. We can't let Chloe Satin anywhere near us." Because knowing my father, he will most definitely screw us over somehow, and I need to be on my toes for when it happens.

'We'll start working harder with the loans and poker games. Maybe expand our slot machines into Vegas and network our name instead of your father's empire while spreading seeds of doubt about Gabriel throughout the empire. Only making ourselves look good. So, everyone sees Gabriel for who he is—a scumbag. We need to gain the trust of everyone around us while simultaneously making them doubt Gabriel,' Shepp signs in agreement.

Fucking Gabriel and his paranoid ass.

"Very soon, we'll have you with us, Little Kitten," Arrow coos, kissing her head again. "I'm going to continue my outreach confessional business." Right. Arrow and his good deeds.

For someone who was born a complete psycho, he cares about the people living on the streets and the downtrodden. Something he inherited from his father. Every Wednesday, he has meetings with people in need. Hell, sometimes they show up to Rave and beg us for help. As long as they have the proper coin, etched with a V, then we invite them in and help them with whatever they may need. Loans. Relocation. You name it, we're there to help. For a price, of course.

And she will be with us soon. We'll prepare our kingdom for her. Then, we'll be ready for her whether she wants us or not.

'Hopefully, something useful besides murder and knives?' Shepp signs with his brows raised. Despite not using his voice to speak, the sarcasm flows off him in waves.

"Judgemental and rude," Arrow huffs, standing naked with Journey in his arms. "Those are my two favorite things, besides my Kitten here."

I'm sure if we tried to steal her away now, we'd never be able to pluck her out of his hands. He's like a feral, possessive dog. Maybe tonight was a bad idea. I'm never going to be able to keep a handle on him.

Only three more weeks.

Then, she's ours.

Permanently.

No matter what she says.

Arrow doesn't say another word as he waltzes to the closet on the other side of the room. Throwing it open with Journey still in his arms, he rifles through it while whistling a tune.

"Well, lookie here," he says, throwing out a few shirts onto the king-sized bed. Then, he moves to the dresser and gathers a pair of sweatpants. "I'll dress you, Kitten," he coos at her gently, setting her unconscious body on the bed. "We'll always take care of you." Slowly, he lifts a shirt over her head and puts her arms through, covering the under corset and any exposed skin. Arrow hums to himself as he puts her feet through the baggy sweatpants and pulls them up until she's dressed.

My eyes dart to Shepp, who furrows his brows. Something as simple as helping to dress her isn't in Arrow's normal wheelhouse. He's ruthless, a little out of his mind, and has no fucking limits. It seems we've found the perfect person to satisfy his urges and level him out.

Now, Journey is completely dressed in a stranger's clothes. Something I'm not exactly thrilled with. In fact, my fingers curl into a fist. If this was my room, she'd be draped in my clothes—or none at all—and no one else's. But we can't exactly drag her out of here in the nude. Then, we'd really have some murder on our hands.

I shake my head when the three of us get our clothes on and secure our masks over our faces once again. Arrow tilts his head, staring down at Journey as she rests fully clothed on the bed, and then, he scoops her into his arms and cradles her there.

"Okay, let's roll." He doesn't wait for us when he walks out the door or down the stairs. "We're going to make a pit stop before the drug wears off, and then we'll tuck her into bed real nice."

'Pit stop?' Shepp signs, following after him.

"What do you mean pit stop?" I ask, following him down the empty stairs and into the equally empty mansion. It seems as if everyone has disappeared from the party. Except for a few stragglers passed out on the couches and party favors and drinks sprawled around on the floor.

"Tattoo shop," Arrow says with a grin, gently cradling Journey's head into his chest.

'A fucking tattoo shop?' Shepp signs with a huff. *'This should be good.'* Or bad, depending on how you look at it. Arrow always has something up his sleeve. Crazy. Good. Bad. Whatever it may be.

Looks like we're going to his favorite tattoo shop and branding what's ours.

CHAPTER SIX
Journey

Blood pools around me. Tears cloud my eyes.

"What did you do?" Her scream shrieks through my mind, forever imprinting in my mind. "What did you do, Journey?"

What I needed to do.

A gasp tears from my throat. My mind swims in the shadows of the worst day of my life. My fucking heart pounds wildly like an erratic drum, beating out of control.

"What did you do?"

Her scream echoes in my mind on repeat. Fuck. I cover my ears, blocking out the shrill cries. But it doesn't help. She screams in my skull until I want to take a hammer to it and never hear her again.

Her screams haunt me. His taunting laughs and smile follow me everywhere.

No. I grunt, slapping the side of my head, forcing the images away.

A sinking, hollow sensation gnaws at the pit of my stomach when my eyes try to flutter open. They're so damn heavy, the feeling of sand rubs against them, refusing to let them open. I dig my palms into my eyeballs, wiping away the groggy sleep.

What the hell happened? And why do I feel like I got run over by a bus? Like my whole damn body throbs with my heartbeat.

I suck in a breath when I move to my back, staring up at the ceiling of my room. It's white and simple, with large cracks working through the walls. I count them one by one, calming the anxiety bubbling through my veins. Something is off. Something weird has happened between then and now. Every inch of my body aches, especially my...

I sit up with a frantic squeak, looking around the room. My room. My goddamn space. How the fuck did I get here? Wasn't I at a mansion, dressed like a cat? Looking down, my brows furrow when I pluck at the oversized T-shirt and sweatpants. Definitely not mine. Where the hell did they come from? Did I sleepwalk again? Shit. I rub my temple as the memories assault me, bringing it all back like a damn horror show.

I rebelled. Hard. Fast. Taking my body and life back into my own hands. I didn't think of the consequences. Didn't think of the future...

I didn't think at all.

Maybe it was the atmosphere. The party. The three of them. With their hands on me. And the orgasms... God, they were so damn liberating. It was so fucking freeing from the dark prison I'm floundering in. With no end in sight. But how did I get back here?

When my body shifts on the bed, a deep pain erupts from my right ass cheek. What the hell? Maybe I fell? Is that why it hurts so damn bad every time I move? I blow out a breath, shifting the sweatpants over my cheek, and examine myself in the mirror beside my bed. Yup. Right there on my butt cheek is a massive bruise. Maybe I did fall, or maybe it's a sex trophy like the other bruises I can see forming on my skin.

Shit. I throw myself back onto my bed and stare at the ceiling again. I need Sunshine back. I need her here with me so I can take care of her. So we can leave and never come back. I had one good night, and now, I need to focus on our escape.

Taking a deep breath, I drop to the ground in front of my nightstand and open the bottom drawer. To the naked eye, a bunch of school papers with A's and A+ sit on top, making one think I'm proud of my accomplishments. Despite being held back my sophomore year and missing a lot of time, thanks to my monster's captivity, I still manage to make good grades and keep up on my work. It's a distraction, at least.

Under the papers rest my toys, discreetly hidden so no one can find them. A girl has to have some sort of release at the end of a shitty day. And if I wasn't allowed to find a man to help me with that, I have B.O.B—my battery-operated boyfriend, to lend a vibration or two.

Working my way through the papers, I manage to find the false bottom I created years before and pull out the contents—two thousand dollars I've managed to steal and squirrel away, and ten letters I've been allowed to receive from Sunny over the past three years. It's the only thing I can save from our interactions. Between rare phone calls and letters, it's all I have left of my little sister.

J!

I love you so much and miss you lots. I know you're probably worrying about me, but please don't. I don't know what's happening on your end, but I'm finally in a hospital. Not sure where, though. They haven't told me. But I've got fluids and lots of tests coming up. They're talking about a heart transplant, Journey! Can you believe that? I'm actually going to be okay... I guess since Mom couldn't afford it, he can? I hope you don't feel guilty for what happened or why I'm here and you're not. I'm fine, and I hope you are too. I love you a lot! He only gave me five minutes to write this out.

Love you!

Your Sunshine.

I suck in a breath, holding the letter to my heart. Tears

threaten to spill, but I hold them back. An ache forms across my chest. I fucking miss my sister. For years, I was the one to take care of her instead of my mom, who'd rather stick a needle in her arm than be a parent. It was Sunny and me. Always. Forever. Even through the heartbreak of her diagnosis. Her heart was failing her, and she needed her first transplant or she'd die. I took her to every doctor's appointment, trying to find someone to run more tests and give us more answers, but the doctors we could see on our medical card were slim, and the care was even worse. If we had more money, I could take her to see better doctors. If her father had stayed in her life, whoever he may be, then maybe we'd have the child support to care for her.

Or hell, even my father, the rat bastard. I swear, Corbin West is more worthless than Sunny's father. At least I know who my father is, she never did. Not that it helped any. My dad wrote us off the second he could, casting my mother back to Briar Cove while he went back to his mansion in East Point Bluff, California. For as long as I can remember, I've blocked his existence out of my life. If he didn't want me, then fine. He wouldn't have me. I'd forge my own way. Fuck him.

I swear the men in my life have done nothing but let me down or taken advantage of me.

I cling to the letter tighter, pretending my arms are wrapped around her. This was one of our last correspondences. The last thing she was allowed to send me a month ago. I read and reread her words on a daily basis, trying to convince myself that she means it. That she's okay and not suffering alone in some cold dungeon like I was. That she's healing and getting better. I thumb over the pictures my monster has handed me over the past three years. Photos of my sister, sitting in a hospital bed with a smile on her plump face, gaining her color back. She's been sick for so long, but my mother was never able to save up to get her the proper care. Until now. Until I fucked up and put all our lives in danger. One quick trade is all it took to make our lives hell.

With a sigh, I put everything back into my false bottom and

secure it tight. My mother will do anything to get her hands on more money to fuel her habit. So hiding anything of value is always on the top of my to-do list. Not that I have anything super nice, but still, this money is my savings. My way of investing in my future and hopefully breaking free of this place with my sister. And since my billionaire father is no help, this is all I have to my name.

Peeling myself off the ground, I limp toward the bathroom down the hall, cringing with every step I take. I guess this is why people shouldn't lose their virginity to three men. Was it worth it, though? You betcha. But every inch of me aches like someone punched their way down my body.

No matter what happens or what my future holds, for one night I was free from the confines of my prison—the rules, the lessons, and everything in between doesn't fucking matter right now. I got out. For just a split second, I reached through the bars and found myself again, under the grips of three masked men.

I relax into a hot shower, groaning when the water flows over my tired limbs. As my hands work down my body, I stiffen when pain takes over my tit, and I look down. Jesus. Mary. And Joseph. My eyes widen at the multitude of bite marks lining my chest and hickies on my goddamn thighs. Holy hell. What did I get myself into last night? A lot, apparently. Those three masked men marked me for the world to see.

I'm as equally turned on as I am terrified.

Even though it's May and warm outside, I'm refusing to wear anything revealing like shorts or a T-shirt until these bruises heal. There's no way I could explain this to my monster without saying—yeah, I had sex—without getting punished for breaking a rule. He'd throw me in his basement dungeon again, lock me up, and throw away the key for defying him. He'd starve me, beat me, and do whatever he wanted if he ever found out. He's done it before.

Shit.

What a ridiculous rule. It's something he can't dictate,

anyhow. How could he know? He wouldn't. Unless someone was spying on me from afar and telling my monster everything.

Sometimes, I wonder what his motive is for keeping my virtue intact. Like why dictate who I can and can't sleep with or touch? Is it a power trip, keeping me on a short leash? Whatever. I've lived by that rule for so long, it almost feels foreign to think those strangers popped my cherry. Three times over.

After washing the stink of last night off, I rest my head against the cracked shower wall, letting myself truly absorb what I did. I defied my monster's orders and did something for myself. If only he had let me talk to my sister. If only he'd let me see her goddamn face. But he doesn't. He knows what he's doing by dangling her health above my head and expecting me to jump when he says so. With one call, he could end her life. And then mine. Fuck him.

My stomach twists, knotting together. Usually, anxiety would have me in its grasp right now, fearing for the inevitable of him finding out and locking me away in his basement.

But not today.

There's nothing wrong with what I did. In my eyes, at least. I swore on my knees three years ago that I'd follow his rules. I bear the mark he carved between my breasts, near my sternum, promising my cooperation. If only I had a choice. Nothing about this was my decision, but last night... I took back control for the first time since he stole my sister away and forced me under his wing, blackmailing me into doing his dirty work.

I did the job he sent me there for. So, why does anxiety continue to bubble in my stomach until it aches?

Finally, I turn off the hot shower as the cool water takes over. I've successfully stayed under the warmth for fifteen minutes, and now, it's time to face the day. Every Sunday I have a list of things to get done: laundry, grocery shopping, and anything for the trailer. Besides, my mother will need some sort of lunch soon to fill her belly and make her feel a little better before she inserts another needle into her arm and falls into a blissful high. I'm her main caregiver, after all. I feed her, make sure she hasn't choked on her puke, and throw her in the shower if she does. Anyone else that comes to this trailer either fucks her into oblivion so she can get high or sells her what she wants—drugs. It's just another day in paradise.

After I'm dried off and dressed in a hoodie and sweatpants, I head back to my room to grab my purse and laundry basket. It's the only day of the week I have to myself. Monday through Friday, I'm stuck at school, gaining my education during the day. Friday and Saturday nights, I'm usually busy working for my monster—like yesterday. I went to school and then prepared myself for the party, which leaves today free and clear. Something I only usually get on Sundays. But I'll take it.

"Seems you had a late night."

I freeze by my bedroom door, fear sinking its ugly claws deep into me. My eyes widen at the figure hovering by my bed. Tall. Dark. Deviously handsome and deceptive in his three-piece suit, not looking a day over forty. His mere presence has my hairs standing on end and my fight or flight kicking in. I want to run and hide, but I know it'll do me no good. He'll track me down in a matter of hours and make me wish I was never born.

He never shows up here. Not in my room. We have a code and a special meeting place down by the docks in a ruined building. He sends me a discreet text with the numbers 4-2-1, and I do the opposite 1-2-4, indicating I need to speak to him.

It's how we've always worked for the past three years.

If he's here, risking it all to be in my bedroom, then I fucked up, and he knows everything about what I did.

CHAPTER SEVEN

Journey

"RIGHT HERE, LITTLE SNAKE," my monster sneers, thrusting the knife into my hands. *"You see here?"*

I shakily nod, my chest caving in when he points to the space between the poor man's ribs. The very man tied to a chair in front of me, begging for his life. My fingers shake when my monster thrusts my arm forward, forcing the blade to penetrate through the buttery skin of the man, wailing for me to stop.

"Please. Please! I'll tell you anything you want to hear!" he shouts through the gag, drooling and nearly throwing up when my monster forces the blade to stay put.

I'm going to puke. This can't be my life right now. This man on the chair... he didn't even do anything to me.

"Keep it still," my monster hisses in my ear before straightening. Despite his warning, I shake like a leaf. Nausea blooms in my stomach, forcing its way up my throat until I'm puking on the ground. Spit hangs from my mouth as I hunch over, knowing what's coming next. "Out of your system, Little Snake? Can we continue to gather information from this fucking pissant?"

I swallow more vomit and nod, hoping when I stand, I look more confident than I feel. I have to. I can't die in this dingy basement with this man.

"Oh, good," he says way too calmly for my liking before straightening his suit and moving forward. "Hands here. Now, *yank it out." With his help, I yank the knife out from between the man's ribs, cringing the entire time.*

I don't want to be here. Why am I forced to do this shit?

Our poor victim's cries fill the dark basement I've called my home for five months now. How no one misses me is beyond me. It's a month into the school year, and no one has come looking for me. At all. I figured my mom wouldn't care. He probably has her so drugged up that she's compliant. So she doesn't give a shit. Not that she would. But I thought maybe... maybe someone else would wonder where I've been. Or where Sunny is. I swallow hard, my heart aching for my sister.

"Now, Eugene. We can do this the easy way. Tell me what I want to know, and then I'll end your suffering. Don't tell me what you know, then I'll make you suffer longer. And so will she. She's learning the ropes." My monster flashes me an evil grin, highlighting his dark eyes and chiseled face. He could give the devil a run for his money.

Eugene stares me up and down with wide eyes, blanching when he sees the blood staining my fingers. His blood. Fuck. I try to ignore the crimson on my hands. I try to ignore the warmth spreading across my flesh from the wound I was forced to inflict on him. Numbness tingles inside me. The real Journey buries herself deep in my mind, fleeing from this situation. It's something I learned from the last time.

If Eugene would just spill his guts, then I would not have to be here. I want to be anywhere but here. Anywhere other than in this room. Give me the cage I'm forced to stay in over this.

"I didn't..."

"You didn't do anything or know anything? Is that why a certain little snake had some interesting things to tell me?" My monster's eyes dart to me, grinning with pride at how I successfully followed Eugene undetected, hid out in his office, and found the information I needed without being caught. At night, I snuck out with video proof, pictures, and an array of files the good lawyer liked

to keep unlocked in his office. "Go ahead, Little Snake. Go a rib down."

I swallow hard at his instruction. My brain yells at me to stop. My feet want to move through the door as my stomach turns, threatening to send more vomit up my throat. But I know what will happen if I don't do as he asks—terrible pain like I've suffered before at the hands of the man teaching me to torture. Just like Eugene is suffering through, I'll suffer worse. No food or water. He'll shut off the lights and leave me to rot until he thinks I've learned my lesson.

My only reprieve is when the music starts above me as I sit in my cage. It quietly whines and weaves its way through the ceiling, wrapping around me like a comforter. It's the only noise that permeates through the walls, killing the silence that sets me on edge.

Without an ounce of hesitation, I shut myself off, becoming a different person. The whine of the violin plays in my mind, locking me away with peace and comfort. I become the type of individual who enjoys torturing, maiming, and murdering as a pastime. Because if I remain Journey, my soul will blacken to the deepest depths of evil. Something I didn't have before I was taken. I'll let the darkness that peeks through, aching to take over, completely consume me. It's something I don't want to give my monster the satisfaction of having. He can make me do whatever he wants. But he'll never strip me of my emotions. Ever. Even though he's the cause of the evil rising inside me.

"Good girl," my monster breathes when I press the blade through the man's ribs.

His screams fill the room again. "Okay!" he shouts, trying to bat me away.

"Okay?" my monster says with a smug smirk. "Go on..." He waves a hand, watching Eugene with a keen eye, never taking them off him.

I suck in a breath when I pull the blade from his ribs, making him scream again. Full sobs wrack his body when he finally breaks down, divulging all the information my monster so desperately *wanted. Numbness fills me for the first time when I step back, letting the knife hang limply from my fingers.*

I've stabbed a man and killed him to save my sister's virtue and mine. And now, I'm stabbing this stranger for daring to side with my monster's enemy. He's not the first. Definitely, not the last, either. Is this my future? Is blood and death and destruction my life now?

"Shadow..." Eugene's voice trails off, and he shakes his head. "I don't know his real name. He only contacts me from untraceable phones."

The man rears back when my monster unleashes a fury of fists on his face and sticks his fingers directly into his bleeding wounds.

"His name! I need his goddamn name!" he shouts, making my body stiffen.

"Don't know," the man chokes out, slumping to his side and stills, falling into the darkness death brings.

My monster's back heaves wildly as he stands above the man we killed together, trying to extract the name of his nemesis moving in on his people.

"For months, this Shadow fucker has been intruding on my town, bringing his filth into my goddamn city! I will ruin anyone who associates with him. Decimate anyone who thinks of teaming up with him and coming into my goddamn city!" He roars every word, throwing his fists into the corpse over and over again until blood splatters all over us.

Vomit rests in my throat when he turns his attention back to me with a sadistic smile. "What a good little snake you are, huh?" he coos, marching toward me and wrapping his bloodied hand around my throat. "Excellent work," he says, squeezing lightly against my neck. "You've earned a reward." Without another word, he holds up his phone, presses a few buttons and turns it toward me.

Tears spill down my cheeks when my little sister Sunny's bright face fills the picture. It's been months since he took her, too. Keeping her captive without telling me where she was. All he could say was, she's fine, and she'll remain fine as long as I'm a good little girl. Her cheeks aren't as swollen as they once were, and bright color fills her face. She looks alive, rather than half dead, like before when I was fighting to get her to the doctors and have someone listen.

"Sunny," I rasp, furrowing my brows when her face turns down.

Her bright eyes run the length of my face, fluttering toward my chest. My heart sinks. It's only then that I realize I'm covered in another man's blood. Something I can't explain to her in her fragile state. It's all for you—I want to say. But I stick to something easier. Something I've been desperate to ask since she left my sight the night I murdered the man taking advantage of her.

"You okay?"

She nods. "Better," her tiny voice rings through the video call with concern. Her mouth opens again, but nothing comes out.

My heart shatters in two when her face fades into nothing. She's disappeared again. In her stead is a black screen of nothing, much like my fucking soul right now. I needed more time. I crave to touch her, talk to her, and find her.

My monster must see the anger lining my face when he smirks.

"She's getting the hospitalization she needs. But only if you continue on this path, Little Snake. Be a good girl. Do as I say, and you'll be reunited with your sister." He pats my head like a dog and then grabs my arm forcefully, throwing me back into my cage with blood staining my skin.

It's on the tip of my tongue to beg for answers to my questions. How long will I be here? How long will Sunny be his other prisoner? When will I get to reunite with her? But it all slips away when the lights fade in my prison, and I'm left in the hole he's dug for me. Sounds escape from the other rooms around me. Moans. Groans. Screams for help. A chainsaw comes to life somewhere in the distance, leaving me to sleep with the sounds of other people dying.

Then, it all goes silent when the music above me starts again. It whines into a perfect tune, something so beautiful my eyes close on their own accord, and I drift off to a peaceful night's sleep to the sound of a violin located somewhere in this house of hell. It's the only sound that truly soothes my soul amongst the chaos of bullshit.

My stomach drops through my ass and runs completely away at the sight of him standing there waiting for me. His presence dredges up long-forgotten memories I've locked away since he took me into that basement and forced my hand.

Much like a predator, eager to take a bite out of his prey, I see the moment he registers my fear. Probably smelling it in the air when I don't dare to move or provoke him. His words from the first few months he held me captive ring in my mind. One of his many lessons he loves to dole out, showing me who had and has the upper hand. Always.

"We show no fear, Little Snake. Now, do what you need to do! One phone call. That's all it takes to end your sister's life!"

"I did," I reply, folding my hands in front of me and standing tall.

I swallow the fear attempting to choke me, replacing it with fake indifference. It's what he wants to see. No fear. No emotions. It's what he's taught me over and over again. No fear. No weakness. No fuel to give to your enemies. Ever. He's taught me so many things over the years, but the most important was how to be invisible.

"You see that man over there, Little Snake?" my monster discreetly asks, cornering me in the crowded restaurant filled to the brim with people in their finest attire.

The same eatery he brought me to after cleaning me up and dressing me in a fancy, sparkly dress with high heels. He painted make-up on me, dressed me up, and forced me to become his living doll. Once he was satisfied, he threw me in my own limo and gave me the address of the place I was to go. My only instructions were: stand in the corner, look pretty, but be discreet. You're to fit in with the crowd, but keep an eye out.

I nod, eyeing the man in question, swallowing hard. The moment my eyes fall on his tall frame, I recognize him. The dark hair and eyes, focusing on what his companion is saying with little interest. There's an air of indifference encompassing his frame, giving him the fuck-off attitude.

"You're going to tail him tonight. I want details on everyone he talks to, what he eats, and what rooms in this establishment he visits. You've memorized the names I gave you?"

What else was I supposed to do in my cage to pass the time? Listen to the violin for hours on end and daydream about my escape? No. I read the twenty pages of names he gave me to memorize in the bleak light he finally allowed me to have, along with the descriptions of their appearance and their spouse's names.

Even his name and his friends.

"Yes, Sir," I say with a nod, keeping my expression neutral.

"Good. Now, go be invisible," he huffs, sipping his drink. As quick as he came, he swivels on his heel and leaves the area I'm stationed in, giving me time to eye the man I'm supposed to watch after tonight.

Jericho Viotto.

We walk the halls of the same high school. Or did. I've missed so much since I was kidnapped. When we were kids, he oddly followed me around with puppy dog eyes but backed off when he was ten. I haven't spoken to him since. He avoids everyone, but his two friends, Arrow and Sheppard.

And now, I'm in charge of following him around this stupid party without being detected. Of course, my monster would want me to tail someone I know. It's all about invisibility and the lesson I'll learn doing this.

He nods several times, walking toward me like he's the lion about to devour me.

"I want to discuss Elias." Right. My job. "Explain this to me." He waves a hand.

I lick my lips, going over what I saw last night in my mind without a second thought or question. Plus, the pictures I had already sent him when my mission was done. Technically, I was instructed to leave the party and come home, but I got a little distracted by slipping and falling on three massive dicks.

Speaking of...

I mentally curse myself when I shift my weight, and pain from my damn vagina flares, igniting my belly. I don't dare make a noise or bring his attention to my discomfort. He reads me like a damn book every time. In fact, why he's here asking me these questions has my hackles rising. My monster is a phone call from a private number kind of man. He's far too busy to track me down and lecture me.

My monster knows it all. He's like a fucking God hovering by the ceiling, seeing what everyone does and thinks. So, him being here can only mean bad things. Shit. Maybe he knows what I did and wants to punish me.

"I got to the party at eleven and found him standing in the corner with the woman pictured. She's from school, a senior, like me. Her name is Jenni Thomas. He left her side and went to the basement, where I followed. Then, once he was done, he came back upstairs and met up with Jenni again."

Never in my life have I seen my monster's lips curl into such a massive grin. He chuckles lowly but doesn't dare explain.

"Go on."

"Um, they talked for a while, but it was mostly flirting, and then they went up to a bedroom on the second floor and uh... banged."

Banged? What the fuck is wrong with me? But I mean, it was the truth. My classmate and this douchebag from God knows where didn't come out of that bedroom for hours. Seriously, I watched and waited. I may have been a creeper outside the door, making sure they weren't conspiring or some shit. It's my job, after all. If I'm not thorough, then my ass is on the line.

"And you didn't see them leave?" he asks, raising a brow.

"They were locked in that room for a long time, Sir."

He nods a few times, flicking invisible lint from the lapel of his suit. Always dressed to the nines when he actually shows his face.

Do this, Journey. Do that, Journey. It's never *hey, you doing good?* Or *hey, that mission didn't go well; better luck next time, Champ.*

Not for me. But I guess I'm paying him a debt. Why would he be nice to me? I'm just another cog in his stupid machine. The little snake he sends into the belly of the beasts.

"And what were you doing during the time they locked themselves away?" He raises a brow, his dark eyes zeroing in on my expressionless face.

Never let the enemy know what you're thinking.

Never show your fear.

"I was a party-goer, Sir. As instructed. I blended in and kept watch, waiting for them to come out."

Not a lie. That's what I was doing after following them around to the basement and main floor again. Then came the dancing and pretending to drink and embracing my damn freedom for one single night as they fucked like bunnies in an upstairs bedroom. Then, they came out with hickies and disheveled clothes, leaving together out the front door, pushing past me and the three men, begging me to go upstairs with them.

I could have followed Jenni and Elias out the door. I could have stolen an expensive car littering the drive, something I've never thought about doing. For one split second, I almost went. I almost said no to the masked men and to the desire flowing through my body.

But my freedom meant more to me than following through with my mission. I came. I saw. I did exactly what he wanted me to do. He never specified leaving the party and following them home. My orders were: go to this address, attend the party in this outfit, and keep an eye on Elias, AKA Blue Spider—a notorious gang member on the south side of Briar Cove, California. Watch who he's close to, and never take your eyes off them.

So, I didn't. For once, I followed my own wants and needs, putting them above everyone else.

"And when they came out?"

Jesus Christ, he's full of questions. It's like he's trying to elude that he knows exactly what I did. Fuck. Can he see that I'm not a virgin anymore? Is it written on my face? I take a deep breath, pretending to look back over the night's events.

"They came down the stairs together, holding hands. They looked like they had just banged." Fuck, again, with the banged.

I swallow hard, tightening every muscle in my body. I know when I say something wrong because his face twists into an awful expression that looks like he's sucked a lemon.

"And then they walked out the front door and drove away together."

"And you didn't follow them?" he asks, zeroing his eyes in on me.

"I didn't know if I should, Sir."

Every person has a tell when they're about to explode. Mine? I ball my fists and a darkness swirls behind my eyes, clouding my judgments. It's swift and explosive. Just how my monster brainwashed me. But I rarely let it happen. I'm more in check with myself these days. It's how I survive.

But my monster? His nostrils flare—like now—his body turns rigid, and a devilish expression passes over his reddening face.

"Following them was your orders, Little Snake!" he shouts, throwing my lamp across the room until it shatters against the wall, leaving us in a darkness so consuming that my hairs stand on end. "You were to follow them EVERYWHERE!" His shouts bounce off the thin trailer walls, no doubt gaining my mother's attention from the other room.

Not that she'd step up and help me through this. This situation was my fault, after all. And she's the one who sold me to him to gain access to her drugs and probably the means to get them. I'm the one who suffers. Not her. Not him. It's my sister and I. All for defending ourselves. And he's made sure I could never run away, by keeping my sister's location a secret. It's something I've never been able to figure out. I'm desperate to know, but he's too smart. He's hidden her too well.

I stand rigidly, keeping my chin up as he advances on me.

Internally, I know what's coming. There's nothing gentle about his corrective ways. I close my eyes when his fist meets my face. Pain explodes, stars burst behind my eyes, and yet, I don't dare cry out or whimper. It'll only make it worse.

My silence continues when his greedy fingers wrap around my throat, squeezing as hard as he can. As the oxygen wanes and my hand wraps around his wrist, I mentally beg him to do it. Just end my fucking suffering and let me be free from the confines of his goddamn prison.

I'm so tired of being tired and suffering at his hands. My sister's beautiful face pops into my mind, wrapping me in a heavenly peace as my limbs buzz and grow limp.

One day, I'll escape this Hell. But today doesn't seem to be that day.

I gasp when he releases my throat, stumbling back over my numb feet.

"Every day, you prove what a goddamn disappointment you are." Me? Really? I didn't do anything wrong. I followed his orders to a T. But nothing seems to please him.

"I'm sorry, Sir," I sputter, coughing hysterically, trying to bring air back into my depleted lungs. "I..." I shake my head, falling to my fucking knees like the pathetic being I am. But I learned a long time ago not to argue with him. He'll only punish me more. Or worse, punish my sister.

My monster looms above me in the shadows, staring down with disgust written on his face. Am I pathetic? Most definitely. But I have to survive somehow. Always fucking survive. I have to pretend to be compliant or he'll fucking murder me. Or worse, lock me in the cage and throw away the key.

My monster reaches into his suit pocket, pulls out his phone, and presses the call button. My heart drops into my stomach, swirling it into tiny pieces. Another tiny sliver of my soul fucking breaks off when he looks directly into my eyes. I let the numbness take me over, hiding my feelings as much as I can.

"Take Sunshine off the transplant list," he demands into the phone without an ounce of remorse.

"No," I croak, tears springing to my eyes for the first time in a long time. "She's innocent. This was my fault."

"It was your fault. And you know who pays the consequence when you fail," he sneers, hanging up the phone and placing it in his pocket. "And here I thought, after three years of training, you were on your way to being a good little snake. Maybe I was wrong. Maybe we should end this now." He lifts his phone again, hovering his finger above the call button.

"No," I breathe, stumbling to my feet. "I promise I'll do better next time. Just please, put Sunny back on the transplant list. You know she's going to die if she doesn't get a new heart." I may not beg for myself or have any dignity left, but for my sister, I'll do anything. She's too young and innocent to have to go through this.

My monster strokes his chin. "No."

"Sir, please," I beg as a tear escapes, running down my cheek.

He grins, stepping forward and swiping the tear away and onto his thumb. He hums when he sucks my tear into his mouth. "I have another task for you. Prove yourself to me, Little Snake, and I'll think about putting dear ole Sunny back on the transplant list. But let that be a lesson to you. Your actions matter. What you do puts your sister's life in danger. You should be more careful."

Everything inside me shuts down. I was careful. I did everything he asked and more, but it wasn't enough. Nothing I do will ever be good enough for him. He'll always have this hold on me, and there's nothing I can do to make him happy. Nothing I can do to fucking live my life. I swallow hard, trying to push those depressing thoughts into a small box in the back of my brain. I can't let them consume me; that's how I'll drown. The old Journey will perish, and the new Journey will emerge as nothing more than an empty husk. A numb little puppet following the commands of her puppeteer.

I can't be her. I have to remain true to myself and not let his constant manipulations and tear-downs get to me.

"What's my new task, Sir?" I ask quietly, resigning myself to the fact I'm never getting out of this. I could single-handedly remove his enemies one by one, and he'd never thank me. He'd find something wrong with it and continually punish my sister for it.

Reaching into his pocket, he pulls out his phone and taps a few times. Turning it toward me, he shows me a picture of someone very familiar to me.

"Befriend Jenni Thomas. Get to know her. Go to family dinners. You are her new best friend. I want all the intel on her family life—her parents, her siblings, and most importantly, intel on that fuck she's 'banging'. Prove to me you can do this simple task, and we'll revisit the Sunny situation." My monster pulls out a handkerchief embroidered with the letter G and hands it to me. "Wipe away your pathetic tears," he sniffs, putting his nose in the air. "Your emotions will never get you anywhere."

I lick my lips and gently wipe the emotion from my face. Guilt rears its ugly head inside me, holding me captive.

I did that to my sister. She's slowly dying without a new heart, and I ripped it away from her when I didn't follow Jenni and Elias out of the party. Not that I had a car to follow them or anything. But still, if I had at least tried. If I had been better. If I... I shake my head, not allowing myself to fall into the trap of his manipulative ways. But how can I not when he's always knocking at the door with his insults and sneers.

This is my life.

"Okay," I say, sucking in a breath and letting it all go. "I will become her friend."

"Hmmm," he hums, taking a step forward, gently running his finger through my curls. "You're a good little snake when you try. This one is important. So, don't fuck this up. I need to know what's going on behind closed doors, and you're going to be the one to bring me that information."

"Of course. I promise I won't fuck this one up," I murmur, rolling my lips together when he finally drops my hair.

"Prove yourself to me and get the job done right," he says, stepping back. "Now, I must be off. Business to take care of."

"What about Sunny?" I dare to ask when he walks by me toward my bedroom door. "Is she..." I trail off.

"Still in the care center I put her in. Sunny will live without a new heart. For now, at least. She's getting the best care money can buy. Another thing to add to your debts."

With that, my monster walks out of my bedroom, leaving me standing in the silence of everything that just happened. The aftermath of my decisions weighs heavily on me when I walk to my tiny window and watch the man who took my life away from me climb into his expensive black SUV, and then he's gone.

CHAPTER EIGHT
Journey

TURNING BACK, I finally let more tears fall and sag onto my bed. The memory of the violin from so many years ago plays through my mind, soothing the crisis rising inside me. Closing my eyes, I relive the night before like a fantasy, reveling in the feel of their hands and basking in the life and light coming back to me. Under them, I was someone. They wanted me. Hell, they used me like I used them. An anonymous hookup that I'm going to hold close to my heart as I make it through high school and then beyond.

I may never get the freedom I crave, but that one sliver of light in my darkening world will anchor me in my most trying times, holding me to this earth.

Whatever my monster has in store for me, I'll survive. I have to. For Sunny. For my fucking sanity. I can't keep living under his thumb. If I do, I'll slowly wither away into the puppet he wants, and I won't give him the satisfaction of it.

I'm stronger than that.

Responsibility crushes down on me as I make my way out of my bedroom, making sure to shut the door behind me and lock it. Not only does my mom have a bad habit of drugs, but the means to pay for those drugs walks through our front door at every hour of the day. She wasn't always like this, bleeding herself dry just to catch a high. I remember a time when my mother read me stories and tucked me in at night. Then, one day the drugs grabbed hold of her and never let go. Even through her pregnancy with Sunny, it was hard to keep her sober and coherent. I blame her for Sunny's health issues. If she would have just stopped for nine months and given it a rest to bring a healthy child into this world, then all would have been well.

When I make it to the living room, I sigh at the sight before me.

"Want some food?" I ask, rubbing the side of my aching face, which will no doubt bruise later.

My mom's bright blue eyes snap to me as she pulls another drag from her cigarette. The smoke blows from her mouth, and she shrugs. "No." She turns away, going back to staring at her phone.

"You have to eat," I sigh, walking into the open kitchen off the living room.

A daughter shouldn't have to do this. I shouldn't have to take care of my mother like she's the child, making sure she eats or drinks. Hell, I even check her breathing at night before I crawl into bed to make sure she's still alive. My fear is one day, I'll come out here and she won't be here anymore. Then, I don't know what will happen to me or Sunshine. I'd be homeless, forced to do my monster's bidding from the streets. And Sunshine? She'd at least be cared for in the hospital she's locked in. It's a future I don't want to even imagine. As long as my mother is alive, I have a home and so does Sunny. From there? I have no clue.

I lick my lips when a package of donuts looks back at me from the counter top. Something I'll eat later after I make my mom and I lunch. My stomach rumbles, thanking whichever John stopped by to see my mom, for bringing these donuts. It happens from time to time. They're probably hoping to get into my good graces. Feed the barely legal adult, then maybe she'll sell herself, too. Fat chance. I've seen what they leave behind after they're done with my mom. I'm not interested in anything more than the food they leave me.

Most days, it's the donuts for breakfast, but occasionally there is sandwich meat, cheeses, condiments, bread, and potato chips that I know my mother hasn't bought herself. She barely eats and doesn't care about feeding me. So, that leaves the other people waltzing into my home.

I spend about thirty minutes in the kitchen making each of us a toasted cheese sandwich and give her a plate. I take mine back to my bedroom without watching to see if she eats. It's terrible to think, but sometimes I wonder what will happen if she just doesn't eat and lives on drugs alone. I know her body will fail her at some point. I love my mom; she gave me life—one that started out okay. We were happy, healthy, and then something happened that changed her into the woman she is today.

After eating my sandwich and contemplating the list I've made myself for the day, I decide to say fuck it and throw myself back into bed. It may only be three o'clock in the afternoon, but I've had about all I can handle today. Besides, the drowsiness that plagued me from the moment I woke up this morning comes back with a vengeance. I might as well sleep the day and night away, ready to start my mission tomorrow—making Jenni my friend.

Standing before my mirror, I sigh, staring over my tired appearance. Twinges of pain spread through me with every move I make. Out of curiosity, I lift my sweatshirt to reveal the bruises resembling teeth marks all over my body; I shudder at the feel of their ghost hands working over me.

Fuck. My soul ignites, coming back to life at the mere thought of my life in those strangers' hands. What I wouldn't give to know who they were so we could redo this time and time again. Fuck me and my stupid rules, but that's how it had to be at the time. No names. No faces. Just meaningless sex. Dropping my shirt, I turn on my heel and stop, frowning when my gaze falls to my much-needed lamp, dead on the floor.

That asshole shattered it to pieces in his anger and then didn't bother to pick it up. Typical. Shaking my head, I pick up the broken pieces and throw them away. My eyes flick to my nightstand and dread fills me at the prospect of spending my savings on a much-needed lamp. But there's no other way around it. When the sun goes down, hours from now, I'll need it to guide me through the night. Nothing gives me more anxiety than opening my eyes and seeing nothing but the darkness of my room.

You can do this. You can conquer the darkness when the sun goes down. Your demons won't be on your ass in the daylight.

I close my eyes, willing the damn memories to fucking leave me alone. But they never do. If it was my monster's goal to make me remember every piece of torture he did inflicted, he succeeded.

"What did you do, Journey!" her panicked voice echoes in my mind the moment my eyes close. "I'll make the call. I can't believe you did that! And to him, of all people. How could you? How could you do that to me?" she hisses, grabbing me by the hair and dragging me out of the room.

Blood.

Red.

It drips off my body.

"What did you do!" she shouts again, tightening her hold.

"What I had to do!" I cry out, shaking my head.

And then, nothing.

It's just one night. Sure, I could go grab another lamp from the store, but I dread leaving the safety of my room. He's out there. Somewhere. Ready to grab me and shove me into the basement again. The irrational paranoia and panic have me in a vice grip, constricting my throat. Even though he was just here and gave me a new job. The thought of him sticking me back in the darkness to rot, has me wavering on my feet.

So, instead of looking at my troubles head-on like an adult, I grab my massive headphones and put them over my ears. Avoidance at its best. Instantly, the sounds of Whispered Words and their tortuous melody fills my ears. I don't know who fucking hurt them, but their new album has me in a chokehold, speaking to me on so many levels. Their rock music helps to drown out my sorrows and chases the ghosts on my heels away.

Without a second thought, I grab the pill bottle hidden in my nightstand and pop three sleeping pills. They're my lifesavers. The tiny, round pills that take me from the nightmares that plague my mind every second while I sleep and eviscerate them. I'm dead to the world once those pills enter my system.

As the pills kick in and the drowsiness takes over, I pull my blankets over my body and settle into the comfort of my mattress. The events of the past twenty-four hours play over and over in my head, haunting me until I'm on the precipice of sleep, teetering in and out. Peace encases me for only a moment.

Nothing wakes me up. Nothing can disturb me.

And that's just the way I like it.

As Kieran Knight growls in my ears, singing the second part of Roaring River's Dead End, I fall into a much-needed sleep, ignoring the world and my responsibilities.

CHAPTER NINE

Arrow

HERE KITTY, kitty. Where have you gone?

I frown, peeking in her window. The guys think I'm out doing some sort of recon. I totally am but of the kitten variety. My aching heart pounds against my ribs when I stand outside her dusty window, watching as she sleeps soundly in her bed, without the blankets covering her body. Her long legs which were once wrapped around my waist, stick straight out, tempting me to lick them again. That needs to change, right? It is a little chilly out here for May. If I'm cold, then she has to be freezing. Right? She really needs me in there to warm her up with blankets and my naked body. I don't think she'd mind. She seemed to really enjoy our time together, and fuck...there goes my dick getting all hard again.

Time to make my grand entrance.

I rub my hands together before slowly lifting the window inch by inch, cringing when it squeaks the whole time until it's wide open. I grin. Silly, Kitten. You're supposed to lock your window every night. Now, the big, bad mafia man is about to infiltrate your space. I poke my head in her window before lifting myself up and climbing in, landing with a soft dismount.

"Oh, Kitty," I murmur, looking around her room as my camera swings from my neck. Something that usually never leaves my side. You never know when a picture-perfect moment will present itself. Case in point, last night during our first meeting with Journey. The pictures would have been magnificent keepsakes, but Jericho is a party pooper and told me to leave it at home.

Rude.

No matter. I have it now, and I'll have to make up for it ten fold.

"Oh, panties." My eyes snag on a bright pink pair just begging for me to take. I swipe them off the ground, holding them up to inspect them. One little sniff won't hurt, right? Her scent fills my nose, and my dick instantly bounces in my jeans. Down boy, we'll play with this dirty pair later.

Yeah, I'll save that for later. And I shove them into my pocket.

Despite her room being filled with clothes and shoes haphazardly thrown around, it smells like her. I suck in a breath, taking it in completely. Messy. Chaotic. I fucking thrive here with her.

"Oh, my Kitten. I can't believe I had to release you," I hum, hovering above her, watching her chest go up and down. I note the large headphones over her ears, no doubt blocking out all the noise around her. "If it were up to me, I would have taken you back to our lair and kept you in my bed forever." I pout, gently setting my lips against hers. Fuck. This is dangerous territory. She could wake up. Oh, yeah. That makes my dick turn harder than before. Whatever. I close my eyes, savoring the gentle one-sided kiss and sigh, pulling back. "One day, you'll actually be awake for that." I grin, gently running my hand through her hair, reveling in the feel of it wrapped around my fingers.

It was such a gamble coming here to see her. What kind of sleeper would she be? Would she wake up when I came inside? I'd hoped not. She slept so soundly in my arms when I drugged her. I hoped she'd be a heavy sleeper.

My eyebrows furrow when I look at the medicine bottle resting on her nightstand. Interesting. Potent sleeping pills. Hmmm. I wonder what they taste like. Probably bitter. I shake the bottle, letting the pills rattle around and finally open it up and pour a pill into my hand.

Yup. I'll save that for later. Anything my Little Kitten takes, I want to take, too. It'll help me feel closer to her. Besides, how fun.

I shove the lone pill into my pocket, promising myself I'll take it later when I'm ready for bed. For now, I soak in my girl's presence, taking in everything. The sweet scent. The way she snores. It's goddamn adorable.

I drop to my knees at the side of her bed and rest my chin on her mattress. I wonder how freaked out she'd be if she found me here, sitting beside her. She'd probably scream. Loud. Fuck. I don't want to scare her away, I'm just desperate to have her in my arms again. It's almost criminal how Jericho made me give her back. She's ours, damn it. No matter what Papa Gabriel has to say about the situation or the other marriage offer he might have on the table. There's no way we're ever going to go for someone else. From the first time I saw my Kitten, I knew she belonged to us, and we belong to no one but Journey.

I sigh, running my fingers up and down her bare arms. I don't miss the way goosebumps pimple under my touch or the way she sighs, relaxing more into the bed.

"So, good," she moans in her sleep, slightly twitching when my fingers find their way to her breasts. I gently circle her nipples poking through her T-shirt. "Mmmm," she hums, smacking her lips together.

"You're gonna make me come in my damn pants, Kitten," I mumble, adjusting myself and pulling my hand back.

Journey shifts in her sleep, turning on her side into the fetal position. Her ass points in my direction, giving me a beautiful view. My mind turns when I slowly lift her long T-shirt and nearly swallow my tongue when she's not wearing any panties.

But that's not my mission. Using the moonlight, I check the spot on her ass cheek now a beautiful black and blue color. Oh good. Her body is sending lots of blood to heal that spot after what I put on and in there. She'll never know the lengths I went to protect her. A giddiness takes over as I gently kiss the bruise, aiming to make it feel better. One day, she'll find out what's adorning her skin. But for now, my lips are sealed.

I could do a lot more to her while she sleeps. Fuck her. Take pictures. Anything under the sun. But I stop myself from going too far. There are limits that I don't want to cross. I want my Kitten to like me when we take her for ourselves. Not hate me or fear me because she woke up too soon.

My gaze lands on her bedroom door, fit with a large chair wedged under the doorknob. Curious. I meander over, doing one last sweep of her room before I leave for the night. Murmured voices ring out from the living room. One male and one female.

"She's... she's not for-for sale," the female voice, who must be her mother, says in a slurred voice. "She's only in high school."

"Next time," he rumbles, making a sucking sound.

My lip curls back as I finger my knife, resting in my pocket. If I carve their beating hearts from their chest, would my Kitten be angry? It's all for her, anyway. Always. I could present them in a clear case for her to see and display above the fireplace. Much like a mounted deer head. Only this would be a human heart from someone inquiring about her.

"Next-next time. Now, give me another hit."

"If that's a promise, Sable."

There aren't many things in life that set my teeth on edge. Torturing assholes? Nah. It's my favorite—a stress release. Tracking down bad guys—fucking bring it on.

But having some strange man, alluding to having fun with my Kitten. Mine. Theirs. Oh, no. That won't happen, asshat. My Kitten is all mine. Here, at least. I'll be here every night ensuring my girl is safe from the men her mom keeps around.

"Yup. A promise. You can have a taste of Journey. Not like she'll-she'll wake up," she slurs again with a sigh, no doubt reaching the high she's been aching for.

"Good," he chuckles, so menacingly my grin grows wider.

Oh, yes. Please, come back here and make my goddamn day.

Jitters spread through my nerves when heavy footsteps move closer to Journey's room. Closer and closer he moves, slowly creeping.

"Stupid bitch," he huffs from right outside her bedroom door, jiggling the knob a few times and growling again.

He seems to be having trouble coming through the door. What a shame. Maybe someone should help the poor man out. So, like the gentleman I am, I unlock Journey's door and remove the chair from beneath the knob. There's no doubt he'll come creeping through and zero percent chance my Kitten will wake up. She's too drugged and sleeping too deeply to even sense him enter.

I step back further into the shadows, concealing my face when the door creaks open ever so slightly. *Come on in, little intruder. It'll be the last thing you ever do. No one touches my little Kitten except the Devils. She's ours now.*

"Fucking bitch," the guy slurs, stumbling in through the dark room toward Journey's passed-out form. "Trying to keep me out."

My kitten doesn't even flinch when he hovers above her, examining her bare legs. Internally, I curse myself for not protecting her flesh with the blanket. That should have been the first thing I did after checking her bruise. But no matter, he won't last much longer. He's looking at something that doesn't belong to him.

The shadows and I move as one, concealing me until I'm standing right behind the man. The smell of rank onions wafts off his skin when I peek over his shoulder. His fingers tremble, resting just above Journey's leg. Hovering there with ill intent. Well, until I grab his wrist and pull it straight back until the bones contort and snap under the pressure of my hand.

My other hand slaps over his mouth when he cries out, filling the room with his agony.

"Ah-ah, you shouldn't touch things that don't belong to you," I murmur, directly into his ear.

His wails grow higher pitched and his breaths pick up.

Tiny hits land on my shins as he kicks me. But I'm not deterred. The pain fuels my anger as I crack his wrist back further, basking in the way his body tenses in my grasp.

"I don't think you'll be touching anything any time soon."

Not that he'll live to ever do anything like this again. He's going straight to meet my growly friends—Maximilian and Nova. My pet lions, gifted to me by Jericho's father for my tenth birthday. What a hell of a way to ring in that year. Through the years, they've aided me in many interrogations. Place a man who doesn't want to squeal in the center of a lion's cage, he doesn't last very long. He'll spill his guts—literally—in a matter of minutes.

"Please!" he cries out in a pathetic voice from under my hand.

"Please what?" I ask, dragging him away from Journey to the corner of the room. Although I'd love for her to wake up and see what I'm doing to protect her, I can't chance her seeing this. "Please don't break your kneecap? That's always been a satisfying crunch. Please don't chop your balls into little pieces? I can't make any promises."

Tears roll down his face, drenching my fingers. Gross. There's nothing worse than tears. Not even blood. God, I love blood. Especially this man's. I can't wait to paint the world with his red life source.

"I wasn't going to touch her... I just wanted a look. Her mom keeps her hidden. She..." I grin, spin him around, and grip the front of his shirt tightly. I rear my fist back and slam it into his mouth until teeth spring from their place and land on the ground.

Oh, gifts for later.

"Ah, no. Think again. She is not for you to look at or touch. That girl is mine. She belongs to the Devils."

Ah. There it is. The paling. The sweating. My fingers twiddle with the fun stabber in my pocket. No, not my dick. Although, I could call him stabber instead of Big A. The little gift in my pocket is the necessary syringe I carry everywhere—the night-night juice. Jericho just doesn't understand why I need it. Well, this is prime example number one. You never know when someone needs to go to sleep in a matter of seconds. Chloroform can't even do that.

"So, you've heard of us? We're pretty notorious. You heard what we did down at the docks, didn't you?" I wiggle my brows when he shakily nods in my grip, and I continue my beautiful story. "That's when we obliterated the people responsible for running bad drugs and guns. We don't take kindly to people like you sneaking into places they shouldn't be and touching things that don't belong to them. You remember their bodies in the papers, don't you? Splattered all over the news. It was a warning. One, apparently, you didn't take seriously." The asshole shakes uncontrollably in my grip, basically pissing himself when he realizes just what he's done. Maybe I should let him go to warn the others traipsing through this house night and day. Or, on second thought, I need some entertainment.

"Then you'll expect this." My grin grows wider when I plunge the fresh needle into his neck, dropping his consciousness like it's fucking hot.

Bye, bye rapey asshole. When you wake up, we'll have some fun.

I throw the fuckhead through the open window with ease and laugh when he rolls on the ground outside. I quickly find his teeth that fell out and scoop them into my palm. Grinning, I take the Polaroid camera hanging from a strap around my neck, snapping a picture of the man on the ground with blood trickling from his mouth.

"Perfect," I murmur, grabbing the picture and waving it around, revealing the black and white image of him on the ground. "She'll love this." I grin when I find a marker on her desk, writing a note at the bottom of the picture. "I'm always watching."

I move beside her bed, placing the picture and his teeth on her pillow. Tomorrow, she'll know I protected her from the hands of this jerkwad. She'll be so happy! I take another picture of her sleeping soundly, remove it from the Polaroid camera, and wave it around.

Shit. I wish I could keep this with me forever. But she deserves to know what she looked like while she slept so deeply. So peaceful and carefree. She'll thank me later for saving her life.

"Goodnight, Kitten," I whisper, leaning down and kissing her lips. "We'll be together soon." Forever and ever. I've had a taste, and now, I need more and more.

My obsession festers under my skin, begging me to do everything under the sun to her. Tie her up. Gag her. Lock her to my bed. But I resist. For now. We've got shit to prove to her over the next few weeks. We'll grow our empire with our queen by our side and finally take everything from the paranoid asshole running these streets.

"No, Sunshine," she mumbles, twitching in her sleep. Her arms flail and her breaths pick up. Her head thrashes back and forth until she shoots up, eyes wide open.

I freeze beside her, taking in her glazed-over eyes darting around the room.

"Sunshine?" I question, waving a hand in front of her face.

She doesn't twitch or move. Hell, her eyes don't focus on me at all. How curious. She's sleep-talking. Sleep-sitting up and doesn't notice me staring deep into her eyes. I wonder if I could make her into my little puppet.

Lift your shirt, Little Puppet. Let Arrow get a glimpse.

"Sunshine!" she gasps, reaching a hand out before it falls back onto the mattress. "Don't leave me again," she cries, tears falling down her cheeks. With a gasp, Journey falls backward into the mattress, and her eyes fall shut. She curls in on herself in the fetal position, sobbing into her pillow. "Please, don't hurt me."

My fascination grows, bursting like a damn balloon. My girl has some secrets crawling beneath her flesh, eager to escape. Well, we'll help in that adventure.

I sigh when my phone buzzes in my pocket.

SHEPP

Recon? Really?

Arrow...

Well, shit. I can practically feel his growl of authority from here.

ME

Prepare the King and Queen! I'm bringing them back a chew toy.

SHEPP

.... What. Did. You. Do?

Ugh. He's so nosy.

ME

I'm as innocent as a flower. Also, set out a tall glass of orange juice. And pickles! I have a hankering for some dills.

I lick my lips at the combination. Murder works up quite the appetite, something only pickles and orange juice can supply. Speaking of...

I glance out the window at the would-be rapist and tut in his direction. Bad boy. Now, you'll pay. Before hopping out, I tuck Journey in, covering her body. I relock her door and place the chair beneath the knob. She can keep others out, but not me. I'll always find a way in. I'll crawl through the damn wall and live there just to get a glimpse of her every night.

I make it look like I wasn't there.

Except I was.

And the proof is in the pudding. Or on her pillow. And definitely will be in these panties I stole.

I grin, clutching my Polaroid one last time, and take another picture of her panties wrapped around my fingers. Bright pink contrasting to my pale skin makes for the perfect goodbye when I set the developed picture over the other.

What a lovely surprise she'll wake up to tomorrow. Too bad I can't be here to see her reaction. Hell, maybe cameras are necessary. They'll keep her safe, that's for sure. But that's what I'm here for.

"No one will touch you again, Kitten. Not on my watch."

I hum, checking the bottom nightstand drawer next to her bed. If I were a girl and had a fun, sexy toy, where would I keep it? Ah, right here that's where.

"You won't need this, Kitten. I'll get you a better one." I grin, plucking her bright pink vibrator from her drawer and putting it in my pocket. There's no way she should be allowed to touch something like this when it's the wrong shape and size—aka—it's not mine. Or Jericho's. Or Shepp's. Ah, yes. I'll get her better ones she can use on herself to prepare her tight cunt for what's about to come in a few weeks.

I make my way out the window and head straight for the unconscious man on the lawn.

"Let's go meet the Queen and King of Viotto manor. I'm sure they have something very important to growl at you while I pull you to pieces for even attempting to touch my girl." If I could take her away from this place without interference, then I would.

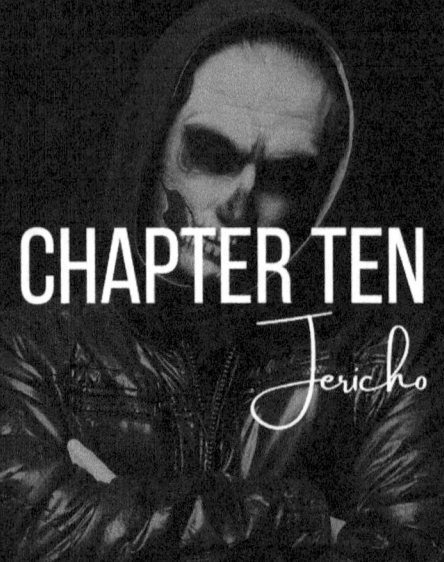

CHAPTER TEN
Jericho

RELIEF FLIES through me the moment I lift my violin from its case resting on the bookshelf in my home office. It's like all the worries running rampant through my mind disappear the moment I touch the smooth wood and cradle it against my chin.

Anticipation runs through my veins, counting down the seconds until I draw my bow over the strings and losing myself in the melodies ringing out through the small room.

For only a moment, my internal fears take hold. The bright futures Arrow, Shepp, and I hold flash through my mind, until they're drowned out by the beautiful music cleaning the room and washing everything else away. My body instinctively sways as I stand, weaving the bow over the strings rapidly coming to a crescendo in my song.

It's hauntingly beautiful. A song of my own creation, created under the duress of my father's watchful eye. Every night as a child, I stood in front of him as he worked, playing my heart out. Until he was done with me. If I fucked up, then there was hell to pay. More time in the darkness, thinking about my misdeeds.

Perhaps it was a lesson in what's to come when the boys and I fully integrate into the organization. In the coming weeks when we pledge ourselves to the family, more responsibilities will fall on our shoulders. Something my father reminded me of earlier today when he dropped by the mansion while the sun was high in the sky. A rarity for Gabriel Viotto. He hasn't walked through those doors since he left years before, giving the mansion to the boys and I. Our meetings always reside in the tower he built to protect himself.

But not today.

"Once you're a man, I want you and the boys in charge of the runners," my father says, clasping his hands behind his back and pacing in front of me. "They've been traveling to your uncle's territories to collect from our casinos and nightclubs."

The runners—men of the family who collect funds from our various gambling institutions throughout California, bringing back the money owed to us.

"Of course, Sir," I say politely with a nod.

"They're being killed off or recruited, Son," he says with a frown as his fists clench at his sides. "Someone is taking them away from their positions, and they're disappearing without a goddamn trace."

"Any leads?"

My father's furious stare drills through me with accusation.

"Shadow," he grits out angrily. "He's the only one who swoops in and steals things that don't belong to him." His jaw tics, and his gaze falls away.

Shadow. Of course.

My eyes narrow at the man continually pacing across my opulent office space. A familiar feeling bubbles to the surface. A feeling I get when a liar stands before me and opens his mouth. He's holding back. There's something else there he's not telling me. Typical.

"Noted. Want me to step up and take responsibility for the runners?"

My father nods. "Smart thinking. You're in charge of them now. Make sure they're staying in line and not fraternizing with the enemy. And find me that bastard before he crosses the line!" He growls the last part as he picks up a whiskey tumbler and tosses it against the wall.

I don't dare move when his chest heaves and his fingers tighten into fists.

My father doesn't lose his shit in front of others often, but when he does, his tantrum is overly dramatic.

Pathetic.

Our main gambling hub is set in the VIP room of my father's famous club—Rave—overlooking the crowds dancing below. It will become our home away from home as we continue to build our side gigs, away from my father's prying eyes. Despite Rave belonging to my father, the boys and I took over the moment we turned eighteen; with my father's blessing, of course.

Despite being semi-initiated near our sixteenth birthdays and having blood ties to my father, we started at the bottom as low-level members, like any other new initiate. The plebs, training under the bosses and doing bitch work. Hard work and determination have sealed our fates. And we'll continue to solidify our role as members of the family until our full initiation hits at the end of May.

Then, the real work begins.

Clinking metal grabs my attention from the doorway of my office, forcing me to still and cease the flow of music. I blink several times, coming back to myself by pushing the memories into the back of my mind. I heave a breath, setting my violin back into its case and securing the bow.

I turn on my heels, facing Shepp's worried expression as he stands in the doorway, watching me intently.

Paint covers his hands, and small splotches dot his cheeks when he tilts his head.

'He brought home a fucking body,' Shepp signs, shaking his head. *'And put it in the cage.'*

Every muscle in my body goes rigid. Arrow bringing home a body? It's not too unusual. But to put them in the lion's den without Shepp and I to supervise. Well, that's a goddamn disaster.

"In the cage?" I question, slowly standing from behind the desk I've been at for hours now.

'Inside, Jer,' he signs with a huff. *'He's going to get himself killed.'*

Possibly. I trust Arrow with every fiber of my being. With my life, my love's life, and Shepp's. In most cases, anyway. When he's riled up and aching to kill, his common sense seems to slip through the window, leaving him soulless with one purpose—death.

I sigh. If Arrow has a body—hopefully still alive—inside his pet lion's large enclosure, then I have to intervene. He's either dangling them by their ankles above growling lions, locked them to the bloodied rock, or he's tied him to a chair, ready to interrogate. The man is unpredictable at best, completely unhinged at worst.

Coming to stand before Shepp, I note the worry hanging in his eyes as he inspects my indifferent expression. I crane my neck, staring up at the large mass I've come to call my brother. He may not be blood related, but he's had my back far more times than anyone with my blood running through their veins. I only wish he'd lighten up in his old age. One day, he'll keel over from a stress-related death. Instead of something predictable, like a shot to the chest or head.

"Shall we?" I gesture for him to lead the way.

He huffs at me, eyeing me up and down. Every worrying thought Shepp has displays on his expressive face, letting me know exactly how he feels about this situation.

'Fine,' he signs, turning on his heel and storms away with me casually on his tail.

Our footsteps echo through the vast hallway leading toward the backdoor. Marble floors, grand staircases, high-class chandeliers. Over twenty years ago, my father built only the best for my mother; when he was so in love he could barely breathe. Then, she no longer existed, taking every ounce of love he had to give with her. Such a pity, too. Losing Grace Viotto made my father a shell of who he once was. Changing him for the absolute worse. Her disappearance sent my father into madness, leaving me to pick up the pieces and take the brunt of his pain. It also left me with this monstrosity of a home, fit with a zoo and multiple rooms I have no use for.

If only I could turn back time and face the ghosts of my past head on. Find my mother. Speak with her. But I can't. They're all gone, buried under a mound of secrets I've yet to dig up.

When the cool spring air smacks me in the face, I focus on the present danger lurking on the back half of our large property. Shepp frowns, urging me into the passenger's seat of our ridiculous golf cart.

For miles, shrubbery, flowers, and large trees decorate our land. Our mansion sits conveniently on a hill, overlooking the town of Briar Cove. Although my father built everything for my mother, he also built it as a status symbol, taking over two-hundred acres of land. He also built her a zoo on the back half of our property. Fit with proper enclosures for all the animals she adored and saved. At one point, he had even hired a zookeeper to keep my mother's prized animals safe.

Then, she disappeared, destroying everything. My father. His sanity. Her zoo.

"Toughen up. You're the heir to this, Jericho Michelangelo Viotto. This is your kingdom. This will teach you to cry over ice cream."

I was five when my father threw me into the dark basement closet for the first time, leaving me there to rot until he saw fit. Rage lived in his eyes, blackening them into oblivion. He etched his cruel words into my skin with every volatile thing he spewed into the darkness, until I was a crying child, begging his father to stop. He didn't, of course. Why would he? That was the day he introduced me to the demon that lived in his soul, loving the emotional and mental torture he rained down on me.

It wasn't the first or last time he punished me for simply being a child. The first time was because I cried over my ice cream spilling off the cone. Another was when I pouted because I didn't get the toy I begged for on Christmas. Every indiscretion on my part had the same outcome—the basement closet, which only started after my mom's disappearance when I was four.

Did he mold me into the perfect, unfeeling monster he wanted? Halfway. I'm still me. I've clung to my humanity for all these years, begging my moral compass to guide me when I was stumbling through the dark.

But I'm still a monster.

There's no denying that.

Shepp maneuvers the golf cart down the concrete path through the remnants of my mother's old zoo and finally parks it in front of the lit up lion's enclosure. Giving us the first peek at what toy Arrow decided to bring home to play with.

Wonderful.

'Here,' Shepp signs, gesturing toward the spectacle.

"Here indeed," I remark, unhurriedly jumping out of the golf cart.

Shoving my hands into my slack pockets, I leisurely make my way toward the enclosure with Shepp at my side. I cock my head at the spectacle before me.

'What the hell is he doing?' Shepp signs, furrowing his brows after clicking his rings to get my attention.

"Whatever he pleases," I mutter, turning back and watching Arrow's pacing form with sick fascination.

A demented look twists his face as he waves around his favorite hunting knife, perfect for piercing through flesh. His tattoos ripple on his shirtless back with every manic step he takes, muttering words to the poor unconscious man tied to a small wooden chair who has no idea what's in store for him when his eyes pop open. Not twenty feet away, rests Arrow's precious cats, watching his every move with interest. They're lazily lying on their bellies with cocked heads and ears alert. Not yet a threat, but hunger bleeds in their eyes.

Max and Nova are simply biding their time until they're the stars of the show, catching their unsuspecting prey until he screams. Or maybe that's Arrow's intention. Either way, the man tied to the chair doesn't stand a chance.

Now, I need to figure out if the punishment fits the crime.

"Care to explain why you're pacing in the middle of Max and Nova's domain?" I ask, raising a brow.

Arrow stops suddenly, darting his gaze to me. Nothing lies behind his glossy eyes, his soul long gone and retreated into a black box. Leaving behind the blood thirsty man staring back at me with a lifeless expression.

"Arrow!" I shout into the void, attempting to grab his arm when the man on the ground stops moving. His chest heaves. Blood smears all across his face. I jolt Arrow around, forcing his tall frame to face me. The blank look in his eyes is something I've witnessed before with my father. He's lost himself in the darkness of murder and debauchery. "I want you to listen to me," I say in a stern voice, keeping my hands wrapped around his biceps. "Do you hear me?" I ask again, gently squeezing his arms.

He blinks several times. There it is. There's the focus I've been waiting for. His brows furrow until he sees the carnage of his darkness.

"You let your darkness eat away at you again," I simply state, stepping back from his shivering frame. "What was his crime?"

His lips curl as he stares at the man on the ground, giving him one last kick to the head. Arrow doesn't utter a word when he leans down, picking the man up off the ground. Even though he's only seventeen, his strength knows no bounds.

I watch in fascination as he begins walking through the middle of town at ten p.m. with a man barely clinging to life on his back. He doesn't speak, too lost in the thoughts most likely consuming him.

But I follow.

I'll always protect him. No matter what.

"No." That is all he says when he punches the man again, knocking his head to the side from the force.

"Okay. Care to explain then who this man is?" Clearly, I won't make any headway down this route. Time to start asking the important questions that will pique his interest.

I hum, eyeing the dirty stranger and taking in his features. He doesn't seem familiar. With simple, worn jeans and a stained white T-shirt, he's a simpleton. Not of our status. Which begs the question as to why he's tied up on our property with a metaphorical sign attached to his forehead saying dead man sitting.

As a general rule of thumb, we do no harm to the general public. A rule created by the first generations of crime families many moons ago. Technically, we're supposed to run under the radar and keep a low profile, never letting the authorities get to us.

Here in Briar Cove, though? We run these streets. The police are in our pockets, paid to turn the other cheek when bodies show up riddled with bullet holes and missing parts. The one good thing my father did for his family before falling into the darkness of grief and paranoia.

"He was in her room." Arrow's jaw clenches as he paces in front of the man, half-naked with his shirt thrown off and his jeans unbuttoned. Thankfully, he's kept his shoes on this time as he wades through the trimmed grass of the enclosure.

Max and Nova were handed to Arrow for his birthday as cubs. And he's raised them ever since. Day after day, he made sure they were taken care of and fed. He even designed their enclosure. Right now, they rest beside each other, eyeing Arrow with interest. They feed off his agitation but make no move to hunt him down. To them, he's their companion. The one who feeds them and loves them.

My teeth sit on edge when he continues his pacing and pulling at his hair, muttering to himself. Whatever this man did, he deserves this.

"He was in whose room?" I ask, rocking on my feet with a pit opening in my stomach. "Arrow!" I shout, making him stop dead beside the unconscious man. His bare back heaves with every breath he takes. "Answer me. Fight through the darkness. Whose room was he in?" I bark out, making him tense at my tone. Good. It's the only way I can pull him out of the abyss.

"He was in Journey's goddamn room! Of course, I have a reason to bring him here! He was... He was... Fuck!" Arrow's booming voice echoes through the land, but only one word reverberates through my mind. Journey. Her room.

Red blurs my vision. My heart rate spikes. I swear my blood pressure shoots so high a headache forms in my skull, pounding to the beat of his yells. Journey's room. My fucking future wife's room! He was there in her room? Where were my men? Watching her on the fringes?

"Fuck!" I roar, slamming my fist into the thick metal of the enclosure.

"Now you see. Now you fucking see why I brought him here! He deserves to lose his fucking balls!" Arrow shouts, punching the man in the nuts.

The pathetic bastard's eyes pop open just in time to realize he's trapped. He yanks at the restraints, eyes darting around, looking for an escape. Arrow bends down, picking up the shiny knife he once held and must have thrown.

"No! No! Fuck!" The man cries out when Arrow slices the sharp end of the knife through the man's right hand. His cries echo, drowning out Arrow's manic growls.

And that's when he absolutely loses his shit. I knew he would when he requested orange juice and pickles. His official celebratory treat after a successful mission. Sometimes, I wonder if the bitter taste helps his humanity return. Or what little humanity he has.

Was he born with morals and humanity? Debatable. Did my father help to mold him into this? Absolutely.

The once unconscious man is now fully awake and screaming as his fingers lie on the grass. Wonderful. We'll have to clean that up later. Or not. The lions lick their lips, inching closer to the mayhem, eager to pick the man apart with their sharpened teeth.

He sees them, of course, screaming more as blood spurts all over Arrow, soaking him in his favorite shade of red.

"Why!" Arrow shouts. "Tell me why you thought you could touch her or be there in her presence! You unworthy fucking worm!" Arrow heaves, shoving the knife through the man's other hand, taking all his fingers off with one blow.

The man cries out again, tears leaking down his face. Snot blows from his nose when he slumps in the chair, his adrenaline taking away the pain of his torture.

"I... I... I wasn't going to do anything!" the man shouts in defense.

"And standing over her about to touch her was your idea of not doing anything?" Arrow grunts, slamming the pointed end of the knife straight into the man's chest. "You'll never harm another person again, you piece of shit."

A darkness clouds my vision, much like seeing red. My wife! My goddamn woman. If the man was still breathing after that last blow, I'd fucking pull his heart out with my fist. No one touches what is ours, especially this low-life piece of shit sneaking into her room hoping to cop a feel. The heat of my anger creeps up the back of my neck. Standing over her? About to fucking touch her? My fingers flex, eager to punch the motherfucker's face in myself. But, I collect myself and let the man at the center of the cage carry out the man's sentence.

"End his fucking life," I growl, clinging to the fencing like my life depends on it. If I don't, I'll march in there with two hungry lions and a serial killer without a second thought.

I squeeze my eyes shut, counting backward from ten. Something Shepp taught me long ago to calm my nerves. I seek him out when he squeezes my shoulder, bringing me back from the brink. We all have our faults. And my darkness is mine. Much like Arrow's. We're one in the same. Yet, so different.

'Fuck that guy,' Shepp signs with rigid movements, his fingers almost looking robotic with every move, displaying his anger. His

nostrils flare when Arrow lets out an animalistic roar, standing above his victim. *'He touched her.'*

"So, he tried to touch what wasn't his?" I reiterate what Shepp said out loud through my contained rage.

Shepp shoots me an appreciative look for voicing his words without having to gain Arrow's attention. Not that he'd be able to. Arrow is too lost in the fog of chaos; he won't come back until the threat is neutralized and no longer an issue.

"Duh!" Arrow shouts. "Did you think I'd bring someone back here for shits and giggles?"

"Quite frankly, yes," I quip, putting my hands behind my back, feeling a calmness rush over me. The man before me is about to meet his end. One less scumbag on the streets or in my future wife's bedroom. "But now I see the full picture. You should have made him suffer more by ripping his dick off and shoving it up his own ass." I grin when Arrow flashes me a demonic-esque smirk and rips the knife from the man's sputtering chest.

"You hear that? I should have made you suffer more." The man's eyes widen as he sputters through the pain of his stab wound and missing fingers. "Tell me or you die." Oh, he's dying anyway. There's no doubt about that. But he's giving the man an opportunity to explain himself.

"She was... was off limits," he wheezes, spurting blood between his lips like a pathetic man on the verge of losing his dick. Oh, wait, he is. "I wanted a taste. I wanted to touch her. I wanted..."

Arrow stiffens with every word and finally puts an end to the man's ramblings. The knife plunges right through his throat until he gurgles, trying to draw in air. His ruined body slumps in the chair, devoid of life.

Arrow's chest heaves when he steps back, dripping with warm blood. A grin spreads across his face. Any normal person would cower in fear, but he draws me in. There's a reason he's basically my brother. He dropped into our laps when we were six, and my father took him in under strange circumstances.

"Priest," my father says, settling in his leather seat behind his desk.

His eyes fall on me as I stand beside him, silently watching the nervous priest take a seat across from us with a little boy in tow. I've seen him before. He's the head priest of the church my father likes to frequent to beg God to forgive him for his sins so he can repeat them the next week. Usually, he's draped in white with a serious expression. But today he's wearing loose jeans and a nice button down shirt. Pain is etched into his expression when he looks at his son and then back at us.

"Have you finally come to your senses?" my father asks with a grin, steepling his fingers.

For whatever reason, the boy has been on his list of people he wants in his inner circle. Maybe it's the crazy that lights up the boy's eyes that has my father interested. He's all for training soldiers young and forcing their loyalty.

The priest licks his lips, looking at the little blond boy, near my age, wiggling beside him.

"Yes," he says softly. "I can no longer contain him within the church and keep him hidden from my superiors. I'm at risk of losing my priesthood if he's discovered. Arrow, calm down," he speaks the last part with loving patience for the boy named Arrow and his wild ways.

Arrow grins up at him, exposing his top two missing teeth. Defiantly, he wiggles more, sticking his tongue out at his dad until the priest sighs, pinching the bridge of his nose.

"The clergy wouldn't approve of your bastard love child?" my father quips.

"No," the priest retorts in a low voice. "I want better for him since his mother ran off when he was born. I can't keep him hidden if he's beside me. I need..."

"Me," my father interrupts. "Well, you've come to the right place. You know the score, Priest."

"I want to see him every Sunday," he demands softly, running his fingers through Arrow's wild blond hair. "For an hour at least, after church for a private lunch."

I blink several times, memorizing the look he gives Arrow. It's full of love and admiration. Nothing my father has ever given me. Just last night he shoved me in the dark closet again, all in the name of making me a tougher boy. The only emotion I feel toward my father is hate and disgust every time he shuts the door, leaving me there until I'm curled in a ball, listening to the sounds of the men he's torturing.

"Done," my father says without objection, which seems odd for him. "The Viotto family will begin attending Mass every Sunday, in exchange for a room in your church, and I'll raise your boy myself." He grins at Arrow who stills, narrowing his eyes at my father. "I'll harness that defiance and guide him in the ways of the family. He'll be the perfect addition. At no charge."

The priest sucks in a breath. "No charge? You're willing to take him with no fee?"

"No fee," my father says with a shrug, rising to his feet. "You see, Victor. Your son shows great potential. He's perfect for this life. One I can give him and you cannot. You walk with God. I walk with the devil. Our deal is this. Arrow is mine. Hell, I'll even give him my last name so he'll be hidden from your precious clergy. You'll be free to run your church and live your life, no longer having to worry about him bringing you dead cats and squirrels." My father grins again when my stomach drops.

He's a psycho kid.

"I... How did you know?" the priest asks, bewildered by my father's statement.

"I have my ways. I always know."

"Okay. He's yours. I just... every Sunday. I do love my son. I just can't risk his behavior or existence getting out. Take care of my boy, please," he whispers, holding back the emotions shimmering in his eyes.

"Always," my father says with a smirk, holding out his hand. *"Let's shake on it."*

"I know what I have to do now," Arrow says, inspecting his blood-soaked knife.

'Bury the body in the woods?' Shepp signs with an eye roll as I repeat his sarcastic quip out loud.

"Beyond that," Arrow grunts, pacing the enclosed space in front of the lifeless man. "I want to wipe men like that off the face of the earth. If I hadn't been there!" He grunts, throwing the knife straight into the chest of the dead man. "He would have hurt her. It could have been my dad or anyone else that he hurt for that matter."

Ah. There's that sliver of humanity that lives deep inside of him. Arrow only cares about a few things—Journey, his loving father, and innocent people.

"He would have. If you hadn't been there," I grit out, squeezing my fingers into fists. This man walked into my future wife's room, attempting to touch her. Then, there's Arrow, touching things he's not allowed to touch yet. No matter that we already did, behind our masks with hidden identities. We need to lie low until we can take her into our arms. Who knows what that fucker would have done to her while she was sleeping. Fuck. My nostrils flare until I turn away, grounding myself.

Deep breaths. Arrow took care of the bastard. He's no longer a threat to Journey. He's no one. Anyone who dares to touch what's ours from here on out will pay the price.

I turn on my heels, watching the lions lying intently near the scene. Blood pools on the grass, splatter so close to them they could probably lick it. They're loose in their enclosure, free to roam the area with Arrow, but they don't. Whatever Arrow says, they seem to listen.

"Stay," Arrow says, pointing a finger at his precious over-sized cats as they tilt their heads and lick their lips with anticipation. "Daddy is going to get you some meat to eat while I clean up this mess." I raise a brow as he baby talks the large cats staring at him with obedience. "You're not allowed to eat this piece of meat."

Arrow huffs and disappears into the roofed shelter, situated inside the vast enclosure. His lions watch his every move from their resting place. Over the years, Arrow has built the large enclosure into a luxury resort for his pets. They have over twenty-acres of land to roam with large fencing stopping them from leaping out. Not that they'd want to. Why would they? Arrow has ensured they're never hungry, have toys to play with, rocks to lie on, and water to drink and play in. He's taken care of everything, ensuring his babies never wanted for nothing. During the day, an expert comes through and helps to continue their care and make sure they're healthy.

It's a win-win.

Arrow comes out of the shelter with a frown, throwing both lions large pieces of raw meat in front of their faces to reward them for their good behavior. He then works to drag the man out of the enclosure completely and throws him into the woods like he doesn't weigh a thing.

"I'll deal with him later. Right now, I have ideas." He grins, rubbing his bloodied hands together.

'And they are?' Shepp signs when we step up to him.

"Cleaning the streets of Briar Cove of people like him. People who could harm my Kitten. I want to take them all out and fucking obliterate them!" he shouts, throwing something against the hard surface of the building.

"And how do you plan on doing that?" I ask, curious to know what's going through his demented mind.

He's always needed something to pull him away from his murderous tendencies. Since my father started training him in the basement, alongside me.

"I have my ways. I need to talk to my father." He marches past us.

"It's the middle of the night, Arrow," I grumble, running a hand down my face.

"It's five a.m.; the priest will be up preparing for the day," he snarks.

"Then clean yourself up first. Shepp and I will take care of the body."

Arrow grins. "By Wednesday, I'll have something set up. Something to show you and my Kitten that I have a plan for the future. I'm taking out the trash. Permanently."

I sigh when Arrow walks out of sight toward the house.

'What the fuck just happened?' Shepp signs as we make our way toward the body Arrow haphazardly threw into the brush.

"No idea," I say, double-checking the lions' cage and locking it. We can't have our prized cats wandering into town and eating people.

I blink several times at the sound of a loud car engine booming to life and then taking off.

'He...' Shepp scrunches his face. *'He's leaving now? Did he even wash up? Father Amour is going to flip his shit.'*

Correct. After witnessing the exchange of Arrow between my father and his, I've come to learn that the good priest is terrified of Arrow's actions and what he's capable of. Understandable. He's got quite the appetite for blood and mayhem. But he has heart, too. Only, as a kid he didn't understand how to articulate his needs and wants. Like now. If I could have held him back, then I would have. But Arrow does whatever Arrow wants. Only bribing and other means keeps him occupied.

"Whatever idea he had must have been important." I shrug, leaning down to inspect the man's bloodied face. "Looks like a junkie," I hum, following the track lines in the crook of his elbow.

"Let's get this over with."

And so we do, burying the body as the sun peeks over the horizon, leaving me to my thoughts. From here on out, Journey will never be alone. My guys will be on her, watching her every move.

"We're taking her early," I grunt, heaving dirt to the side as the hole gets bigger.

Shepp stops abruptly with his shovel in the dirt, eyeing me. Moving his shovel to the side and leaning it on his chest, he huffs.

'What do you mean take her early?' he questions, raising his brows.

I grin, forcing the shovel into the dirt again and heave another shovel full to the side.

"Journey West is ours. She is meant to be by our side. No matter what. We could wait until she graduates to please my father. But she doesn't have the time. Men are sneaking into her fucking room at night because her mother can't make a buck doing a real job. She's putting Journey in danger, and I won't fucking stand for it anymore. So, yes. We're taking Journey early," I grunt again, the night's frustrations festering inside me.

'How?' Shepp signs.

Well, that's the question, isn't it. "I've got ideas, but none that are concrete. I'll figure it out," I say confidently, heaving more dirt out. "Now, let's throw this body into the hole, set it on fire, spit on his fucking face, and then brainstorm."

Shepp rolls his eyes, kicking the body into the hole. *'Don't we have men to do this for us?'* he signs.

I snort, a feeling of elation roaring through my veins. For so long, I've itched to have Journey in my arms and in my bed. Now, I almost have her.

"Yes. But why bother them when we can have a bonding moment?" I quip.

CHAPTER ELEVEN

Journey

MUSIC CONTINUALLY BLASTS in my ears the moment my brain comes back to the land of the living, clearing out the thick fog of my nightly sleep meds. I groan, wanting to head back into my dreamless sleep without interruption. Like that will happen.

Now that my brain is back online, there's no hiding under my covers until I can fall back to sleep. I've been in bed for over fourteen hours. It's time to move and go buy a new lamp. Thankfully, there's no school today. If I stayed in bed, then my brain would torture me over and over with past events I can't outrun. And taking more pills to block out my shitty life is not an option.

Warmth spreads through me as I stare up at the blank white ceiling, taking several deep breaths, enjoying the last moments under my warm blankets. Do I really have to leave? Can't these blankets adopt me and keep me safe forever? Fuck.

Without another thought, I take my headphones off and sigh at the ringing in my ears—the leftover evidence Whispered Words sang to me all night long on repeat. Man, I just can't get enough of their music. One day I'll see them live—when I'm free from this hellhole.

As the ringing subsides, the silence sets in. And when the silence sets in, my thoughts begin to wander, taking me to dangerous places. Somedays, I wish waking up wasn't so hard and that I could go back to my good dreams whenever they grace me. There, I'm a princess with a long dress and a charming prince who caters to my every need. I'm valued for more than what I can do for someone else.

One day, I'll be out from beneath my monster's shadow. Then, I'll disappear with my sister and never come back. We'll live on a mountain, in a small cabin where no one can reach us. Well, a girl can dream. Once she's healthy. Until then, I have to work my ass off to prove myself and get Sunshine back to where she belongs. Out of the hospital with a new heart and back in my arms, safely away from anyone who can harm us.

My toes tingle when I kick off the blankets and slowly sit up on the edge of the bed. Blindly, I grab my phone from my worn nightstand and scroll through social media. It's my morning routine. For the first ten minutes after my eyes open, everything feels sluggish and groggy.

Well, until my heart jolts at the pictures coming across the screen. It's me. Them. Together at the fucking party. No one can tell it's me, though. There I am in my cat mask, surrounded by the three masked men, hovering around me like predators trying to capture their prey. It's there in their eyes. Every emotion they didn't want me to see. Their eyes shine with want and drip with lust. The way they look down at me and have their hands on my waist sends goosebumps down my arms. I swallow hard, inspecting the four of us huddled together in the middle of the dance floor, staring at one another like we're the only people in the room.

Fuck.

Tingles work up my legs and straight into my sore pussy that convulses from the memory of their hands on me and their dicks plowing into me. The amount of mercy they didn't show was the best thing I had felt in years. Bring on the pain. Bring on the feelings of not being a girl made of glass. Fucking shatter me. Fuck. I blow out a breath when my pussy slickens at the thought of them. Me. Us. Circling each other until we landed in bed, and they made all my wildest dreams come true. They're the epitome of freedom for me.

My breaths pick up when my fingers run over the bite marks lining my legs, stomach, and breasts. They're still here. More than a day later, marking me as theirs. How long until they fade away? Rampant thoughts about the way their mouths moved over my body has me reaching for my pussy and making small circles around my eager clit. My hips buck up, chasing the feeling my fingers provide, which doesn't seem to be enough. I grunt, leaning over to my nightstand and pull it open, revealing...

"What the fuck?" I murmur, looking at the empty contents of my drawer. Well, not empty. But empty of what I was looking for —my goddamn vibrator.

I frown, moving the papers around, and finding absolutely nothing there. Did I sleepwalk somewhere? Shit. It's not out of the ordinary for me to cum while I'm sleeping, thanks to the pills I take. But to actually grab my vibe and have a good time while I'm not exactly conscious? Weird. I shake the feeling off and shut the drawer. When I go to stand, I pull my long shirt down over my ass and turn to make my bed. I freeze when three Polaroid pictures and two hard, white pieces of what suspiciously look like teeth, stare back at me from my unused pillow.

I cover my mouth when heat fills my cheeks and pick up the pictures with trembling fingers. One picture is a large tattooed hand with bright pink panties wrapped around it. Another is me, sleeping soundly with my headphones and the very shirt I have on. And the last is of a man I've only seen a few times, sniffing around my mom. He comes and goes. He's a regular with her. But to see him slumped in my fucking bedroom with his hand mangled and what looks suspiciously like blood dripping down his face creeps me out. Adrenaline pours through my veins when my eyes find the words written in marker on the front of the picture. "I'm always watching."

My mouth dries out. "What the fuck?" I whisper as my eyes dart around the room and finally land on the window.

On shaky legs, I march to the window, make sure the lock is secured, and double-check again.

Someone came into my room. Someone took pictures in my fucking room. And whoever they were, saved me. But from what? The man in the picture?

My hand covers my mouth as my stomach sloshes. Who would come into my room like this? Who would do such a thing? Fuck. Fuck. I can't go to the police; they'd never fucking believe me. I can't do anything but lock my damn windows and maybe sleep with a knife. But what good is a knife when I sleep like the dead? That's the thing of it all—I can only sleep with my pills, and if I don't take them to watch for an intruder, then my nightmares will catch up to me like they always do.

I slump to the floor, holding my face in my hands. Deep breaths, Journey. You have to remember to breathe through situations like that. You can't let this fear overtake you. You have to stay vigilant. You have to fight this so no one else can enter this room except you.

"Journey!"

I jolt when my mother's slurred voice echoes through my room, knocking me out of my tormented thoughts. I have to take myself away from the darkness plaguing me and focus on something else. Like my mother.

"Yeah?" I call out as I stand on my shaky legs.

I throw the pictures and what look like teeth into my nightstand drawer, shuddering when I put them away, refusing to look or think about it too hard. If I do, I'll spiral into the darkness that is eager to pull me under and hold me captive. It's the part of me I refuse to meet. The part of me I don't want to acknowledge. But it's that piece of me my monster created in the four months he held me in the dark and carved away at the pureness of my soul.

"Mom?" I call out again, listening for any sort of reply, but I'm greeted by silence.

I huff. Typical. She always does this. She's either hungry or is too high to get up and get what she needs, usually the bathroom or a shower, leaving the responsibility to me. If I don't get up and go assist her, then she'll possibly burn the house down or fall over and break an arm.

Worry gnaws at me, so I quickly dress in jeans and a baggy shirt and make my way down the narrow hall with shag green carpet and into the living room. The small TV plays softly in the background when I make my way toward my mom, resting on the oversized couch with worn-out leather and cigarette burns. Her head slumps forward, with her chin almost resting on her chest.

I stop right before her as she nods off with a cigarette in her mouth. Old puke rests on her chest and down the front of her, reeking of stomach acid. My stomach turns at the scent of her. Quickly, I cover my nose with my shirt, blocking out the rancid smell. Fuck. She needs a shower and soon. Her dingy brown hair sticks up every which way from lack of washing.

"Mom," I grunt, shaking her shoulder until her glazed-over eyes pop open and narrow at me.

You're the one who called my name. Not the other way around. I grumble internally when I raise my brows, expectantly awaiting her answer. She huffs, looking around with furrowed brows.

Watching her confusion morph into anger has guilt eating away at me. For as long as I can remember, she's been doing this to herself. Drugs every morning for breakfast and then again at lunch, and then she tops it off for dinner, too. For God knows why. Sometimes, people can't help the addictions they find themselves in. Once a drug takes hold, it's literally a disease eating away at its very core, dragging them further and further into its grasp. It's unstoppable. Uncontrollable. And ultimately, becomes their downfall.

My mother is the perfect example of this. Even if her addiction is the reason I'm in this mess. Sometimes, I want to lash out, hide her drugs, and lock her away. Other times, I want to pull her into my arms and remember the woman she used to be before she fell into this.

"I love you, my angel," she murmurs to me as she pulls me up

into her bed. *"How about we read this tonight?"* she asks, putting an arm around my shoulders and tucking me in to snuggle into her side. *"You're the most important person to me, Journey girl."* Her grin widens when I look up at her and snuggle into her more.

"Please read, Mommy."

"Need help?" I ask, gesturing to the puke in her lap that turns my stomach over and over.

Her glassy eyes fall to her lap when she blows out the smoke in her mouth. "Sure," she says with tears falling down her cheeks now.

"Don't worry, Mom. I got you."

"Don't fucking call me that," she grunts when I slowly lift her shirt over her head, careful that the puke doesn't fall in her hair. But after a comment like that, one she's made so many times, I'm tempted to say fuck it and let her stay dressed in her own puke. Why should I help when she doesn't give a fuck about me anymore? Because she's my mom, that's why. And for some fucked up reason, no matter what she's done, I can't give up on her. One day, I'll pull her back to shore from drowning. Just not today.

"Sure, Sable," I grumble, using her first name with reluctance. She flinches at the sound of her name, grumbling something unintelligible under her breath.

Since her drug addiction took hold, the woman has refused to let me call her mom. It's like she doesn't want the reminder of who I am. Or maybe it's who my father was. Corbin West. What would my life be like if my father had taken me away like I longed for him to do? I'd be in a mansion with no worries about where my next meal was coming from. I'd never have to shiver in the cold of night because my mom forgot to pay the heating bill or spent that money on drugs. Sometimes, I wonder how we've survived for this long. But then again, she always turns to the one man she shouldn't. My monster. The man she gave me to three years ago, who continues to pay for her habits and bills.

"That's better, you little twat," she mumbles, leaning on me in just her bra and panties as we head down the hall to the bathroom.

"Want it hot?" I ask, setting her on the toilet, getting a grunt in return. "Okay," I mumble, reaching into the standing shower and setting the water in the middle.

"Now go away," she hisses, tossing her spent cigarette into the toilet, and starts to undress.

"Aye, Aye," I grumble, flipping her off, and then shut the door.

Nothing makes me feel like shit more than having my own mother disregard me, especially when I'm helping her. She blames me for everything that's happened in our lives. Rightfully so, I guess. The feelings consume me more as I make my way to the kitchen, searching for breakfast. Fresh donuts sit on the counter. Peering around, I look for anyone here and find no one lurking in the shadows like I expect. The hairs on the back of my neck stand on end when I walk around the kitchen, the feel of someone's eyes on me, watching my every move. Or maybe it's the same eyes that walked into my bedroom when I was fast asleep. I shiver, shoving a donut into my mouth, and make my way back to my bedroom. It was my only sanctuary from the bad shit happening around me. Now, I don't even know if I can trust sleeping here.

The sound of the water shutting off and my mother moving around the bathroom has me hightailing it into my room and shutting the door. If Sable doesn't want my help, then she won't get it. I'll lock myself away, contemplating the rest of my day, and then, onto my newest mission—befriending Jenni and learning her schedule.

CHAPTER TWELVE
Journey

FIND JENNI AND BEFRIEND HER—EASIER said than done. It's been one week since my monster stole my peace and demanded I work my way into her life. How? I have no fucking clue. One day she's in class, and the next, she's out of school, doing God knows what. Usually, when he sends me on missions, there's a time and place for me to spy. But this? God, this is all up to me and my sparkling personality. Or lack thereof.

It's been exhausting, to say the least.

Wherever Jenni runs off to, I know she frequents those parties quite a bit. Especially hosting her own. Fuck! They're my least favorite places to be, especially when I'm working.

I hate the people crowding around. The loud voices. Just everything in between. I'd much rather be at home, wrapped in my blankets, and reading a book. Especially today. It's Saturday morning and the sun is shining bright in the sky above our trailer, illuminating my messy room. More pictures showed up last night on my pillow, leaving a hollow feeling in my stomach, but it's not fear. I can't even place it. Maybe it's a comfort to have my stalker sneaking in my window and watching me as I sleep. At least they look out for me, eliminating the threats sneaking into my room.

I longingly look at the book sitting on my nightstand, staring at me and begging me to crack it back open. *Gabby and The Gobblers*, a Thanksgiving-themed book. Nothing says take my mind off my dismal life than reading about a girl getting railed by three triplet turkey shifters in an alternative world of fated mates. How I wish I could, but I've got work to do. Jenni will no doubt be attending a party or hosting one herself.

I pick up my phone and begin scrolling social media again, looking for the girl I need to spy on. And there she is, smiling in her profile picture with a beautiful mountain backdrop. Her red hair glistens in the sun, almost matching her bright smile, showcasing her pearly white teeth. She's an absolutely beautiful girl inside and out, which is rare to find. I've talked to her a handful of times in math class, when her brows furrow and she stares at the board like she doesn't have a clue as to what's happening. I've helped her, and she thanked me by inviting me over for parties here and there in passing. She's social, nice, and very friendly—which will ultimately be her downfall.

"What does that say?" she asks, squinting at the board.

"It, uh, says solve the equation. Here," I say gently, handing her a page with the problem written down and a nice explanation of how to solve it. A little kindness in the world never hurt anyone.

"Oh my God. Journey! You're a lifesaver!" she says with a large smile. "So, what're you doing this weekend?" she asks when the bell rings, and we stand.

"Oh, uh. Nothing," I say with a shrug.

"My daddy is going out of town. I'm throwing a huge party. It's almost an every-weekend kind of gig. You should stop by and drink with me." She grins.

"Oh, thanks," I say. "I'll think about it."

Jenni Thomas—a girl so connected she probably won't ever work a day in her life. Her father, Kent Thomas, is the CEO of his own fucking plastic company. He's also a top dog in the damn Viotto Crime family. A shiver runs down my spine at the name Viotto, and I squeeze my eyes shut, blowing out a big breath.

"Party tonight at my house :)"

I read and reread the post Jenni sent out to all her friends on social media with my heart pounding. Fuck it.

Journey: Girl, I'm in!

I roll my eyes when I reply to her post. Fuck. I sound so lame. My face twists as I repeat out loud what I said.

"Girl, I'm in," I mock myself, slamming a palm against my forehead and repeatedly smacking myself.

Well, until my phone dings with a new message through social media.

Jenni: Journey fucking West! FINALLY!!!

I can practically hear her squeal through the message.

Journey: Haha! Yup! It's so close to finals that I figured I needed some time off to party...

Jenni: Well, girl! You need to come right now and drink with me! And then we can discuss how you want to help me study...

I snort. Of course, that's my way in. She needs me to help her with math. I can tutor and party with her to get closer to her. Not that she's that hard to get to know.

Journey: Girl. I got you, okay? We can def discuss studying. But get me drunk first...

Jenni: *laugh emoji* Come over. I have some shots with our names on them! And pack a bag, you're staying here!

Journey: Let me get dressed, and I'll be on my way!!!

Jenni: Get here fast, bestie! I can't wait to hang out... Here's my address...

I blink several times, staring at the address. Millionaire's Row. Again. Just like the last party. Those houses are more exclusive than a damn VIP night club. And I've been invited. Time to pull up my big girl panties and slink into a tiny dress. Just like last time.

Fuck. I make my way toward my closet, staring at the minimal pieces staring back at me. Half of my wardrobe is on the ground and piled up on my dresser. But the ones I barely wear, hang here, staring at me.

My fingers run over a few short dresses from my past spying adventures, and I sigh as memories run through my mind.

Longing hits me hard. Why do I crave three strangers I saw one time for only a few hours? I want their hands on me. Their tongues in my mouth and their dicks in my pussy. Crap. I rub my thighs together, trying to ease the urges growing inside me.

I want them again. Desperately.

But I can't. Because I don't know who they are or where they came from. The only remnants I have of them are their deep voices and the fading marks on my body from their teeth and wandering hands. A thrill runs through me when I pluck a violet dress from the hanger. It barely covers anything and sparkles under the lights.

I wonder if they'll be there tonight, watching me from the shadows, and want a repeat of what we did.

God, I hope so.

I throw myself into my bed, staring up at the plain white ceiling as I contemplate the evening ahead. Looks like I'm going to finally take her up on her offer and show up with fucking bells on.

This should be an interesting night of partying and cozying up with Jenni.

CHAPTER THIRTEEN

Jericho

IT'S BEEN TOO long since I've laid my eyes on Journey West. The distance puts my teeth on edge. Albeit, necessary. We can't be hovering around her like we want. If it were up to me, my Little Chaos would be anchored to me forever. Not a bad idea for the future. But I'm working on that. Ever since we buried that body, I've been racking my brain and trying to figure out how to chain my future wife to my side, earlier than we anticipated. And hopefully with my father's blessing. Despite that I don't really need it, I want him to be onboard with it.

Although, Arrow, ever the obsessive stalker, has been sneaking away night after night, checking in on her in her room and coming back with pictures, of course.

My skin crawls when I settle myself into my father's leather sofa, located in his posh office, fit for a mafia king. The title he's come to love and sink comfortably in.

It's not often I'm summoned via text to his office. But when I am, I'd rather pluck my eyeballs out than be in his nauseating presence.

I scoff to myself, curling my lip at his overly opulent decorations, including original paintings costing upwards of hundreds of thousands of dollars and imported furniture.

If he appropriately spent his money, rather than squandering

TwISTED IN OBSESSION 121

it away by decorating his buildings with the fanciest designs, then maybe he wouldn't be so damn broke.

Or have a resistance on his hands.

Perhaps he wants to reprimand me for skipping out on the initiate's ball in favor of going to a masked party. Or perhaps, he wants to discuss the man I found sneaking around my mansion's property the night before, wielding a few answers we've been seeking. If my father had been present and still living at the home he built, then he would have seen firsthand what happened instead of calling me downtown to the stupid tower he built to get away from the property.

Not that I mind. I'd rather him be there and away from my day to day activities.

"Please!" the intruder cries out in heavy breaths the moment Arrow catches him and throws him to the ground.

"I love a good chase!" Arrow beams with a sadistic smile that could melt the flesh off any mortal in his proximity. "Whether it ends in fucking or cutting throats, it's my favorite activity. And seeing as you're not my type, maybe I should cut first." Arrow unsheathes a large knife strapped to his thigh, bringing it to the wailing man's face. Picking him up by the shoulders, he forces the man to kneel before us while staying at his back to incapacitate him.

"Perhaps we should let him speak," I say, burying my hands into my pockets.

Shepp nods in my direction, finishing our circle around the man.

"You two are no fun. Just a little cut?" Arrow asks, batting his eyelashes and pressing the tip of the blade to the man's cheek.

"One cut won't hurt." I shrug, knowing Arrow won't let himself get too carried away with us here.

We're his keepers after all.

The man cries out, collapsing back to the ground in pain when Arrow uses the tip to cut a straight line down his cheek exposing the bone.

My skin tingles with the destruction and blood pooling on the grass beneath him.

"Tell me who you are and why you're sneaking around my lions," Arrow grunts, pulling the sobbing man back to his knees and hovering above him.

"I'd answer him if I were you," I say coolly, stepping forward until I can tip his chin up.

Fuck.

I shiver at the blood pouring from his wound and nearly groan when I run my fingertips through the mess, staining my flesh red.

"I won't fucking talk!" he hisses, spitting blood and saliva everywhere.

"The itsy-bitsy coward fell to his knees on the grass. Arrow took a knife and carved out his ass. The itsy-bitsy coward no longer had a life," Arrow sings to the tune of the itsy-bitsy spider song, loudly for the entire property to hear. "Because the itsy-bitsy coward leaned too hard on my knife. God, I love singing nursery rhymes in the middle of murder." Arrow grins again, humming it under his breath as he traces every vein protruding from the man's neck with the very sharp edge of his knife.

What a wonderful father he'd make one day.

"Jericho, Sir!" my guard reports, running up behind me with furrowed brows. "The rest of the property is clear."

"Very well, Stewart. Thank you for your hard work," I say with a nod, sending him back to his post.

'We should fire him,' Shepp signs with a frown.

"We'll deal with Stewart's incompetence later. Now, to you," I say, pressing my finger into the wound on his cheek. "We can make cut after cut, straight to the bone. I can play in your bloody holes all night long."

"Sounds dirty, Jer. Will you play in my bloody holes?" Arrow quips, tightening his hold on the spy.

I ignore his comment, not falling into his dirty innuendos when he's at the crest of losing all control. If we're not careful, he'll stab him so many times he won't be able to speak.

"How about another one to match?" I ask with a grin, chuckling when the man screams again and pisses himself the moment Arrow slices through his other cheek as if it were made of butter.

"You're beautiful now," Arrow says, patting the man's bloody cheek. "A damn masterpiece. Sheppy, do you want to paint his portrait?"

Shepp shakes his head with a huff.

"A shame," Arrow says with a grin. "Then, I'll memorialize my prize. Take a pic?" Arrow thrusts his Polaroid camera into Shepp's hands, not taking no for an answer. "Say cheese, Coward. Then we can really get down to business." Arrow's grin lights up the space as he holds the crying man's head between his palms.

Pathetic creature. Who cries in the face of danger? Weak, pissant humans who can't take the pain they were so eager to dole out.

Shepp huffs again but doesn't protest in taking the picture. Once it pops out of the camera and develops, Arrow nods with satisfaction. Another one for his wall of trophies.

"Tell me who sent you, and maybe I'll spare your dick," Arrow whispers into his ear, running his knife over the man's crotch.

The man shudders several times, clamping his lips shut, until Arrow unzips the man's pants.

"Shadow!" he cries when Arrow shoves the knife down the front of his boxers, threatening his manhood directly.

"Shadow, of course.They've had a hard-on for us for years now. What does he want, Coward?" I grit out, slipping my fingers into his wounds again.

He cries out. It's music to my ears, like a full symphony of violins rejoicing in his pain. My stress melts away when he opens his mouth and sings like a little birdy.

"Shadow! He sent me! He wanted me to get close to your house and set this!" the man shouts, clawing at his shirt before throwing it open and exposing a small bomb attached to his chest.

"Restrain his hands," I shout, gesturing to Arrow until he grabs

the man's shaking hands, attempting to set off the device lighting up and ready to blow.

Shaky hands, sweaty face, and piss staining the front of his pants. Yeah, he's no trained assassin. He's a goddamn scapegoat.

Arrow grunts, shoving the knife straight into the man's stomach.

"Hold that for me, would ya?" he chuckles, yanking the man's arms behind his back.

"Let me go," he cries out, struggling in Arrow's hold.

"This is boring. I want explosions!" Arrow shouts into the man's ear. "But first, I want to know why you want to blow us up? We're just children," he quips, pouting slightly.

"Children?" the man scoffs, rolling his eyes despite the situation. "You're murderous assholes who think you own this town," he sneers. "And Shadow wants to wipe every single Viotto off the planet."

"That's a hefty order, Coward," I chuckle, pacing in front of him as he continues to thrash in Arrow's hold.

But I'm not worried. Arrow's strong. He could hold the man for hours without complaints. Well, that's a lie. His only complaint would be the lack of blood and carnage.

"Oh, his name is John," Arrow says, wiggling his brows and holding up a wallet. "John Baily. He lives at 547 North McClellan Ave in, oh, Briar Cove."

"Briar Cove?" I raise a brow.

'This is a two-handed operation, Arrow!' Shepp aggressively signs, snatching the wallet from his hands.

I snort. "He has a point. Two hands around the man's wrists before he blows us to bits."

Although, I'm not technically worried.

"So, you're in Shadow's gang?" I inquire, pacing in front of John, the dead man walking, or should I say kneeling.

Of course, I don't know if it is a gang. Shadow's been recruiting people over the past few years. He's been a pain in the ass, stomping all over our territory with his drugs and guns on the streets. But we know nothing about him. Only that he apparently wants to blow us to bits.

But that won't happen.

"You've cut my face and stabbed me!" the man shrieks, slumping in Arrow's hold. "I won't tell you anything else," he hisses, baring his teeth.

"Let's blow him up," Arrow says with a grin, peering down at the trembling man.

John. He was a runner for us last year. He went to fucking East Point and back,' Shepp signs with a frown, shoving the wallet in his back pocket. *'Then he disappeared from our service.'*

"Well, It doesn't look like he's a Viotto runner anymore, does it? Tell me, John. Did you get recruited by the enemy?" I raise a brow.

John swallows hard, staring at me with hardened eyes. "Fuck you. Fuck Gabriel. Fuck the family. I hope you all burn in the Hell you deserve!" he shouts, spitting on the ground in front of him.

"Here's the deal, John. Tonight you die. Whether it's by the bomb ticking on your chest or by the wound on your stomach. We're going to walk away..."

"We are?" Arrow shouts in outrage, grabbing the knife he left inside him and yanking it out. Blood flows from the wound, tinting our grass a beautiful shade of red.

"We are." I nod, gesturing for Shepp to take a step back. "John, you can lie here and die from blood loss." I wince when Arrow stabs him again in the gut, opening another bloody wound. The color on John's face slowly drains away. "Or you can do us all a favor and blow yourself the fuck up and cease existing," I growl through clenched teeth.

John heaves a breath, staring between the three of us as we wait for his answer.

"Blow yourself up, Johnny Boy. Do us all a favor and end it before I drag you to my lions and let them gnaw on your fucking bones," Arrow snarls, letting the man's hands go. Stepping back, he points the bloodied knife at John's face with a sadistic smile lighting up his face at the thought of destruction.

John kneels before us in a weakened state and licks his lips. "One day. You'll all be in Shadow's grasp. One day, he'll end your *existence like you deserve. All of you!" he shouts weakly, losing his grasp on his fucking life force.*

A pity.

I take a step back. After inspecting the explosive attached to his chest this entire time we've spoken, I noted how small it seemed. Meaning, we would need a small radius to be out of its blast. Of course, that's never foolproof.

I jerk my head, instructing silently for Arrow and Shepp to follow, giving the man a wide berth. We've given John his choices. Either way, he's dead and not our fucking problem. Shadow is though. Whoever they are, they're getting more brazen with their attempts at our lives.

It ends soon. "No matter what you choose. You're dead. Shadow will know you failed in your attempts to end us. Any last words?"

John's chest heaves rapidly, spiraling him into death's hands as we step back far enough to hopefully get out of the blast range. I cock my head when his trembling hand reaches toward his vest, and he hits a button.

A small beep emanates from him, and then, he's no more. The deafening blast rocks the land like a mini earthquake shaking beneath us.

Bits and pieces of coward sprinkle on top of us like rain, smacking into the grass with a sickening splash.

"Arrow!" *I bark, jumping to my feet with furrowed brows when he's nowhere in sight. What the fuck? He was just here!* "Arrow!" *I shout again with my heart slamming against my chest until he skips toward me with bits of blood and guts hanging from his blond locks.*

"That's the most fun I've had in ages!" *he whoops.* "Maybe this Shadow fucker will send another bomb our way. Poor Coward. He went and martyred himself for the wrong side," *he tsks, kicking a fallen limb blown off by the blast.*

Shadow.

The man. The mystery. Whoever the hell he is.

Years ago, his name began floating through the streets of Briar Cove as a threat to our livelihood. Competition for my father and his underlings. Threats of hostile takeovers and murders whispered on the wind, aimed in our direction. Slowly but surely, the man without a face has made his rounds, gathering up our disgraced members and luring them to the dark side. And taking out anyone who dared to fight back against him.

Including us. We're the main focus of his crusade to end the Viotto Crime Family.

Whoever he is, he's ruthless. And a goddamn mystery. How can you take out the man gunning for you when you don't even know who he is? Or if he's a man. He could be anyone, and we wouldn't have a damn clue.

It's been so wonderful for our family. Not.

I sigh, grounding myself as I continue to wait on my father. I texted him immediately after the bomb situation, letting him know what happened and who was to blame. For a man so desperate to wipe out his enemies, he's always exceptionally late and unbothered. Especially with me. The son he loves to hate and hates to love.

He's never loved anyone in his entire life, except himself. Grace Viotto may have been the exception. But my mother is gone now.

My eyes wander over the multitude of cameras set up in his office, pointing in all directions. Of course, it's not just here, in the tower... It's all over his precious town. Everywhere my father has touched, a camera is left behind. Leading Shepp, Arrow, and I to be very careful about the things that fall off our tongues in his places.

Anywhere really. My father has spies in every business, street, and home. He's not dumb. You don't rise to power without watching your back.

He's just excessive.

As I wait for my father, my mind drifts to the girl I can't wait to get my hands on. Again. My Little Chaos has no idea what I have in store for her.

Finally, the door opens, and my father saunters in without a care in the world.

"Good, you're here."

"You texted. I came." Like the good, dutiful son he expects me to be.

"Tell me every little detail about last night," my father demands, raising a brow when I shrug a shoulder with indifference, referring to the man we caught sneaking around our property.

Those dark eyes zone in on me with a wicked gleam, examining every facial twitch and movement I present. Jokes on him, though. I never give myself away to my enemies—and he's my biggest one.

Even if I had found something important, the last person I'd divulge all the details to would be this man. The most notorious, ruthless mafia man in California. If he didn't have the law in his pockets, he'd be in prison right now, and my life would be a whole lot simpler.

"He only mentioned this Shadow guy as the person he was working with," I say with a straight face, sitting across from my father's desk at his office, high above the people below. Nothing but the blue skies, clouds, and the sun streaking through the windows behind him.

The light streams in throughout his modern office, illuminating his facial features. Dark eyes look back at me with malice resting behind them and trimmed facial hair running down his sharp jaw. To some, he might look like an angel— innocent and giving. To me and others, he's the damn devil hiding behind flawless flesh. Only, others haven't received the brunt of his lessons with fists and kicks and dark basements. That was reserved for only me. Imagine being five years old and getting woken up in the middle of the night, dragged down the stairs by your hair, and thrown into your dingy basement.

"Hmmm," he says, stroking his jawline, deep in thought.

"Well, I'll be glad to have him out of the picture. Now, we need to figure out who is really moving in on our territory."

Right. There's more resting in the depths of his eyes. He knows something he's not telling me. It's right there in the way he strokes his chin and avoids eye contact. I can read this man like a magazine. Only he hasn't a clue. There are a lot of things in my life he doesn't know about. Not yet, anyway. One day, I'll reveal it all to him when he's on his knees, chained in a dark basement, at my fucking mercy.

My teeth grind together, and I blow out a breath. Fuck. Some days, I get myself way too worked up. I can't let that happen. He, too, reads people like it's his goddamn gift. And it is. Give him an inch—he'll take a mile.

"Agreed," I hum, keeping my words short and concise like my father likes it.

It's odd sitting in this oversized lounge chair, resting in his overly done up office with expensive decorations. Something he never used to care about. There he sits behind a large oak desk, gleaming under the sun's rays. Leaning back in his equally expensive office chair, his eyes wander around the room, seeming to get lost in thought. Something he doesn't do very often.

Gabriel Viotto is usually too focused to ever let his mind wander. It's a weakness in his eyes.

My father's setup hasn't always been like this. Over the years, his paranoia has ramped up to an all-time high. Constantly feeling like someone was right around the corner with a gun, ready to end his life, or simply following him wherever he went. In some aspects, I guess he was right, especially after the attempt on his life.

Many years ago, he was a lot closer, living under the same roof as me—and Arrow, who has roomed with us since he was six, when my father took him under his wing and away from the priest.

Then, it all changed—after someone bombed our mansion and

attempted to take his life. Or mine. Who knows? His paranoia ate at him until he packed up all his shit and left the premises without looking back. Including leaving Arrow and me behind. It wasn't sad for me. I'd never miss the lessons he insisted on teaching me. Ever. They may have built me into the heartless asshole I am now, but he ruined my innocence long before I even knew what that word was.

No. My father is a coward. Always has been. Always will be. Even now, as he sits behind his massive desk, with all his false power he's built up around himself he's still afraid.

Sometimes, I wonder if he would have turned into a better man if my mother was still here. Sometimes, I wonder a lot. What would my life be like with her in it? Would it be like Shepp's when his father was still alive? Where his mother couldn't stick up for him or anyone, always cowering in the corner. Now, she's married to my father—for some fucked up reason that can't be love—and is so drugged up on whatever he gives her, living her life like nothing has happened. She just walks around, spending his money with a dopey smile on her face. Not even caring about her son.

I sigh, mentally shaking myself from the past. There was nothing I could do about it back then. And now, I'd rather him be here than at the mansion, which has become our home. Not only does it make our lives easier not having to listen to his every demand, but for the plans we have in overthrowing his ass from power, well—it helps he's out of earshot.

"Fine then," he finally says, leaning over and opening a drawer. "I wanted to offer you a piece of the pie in celebration of you coming into the family completely and taking your oath soon. You're a man now, Jericho Viotto." Those stern eyes eat away at me when he looks me up and down. "And I want you to officially take over as the owner of Rave."

I blink several times when he slides a piece of paper toward me, detailing the contract, pay, and rules of my newest role as sole owner of the entire nightclub we've built up.

Suspicion rolls in my stomach while I look him over, trying to hide the stunned expression on my face. My father doesn't just hand over operations without stipulations.

Sure, he lets Arrow, Shepp, and I run the poker games from the VIP room of the club. Of course, he gets a cut of our profits and checks over our books every chance he gets. He keeps us in charge of loans given out to the people of the city, but there's always something he wants. A little off the top here. A little off the top there. He doesn't think we pay attention to what he does.

We do, though. Others may not. How's that saying go? The Devil's in the details.

But we're not fucking stupid. Gabriel Viotto always has something up his sleeve. He's always two steps ahead of everyone else.

Or so he likes to think.

"You're giving me Rave?" I ask with true appreciation.

I've been basically running the club for three years. From the moment I turned eighteen, the club became our favorite place to conduct our own business. We found our tribe there, gaining loyalty through the foot soldiers my father placed around us. Some are untrustworthy. But the others? They're ours. Not his. Their loyalty lies with us and no one else.

"Of course," he scoffs. "What else would I give you? You've been conducting your own sect of the family there for years now. You're growing your own. You've made me proud, son." He tilts his head as a wistful smile pulls his lips apart. "And now, it's yours."

"I appreciate it, Sir," I say, running my finger over my name listed as the new man in charge of operations and, well, everything.

I'm the new owner with deed in hand.

"As my only son and heir, I figured you needed a little piece of the action." I swallow hard, staring at my father, maybe for the first time.

My relationship with him has always been a little strained. More on the professional side than personal. I'll be forever grateful that he brought me into this world, but I've seen how he handles his business.

"I've viewed the numbers on several occasions. It's a booming business, Sir. It's very generous of you to trust me."

"A present," he says, waving a hand. "A sign of my trust in you."

Pfft. Trust in me?

This new adventure he's handing me on a silver platter is more likely a way for him to anchor me to this place and watch my every move—ever the paranoid asshole. My father may think I'm just a child, still only twenty-one, but I have my head screwed on better than anyone else I know. Besides Shepp, and maybe Arrow on a good day. They're my family. The men who help me on this journey through life.

My eyes wander over the contract trying to find the holes he may have placed there. I swallow hard, skimming the words and finding everything straightforward and present. I sign my name and hand it back to the man with his hand out.

"And what about Journey?" I ask, masking the hope I've held onto when he first presented me with the arranged marriage he somehow set up with her mom.

"After the initiation ball, the wedding will commence. And other announcements will be made," he says, cocking his head. "Maybe bring her along? After your initiation, she's yours for the taking," he questions with a smirk.

My heart pounds against my ribs. He's giving me the green light to take the girl I've been forbidden to speak to or interact with for years. But other announcements? Maybe he's referring to Chloe Satin and her family. Although, I'm not quite sure how she fits into everything. Surely, he'd mention her being presented to Arrow or Shepp. Right?

"I can make her come," I say, grinning at the prospect of holding her close to me and dancing the night away.

"Then, it's settled. Enjoy the nightclub. I'll see you, her, and the boys when we celebrate the men you've become," he says, standing up. "Now, if you'll excuse me. I have a Shadow to track down. Keep your nose to the ground, boy, and ears open."

"Yes, Sir," I say, standing as he walks out of his office without looking back at me.

For someone with so little trust in people, he really has no problem turning his back on me when I'm in his domain. No matter. The cameras everywhere prove I won't snoop through his desk.

Besides, I have a nightclub to take ownership of.

CHAPTER FOURTEEN

Shepp

MUFFLED music leaks through the large window overlooking the crowd below, as I settle back into the oversized leather chair with a frown. I gently twirl the lit cigar between my fingers, watching as the smoke drifts from the hot cherry end.

The club below us is packed with bodies dancing and gyrating to the thumping music vibrating straight through me. It's our usual spot on nights when the family business doesn't need us—Rave. The very club we've run as a team since we were eighteen, taking over day-to-day operations from Jericho's father.

And now? He's named Jericho as the owner and operator.

Our VIP room never fails to settle the discourse rattling around in my brain. It seems to be the only place I can outrun the demons, constantly gnawing at my mind. Between the chips on the poker table or the money exchanging hands with loans, this is my home away from home—my sanctuary.

"I don't understand the appeal," Jericho mutters, sucking in the flavor of the cigar and then blowing it out with disgust.

"It makes you look important," Arrow offers, eyeing his like it might bite him "See?" He grins, bringing it up to his lips and leaving it there while he sits back on the leather sofa, resting next to me.

"There are no listening bugs in here, Sir." My eyes find Aiden standing at attention with a detector in his hand. "This room is clear." He swallows hard, looking between the three of us with an unwarranted amount of anxiety.

He's agitated and possibly a little frightened.

Strange.

Jericho nods in his direction with gratitude. Good. I wouldn't put it past Jericho's father to bug the entire place in hopes of catching us doing something behind his back. Or saying something he may not like. His paranoia will eat him alive one day.

"And the rest of the club?" Jericho asks, raising a brow.

"Brandon and I will sweep the entire premises when it closes and everyone has left. We know Gabriel has always had heavy security, including guards and cameras throughout the place."

'But none in here,' I sign, eyeing every nook and cranny. *'Maybe he trusts you.'*

'Doubtful,' Jericho signs back, not wanting to alert anyone else in the room of our conversation.

Arrow and Jericho are the only ones in the family that have bothered to learn ASL for my sake. Even when my father took my voice, he still expected me to answer him when spoken to. Too bad he never got that. I refused to use a voice he didn't want present. Screw him.

"Use your voice, boy!" he booms from the dining table, ripping into his steak like an animal.

I swallow hard. Or try to. It's difficult these days when he's taken so much from me. I refuse to bend to his will any longer.

He narrows his eyes at me, gulping down another beer.

"I see," he says coldly. "How about a trip to the basement again?" A sadistic grin pulls at his lips, and my mother and I are too weak to stop him from hurting us both. "You, too, Aurora."

'The day that man trusts anyone, Hell will freeze over,' I sign with a grimace.

Gabriel Viotto trusts no one, ever. He barely trusts us but only does it because Jericho is his son, his heir and prodigy. He's under the impression he's trained Jericho without default, expecting him to be his copy.

Oh, how wrong he is.

Arrow snorts and signs, *'Facts.'*

I sit back in the leather seat, watching as they converse in sign language. My language. The one I had to pick up when my father... I suck in a breath. I hate those memories. I hate how they're laced with violence and abuse from the man that was supposed to protect me.

Tears roll down my cheeks, but I quickly wipe them away. Pain gnaws at my mouth where my tongue should be, an empty space near my teeth. More pain tears through me when I attempt to move the back of my tongue, it's the only part that's left, but makes me feel useless. It's a reminder of what was taken from me in the dingy basement of my parent's home. I squeeze my eyes shut, trying to compose myself before I have to face the world. He allowed me five days of recuperation. Only five days to live with the fact I lost a piece of myself. All for telling the truth.

"Shepp," Jericho breathes, staring me up and down when I meet him in the halls of our elementary school. Concern laces his expression when he steps forward, examining my bruised-up face. "You've been missing." He raises a brow.

I nod, unable to utter a word. Instinctively, I open my mouth to tell him what my father did now and how he took the one thing from me that I needed. That his suggestion to speak with his father about what's been happening in the middle of the night went south, and now, I'm voiceless.

Broken.

I swallow hard or try to. It's hard when you've lost the majority of your tongue. I've had to learn how to eat, swallow, and breathe without it. There's so many things I can do without my tongue. Even speak without it, but I refuse. This is what he wanted. He took it from me for the sole purpose of keeping me silent. So, I will be silent for the rest of my life.

Jericho must see the anguish written on my face when he pulls

me into a small room and shuts the door. For someone so young, he's
smart and awfully observant. Just how his father raised him.

"What happened?" he asks, nibbling his bottom lip. "Did my
father..."

I shake my head, opening my mouth again. But the pain stops
me. With a sigh, I take out my notepad and jot down a quick note
and hand it to him.

Standing silently, Jericho stares at the note with wide eyes. The
only sign his emotions are taking hold is the tremble of his hand.
Quickly, he crumbles it up with a growl.

"It's gone?" he whispers, looking me over.

I nod.

"And your voice?"

I lick my lips and write a note.

Gone.

Of course, my voice still exists. It's just broken and locked
away like the rest of me. I refuse to use it. My father worked so
hard to crush my existence; in this one moment, I think he did.

And I let him.

The moment I came to Jericho with a notebook and pen,
looking like someone had run me over with a truck, he didn't
hesitate in dedicating himself to learning sign language with me.

Through tutors and many months of studying, we learned the
language one word at a time. It's come in handy through the years
in keeping our conversations private in front of prying eyes. Even
Gabriel never had the motivation to learn, despite the
encouragement he gave us.

I was born to be Jericho's best friend and right-hand man, and
how my father stole from me was our wake up call. From that
moment on, our faith in Gabriel Viotto and Thomas Mondelli
dwindled into ash.

Now, we only trust each other.

"You say he's been sneaking into your room at night?" Gabriel asks, peering at me with an unreadable expression.

"Yes, Sir," I whisper through quivering lips.

He was the first adult, besides my mother, that I could think of to tell and would help me fight him off.

Gabriel sits back in his office chair, shifting slightly as he looks me over with a sharp eye, taking in everything.

"And?" Gabriel responds with a roll of his wrist without an ounce of care.

"I... I... Want him to stop. He touches me, Sir. He..." I swallow hard, shame rearing its ugly head inside me.

Gabriel shrugs. "If that's how your father takes care of things."

I blink several times, and my fists clench at my side. Coming to him for help was the biggest mistake of my life.

When my father met his end, I rejoiced. My mother celebrated. We had a party after we buried his ashes at the cemetery. Never again would we have to deal with his bullshit ways.

No one on this planet misses Thomas Mondelli except Gabriel Viotto.

"Thank you for trying, Aiden," Jericho says, dipping his head with respect.

It's the one thing Gabriel never shows his men. Respect. Admiration. Loyalty.

He uses and abuses, throwing away perfectly good, loyal men without a second thought. Blackmail. Underhanded dealings. Murdering in cold blood. He's done it all. Everyone in the family is beginning to suspect how unhinged he's become. Even his competence as the great ruler of Briar Cove is coming into question. His brothers, Jericho's uncles, have questions—ones Gabriel refuses to acknowledge.

No matter. We've been building an army of our own, collecting loyal soldiers right under his nose. He'll never see it coming. Like Aiden and Brandon, our lead security at Rave.

"No problem, Sir. We'll keep guard outside for now," Aiden says, dipping his head again and then turning on his heel.

Aiden disappears behind the large doors separating us from the rest of the club below. Briefly, the music filters through on full blast, washing over us with its rhythmic beat.

Ah, to be young and carefree, dancing your life away as alcohol affects your ambitions. It's something I've never had the pleasure of being—innocent, carefree, and ignorant of the world around me. Instead, I'm a broken soldier raised in the darkness of the basement with only a monster to guide me down the twisting paths of life.

"I like him," Arrow says, puffing his cigar and wrinkling his nose again. Funny. Arrow doesn't like anyone but us. And, of course, Journey. "And I don't like this. Why do all the old men celebrate with these things? They taste dreadful. And they don't make us look as important as I thought."

'He's our most trusted,' I sign. *'He never rats.'*

"He's proven his loyalty to us," Jericho murmurs, puffing his cigar again.

"Excuse me, Sir." Aiden's voice catches me off guard as he peeks his head back into our windowed room. "There are more players here. They have the golden coin."

"Thank you, Aiden. Let them in," Jericho says, rolling his wrist with feigned indifference.

Settling back into the oversized leather chair, I watch the door with a careful eye. In this business—money and mafia—you never know who is about to walk through your door. Could be hired guns, ready to fire rounds into our chests. It could be just simple poker players gambling their life savings away. Either way, we have to be on our toes and have our wits about us.

I'm sure Aiden checks them thoroughly, even taking their cell phones into a basket so they can't make any calls, but there could always be a traitor in the mix.

Somewhere.

Three men, maybe a little older than us, waltz into our perch with smirks on their lips and a stagger to their steps. Cocky. Greedy. They reek of desperation. Perfect for our table. They will eagerly set their life savings on the line, betting it all away and lining our pockets. At least, they have enough common sense to dress for the part in three piece suits, expensive watches, and shiny white teeth.

"Hello, Gentleman. Have you come to play a game?" Jericho asks, tilting his head as their attention snaps to him with surprise.

I'm not sure what they expected to find when they walked in here.

The blond one in a black form-fitting suit holds up the gold coin with a V etched into it.

"We were invited," he says smugly, flipping the coin in his hand.

It's the only way someone can get invited into our little slice of Heaven.

No coin. No entry.

"It seems you were," Jericho says, holding out his hand. "These were your invitations."

"Yes," a dark-haired one with the same suit on says, stepping forward. "Our invitation," he says, holding up his gold coin, too.

"Wonderful." Jericho collects the coins and places them down on the table. "You understand this was a one-time invitation. You can earn more by playing fair and not causing trouble. Win a few hands and get your names thrown back into the game. You're going up against the best players in the country. No weapons of any kind are allowed inside. Bring one, and well, you won't like the consequences. The buy-in alone is one hundred thousand dollars. You'll pay the man back there once we escort you in. The game is set to start in..." He flips his watch over, eyeing the time. "About thirty minutes. Right at midnight. Are we clear?"

"You run this?" The blond-haired guy asks skeptically, raising a brow. His light eyes search Jericho up and down, eyeing his shiny dress shoes, slacks, and white dress shirt.

Dress the part. Be the part. It's something Gabriel installed in us, time and time again.

"You gotta problem with that?" Arrow asks, standing up to face the men who blanch in his presence.

He crosses his arms over his chest, flexing his muscles against the three douchebags questioning us.

I smirk when the color drains from their faces. Their eyes pop wide, and they instinctively take a step back. That's right, you cocky assholes. That's Arrow Amour. One man you don't fuck with or ask questions to.

Arrow's knack for violence and blood has given him quite the reputation.

"No. We just wanted to make sure we were in the right place," the third man, who has been silent the entire time, says as he steps forward. His black-rimmed glasses gleam under the soft lights of the room. "Here," he says, offering his coin. "All the rules. The buy-in. Everything is fine. We're just here to show off our skills."

"Exactly," the cocky blond one says, putting his hands in the air.

"This is your way into the room. Brandon here will escort you to your seats and take your payments. Have fun, Gentlemen. But always remember the rules." Jericho grins, giving them their coins back and watching as they walk through the steel doors of the gambling room behind our seats.

They're scared fish, hiding behind cocky attitudes but swimming straight for the world's biggest sharks.

They're going to get eaten alive,' I sign with a huff after clicking my rings, then taking another puff of my cigar, really breathing it in and blowing it back out.

"More money for us," Jericho quips with a shrug, getting up from his chair.

We may have the inclination to clean up the streets of Briar Cove, but we've always had the business bug running through our veins. From an early age, we were taught to be the providers for our wives and children, working long hours to conduct whatever business must be dealt with. Whether it's loaning out money to the townspeople with lower interest rates than banks, which encourages them to come visit us. Or the high-stakes poker games and slot machines—that's our empire. We build steady relationships with the townspeople and bring in steady business opportunities with the men and women who seek to play our games.

"Excuse me, Sir." Aiden draws my attention again with a grimace. "Sorry to pester you. But there's an older woman here with this," he says, holding up a silver coin etched with a V on one side.

My heart beats rapidly against my chest at the significance. Normally, people with these wait until Wednesday nights when Arrow makes his presence known in the confessional booth at his father's church. It's there that people ask for help against others who are doing them wrong. Or brokering for a loan to get out of sticky situations.

"Of course, send her in," Jericho says, waving a hand as he stands securely by the glass window overlooking the chaotic nightclub party in full swing. Taking one last look at the people moving as one to the music, he turns on his heel and heads to his chair.

Business never sleeps.

Aiden opens the door wider, providing ample room for a weary-looking woman who appears to be in her mid-forties and smaller than a stick. Brown hair. No make-up. Sagging skin. She's definitely seen better days.

I sit up in my seat, taking her appearance in. Her entire body trembles under her baggy jeans and oversized shirt, probably hiding more bruises than the ones under her sunken eyes and neck. Her fingers play with the silver coin she must have gotten from the priest as she makes her way fully into the room.

"Please have a seat," Jericho says, gesturing to an empty chair, letting her know it was okay to speak to us.

"Thank you," she whispers so softly I barely hear her voice over the drumming of my heart.

"How can we help you today?" Arrow asks, placing his elbows on his knees. "You brought the silver coin."

She swallows hard. "Someone gave it to me and said I'd know where to go when I needed help."

Jericho rubs his chin. "Yes, you came to the right people."

"It was the priest wasn't it?" Arrow asks, leaning in more with a gentle tone. "He knew you needed something..."

"Money," she mutters, darting her eyes to the floor in pure shame.

"We do offer loans," Jericho says.

"And sanctuary," Arrow says with a nod.

"My husband..." She sucks in a breath, on the verge of tears. "He drinks too much and takes it out on the kids and me. I need a loan. I need to get away from him." She discreetly swipes a hand under her eyes, shaking more as she does.

"Don't worry. We'll get you all set up," Arrow says with compassion, lighting up at the thought of helping an innocent woman run from her husband.

That's the thing about Arrow Amour that no one seems to understand. Is he a ruthless killer willing to take off the fingers of any man who touches his woman? Yes. Is he willing to take down the enemy with everything he's got, even if it gets him killed? One-hundred percent. But there's another side to him, only the individuals down on their luck and the ones who seek him out in the confessional get to see—his compassion. He may not have a loving bone in his body, but he deeply cares for the unfortunate. Maybe it's his father's influence from being raised in the church as a child. Or maybe, it's who he truly is deep down.

Arrow rushes about, explaining the process to the poor woman—Lori Heins—as she later tells us. Much like a bank, we keep records of everyone who takes money from us. Even the ones who give us a sob story. They sign the papers, and then, they're on their way with a wad of cash from our vaults to start their new lives. Some pay us back in full within the time limit we give them. Others, we have to track down and give a reminder of their promise.

"Yes. I will pay you back when I get back on my feet," Lori says, nodding her head with gratitude.

"And you understand," Jericho starts, slowly getting to his feet and putting his hands in his pockets.

The last thing we want to do is intimidate the small, fragile woman. We know the circumstances she's led us to believe. She's gotten the coin from the Pastor at church. But if there's one good piece of advice Jericho's father taught us, no one is as they seem.

Snakes live in the deepest part of the pits, but when they come out to face you head-on, they'll bite you so fast—you wouldn't have seen it coming.

"That we know who you are. You've handed us your information. Your husband's name. Your children's information. We don't operate entirely in good faith, Mrs. Heins. We operate on money. This is a loan. Not a charity case. We'll gladly help you in every avenue of getting you back on your feet..."

"A house, a job, a car, and anything else you might need. But my brother is right. There is a time limit to this, okay? No horse shit," Arrow interrupts with passion.

"No!" she gasps, holding a hand to her fragile heart. "No horse shit, absolutely not. I will pay you back! I just need to get away from him and save my children before... It's too late," she says, sniffling and wiping her nose.

"Understandable. Then, take this as your key to freedom. Your repayments start in six months as a courtesy for your situation. Don't mistake our kindness for weakness, though. We will find you if you run or don't pay."

She nods. "I understand! I promise. I just..."

"Now, go and start your new life," Jericho says, nodding his head toward the door to get her moving.

"Thank you again. This is going to get us so far in life. You don't understand." With that, Lori scurries her way out of our suite with the cash and on her way to a better life. I hope, at least.

"Can I take her husband's fingers?" Arrow asks, standing up with a sadistic smile.

I snort, getting to my feet. My cigar burns between my fingers when I slowly make my way toward the large window overlooking the crowd to indulge in my favorite activity—people watching. Observing others has always been somewhat of a pastime of mine. I could watch for hours, taking in a stranger's habits. Even now, above them all, they fascinate me.

'We'll watch her and make sure she gets settled in. And make sure her husband hasn't followed her,' I sign with a shrug, turning to look out the window.

"And then, I can pay him a visit to remind him how to treat women," Arrow hums.

Something tugs my eyes through the mass of people like a target, calling to me from below.

Down there, hundreds of elites gyrate, drink our liquor, and party their lives away. My eyes scan more of the crowd, stopping when my heart soars into my throat.

The moment my eyes connect with the woman who has had my heart in a vise since I learned she was promised to us. Journey. The girl I've been protecting and feeding for years now. Lightning soars through my body. The hairs on the back of my neck stand on end. The girl with moss-green eyes and a story to tell—secrets to unravel—dances before me.

My lips roll together when I stand outside the door of Journey's trailer. A habit. Something I promised myself I wouldn't continue, but I can't stop. Not now. She needs me to continue bringing food and water so she can live. As the sun begins to peek over the horizon, illuminating the world around me, I listen for any sort of noise inside Journey's home. Again. The TV blasts some news story about the rising crime in Briar Cove, blaming the gangs surrounding the area.

Typical.

They always blame the gangs and the mafia ruling the city. Granted, we do bring crime into the area, we also help to clean the streets. There's more to us than meets the eye. But the public will never know.

Reaching into my pocket, I pull out the key I copied last year after stealing it from Journey when she wasn't looking and slowly enter their domain with measured footsteps.

Sable, Journey's mom, rests on the couch like she usually is, with a cigarette trapped between her lips, barely staying in her mouth. Her head slumps forward, her chin almost resting on her chest.

I shake my head, silently marching forward and plucking it from between her lips. If I wanted to speak, I'd tell her she's a waste of space and doesn't deserve a daughter like Journey. She doesn't deserve anything but a jail cell.

I sigh, moving into the kitchen and setting my homemade donuts down on the counter. If there's one thing that gets me moving in the morning, it's making food. And Journey. Always her. She'll never know I was the little shadow following her around and making sure she's okay. Especially when she needed it most.

After she disappeared and changed, I took more interest in finding out what was happening to her. Nothing seemed out of the ordinary, though. The only mishap was how often she snuck away from home. When I followed her, she'd sneak out of the grocery store with food under her clothes. Or she'd scurry to the church down the road that headed the food pantry for the city and bring back a big box of food.

She was starving.

So, I decided to secretly care for her. Fresh donuts every morning. Food in her fridge and cupboards. Anything she needed to survive, I helped.

CHAPTER FIFTEEN

Journey

Two weeks have passed since my monster assigned me a new mission. I take a deep breath, sitting outside the club of my nightmares. People suck. Hard. Not to mention, I hate crowded places. Touching shoulder-to-shoulder with people I'd rather push off a cliff isn't my idea of a good time.

You know what is?

Being at home curled up with a good book, reading about a girl getting railed by multiple lovers. Or one lover. I'm really not that picky. Although, how one girl can handle so many dicks, is beyond me. Four at a time? God only gave you three holes, sister. I guess that's what hands are for. And the girls are always so pampered and loved with multiple men.

I know I was.

Who knew losing your virginity to three masked men would be such a damn thrill. Not this girl. Besides, unlike the books, they each took their turn with me. There was no backdoor play or blowjobs while I was being plowed.

Maybe next time...

My thoughts drift off to the powerful men who exuded so much big dick energy, it nearly choked me to death. I may not have seen their faces, but God damn, their bodies did a lot of talking to mine that night while I was blindfolded. A rude disadvantage, if you ask me, even if I was the one saying I wanted to remain anonymous. I wonder if they'll be here or if I'll recognize them by the sound of their voices. Or maybe by the way they stand or move around. Their voices were deep, enchanting, and sucked me in. Fuck. Knowing my luck, they're probably from out of town, living dangerous lives, and haven't thought about me since.

Bummer.

I pout to myself at the loss of men I never had. That's why I've been losing myself between the pages of books in my spare time. It doesn't really matter to me what type of romance book I'm reading, I love them all. Whenever I have an ounce of spare Journey time—which is rare when I'm constantly working for that asshole who thinks he owns me—I stick my nose into a book and forget it all.

As pathetic as it sounds, it's my only escape from reality. I'd much rather do that than hang out with Jenni in a crowded elite club. A club I'm not sure how we're even going to get into. She's eighteen, and I'm only nineteen. Although, the dress she picked out of her closet and basically forced me into helps. I swear my boobs are plumper and bigger than I've ever seen. Nearly at my damn chin.

Jenni did a damn good job of dressing me up like a doll, tossing all my insecurities in the trash. Well. Minus the one peeking out from between my breasts in dark swirling colors, surrounding the key hiding my scar. Jenni didn't mention going out to a club when she picked me up and took me to her house to hang out. It was a split-second decision. Meaning, I left my damn corset at home, which keeps my insecurity hidden.

So, I'm already over this, and we haven't even gone into the club yet.

I'm going to need a lot of alcohol to make it through the night.

Jenni pulls me out of her car with a grin, staring up at the massive building nestled in downtown Briar Cove. It covers at least three city blocks. Gigantic spotlights twirl back and forth, beckoning people like the damn bat signal to come and drink. And they do. Rave is famous for bringing in very wealthy clientele and catering to their needs.

How we're going to be permitted in, I'm not sure. Well, Jenni could be. Her father makes millions upon millions every year. And me? I'm just playing the part of a rich bitch tonight.

"You look so hot, Journey!" Jenni squeals from the sidewalk, curling her fingers around mine as we slowly walk.

And I do mean slowly. This bitch put me in six inch heels, helping me tower over the other people walking around me. Even though I wobble with every step. I'm probably going to have a broken ankle by the time this night is through.

Oh, the things I do to protect my sister.

I snort, "You, too." I grin when she hip-bumps me, raising her chin and showing off the shortest dress I've ever seen.

I think her vagina might flop out. I guess that's why I insisted on wearing something that at least hits mid-thigh. I had to concede the fact my tits were about to bulge out the top. But she taped those puppies down and made sure they wouldn't fly out. I can't say the same about her ass.

"We're two hot bitches marching into this club like we own it. Oh! Here's your ID," she says, reaching into her cleavage and pulling out what looks like a driver's license.

I raise a brow when I inspect the picture of me, but the birthdate and everything else are completely wrong. "Cherry Longlegs?" I gape at the name on the ID.

"Yup! You're Cherry, and I'm Destiny Glideswell." She grins at me, holding out her ID. "It's very fitting." Her brows wiggle when she puts her ID back, and we continue our walk toward the thumping club, practically vibrating my chest with the bass coming out of it.

"Well, Destiny," I quip, shoving my ID into the little black clutch Jenni made me bring. "Let's get our dance on." I insert false bravado and happiness into my tone, making her squeal again.

I like Jenni. I really do. She's been the kindest person I've met so far in my spying adventures. Over the past week, I swear she's taken me under her wing in appreciation for helping her bring her grades up in almost every subject she needed help in. Especially with math. She's been a quick study, though. Proving to me that she's a very smart girl, but rarely shows it.

"Elias is out of town tonight." Jenni pouts for the hundredth time when we get to the back of the long line, stretching past the corner of the brick building. "I just wanted a nice Saturday with him. He's been so busy lately. It makes me sad." A gloss forms over her eyes, and she sighs heavily.

Right. Elias. My original job and her boyfriend. A man she seems to love very much. And from what she's told me, he loves her, too. I haven't had the chance to meet him just yet. But I know in time I will.

"You love him, don't you?" I question, staring at her slumped shoulders.

She offers me a sad smile and nods. "From the first time I saw him, I knew he was it for me. Which sounds crazy for some teenager to say. But it's like fate or destiny," she giggles at the last word.

I bump my shoulder against hers as the line advances a few steps, and we come to a halt. "I think it's romantic. You're like Romeo and Juliet. Minus the suicide at the end." I grin when she perks up a little.

"I like that," she says, offering me a genuine smile. "Two lovers on the opposite side of things. Ah, yes. That's us. He's my handsome Romeo." She pauses for a brief second as grief flashes across her face. And then, it's gone when she smiles, wiping everything away. "But that's why we're here. I just want to dance the night away and forget that he's out there doing something dangerous."

"What's he up to tonight? Does he ever tell you?"

Please say no. Please don't tell me it's something sinister against my monster. Please don't make me go back to that evil man and make me tell him everything.

A smirk pulls at her lips when we move again. "Girl, you have no idea," she murmurs, leaning in really close. "He trusts me with his best kept secrets. Can you believe that? Tonight they're meeting with their big boss. He's some mysterious man living in the shadows or something. He has an island fifty minutes off the coast. Elias told me all about it. It's tropical. People are everywhere. It's wild."

My heart sinks. "Holy hell! An island? And I thought Elias worked for himself?" I question, leaning in further.

"He does and doesn't. He's teaming up with more people around here." Her eyes widen, and she looks at me with worry. "But I didn't say that, Journey. You have to promise me that you won't tell anyone, okay?"

"I won't. Cross my heart and hope to die," I say, offering her a soft smile and squeezing her hand in mine.

Should I cross my fingers behind my back? Probably. Because I'm a big fat liar. Hell, maybe I shouldn't make these promises at all. One day, Jenni will wake up and see my fangs, seeing me for who I truly am—a goddamn snake in the grass, ready to turn her and her boyfriend over to my boss.

We fall into a quiet calm, advancing through the line quickly. Several people walk by us with frowns on their faces, bitching about the uppity security guard not letting them go in because their clothes weren't up to par. One woman cried because her shoes were so last season, and they wouldn't let her gain entry.

What the hell am I walking into? A nightmare, that's what. Give me knives and blood any day over this hellhole. On second thought, I don't want that either.

"What kind of place is this?" I frantically whisper, eyeing the big guards at the front of the line.

"Very elite. But don't worry. I have the proper coin to gain entry," she murmurs, digging into her boobs once again. She grins when she pulls out a coin with a large R stamped into it with an intricate design all around. "R for Rave. Those people being turned away? They have to have this to get in. It's only given to the best of the best. You can thank my daddy for that." She squares her shoulders with pride as we take another step forward. Only two more people to go, and then we'll be at the head of the line. "He's the head of Thomas Plastics. That's how we got this." She grins at me like I don't know her father is one of the bosses in the Viotto Crime Family.

Whatever.

I'll pretend not to know a lot of things for her sake and mine. The faster I can gather information, the quicker I can hopefully get out of this stupid town. My fingers brush the exposed tattoo in the middle of my chest, following the sharp scar between my breasts. The skin tingles under my touch, reminding me of the night I finally graduated from my torture room and became the woman I am today.

Peering down, I shiver, pulling an arm across my body and lean into Jenni for support. A bone-deep vulnerability at how exposed I feel standing on the sidewalk in a barely there dress and heels, hits me in the chest. My breaths turn shallow, and heat rushes up my spine.

I want my hoodie, sweatpants, and my bed to sink into. Anything to soothe my skin crawling at the prospect of rubbing necks with so many damn people. But I'm here for a reason, and that reason is standing beside me. No matter my discomfort, Jenni comes first.

My mission trumps all.

"By the way, I love your tattoo," Jenni beams, gesturing toward my fingers running the length of my scar underneath. Thankfully with the key and vine design I picked out, It's barely noticeable sometimes. Although I usually protect it with an under-boob corset, I couldn't tonight.

"Thanks. I got it when I turned eighteen."

"Next!" the security guard hollers, beckoning us forward.

"We're good," Jenni says with a grin, showing the man the coin.

"And your IDs?" he asks, raising a brow when Jenni plucks her from her cleavage, and I grab mine.

He inspects them for a split second with a scoff. "Okay, Destiny and Cherry, you're in," he says, nodding toward the loud club, basically vibrating from the inside out.

"All right, Bitch. Let's go dance our asses off," Jenni giggles, pulling me forward toward the red double doors.

Dancing in six-inch heels should be illegal. So should the strong alcohol coursing through my underage veins. Oh, wait, it is. It's stupid how it tastes so damn good on my tongue. I want to swim inside a glass of it and never leave.

"Oh my God," Jenni slurs, swaying beside me with her arms in the air. "I think the Devils are in their little hidey hole," she giggles at that, doing some awkward dance I can't quite put my finger on.

Is she twerking? God, I hope not. Pretty sure that's not how twerking works. I tilt my head in fascination as she giggles, putting her hands on her damn toes. Her ass sways in the air back and forth, garnering attention from a group of guys from across the bar who scream bad news and danger. Oh, God. I stiffen. My fascination turns into horror when she jiggles her damn peach too close to the sun, and her ass cheeks fall completely out of her dress, flashing the entire club her goods. Shit. The guys from across the way rearrange their junk, watching her with lust in their eyes. Fuck balls! Not today, Satan! I lean forward, pulling her itty-bitty dress over her round peaches, and huff at her antics.

"Jenni, stand up. You're flashing your cock pocket to the entire damn club," I hiss, reaching down and helping her stand up. She grins at me and kisses my cheek with appreciation.

"You always look out for me, don't you?"

Mmmhmm. Something like that.

"Of course. You're my bestie," I say, fixing her red curls as we begin to dance together. "Just don't bend over again. Unless you want Elias to murder half this place."

Her cheeks turn pink. "Mmm. I think they like you. They're watching you," she hiccups, leaning her forehead on my shoulder like we're slow dancing at our middle school dance.

"Who?" I ask, pulling her closer as she stumbles over her feet.

"The Devils, bestie. They're watching," she hiccups, nodding in a weird direction. "In their hidey hole," she sings, throwing her head back with a laugh.

Jesus Christ. She's drunker than a skunk. Hell, she acts like she's about to collapse in my arms and black out. Or, God, puke.

Wait.

"The Devils?" I ask, looking around the dance floor, trying to find them. "And a hideout?" My eyes continue to look around the packed club, filled to the brim with half-dressed people dancing to the DJ standing at the front. My heart pounds at the sound of their name and the danger they bring with them. "Jenni, concentrate," I grunt, trying to stay on top of her as she moves again.

Lord help me. I'm going to have gray hair by the time this night is over. My drunk friend is going to get herself into so much trouble. Between her ass playing peek-a-boo and the amount of drinks she's had, I'm going to play babysitter soon. Or have a puker on my hands.

I should not have let her have that fourth shot of tequila. Not to mention the weird mixed drink she ordered and promptly chugged, begging for another. And another. This girl clearly had a mission when she came to the club—get drunk as fast as possible and forget about her boyfriend not being here.

"Hidey hole. Hidey holeeee!!" she screeches, throwing her hands all around in the air.

"No more drinks for you," I grumble, shifting her as she sways with the music and leaning against me.

"They're up there. Shepp is watching you," she whispers right in my ear. And somehow, she is conscious enough to turn us around until I'm facing a certain part of the club. "Look up, Bestie."

The moment my eyes connect with Shepp's through a large window hovering above the club, shivers roll down my spine. He watches me like he owns me and wants to possess every inch of my flesh. Hell, maybe I'd let him. Let freedom ring with a big dick and...

"I'm going to be sick," Jenni hisses, covering her mouth.

Fuck.

Jenni takes off in a frantic run with me not too far behind her, pushing through the gyrating crowd.

"Puker on the run!" I shout, waving a hand and pointing to the tall redhead, maneuvering through the sea of people like she's done this before.

Shit. She probably has. I try as hard as I can to stay on Jenni's almost exposed ass, but my stupid heels get caught in what feels like a sticky substance, and I tumble to my knees and slam into the gross floor of the club. Thankfully, I'm out of the main pocket of people dancing, so I don't get trampled.

"That had better be gum," I whine to myself, dusting off my hands.

In the distance, the bathroom door swings open and slams shut, letting me know my girl made it. Several girls fall out of the bathroom, looking equally as drunk as Jenni. One lady even pushes through the crowd with her arms around her friend's shoulder, completely supporting her weight. Now, I need to check and see if she called Ralph on the big white phone or if we need to call security and clean up her mess. Just as I'm about to get up on my own, a warm hand wraps around my bicep. I squeak, ready to tell the perv off, but I don't have a chance.

"What the fuck are you doing in my club?" Jericho hisses, dragging me to my feet.

I grunt, stumble over the stupid heels, and cringe when I

don't see gum on the floor. Fuck. Replace the G in gum with a C, and I think I have that on the bottom of my borrowed heels.

"And in that!" Jericho shouts again, shaking me slightly until I pay attention to his face.

I stop dead, stiffening when those familiar brown eyes speckled with gold glare at me. He utters something else, but I don't hear the words falling from his lips.

I've known of Jericho Viotto for years now. We walked the same halls. Took the same classes. But we were always separated by an invisible wall of society. Him with his security guards and riches. And me, with everyone else, barely surviving. Jericho, Arrow, and Shepp were a cut above the rest of us. Better. Wealthier. They're heirs to the throne of Briar Cove.

My eyes fall down his tall frame, taking in the muscles hiding beneath his white dress shirt. There's little left to the imagination. Even under his tight pants. He towers over me, still babbling about being in his club and how I'm underage.

It's odd to me that someone like him could come from my monster—Gabriel Viotto. The king of the city. Someone who takes little girls and hides them away from their sister, who he keeps under his thumb, forcing them to murder and maim under his rule. Even thinking his name has shivers rolling down my spine.

No. Gabriel Viotto is rotten to the core, someone who deserves to catch a bullet between the eyes. He doesn't deserve a name. He deserves a title—that's all he'll ever get from me. No respect.

Jericho and his father look so much alike. Tall. Dark. Devastatingly handsome. Only Jericho isn't him. Not like his father at all. At least, I don't think he is. I've had to watch him before on many occasions, tailing his every move. I think he only saw me once before I darted into a dark hallway.

"Why are you in my club?" he hisses again, practically shoving his face into mine and drawing me out of my rampant thoughts.

Fuck. I'm way too drunk to deal with him. He could skip off to my monster and tell him I was here.

"You're judgmental and rude," I growl, attempting to peel his fingers from my arm, but he relents.

"And you're a bad fucking girl, Little Chaos," he hisses, getting right into my face with his handsome sneer.

"Who the hell do you think you are?" I grind out, wanting to stab him in the eye with my cum shoe. In fact, I bend down, ready to take my spiked heel off and push it through his eyeball, but another hand catches my other arm.

Wonderful.

I'm surrounded by the Devils in a crowded nightclub while my best friend pukes her brains out in the bathroom.

Could this night get any worse?

CHAPTER SIXTEEN
Journey

IN THE HISTORY of all that's history, no one should speak the phrase *could this get any worse* and expect a better outcome.

I stare Jericho down with a defiant gaze. Now that I'm steady on my feet, thanks to their hands, I can manage a mean expression. Instead of falling over onto the cum-stained floor. Again.

"How did you get into my fucking club?" Jericho barks again.

Finally, his hand unwraps from my bicep, leaving Shepp holding my other arm. No one should be allowed to manhandle me. Ever. And... Shit. I think I'll have a Jericho-sized bruise there. But oh crap, my breath completely leaves me when he wraps his hands around my waist and brings me flush against him. He smells way too good to be this close to me. I might just eat him alive.

Add Jericho Viotto's sinfully hard body against mine to the list of illegal offenses for the evening. I swear to all things holy, I can feel every inch of his hard muscles through his tight white dress shirt, and it goes straight to my damn pussy.

"To answer your question, they let me in. Besides, I'm having a girl's night out. And you were not invited." I lift my chin, meeting the darkness in his eyes. It fucking calls to me to poke the damn bear and rile him up.

Even Arrow agrees when he chuckles at my side, rudely

running his fingers through my curly, disheveled hair and snagging on knots. He pulls and pulls until his fingers are free. But I never flinch from the pain pulling at the roots. My toes may curl, and a moan may lie on the back of my tongue, but I hold back.

My freedom beckons me to rebel against my monster once again. To let these three take me somewhere dark and dangerous and have their wicked way with me.

Where this sass is coming from, I have no idea. This is Jericho Viotto—mafia heir, and his two cronies. And apparently, his club. But he's in my face, looking all handsome and angry at me. So, I have to fight back, right? I can't let this tall bastard win. Huh. I guess six-inch heels are good for something. They give me a leg up and put me about as tall as Jericho's chin. Eat that, asshole.

"I need to go check on my bestie and make sure she's still in the land of the living." I grind my teeth when his hands move up and down the sides of my hips, getting dangerously close to the flesh of my outer thighs.

Touch me—my brain sings. Touch me until I come so violently I black out and forget about all my problems. A little voice rings in my head over and over, begging me to claim my freedom again. Memories of the night with my three masked men spring to mind, and a familiar warmth encases my flesh.

If I stay like this, I might just drink his dangerous aura up and get drunk on it. Not that I'm not tipsy. I am. Just a little bit. Jenni insisted on fruity mixed drinks and shots to get us started. Me and shots? We're not well acquainted. I stopped after the first one and went to sipping my mixed drink because fire burned down my throat. Hence why she's four tequila shots deep and at least four mixed drinks, too.

Damn. I'm a terrible drinking bestie. But at least I made sure her vagina stayed covered, and she didn't get herself into any trouble. It's what friends do, right?

"Call security," Jericho says, eyeing Arrow, who stands silently beside us with a grin on his face. "Let them know there's a girl who needs looking after in the restroom. In fact, call Nichole from security. She'll help clean Jenni up, and then, we can kick these two out."

"But my Kitten," Arrow whines with a frown.

"Arrow," Jericho barks through clenched teeth. "Don't fucking test me right now."

Arrow scoffs, leaning into the side of my face. I stiffen when his flat wet tongue runs up my cheek, leaving nothing but wetness behind. "I licked her, she's mine," he says with a pointed look when he pulls back.

I frown. "I belong to no one," I hiss, shoving at his chest and then wipe my cheek off. Well, as best I can when one asshole is holding my arm and the other has my front plastered to his. If I didn't know any better, I'd say... they want me.

I swallow hard, ignoring that thought in my brain. It's the alcohol's fault. Yup, that's it. There's no way these men dressed in fancy clothes, smelling like cigars and a mix of whiskey, who belong to the damn mafia—would ever be interested in little old me.

"What are you doing?" Jericho grunts in a low voice next to my ear. "Are you sniffing me?" he whispers.

I shiver when his lips brush against my jawline in a soft kiss.

"No," I retort, taking another deep breath. What's one more, right? He smells divine. "Maybe," I huff, craning my neck when he runs his nose down my flesh in a groan. "Are you sniffing me?" I retort sarcastically. Or at least I think I did. It came out as more of a breathy moan.

"Yes," he says directly next to my ear. "I'm going to give you an order, Little Chaos."

My Kitten? Little Chaos? It tickles something in the back of my squishy mind, but I can't fucking recall it. I wish I could. It makes my pussy weep with want. Especially when his voice dips so fucking low that all my nerves go on high alert.

"Acknowledge my fucking words," he demands in my ear.

But I can't focus on anything. Not when his fingers wander

across my inner thigh, heading up, up, up—straight for the promised land. Another set of fingers run up and down my arms.

"I acknowledge your fucking words," I garble out in a rush of words that were supposed to hold meaning and sound snarky, but it all falls flat when his palm bumps against my panty-clad clit. At least I did one thing right tonight and insisted on underwear. Unlike some other girl I know who decided going commando was the way to go. We all saw how that went. Flash city!

"Cover me," Jericho says to someone. I don't know who. And I don't give a shit when his palm grinds against my clit and sparks of joy run through my body. Who needs my three masked men when I have the most dangerous one of all about to make me cum in the middle of a crowded room. "Good, girl," he murmurs. "Now, I want you to come all over my fingers. That's an order."

"Fuck, Kitten," Arrow moans from beside me, reclaiming his spot. His fingers run over my lips, tasting like smoke and whiskey. "Suck my fingers, Kitten. It'll stop you from drawing attention to yourself."

"What's the status of her friend?" Jericho asks.

Right. Jenni. My bestie. She's slumped over on a toilet, puking her brains out. I should care. I really should. But it seems like these fellas have it under control. Besides, there's a fireworks show happening behind my eyes, and my pussy is ready to devour Jericho's fingers as he slowly eases them under my panties and his palm hits the magic button over and over in slow motion.

"Nichole is cleaning her up and will have her sleeping in the car with a bottle of water. She'll be there when we're ready. And we need to have a talk after all this," Arrow confirms in a serious voice as he shoves his fingers in my mouth. "Suckity suck, Kitten. Show me what you can do with that wicked little tongue of yours besides mouth off and piss Jericho off." He chuckles at that when I run my tongue over three of his fingers he so rudely stuck in my mouth. I hum against him, drool dripping down my lips.

"This is a claiming, Little Chaos," Jericho murmurs, grunting when he shoves three fingers into my pussy, curling them right against my G-spot.

Holy mother of Devils. My hips buck, begging for friction when he leaves them there.

"What do you mean a claiming?" I mumble out around Arrow's fingers as he slowly inches them in and out of my mouth, leaving me full.

Jericho grins. Arrow grunts. And Shepp, well—he stands there with his hand wrapped around my arm still. My eyes drift to his as best I can, staring into their depths. My chest heaves, and his eyes drop to my tits with want.

What the hell is happening right now?

"Do you want to come, Little Chaos?"

I nod my head with vigor, nearly biting Arrow's fingers off when my teeth clamp down. He moans, throwing his head back. The unmistakable tent in his pants juts forward.

"Fuck this. We need to take her to our office, bend her over a goddamn chair, and fuck her brains out," Arrow says, bouncing on his toes. With his free hand, he grabs mine and shoves it down his pants, wrapping my fingers around his bare length, pulsating against my palm.

"You know we can't," Jericho's deep voice does funny things to me.

But wait. Why can't they? I'm down to fuck. Bend me over! Relieve this stress and help me feel again. Give me the freedom I ache for.

I swear my brain melts when he thrusts into my hand. "Fuck yes, Kitten. Tighten your fist like that," he moans right in my ear. "Yes, I'm going to come in your hand now. I want you to come with me. Make her come, Jer. So we can get the fuck out of here," he says, thrusting faster and faster.

"You heard the man, Little Chaos. I want you to come all over my fingers now. Fuck, that's a good fucking girl," he whispers, clamping onto my neck with his teeth and sucking hard as my orgasm hits me like a fucking train throwing me down the tracks.

I would have screamed. But Arrow shoves his fingers further down my throat, effectively blocking off my oxygen and making my gag reflex kick in. Then I feel the warmth spread through my hand in Arrow's pants as he gasps for air.

"Yes, Kitten. Fuck. You milk me so goddamn good," he whispers straight into my ear as I come down from my high.

I suck in so many breaths, trying to pull oxygen back into my lungs, that my brain almost goes black when he removes his fingers from my mouth, soaked with my saliva.

"That was a claiming," Jericho whispers.

When I peek my eyes open, he grins, sucking his fingers soaked with my release into his mouth with a satisfied hum.

They do this all the time, right? Pick girls from the club and maul them on the busy dance floor. Shit. The busy dance floor. My eyes pop open wide when I peer around at the crazy crowd growing rowdier by the second, but they're barely visible through the low lights of the club.

"They're all so drunk and busy, Kitten. They don't have a clue we basically fucked on the dance floor. Plus Shepp was blocking you from view." Arrow grins at me, keeping his hand wrapped around mine in his pants. Ever so gently, he lifts them out of his waistband but doesn't let go. His warm cum slathers over my fingers and palm. "You're going to do something delicious for me right now. You're going to stick your cum-coated fingers into your pussy until every last drop is inside you," he says with conviction, eyeing me when my brain short fucking circuits.

"What?" I gasp as he wrenches my hand—which is full of his cum—under my skirt with force. Like I don't have a say in the matter.

"You heard him," Jericho says with blown pupils. "Finger yourself in the middle of this club and lubricate yourself with his slick cum. Then, you can go home."

Well, home does sound quite appealing right now. Nothing like a few drinks and an orgasm with fingers down your throat to make me sleepy as fuck.

I lick my lips as they stay on top of me, surrounding me and blocking me from the view of other people. There's truth in their words from before. No one pays us any mind. They're all too busy getting hot and heavy with their own partners to notice what happened here. Fuck. I swallow hard when moaning starts happening around the club. People start fucking everywhere, high on the heady lust floating in the air.

Okay. This is really happening. They won't let me go until I fuck myself in front of them with Arrow's cum coating my fingers. Good thing I have an IUD.

Jericho's fingers wrap around my throat, and he pulls me closer. He sinks his teeth into my bottom lip as my fingers work through my wet folds. My cum soaks every inch of my panties, and now, it's about to get messier.

The moment my fingers enter my pussy, my eyes practically roll back into my head from the sensitive sensation. I want to squirm away. But yet, I'm still too fucking aroused to say no. I want this, I realize.

"Oh fuck," I moan right into Jericho's mouth as he overtakes me. Someone grabs my arm, squished between the two of us, and helps me pump my fingers up and down.

"Fuck yes. Get all my cum inside you, Kitten. Coat your pussy with it," he groans in my ear, nibbling on my lobe.

My breath stalls when my pussy convulses again around my fingers, dragging them further inside. White dots sparkle behind my eyes as I deepen the kiss with Jericho and moan into his mouth. As soon as it's over and I've ridden my high, my body slumps against his.

"See, you can be obedient when orgasms are on the line. I'll remember that. For now, let's get you home and away from this club before it turns into an orgy for the night," Jericho murmurs, helping me remove my fingers from my pussy.

And then he picks me up.

I'd protest that I can walk, but with the way Jell-O has replaced every bone in my body, I think I'll stay in his big, strong arms. He's like a knight in shining armor, except he's the devil in disguise.

A burst of warm air brushes against my flesh when we finally make it from the darkened, noisy club and come outside. Only stopping once.

"You see this face, Seymour?" Jericho's deep voice grunts, showing the poor man my face.

"Yes, Sir," he says hesitantly.

"She is no longer allowed in here. Along with her little friend. Unless they're accompanied by us. Understand?" The man has so much authority in his voice that I can practically see the big bad security dude's balls shriveling up from being chastised. But I don't. Because I can't really open my eyes. They're permanently shut for the night. And apparently, so is my mouth. I'd have protested that we should be allowed to come in, but my jaw hurts. My pussy throbs. My legs won't work from too many orgasms. I'm a sack of potatoes in Jericho's arms.

"You didn't?" Jericho asks lowly with accusation.

Didn't what? I have no clue what they're even talking about.

"No, Daddy Jer. That's all the orgasms and drinks," Arrow chuckles.

The sound of a car door opening rattles my ears, and then, we're inside a vehicle with me still secured on Jericho's lap. He pulls my head into his chest and runs his fingers softly up and down my calves and thighs, soothing me even further. I swear, I melt into him. A man I shouldn't even trust. But, something in my gut has me swooning over him.

"How's Jenni?" I grumble, peeking an eye open when a second set of hands peels my heels off. Arrow grins, shoving his thumb into the arch of my foot. "Marry me?" I mumble jokingly when he rubs my feet with expert pressure.

"You don't have to ask me twice, Kitten. I'll put you in a black dress, march you up the aisle, and say I do before you can even realize what's happening," Arrow quips.

"Why black?" I ask, not daring to move from between the two men who are so lovingly taking care of me.

"Because we all know you can't wear white," he says with a shrug, continuing his beautiful massage movements on my feet.

I don't bother asking why he said what he said. Instead, I close my eyes, blissfully loving the attention. Even if it's from the wrong people.

"Go to sleep, Little Chaos. We'll take you home and tuck you in," Jericho murmurs, gently kissing my forehead.

What a weirdo. I should ask more questions like—how do you know where I live? Or why are you being so kind to me? But whatever. Sleep never clings to me this damn hard. So, I fall into the abyss of darkness and let myself freely fall in front of three strangers who just made me come in the middle of a dance floor.

What a weird ass night.

CHAPTER SEVENTEEN

Shepp

IF THIS BONER doesn't go away, I'm going to have to finish myself off in Journey's shower before we leave. It's trying hard to punch through my damn jeans.

"Just stand over her, Sheppy Boy. She'd love a cum shower," Arrow says with a grin, staring down at the sleeping girl tucked away in her bed.

'That's a you thing. Not a me thing,' I sign with a frown. *'Besides, that's creepy.'* I roll my eyes when he lies beside her, staring at her face with a grin.

"You wouldn't mind, would you, Kitten?" he hums, tucking a wild curl behind her ear.

Jericho paces Journey's disaster of a bedroom with his phone glued to his ear. He frowns, and his nostrils flare wildly. Whatever is happening back at Rave needs our attention immediately.

"What the fuck do you mean there's been a problem? Two goddamn problems?" Jericho bellows into the phone with a scowl. "Secure them. We'll be there."

Arrow sighs, placing his lips on Journey's, and removes himself from beside her. I glare at him when he waltzes through her bedroom like he owns it, heading straight for her messy dresser.

Arrow rummages through Journey's dresser, humming as he

pulls several things out. Sweat pants, a T-shirt, and fresh underwear.

'*Why the underwear?*' I sign with a frown, standing guard next to Journey's bedroom door so Sable doesn't get any bright ideas about entering.

Arrow doesn't respond as he sets them on her bed, eyeing her passed-out form.

"There's an issue with the game," Jericho curses, putting his phone into his pocket. His eyes dart to Journey with furrowed brows. "And apparently, there's something we need to see on the surveillance videos."

'*What kind of issue?*' I sign.

"It was those new money-rich assholes, wasn't it?" Arrow asks, slowly removing one of Journey's high heels and bringing it up to his nose. "Even her feet smell delicious." He sighs a little, turning the heel upside down, sniffing the bottom. "And salty."

I blink several times in disgust. '*Gross,*' I sign, knocking the shoe out of his hands. '*Stop sniffing shoes and pay attention.*' This is his problem. He never pays attention when Jer's in his angry place, earning him more glares.

Arrow frowns, slipping her other shoe off and throwing it to the ground. "Happy?"

'*Yes.*' I nod. '*You were saying?*' I sign to Jericho.

As I turn my attention to Jericho, I purposely tune out Arrow and his obsession with her scent as he leans in and licks her toes with a satisfied hum. I discreetly watch him as he works his way up her leg and around her knee, using his tongue to taste every inch of her. My dick begs to pop out of my pants when he slowly lifts up her skirt, but that's where I draw the line. I grunt, grabbing him by the back of the shirt and shaking my head.

'*Stop licking her,*' I sign after letting him go.

He grins. "But she's mine. I can lick what's mine."

He shrugs like it's the most logical thing he could have said.

"Cheaters," Jericho remarks, without any emotions on his face, bringing us back to the conversation. "Security watched the tapes and said they were not only counting cards but hiding some up their sleeves. It's an elaborate scheme to fuck us over and steal our money." He swipes a hand over his creased forehead. "Someone went missing from within our club. A woman. The police are in our fucking office with questions. More shit piling up."

If there were more than just the four of us in this room, everyone would be giving Jericho a wide berth. Rage wafts off him in waves. It's so potent I can practically smell the fury from within him.

"I want to take their fingers," Arrow says, standing tall with renewed focus on the situation. "I can strap their hands down and chop them off one by one until they confess to their sins."

"That won't be necessary. But we do need to head back and dispose of the troublesome group. They'll never come back to Briar Cove if they know what's good for them," Jericho growls, squeezing his fingers into fists. "Arrow, you'll take care of them. I'll placate the police and get them moving."

"Fuck yes. Bring on the blood and mayhem! If I can't fuck my lady properly, I want absolute destruction."

Jericho sighs. "Then, shall we? We can't keep our victims waiting. They're in the basement of Rave, ready for their talking to." He sweeps an arm out, gesturing for us to get moving.

My eyes fall on Journey, deep in her slumber. A protectiveness takes me over and calls me to stay by her side. Besides, destruction and blood are not my forte. I'd rather watch her peacefully sleep and stay by her side than chop off dicks and fingers.

'I'll stay here and keep an eye on her. She could vomit in her sleep,' I sign, swallowing hard when Jericho narrows his eyes.

"If you jack off, make sure you come on her. It'll let others know she's spoken for," Arrow says, grinning when he adjusts himself." And rub it into her skin really well. It's a natural moisturizer."

'Please don't tell me you've been coming on her while she sleeps,' I sign, alarm bells ringing in my head.

"Okay, I won't say," he quips, opening her window and hopping out. "Which reminds me," he trails off, looking toward the sky as a grin spreads across his face.

'He's coming up with some diabolical plan,' I sign in a frenzy, nodding toward Arrow.

"What's new?" Jericho sighs, looking down at our girl. "Take care of her, all right?"

Always do. *'I will,'* I sign with confidence on my face. *'Don't worry.'*

He nods, joining Arrow outside the window.

"We'll text you with fun updates," Jericho quips, wiggling his brows. Whatever tension had him by the balls five seconds ago, has released as they leave.

No doubt, he's excited at the prospect of bleeding the cheaters dry.

"I'll take so many pictures for you, Sheppy Boy. It'll be like you didn't miss a thing." Arrow grins, waltzing off toward the SUV with a swagger in his step.

Always ready for the destruction of our enemies. Even the ones attempting to cheat at our highly secure games. But not me. I'd rather stay behind and not have to witness the bloodshed. There's just something about the violence I've never got used to.

"Protect her with your life," Jericho murmurs, glancing at her one last time before walking from view.

'Just you and me,' I sign to the girl snoring, sound asleep on top of her comforter. *'You just lie there, I'll help you get changed.'* I snort to myself, taking a step away from her and letting my eyes wander.

There's clothes everywhere on the ground and covering her dresser. Soda cans lying near the overflowing trash. Papers strewn in the corners. I sigh with the urge to pick everything up and tidy her room. She'd probably sleep through the whole process.

No. First things first.

'Sorry, Sweetheart. You need out of this dress,' I sign, leaning

forward and memorizing every imperfection on her body, especially on her face.

The freckles across the bridge of her nose. The dip in her skin next to her lip where a scar sits. Fuck. I suck in a breath, shaking away the feelings uncoiling inside me.

I want to strip her bare. But I'm not Arrow. Not really. He takes what he wants, regardless of her consciousness. And me? I sit back and try to do things the right way. In some regards, though. He and I are one and the same. He, the loud stalker. And me, the silent predator, freely walking into her home.

I'll protect her with my life.

Thoughts of the night we had filter through my mind. Not an hour before, we were on the dance floor, bringing pleasure to the woman before me. Right now, she's passed out. But before? God, she was so damn alive under our fingertips. I wanted to caress her heaving tits and pinch her nipples between my fingers.

I squeeze my eyes shut. The imagery is not helping my raging boner begging for relief. I swear my balls ache when I think about what I need to do. Journey came in her panties. Then, she used Arrow's cum to get herself off even more.

Every inch of her clothing needs to come off her body. But my morals scream at me. We never take advantage of a woman while she's sleeping in her own bed. Ever. This is her sacred domain, where she feels safe from the men that come in and out of her trailer at all hours. She's even safe here from her mother's abuses.

I blow out a breath, trying to picture football or even my father's face. Anything to make this boner deflate and leave me until I can truly take care of it. My fingers tremble when they trace around her knee, slowly gliding up her thighs toward her soaked panties. My dick throbs harder when I grip the sides and bring her thong over her knees, ankles, and feet. Finally, they dangle from my fingertips, and I'm transfixed by the wet spot staring back at me. My breath quivers in my chest when I shove them in my pocket and promise myself I'll use them later. No matter whose cum is dried to the fabric.

I swallow any future regrets and reach down, grabbing the new pair of panties first. I slowly bring them up her legs, keeping my eyes diverted away from her center, and settle them on her hips. The sweatpants Arrow set out come next, and I slowly pull them up her legs with a grunt, getting snagged behind her knees. After several heaving breaths, I secure them to her hips.

That was the easy part.

Journey doesn't stir. Not even flinching when I move some wild hairs away from her forehead. She's dead to the world—to me. How I wish she'd open her eyes and see me standing before her, ready to protect her at the drop of a hat.

Dread unfurls inside me. What would have happened if we hadn't seen her? Or gotten to her? If she had stayed at our club? Maybe she could have been that person that went missing. Some other guys could have tried to pick her up. Not like Arrow wouldn't have been able to track her down and drag her out of their clutches. That's easy. But who would have taken advantage of her?

My fingers curl into fists, as I will the images of the what ifs away from my mind.

Journey was drunk but not as bad as Jenni. She was out of her mind, swimming in alcohol. Something in my gut says there's something odd going on in our club. Why were these two even permitted? I'm sure Jenni got a VIP coin, allowing her entrance. But they're too young to be inside the walls of Rave.

I shake off the weird feeling brewing inside me and reach down for her plain black shirt on the edge of the bed. I freeze when her hand snatches my wrist away from her shirt, holding it tightly.

"Don't take her," she says through a rasp. "Leave Sunshine alone," she begs with tears glistening in her glazed-over eyes.

My body stiffens at the fear in her eyes. Her tone leaves no room for arguments as she pleads again.

"Dude, you grunt in your sleep," Jericho remarks with a frown,

sitting opposite of me. "Are you sleeping all right?" He raises a brow when I push my breakfast around on my plate.

'Fine,' I sign, refusing to look him in the eyes.

"You... speak, Shepp," he says in a low voice. "I hear your screams."

I hear your screams. It repeats in my mind. My screams? My fingers caress my throat as I ponder his words, and my eyes shut on their own. The dreams that plague me when I close my eyes send shivers down my spine. It makes me not want to sleep at all. But I have to.

'I said I'm fine,' I sign with a scowl, wishing he'd back off. Since I lost my voice, I've been plagued with nightmares of the night over and over again.

"I did it! It was me! Leave Sunshine out of this!" She sobs now, shouting in my face with a pleading look twisting her features. "Please."

Her words stab me in the heart. Her heartfelt pleas, begging an invisible villain.

But why? What's happened in her life? And how do we not know about it? We know almost everything about her. Well, whatever we've dredged up over the years through our lawyer.

I wave a hand in front of her face, attempting to catch her gaze and bring her back from the brink of falling. She doesn't flinch again. She's completely lost to whatever nightmare is holding her in its grasp.

I have to let her ride it out. Never wake a person in the midst of a nightmare.

"Please don't hurt her. She's just a little girl. She didn't do anything wrong! I did it!" More tears leak down her cheeks, dripping down her chin and landing on her fluffy comforter.

What is she talking about?

My breath stalls when her fingers loosen from my wrist, and she winces.

"Please don't leave me in the dark, Sir. Please don't leave me here to rot! I'm sorry! I didn't mean to."

She scuttles away from me, moving back on her bed until her back hits the headboard with a loud thud. Through the darkness of the room, I see her trembling form, attempting to get as far away as possible from me. Her glazed eyes look me up and down with fear written across her expression.

Desperation spears through me to gather her in my arms and soothe the ache clawing at her. My mind races a million miles a minute. My hands reach out and then retract, torn between wanting to scoop her up and hold her. And staying back while silently hoping for her nightmare to cease.

"I didn't mean to," she whispers again, shaking her head. I freeze at her confession. "It was all for Sunshine. She's my sister. All for her. She didn't deserve that. Please..." she trails off with the please, shaking like a leaf in bed. "Please! Sir! Please don't hurt her! She's only a kid, and her heart. It's bad. She needs her medicine." Snot and tears flow freely down her cheeks as she makes no move to swipe them away.

She draws her knees into her chest, hopelessness settling in on her dropping face.

"I was protecting her."

Fuck this.

My heart thumps wildly when I slowly move forward, aching to soothe her dreams away. My fingers brush through her hair slowly, combing through her curls when her eyes connect with mine.

The lights are off, and no one's home inside her mind. She's fallen down into the dark abyss, unable to resurface.

"Please!" she shouts in my face with desperation, attempting to flee from my grasp. No, Sweetheart. You can't escape me. I'm here to protect you. "Please don't. I'm sorry." Her sobs echo through the room.

I pull her into me, but she fights me off, pounding her fists into my shoulders and chest. With each hit of her fist, my resolve flushes down the drain.

I open my mouth, willing my voice to work for once. I haven't... I can't...

I squeeze my eyes shut. If I could just soothe her with words. If I could just hold her tight and whisper in her ears that she's going to be okay. That we'll find her apparent sister, Sunshine, and bring her back.

"Please, bring her back!" she shouts, pushing off me. "Give her back to me!"

Journey's tears reach into my fucking chest and yank out my heart. She owns me—my beating heart and fucking blackened soul. From the moment I laid eyes on her, I knew. I knew what she'd bring to the table. I just didn't know I'd be sharing her with my two best friends.

No matter. I'm keeping her forever.

Her panic rises, her cries growing louder and louder until her breaths come in heavy pants. Shit. She clutches her chest, turning red from the lack of oxygen. Her gasps ring in my ears as she continues to cry and beg for air.

I open my mouth again, sucking in a breath. Mentally, my mind tumbles with indecision. Do I? Can I? It's been so fucking long since I've used it. Or had the desire. Not since he took my tongue, effectively muting me.

"Now, you'll never be able to utter another word to Gabriel ever again." His sickening smile haunts my dreams.

I open my mouth, feeling the hollowness where my tongue should be. On instinct, I try to move it, but I only work the base of it where it still rests at the back of my throat.

It's gone.

He took it.

Without my permission.

And now, I'm voiceless amongst the loud.

Just how he wants me.

I shake away the memory. One filled with probing hands and hateful looks. Thomas Mondelli was never a father. Especially not mine. He didn't deserve the title. Ever. He deserves to rot in the deepest part of hell, sizzling for eternity. I'm glad someone killed him in the line of duty for Gabriel. I'm glad he was shot straight through the chest and choked on his own blood. He deserved to hurt.

I've never had the desire to speak since my father cut out my tongue. He took my voice. My way to communicate. Right now, I need it more than ever to cut through her cries and panic.

In a futile attempt, I sign loving words in front of her eyes. Not that she'd know what I was saying, but maybe it'd knock her from her stupor. But it doesn't do anything at all.

There's only one thing I can do to soothe her. Only one thing to do before she crashes and burns before my eyes.

Even if everything inside me squirms and my skin heats from the uncomfortable feeling of clearing my throat and producing the unmistakable sound of my deep voice. Little noises erupt from my vocal cords, and the webs from disuse fall off, giving way to something I completely forgot about.

My voice.

"It's okay," I rasp out as best I can without the support of my tongue.

I freeze. It's odd to hear a piece of me that I haven't experienced in years. My eyes widen at the sound of my scratchy voice, barely above a whisper. It's low, raspy, and airy. A forgotten entity I've buried for so long, hellbent on burying the memories of the man who took this from me.

"You're okay, I swear. I won't hurt you, Sweetheart. I'll protect you forever." That's a goddamn pledge I can get behind. "We'll never let you go."

Journey's body continues to tremble, her glazed-over eyes zeroing in on me when I bend down in front of her, clutching her cheeks in my palms.

"Wherever you're lost at, I'm the lighthouse bringing you back. Fight through the fog, Sweetheart," I rasp in a whisper, forcing her sleeping form to stare at me. Even if it doesn't register. "Fight to get back to me."

Journey's lip quivers as more tears spill. "I just want to go home," she whispers with desperation. Her fingernails dig into my forearms where she hangs onto me like a life raft. "Please. Don't let my monster come back. He'll hurt me."

"I am your home," I whisper again, pressing my forehead into hers. "Let go, Sweetheart. You're safe here. Not there. Follow my voice and leave the darkness."

She nods like she understands, loosening her grip and falling limp.

"I'm safe," she whispers, shivering in my grasp.

"Journey?" I murmur, catching her cloudy eyes.

"Hmm?" she hums, growing weaker and weaker in my arms.

"Who's Sunshine? And who has her?" Tears sting my eyes when a small smile pulls at her lips, and she sighs wistfully, almost seeming awake. But I know by the glazed look in her eyes, she's still not with it. She's sleep-talking. She'll have no recollection of this in the morning.

"My little sister. But he has her. He holds her over my head. My monster." Her words ring through my mind long after her head lolls to the side, and the nightmare fades away into nothing.

Tears cloud my eyes when I pull back, and her sleeping face greets me. Tears stain her reddened cheeks as she takes a deep breath, snuggling into my palms on her cheeks.

She's home. She's safe.

And I'm never letting her forget it.

Without hesitation, I pull her into me for reassurance. Her head rests into my shaking chest, and my fingers run through her curls, careful not to snag. Together, we fall onto her mattress, lying side by side. My arm tightens around her, dragging her back to my chest and settling her ear against my thumping heart. Quiet sighs of contentment fall from her lips. Her arm wraps around my middle, clinging to me as she sleeps away the fear she once felt.

This is what Arrow does when he sneaks in. And now, I understand why. But has he seen the way she thrashes and calls for Sunshine?

I'm her goddamn anchor in the storm, bringing her back from the brink of a hurricane. She's my fighting tempest, blowing through the land and taking down whatever is in her path.

I'll forever hold her and anchor her.

As I stare up at the cracked ceiling, a sense of rightness falls over me. No regrets. No wanting to turn back the clock and put my voice back in a dark box I hid it in for years.

I soothed her—my girl.

I comforted her when she needed someone in her corner. I wonder if Sable ever hears her cries in the middle of the night and is too high to notice the fear laced in her screams. Probably. The walls are too thin. But she doesn't care. Not about Journey and definitely not about herself. Only her addiction.

But now I want to know why her nightmare happened in the first place. Who is this *Monster* she's referring to? And why is she so damn afraid of the dark?

Something happened to Journey West, my Little Tempest, and I'm going to find out what.

CHAPTER EIGHTEEN

Journey

I BLOW OUT A BREATH, lazily following my peers, lost in my thoughts as we make our way into math class. One last Friday. One last day until freedom. Then, Sunday, is our graduation. The moment I walk across the stage and grab my diploma, I'm looking harder than ever for Sunshine. There's been a few clues in her letters here and there. I know she's trying to help me find her, but I'm still stumped.

I rub a hand over my forehead, fighting the headache forming in my skull. I swear, I never want to see another party again. Booze? Nope! Don't need it. Wine? God no, I might vomit before I do that again.

You know what I want? I want my books, bed, and solitude. Instead, for the last couple of weeks, I've been indulging in parties with Jenni in hopes of gathering information for my stupid monster. How's it going? Well, I've drank my weight in more alcohol than I could even imagine, and I've managed to get bits and pieces of what her life is like. She's really opened up since we danced at Rave, and she completely tossed her cookies. Oh, and I practically fucked the Devils on the dance floor.

I can still taste the whiskey and smoke on Arrow's fingers as he gagged me into an orgasm. But I'd never admit that to him. They cross my mind here and there when I lie down to go to sleep. And in the morning, the evidence of my stalker rests on my pillows. It's mostly photos of me sleeping or their hands on my things. Specifically, my underwear. The fucker has a knack for stealing my panties, and soon, I won't have any left. Whoever he is, he better start leaving me some new underwear. Somehow, though, deep in my gut, I feel like I know him. Does it bother me that someone is coming into my space and watching me sleep? Yes and no. Which makes me crazy, right? I'm fucking insane for semi-enjoying his presence. So, I try not to think about it too much.

Jenni and I have also been studying like crazy, almost every night—when we're not partying, of course—leading up to finals. Sometimes it's like talking to a brick wall, but I think I've chiseled away at a lot of her defenses and opened her up. Hopefully. She's a pretty easy person to be around. And honestly, I like her. She doesn't seem to have any other close friends, besides me now. She's one of those—everybody knows her, but no one really knows her—kind of girls.

Now, the end of high school is near. Today is our last day of final exams, and then we're free. Well, they are. I'm still a little puppet for a deranged psycho. But that's the least of my worries. I have to take a test on a full-blown hangover. Jenni and I indulged in way too much wine last night as we stuffed ourselves full of cheese and watched movies while last minute studying. If you could actually call it that. It was nice to share a laugh with someone else and lose myself in the stupid comedy she put on.

Whatever I've done so far has worked. I've gained her trust. Somewhat. I've been snooping in her mansion, looking for any clues. Her father has an office he keeps locked up. He never seems to be home. Neither does her mother. Leaving Jenni to her own devices. It works for me, I guess. There's no cameras lurking in the corners of the rooms or watching from secret places, so it's given me plenty of time to get the lay of the land, memorizing the house and everything in it for future reference.

"No more white wine," I grunt, plopping down into my seat next to Jenni.

She grins, twirling her pencil, not showing an ounce of alcohol-regret. She looks as beautiful as ever. Shiny red hair, tight jeans, beautiful top. Hell, even her face is painted perfectly. And me? I groan, looking down at my ratty jeans and T-shirt. I managed to throw my messy hair into a ponytail this morning.

"And why are you so chipper and pretty?" I lie my head on my arms, groaning into my desk.

"Oh, you're so dramatic," she giggles, waving a hand. "I have news, and I need you. My father is going to be in town this weekend," Jenni pouts.

"No rager?" I quip with a grin.

"Not tonight. So, I need you to help me." She claps her hands with excitement. "So, you've met Elias."

Yeah, he's her boyfriend. Once, when we were hanging out at her house, he popped by for a quick visit. I stayed in her living room studying my textbook. While she studied his dick. Loudly. In her bedroom.

Good times.

I know who Elias is because I've had to study him, too. Just not his dick, thankfully. I know exactly what he does on the outskirts of Briar Cove. Gangster. Drug runner. Gun seller.

He's about as dangerous as the Devils are. About, being the keyword. They still rule this town. Somewhere in my gut, though, I get this twisted feeling that Elias is looking to take this town over. One step at a time.

"You will follow this man, Elias White." I swallow hard, coming to stand by my monster, who rests at six-foot-two, towering over me. His manicured finger points at the man staring back at me from a black and white photograph. Leather jacket, neck tattoos, an eyebrow piercing, and deep, soulless eyes.

"Whereabouts?" I bravely ask, sucking in a breath when he turns his glare to me.

"Elias White runs the Blue Spider Gang. They're notorious for selling potent drugs, something I've allowed on my streets. But now, the people of my town are turning up dead. It's all pointing to him

and his shitty operation. Is that enough information for you, Little Snake? Or do I need to do this entire mission for you?" He raises a haughty brow, glaring at me.

Well, it'd be a lot easier if he did this himself. Obviously, he knows the information better than I do.

"I want to know who he's seeing, what he's doing, where he's going. Bring me back photographic proof. Follow him to the ends of the earth. But..."

"Don't get caught," I say with a sharp nod. "Of course, Sir."

He nods again, slapping a piece of paper into my hands containing an address, a full legal name, and the photograph. Great, so much to go on.

Hopefully, this all ends soon. My monster has never combined my missions or extended them before, except for this one. Once he found out Jenni was my classmate and knew I could use her to get closer to Elias and spy on her father, my fate was sealed. Although, this mission is by far the tamest I've been on. So, I just nod.

"He's meeting my father this weekend."

My brows furrow. "Is that a good idea?"

One mafia man and a gang member notorious for using force to get what he wants. Yeah, that doesn't sound smart at all. Unless they're up to something—and that's what my gut is telling me.

"Pfft. My father is coming around to the idea of him. In fact, they might be striking up a little deal." She wiggles her brows with a grin.

"Which would be amazing because if they don't..." Her eyes dart to a figure in the front of the class, goofing off with his friends—Leighton LeMaster—the governor's son.

Jenni swallows hard, quickly looking away from him. Jenni is an open book, never shying away from informing me on everything her father does. In fact, if the mafia wanted someone in their organization to tell everyone their dirty business, Jenni would be their gal. The number of times she's let it slip about what her dad does within the organization, is wild to me. He's running from town to town, selling their services in exchange for safety. And now this. Her father is willing to turn his back on the mafia for the leader of the Blue Spider Gang? Why?

"What kind of deal?" I ask with interest.

She shrugs. "No idea. But Elias told me that my father contacted him and invited him over for dinner. So, could you come be my buffer?" She grins again, wiggling her brows. "Make it less awkward." She folds her hands together in a pleading manner.

"Okay," I say with a shrug. "What time?"

"I'll pick you up at seven?" There's so much hope and trust in her eyes. What she doesn't realize is, I'm the damn snake about to take her down. As cold as it sounds, she doesn't matter. My sister does. This is all for Sunny and her damn safety.

I nod. "Yeah."

Just then, our teacher meanders into the room with a stack of papers and sets them on his desk, ready to begin our final exam.

I sigh, digging into my pocket and pulling out my phone. My finger hovers above the contact name. It's inconspicuous—Landlord. Because I can't very well type his real name in or label him as the monster he is.

So, without a second thought, I type in our secret code meaning I have information without spelling it out.

ME

1-2-4

I anxiously wait for an answer all through math, finally getting one after class releases.

LANDLORD

Five p.m. That's all I can spare.

And yet, if I didn't relay this information in a timely manner, he'd have my ass and throw me away.

CHAPTER NINETEEN
Journey

"I WANT you to gather more information," my monster says, pacing the creaking floor with his hands behind his back. Anger rests on his face. Whatever he came from thoroughly pissed him the fuck off, and now, I'm about to experience his wrath.

Yay for me.

The building around us smells of decay and soot, having gone through a fire years before. The water from the cove sloshes against the outside, drowning out the world. I heard stories about this place and how many men died right in the room we're in. An eerie feeling settles over me when my eyes settle on the many old blood stains littering the floor, not drowned out by the blackened ash. Funny how blood never leaves a place.

"Journey! What did you do?" she wails, sobbing beside me. "What did you do?" she screams again, filling my ringing ears.

"I don't know," I choke out, shaking my head. "I..." My eyes find the blood pooling around us and the dead eyes of the man before me.

I shiver, looking away from the blood stain.

I don't know how this building has remained standing. Maybe its darkened insides hold it together. Or maybe the foundation is too strong to ever let it fall. Its walls may be crumbling, but it's a mighty building that'll take more than a tragedy to make it collapse.

I startle awake, banging the side of my head against a hard metal with a shout. Pain blossoms from the bump and thumps through my skull. I hold my hand there as the visions of my night fly through my mind like a movie, and tears stream down my face.

"Sunny!" I sob, squeezing my eyes shut, and take a deep breath.

When my eyes open, the man who took me stares back at me with a small grin from outside the bars of my new prison. I cringe, taking in the small cage, hanging from the ceiling, suspended over the floor. My legs barely have space to stretch out, and there's no way in hell I can stand.

"Welcome to your new home," his voice rings through the dungeon he's stuck me in. "Get comfortable. You'll be there for a while until I can decide what you're good for." He eyes me up and down, sending spiders crawling over my flesh. Something flashes in his eyes, and disgust rolls through me.

"What about my sister?" I ask when he turns his back to me. "Please! She has a heart condition. She needs help and her meds!" He stops abruptly but doesn't turn to look at me. "I'll do anything if you keep her safe," I whisper, pleading with my whole fucking soul for him to comply and keep Sunny safe. She has to be.

He doesn't say another word when he saunters out of the room, leaving me in a small cage with nothing but the bloodied clothes I wore earlier.

And then, every ounce of light in the room disappears with him, leaving me in the soul-crushing darkness to contemplate my shitty life decisions.

As I'm sobbing alone in the darkness, a spark of hope ignites inside me. The high-pitched whine of an instrument starts through the walls, drawing me into the beautiful tragedy unfolding before me.

Two and half years ago, when my monster let me out of my captivity, this became our meeting space. We're always undisturbed here. No one bothers to come to the docks where so many men lost their lives at the hands of the Devils.

"Of course." I nod, keeping my eyes on the viper moving through the room.

What else did he expect me to do? Ignore it all? Not enlighten him about what was going down? I'm doing the job he asked me to do.

"Pictures, videos. The more evidence you can get against Jenni and her father, the better." He strokes his chin as he moves, deep in thought. "I want them tonight. I want everything you have. You understand, don't you, Little Snake? That if you get me this..." A creepy smile pulls at his lips when he pulls out a small piece of paper and holds it in front of me. "You get this information for me, and I'll give you more than just a little piece of paper to remember your sister by."

My heart stops in my chest when he throws it at me, and I catch it, clutching it to my heart. For one minuscule moment, I show my emotions, letting the feel of my sister's letter touch my heart. She wrote this. She held this.

"And the transplant list?" I whisper with hope.

"Prove your worth, and I'll elevate your sister Sunny to the top of the list. Get this done tonight, Little Snake." He raises a brow, zeroing those dark eyes in on me.

"Yes, Sir. Of course," I say with a nod, holding my breath when he checks his watch.

"Now, I've got business to attend to." With that, he walks out without saying goodbye, leaving me in the darkened space of the warehouse with my sister's words.

Tears fill my eyes when I slowly unwrap the lined paper.

Journey,

It's been a long time since I've been able to write to you. I've asked and asked, but they keep telling me no. He came by again today at 3:00 p.m. and handed me this page and this pencil. He gave me five minutes and told me he was going to meet with you. I wish he

*was taking me with him. I'm still here... where he put
me. I'm still safe, too. My treatments have ramped up.
He said... that you caused me to be pulled off the
transplant list, but you have a chance to fix that
tonight. I... Be safe, J. Please. I'm a lost cause. Don't
do anything for me. Do it for you. Please. I love you so
much. I'm running out of time. He says he has to leave
to make it to you. Don't get yourself hurt. Be careful.
One day, we'll be together again.*

    Pinkie swears and promises.

    xoxox

    Sunshine

"Pinkie swears and promises," I whisper to the empty room, hugging the letter for dear life. Tears cascade down my cheeks, and I let it all go.

I sigh, walking into Sunshine's bedroom beside mine, and gently close the door. "Mom's at it again," I grumble, locking the door behind us.

"But you got it?" Sunshine asks with a toothy smile, placing her book down on the bed.

"I shouldn't give you this," I say, shaking my head.

"Please, Journey," Sunshine begs, folding her hands together.

"One piece," I say, tossing her the Reeses peanut butter cups. "Your doctors are going to kill me."

Sunshine grins with chocolate-filled teeth, beaming up at me as she bites into another cup.

"So, where are you going tonight?" she asks, munching on the candy like it's the best thing ever.

"Down by the river. We're having a bonfire and hanging out. I should be back by midnight." I eye her as she nods.

"I know the rules, J. Lock my door, put a chair under it. I'll be

okay. You don't have to worry about me." She gives me a toothy chocolate grin again, giggling when I roll my eyes.

"You know I worry about you and..." My eyes stray to the door and to the person beyond the door passed out on the couch.

"She's sleeping, right? I'll be fine, J. I swear it. Pinkie swears and promises." She holds out her pinkie.

I blow out a breath with an uneasy feeling taking me over. But despite that, I latch my pinkie with hers. I'm young and free, and I deserve a night out.

"Pinkie swears and promises." In unison, we make an x over our hearts with the pinkies we swore with.

"You worry too much," she says, licking her fingers.

"You're my baby sister. I'm supposed to worry."

She smiles. "Go have fun. You deserve it. I'll be here watching Grey's."

I roll my eyes. "There's no way you should be watching that. You're way too young to understand."

"Okay, Mom," she teases, turning the show on with the click of her remote. "I'm eleven, not a moron. Besides, I'm reading at a college level and have straight A's. I'm mature for my age." She sticks her tongue out at me.

She's right. She's smart as hell for an eleven year old and so mature. Sometimes, I think if she wasn't so sick and stuck on the sidelines, that she'd master everything around her. But she's sick and stuck in this bed.

More tears fall. That was the last time I truly spoke to her. I stupidly went out to a bonfire on the banks of the river, and she endured something no eleven-year-old should. Something my mother never should have allowed or been in on.

I swallow hard, sneaking in through my window with ease. Alcohol dances across my breath, and I giggle when I fall through to the floor. Tonight was a good night hanging out with my friends from school. We sat around a fire on the banks of the river, drinking some wine coolers Mary's parents had left out, and talked until two in the morning. I lost track of time, realizing I had left my little sister alone for too long. But it's been one of those nights that brings joy to my heart. Plus, it got me out of this house and away from my mom. I can only handle being the only conscious adult in the house for so long before I lose my shit. So, once a month, I try to go out with my friends and just be a kid. My sister seems to understand. Even if the guilt from leaving her behind eats away at me.

She should be able to be a kid, too. Not just lie in bed while she wilts away. I swear, I've taken her to more doctor's appointments than I ever thought possible, and they never had good answers for me. The good doctors are unattainable because of our shitty health insurance from the government. We're stuck with long waitlists and doctors who don't give a shit about us. I'm doing the best I can for her, but it never seems to be enough. She needs a heart transplant, that much I know. Hell, she's even on the list. But each day, her health is getting worse, and I fear she's going to die before I can ever get her to a proper doctor that won't cost an arm and a leg.

"Please don't," Sunshine's fear-filled voice quivers, echoing off the walls.

I freeze, fear slithering up my spine, and I break out in a cold sweat.

"Shhh," a man's deep voice booms through the paper-thin walls of the trailer.

My breath catches in my fucking throat. Every muscle in my body locks up when he grunts something out. My thoughts run rampant, my heart speeding up as I make my way out of my bedroom door and into the hall to investigate, being as quiet as possible.

"Hurry up," my mother's impatient voice calls out from the living room. "I'm sure she'll be home soon. You need to give me what I want and fuck off," she hisses, more than likely referring to me, which means she knew I wasn't in my bedroom like I said I'd be. Meaning she doesn't give a fuck whether I stay or go.

But I'm home. What...

"Shut up and take this," he grumbles, and my mother giggles with glee.

In a daze, I walk further down the hall, making sure to miss the squeaks and creaks of the floorboards. My heart hammers in my throat, and vomit rests on the back of my tongue. Sunny pleads again for whoever it is to stop doing what they're doing, but the man doesn't listen. He doesn't fucking listen when she starts to cry and doesn't listen when she begs more. Fear races through me for the safety of my little sister. I've told her over and over again to lock her door. But I wasn't here to protect her. I went out with my friends instead. Fuck. This can't be happening to her.

I peek into her bedroom, finding it dark and disheveled. No sign of them. Her cries increase from the opposite side of the trailer. Maybe if I wasn't so fucking drunk, I could have realized she was in my mom's bedroom and not in her room. Fuck. I sway, walking down the hallway again, and stop in the living room, staring at the woman who never should have become a mother in the first place.

My mom rests on the couch with a fresh needle hanging from her veins as Sunny's cries get louder and louder, filling the space with her unmistakable pain. Her heart can't handle that amount of stress without triggering something that could possibly put her in the damn hospital. She's too young to deal with this shit I've tried to protect her from.

As I pass through the open kitchen, peeking behind me and making sure my mom hasn't woken up from her stupor. I grab a large knife from the block. If anyone is hurting my baby sister, well, I'll hurt them too. Damn the consequences. When I peek around the corner, my heart drops into my ass, and the knife nearly slips from my fingers.

"Sunny," I choke out, tears falling down my face when she's face down on the bed and a man is on top of her, trying to rip her clothes off, but she's struggling against him.

"Journey!" she shrieks, drawing the man's eyes to mine.

"Another one?" he rumbles with pleasure as his devilish blue eyes blow wide, watching me with interest. He's high as shit, too. Fuck.

"Why don't you come here and join us?" His grin widens. "I won't even have to pay your mama twice." The devil rests in his eyes when

he undoes his belt and stands, finally removing himself from my sister's tiny body. She curls in on herself, crying hysterically into the mattress.

"What did you do?" I hiss, clinging to the sharp knife behind my back.

He adjusts his white button-down shirt, popping the first few buttons, and shrugs.

"Nothing yet, Dollface. Her clothes are still on, aren't they? But something more interesting walked in," he says, sinking his teeth into his bottom lip. "How about you and I have some fun?" he reaches out, brushing my hair from my face and looking me over.

"I know you," I mutter, staring into his eyes. "You're..."

The moment his hands begin to wander down my body, I dissociate and float away, refusing to live through the moment. He can't hurt me. He can't hurt her. This is for Sunshine. Everything is for Sunshine. Making sure she's safe. Making sure she has food in her belly and a smile on her face. Making sure her medicine runs through her veins.

All for Sunny.

It isn't until my mom's screams echo through the room that I come out of my fog, drifting back into awareness.

"What did you do, Journey? What did you do?" she shouts, shaking me as she stares down at the blood pooling around me.

And him.

And her.

I blink several times, staring down at his unmoving body. His face and torso are littered with stab wounds. The knife is still protruding from his stomach.

"What did you do!" She sobs now, pulling me away and frantically shoving me onto the couch. "You killed him! Oh my God, you killed him! I can't believe you killed him!" she shrieks more.

My eyes float to the door when another man enters with a stern look.

"She did it! She's the one I called you about!" my mother shouts.

"She fucking murdered him!" Tears stream down her face when the man moves past me and checks the other's pulse.

"Don't worry. We'll take care of it, okay? I'll call the boss. You can work it out with him." Him? Who is him? No. I can't. But I did it to save Sunshine. He was going to rip through our innocence without a second thought. I protected her.

"I did what I had to do," I tell my screaming mother, sobbing uncontrollably in the corner of the room. "I had to. For Sunshine." The second man carries the bad one out with a grunt, shoving him into a vehicle, probably in hopes of getting him help.

But he doesn't. He dies en route, at least that's what I'm told. Rightfully so, too. No man should put his hands on a vulnerable child.

At the age of sixteen, I murdered a man to protect my sister from his devilish ways and wandering hands. Giving way to the real devil—my monster—who took me that night as payment for my crimes—killing his best man—and left me in the darkness for three whole days before he decided what to use me for. Some days I wished he had just killed me for what I did. Then, I wouldn't be a prisoner in my own damn skin. Others, I'm glad he built me into a stronger woman because someday soon, I'll use that strength against him.

I sit rigidly on the ground of the warehouse, so lost in my memories I don't notice the sound of something slamming in the distance. Whatever it was knocks me out of the darkness that's plagued me for three years. I try hard not to think about that night and what I did to land me in this position.

I'm a murderer.

I took someone's life.

But it was necessary. I'd do anything for my sister. I'd protect her to the ends of the earth.

Whatever my monster did to me in the pits of his basement, I deserved it. For leaving my sister when she needed me the most and coming back in time to slaughter her assailant.

Fuck.

I need to peel myself off the ground and stop dwelling in the past. I need to move forward and do my mission.

All for Sunshine. Always.

I check my phone, noting the time. Jenni would be outside my trailer soon in her fancy jeep, beeping at me until I got in. I need to get back home, clean up, and keep my mind on my sister's life.

No more funny business.

CHAPTER TWENTY
Journey

"Daddy! This is Journey," Jenni says with a grin, wrapping her arm around me. "She's my best friend."

Kent Thomas peers at me with narrowed eyes, evaluating every inch of me as I do the same to him. Typical man in the mafia, lounging around in his fancy suit with shiny shoes and a nice watch adorning his wrist. The aura around his body exudes danger, making the hairs on the back of my neck stand on end. My mind screams to run away, but I remember everything my monster taught me.

"New friend?" Jenni's father asks, getting up from his armchair with a small drink in his hand, containing an amber liquid. The ice clinks with every step he takes toward us.

"It's very nice to meet you, Mr. Thomas," I say, extending my hand with a smile.

He nods, firmly shaking my hand. "Nice to meet you, too. Are you the one who's been keeping my Jenni company and out of trouble?" he asks, raising a brow.

"I suppose so," I say nervously, darting my eyes to Jenni with a smile.

"She's my best friend, Daddy. No need for the third degree." She waves her father off, dragging me toward the dining room. Thank God. "I'm sorry," she hisses, looping her arm with mine. "He's so overprotective sometimes. He thinks I'm just going to spill all his secrets to the wrong person." She giggles, leaning her head on mine.

Guilt slams into me again at the truth of her words. She *is* telling the wrong person all his little secrets. Never shy in telling me what he does for business or where he is for the weekend. If they wanted to keep things discreet, well, they're failing with her. She'll tell practically anyone, anything at the drop of a hat.

I'm a terrible person.

Jenni freezes when the click of the front door opens, and two male voices rise in the air.

"Mr. Thomas."

Instantly, I recognize his voice drifting through the house. Elias White. Jenni's beloved boyfriend.

"I'm not really supposed to be with him," Jenni says, sipping her wine.

"Why?" I ask, looking away from the movie as she settles back with a frown, shrugging.

She nibbles her lip. "You won't tell anyone, right? I can trust you?"

I nod, lowering my gaze. She's genuinely a good person, and I'm lying to her face. Whatever she tells me is not safe with me. I have to tell my monster what she says or my sister is dead. No matter what, I can't leave any details out of it. Because he'll find out, he always does. I'm like his little spy who has a spy on her ass, too.

"Since birth, I've been in an arranged marriage," she murmurs, immediately gulping down more wine.

"What? That's..." I trail off, unsure of what the proper word is for it.

"Sexist? Stupid? You name the word, and that's what it is. But I swear on my life, Journey. I'm not marrying my chosen guy. There's no way. I'm... Elias is going to carry me away," she whispers, leaning in close with a gleam in her eyes. "After graduation, we're running away together. Unless he strikes a deal with my daddy."

Sadness passes over her face, but she shakes it off.

"Well, you should be able to," I murmur. *"Who are you supposed to marry?"*

Her nose wrinkles. *"Leighton LeMaster. My dad made a deal with his dad. It's gross. He's gross. I don't want to even think about marrying him. He follows me around with a sick look in his eyes."* She shakes her head and squeezes her eyes shut. *"I have to leave with Elias. I have to,"* she sniffles, wiping away her eyes.

These emotions catch me off guard. Jenni is a real human being. She doesn't hide anything from anyone except her tears. Usually, she's happy-go-lucky. Never like this. Not with her mask off and her smile gone.

"We'll make sure you get carried away by the man of your dreams, okay?" I say, hitting my shoulder against hers.

"He's here. Oh my God. Do I look okay?" Jenni asks, twirling in her tight, little black dress with matching shiny heels. Her make-up is done to perfection, and her red hair is expertly curled. She looks like she's about to hit happy hour with her fellow millionaire friends on a yacht.

"I hate you because you're so gorgeous," I quip, earning a giggle in return.

"I don't know where you've been all my life, Journey West. But I'm glad you're here. You're a real friend, aren't you?" she says, not hesitating to throw her arms around me.

That same shitty feeling strikes again when she squeezes me tight.

"Well, I'm here now. We got this!" I whisper with a false smile, trying to comfort her as the two men round the corner, murmuring to one another.

"How about we head to the table and eat?" Mr. Thomas asks, clapping Elias on the shoulder with a grin.

Well, that's good news, at least. They're in good spirits.

"You look beautiful tonight, my love," Elias murmurs, kissing Jenni's pink cheeks and taking her hand. "And you must be the new best friend," he says, raising a brow when I nod.

"You've met before," Jenni chuckles. "This is Journey."

"Ah, we have," he says with a sharp nod, taking in my appearance.

Jenni, bless her soul, immediately took me into her closet and forced me into a nice mid-thigh black dress, almost matching hers. She even insisted on shoving my feet into her too-big heels, bringing the look together. When she said she'd pick me up, she meant an hour early so she could doll me up appropriately.

"Nice to see you again," I say with a wide smile, tucking my hands in front of me.

"So, shall we?" Mr. Thomas says again, leading us all into the dining room.

We all follow him into the large dining room fit with an extra large table. I don't hesitate to sit across from Jenni and Elias as they snuggle close to one another in front of two place settings while Mr. Thomas sits at the head of the table next to us. He watches their exchange with interest, noting the way they hold hands and especially the way Elias takes care of his daughter. True love rests between the two of them, and it's not hard to see. Even if Jenni is only eighteen.

"Let's get started, shall we?" Mr. Thomas says with a straight face.

The moments the words leave his mouth, round after round of food filters in like it was made for an extensive dinner party and not four people. We don't really speak as we eat, sitting in an uncomfortable silence.

"Elias," Mr. Thomas says after setting down his fork and wiping his mouth. "I think you and I need to leave the ladies and have a discussion." He eyes Elias with a knowing look, standing abruptly without another word.

"Of course," he says, kissing Jenni's cheek. "I'll see you later," he says with promise in his voice. Standing tall, he adjusts his suit jacket and follows in the same direction as Jenni's father. The sound of their footsteps trail off up the set of stairs leading to the second floor of their home. Judging by the opening of the creaking door, they're heading into Mr. Thomas' office and closing the door behind them.

"This is it!" Jenni says with a small clap. "He's going to talk to Daddy about marriage and something else." Her grin widens with happiness at the prospect of getting away from Leighton. Not that I can blame her. Elias seems more devoted than anyone I've ever seen. He worships the ground she walks on. All I got was a crazy person who sneaks into my room and takes pictures of me while I sleep. And some John who leaves donuts and fills my fridge.

It could be worse, I guess. My stalker could kidnap me and shove me into a hole in the ground. But I digress.

Someone's coming into my house while I'm vulnerable and dead to the world. If I were richer, I'd install cameras and watch as the pervert enters through my window or door or wherever. The only confusing part about it is I don't know why they're doing it. They don't seem to mess with me. Or maybe they do. But it's always the same when I wake up from my drowsy state. Pictures of me sleeping through the night right next to my head with the same note: I'm watching you. Maybe it's my monster being a creep and trying to keep me in line. Either way, I need to find a solution to my picture-taking stalker.

Maybe I'll stay up all night long and confront them.

I shake myself out of my thoughts when Jenni grabs her phone and begins scrolling through social media. Another lady enters the dining room carrying a tray of coffee and some cakes for dessert.

"While you wait, misses," she says with a smile and sets them in front of us.

"I'm going to go use your bathroom," I say to Jenni, who waves me away without looking up from her phone.

"I'll be here," she says, sending me a smile as I rise from my seat with shaky legs.

I swallow hard, looking over my shoulder at Jenni at the table. This is why I'm here. I'm spying on her and her father for this very reason; I feel it in my bones. Her father is upstairs making some sort of deal with Elias. But what could it be? There's only one way to find out. I drag my phone out of my pocket and hit the record button in video mode. Whatever they say now will be on video for my monster to hear.

As I hit the top of the stairs, I hold my breath and listen to the discussion happening to my left. The door is ajar. He didn't even bother to hide his indiscretion. I tip toe over the hardwood, weaving away from the creeks that would surely give me away. I've slept over here enough times now to know where to step and how to stay quiet.

"I want in," Mr. Thomas says. "The thing we discussed before."

I silently stand where I am, praying they don't peek out the door and find me standing there with my phone in my hand. I'm invisible—no one. I take a deep, relaxing breath, slowly move past the open door, and lean against the wall with my phone out.

"Right. What we discussed before. What I brought to you six months ago. You're still good for everything we talked about? Or should I get a contract over here for you to sign?"

"My handshake is my word," Mr. Thomas says in a cool tone. "I'll fund your expansion into our territory."

"Where I'm not supposed to be," Elias chuckles. "How is your big boss going to feel about that?"

"He won't know," Mr. Thomas answers quickly.

"He won't notice our product on his streets? He's threatened me before, you know?" Elias doesn't sound the least bit concerned that Gabriel Viotto has threatened him. In fact, when I peek through the crack in the door, I'm greeted by a smirk on his face. He's confident this deal will go his way.

"I'll cover your tracks," Mr. Thomas says.

"And Jenni?" Elias's voice tightens when he asks the question.

"She's yours. That was our deal. I'll help with your expansion, have my men help distribute your drugs into our city, and you also get my daughter's hand in marriage. In return, I'm asking for a fifty/fifty split of the profits."

My brows furrow. It doesn't even sound like a fair deal. Mr. Thomas is losing a lot by funding this adventure and handing Jenni off to Elias. Maybe I'm overthinking this, and it is something for the future, but I can't imagine.

Elias is quiet for some time, leaning against Mr. Thomas' desk with a straight face. "It's a deal," he says, holding out his hand, which Mr. Thomas gleefully takes.

"Then it's settled," Mr. Thomas says with a laugh.

I blow out a breath, leaning back against the wall, and stop the recording. They don't say anything else when I walk away and find myself in Jenni's bedroom, heading straight for her connected bathroom. Once the door is shut and locked behind me, I slump to the floor and squeeze my eyes shut. This is it. This is the moment I feel like the scum on the bottom of Jenni's fancy shoes.

ME

1-2-4

I hit send with shaky fingers, attaching the video with the message. I swear bile rises in my throat when it's received, and he opens the message right away.

LANDLORD

What a good little snake you are. Tonight.
Don't be late.

I don't feel like a good little snake. I feel like a piece of shit on the lawn, left there to rot and decay. As I should. I'm the worst of the worst. She invited me as a buffer for her family meal, and I only came to spy on her and her father's conversations. Whatever tonight brings will live within me for years to come. I can't rectify the damage I've done to them.

I've sealed their fates.

And death is on the horizon.

When I walk down the stairs and sit across from Jenni, she smiles at me.

"Thanks for coming tonight. You seriously are the best."

"You're welcome," I say with a sinking feeling in my gut.

"So, hey. Sunday night after graduation, do you want to come over for this massive party I'm having? I swear everyone is going to be here."

"Your dad won't?" I ask, raising a brow.

"Nah. Business again," she says, waving me off.

Of course. Business. That's what he's always off doing. Although, he seems to really care about Jenni and seems to love her as his daughter. But he literally just handed her off like a chess piece, moving her for his own gain. Despite the fact that she likes Elias. I can't imagine what it would have been like if she hadn't liked him in the first place. Would this still have been a thing?

Fuck.

I need to prepare myself for the ultimate fallout and distance myself from everything.

Once we've had our dessert and coffee, I excuse myself and ask her to take me home, feigning a stomach ache.

When I'm finally alone in my room, removing the dress and shoes she told me to keep, I fall into my bed with a sigh, counting down the minutes until I have to walk the mile down to the docks and discuss my evening.

What fun.

CHAPTER TWENTY-ONE

Journey

IT'S odd standing in the middle of a crowded party with knots in your stomach and a fake smile on your lips. A few hours before, we walked across the stage and stuck our middle fingers in the air, saluting our principal and teachers with smiles.

We're done.

Goodbye, high school. Hello, real life.

My eyes dart around the room, taking in my former classmates who are getting shitfaced in celebration. After dropping the bomb about Jenni's father to my monster, nothing has happened. I suspected within a few hours my best friend would stop texting me, but here I am, standing in the middle of her kitchen, celebrating our graduation and freedom from high school with my very alive best friend. She's still in the same spirits, smiling and laughing. Hell, she's even shown me the rock on her finger that Elias gave her yesterday after getting down on one knee.

"You should run away with him," I giggle, nudging my shoulder into hers.

"No need to now. Oh my God, will you be my maid of honor?" she squeals, pulling me into a hug.

"Just go to Vegas," I laugh. "I'll come with you." Anything to get her away from here and away from my monster waiting in the wings with whatever he's going to do. Please. Just run away with *him and get away from me. Leave here. I'm desperate for her to just go.*

"Take another shot with me!" Jenni yells over the music pumping through the speakers all through her house.

Why did I think coming to a party full of people was a good idea? Oh, right. It wasn't really mine. Despite doing my job and getting him the information he requested, I'm still on her tail, reporting anything of interest back to him.

"Befriend Jenni. Tell me about her family life." For fuck's sake. Do it yourself, asshole.

I sigh, fake grinning in her direction. This entire situation has drained more out of me than I ever thought possible. Before I was made to follow people around and gather intel on them while being the invisible girl. Not this time. I had to put myself out there and make a new friend, someone I oddly have come to care about. Jenni is a magnificent person with so much going for her, and I've taken her future away with my lies and spying ways.

The darkness within me swirls in my brain, attempting to shut my feelings off and do my job. But I don't allow it to. If I can still feel the guilt and the shame in the back of my mind, then I know I'm alive.

It's the day I stop feeling that I'll know I've died inside and no longer care about my humanity, which slips through my fingers faster than sand.

I wrinkle my nose and pull down the back of the tight dress that Jenni insisted I wear when she picked me up at my trailer earlier. Why did I let her convince me to wear this tiny monstrosity? I have no idea. In my mind, it was the best thing ever. Look hot. Grab everyone's attention and maybe have some fun with someone like I did the night the masked men took me.

And it worked. Almost too well. Everyone's eyes—or that's what it feels like—have been on me since I walked through the door. God, I hate being the little snake in the grass feeding off everyone's information. I'd rather hide in a hole and bury myself alive at this stage of the game. Maybe more alcohol will help to loosen me up and relax.

The clock is ticking away on Jenni's life. I have to convince her to get the fuck out of here before my monster strikes.

"Sure!" I shout over the music, taking a shot glass from the counter and raising it in the air. "A toast to our friendship!" I say with a blinding smile, causing her to laugh.

"We've gone to school together for so long! I can't believe we're finally friends, and it's the end," she shouts, dumping the shot down her throat and cringing at the taste. "God, I hate tequila."

Yeah, me too. Oh, the things I do for these assignments from my monster. Like drinking tequila, wearing uncomfortable dresses, and drinking until I can't feel anything anymore. What a dream come true. The only downside? I have to report all this back to him and take pictures and videos as proof that I was here.

"Yeah," I croak after swallowing my mouthful and setting the shot glass down. Fucking gross. "Tequila is terrible." I stick my tongue out, trying to remove the taste from my tongue.

It burns like damn gasoline lining my throat. I'm really not that big of a drinker. I have hardly touched a sip since the night my sister was savagely taken from me and I was too busy drinking to protect her. It haunts my every waking hour. It also doesn't help that my mom is barely ever conscious on her diet of drugs. I've stayed away from it to keep my wits about me, except with Jenni. With her, I've had to play the part and drink my life away. It's the way to her heart, after all. Not to mention, it's freeing to let go and giggle at nothing in her company.

My eyes scan the party when she pours us two more shots. Everyone is here from school, including my damn nightmare—Leighton LeMaster. The boy who can't take no for an answer and never has been able to.

"You good, Journey?" he asks, *leaning in close so his breaths brush against my cheek. His hand wanders up and down my back*

as I sit at a table in the library, trying to figure out my English homework.

I cringe, shifting away from his touch. He just smiles at me, leaning against my table and invading my space.

"Oh, my God! He came!" Jenni squeals, jumping up and down and clapping her hands together, knocking me out of my thoughts.

Fuck Leighton and his wandering hands. He's so damn touchy and insistent with everyone.

"Who?" I ask, scanning the crowd.

I don't have to search for too long when my eyes find him. The man with the blue spider tattoo painted near his thumb.

Elias.

The man who has no clue my monster is onto him. And Jenni... I swallow hard. This is the worst thing I've had to do.

"You no longer feel guilt, Little Snake." My monster's eyes burrow under my skin as I kneel before him just outside my prison. A knife rests in his hand, twirling with every step. "Now, let's learn how to hold in your emotions."

"My fiancé," she giggles, putting her manicured nails over her lips, displaying the gorgeous pink diamond nestled on her ring finger. "That's so strange to say, right?" she murmurs to me with a huge grin. "He wasn't supposed to show up. But since my daddy is out of town on business, he must have decided to surprise me!" She sighs, watching him dreamily as he greets other partygoers with hand shakes and head nods. "Ew, Leighton," Jenni scoffs, eyeing him as he saunters up to Elias, and they shake hands, looking as if they're exchanging something.

"Why is Leighton here?" I ask, eyeing Jenni as she straightens. "Does he know about your new engagement?"

"Because he's a leech who thinks he's owed something," she hisses, tightening her fingers into fists. Then, all the anger drains out of her, and she blows out a breath. "Help me avoid Leighton?" Her eyes turn pleading when I nod in agreement.

Without waiting for my response, Jenni grabs me by the hand

and pulls me through the crowd and toward the foyer. I feel like a fucking ragdoll until she stops in front of him.

"Baby!" she says, dropping my hand and throwing her arms around his shoulders.

He smiles at her. Like genuinely looks at her like she's the love of his life and smiles. "Hey, Baby Girl," he mumbles, kissing her lips with passion.

"Oh! This is my friend Journey. You remember her, right?" she excitedly says, gesturing to me.

Elias' eyes narrow at me like he knows what I've done. Like he can see right through me, and knows who I secretly work for, and is prepared to take me out.

"Hi," I say with a small wave. "It's nice to see you again." Double lame.

Parties are not my forte. Neither is socializing. This is damn humiliating. But I grit my teeth and fucking fake it till I make it. I have to.

All for my sister, Sunny.

All for my freedom.

He chuckles, putting a hand on her ass and gently squeezing. "Any friend of my girl's is a friend of mine." He nods in my direction with a sparkle in his eye, searching for a deception. "Nice to see you again."

Yeah, I wouldn't trust me, either.

"Let's go drink!" Jenni says, grabbing Elias hand, leading us back to the kitchen we had abandoned.

"So, how'd you two meet?" I ask, downing the rest of the shot I left behind, begging for liquid courage.

Technically, I shouldn't be consuming any sort of alcohol that inhibits my job. *Never let your guard down, Little Snake. Always have your fucking wits about you.* His voice rings in my mind among the many lessons he bestowed on me with his fists and cruel words. But fuck it. Freedom claws just beneath my skin, begging to come out and play. The shackles of my prison fall to the ground with every drink I take, bringing me to the normalcy I crave. Fuck my monster. Fuck this mission. For the night, I'm not a damn puppet on a string for him to swing around and force into stupid situations.

I'm Journey fucking West. Normal girl, hanging out at a party and living in the moment.

"Ohhhh," Jenni giggles, waving a hand. "It was just one of those chance meetings." Her eyes slide to his, and he chuckles, shrugging.

"Just one of those things you had to be there for," he says, kissing her cheek.

"Another shot?" Jenni asks, getting a large bottle with no label on it and setting it down. "It's definitely not tequila." She grins when my expression turns soft, and I nod.

I thought she'd never ask.

"Pour us all one," I say, hoping the effects of alcohol will loosen their tongues and make them more likely to spill their guts. The less I have to be here pretending I'm someone I'm not, the better my night will turn out to be.

"I can't believe you came, baby. I thought these parties weren't your thing," Jenni says, puffing out her bottom lip slightly.

"They weren't. But my girl's all alone in her big old house with a bunch of horny teenage boys. Besides, Baby Girl. I have some things to discuss with certain people." He plucks her lip in a loving way, swooping in to kiss her lips before she can even respond.

I longingly watch them with an ache in my heart. Is this what love looks like? Kissing? Googly eyes? Hearts in their throats? Fuck. I've only dreamed of feeling the loving hands of someone who cares or adores me. I long to see the light of love shining through in someone's eyes when they look at me.

Much like the night with my strangers in masks and their rough hands on my body. I'm nearly knocked back a step when a craving hits hard and takes my fucking breath away. Images of our roll in the sheets grabs me by the throat, thrusting me into my memories of the night I let everything go and won.

"Give yourself to us. For tonight. We'll bring you to your fucking knees. But know I'm in control," his whispered words ring through my mind over and over again. *My knees knock. My pussy fucking grows wet with every thought.*

Their hands, tongues, and husky voice. Their smells and the euphoria they brought me.

God, I need a damn repeat. Over and over again to help me feel something. Anything. I came alive under their fingertips, like my soul had reignited. Feelings came back to life after lying dormant for so long under my monster's cruelty.

They breathed life back into me for the first time in three years. I was free, floating, and fucking invigorated. I was no longer the girl imprisoned in a cage, held captive by the menacing monster in the dark. I was alive. Glowing. Heart pounding. Fresh oxygen entering my lungs. The moment I stepped away from them and woke up in my own bed, it felt like a dream. Good things only ever happened to me in my dreams.

Even if I failed my mission. Even if I failed my sister and got her off the list, I'll fix it all. I'll get her back on there.

Fuck, I need my masked men to come back into my life and steal me away for good. How I long to be the princess with a white knight, or three, taking me from this hell. Me and Sunshine.

But that will never happen. They were strangers with masks. Men I'll never have the pleasure of seeing again. Even if I did, I wouldn't have a clue. The only thing I saw in the dim moonlight was their eyes before they blindfolded me, blocking out my vision. And then, their fingertips did the talking.

I shake off my morbid thoughts, trying to focus on the present. Not the masked men. I fumble with my shot glass, trying to find something to do with my hands as Jenni and Elias continue their conversation.

"So, you'll stay the night?" Jenni breathes, folding her hands together when he finds her waist and pulls her in.

"As long as your big, bad daddy ain't here. I'm here. Me and the boys." He nods to the other two silent men standing behind him with smiles on their faces. I swear Jenni's face turns three shades darker, and she nods.

Interesting. There's a story there.

"He's gone all weekend on business. Now, how about some shots!" she shouts, scooting out of his grip, and pours the liquor into five shot glasses. "Cheers!" she shouts before downing her drink, and I do, too.

"Fuck. Worse than tequila, you bitch," I hiss, sputtering on the gasoline she handed me.

I didn't think it could get worse, but that shit is way more potent than what she handed me before. Way higher alcohol proof, too, just from taste alone.

Her twinkling laugh spears right through me when she gently pats my back. "Yup!" she squeals, popping the P. "But it made you feel good, didn't it, bestie?"

"Yup!" I grin, wiggling my brows at her while we laugh together.

I'm going to enjoy these moments while I have them. Before my monster takes them from me. He'll ruin their lives. Like he's ruined mine.

At the moment we each finish our shots, something in the atmosphere changes. The music softens to almost nothing, and murmurs rise into the air. The hair on my arms stands on end like electricity is trickling through the room.

Then, I find the reason why.

Them.

The Devils all standing side-by-side, standing in the foyer. They're tall, dark, and so fucking handsome. Albeit, untouchable in many regards. They're something every woman in the room wants but is too afraid to throw themselves at, because they know the outcome. The three of them don't socialize with the likes of us. Let alone fuck any girls from high school. They never have, no matter how much the girls try. They've never seemed to have an eye for anyone. Well, except me as a kid. I remember when I punched a boy and how proud Jericho seemed to be. He even claimed I was theirs. But after that, it all fizzled away, and we never spoke again.

Well, until that night at their club when they got me off and shoved their cum inside me.

"And there's my meeting," Elias says, wiping his lips with the back of his hand.

"With them?" Jenni asks with her mouth agape. "I..."

"Remember our deal," he says, cocking his head. No emotions rest on his face like he's mastered his feelings for years. But of course he has; he is the most notorious gang leader around.

The leader of the Blue Spider Gang. They run the south side of things, just over the bridge and outside of Briar Cove. It's their territory and domain, given to them by Gabriel Viotto—Jericho's father. They struck a deal a few years ago, allowing the gang to get this close to his operations. With rules, of course. What those are, I have no idea. I've snooped enough to know the basics. They stick to their side of things and Gabriel will allow them to stay there. Doesn't seem like Elias is sticking to his deal, though, considering the deal he made with Mr. Thomas this past week.

"I know. But them? The Devils?" Her eyes turn to them with concern when they spot all of us standing at the island.

They freeze, locking eyes with me. All three of them. The mafia heir, his silent partner Shepp, and Arrow, who always seems to be up to something.

I swear their eyes eat me alive and swallow me whole. My stomach drops. Adrenaline pours through my veins. *I'm fucking alive under their gaze.* I don't dare move or make a peep. I'm the prey. They're the predators with sharp teeth. Every hair on the back of my neck and arms stands on end in their presence.

They're bigger than life.

CHAPTER TWENTY-TWO

Journey

JERICHO RAISES a dark brow when his eyes run the length of my body, reminding me of the night at their club with his disapproving look. His chiseled face tightens when he appraises my dress. I swear to God his dark eyes turn completely black under the soft lights of the party, and a sneer pulls at his lips.

Rude. I look fine as hell in my little blue dress that barely covers my ass. He snarls, turning to Shepp, who signs something with his massive hands. I swear that man is as tall as a building, and as thick, too. Rumor has it, he's at least six foot six inches, and he hasn't spoken a word since he was ten. And Arrow, the blond Viking giant who grins in my direction. His eyes slide up and down my body with interest, approving of the dress fit around my body. A dress I carefully picked out to help me blend in with my peers.

"You might be drooling," Jenni says, elbowing me with a grin.

I frown. Shit. I lost myself in their presence instead of staying aware of my surroundings. Something I have a hard time doing these days. Dissociating from my existence has become the new norm. Books. Movies. Fantasies and new worlds within my own mind. Anything to take my mind off my shitty life.

"I am not," I quip, wiping my mouth with a grin.

Yeah, I was definitely drooling. But they're hot as sin. They've left a lasting impression on me.

Jenni grins. "So, the Devils, huh?" she says, wiggling her brows and leaning in closer. "They're untouchable, Journey. Completely out of anyone's league. But you can try. I know I have. Well, before Elias. My dream boat," she giggles at that, topping off mine and her shot glasses. "Rumor has it, anyway, that they're already promised to someone." She shrugs. "Some big alliance. But my father wouldn't say," she says with a slight slur. "Careful with them," she whispers with a grin, eyeing them when our connection finally breaks.

They move forward as one. Shepp and Arrow on either side of Jericho. An impenetrable wall of muscly men. No doubt protecting him from potential harm. Whatever that might be? They're his second and third-in-command and will be as he ascends to the throne his father has created for him. The mafia scene in this town is fascinating. Almost as fascinating as the men walking toward me.

And wait, what did she mean?

"Promised to someone?" I mumble.

"Ah, yeah. Like I was. You remember? I told you," she slurs, taking another shot without me. "The men of this town still have this arranged marriage and remain untouched-bullshit. Normally, we're not supposed to know until they're inducted into the mafia. But my daddy told me. You know, you marry her because her daddy is the CEO of some plastic company and remain a virgin for some asinine reason."

Oh, like her dad. Interesting.

"Like you were promised. Right, I remember," I trail off.

She frowns then, hurt crossing her eyes.

"Not anymore." She shakes her head, downing another shot. I'd stop her from drinking so much, but I don't think she would. Besides, she's teaching me important lessons from a world in which I'm an outsider. Almost. "Once my diploma hit my hand, I was supposed to marry Leighton, you know." She sticks her tongue out in disgust, eyes darting to Leighton LeMaster from across the room. "He'll get initiated into the Viotto Crime Family.

Just like them." She nods to the Devils. "It's a big to-do around here. They even have a damn party where they announce the weddings." She rolls her eyes. "Thankfully, Daddy got me out of that with this. So, Leighton is up for grabs and being assigned to someone else."

I frown, looking at the disgraceful man himself, Leighton. Tall. Lanky. Scraggly teeth. There he sits, laughing it up with three girls surrounding him and his man posse hovering nearby. He'd be somewhat handsome if he wasn't a fucking psycho, who pressures girls into doing shit with him. But have no fear, his daddy, who is the governor, gets him out of every sticky situation he gets into. He's also a part of the Viotto family, just like every other prominent man in this town. There must be something in the water. Or maybe, they're all after the power of the position.

"I was also supposed to be a virgin," she giggles, breaking out of her sadness with a grin. "But that didn't happen." Her eyes float to Elias, who greets Jericho with a handshake.

The way he looks at her has my heart reeling for the love they have. Whether it's superficial or puppy love. Whatever. What they have seems to be real.

I blow out a breath. "Good." I flash her my best smile, but it disintegrates at the look on her face.

"Another shot," I rasp, tapping the countertop with urgency. If I'm going to make it through this, I need more liquid courage.

"That's my girl," she quips with a slur, pouring two shots and overfilling the glasses. She giggles when she raises hers, and I do the same. "Seriously, where have you been all my life?" And we gulp down our next shot.

"I have an office, you know," Jericho's deep voice booms through the kitchen. "But you insisted on meeting here." He folds his arms across his body, standing stock still and watching Elias with a sharp eye. So cold and calculating. Just like someone else I know. In fact, he's the spitting image.

I side-eye him standing tall next to Elias as he sends him a death glare. Those dark eyes, turning menacing when Elias laughs in his face. *Okay, maybe not a happy meeting.*

Elias grins and shrugs. "Your office at the top of your fancy little club. Why would I go there and disappoint the people of Briar Cove? Look at them; they're all pining for your damn attention." He spreads his arms wide in the direction of all the partygoers, dancing and eyeing the devils with lust in their eyes.

Seems I'm not the only one affected.

Arrow and Shepp stay firmly planted at Jericho's side when he scoffs. "Ah, a power play and a show. Genius." Jericho scrunches up his sleeves, pushing them up his veiny forearms. "Why don't we discuss this away from prying eyes?"

Holy hell. Forearm porn. Whoever said the best part of a guy is their eyes, has never seen forearms protruding with veins. It's a beautiful sight.

"You're drooling again," Jenni giggles, thrusting her elbow into my side. "How about we take one last shot and then go dance?"

Dancing sounds about as appetizing as the damn tequila. Do I want to shake my ass on the dance floor? Fuck no. Do I have to? That's affirmative, which annoys the hell out of me. But fake it till you make it, right? Jenni is my best friend.

"Sure!" I cheer, throwing my arm in the air.

"We'll be right back," Elias says, kissing Jenni's cheek. "Be a good girl," he murmurs, causing her to giggle more and turn bright red.

"Always. Me and my bestie are going to dance."

As she says those words, the three devils turn at once to stare at me. Jericho's jaw tightens, and his nostrils flare angrily, looking me up and down again. Leaning in, Arrow whispers something to Jericho, and his chest deflates.

"Let's get this over with," Jericho says, gesturing for Elias to lead the way down the hall to the right of the kitchen.

"Use Daddy's office!" Jenni shouts, searching in a drawer for a lone key and tossing it to them. "But don't touch anything." I make note of the key she tossed and which drawer it was in.

Something I might need for later. There's a reason I was told to befriend her and spy on the family—something is up with Kent Thomas beyond him fucking around with Elias and making deals. There's a reason I'm still here and not assigned somewhere else. And I'll be the one to figure it out for him. I'm not an idiot.

"Now, let's dance!" she shrieks, grabbing my hand and pulling me onto the dance floor just in time for all the booze to work through my system.

The moment we make it through the crowd of people, my head starts swimming in a delicious fog of alcohol. Finally, it courses through my veins, taking me away from the guilt, shame, and every other emotion rushing through me. Little Snake who?

I'm Journey—the dancing girl, losing myself to the music and body heat pouring all around me.

CHAPTER TWENTY-THREE

Journey

M Y H I P S S W A Y back and forth as the music consumes me. Everyone fades away as I lose myself on the dance floor with Jenni by my side. Warm hands glide over my hips, helping me to move back and forth. Sparks fly over my flesh, igniting a fire deep in my gut, spreading under my skin. Warmth encases me. Fingers dig into my side, pulling me into a hard body. Fuck. My eyes pop open, and breaths pour from between my parted lips.

Then, their intoxicating smell wraps me up in them. I don't want it to ever go away.

"Don't stop," he murmurs in my ear, tightening his grip. "Keep moving your ass, Kitten. Fuck. You feel so damn good." Shivers roar through my body when his hand comes around my front, gripping my abdomen hard like he doesn't want to let me go.

Kitten. His words vibrate in my damn mind, ricocheting off my skull. Why it sounds so fucking intoxicating, wanting me to stay right here, and yet, so damn familiar at the same damn time.

"Arrow!" Jenni giggles, throwing her head back with a laugh.

"Arrow?" I question in a slight moan. "What are you doing?" I ask, trying to shake the fog from my brain, but it clings on, much like Arrow. He grins, putting his face in my neck, brushing small kisses along my flesh.

I never want this to end.

Another warm body presses to my front. I don't have to open my eyes when his large hands sit on my hips below Arrow's. My vision blurs when I look at the towering figure hovering above me. A pained expression crosses his features when he takes all of me in. Flushed face. Moving body. We continue to sway to the music, grinding against each other. Murmurs happen all around. Other people take notice of the two Devils taking me for themselves. We're a spectacle under the dimmed lights. And for some reason, I don't fucking move or tell them to fuck off. No. I revel in the feeling of their hands on me. Their bodies against mine. The heat between us simmers to higher levels that I don't want to escape. Looking into Shepp's eyes, I fucking melt into a damn needy puddle. Every touch. Every fucking move starts more fires inside me, needing something—or someone—to put them out. So much lust rests behind his light eyes. My breaths escape me when his hardness pokes my front.

Freedom claws at my psyche, aching to come out again. I'm so fucking tired of being repressed and held back and shackled to my duties. To my fucking monster. This freedom right here gives me a tiny taste of what my life will hold when I'm out from under his thumb.

Tonight. For right now. I'm living in this moment and forgetting that my actions have consequences. Dire ones if I'm caught.

But I won't be.

I need this more than breathing. More than anything.

I need to feel alive.

Like the night at the club.

"Keep dancing. Whatever you do, don't fucking stop, Kitten," Arrow whispers in my ear. His hot breath pours over my flesh when his lips meet my neck, peppering small kisses.

"Why?" I breathe. "What are you going to do?"

Arrow's smile disarms me. "I'm going to play hide the fingers," he says directly in my ear. "They need a warm place to go, and I want to see your face when you come on them." Shepp stiffens and not just his cock. His hands move from my waist in what I can only assume is him signing something. "Sheppy doesn't want me to do this in a crowded room in front of others," Arrow says, tsking Shepp, who frowns and signs something more. "He says you deserve a nice big bed to spread your legs on. Do you agree?" Arrow nips my ear.

Holy fucking shit. Every inch of me is on high alert when Arrow cocks his head, watching my expression. I feel the heat shooting up my neck and cheeks. Do I want to do this? Get fingered in the middle of a crowded room again? No. I can't do it in the crowd. Not this time. It has to be in private where my monster's other spies can't see it happening. Fuck, what am I thinking? I have to stop this, but I fucking can't.

"Bedroom," I blurt with wide eyes.

Arrow's grin widens, showing off his pointed teeth. "I'm going to eat you alive."

"By all means," I slur a little, gesturing for him to lead the way.

"Which room?" Arrow isn't asking me; his eyes lock on Jenni.

"Up the stairs and to the right, there's a guest bedroom with your name on it!" she shouts from behind Shepp.

"I was dancing, you know!" I screech as he hauls me into his arms and lifts me off the floor. If I even thought about putting my legs around his waist, I'd moon the entire party. I may be comfortable with my body, but I'd rather not have everyone seeing my ass. "I can walk!" I hiss, clinging tighter to his T-shirt and digging my nails into his shoulders.

He grunts something unintelligible in my ear when he pushes through the crowd. His head swivels from left to right.

God, what am I doing? Why am I letting Arrow Amour carry me off and lock me into a bedroom? I think I've lost my damn mind. In fact, I know I have. Normal Journey would never let anyone carry her away, especially in public. Especially not them. Again. Anyone could see this. Anyone could report this back to my monster, and then I'd be fucking toast. Scratch that, my sister would be. She pays the price for every indiscretion I cause.

Yet, I can't stop myself from chasing the freedom at the tip of my fingers. Some would run away from the danger of being in the arms of a dangerous man. Some would willingly dive into bed with them at a moment's notice. Me? I'm somewhere in the middle. A few weeks ago, I took a chance and fucked three strangers with our masks on. It was one of the most freeing nights of my life. Even after everything was ripped away. No. I can't think of that right now. My sister wouldn't want me wallowing in my fucking misery for the rest of my life. She'd tell me to keep my chin up and follow my heart.

But my heart isn't in control right now. It's my pussy. And what she wants is for this man to lick her clean and give her the best damn orgasm of her life.

Looking over his shoulder, I spot Jenni hysterically laughing in my direction. She gives me a little wave, sending me off, and then goes back to dancing by herself. No one around her dares to lay a hand on her as she sways her hips to the beat.

Arrow takes the steps two at a time, continuing to hold me tightly to him. Shepp remains on our heels. Glancing at his face, I note the indecision playing across his features.

"There will be no more shit in our territory..." Jericho's voice booms from behind a closed door to our left when we finally make it up the stairs.

Arrow stops, narrowing his eyes at the wooden door with interest.

"That's not up to you. You're not my partner in this endeavor," Elias replies in a cold tone.

"And who is your partner? I'd love to have a discussion with them as well on why you're releasing dirty, potent drugs into my fucking town without speaking to me first." A loud bang echoes through the hall when Arrow and Shepp exchange looks. "You're murdering your consumers." His voice is downright deadly, sending tingles down to my toes.

Elias' laugh booms from the office. "You're merely a prince to the mafia crown. You have no authority here, Little Heir. You can't tell me when I can and can't do something. Your territory? Maybe it was cleared by the big man himself," Elias says in a condescending tone, deepening with every word he spouts.

"That's our cue," Arrow murmurs, pushing through a bedroom door and into a pitch-black room.

I blink several times, letting my eyes adjust to the darkness. The only light source is the small amount of moonlight coming from the open window across the way, leaving me to stare at the outline of Arrow's face when he walks further into the room.

Shepp follows behind, albeit reluctant and dragging his feet.

"All right, Kitten. Spread your legs. I'm a starving man. Slather me in your juices," Arrow says, tossing me onto the made king-sized bed with an umph.

"That's the least sexy thing anyone has ever said," I grunt, landing on my back on the soft bed. I sigh, darting my eyes to Arrow, who rubs his chin.

"Let me eat your pussy and make you come?"

"Warmer," I giggle, placing my hands behind my back.

"How many licks does it take to get to the center of your pussy and make you come?" he spouts off again, removing his shirt over his head with a grin.

"Mhmm," I murmur when he steps up to the bed and gets on all fours, crawling toward my sprawled-out body.

A clicking sound coming from Shepp stops Arrow in his tracks. His blond brows furrow as he watches every hand movement Shepp does.

"Who cares," Arrow says, waving his hand. "Let Jericho find out." He grins when he crawls over my body and presses his hips into mine, letting me feel the hardness trapped in his pants. "He's worried Jericho will burst in here and take us away from you." Arrow's soft lips work over my neck, sucking my flesh into his mouth. No doubt leaving hickies in his wake. "This marks you as ours, Kitten." He works his way down, biting at my clothed breasts with a grin until he's between my legs. He works my dress over my hips, exposing my black, lacy thong. "Journey," Arrow murmurs when he's at eye level with my clothed pussy.

I shiver when his warm breath blows across my wetness. "Yeah?" I choke out when his finger swipes through my folds and his breaths warm my pussy.

"Take Shepp's cock out and give it a little kiss. He just asked." Arrow chuckles against my cunt, teasing it.

My head swivels to Shepp, who blinks rapidly and moves his fingers even faster. A redness takes over his cheeks, and he stomps a foot, gaining Arrow's attention.

"Oh, he says balls deep. Can you take him all the way back into your throat?" Arrow says, grinning when Shepp marches forward and shoves Arrow's face into my pussy.

"Oh fuck," I breathe when Arrow's tongue swipes rapidly across my clit, aching to feel more. "More," I moan, shoving my fingers into his hair and pushing him further. My back arches when he inserts a finger into my dripping pussy, pumping it in and out at a slow, agonizing pace. Thank God it's so dark in this damn room, and we can barely see one another. Heat takes over my cheeks when he dives in harder.

Arrow finally relents when Shepp takes his hand off the back of his head. "That wasn't really a punishment," he says with a large grin and licks his lips. "You taste absolutely delicious, Kitten. I could live and feast off your cunt every day. Let's make that happen. I'll take you home, tie you to my bed, spread eagle, and eat you for breakfast, lunch, and dinner. What do you say?" Arrow wiggles his brows but grunts when Shepp smacks the back of his head again. Arrow frowns. "Soon," he reassures me while blowing hot air across my throbbing clit. "You'll be ours soon. You know that, right?" He stares up at me from below, his blue eyes sparkling in the low moonlight.

I swallow hard at his statement. "Yours?" I ask with confusion, making his smile grow wider and more blinding.

He makes a show of running his long tongue over his

glistening lips and nods. "You really have no idea what we have in store for you. But yes. Ours. The Devil's little slut. You want to be ours, baby?"

I moan when he spreads my lower lips and sucks them into his mouth, darting his tongue straight into my dripping cunt with enthusiasm.

"Your pussy agrees. Now, beg me," he whispers, flicking his tongue over my clit. "Beg me to let you come on my face. If I'm lucky, you'll soak me to the fucking bone. Now..." He raises a brow when my cheeks heat.

I'm not a goddamn beggar by any means. For this man, though? He makes me want to drop to my knees and smother his face with my pussy until I explode all over him. So, I'll beg. I'm desperate enough to shout my next words.

"Please," I beg.

"That's my good whore," he says, licking me again. "Shepp, you might want to make her quiet. I'm about to make her scream. We can't have Jer marching in here before our girl comes."

Shepp swallows hard, turning his eyes to mine, and signs something.

"He wants to know if you're okay with him shoving his dick down your throat."

Shepp grunts unhappily, rubbing the back of his neck. But nods.

I lick my lips. "I've never..." I shake my head. "I..." My breath leaves my lungs when he kneels beside the bed, getting eye level with me. His fingers run through my hair so gently, I'm nearly thrown off my axis when he leans in, brushing his lips against mine.

"Thatta boy, Shepp. Take what you want. Journey West is on the menu," Arrow chuckles, diving back into my pussy and licking me back and forth until I'm moaning into Shepp's mouth.

Pulling back from our kiss with a heavy breath, Shepp furrows his brows. His fingers trace over my swollen lips with interest.

"You're good with this?" he mouths, not making a sound.

Surprisingly, I understand him, reading him with ease.

I nod once, and that's all it takes for him to step back and undo his pants. I nearly swallow my tongue when his dick jolts out and then bobs, after it is released from the confines of his zipper. Glistening with precum, he runs his massive hand up and down his length before stepping forward.

My lips pop open, and I take him into my mouth, swirling my tongue around his tip as best I can. I breathe through my nose when he thrusts forward and wraps his hand around my hair, holding me still.

"Look at my good little Kitten taking Shepp's cock like a pro. Now, hang on. I'm about to make you come, and hard. Come for me, Kitten," Arrow croons, twirling his tongue around my clit.

His fingers pump in and out of me at a rapid pace, curling inside me. I swear I see stars the moment my pussy contracts around him, and I moan around Shepp's cock.

A groan erupts from above me, and before I know it, the salty taste of his cum slides down my throat. I breathe through my nose rapidly, trying to swallow the taste of him and nearly gag. But I take it all until he pulls out with a dreamy look on his face. Without warning, he leans down, putting his lips on mine.

"He wants to marry you now," Arrow quips, wiping his mouth. Shepp pulls away, shooting him a dangerous look, promising hell later. He only smiles at him and then slaps my satisfied cunt as I cry out. "Good girl."

What the hell did I just let happen? No matter. It's fine. I'm fine. Everything is fucking fine.

Or not.

I just got into bed with two of the three Devils. I let them lick me, suck me, and almost fuck me. What is wrong with me lately? Drunk. That's it. I'm wasted on shitty tequila and whatever else she gave me.

Why am I pushing the limits of everything I've known for the past three years? Fuck. I know why. Because what the hell else do I have to lose? My sister? She's gone. He took her without letting me say goodbye. My sanity and innocence? Nah. I gave that up the moment my monster forced me to shove a knife into the chest of his enemy.

All in the name of his wicked lessons.

I can't let my anxiety get the best of me, though. I made this bed, and I'm going to lie in it. First, the masked men, and now these two. I'm headed down a dangerous road Sunny might not recover from. Shit. No. Don't think about your sister right now. She's safe in a hospital. He would never hurt her. Not really.

Arrow chuckles, righting my dress over my extremely sated lady bits that beg for another go with his tongue or dick. He doesn't bother to put my underwear back on, though. Instead, I see him discreetly put them into his pocket with a wicked grin. I should care. Should, being the keyword. But I don't. He can keep them and do whatever he wants with them.

I never want to move again. I can lie here forever. That man should get an award for pussy eating. He'd be number one. Arrow crawls up the bed to lie behind me. The feel of his body heat against my back as his hand rubs over my stomach is very soothing.

"You're such a good girl, Kitten," he whispers in my ear, sucking my ear lobe into his mouth. "I'd bend you over right here and please you until the sun comes up, but my handler will be smashing through that door at any second." I feel his grin against my skin.

"Your handler?"

"Normally, it's up to Shepp, but seeing as how he can barely stand—good job, by the way—I think you sucked his soul from his cock. You good, Sheppy boy?"

I snort when Shepp lifts his middle finger in the air for Arrow and then is suddenly in my face, locking his lips on mine. I groan into his mouth.

"On second thought, he's caught his second wind," Arrow chuckles, palming my breasts and grinding against my ass. "I want to fuck you, Kitten. So fucking hard you can't walk straight for days. I want to claim every crevice on your body, including your tits. We'll paint you in our cum when the time is right."

"When the time is right?" I ask through the haze of hands wandering down my body and squeezing every part they can sink their fingers into. I'm on fire, igniting from the feeling of the both of them like I was meant to be the damn ham in their sandwich.

"You'll learn soon, Kitten."

"Why Kitten?" I gasp when he tweaks my nipple through my dress, causing my hips to buck forward. But I'm too far gone to inspect every fucking thing he's said.

"Because you..."

"Arrow! Sheppard! I swear to fucking God," Jericho's loud voice booms outside the locked bedroom door with such venom I swear my soul shrivels away.

"Party pooper," Arrow grumbles, kissing my cheek one last time. "One day," is all he says before lifting himself off the bed and standing side by side with Shepp, who signs something to him. "Oh, sure. Blame it all on me Mr-I-got-my-dick-sucked," Arrow scoffs, looking like a shadow standing before me as he puts his shirt over his head and squares his shoulders. "You let him in," he responds to Shepp's silent demand. "I'm not. He's going to punch my face in. He'd never suspect you. You're Mr-I-have-a-conscience."

I take a deep breath, flopping onto my back. Every inch of me is so sated and relaxed that I lose track of time, and I don't even care when the door is thrown open and the lights flipped on, illuminating the entire bedroom we landed in.

"Unbelievable," Jericho grunts, slamming the door behind him. "I had to track fucking Jenni down to get a key. Locking yourselves in a bedroom with her?" My teeth sit on edge at the way he says her like I'm such a goddamn disappointment. "Get up, Journey. Walk out of here," he fucking demands, coming to the side of the bed with rage written on every inch of his face.

He's so goddamn rude.

"You know what? You're fucking bossy," I say, forcing myself to sit up as the damn room spins. "And you yell a lot." I rub at my temple, sucking in a breath at the sudden dizziness taking me over. "And you're rude," I ramble, talking through the headache forming in my skull.

He bends at the waist, getting eye level with me. Those dark eyes look over my face. His fingers snatch my chin, forcing me to stay still.

"You've mentioned how rude I am before. Are you drunk?" he grits out, rage consuming and twisting his expression.

"A little." I hold up my thumb and pointer finger, showing him the itty bitty space between them. "Maybe it was the orgasm." I grin when he stands tall and shifts on his heel to face Arrow.

"What part of the rules for tonight didn't you fucking understand?" he growls, getting right into Arrow's face. They stand nose to nose. Neither of them backing down. Shepp grunts, putting a hand on each other's chests and pushing them back, signing something. "You, too, huh? We came here for..." Jericho swivels his head in my direction with a frown and then huffs, zipping his lips.

"For business!" I say gleefully, getting to my feet and swaying a little. "Maybe I should sit down."

But I don't. I stand beside the three of them, staring at me with varying degrees of expression.

Arrow grins like a maniac, licking his lips. Maybe he wants dessert? I sure do. Shepp's chest heaves when he looks me up and down with concern and stars in his eyes. Maybe I did suck the soul from his dick and make him fall in love with me. And Jericho... He looks like he wants to turn me over his knee and show me what a bad girl I've been.

"I gotta go," I murmur, pointing toward the door, leaving them to their now whispering argument. They don't try to stop me or make sure I won't fall down the damn stairs.

CHAPTER TWENTY-FOUR

Journey

As I leave the room, shutting the door behind me, the distinct sound of a fist hitting flesh pierces my ears. My eyes widen, but I'm not stupid enough to get between three mafia boys and their weird argument. That's a no from me.

I'm fucking out. I need to get a grip on myself.

Once I'm in the hallway, reality sinks my stomach to my feet. I hooked up with Arrow and Shepp. Hooked the fuck up. The Devils. The most notorious mafia men around town. I let them... Jesus. I let them in. Again. I put my walls down for them. Again. And damn does it feel good.

I'm so fucking alive right now, it seems impossible. The air is crisper. The lights are brighter. Everything is better.

The feel of his warm mouth lingers on my pussy. Goosebumps prickle at my skin. The way their hands ran down my body, gripping anything they could. Even the salty taste of Shepp's cum spurting into my mouth when I brought him to completion.

Shit. My face flushes from the memories. I need a second to breathe before I go back to the party and mingle with the crowd. Or before I face Jenni.

I rush to the bathroom to my right and walk in, splashing water on my face. I need to walk back into that party, find Jenni, and drink some more. Maybe do my damn job and spy on her and

Elias, if they haven't disappeared, too. Jericho is obviously done with the meeting. So, that leaves them in the wind. Great.

Water drips from my face when I greet myself in the mirror. Flushed cheeks. Hickies lining my neck from Arrow's over-aggressive biting. My fingers run over the marks, slowly fading in the light.

"This marks you as ours, Kitten."

I shiver at the memory of his words from tonight and squeeze my eyes shut. Fuck. I need to get back out there and make an appearance. Hopefully, no one else saw our joined exit. I can only hope they were all way too drunk to comprehend what was happening. The fear of having my monster find out sends waves of terror through my body, but also excitement. If he finds out... He'll punish me. But it's a him problem. He has this control over my body and my time, and he's slowly losing it each and every time I defy him.

I shake it all off and put on an indifferent front. I don't fucking care. Not one bit. I can't afford to care.

When I'm done washing my face, I exit the bathroom and make my way down the hallway to the top of the stairs. Before I leave the second floor, I peek over my shoulder, noting the bedroom door is still shut.

Must be having some kind of meeting in there. Or maybe they're really fighting. Who knows. I need to get as far away from them as I can before I fall on my back and let them do something more, like fuck me senseless. God, that would be delicious. I finally get to the bottom of the stairs and blow out a breath. I half expected Arrow and Shepp to follow me down with an angry Jericho on their heels.

My eyes scan the rambunctious crowd, still dancing against one another. Some plant their lips on their partners. Others grind so hard it's like they're practically having sex on the dance floor.

Through the crowd, I attempt to find Jenni, who should stand out like a sore thumb with her red hair and tall stature, but she doesn't emerge. I don't blame her. She probably has more important things to do, like Elias. Half of me wants to march back upstairs and rummage through her father's office for evidence. Of what, though? I have no clue. I was only instructed to keep an eye on them and relay anything of importance back. Well, nothing important has happened tonight. Kinda. Fuck. I rub at my temple as I make my way through the crowd, examining everyone around me. They're too lost in themselves to notice I've disappeared or reappeared.

Good.

I make my way through the vast house, wandering away from the chaos. As I meander down the long hallway past the kitchen, a few lingering people are having conversations around me. My heart speeds up when I walk past an open door, revealing massive bookcases from floor to ceiling, lining the entire room. My favorite room in her house. I peek over my shoulder and then wander in, running my fingers over the leather-bound books. What I wouldn't give to get lost in the pages of any of these books. For just a second to forget who I am or where I am in life. Like the book on my nightstand, begging for me to finish it. I just got to the part where she throws a giant dildo at a peeping turkey.

Why can't I go back to that?

"Journey West."

All the saliva in my mouth dries at the sound of my name on his lips. True fear runs through me when I whirl around, facing the boy who dared to say my name. Leighton LeMaster. The boy who can't take no for an answer. Ever. He's relentless in his endeavors; I'll give him that. He could seriously have most girls around school without a fight, but that wouldn't be good enough for him. He likes the fight.

"Come on, Journey! Go out with me." I always say no.

"It's just a little kiss, Journey," he murmurs, trying to plaster his lips against mine in the hall at school. It's like the moment I slipped away from the cafeteria to escape the masses, he attacked, cornering me against the wall with his body weight. "Come on, girl. Make this easy."

"What are you doing wandering around alone? Did they not satisfy you enough?" He saunters in, thrusting his hands into his jean pockets.

The sleazy grin on his face has my hair standing on end. His glazed-over eyes take in my body with appreciation when he advances on me more, finally stopping before my frozen body. Shit. Why can't I fucking move from this spot and get away from him?

"You're so fucking hot," he murmurs, attempting to lean in for a kiss.

"Stop it, Leighton," I grunt, pushing his face away from mine. Finally, I move. But it wasn't fast enough.

I have to find an exit. I peer around, looking for the door, but somehow I lost myself in the shelves, and he shut it behind us. This isn't good. Darkness swirls in my mind, threatening to drown me in its clutches. No one understands what my monster did to me in the basement of his home, locking me away and forcing the darkness inside me to reveal itself. Turning me into the same monster I see in him. The perfect little weapon he wields on unsuspecting people.

"This is for your crimes," my monster calmly says, smacking the side of the dangling cage I woke up in just a few minutes ago, bleary-eyed and confused as hell with my mother's screams echoing in my head.

The last thing I remember... Crap. Bile shoots up my throat and through my lips before I can even beg for my life. Memories assault me, forcing me down the deep, dark rabbit hole of the crime I committed. I swallow down the rest of my vomit, meeting the disgusted eyes of my captor. His lips twist up, and he shakes his head.

"Please," I beg, shaking my head. "I'll... I'll..."

"You'll what? Give back what you took?" His blue eyes narrow on me, basking in the tears rolling down my reddened cheeks. "I didn't think so, Miss West. Everyone has a price to pay, and yours is greater than money or begging. Live with the consequences of your

actions." His grin burrows into my mind as he flips off the lights, blackening the room.

How I ache to grab Leighton's hand and break his fingers. Or punch his face to make him back off. But he never does. No matter what. Leighton LeMaster is a relentless creep, pushing himself on people.

"Come on, baby. You gave it up to those assholes. Why not me? Why're you always denying me?" he grunts, pushing me up against the bookcase.

Vomit rests in the back of my throat when he presses his disgusting body against mine, letting me feel his attraction pushing through his jeans. Someone needs to chop it off so he can never hurt another girl again.

"Because you're a goddamn creep!" I grunt, attempting to push him away, but he chuckles.

"Eh. I just take what I want, baby doll. What are they going to do to me? Now, open your legs for me."

Darkness completely takes over my vision when his fingers run up my leg and then settle between them.

"What are you doing?" I growl, grabbing his wrist in my death grip. Like fuck am I letting another man take advantage of me. Never fucking again. My monster may not fuck me like this, but he finds other ways to completely screw me over. And now this man? No... he's a boy. Only boys don't take the word no seriously.

"Just let this happen," he murmurs, pushing harder into my body and forcing my legs further apart.

I close my eyes at the feel of his fingers in places they shouldn't be. Places I don't want him to be. No matter how hard I push against him, he pushes harder back, grunting when he enters me with his fingers.

The dark cloud tarnishing my soul clouds my vision. The room disappears. He disappears. The feel of him vanishes into thin air.

"Get your hands the fuck off me," I hiss, rearing back and

throwing my fist into his face. The satisfying crunch of his nose fills my ears, and the darkness in me revels when he falls back with a loud shout. How I had the room to throw a punch, I'll never know.

My chest heaves when I push my dress back down, covering myself from the carnage he had left behind. The bookcase digs into my back when I finally push myself off it and step up to Leighton, who lies on the ground. Where he fucking belongs for ever thinking he could put his hands on me.

He stares at me with wide eyes, holding his bloodied nose. "What the fuck, Journey?" he hisses, slurring his fucking words.

"What the fuck indeed."

My head jerks up when Jericho stalks through the room with the other two on his tail. Fury twists his face, and his fists curl at his side.

I swallow hard at the broken door lying in pieces on the ground. How did I miss him tearing through the hardwood? How did I black out so much that I don't understand how I got to this point?

The darkness, my mind screams. That's what happens when it takes hold. It suffocates existence from my vision and merely takes over like another person is inside me clawing for dominance. It only happens in precarious situations when danger flashes before my eyes.

Like when Leighton had his hand inside my vagina, violating me. Something switched in my brain. But now, I'm back to me.

My jaw clenches when I stare at Leighton, pitifully groaning. "She punched me!" he whines, holding up his bloodied hand. "Bitch—"

My eyes widen when Jericho smashes the heel of his foot into Leighton's nose, flattening him again. Danger wafts off him like he's two seconds away from tearing Leighton to pieces. Not that I'd mind. In fact, I'd love it. Get him, Jer man!

"Watch what you fucking call her," he hisses, raising a brow when Leighton dutifully nods. "Now, fucking explain," Jericho demands, narrowing his eyes at me.

Well, I narrow mine right back. How dare he speak to me like I'm a goddamn child. I huff, marching forward and standing right over Leighton as he remains on the floor. Honestly, I'm surprised he hasn't pissed himself in Jericho's presence.

"I was minding my own business. Wasn't I, Leighton?" I spit his name when I lean down, taking in the utter fear in his glazed-over eyes. He's more than just fucking drunk and stumbling around this party. He's high as a kite, taking what he wants from girls. Well, it's about time I take what I fucking want, too.

"You were begging for it," he slurs, showing off his bloodied teeth. "Walking around here in your little dress and..." He grunts when I slam my fist into his mouth, turning his head to the side.

"Little Chaos," Jericho tuts, taking my hand into his before I can shake away the pain. "Your thumb does not get tucked in. Leave it out to prevent breakage."

I know that. But fuck. This asshole just tried to take what wasn't offered freely.

Sparks fly up my damn arm when he strokes his thumb over the puffy skin forming on my fist. Now is not the time to get turned on. Especially with Leighton in the room, and after he violated me so crudely. But I can't help it. Since Jericho kissed me on the dance floor and claimed me as his, I've been hopeless.

"Now, continue. You were minding your own business and apparently asking for it. What were you asking for?" he raises a brow when I remove my hand from his and shake off the desire running through my veins.

Leaning over Leighton, I inspect the bloodied mess they created on his face, and I grin. "Apparently, he thought his fingers should go in places they weren't meant to be."

Three growls erupt in the room.

"He fucking what, Kitten?" Arrow asks with a deadly tone, gliding forward with a darkness encompassing his eyes. A demon seems to take him over as he stands above Leighton with ill intent.

And I'm here for it.

"Don't worry. He took something from me. So, I'll take something from him." Without further explanation, I dig through Leighton's pocket and pull out his keys.

"No!" Leighton squeals, reaching up for the keys in my hand, dangling just out of his reach.

"I think I'll go for a joy ride," I say with a shrug, desperately needing to get out of this room and away from him and them.

Their fury sits like a dangerous cloud seeping through the entire room. I need to break away from this entire night and not succumb to the darkness peeking through the edges of my eyes like a demon attempting to infiltrate my soul. I shake off the numbness in my fingers and toes. I shake off the evil residing inside me and push it to the back of my mind.

Because that's what it is. My monster put evil inside me when he forced me to murder people until they spilled their guts. Literally. What happened in that basement changed the very DNA in my body.

Fuck Leighton. Fuck everything.

Now is the time to feel alive and grasp my freedom by the balls.

Sparks fly through me when I push past Jericho, Arrow, and Shepp, leaving Leighton on the ground. Bellowing about his precious car that he loves to show off, attempting to get anything with a pussy between their legs to ride fast with him. It's his signature move.

Oh, boohoo you wannabe rapist.

"Need a ride home, Journey?" he asks, leaning against my locker with a grin, dangling his keys in my face. "It goes from zero to one-twenty in eight seconds. It could knock your panties right off, Baby Doll." Inwardly, I spew my guts at his suggestion.

"I'm good," I retort, shutting my locker and hoping to lose him. But no dice. He follows so close I swear he's implanted himself up my ass.

"Come on, Baby Doll. Take a fast ride with me. I can get you all wet and hot and..."

"Does that really work on girls, Leighton?" I sniff, raising my chin. *"If I were even interested, I wouldn't want it to go fucking fast. Slow and steady wins the race, assbag. Now, kindly fuck off for eternity."* With that, I spin on my heel and book it out of the high school before he can register what I said.

On my peaceful walk home toward the trailer park near the middle of town, a loud car rushes by me, splashing water on my dingy shoes. I raise a brow when a middle finger protrudes from the driver's side window.

Huh. Must have wrecked his little ego.

And now, I'm about to wreck his fucking car. First, my monster, now Leighton, and then the Devils trying to play hero. I'm so goddamn tired of men running my fucking life and ruining it. Or trying to save me. I can do that myself.

This is my life. My fucking body. And my fucking revenge to seek.

CHAPTER TWENTY-FIVE

Journey

"Whoa, whoa, Kitten!" Arrow catches up, stalking beside me as we weave through the crowd and finally make it outside. "What's the plan?" he asks, rubbing his hands together.

"Just because you ate me like a meal doesn't mean you can tag along," I huff, marching toward the monstrosity Leighton calls a sports car.

"And what do you plan on doing, Kitten? Drive it until it doesn't work anymore?" he asks with a grin evident on his face.

I huff, immediately turning toward him and stopping our advance. "Do you have a plan, Genius?" I ask, folding my arms over my chest.

Because... he makes a fair point. To be honest, I didn't have a plan. I wanted to scare the ever-living shit out of Leighton by taking his keys, but beyond that? I don't have a clue. I'm more prone to hanging in the background and collecting information. Not banging up expensive cars for a good time.

Arrow grins. "Kitten, I have the right tools for you." He holds up a finger before disappearing down the long driveway filled to the brim with cars from the other party-goers.

"I've taken care of Leighton," Jericho says in a smooth voice, sauntering up to me without a hair out of place.

His fancy clothes aren't even wrinkled when he stops beside me, eyeing my stiff stance.

"I didn't ask you to," I growl, clenching my teeth.

"You didn't have to, Little Chaos," he says, assessing my body. "Now, I want you to tell me every little detail of what Leighton did." He rolls his wrist like a jackass, egging me on to divulge the lengths of my trauma with Leighton.

"What gives you the right?" I ask, turning to him and squaring my shoulders.

Right now, he's not the mafia heir. He's the asshole who thinks he has the right to climb inside my skin and know everything about me.

"The right?" he chuckles, stepping up to me. "Everything about you gives me the fucking right. You're mine." A possession I haven't seen before rests in his dark eyes. "I claimed you. Don't you remember when you rode my fingers in the middle of the dance floor? Or when your cum soaked my flesh? I marked you as mine when I sunk my teeth into your neck and left a beautiful reminder of our time together."

Fuck. His words shouldn't affect me as much as they do. He smirks. I'm sure my pupils dilate remembering that time together. But I've been satisfied tonight. I came on Arrow's face like a champ. So, his pretty words can't make my pussy weep for him. Not right now.

Instead, I raise my chin in defiance, looking the Devil in the eyes.

"I am no one's," I hiss, poking at his chest hard with my index finger.

He doesn't budge. Not even an inch. He just stands there staring at me with unblinking eyes. Every emotion seems to vanish from his chiseled face.

A strangled noise comes from Shepp when he shakes his head, signing something to Jericho. Quicker than lightning, Jericho's fingers wrap around my throat, and he pulls me into him.

I shiver in his grip. For some reason, I don't feel threatened in the least. Sure, there's fury on his face, reddening it with every second that passes. But he doesn't want to harm me. He simply wants to control me.

And that fucking pisses me off.

"A few more days, Journey West. That's how long you have until your freedom is mine. Everything that concerns you is mine and theirs," he growls, pointing to Shepp and Arrow.

My lips pop open when he squeezes again, letting just enough air through my windpipe to keep me upright.

A few days? Why that length of time? And what the hell will happen then? Schools over. I graduated. Now, my focus is finding my damn sister. I've been trying for so damn long to get it done, but I'm never successful. All bets are off now.

"Please tell me what he did to you so I can chop every fucking digit and appendage that touched you without your consent." He raises a brow when my fingers wrap around his wrist.

"Why don't you wait until after we dismantle his car?" Arrow pipes in, letting an armful of weapons fall to the ground with a clatter. He grins at me, gesturing to the pile. I wrinkle my nose. Geez, do these boys do this a lot? Mentally, I tally the pile—a metal baseball bat, an ax, two lead pipes, and a samurai sword. Who needs a samurai sword? But also, what do they use them for? Also, where can I get one for myself?

"All right, let's fuck shit up," Arrow says, rubbing his hands together with glee. "Pick your favorite piece, Kitten. Personally, this is mine." He reaches down and grabs the ax. "It slices through metal and flesh—no problem."

I stiffen at his words, still stuck in Jericho's grasp. My eyes fall to Shepp, who gently nods in Jer's direction with a pleading smile.

"Fine," I rasp, peeling his fingers from around my throat. I need to get this destruction done and over with before Leighton decides to call the cops and have me fucking arrested. Worst outcome ever. "He assaulted me. Okay?"

"Assaulted?" Jericho growls, turning a deep shade of red. "I'm going to..."

"Help us wreck this piece of shit. Come on, boys. Grab a

weapon." Arrow doesn't hesitate when he hands me a lead pipe. "Let's cause some mayhem!" he howls, throwing back his head with a demented laugh.

I focus on nothing more than the destruction of Leighton's car.

"Ladies first," Arrow says, gesturing to the window.

Nothing beats the taste of destruction in the middle of the night under a full moon. Much like Arrow, I let it all go and fucking howl one time before I get started. Nothing runs through my mind but the retribution I'm owed. Even my darkness joins in, taking over as my grip tightens on the metal pipe. Men like Leighton don't deserve nice things while they shove drugs and booze down their throats and take advantage of women.

This is his goddamn reckoning.

I kick off my heels into the bushes that decorate the mile-long driveway and make my way onto the hood of his car. I rest the lead pipe on my shoulder, staring down at the beast beneath me.

"Hold it right there, Kitten," Arrow groans, shoving a Polaroid camera in my direction. The bright flash momentarily stuns me. Then, a picture spits out of the device he now has hanging around his neck.

I swallow hard, my heart pounding wildly in my chest when he shakes the picture and then looks it over with appreciation. My eyes connect with his as they sparkle with a knowing look, and he nods. The grin on his face sends shivers down my spine.

So few people carry instant cameras these days.That's what cellphones are for. Instant. Digital. Well, everyone except Arrow and the man who enters my bedroom each night and leaves them on my pillows before he leaves.

"You," I mumble through a breath, momentarily losing traction.

He winks at me, nodding his head toward the car like he knows I'm about to lose my mind with the facts surrounding me.

But I don't have time to truly dissect what's happening right now. Is he the one leaving photos by my pillow each night? Probably, yes. He's proven to be insane enough to do that.

But I've got a car to destroy. Then, I can accuse him of being a stalker.

"This is for my spank bank later. Destruction gets me so fucking horny, Kitten. Now, show me what you got." He gestures for me to continue and takes a step back, grinning from ear to ear.

My heart pounds under the glare of the stars as metal groans beneath my bare feet. Taking a few steps across the hood of his precious sports car—how goddamn cliche—I spit on the windshield in disgust.

"Fuck you Leighton," I grunt, sticking my middle finger in the air. Another bright flash accompanied by a moan follows when I spit again. "This is what you get!" I shout, heaving the lead pipe into the windshield.

Spiderweb breakage takes over the glass, splintering in every direction.

One by one, I'm breaking my rules. Double fuck him with a soldering iron. Another step toward freedom. Another day that I'm taking my life in my hands and not caring what he thinks. I'm so desperate to be out from under his thumb and just be myself that I'm willingly committing a crime. Screw the fucking consequences. Let the cops haul me away. Let the neighbors in this hoity-toity neighborhood call this in.

Let my monster in on the illegal things I've done. What more can he do? Kill me? I don't think he'd ever truly hurt Sunny. She's innocent. But I'm not. They have a moral code that rules their decisions. As fucked up as it might be, they don't intentionally harm civilians. Me though? I fucked up long ago. I'm fair game. Guilty of the crime I committed.

My fingers brush against the large scar hidden between my breasts. The mark is an everlasting reminder—a brand of my survival. An infinite wound that won't ever heal. Numbness greets my fingertips as I run over the thick, corded skin. It may not bleed any longer, but the pain resides behind my lungs.

Once my mind spirals back to the land of the living, I return to the destruction I've meticulously planned since that creep Leighton put his hand between my legs without even as much as a how ya doing, Journey.

Let Leighton reap the consequences of his fuck boy actions.

Looking up after losing myself for several seconds, my breath hitches at the beauty of Shepp standing just behind me on the ground. His light gray eyes sparkle in the moonlight, hinting at a bit of mischief and knowledge. With grace, he taps at the edge of the glass repeatedly, like he's trying to prove a point. He huffs, turning to Jericho with his fingers moving a mile a minute.

"He wants you to tap the edge of the glass," Jericho helpfully adds from my right, appearing out of nowhere. "Right here," he murmurs, pointing to the same spot. "You can't hit the middle. It's made to take blunt force. But the edges? That's where it's at. Hit those, and Leighton's windows won't exist anymore." Something sparkles in his gorgeous but deadly brown eyes, making my breath catch in my throat.

Danger—my mind screams. Run—another voice yelps with desperation. Yet, my feet root in the spot, and my body soaks up their warmth as they stand mere millimeters away on the ground, watching with admiration.

Shepp nods at Jericho's statement without uttering a word, leaving his eyes glued to me. Nearly knocking the breath from my lungs. There's something so beautiful yet devious lying in the depths of his pupils, sucking me into his presence.

Without wasting another second, I hit the edge of the windshield and whoop when it collapses into the car, breaking into several large pieces.

"That's my Kitten!" Arrow whoops in victory.

"Get down, Little Chaos. Before you hurt your damn feet," Jericho growls, reaching out to grab me from the hood of the car. I screech when he pulls me into his tight grip and cradles me in his arms.

"Why'd you do that?" I hiss, hitting him with my free hand

and wiggling out of his grip. Okay, I don't wiggle as much as he
lets me go. With his strength, he gave up easily.

"Glass," he grunts, gesturing to the pieces. "You don't have
any fucking shoes on. You could hurt yourself!"

"I'm a big fucking girl!" I shout back, pushing his chest with
my hand. "I'm a grown woman! You can't dictate my goddamn
life. No one can. Not anymore!" I shout into the void.

This time, he stumbles a step back, staring at me like I've lost
my fucking mind. Maybe I have.

"Have at it," he says with an indifferent expression, nodding
toward the car. "Break his car to pieces. Get glass in your
goddamn feet. But don't come crying to me when the
consequences of your actions come back to bite you in your sweet
ass."

My next step is breaking every single fucking piece of glass on
the car. Windows, headlights, and back windshield. They don't
stand a chance with me solely taking down his fucking piece of
shit car.

"Yes, Kitten! Destroy it!" Arrow shouts with a grunt, shoving
the head of his ax right through the metal of the hood.

I grin when he joins in, completely obliterating every inch of
Leighton's car.

"Now, for the final touch," Arrow says, handing me a can full
of gasoline.

I blink several times. "You want me to light it on fire?"

And why did he have this on hand? I have so many questions,
but I'm way too tired to do this shit. The only thing on my mind
is the destruction I need to finish.

He shrugs. "Up to you, Kitten."

My eyes pass over each of the Devils, watching me from the
sidelines with tiny smirks and then to the house fifty yards behind
us. The party rages on. No one seems to notice what's happening.

Where the fuck is Leighton?

"He did put his hands on you, Little Chaos. He did this to
himself." Jericho shrugs, pulling a lighter out of his pocket.

"Light that bitch up, Kitten!" Arrow howls again, stomping his feet.

"Did you beat his ass? Leave him unconscious?" Uneasiness fills me when I uncap the gas cap, letting the fumes rise into the air.

A grin splits Jericho's lips. "Black and blue until blood spilled. See?" He gestures toward his shoes, where shiny spots of dark red glisten under the moonlight.

I nibble my lip with uncertainty. Sure, I just committed a major fucking crime, but adding fuel to the damn fire? Literally. Why not? Revenge beckons me forward, eager to punish the boy—not a man—who dared to put his hands on me.

"Go big or go home, right?" I murmur to myself as I turn on my heel and march toward the car, soaking almost every inch of the inside with gasoline.

"Now, for the boom," Arrow whispers in my ear, wrapping his arms around my body. "Let's step back so the fumes don't get us." He kisses my cheek, dragging me back between Jericho and Shepp. Thankfully, no one else has gathered around outside, giving us good distance from the wreckage.

"I'll do the honors," Jericho says, flicking the flame to life and then throwing it straight into the car.

A bright, hot fire whooshes to life right before our eyes. Heat hits our faces as the car is devoured by the ravenous flame eating away at the metal we destroyed.

"Holy shit!" I gasp, sinking back into Arrow while shielding my eyes.

Freedom and liberation soar through me. Nothing can touch me now. I finally took my life back into my hands. For once in my life I've done something to a man who took a piece of me.

"Show time," Jericho says over the road of the fire consuming the car. My eyes flash to him, and he smirks.

"What the absolute fuck!" Leighton shouts, staggering toward his car.

"Here's the keys," Jericho chuckles, tossing the keys toward Leighton, but they fall to the pavement.

"Don't think you'll really need them anymore, Bro. Journey really did a number on it." Arrow grins, holding me hostage in his grip.

"You," Leighton growls, turning to stare at me with a snarl. "You fucking..." He shakes his head, watching his car turn into nothing but a fiery hunk of melted metal. "You... lit it on fire! My father is going to lock you away and..."

"Tsk. Tsk," Jericho says, shaking his head. "He'd love to know what you've been up to, wouldn't he? How's your promise going?" Promise? What promise?

Leighton fucking pales. "I could say the same for you assholes."

"My dick has never been wet. How about yours?" Arrow quips, squeezing me again. "My mouth, on the other hand..." he trails off with a vibrating chuckle, spearing right into my back. My cheeks heat at his implication, and my eyes dart to Leighton. Fuck. I can't take my eyes off him as anger roars through his system.

Sirens ring in the background, traveling somewhere fast and close. My heart rate kicks up. My eyes widen when the red and blue lights pull up down the drive. The sound of a heavy engine braking echoes off the mansion. Several people stumble down the large stairs, coming to see the spectacle in the driveway.

I swallow hard at the sight of the officers marching up the drive with concern etching into their features.

Leighton's nostrils flare. "Well, it's too goddamn late. It was her!" he shouts when two policemen walk up the long driveway, accompanied by firemen dragging a hose. "She did it! I saw her!"

"What the fuck," I grunt, trying to get out of Arrow's hold, but he doesn't let me go. "Let me go!" I turn to look at him, and he grins, leaning down to kiss my cheek.

"No can do, Kitten."

Jericho saunters in front of me. "You're a big girl, right? You can take care of this situation yourself. I don't dictate your life, right?" He gestures to the two cops, leaning over Leighton's phone as a video plays.

My heart completely drops. My fingers tremble. No. No. God no. This can't be happening. I can't be the only one to get blamed for this.

"See, she fucking did it. She tore my car up and lit it on fire. I have it all right here," he says with a sinister grin.

The two police officers turn to me with their hands on their hips.

"Miss, I'm going to have to ask you to turn around and place your hands behind your back. You're under arrest for destruction of property."

My heart pounds against my ribs, echoing in my ears, when Arrow forcefully turns me around, and the cold shackles wrap around my wrists until I'm hauled backwards out of his grip.

He grins at me, giving me a little wave. "Have fun in the slammer, Kitten!"

I'm so fucking fucked. Beyond fucked.

My monster will most definitely hear about it. There's no way he won't. He knows it all. Hell, the cops are in his fucking pocket. And when he does, he's going to lock me away in his own fucking prison where I won't see the sunshine for months at a time.

Just like before when he took me for my crime.

"The art of being invisible begins now," my monster's voice rings out through the dark room as the lights above flicker on. "Good morning, my caged little snake." His manic grin darkens the room as I blink rapidly, trying to adjust to the light infiltrating through my eyelids.

I swallow hard when he stands before my prison in his ever-impressive suit. Always looking immaculate when he stands outside the bars of my home, staring at me with deep interest resting in his evil blue eyes.

No soul resides behind them. Nothing. No life. He's the devil in disguise, holding me captive for my crimes.

Four months, Sixty-two hours, twelve minutes, and fifty-four seconds. That's how long my hell has been going on. Believe me, I've watched the glow in the dark clock on the wall tick away. When it will end, I have no clue. Hopefully soon. I don't know how long I can cling to the rest of my humanity he hasn't chipped away. I want to go back home and go to school. Surely someone has noticed I've been absent?

My monster's shiny black shoes click against the cement basement floor as he walks around my swinging cage. His fingers wrap around a piece of metal, keeping me inside.

"How are you feeling today, Little Snake?"

I adjust my body, bringing my legs to my chest. "I'm fine," I say, avoiding his eyes.

"Mmm. Well, we have several lesson plans today to go over," he says, lifting the key out of his pocket.

Yay. More lessons. More ways for him to break me down and build me up again. I can already feel the effects of my imprisonment taking hold. He's beaten me down so hard already I don't know if I'll survive anymore. I don't know if I'll leave this place the old Journey West I was before.

"What's the lesson today?" I blink several times when he swings the door open to my cage and smirks down at me.

"Eager already, Little Snake?"

Eager to get out of this cage, but I don't dare talk back to him. I learned that lesson within the first week of being here. I can still feel the remnants of the gag he shoved into my mouth for two days straight, refusing to feed me until I learned to hold my damn tongue. So, I hold my tongue. For now, anyway.

"Yes," I say with apprehension, moving to step down from the cage hanging from the ceiling and suspended above the cement.

The room's cold air seeps through my damn bones, despite the ratty sweatpants and T-shirt I've been allowed to wear. My bare feet hit the ground, sending shivers through my emaciated body. My stomach grumbles at the thought of the last meal I had. It wasn't anything substantial. A peanut butter and jelly sandwich with a bag of chips.

"Then, let's get started, Little Snake." He grabs me by the back of the neck, forcing me toward another room at the opposite end of the basement. Or warehouse. Or wherever he has me. I've never been able to figure it out. All I know is it's dark at all times. It's cold and damp and constantly smells like mildew. If I ever make it out of this prison he's so gleefully thrown me into, I'll never fuck up my chances again.

I take a deep breath when we walk into a brightly-lit room filled with fluorescent lighting. They hum in the small room, highlighting the array of torture devices hanging from the walls and resting on a metal tray. Oh, and the man tied to a metal chair, strapped down by his hands and feet, unable to move. A gag rests in his mouth as he squirms, probably begging to be free.

"Oh, I almost forgot." No, he didn't. Whatever it is, he's always two steps ahead of me. "Your sister has written you a letter." He grins down at me, forcing me to face him. God, how I wish I could pluck his beady blue eyes out and put them on a stick for all to see that I killed the monster holding me hostage. He doesn't deserve a face or name.

My heart pounds double time. I haven't seen Sunshine in four months. Not since... He promised me if I complied with everything that he'd save her. That this was my repentance for being a bad girl.

"Can I?" I ask, licking my lips, which draws his attention toward them. Interest flares in his eyes, and I want to shrink back away from his gaze.

"Why don't we interrogate him first? Then, I'll see about handing over the letter. Be a good little girl today," he says, running a finger down my jaw with interest. "Then, we'll see."

CHAPTER TWENTY-SIX

Jericho

OUR PROMISE to the Viotto Crime Family is this: we will remain pussy free until our initiation commences. Then, we will have someone special for us—an arranged marriage. Normally, each member of the family has their wife selected for them from an early age. Seeing as Arrow's father wasn't in the family, he was never truly considered. Or Shepp, whose father passed on before any connections could be made. And then, there was me. At eighteen, I was provided with who I was supposed to marry on a slip of paper and told to keep my nose clean.

The boys and I decided right then and there, we would share her. Seeing as we were each intrigued and heavily interested in one girl—Journey West.

Is the practice barbaric and outdated? Absolutely, yes. It's something we shouldn't have to deal with in this day and age. Yet, my father pushed, and I conceded like the dutiful son I was. Nowadays, I'm far from his puppet on a string, the boy he threw into the dark basement closet because I reminded him of my mother.

I'm Jericho fucking Viotto, heir to the mafia throne. I no longer believe my father's words of contempt or strictly follow his rules.

I make the rules now.

And I say, Journey West is ours and forever.

Not Chloe Satin or whoever else he'd like to throw in our laps.

"I wouldn't have ratted you out, you know?" Leighton says in a smooth voice, waving off the firefighters and police officers as they haul away his burnt-out car as evidence against Journey.

Evidence that's going to promptly disappear. Along with her conviction. Right after I convince my Little Chaos that she does, in fact, need me. She can pretend she's a strong, independent woman, all she wants. Not under my thumb. She's mine. Ours. And she will abide by what we have to say, no matter what.

"Of course not," I say, side-eyeing him. "You wouldn't rat out your own."

He snorts, eyeing the carnage with hazy eyes so clouded by the drugs and alcohol in his system that he doesn't feel the danger crowding in on him.

"Fuck no," he says, digging in his pocket. "I didn't really like that piece of shit car, anyway." He shrugs. "She did me a favor. A hot as fuck favor. How'd you get so lucky to get that? Wanna trade?"

The urge to punch the cigarette he's currently lighting straight into his mouth and watch as the flames eat away at his tongue rides me hard. But I resist. For now. Leighton will pay for his crimes.

"Trade?" I ask gruffly, shaking my head.

"Jenni's going to run off with that dickhead inside, leaving me with no one. It's stupid as fuck," he grunts, blowing smoke into the air without a care.

"And what do you know about that dickhead inside?"

Leighton snorts, closing his eyes and swaying on his feet. "Elias—the leader of the piss poor excuse for a gang. The Blue Spiders. Who the fuck names themselves that? It's fucking stupid. What's more ridiculous is your father gave them the right." He rolls his eyes.

Yes. My father gave Elias the right to settle his drug empire on the south side of Briar Cove, manufacturing copious amounts of weed and pills. As long as he shared the wealth with the man who okayed his adventure. From what I've seen, my father hasn't been getting his fair share. Or so he thinks. If my father knew how to spend his money wisely instead of throwing it around like confetti, then he'd be in a better situation.

I discreetly nod when Arrow sneaks up behind Leighton when he's thoroughly distracted. "You messed up," Arrow whispers in his ear right before depositing a needle into his neck.

Leighton's eyes widen, darting to me as he clings to the few precious seconds of consciousness he has.

"You touched something that didn't belong to you. Now, you'll lose something, too." I shrug when Arrow pushes Leighton's body forward as he crumples and lands directly on his face.

Arrow grins. "And you tell me carrying this around is a waste of time. Look at me now, Daddy Jer." He wiggles the spent tube several times as I cringe.

"I am not your daddy," I say, sticking the pointed toe of my shoe into Leighton's side, checking for life.

Shepp clinks his rings a few times, looking up from his phone. "Word is she's not cooperating. They've left her alone for now in a holding cell by herself." He turns the phone toward me as an image flashes before my eyes.

Right there is my beautiful future wife, sitting on a bench dressed in stripes. I grin. "I hope they burned that dress," I growl, clenching my teeth so hard I'm afraid they'll crack from the pressure.

That fucking dress can burn in the depths of hell, for all I care. I'd much rather rip it off her body and show her what happens to her when she insists on wearing such revealing clothing.

No matter.

My future wife will never wear a dress like that in front of anyone else again. Ever. From here on out, I've procured her a wardrobe full of modest clothing for public outings and indecent clothing for the bedroom.

A win-win.

Shepp snorts, tucking his phone away.

"It was easy access, though. You missed out, Daddy." Arrow grins again when I turn on my heel and promptly punch him in the shoulder. "Fine. Not daddy. But for real, dude. You missed out on the best-tasting pussy in Briar Cove. I can't wait to fill her with my cum every day until she's nice and plump with our baby." He wiggles his brows.

Obviously, he's thought that plan through. Not a bad idea. Tie her to us for eternity. She'll never be able to escape. Especially if our child is in her arms.

"Then we can really lock her down," I say, rubbing at my chin. "Check her health records for birth control. We haven't checked them in a while."

Shepp nods and signs, 'Of course.'

Ah, my dutiful best friend. The only one I trust to look into her past. Which we've done from time to time. Journey's records and life have been something I've sought out for years since I learned she'd be mine.

I want to crack every crevice of her existence. Know everything there is to know about her. And apparently, that's an issue. Her records hold nothing of interest as to why my father chose her. There has to be something. A secret tie to our society that holds value. Money—which she has none of.

That'll all change soon. The world is her oyster. No matter the outcome of this. She's officially property of the Devils.

"I hope not," Arrow grunts, heaving Leighton over his shoulder without wincing. "Just imagine if we knocked her up already. God, she'll be so fucking pissed. I'll make Shepp stick his dick in her mouth again to calm her down."

Shepp turns bright red, narrowing his eyes. 'Asshole,' he signs and then gestures with his middle finger.

My brows raise at Shepp when he darts his eyes to the ground. Ever the secret keeper.

I contemplate everything Arrow has said, mulling over his words. "Let's get him into the back of the SUV."

"Are we taking him to my basement lair?" Arrow asks with a grin. "I want to tear his fingers off for ever touching her." *The feeling is mutual.* "Or Max and Nova?" He wiggles his brows at the prospect of feeding Leighton to our lions.

Not a bad fucking idea. They'd enjoy chasing him through their enclosure. Something we've done many times to our victims.

Need answers? Introduce people to a couple of ravenous lions. They'll spill their guts. The same guts that will later splatter the grass when we're done with them.

It's a win-win.

I nod. "Straight to the special chair for him. Maybe the lions. We'll see how much he cooperates when he wakes up."

'And if your father finds out?' Shepp signs, scrunching his brows. *'As much of a piece of shit as he is, he's still a part of the family. And his father...'*

I roll my eyes, slapping his hands down and holding them between mine. "My father can choke on a cock," I hiss, squeezing his fingers between my hands. "And his father?" I spit at the ground. "He can also choke on a fat fucking cock for all I care. Leighton LeMaster is a goddamn dead man. I'm going to chop every fucking finger that entered my girl without her permission. Fuck his father. And fuck my father. They can duke it out. But I'm the goddamn heir of this city, and I'm going to make sure no one forgets it."

They certainly won't when I'm through with Leighton. When they look at his hand, there will be a constant reminder of who he fucked with. Then, no one will do it again. Ever.

"And then, we're going to give them to her as a present. I have the perfect box!" Arrow grins, rubbing his hands together. "We have like maybe two hours until fuck boy wakes up. So, we might want to get a move on."

'You're way too happy and eager to take fingers,' Shepp signs, stepping away from me and my iron grip. *'Let's get this over with. We'll have to get Journey out of jail.'*

I grin, stepping up beside Shepp and clapping him on the shoulder. "She can sweat it out a little bit. Besides, we need to speak with our lawyer."

Shepp stiffens. *'A lawyer?'*

"When Journey West gets out of jail, she'll no longer have a few days to get used to the fact that we're her future."

No. When she gets out of jail, she's going to be released into our custody. Those are the terms. My Little Chaos will never leave my sight again. Ever. I won't allow her to. And if my father has anything to say about it. Well, he can shove it so far up his paranoid ass that it comes out his throat, for all I care.

I've followed my father's rules to a T since the moment I was born. He never had to worry about his little brainwashed boy disobeying him. Unless he found something to be disappointed over. Lately, I've learned to control myself around him. I'm his perfect little soldier under his eye. But in the shadows?

Now, that's a different story entirely.

'What the hell did you do?' Shepp signs, chasing after me when I meet Arrow, who bounces on his toes with excitement at the SUV.

"I'm binding her by contract. She's no longer Journey West, a free woman. She's ours. And the sooner she gets used to it, the better off she'll be."

"Now, let's choppity chop off some fingers." Arrow's gleeful laugh echoes through the private lane as I take one last look around the property.

After the commotion died down and Leighton's car was wheeled away, everyone stumbled back inside to continue their partying. Even Jenni poked her disheveled head out the door with furrowed brows and bedhead, checking to make sure everything was okay with her little boyfriend behind her. The same man whose drugs are currently killing one in ten people in my goddamn city as soon as they consume the pills. I tried to be nice and get him to back off, but now I'll have to resort to more desperate measures. Starting with his little girlfriend.

"Let's leave," I comment, hopping into the passenger's side.

Shepp huffs when he puts the car in drive, pulling in the direction of our mansion fifteen minutes away.

Far away from here. Far away from my father's stupid tower downtown. And far away from my beautiful blushing bride resting in a jail cell.

"Tell them to keep her in holding until we get there. No more questions."

CHAPTER TWENTY-SEVEN

Shepp

"It should be any second now," Arrow croons, grabbing his skeleton mask and placing it on top of his head. Arrow turns over his watch, staring at the hands ticking away around the numbers.

Two hours ago, Arrow stuck Leighton with a needle, knocking him unconscious. It's too bad his nose is twisted and bloodied from falling forward and directly on it, scuffing his face, too.

Such a damn shame.

I blow out a breath, centering myself before the mayhem Arrow loves so much begins. Blood. Chopped off fingers. And anything in between. I've seen it all my life. Lived it. Breathed it. But it never gets easier. Blood makes my stomach curdle. Violence makes my hair stand on end. I'll endure it, though. It's my life. So, I try to make the best of it and help my brothers.

My ears tingle when a groaning from the room next to ours intensifies, turning my damn insides. I squeeze my eyes shut, visions of my past roaring through my mind. Fuck. This is so stupid. You'd think a guy who seems so big and is covered in scars would know how to handle this sort of thing. Blood? It should be easy! I grew up watching my father perform surgeries for years in our basement for the boss. Time and time again, my father cut someone open for the sake of torture, luring out the information one piece at a time.

Over and over, he made me watch from the shadows. Every moan of pain. Every cry, begging for their lives. I was there. Waiting for it to end, which it always did. By death.

His face flashes through my mind.

"Sit up straight, boy. Tonight is my damn coronation." My father's beady eyes examine the stage in front of us, where an old-time jazz band plays for the best of the best.

Every single person lining this room has a kingdom waiting for them throughout California. The Viotto Crime Family. Five brothers in charge of their sections. This happens to be Gabriel's domain. My father's Commissioner—the man he's about to become second-in-command for. He's thoroughly proved himself over and over again.

Just great. I hang my head.

The lead singer steps up to the microphone, hits us with his deep voice, and sings to us in the middle of the meal provided for everyone. People murmur to one another, decked out in their best clothes, dripping in diamonds. The amount of money slithering through the fancy ballroom would have me swallowing my tongue— if I had one.

My eyes find Jericho, my best friend since birth, standing stoically next to his father, who shakes the hands of several suited men. His cousin, Olivia, wrinkles her nose next to him as her father, Gabriel's brother, and Gabriel himself talk with straight expressions.

"Fucking Rafael," my father growls, stabbing his fork into his juicy steak. "Always brown-nosing and trying to get back into his brother's good graces," he scoffs. "The best thing Gabriel ever did was send him and his whore wife away." My father rolls his eyes, shoving a large piece of steak into his gullet, chewing loudly.

My mother darts her eyes toward my father and places a soft hand on his wrist, silently telling him to cool it. He never does, though. Nor does he listen. Ever.

"*Don't fucking touch me,*" *he growls at her, tossing off her hand. She nods. That's all she does these days, setting her eyes on her minuscule plate of salad and carrots—all he allows her to consume to stay thin. Even though she's perfectly fine.*

I stare off at Jericho again, who connects his eyes to mine. Nothing rests there. No emotions. Just like his father has trained him to be. Stoic. Emotionless. Heartless. But what his father doesn't know is it's all a facade. Has been for years. Thank God. I need someone by my side when we rise to the top after our own initiation. That's where we're headed. Jericho is the son of the leader of the mafia. And in turn, that's where he'll be with me and his adopted brother, Arrow. My other best friend.

"*Pay attention, boy,*" *my father growls, elbowing me when Gabriel takes the microphone, droning on and on about the three men around him on stage with their shirts open, revealing the wound across their hearts.*

Their initiation party. A celebration of the day they dropped to their knees, after years of training, and pledged their souls to the very organization that will lead them astray the moment they fuck up.

"*Your time will come, boy,*" *my father's deep voice penetrates through the fog in my brain. "You're only twelve, but it'll come before you know it. Then, you'll make me proud."*

I nod. That's all I can do these days. Nod. Write notes. Just like he wanted. Since the night... I squeeze my eyes shut, refusing to live through the trauma once again. Panic blooms through me when he places a hand on my shoulder and squeezes.

"*You'll make me so damn proud. Won't you?*" *No. Never. I don't want to make him proud; I want him to leave me the fuck alone.*

I shake myself out of my memories, laced with nothing but pain. The only memory worth noting was the best day of my life. When the light in my father's eyes faded, and we lowered his body into the ground, encasing him in a coffin and six feet of dirt. I never had to look at him again. Or see the cruelty in his eyes or the hate he projected on me, his son. The man who was supposed to protect me fed me to the wolves. Over and over again.

"Don't worry, Sheppy Boy. The good doctor in the next room is on his last leg. I got him good last night," Arrow says, waving a hand in the direction of the sounds coming from the doctor situated in a make-shift jail cell, hanging from the ceiling.

The man couldn't keep his hands to himself and injured his dental patients when they trusted him. He'd put them to sleep and then take advantage of them. They never knew until a few days ago. It all came out when someone came forward to Arrow and spoke her truth, begging The Devils to do their worst.

This is his lesson. One he won't live through. Courtesy of Arrow and his ambition to be good for the community.

Some would say Arrow is nothing more than an unfeeling psychopath. In part, they're right. But what he does with the town's scum since he killed that man for Journey has ramped up. Sure, he always cleaned the streets of the worst to tamp down his insane blood lust. Now, though? He's taking it seriously, putting his focus into something our girl will be proud of.

My heart leaps at the thought of her—Journey West. Our girl.

"If it isn't silent Sheppard Mondelli," Jaxson, a boy from class, sneers in my direction.

I swallow hard, trying to accommodate myself to the new reality my father thrust me into over six months ago. By now, the swelling has ceased, and I can at least eat normally. But it doesn't stop the teasing or the put-downs. Even when our bodyguards hover in the corners of the rooms, watching. But they do nothing to save me from this torment. Probably an order from my father to let me suffer more than I already have. They won't even defend me when Jericho and Arrow are around. And right now? They're in a separate class, leaving me to fend for myself.

"What's the matter, Little Sheppy?" he sneers again, poking at my chest.

My fists curl at my sides. I open my mouth to defend myself, but then I remember. The art of language was stolen from me. My voice was clipped and taken right before my eyes.

"Leave him alone." It's a scoff, and a small figure pushes in front of me. "You're so pathetic, you know that? Picking on a guy who can't speak."

In the shadows, my bodyguard finally advances toward me, eager to hurl Journey away. My stomach twists. They're never concerned when boys step up to me, eager to put me down. But her? That's a different story.

Jaxson narrows his eyes at her, ready to open his mouth, but doesn't get the chance. Journey punches him right in the dick, sending him to his knees with a squeak.

"Next time, just punch them in the balls. It's their weak spot," she says, turning to face me. Her neck cranes back as she stares up at me with pursed lips, and then, she walks away as quickly as she came. I don't know what got into her or why she stood up for me, but I watch her from then on out. We hadn't been allowed to speak with her or anyone else, really.

And that was the moment, when I was twelve, that I fell in love with the girl who stood up for me. I vowed to return the favor tenfold, by secretly looking out for her. I never want her to suspect it's me leaving donuts every morning. Or that it's me that stocks her fridge with essentials to get her through the days. I was so damn tired of watching her scurry to the food pantry and bringing back minuscule amounts of food, that I had to do something. That day she didn't have a clue what I had been through. No one did. Not even Jer. She knew who I was— everyone did. Sheppard Mondelli. A boy destined for bad things within the mafia. But she didn't know the voice she gave me that day.

The voice with my fists.

Speaking of...

My phone buzzes in my pocket, taking my mind off the small basement room we've found ourselves in.

I shiver when I look around, trying to hold back the bile in my throat at the sight of Arrow holding up his torture saws with glee.

Get a damn grip. You're in the goddamn mafia. Feeling faint at the sight of blood and guts. It's ridiculous. It's something I have to cope with. I just sail away in my mind until I'm no longer standing in the room.

"First, I'll take the fingers that entered her. No one can have anything with her pussy juice on it."

Jericho groans at his dramatics but nods in agreement. So do I. No one can ever touch her without us knowing about it and taking action. Grabbing my buzzing phone, I check my messages.

> **CHIEF**
>
> Still good on our end. She'll be here whenever you three are done. We'll keep this just between us.
>
> She hasn't spoken a word, either... The detective is sniffing around. I'd hurry...

> **ME**
>
> Thanks, Chief. We owe you. We'll be there to sign her out shortly.

The more secretive this is, the better off it will be. We're moving forward with our long-awaited plans a few days prematurely. All for her. Our girl.

Turning back to the other two, I click my metal rings together, instantly gaining their attention. Shoving my phone into my pocket, I sign, *'Chief texted.'*

Police Chief Anderson has always been on the mafia side of things. Considering he's a part of the Viotto Crime Family, it should come as no surprise. His alliance with us, though, would drive Gabriel cuckoo. He hasn't a clue, which works in our favor. Anything we need, the chief is there to aid us on the sly.

"How is she?" Jericho asks, rolling up his sleeves and exposing his tattooed forearms.

'They say she's fine, not talking still, and she'll be there... But

that douchebag detective is sniffing around,' I sign. *'And it's on the down low.'*

Jericho's grin grows in a Grinch-like smile. I swear if he weren't my brother by bond, I'd run in the opposite direction. As it stands, he doesn't scare me. Only his plans do. They fucking terrify every molecule in my body. But that's what we're supposed to do. Go against the status quo. Rise up and take over what rightfully belongs to us, reclaiming it from the tyrant king who only cares about himself.

That's our job.

And now, we're enacting it by taking Journey earlier than planned. To keep her safe and with us at all times.

"Did you really think she'd squeal?" Arrow asks, peeking over his shoulder and rummaging through the sterilized toolbox behind the chair. "I didn't. My little Kitten would never tell them anything." He grunts, rustling through the box, only stopping when he finds the perfect tool.

'She never has before,' I sign, raising a brow when Leighton moans, coming out of the drug that knocked him out.

"Wakey, wakey, Leighton LeMaster," Jericho hums, slapping his cheeks repeatedly. "Finally." He grins, stepping back with glee when Leighton's beady eyes pop open. He looks around with heaving breaths, taking in the small room.

"What the fuck?" he slurs, pulling at the restraints that hold him to a chair that is bolted to the floor. "What the hell?" The sound of the metal cuffs clanking ricochets off the walls, just barely quieter than his incessant wailing.

Poor fucker. I can tell by the drop of his face, he's about to shit his pants and beg us for a second chance. Not likely.

"We have a code, Leighton," Jericho states, placing his hands behind his back. "A moral code within the family." Leighton stiffens when Jericho leisurely stops in front of him, leaning down to bring himself to eye level. "You're a part of the family, are you not?" He raises a brow when Leighton pales. "The Viotto Family takes their oaths and promises very seriously."

Convenient, I want to say. Our promise to keep our dicks in our pants to focus on our future was obliterated at that party. Not that I'm complaining. The moment I entered my girl, I knew it was written in the stars. I wanted to keep her at my side. But I knew the consequences of Jericho's father finding out we didn't stay true to the rules—severe punishment.

"A code? Really? This is what we're going with?" Leighton slurs again, darting his eyes all around the room, taking in the exposed brick and weapons hanging from hooks. "What is going on? Where the fuck am I?"

"What's going on is you put your hands on and in someone that doesn't belong to you. She never has."

"She's too fucking good for you," Leighton hisses, spitting in Jericho's face. "She should have been mine."

"So disrespectful for a boy tied to a chair." Jericho stands tall again, swiping the spit from his face and flicking it to the ground with disgust. "You've always walked the line, Leighton. Skated on thin ice. You swore my father wouldn't do anything to you because your daddy gets you out of every little indiscretion you get into. But you're in my house now." Jericho grins, opening his arms wide.

"What? No! You can't..." Leighton screams when Arrow pops up in front of his face, bringing his skull mask down and hiding his grin.

"I'd stay still, Leighton. And answer every question Arrow has to ask. He's very testy right now, so I wouldn't provoke him."

"What! She-she hit my fucking car! I didn't say anything to the cops about you..." Leighton tries to shake his head and pull away from Arrow as he holds up a Gigli saw with glee.

"Which fingers did you use on my Kitten?" Arrow growls, running his finger over Leighton's.

I swallow hard at the demonic sound emanating from him. He means fucking business, and he won't stop until he takes a finger and shoves it down Leighton's throat.

"What are you doing?" he asks again with a slight tremble in his voice. "You can't do this! My father will burn all of you and the organization to the ground," he hisses through several heavy breaths as sweat pours down his neck. With satisfaction, I watch the color drain from his face as the realization of what's happening hits him like a truck.

"And my father will make sure your family ceases to exist," Jericho says, calmly approaching Leighton's side. "Leighton who? Governor LeMaster, who? Everyone will forget your existence the moment my father says so." He snarls at Jericho, ready to spit more volatile words his way, but Jer cuts him off. "I'm curious. Which hand did you use to assault her?" he asks again, lifting a small knife from the table to his right.

Jer hums, running the sharp blade across his fingertip, turning my stomach until it knots, charging toward him with vengeance in his eyes. Deep red coats his fingers when he stands before Leighton, examining the shiny knife he loves so much.

Jericho and Arrow are two peas in a pod. Arrow loves destruction. Jericho loves the blood on his hands. Together, they're mayhem. And me? I'm the silent guy on the sidelines, using my strength for whatever they need me to. Silently protecting our future wife and providing for her as quietly as I can. Like now. My strength is staring Leighton down, enforcing the message Jericho is trying to convey.

Pain.

"I didn't," he squeaks, watching as Jericho advances on him more. His beady eyes soak in the sharp knife nestled in Jericho's hand, ready to stab Leighton at any second. "I swear. I didn't do anything," he begs again, with snot bubbles popping out of his nostrils and tears dampening his eyes. Fucking pathetic. "I didn't," he cries again, trying to shake his head, but the restraints hold him firmly in place.

Swallowing my disgust, I move forward, standing beside Arrow as Jericho leans down, getting into Leighton's face.

"Right. Of course, you didn't. She was lying, right?" His

breath hitches when Jer brings the sharpened blade near his right eye.

Vicious thoughts of removing it from his skull for the simple satisfaction of watching him navigate this world without it cross my mind until I shiver with rage. I'm not one to inflict pain, but watching him squirm under Jericho's eager stare has a demented smile crossing my lips.

"It wasn't you?" Jer hums again, dragging the blade down Leighton's left cheek and digging it in until their blood mingles on the sharpened edges.

I swallow hard, running the tips of my fingers over the scar on my own face. Whatever Jer does to him now, it'll leave a scar—another reminder of who he shouldn't fuck with. Us. The family he's pledged to serve for the entirety of his life.

The only way out of The Viotto family is through death and death alone. There's no sneaking away once you've started training. You can run and hide, but they will find you, drag you back, and sentence you for your crimes.

They're so old school it's hard to breathe sometimes.

Arrow chuckles, holding up the Gigli saw higher, pulling the metal thread tight, and grasping the handles in each hand with a menacing smile, depriving the room of warmth. His favorite toy. The one tool that causes more pain than anything in the room. It's slow and meticulous and makes people talk quicker than anything else he could do. The intended use for this tool is to surgically cut through bone to amputate limbs, but Arrow thought it made better use as a torture device instead.

"Which hand did you use?" Arrow growls in a lifeless voice, bending to gaze into Leighton's eyes through the slits of his mask. "Tell me now before I cut your fingers off one by one and then work my way up. I want to see the life drain from your eyes when I wrap this around your throat and stop you from begging." Leighton trembles so hard that the entire chair rattles with the remnants of his fear.

For someone in the life, he sure acts like he's never been through this before. Maybe his father sheltered him for too long. Arrow's deep laugh vibrates through the plastic mask. The only thing visible are his vibrant light gray eyes, blazing with destruction and dilating at the sight of blood.

"One last warning," he growls, wrapping the metal wire around Leighton's middle finger and securing it tightly. Slowly, he works the wire back and forth, eliciting a pain-filled cry from Leighton's mouth.

"Yes! I did it! With my right," he sobs, sucking in several relieved breaths when Arrow stops. "I-I wanted her. And... And... I was on some new kind of Molly. My fucking mind, man, was... I just wanted to fuck her."

Of course, he did. He always wants to fuck someone. Especially Journey. The amount of times I've followed behind her and watched as she waved him off is astronomical. I would have beat him back, but she defended herself just fine. She always has. Journey can handle anything. I don't have any doubts about that. I've been hopelessly following her around for years, watching in the shadows as she lived her life. I realized when I was a little older that her home situation wasn't good. That's when I started feeding her and making sure she had what she needed.

Jericho growls, losing himself to the bloodlust while inflicting pain on Leighton. Hit after hit, he slams his fists into Leighton's face until blood spurts from his mouth, and his nose twists to the side worse than before.

Blood drips from his split lip and bleeding gums, flowing down his chin and onto his pants. With fascination, Jericho watches it pool there as Leighton groans, begging him to stop through garbled mumbles.

Jericho's head snaps to the right when the click of my rings brings him back from the brink of murdering Leighton where he sits. Not that anyone would miss him. Maybe his miserable father. But that's it.

'*Molly?*' I sign, holding up a finger to stop us from damaging him any further. *'Where did he get it from?'*

"Where'd you get the Molly from?" Jer calmly asks, rubbing the blood over his knuckles.

"Come on," Arrow whines, moving the hand-held bone saw back and forth again. "Let me take his finger."

I huff, hearing the fucking pout beneath his mask, pleading with us to stop asking so many questions. He's a shoot-first, ask questions later, type of guy.

Jericho narrows his eyes at Leighton. "Where is it from? Is it from…"

"That Blue Spider fucker Jenni is always fucking around with. He comes to the parties and sells them like candy." Leighton shakes in the chair when Jericho strokes his chin." The only good fucking thing that piece of shit is good for."

Pinching the bridge of his nose, Jer sighs. "Take his finger. But let this be a warning for you, Leighton. Don't fuck with what is ours. We'll be discussing this in detail later."

He nods, taking a step back, and Arrow gets to work, taking his prized possession—his middle finger. With victory, he holds it in the air, ignoring Leighton's pitiful cries and the piss that leaks through, soaking his jeans.

Pathetic asshole.

I clink my rings together. *'You know we're going to have to discuss this with your father. He's going to run straight to his daddy.'* I raise a brow when Leighton goes limp.

"Of course we will," Arrow says, grinning with the finger in his hand, holding it up. "It's a thing of beauty, isn't it? I think my Kitten will love this present."

'No presents like that,' I sign, growling until he shrugs, tucking it in his pocket.

He's going to sneak that to her. I can feel it in my gut.

"We'll talk to my father and explain the situation," Jericho says with a smirk, straightening his shirt. "Now, let's get him on his way; we have a Little Chaos to retrieve from behind bars. But first, drop that asshole on his lawn."

CHAPTER TWENTY-EIGHT

Journey

"This is such bullshit," I growl to myself in the lonely holding cell the cops threw me into. Small, cramped, and smelly—that's what it is, also, pure bullshit.

Assholes.

"I didn't even do anything!" I hiss, trying to convince myself more than anything that it didn't happen. That I didn't let myself get pulled into the Devil's bullshit just for them to let me get arrested when they took part, too.

Now, though, it's me against Leighton's word and that stupid video. And, well—I'm fucked harder than ever before. I've been through some shit. But this? This is a whole new level of *Journey is screwed.* This wasn't in the job description I was sent on at the hands of my monster.

This situation is entirely my fault.

I got swept up and away, letting my freedom and darkness take control.

Leighton's precious daddy—the damn governor of the state of California—has so much power in this town that they'll probably throw me away, lose the key, and praise God Journey West is finally off the streets.

Only time will tell.

I pray my monster doesn't find out. Who am I kidding, though? He knows it all. Has eyes and ears all over this city. I'm one little spy amongst a million he probably has. How I thought I could have my freedom and eat it, too, is beyond me.

My eyes catch the clock loudly ticking away against the white wall next to the sealed metal door. Three a.m. Two and a half hours since I whacked Leighton's car into oblivion and lit it on fire. Two hours of sitting here on this bench with nothing but a striped onesie and white socks, watching the time tick away.

Half of me hopes I can get out of here before they find a permanent place for me. The other half hopes I'm here for good, away from the man dominating my life and the mother who'd rather whore herself out than care for me.

My eyes snag on the large mirror hanging on the wall, showing my rough reflection. Dark streaks mark my cheeks, courtesy of the soot and ash from the fire.

My brown curls fluff, proofing out and standing on end from my wild night of drinking and a nice roll in the hay.

Shit. I squeeze my eyes shut.

I would have been five blocks out if Arrow hadn't held me down and forced me to stay when the cops showed up. If only he had let me run, then I wouldn't be here in this position.

You can bet your ass that they'll pay for that indiscretion later. No one screws me over. No one. Not ever again. Especially since I wasn't the only one who tore Leighton's car apart piece by piece. He did, too. And wouldn't you know it? He didn't go to jail, just like I said they wouldn't.

But I did. In that circle, I'm nobody. Not connected to any sort of family with money who can get me out of every indiscretion.

So, I'm totally screwed here. I blow out a breath and lean my head back against the cold cement wall. Despite my self-loathing and unsure future, It was all worth it. Every single hit. The fire. The orgasms.

My goddamn freedom.

A spark of life flickers inside me. For the first time in three years, I'm alive. Wishy-washy, yes. Scared shitless, absolutely. But my eyes are wide open, and the world is in vivid color. There's no longer a thick fog infecting my thinking. I see everything now.

Sitting in silence does nothing good for my psyche. This is why I always have music or noise on hand. My brain tends to fall down the inevitable rabbit hole of bullshit.

Darkness surrounds me once again. Night after night since the man stole me from my home after... I squeeze my eyes shut tighter as the feel of sticky, hot blood rushes over my fingers. Just like that night when I held the knife tight in my fingers. Bile rests in my throat, threatening to spill over. Again. The amount of times I've heaved from stress and lack of food, creating a puddle under my cage, is pushing me over the edge.

But it's the darkness crashing in on me that has my heart pounding and my mind eating itself.

A faint noise tickles through the walls. It's barely there. A beautiful melody, capturing my attention. It's the first noise I've heard since I was thrown in here and left for dead.

It's music.

Sweet, beautiful, melodious music pierces through my ears. The hairs on my arms stand on end when it intensifies. It whines. The notes grow higher and higher until the crescendo hits and falls, sinking into low, passionate, and soothing melodies.

It remains by my side for hours, soothing my heart rate and taking the memories away from my rampant mind.

The violin suddenly stops. Voices murmur beyond the wall. And then, they're gone.

I shiver, covering my eyes when the bright, fluorescent lights kick on above my prison, giving me a glimpse of the small, basement room I'm being kept in.

"Good evening, Little Snake!" the same man's voice from before bellows as he enters the small room and toward my cage. His thick fingers run across the metal, taunting me when he stops and pops open the front of my hanging cage. "I think I've finally decided what I'm going to do with you." His grin has my soul fleeing my body, looking for the heavenly light of the Lord.

Not the darkness of this devil promising me pain.

"My sister..." I trail off, unable to get another word in when he grabs me by the throat and throws me onto the ground.

"Here's the deal," he says in a smooth voice, standing directly above me. "Your sister is safe. Do as I say, and she'll remain there. We may even think about getting her further up the transplant list. You know, she has a bad heart and all. Do you understand where I'm going with this?"

I do. She's needed a new heart for months now, but we can never manage to find a match. Or people who have been on there longer, rightfully get the heart. Sunny is in waiting.

I swallow the lump in my throat refusing to move from my position on the ground. I'm smart enough to know if I try to get back up and face him, he'll only throw me down again.

"Yes."

"Then, repeat it back to me, my little snake." He waves a hand, beginning to pace.

"If I do as you say, you'll help my sister."

"And if you're a bad, bad girl?" He cocks a brow, placing his hands behind his back.

"You won't help her." I swallow hard.

What a fucked up agreement. Sunny was getting help. She has a doctor and medication. But she was so far down on the list, she wouldn't have seen a new heart.

"Precisely. Now, let's get started with our new arrangement."

My eyes widen when he pulls out a small dagger from his pocket, unsheathing it from its cover. The metal edges beam the light off it as he holds it in the air with a smile.

"Shirt off. On your knees with your hands behind your back." It's an order. One I want to refuse. "Times ticking, Little Snake. One measly call will pull all the drugs currently keeping your dying sister's heart pumping. Do not test me when generosity is pouring out my ass."

I shake, pushing myself up from my position, and get onto my wobbly knees. Spots blur in my vision when the reality of what's *happening slams into me. Shirt off. On my knees. He's going to use me. He's going to... I shake it off. This is my punishment for the sin I committed.*

This is what I get for stabbing a man.

My fingers poke at the healed scar resting between my breasts as I lie back on the uncomfortable hard bench with my knees bent, staring at the dotted ceiling. I lose myself in the memories of my past as my fingers twitch over the deep mark that was forced upon me when I fell to my knees. Much like a graduation, he pressed the sharpened blade against my flesh, leaving his stamp on me.

But I got the last laugh when I walked into a tattoo shop once it healed and demanded my tattoo. I wasn't scared when he pulled out the tattoo machine. I wasn't frightened when I had to take my shirt off and my bra so he could access the scar between my breasts.

He stiffens, staring down at me after helping me cover my breasts with coverings. "Wow. That's a hell of a scar."

I swallow through the trauma attempting to take me under. "Yeah," I rasp.

I'd rather not elaborate further as to why I have a sword wound on my chest. Or why I want to cover it up.

He gives me a soft smile, resting on his stool as he stares at the stencil on my skin. "I really love the design we came up with," he hums, pressing the tattoo machine to my flesh and begins with my beautiful tattoo. "You know what the key represents?"

I smile for the first time in probably a year. "Freedom," I whisper, staring at the ceiling as he continues on the piece.

Even though my tattoo covers the scar, my insecurities about it hold me hostage. My monster forces me in low cut tops and slinky dresses so I'm playing the part he's selected. Whenever I can get away with it, I cover the tattoo and scar with my corset for my own peace of mind.

He didn't use me. Not sexually, at least. He carved his mark deep into my skin, marking me as his. His little snake. The person he sent out to do his dirty work. It's a permanent wound that doesn't bleed. A reminder of what I did on that night three years ago.

For the remainder of my six month stint in hell, I leaned on the beautiful tunes of the violin that played every night at six p.m. sharp. Those tunes eased away the lessons of my days. Some harder than most.

The door to my small holding cell buzzes, swinging open. My heart pounds with unease as a man I've never met before waltzes in with his hands in his pockets. I immediately sit up, examining his swagger.

You can spot a lie from the way a man walks, Little Snake. Look in his eyes. Watch the crooked grin.

"Journey West," the man says, coming to sit right beside me.

He's attempting to seem less intimidating by getting on my level and squishing his tall frame down in the chair.

Amateur.

"Yes?" I question without really confirming.

He smiles. It's supposed to exude warmth and understanding. But it doesn't. This man means me harm in any way possible. Whoever he is.

"I'm Detective Alexander," he says, sticking his hand out for me to shake. Begrudgingly, I take his hand, gently shaking it for the sake of fake politeness.

"Nice to meet you," I say, taking my hand back and wiping it down my leg.

"You've gotten yourself into quite the pickle here, haven't you? Leighton LeMaster's car," he says with a whistle, nesting back into the seat. "That was a big fish to fry."

Silence.

I won't give him a single word of confirmation or time to make me confess my crime. So, I cross my arms and tilt my head, continuing the silence between us. The bulbs buzz above our heads, filling the room with their hums.

And I don't say a single word.

He cocks his head, running his eyes over me. "Nothing to say for yourself?"

I huff, sitting back on the bench and shutting my eyes. Not a single fuck was given. Maybe. Okay, internally my heart is racing, my palms sweaty, and I kind of even want some of my mom's spaghetti. But I continue to keep my lips sealed, listening to his breaths.

Choppy. Heaving. Irritation is rising inside him. He's letting his emotions take hold when he should be calm. Good.

"You're going to go down for a long time, Miss West." I peek open an eye, sizing him up. He grins. He thinks he's won something special. "Destruction of property is a pretty hefty charge. Especially when you did it to the governor's son. Governor LeMaster is on his way right now. Hell hath no fury." He clicks his tongue, spouting off his lies like they'll embed in my skin and take root.

Not a chance.

I shrug. Bring on the governor. I have a way scarier man in my corner probably on his way now.

"Silence, huh? How about we put you into a nice cell for the night and let you think it over? I have the perfect roommate for you, too."

I shrug. Literally can't he take a hint? I'm not saying anything. I'd rather him throw me in there with a new roommate.

He sighs loudly, running his hands through his perfectly styled black hair. "It's a shame, Miss West. Such a shame a beautiful girl like yourself is taking the blame for something you didn't do." His eyes scan his nail beds nonchalantly. He wants me to take the bait and ask him questions.

I huff again, shaking my head.

"If that's how it's going to be. If you're going to continue helping those three Devils, then that's on you. Why don't you stand up and put your hands out in front of you."

I do as he says, not uttering a word when he slaps handcuffs on me and walks me out of the room, down a long hall, and into another room fit with a table, a large mirror, and four uncomfortable chairs. So much for going to my new jail cell.

"Sit. More officers will be there to speak with you. They need a statement." He secures my wrists to a metal piece at the side of the table. "Remember my name for when you want to divulge all the secrets about those three boys you're protecting. Detective Alexander. You and I could work out a deal to take them down."

I wrinkle my nose when his hot breath blows across the side of my neck. Once he steps back, he puts his hands back into his pockets and meanders out of the room without a care in the damn world.

Fuck him.

I'm not protecting anyone but myself. The Three Devils of Briar Cove will never see the inside of a prison because their organization owns everything in the town. Their vast fortune and rule reach every inch of this ivory city. The casinos? Theirs. The rich clubs and gambling institutions? Theirs. The plastic company, pharmacies, and everything in between are theirs.

No one could shake their foundations because their roots run deep into the ground.

The clock ticks by again, wasting my time. I'd rather be in a cell, on a bed, and attempting dreamland by now. It's so early in the damn morning, my mind reels over my night. My breath stalls in my chest at the thought of laying my head on an unfamiliar pillow in a quiet room. My nightmares knock, begging for permission to take over. Which I won't let happen.

I sigh when the door opens, revealing another suited cop, waltzing into the room with confidence.

"Miss West, we'd like to speak to you and go over the events of the night." He doesn't bother looking at me when he sits across from me and opens a folder, revealing photos of my crime.

Right there in vivid color, revealing the car bashing and the sizzling fire. With me at the center of it all. Where's Arrow and his ax? Where are the other two watching with lust in their eyes?

Nowhere.

He slides them over one by one. Emotions fade from my features. My darkness trickles in like a shadow darkening everything in its presence. I take a deep breath, centering myself as I stare at the pictures.

"Never show your emotions to the enemies, Little Snake. That's your next lesson." The memory of his grin sends shivers down my spine. *Pure, unadulterated evil rests in his eyes when he twirls a large knife in his hand.* *"You'll earn a scar for every emotion you display."*

My fingers rub against several scars on my fingers and forearm, anywhere I can touch with my cuffed hands.

"It appears, Miss West. That you had some fun tonight." His finger pokes at the photo several times, emphasizing how fucked I truly am if this is the evidence they have.

I lean in, pretending to examine the photos again with a blank expression. At least I looked cute doing it. Bonus points for my ass not falling out of that dress. I raise my eyes to his and don't utter a word. I taunt him with my indifference. Judging by the red creeping up his neck, it's working.

Even though the last thing I want to do is fall asleep here without my comfort items, I'm ready to be left alone. I'll force myself to stay awake until I can go home and curl up in my own bed with my pills and Whispered Words screaming in my ear.

"You—" the words die on the officer's tongue when his gaze snaps to the door thundering open and slamming into the wall.

My heart beats double time against my ribs when he leisurely walks in with an over-confident smirk. Definitely not who I expected to see stalking through that door, but I'll take it.

Jericho Viotto.

His aura exudes power, drawing every person's eye in the building to him. Even Officer Fuckface cowers before the mafia prince towering above him with a menacing glare.

"Holloway." Jericho nods at him, raising a brow when the good detective scowls.

"Mr. Viotto," he growls through clenched teeth.

I blow out a breath, cooling myself off. They did this to me. He threw me to the wolves and watched with glee as they caged me. I want to rip their smug faces off with my bare hands. But I won't. Swallowing down my anger, I permanently bury it, focusing on the tight attire hugging his body like a sexy second skin.

Jericho is a walking, talking sex god in his tightly fitted suit that clings to all the right places. And he knows it. Somewhere between the party and now, he's changed into a fancier suit and shiner shoes. Show off. I may want to shove a rusty fork up his ass and watch him flail in my hatred, but I'm never too good to admit when someone is easy on the eyes. And that man is a delicious steak dinner with cake as a dessert.

Clearing his throat, Jericho drags my eyes back to his, giving me a knowing smile while fixing the cuffs of his sleeves. I lift my chin and settle my shoulders back.

"Wonderful," Officer Ding-Dong says, glaring a hole into the side of Jericho's head with a resigned sigh.

"Good evening, Officer. I believe you have something that belongs to me." Those cold brown eyes sweep over my ragged appearance with interest and possession.

My fists clench at the sound of his possessive nature, hardening his face when he looks directly into my eyes without missing a beat. His? I belong to no one but myself.

The cop across from me silently broods, turning bright red when Jericho comes over to the table, eyeing the pictures.

His tongue clucks when he rips each picture in two.

"You can't do that. That's evidence," the officer says through clenched teeth.

Jericho throws the torn-up photos back in his face with a grunt. "You have no evidence," he says smoothly, sauntering around the table. "You'll leave now."

"You—"

"Leave, Officer Holloway," comes a man's deep voice from the doorway.

"Chief," Holloway balks, stiffening in his seat. "You can't be..."

"I'm deadly serious. Mr. Viotto has the room." He gestures with his head for the officer to follow him out, which he does while stomping his feet.

Then, it's just Jericho and me.

I sit back in my chair. Well, as much as I can with my hand secured to the table. The door opens again, and a portly man enters, hands Jericho a stack of papers with a nod, and then leaves.

"Little Chaos," he basically purrs when he sits across from me, eyeing me with a sparkle in his deep, dark eyes.

"Asshole," I quip, raising a brow.

He chuckles—fucking laughs at me, rummaging through the papers in front of him, until he finds what he wants and places it in front of him.

"You're being released."

"Released?" I question, raising a brow.

On the outside, I'm relaxing into the chair without an ounce of anxiety on my face. On the inside, though? My heart pounds. Speculation rises inside me, mixing with unease as Jericho's smile grows.

"To us," he says in a deep, depraved voice promising something sweet and painful.

"To you?" I breathe.

"Us."

"Us?" I swallow my tongue when he opens the paper in front of him, producing a pen from his suit jacket.

"To us. The Devil's. To our mansion. There are some rules, though." He lifts a brow when I suck in a breath. This is too much. This is fucking crazy. "Rule one, you'll be bound to us so we can keep track of you."

"Like... house arrest?" I blurt.

Ain't no way that's happening.

He grins. "Precisely, Little Chaos. So, you'll sign this, and you're not allowed to leave our sight. Or us. You'll be ours."

Theirs? Not allowed to leave? What kind of stalker shit is this? This feels more like a prison sentence than what I'm already facing. Maybe this place is better than being with them.

"I have a life," I hiss, jumping to stand, but my cuffs hold me to the table. "You can't just..."

"I can. I take what's mine. I refuse to wait any longer. Now, sit." He points a finger down like I'll obey.

My nostrils flare at his demand. Like fuck am I going to follow his orders. He can suck a cactus and then stick it up his ass for all I care. There's no way I'm locking myself away in their creepy as fuck mansion on the hill.

He grins, something flaring in his dark eyes. "I always knew you'd be hard to control. Run from me, Little Chaos. I'll chase you. Always." I swallow hard when he snaps his fingers and points down again. "Sit."

"I'm not a dog," I snark, staying on my feet.

I refuse to bow to the mafia heir like everyone else.

"No, you're not. They're a lot more loyal and obedient. One day, I'll fuck the disobedience out of you, and you'll never say no to me again."

Shivers run through my body at his threat. Or was it a threat? Did I secretly like the scathing look he's giving me for defying him?

He clicks the pen, setting it on top of the papers. "This is my one-time proposal, Little Chaos. You're looking at a long time behind bars. Fifteen years, maximum. That is if Governor LeMaster doesn't make an example out of you and your destructive ways. Not to mention the other crimes they're tacking on. As it sits, if you sign on the line here, your sentence is with us, under our roof and protection."

My mind rolls through everything he's said. Fifteen years? Jesus, that's a long time for a measly car dismantling. Wait...

"Other crimes?"

Jericho smirks, folding his hands together. "They're throwing the book at you, Little Chaos. Endangerment. Possible murder, missing persons. You name it, this police station has written it up. Would you like to see?"

He doesn't give me a chance to answer when he slides a single piece of paper under my eyes.

Murder. Kidnapping. Extortion. Arson. The list of offenses goes on. Crimes that have nothing to do with Leighton's car. Crimes I haven't committed.

"This is bullshit," I whisper, tossing the paper across the table, hoping to poke his eye out. Too bad it fucking misses its mark. "I didn't do any of that!" I shout, my emotions winning the war.

He grins. "There's a mountain of evidence I've submitted against you, Little Chaos."

"What evidence? Are you insane? You can't... They can't..."

"I'm the law, Journey. Everything I give them, whether it's false or not, will take you to court. They'll use it against you and lock you away forever. Is that what you want? It's your move, Journey West. Take my offer or rot."

Rot. He'll let me stay behind bars. Forever. Then, I won't be able to get my sister. Sunshine. She'll rot, too. My monster will pull everything that is helping to keep her alive. Would he let me stay here for eternity? Honestly, I don't know. I'm only his spy. But am I important to him? I'm sure he could sweep in, snap his fingers, and get me out. My only question is. Would he do it? He has the power. But is there want there?

I slump in the seat, inadvertently following his ridiculous command.

"You'd really..." I trail off.

"Blackmail you?" he questions smoothly, thoroughly enjoying the panic rearing up inside me. "Anything to get what I want."

"What do you want?" It surely can't be me. I'm no one important. I've got no money, no real job, and I'm trapped in an invisible prison playing puppet to a master.

I'm simply Journey West, daughter of a neglectful mother and a deadbeat dad who forgot my existence the moment my mom said the words, "I'm pregnant." Fuck Corbin West. If I had his kind of money I wouldn't be here. Sunny wouldn't have been taken from me. She'd have gotten a new heart years ago.

"You," he says easily without hesitation.

"I don't understand," I weakly admit, giving him all the ammunition he needs.

Long gone are the lessons that were drilled into my head about holding my emotions and taking in every small detail for later. Fear sinks its claws deep into my flesh, pulling me under the water and depriving me of oxygen.

"You don't need to. Over time, you will, though."

"You wouldn't," I breathe. "You..."

Jericho shrugs, collecting the papers from the table and stacking them together. He hums a tune under his breath.

"I would," he says, standing tall and straightening his suit. "It was nice knowing you, Journey."

The way he says my name chills the room. All the oxygen leaves it, depriving me. There's no humor. No love lost. He's simply packing his things and slowly walking toward the door.

The decision is now. It can't wait.

"Wait!" I shout, heaving a breath. Desperation claws at me—an unfamiliar feeling taking hold of me. "What is in the paperwork?" My voice drops into a shameful abyss pulling me under.

I'm not one to beg. But he's got me over a barrel. Apparently, where he wants me to be.

He stops, checking his shiny watch. "I don't give second chances." His voice dips so low that I sit straight up in my chair. Those eyes flash to me from over his shoulder, taking me in.

How's that saying go? It's better to be with the devils you know than the devils you don't.

And I know them. Kind of. Not the legal system I'm about to be foisted into. The Devils and I have a history together, spanning months now.

I take a deep breath, confusion soaring through me. I don't

know what the fuck is happening right now. But I know I have two choices: them or prison for crimes I didn't commit.

"This is your only chance," he warns, coming toward me again. "I will walk away if you question me again. I want your complete and utter compliance." He sets the pages in front of me again.

"A contract," I state.

"Indeed. Read through it if you'd like, but it won't change anything. This is non-negotiable."

And so I do. I read through the contract for over an hour, trying to take in all the legal mumbo jumbo and decipher the words. They melt together. Not making a lick of sense. The only words I see are the ones he's mentioned—the rules. I'm being released into the Devils' custody for an undetermined amount of time. I'm only allowed to leave the property if one of them escorts me.

"Time is ticking, Little Chaos." A pen clicks in my face, and before I can even question what I'm doing, I sign the contract without knowing what I'm getting into.

CHAPTER TWENTY-NINE
Journey

"Stand," Jericho demands.

Again.

He's always fucking demanding things with that stern face and fire in his eyes like he wants to bend me over his knees and punish me. Fat chance. There's no way in hell I'm letting this man get anywhere near my ass with his hand.

Maybe.

No. I'm fucking pissed off. First, they let me get arrested, taking the blame for Leighton's car. Then, I had to sign the contract. I was set up. Bamboozled. Fucking played. And for what?

We want you.

Why?

"I'm attached," I grunt, getting to my feet and pulling at the cuffs attached to the table.

"Never underestimate me, Little Chaos," he says, digging into his pocket. "It'll be the worst thing you can ever do."

I stiffen. It's a warning. Why? For what? I haven't a damn clue. But I take note as he undoes one loop of the cuff from the table and then attaches it to his own wrist, leaving one secured to me.

I'm fucking trapped, attached to him. Bound. Forced to be by his side. I want to cry and whine like a fucking baby.

There goes my quick escape. Not that I would have gotten very far. I'll bide my time and figure this out one day at a time. There's no way in hell they can keep me in their mansion for the next few months. Or, God forbid, years.

Shit. I'm a damn prisoner.

A-fucking-gain. I'm sick and tired of being someone's prisoner.

I need out. Time to suck it up and formulate one hell of a plan.

"Noted," I grumble, eyeing his movements.

This entire interaction feels like a damn test. Him locking me to him, leaving the key conveniently in his suit pocket, accessible to my sticky fingers. I could reach my grubby hands right in there and take it before he even felt it. My skills? Yeah, that's courtesy of my monster and his stupid lessons. Something I'll take care of later. I'm sure word will get back to him that I've been arrested and now taken by Jericho. I can't assume anything, though. I'll need to free myself and go to him and explain.

"Come now," Jericho murmurs, tugging at my wrist and pulling me from the interrogation room with force.

Outside the room, Officer Dumbass leans against the wall and slowly follows behind with a disapproving look, throwing a fit about losing my confession. Sucks to suck, asshole. Don't be in the mafia's pockets if you don't want them to bail people out then.

"What about my stuff?" I grunt, attempting to keep up with his long legs.

I'd really like to not have my phone left behind. The dress? Meh. I don't really mind that or the shoes. But my phone. Now, that's another story.

"Taken care of," he says without looking at me.

I narrow my eyes at him, ready to retort, but he yanks me forward. Bastard. I stumble over my feet, barely keeping up with his quick pace as he pulls me through the crowded police station. Out of the corner of my eye, I watch as he nods to the chief, standing behind a desk with narrowed eyes. Interesting. That must be their go-to guy. I'll file that away for later.

Relief slams into me as we step outside into the night air. Long gone are the close quarters of my cement prison. Now, I'm in wide open spaces. My chest swells when I take a deep breath and blow it out with relief.

This is what momentary freedom feels like.

"Kitten!"

My head jerks toward the sound of Arrow's joy-filled voice floating from a dark SUV parked on the side of the empty road, in front of the police department.

Great. They're all here to witness this humiliating walk of shame.

Shepp rests in the driver's seat with the window rolled down, watching my every move with interest-filled eyes. There's something about him. Something mysterious I want to unravel.

Yet, I try not to care. I can't let them wrap me up in their crazy when I have plans of my own. I want a true escape from this hell I've been thrust into by one simple mistake.

Seems I've been making a lot of mistakes in my life lately. Time to be a good little Journey until I can get the fuck out.

Inwardly, I groan at the sight of Arrow jumping out of the SUV with excitement. He's basically an overgrown puppy dog, bounding toward me with a massive grin plastered on his deranged face. Running forward, he opens his arms, engulfing me in an unwanted hug.

I need a shirt that says "No touchy".

"Arrow," Jericho warns with a growl when he's yanked forward with the handcuffs.

Note for later, do this more often and yank him around. That'll serve him right for handcuffing me.

"Oh, Kitten. You didn't think we'd leave you here, did you? We could never," he confesses, snuggling into me and running his nose up and down the side of my neck with a pleased groan— with an unhinged possession.

Shivers erupt, skittering down my body. Why does something so simple and unwarranted have me in a chokehold. I should be pushing him away and kneeing him in the balls.

Yet, I can't.

"Um, thanks for the bailout," I say, scrunching my nose when he squeezes the breath from my lungs. "Too much hugging," I gasp out, punching his back several times with my free hand until he loosens up.

Finally, he releases me with a deep chuckle vibrating his chest. "Ah, Kitten. It's so good to see you again. Next time, invite me to your parties before you start." He winks and steps back, only for Jericho to yank me by the wrist attached to his.

I send a scathing look in Jericho's direction when I stumble back into his side. He smirks, fire brewing behind his dark and devious eyes.

Asshole.

I focus on Arrow's words, remembering his arms circled around me and holding me in place just so the police could take me away. Rage consumes me like an explosion. Darkness wavers in my vision. Most people see red before they lash out. I see darkness trying to take over.

Like the night my sister was taken from me.

"Next time? There won't be a next time. You assholes got me thrown into the slammer," I snarl, trying to throw Jericho off me.

Trying being the keyword. Instead of letting me go, Jericho pulls me closer. More threateningly, this time. Dominating me without saying a word. The cuff tightens on my wrist, cutting into my flesh.

I wince, swallowing hard, refusing to show the fear bubbling to the surface. Be courageous. Face this like you've faced everything else before. They can't do anything worse than what your monster has done.

Question after question slithers through my mind. What will their bailout cost me in the long run? What will this contract actually entail, besides the handcuffing?

"Now, now," Jericho says in a patronizing tone. "Let's get you home. No need to blame us because we came and got you, didn't we? Did they hurt you? Touch you?" As he speaks, his voice reaches new depths. Agitation and possession hold him hostage as he stares down at me with pure evil resonating in his eyes.

"I'll chop their balls into tiny pieces!" Arrow shouts in hysterics.

Turning on his heel and marching in the opposite direction toward the front doors of the precinct, determination lines his face.

"Arrow!" Jericho barks, his voice snapping out into the night air like a whip, wrapping around Arrow's wrist and stopping him cold.

A shiver runs down my spine at Arrow's deadly look. His jaw clenches, forcing his veins to protrude. Oddly enough, he waits like an obedient puppy until Jericho speaks again.

"Did they touch you, Little Chaos?" Jericho asks in a low, vicious voice, ready to prowl into the police station, too.

"Touch me?" I ask incredulously, furrowing my brows. "You're serious right now? They handcuffed me in front of you, shoved me into a police car, and tied me to a fucking table. Of course, they touched me. And you assholes enjoyed the show!" I shout, tearing myself out of his death grip. My eyes scan the psychos standing around me with blank expressions. "So, what are you going to do about it?" I goad, cocking my head, examining the darkening of their eyes, filled with deadly intent.

Jericho steps forward, gently running a finger over my cheek in such a loving manner I almost believe it. Almost. I snap my teeth at him, baring them.

"My feral, Little Chaos." He grins, not deterred that I nearly bit his damn finger. He grips my chin in a tight hold, gnashing my teeth together.

"I will bite you," I hiss, attempting to break from his hold.

"I count on it," he says with a grin. Talk about being feral. It's certainly not me. Stepping back, Jericho eyes Arrow who remains frozen in rage. "Now, Arrow, we'll make sure to address it at our next meeting." Those eyes stare into mine with such intensity that goosebumps spread across my flesh. "But you can't march into the police station and hang them all without warning. Next time, Arrow. Then you can take them into your special room. Besides, didn't you have a present for Journey?"

"Present?" I grunt when Jericho waltzes forward without a care. He doesn't even gently tug me along, I'm more like a puppy forced to follow her new master. "Would you slow down, you long-legged asshole!" I shout, tugging at my restraint to halt his speed. It doesn't. He continues to move at his own pace, disregarding me again. "Fucking prick."

That does it. He halts, turning on his heel, and pulls me into his chest. His free hand tangles in my dried-out curls, yanking my head back.

"I can't wait to harness your defiance." His nose presses against mine, his eyes glaring holes right through me. "But right now, it's pissing me off. You don't want to piss me off, Little Chaos. You think you're stuck with me now. Just wait." His lips press into mine with force, grunting when I kick his shin. Those sharp teeth sink into my flesh until crimson coats his lips, glistening like chapstick. He grins, smearing it around with the back of his hand. "You're going to drive me to fucking insanity. Now, get in the car, Journey," Jericho demands, leaning back. "You're coming home with us."

"I'm not a stray dog," I say, licking my lips. "Besides, my momma always told me I shouldn't get into cars with strangers."

"Did she also mention you shouldn't let yourself get filmed while committing several felonies?" Jericho asks with a blank expression. I scowl, attempting to cross my arms. "That's what I thought," he says with a grin.

Shepp grunts, climbs out of the SUV, and opens the back door, signing something while eyeing me.

Jericho grins back. "We've got something to show you, Little Chaos. Time to take a tour of the town."

"I don't need a tour of the town. I need my shower and my bed." Facts. I'd rather go to sleep and forget this mess happened. Maybe when I wake up in the morning, this will all have been a bad dream.

Who am I kidding? I'm Journey West. I'm like a magnet for trouble.

"Later," Arrow sing-songs, hopping into the back of the SUV. "You're such a good little driver, Sheppy. Ow!" he yelps, holding his stomach. "Asshole, too."

Shepp flips him off with a scowl, turning back to us and gesturing to the vehicle. Great. Looks like I'm getting dragged into a car I don't want to be in. With men I don't necessarily want to be around. Maybe. They're beyond dangerous. For my health. For my body. They'll destroy me. Leave me raw. I feel it in my bones.

But for some reason, this ache in my chest is pulling me toward them with red flags waving in the wind. Why do I hate them, yet feel intrigued by them at the same time? Like I know them.

Jericho pulls me into the car between him and Arrow with a satisfied grin. His hand falls to my thigh, like it belongs there. I narrow my eyes, trying to peel his fingers off my leg, but it doesn't work. He digs harder, probably leaving thick bruises.

Wonderful. This captivity is going to go smashingly.

"Welcome to the backseat, Kitten. Maybe we can dirty up Jericho's fancy leather with our body fluids," Arrow murmurs in my ear, lightly brushing his lips along my neck. His hand lands on my other thigh, squeezing softly.

Humming encases my body the more he touches me. Like he was meant to be touching me at all times. It feels good. Too damn good to have him wrapped around me. My eyes fall shut. What is happening to me? Why am I letting him touch me? Freedom— that's what it is. A little taste in the midst of chaos and captivity.

"Sure," I rasp, leaning my body further into his and soaking in his heat. For one split second, I revel in the feel of him.

Somewhere behind the crazy mask he wears, I feel the security he could provide for me.

"Off," Jericho barks, shoving Arrow's body away from mine. "Keep your tongue to yourself."

Arrow grins wider, settling back. "Later," he murmurs playfully.

I can't help the laugh that falls from my lips when he wiggles his brows. I blame the delirium from lack of sleep for my outbursts.

"Enough," Jericho growls, curling his fingers into a fist. "Sheppard, drive us to the first location."

Shepp blinks and nods from the driver's seat, like a good soldier, and throws the car into drive. The darkened streets of Briar Cove blur by as we make our way through the downtown area.

I swallow hard when a large skyscraper comes into view. Standing tall with lights making the outside appear dark blue and then, turning pink, highlights the massive headquarters of Jericho's father—Gabriel Viotto. The place they run their empire out of. I would give anything to stick a bomb on every floor and watch it fucking burn.

"Oh, Kitten! I got you a present," Arrow says, poking his tongue out as he digs into the depths of his jean pocket.

"A present?" I ask when he finally shoves a tiny, lidded jar into my hands. I hold it up to my face, my eyebrows furrowing. "What is it?" I ask, shaking the two tiny white objects around until they clink against the glass, looking suspiciously like two large teeth.

"Leighton's teeth," he says with a smug grin and straightens his spine. "He parted with them so easily, unlike his finger," he grumbles the last part, delivering the news like it's no big deal. "They really do make the best presents. Teeth especially. Just call me the tooth fairy."

A goddamn finger? Shit. I swallow down the bile rising in my throat. I've seen this before. This doesn't affect me. I can do this.

"How did these come out so easily?" Shaking them around a bit, Arrow's smile returns, and he beams at me.

"Nothing beats a good punch or two. And then bam! They rolled right out of his head. They're nice presents, right? I'll always have presents for you, Kitten," he says in a low voice, running his fingers through the bushy mess my hair has become since this morning when I fixed it up after work. "You should see the one in my room. You'll absolutely love it," he purrs.

"So, you beat his ass?" I ask, leaning back into the seat.

"More than—"

"Arrow, I don't think Journey needs to hear about your extracurricular activities with sharp objects," Jericho reprimands, undoing the first three buttons of his white undershirt. He inhales a deep breath, seeming to relax into the seat.

"Next time," I stage whisper in Arrow's direction, earning a chuckle.

"You got it, Kitten," he says, winking when Jericho clears his throat, drawing my attention back to him.

"We have a few things to discuss with you," Jericho says, demanding the attention of everyone in the vehicle, including Shepp. Without warning, the car veers down a familiar road, leading directly toward the trailer park I grew up in.

My fucking hell.

It's located in the heart of the city. A forgotten lot, filled with old trailers from the 1960s. And surrounded by massive businesses on either side. Only a tall, wooden fence blocks the sound of the growing city and the people running it. For me, it was always convenient. School was three blocks away. The laundromat was less than a mile. Anything I needed was at my fingertips. Which also meant my mom had access to her clients and drugs.

Shepp pulls the car directly in front of my dark yellow trailer, faded from the years of sitting here. Usually, the living room light leaks through the windows to outside, giving me an indication as to what my mother's up to—men, usually. But tonight? Even her shitty car is gone and everything looks devoid of life.

I swallow hard. "What kinds of things?" I ask, cocking a brow as I settle against Jericho with eager eyes, awaiting his direction. Because I'm sure whatever this asshole has to say will be as pretentious as he's acting.

I'll play the part of the dutiful little prisoner until I can grab the key from his coat and run for my life.

"Follow me," he says cockily, pulling me out of the backseat and toward the side door of my trailer.

"Like I have a choice!" I grit out, stumbling over my damn feet as he drags me through the rock driveway and onto the small wooden deck. My brows furrow. My eyes lock on the large red sticker on the front door. "Condemned?" I breathe. "There's no fucking way!" I glare at him. "What did you do?"

"I'm the law, Little Chaos," is all he says as he stares at the sticker with pride. I swear his chest puffs out. Like he did something fucking good.

"You're not the goddamn law, you're..."

An asshole. A fuck nugget! So many words bounce off my skull, but I'm silenced by fucking Jericho Viotto. Like lightning, he reaches out, squeezing my throat in his massive hand. Rage soars through me at the feel of his skin against mine when I reach up and squeeze his wrist in warning.

"Oh, Little Chaos. I am the goddamn king of this kingdom. Your king. The fucking law before your eyes. One day, you'll bow to me on your hands and knees." With every word he says, he tightens his grip on my neck until my lips flop open, begging for air. Finally, he lets loose and presses his lips against my cheek.

I narrow my eyes, taking in much-needed air. "Where's my mom?" I croak.

He licks his lips, searching my face again. "Rehab. Thought that might make you happy."

"Rehab? Happy?" I sputter. "Since when do you care about my happiness?"

"You're a runner, Kitten," Arrow coos, stepping onto the tiny deck with a grin. "This is our insurance." He waves a hand at the empty trailer like I'm sad my mom is out of there and I don't have to deal with her anymore.

"Insurance?" I ask through gritted teeth.

"Runner," Arrow sings again, leaning against the wooden railing. "If we didn't take away your home, you'd come running here the first chance you got and hide out. Not that I wouldn't know where you are." His smile sends shivers down my spine like he's trying to tell me something I don't know. He's hiding something.

I stare him down. Nothing is stopping me from crawling through the window and sleeping in my own bed.

"Don't worry, Kitten. I got all the essentials out of your room." He wiggles his brows.

"We threw the rest out," Jericho says with arrogance. "Everything inside is gone. Your mom is gone. You have no home. No possessions. Well, with us you do."

"You can't just... just take my home from me!" I suck in a breath, bringing my hand over my heart. Panic roars inside me at the loss of control. Why do the men in my life think they can just take things from me? Or take people from me and hold them over my head?

"You signed your life to us." Jericho grins. "You're ours now."

Shepp nods from the top step of the porch, reiterating their thoughts. A grim expression crosses his features when he looks at me, staring deep into my soul. Panic must consume my expression when I stare at them with my mouth agape. Shepp huffs, signing something to Arrow, who rolls his eyes. Licking his lips, he reaches into his pocket and pulls out several pieces of paper. They wave around in the slight breeze, but he keeps them in his grasp before putting them away.

"Why do you have those?" I rasp, willing the heat behind my eyes to go away. I can't cry in front of these three. Then, they'll see what's hidden beneath the mask I wear. They can't ever know about my sister or the letters she's written to me. Then, they'll know about the monster lurking in the background. Sunny has to be my secret, my monster said so.

"*Your sister's existence has been wiped from every database,*" my monster says, pacing in front of my cage with a slight smirk.

"*No,*" I rasp, flinching when he whacks the bars, rocking my cage.

"*Yes,*" he sneers back.

It's the first time he's come back after shutting the lights off and leaving me here to rot. I thought for sure I was going to die of starvation and dehydration before he strolled back through the doors, claiming he had a job for me.

"*B-but is she o-kay?*" I stutter, praying she's safe wherever she is.

"*As safe as she can be.*"

Shepp signs something, but I don't know what he said. I look to Jericho and Arrow who stare at Shepp's words, but they don't utter a sound.

"Why?" I shout, attempting to lunge forward and yank them from his coat.

He steps back, giving me a sympathetic look before heading down the few steps and toward the SUV, where he climbs into the driver's seat.

I heave a breath.

"I take it those are important to you?" Jericho asks, eyeing Shepp as he rests in the vehicle.

I roll my lips together, refusing to give him more ammunition to fire with. Of course they're important to me. They're Sunny's letters. The only piece of her I have left until I can get her back in my arms.

"No answer then. Hmm," Jericho hums, tugging on the handcuffs. "Let's go then."

"I can pry the answer from you later, Kitten. With my tongue," Arrow says with a grin, trailing behind us before we get into the backseat.

Jesus. How fucked was I? I mean, at least I wasn't in prison

ALY BECK

for all those made-up charges. But what the hell had I done by signing that contract?

Fucked myself. That's what.

My eyes slip to the handcuff right around my wrist and Jericho's. His words ring in my mind.

Don't underestimate me, Little Chaos.

Well, I could say the same to him. But I'm not one to lay my cards out on the table for all to see.

I'm sneakier than that. They can trap me in a contract all they want. One way or another, I'm breaking free. I have to. My sister's life depends on it.

CHAPTER THIRTY
Journey

"WELCOME HOME," Jericho snarks when the SUV stops beside a large mansion. "This is our palace. No one else is allowed here except the three of us and now you." With indifference, he stares up at the mansion.

Welcome home? I think not. There's no home about this place. No warm and fuzzy feeling taking me over. If anything, I want to run in the opposite direction. This home, as he calls it, is enormous. No, beyond enormous. It's a goddamn fortress spanning what feels like miles. I crane my neck, looking at the four stories lifting into the sky. Fuck me, they've taken me to an elaborate prison straight from the bowels of hell. This will make my escape a little more complicated later, but it's still happening. I'm running away from this place no matter what.

"So, no big, bad daddy living here?" I snark.

Jericho's gaze moves to me with interest. "Not for a very long time. But don't concern yourself with that, Little Chaos."

Oh, I will concern myself with that. Especially when this place fills me with utter dread and bad omens. I swear to God, a feeling of deja vu smacks me in the face, rendering me breathless. There's just something about the formidable mansion, making me want to turn and run away.

Although my mom sucked, that trailer they decided to condemn has been my home since I was four years old, when my father told my mom to officially fuck off after years of hounding him for support.

"Your father never wanted you. I did, though. I fought for you. That's why we're here," my mom sighs, sitting on the couch, running a finger through her long brown locks. *"But we'll be okay."* She smiles wearily at me as my little eyes look around the trailer. *"I just have to keep going to work, cleaning that mansion and..."* she chews on her bottom lip. *"We'll make this work, Journey Girl. Okay?"* She runs her fingers through my hair, looking at me affectionately.

My heart pounds at the remnants of her voice ringing in my head. Journey Girl. She hasn't called me that since I was... Fuck, I don't even know when she stopped. I don't know when she stopped being that mom and turned into the lady she is now. The woman who doesn't give a flying fuck about my existence.

That moment was one of the last times I saw her healthy and glowing with life. I was little—maybe four—but the memory sticks out so vividly, crashing into me. Why it's haunting me now, I have no idea.

"Come on, Little Chaos. It's been a long night." He yanks at the cuffs, jolting me out of my thoughts.

"No thanks to you," I mutter under my breath.

How this shitty night went so damn wrong, I'll never know. I'll blame the alcohol I consumed to wash away the scuzzy feeling of spying on someone who seemed so genuine. Fuck. I'm never going to get more information on Jenni if I'm tied to Jericho for fucking eternity. And my monster? Fuck. I don't know how I'm going to get to him and let him know. Worry consumes my thoughts as I follow behind him, staring up at the gigantic mansion before my eyes.

How will I save my sister now when I can't leave Jericho's sight? *Escape.* That's how.

And then, hide forever. Easy peasy lemon squeezy.

"Wait until you see your room, Kitten!" Arrow bounces on his toes the entire time Jericho drags me down the driveway toward a side door.

"My room?"

"Your room, Little Chaos. You didn't think I'd secure your soul without facilitating amenities, right?" Jericho purrs, stopping outside the door expectantly.

Secure my soul. This mother fucker is going to get a dick punch in the middle of the night. I smirk. Imagine that. If he forces me to sleep beside him, he's going to get quite the wake-up call.

My pills not only stop the nightmares, but they keep me in place, too. My trauma was a hell of a thing, causing thrashing, vivid dreams, and sleepwalking. The amount of times I've woken up in the closet, on the floor, or in the bathtub is more than I can count. And it's all thanks to my monster and the prison he threw me into when I was sixteen.

Jericho Viotto will rue the day he handcuffed me to him.

My nostrils flare. "What did you bring from my old room? I need..."

"Nothing." Jericho raises a brow, stepping back for Shepp to unlock the door for him, and holds it open. "You need nothing from your old life. I'll give you the clothes on your back and the food in your belly." He says it so matter-of-factly that my heart drops. It's no-nonsense. Impossible to fight him. Especially when he tugs me through the door, leading into the massive kitchen.

"Don't worry, Kitten. I got you a fun surprise," Arrow murmurs, brushing past me. "It's life-size and perfect for when you're in need." He winks, settling on a kitchen stool pulled up to a large island in the middle of the chef's kitchen, fit with the best appliances and marble countertops.

I stop dead, pulling Jericho with me. My eyes flutter around the illuminated space, rich with everything under the sun. This kitchen is about as big as my damn trailer.

"You're gawking," Jericho states, putting a finger under my chin and closing my mouth. I glare in his direction, earning a blinding smile. "As I said, welcome to your new home." He waves a hand toward the darkened house beyond the kitchen.

Right. The sun is still down. But it won't be for long.

Shepp clicks the rings on his hands together, gaining Jericho's attention. His fingers move rapidly as he signs something. But those bright eyes, focus on me.

"What did he say?" I ask when they all turn their attention to me.

"He's going to do what Shepp does best and make you a gourmet breakfast with all the damn fixings." Arrow grins when Shepp huffs but nods in my direction. "It's his love language. Stuffing you full of food and other things." He wiggles his brows.

I'd argue that I want to go to bed and take nothing from them. But my stomach, ever the hungry beast, growls loudly.

"His point," Jericho mumbles sarcastically, pulling me onto an empty stool between him and Arrow.

For the next hour, we sit silently, watching Shepp work the stove like a five-star chef, pulling together a beautiful breakfast of eggs, bacon, sausage, fruits, pancakes, and French toast. Some of my all time favorites. But how does he know? Has he been watching me or something? That'd be weird as hell. So many questions run through my mind, but my panic forces me to come to a conclusion that it's a lucky guess. Everyone loves pancakes, French toast, and eggs. Now, all that's missing is the delicious donuts I found every morning on the countertop of my kitchen.

I watch his back as he cooks with ease. Every muscle in his body seems to lose the tension that's always there. The smell of the food ramps up the gurgling in my stomach.

Beside me, Jericho aimlessly scrolls through his phone with his free hand, leaving the one attached to mine, rubbing my fingers with his. Arrow hums to himself, munching on an apple to the seeds before flipping it to the uneaten side as he waits for Shepp to put the food in front of us.

"Where's my phone?" The last place I saw it was at Jenni's party. Somewhere. Fuck. I can't even remember where I left the damn thing. Last I knew, it was in the pocket of the dress. I didn't come with much, just myself and my phone.

Jericho stops his scrolling to gaze at me with an unimpressed gaze.

"We have it."

"And? Can I have it? People will be worried when I go missing, you know." People, as in my fucking monster who no doubt is messaging me, demanding updates.

Bossy, dickface.

My vision blurs as panic roars inside of me. Deep breaths, dummy. You have to focus on staying calm and getting out of here. It's not like they can see anything on my phone, anyway. Years ago, when I was captured and given that phone, some fancy programming was installed on it, effectively wiping out all evidence of calls, text messages, emails, and anything in between. My monster calls it AntiEyes. I call it burn after reading. Like any good spy, no one will ever know what someone sends me.

Thank God. The last thing I need is Jericho to discover the shameful secrets I've been hiding from the world for three years now.

"Your mother's in rehab. You have no daddy who cares. You have no job. You've graduated. Who exactly will notice that you're gone?" Jericho raises a cruel brow, eyeing my unmoving face.

The realization takes root in my gut. No one. That's the answer. No one, but my monster will know I've dropped off the face of the planet. Not even Jenni. She's probably... No, not probably. Jenni is definitely dead with the information I handed over to my monster. Fuck. My only hope is that Elias was able to sweep her away in the middle of the night before my monster could get his hands on them.

"Exactly. Now, focus on feeding yourself so we can continue with our morning," Jericho hums, waving Shepp on.

Don't panic. If they have it, I can find it. No matter where they hid it. I'll get out of here.

I lick my lips in anticipation when Shepp turns, serving the first round of food. Arrow grunts, grabbing each piece of food with his hands and putting it onto an empty plate. He groans, eating bite after bite, not bothering to clean his lips.

Shepp stops in front of me, bringing his fingers to his lips.

"He wants you to eat," Jericho comments, setting his phone down. He starts plating food and puts it in front of me. "Eat," he huffs again, getting his own food.

"So bossy," I grumble, earning a snort from Shepp. He watches with bated breath until the first piece of homemade French toast hits my taste buds.

Fucking hell in a hand basket. I stare at the food with wide eyes. Is it possible to marry a piece of French toast?

"Where'd you learn how to cook?" I moan like a damn hussy, tucking into my pancakes next and savoring the flavor on my tongue.

They remind me of the premade pancakes I used to find in my fridge as a teenager. Sometimes it was pancakes. Sometimes it was French toast. Other times it was sub sandwiches and chips. Either way, these blow those out of the water. Wherever those came from.

I swallow my bite, snapping my eyes to Shepp and examining him closely. What people would do for a Klondike bar, I'd do for Shepp's pancakes and French toast, which says a lot about the amazing flavor exploding on my tongue. Good God, he should be in the kitchen of a King. Not bound here to these bastards.

He raises his eyes to mine, pride shining from their depths. He licks his lips, looking at Arrow as he signs something I can't understand. I wish I did. I wish I could speak his language so he didn't have to rely on others and I could understand him. If he mouthed words at me, I'd probably have better luck lip reading. It's something my monster instilled in me for missions he sent me on.

"It's a hobby," Arrow snorts, biting the last of his apple. His brows furrow. "Fine. Not a hobby. A lifestyle, Mom."

Shepp grunts, rolling his eyes with frustration. His teeth sink into his bottom lip when he stands in front of me. A vulnerable look takes over his expression when points to his lips.

"*I like to cook. Now eat the food,*" he mouths without making a sound. Not that he could, from what I understand. But what do I really know about these three men? Practically nothing. And Shepp is the most mysterious one of them all.

"You enjoy it," I say, reading the words straight from his lips. He grins with satisfaction, nodding. "And you're bossy, too. Wonderful. Three bossy assholes."

Maybe I should be thankful I can't understand his language. He'd be another bossy douchebag, telling me what to do. I already have two dicks on my tail, barking at me to do this and that. However, learning his language on the sly might be helpful when they make plans right in front of my face without wanting me to know.

Shepp's light eyes devour me when I eat another bite and hum in response. I'd dance in my seat with satisfaction if I could actually move without Jericho bitching. I watch in fascination as Shepp finishes cooking the rest of the pancakes and stacks them on a plate in the middle of the island. Finally, he digs into his own food, and silence descends on us again as we stuff our faces.

Part of me is wary that they've slipped something into my food. Sounds like something these domineering jerks would do. Drug me so I don't run away. Then, they'll handcuff me to a damn bed and keep me forever. I glare at them again, trying to pick apart their brains. Crap. I can't think like this. I need to shake it off and finish my plate. I'd never tell Shepp, but his food is the best home cooked meal I've had in days, filling me up, and taking me back to a simpler time. Which hasn't happened in years.

Sable, who refuses to be called mom, has never had enough money to stock our fridge or cabinets. A shame, really. Even when we got food stamps. She'd sell the funds loaded on her card for cash in hand, getting more drugs to feed her appetite. But not mine. She never cared about my growling stomach and left me with no choice but to grab things from the food pantry. Or hell, I even had to steal a few things from the grocery store. Even when I was seven, I remember sneaking out after she had locked me in my room to find food anywhere I could. Then, food magically appeared over the years in our fridge. Sometimes loaded with my favorite meals. Lasagna. Eggs. Pancakes. Sandwiches. You name it, it was there. Somewhere out there a true angel appeared before my eyes and helped me fight off the hunger that plagued me. I always suspected it was one of my mom's regulars coming through the door and helping me out. I never saw them with my own two eyes. But I had my suspicions.

But now, after eating these familiar-tasting pancakes, I'm not too sure about that suspicion. Shepp bustles around the kitchen, stacking pans and empty plates into the dishwasher. He puts the remnants of the leftovers into containers and places them into the fridge. Turning on his heel, he faces me with a soft smile.

"Eat what's leftover later," he mouths without a sound again, and I nod, thankful for the years I've learned to read lips from my spying adventures.

I swallow my last bite as a heaviness consumes my eyes, threatening to pull them closed. A yawn breaks through, and I groan with tingling limbs taking over. Maybe they did drug this food.

"You're a tired Kitten," Arrow murmurs, brushing some of my wild hairs out of my face.

No shit, Sherlock—is what I want to say. But I nod with defeat. The sooner I can "go to bed" the sooner I can break free from this contraption around my wrists.

"That's our cue," Jericho rumbles, pulling me to my feet without asking me to move.

I grunt, yanking the handcuff. "You can't just drag me along like a rag doll," I hiss, running into the back of him when he halts suddenly. "I have ears, asshole. Speak before you move." My jaw tightens when his broad shoulders stiffen.

Turning on his heel, he faces me with pursed lips. "You're under the impression that you have a say." He raises a brow when anger sweeps through me. "Now come, we need to clean you up for the night before we rest."

"Communal shower?" Arrow pipes in, bounding up the large set of stairs in front of us. My eyes drift around the large foyer, if you could even call it that, until I'm dragged again.

Wait. Shower?

"Shower? You'll uncuff me, right?" I ask, getting dragged up the stairs. And leave me alone for just a damn second. I'm used to looking over my shoulder, but this is ridiculous.

Jericho's chuckle is the only thing I hear when I'm pulled in front of French doors.

"Did you even read the contract?" Jericho asks, raising a brow when he opens the doors, revealing a massive bedroom that doesn't even look like it's been touched.

"That legal mumbo jumbo you gave me like five seconds to look over without a lawyer?" Technically, I had an hour to get acquainted with what it said. I tried. Hard. Maybe I should have asked for legal advice. "If I had a chance to get a lawyer, maybe I would have understood what you forced me to sign," I snap back, stumbling into the room with Arrow and Shepp behind us and closing the doors.

Jericho rolls his eyes. "You had one hour, Little Chaos. But you simply chose to sign it without actually reading over everything. Your mistake. Not mine. Now, you'll follow the rules."

It's at the moment I hear the click of the lock, and fear truly sets in. I don't show it, of course. I lock it away, forgetting it exists. Not letting it affect me when I'm surrounded by three dangerous mafia men who essentially kidnapped me. No! They did kidnap me! Hiding behind a legal document, granting them custody of me from the damn county. Like I'm a fucking piece of property.

Show no fear, Little Snake.

His voice rings through my skull, and for once, I'm grateful for his intrusiveness. It's one of many lessons I learned under his cruel hand, and thankfully, I can apply many of them here.

I blow out a breath and stiffen my body, feigning annoyance, which isn't too far off. I'd rather slap all three of them and run away than be here under their expectant glares.

"Isn't it pretty, Kitten? We designed it just for you!" Arrow says, jumping on the enormous bed at the back of the large bedroom with an oomph.

The oversized black comforter hugs his body like a damn cloud, almost sucking him completely in. And that's not the craziest part. The bed he dove into could hold five people easily.

Or more.

If I thought the kitchen was big, this room knocks my fucking socks off. Huge bed, dressers, a fucking couch, and big screen TV. Shit, there's a bar with a mini fridge on the other side. This is way bigger than anything I've ever seen. It could be its own damn apartment. I'd be impressed if I wasn't so pissed that I'm still attached to Jericho fucking Viotto.

But also, what did he say?

"Wait. For me?" I ask, stumbling again when the asshole pulls me toward another door and throws it open without checking to see if I'm following. Not that I have a choice in the matter. I'm still attached to him. "Words, asshole! You can't just drag me around," I huff behind him, earning nothing more than a shrug.

"Time to remove the prison suit, Little Chaos." Jericho doesn't hesitate to unbutton his shirt the rest of the way without a care, letting it hang open and exposing his impressive body filled with art pieces.

Men like him shouldn't look so goddamn lickable. I should want to stab him with a screwdriver. Not lick him.

"You have to remove this then," I say smugly, holding up our joined hands.

"For a time," he says with a shrug. "But understand the rules, Little Chaos. Until we trust you, you're attached to us in one way or another. Or, I could send your ass to prison and let the judge know you were a naughty girl."

My heart pounds when he reaches into his suit jacket and removes the key, unlocking our cuffs.

Fucking finally! Freedom is on the horizon!

I could run, dart out the door, and take off. But I won't. That's expected. They're not dumb. This is some sort of test, so I take note of him putting the key onto the counter, waiting for my time to grab it. And I will. You and I have a date later, Mr. Key. I just have to make it through this first. Whatever we're about to do.

"What rules?" I question, rubbing at my raw wrist.

Bastard. When I'm free, these assholes are never catching me again. I'll hide in his daddy's precious tower for all I care. Well, maybe not. He's a psycho, too. More so than the boy he raised. Just as long as I'm not handcuffed to these fuckers ever again.

They may be hot as sin, but they're walking, talking red flags. But somehow, I always go full speed ahead toward the wrong people. Like the masked men I let hump and dump me. That night was perfect, but the warning bells were spot on. But God, did they fuck me into oblivion. So much so that I don't remember getting home. How the hell did I get into my bed? I wouldn't put it past me to stumble home and climb through my window. Still, it's a mystery to me. One I don't intend to solve. Ignorance is bliss, sometimes.

"So many," he says with a devilish grin, shrugging his suit jacket off and folding it on the large countertop. Next comes his button-up shirt, leaving him in a white undershirt and slacks.

My eyes widen as he peels off clothes, unable to turn my eyes away. This is the man who handcuffed me to him without remorse. He let me get arrested despite his status with the police department. So, I shouldn't find his muscles enticing to look at. Nope. Okay, that's a lie. He's hot, dangerous, and deranged, and I'm totally pissed at him, but that doesn't mean I can't peek at what he's packing. Right?

Not to mention those tattoos lining his flesh, depicting all sorts of scenes across his body. He's covered in them. The largest one catches my eye, shining through from beneath his undershirt. A large bird, resembling a raven with beady eyes stares back at me, mid-flight, and mouth open. Its feathers stretch down the outside of his left arm and the beak pokes out on his neck, which is usually covered. Lost feathers fall from the bird down his left arm, almost to his wrist. Painting a beautiful picture of a creature that means nothing but bad omens in myth.

To some though, the raven represents intelligence. Even being in the presence of one can mean rebirth and starting anew. Whichever Jericho believes, I'm not sure.

"Do tell," I mumble, averting my eyes to the floor when the sound of water startles me from my stupor. Shiny shoes enter my vision when my chin is lifted, and I stare into dark, devastating brown eyes. He examines my tight expression with a cold stare.

"You're going to take this off and climb into the shower." He pulls at my stupid jailbird suit they forced me into after taking the only nice dress I actually liked. Fuck. I'm going to have to break it to Jenni later that they ruined it. If she's still around, of course. That's just another person I'm adding to my list to talk to.

I swallow hard, holding eye contact. It burns through me until I shiver under his stare.

"Step out of the room, then I will." I lift my chin when his lips quirk up in a smile.

"If you thought I was leaving you alone, you're mistaken. You will strip every inch of clothing off your body and step under the shower, while I watch to make sure you stay put. I've got my eyes on you, Little Chaos. Always."

Infuriating asshole! Rage swirls under my flesh when he quirks a smile at me. It's off-putting. Skin crawling. Fucking mocking. Jericho doesn't care that I don't want to get naked in front of him. He wants to watch me squirm.

I swallow hard, stiffening my shoulders. "No. You can't do that. This is my body, and I won't have you in the bathroom while I get clean." No peep show for you, douchebag.

He shrugs. "You signed the contract. I'd be happy to escort

you back to prison, where you'll stay until you die. Either strip your clothes off or..." He leaves the threat hanging in the air with a cocky smirk on his lips.

No remorse. Nothing in his tone but amusement as I fight to think of what to do next. Is this fight even worth it? Yes. Yes, it is.

"That contract is bullshit! There's no way that would hold up in court."

Jericho licks his lips, moving into my space. Those long fingers wrap around my throat, clinging to it like he loves to do.

"It may not hold up in the courts of the government, but in this house, that contract is binding. You should have read it better if you didn't want me to see you naked in the shower. Every inch of your flesh is ours to suck, fuck, dress, and play with. You're our fucking property, baby."

I hold in the sputter threatening to release. *Show no emotions. Your enemies will play off them.* His property? What the actual fuck do I look like? Definitely not someone who is owned. Not by him at least. Shit. How the hell do I end up in these situations? The last thing I need is some man telling me I'm his. Again. I will no longer stand for it. I'm my own person.

Yeah, this fight is so not worth it. Although, I do enjoy riling him up. What I don't enjoy is him practically eye fucking me when he steps back and takes his white undershirt off, folding it with the others.

Fuck his stupid muscles and arrogant, handsome face.

"I don't belong to you," I breathe. "I'll never fucking belong to you or anybody else." I grit my teeth with every word, making that promise to myself over and over again.

I don't want or need them. I only need myself and Sunshine. I learned a long time ago that I can't depend on anyone.

"You can think that now, Little Chaos. But I'll show you day in and day out who you fucking belong to. Me. Them. You're our little puppet to play with. Now, be a good girl and take that hideous reminder off. I'm going to clean you, and then I'll show you your closet."

So many questions rest on the tip of my tongue, but I hold them in. There's a time and place for it, and right now is not the time. Shivers roar through me when he unbuckles his slacks and kicks his shoes off, standing before me in nothing but tight black boxers, and even those disappear.

Leaving him completely naked. In the buff. No clothes on.

Shit. I think I'm short-circuiting, and I'm supposed to be a rage-filled bull, ready to show him. Instead, I'm staring straight down at his dick.

Goddamn. I avert my eyes, heat filling my face. Holy shit, he's got a dick. A big, big dick. My gaze goes right back to it like it's a bad train wreck, and I can't look away. Standing loud and proud at attention halfway up his abdomen. Holy shit! Of course, he does. He's a man. A man who is packing. Jesus. How does he fit that in his pants?

Okay, deep breaths. I totally have this.

I blush, trying to look away from him as he stands before me in all his glory. God. He's so, so fucking fit and trim. And rude. So fucking rude to stand before me in the nude when I didn't even ask him to. In fact, I asked him to leave the room. And instead of turning around to go, he dropped trou.

My eyes widen. Is that a damn tattoo on his dick? Look away! Abort! Abort!

My eyes fall to the side again, where I focus on the fancy tile on the walls. It's a pretty blue, mixed with black, bringing the whole room together. It's beautiful and fancy. And so not a dick. It even has five lines that run through it. Maybe. I count again, ignoring the man with the raging hard-on.

"Your turn," he rasps, wrapping his fingers around his length and pumping it a few times until precum glistens over his slit.

Okay. So maybe I didn't focus on the tile well enough. Somehow my eyes keep falling on his massive fucking dong. I groan, getting myself together. Of all the things that happened tonight, this is the one that sent me into a tailspin.

He kidnapped you, Journey. Kid. Napped. You. Say it with

me now and breathe. Before you have a damn panic attack from a veiny, thick dick.

I shake it all off and remember my exit strategy. Focus. Be good. And then, get the fuck out with your dignity intact.

"Fine," I say through gritted teeth, yanking at my stupid outfit's buttons and letting them fly throughout the bathroom. Cold air rushes over my bare chest and abdomen. "But I can wash my own damn self." Through pure determination, I yank the jumper down my arms and over my legs, kicking it to the side in his pristine bathroom along with the pair of socks on my feet. His jaw tics at the mess, but his focus on the piece of clothing doesn't last long.

The thing they don't tell you when you go to jail is that everything you have on that isn't white gets confiscated. Panties? Bra? Not white when you get booked in? Well, the jail seizes them and gives you county-issued pairs. Or, in my case, they didn't fucking have any. Usually, when you're bailed out or released, they give you everything back. Something the Devils claim to have. I have no doubt in my mind that they burned it all without a second thought—especially that dress. And hopefully not my phone. Even if they wanted to go through it, they couldn't.

So, here I stand under the bright lights of this freakishly large master bathroom, under his intense gaze, entirely and utterly naked.

Goosebumps pucker over every inch of my bare flesh. My face heats at his stare. His eyes greedily take me in like he can't get enough. Every imperfection. Every inch. Standing before him in nothing but my birthday suit, has every insecurity rising to the surface. My scars. My sins. Especially when his gaze darkens on the tattoo between my breasts, locking on it with interest. My war wound. The infinite mark, holding my ghosts. His jaw tics, anger taking hold and swirling in his eyes. Like he's ten seconds from losing his shit.

Shit. My breath stalls. It's a part of me that I don't usually show off, hiding it with the underbust I usually wear. I may have tattooed over the knife wound scarring me there, but it's still a reminder I like to hide away. He doesn't have a clue what I've been through. If he did, he'd have more to say on the subject.

Stepping forward, I don't dare flinch when he rubs between my breasts, examining the tattoo hiding my pain. Thick, callused fingers trace the slightly raised mark, hiding the sins of my past. Over and over, my flesh tingles from his touch, taking me beyond this room, so I almost forget I'm naked and vulnerable in front of him. My body shivers when he brushes the side of my breast, continuing to trace the outline of the vines and flowers on the side of the key.

Until he steps back with a grunt. My eyes fly open, greeting his empty stare.

"Get under the water. Wash the stink off your body," he demands, wiping away the momentary moment of serenity.

I'd love to say it's the only part of him affected, but that would be a lie. Maybe if I distracted him a little, I could...

"Shower, Little Chaos," he hisses, grabbing my arm and hauling me forward.

Okay. Never mind. A distraction is not in his future. Even without the cuff, he's a controlling asshole, pulling me along like I weigh nothing.

I gasp when the warm water falls over my flesh, and the glass door shuts behind us. Maybe I needed this more than I thought. After the party and drinking and destroying a car, I'm sure I'm filthy and, yeah, smelly. But that gives him no right to manhandle me to wherever he wants me to be.

"Would you fucking stop!" I shout, wiping the water from my eyes. I growl when he smirks down at me, dipping his head back under the spray of a second shower head. Fuck it. I push at his chest, making him stumble back, and he laughs at me. Just fucking laughs in my face no matter how many times I punch him until I'm out of breath.

"Stop fighting me, Little Chaos. It'll do you no good. Wash

your hair, and then we can rest," he says it nonchalantly as he lathers his hair with shampoo, humming a tune.

He's a goddamn psychopath. And I'm stuck with him.

Once we're out of the shower, Jericho insists on drying me off. He even runs the towel through my hair and then scrunches it like I would to maintain my curls near the counter where he had folded his dirty clothes.

"Be a good girl, Little Chaos. And we'll make all your dreams come true. Don't fight this connection we have." As he says connection, a rough handcuff falls on my wrist again, clinching shut. This time, though, he doesn't connect it to himself, leaving it hanging.

Right. Connection. If that's what he wants to call it.

"Now, it's past your bedtime," he hums, pulling me by the forearm toward another bathroom door and pushing it open.

"I didn't realize I had a bedtime," I huff when the lights turn on, and my jaw drops. "What the..."

"This is your closet. It's filled with everything you might need."

That's an understatement. Rows and rows of dresses, nice pants, T-shirts, and everything in between line the space.

"You..." My brows furrow when he unhands me, and I wander away toward a rack of clothes, running my fingers over them. "How..."

"Our union was inevitable," he says, leaning against a center island with drawers and a shoe rack making it up.

"Inevitable?" I ask, swallowing hard. "What do you mean?"

"You were always meant to be ours, Journey West. It was written in the stars. The universe knew who you belonged to. So, I prepared your spot by our side." His eyes wander the closet with pride, taking in the clothes and shoes.

I blink several times when he shrugs and rummages through a drawer, pulling out the smallest pair of underwear I've ever seen. I don't even have the time or the energy to ask questions. So, I bite my tongue.

"Wear these." He tosses them at me, but I refuse to catch them, letting them fall before me. He rolls his eyes, digging through another drawer and grabbing a deep, purple, silky nightgown.

"You're awfully fucking bossy," I growl, letting them drop to the ground. "I can dress my fucking self."

For a beat, I don't hear anything from him, and then he chuckles.

"Put the fucking clothes on, Little Chaos."

"Or what?" I huff, watching his predator-like movements as he grabs another piece of clothing from a hanger and comes toward me.

"Or you'll regret ever defying me. Play with me. I play back harder. I'll spank your ass so red, your blisters will have blisters. Then you'll recognize your king."

I blink several times when he falls to his knees in front of me, grabbing the tiny pair of panties.

"Fight me, and I'll punish you like you deserve. Submit to me, and I'll treat you like the queen you are," he murmurs, pressing his lips against my bare thigh. "Now, lift your leg so I can dress you." It's a small demand, tinged with exhaustion. Hell, it's even in his eyes when he stares up at me. So, I give in, deciding clothes would be nice.

I can fight him tomorrow.

CHAPTER THIRTY-ONE

Jericho

JOURNEY WEST WILL BE the only woman in history to bring me to my knees. Not that I mind. There are a lot of things I can do in that position with my tongue and hands. I'm finally getting the girl I've been obsessed with for years. Since that fateful day when I saw her punch a boy. Then, much to my dismay, I had to walk away from her altogether. I'll never forgive my bodyguard at the time for squealing to my father. Thankfully, I got him fired a few months later, but the order still stood: Journey West was off-limits.

It only made me want her more.

I rub my temple, standing above her as she restlessly sleeps. She'll be the death of me one day, driving me into the arms of my final resting place. But, in the same breath, her fighting spirit is the oxygen to my lungs.

Everyone around me bows their heads, scuttling off to do my bidding. I may not be the king of the city, but I am the dutiful prince in waiting.

Dutiful.

I scoff. I haven't been dutiful for years. Not when the memories of his torture live behind my eyes. At any given moment, they prepare to show me what I lived through.

Alcohol wafts off my father's breath when he finally ceases his movements. No light resides in his eyes when I look up at him from the floor, shivering from the cold cement.

"One day, you'll thank me for this, boy," he slurs, shoving me into a tiny closet near the back of the open basement. "One day, you'll say thank you, Father, for preparing me. You're my heir. My only boy. One day, my kingdom will be yours. You'll rule it like me. I'll make sure of it."

I blink rapidly, calling out to my father when he shuts the closet door and locks it from the outside. Like he's planned this torture all along. I swallow hard, pulling my knees into my chest, whimpering when his footsteps retreat upstairs. Then... Nothing but static fills my ears, and the silence beats down on me.

I'm his heir—his only child. I'm the one who will carry on his name and the family. At least, that's his excuse. He probably got off on watching me suffer alone in the darkness, chuckling as I begged for him to let me go. But begging never stands a chance against Gabriel Viotto. He'll gladly throw you to the wolves.

My father may not have laid a hand on me physically. Not like Shepp's father. Psychological torture was his game. Locking me in closets, leaving me in the damn dark. He didn't care what he did to me as long as it made me stronger in his eyes. Sure, he got the results he wanted after years of mental and emotional torture. But not fully. I'm still me. Only a slightly bent and broken version. One I'm improving on every day.

"Watch as I make him squeal, Jericho. He'll tell us anything he knows." I swallow hard, holding back my gag when my father plunges the knife in between his captive's ribs.

The man's screams echo off the basement walls. Oh, what these walls have seen. If they could talk, our family would have been in prison many moons ago.

The man's crime? Knowing too much. Not a single thing more. My father used to live by a code. Our entire crime family did. But he has slowly pushed that aside, making room for new plans— his own.

I blow out a breath and focus my eyes on the beautiful

woman attached to my best friend lying in bed. Her curly hair is splayed like a halo around her head on the pillow. Occasionally, she twitches in her sleep, her brows furrowing and tiny groans escaping. Getting her relaxed enough to fall asleep in a strange place was a feat in itself. Nevertheless, we coaxed her under the covers, and then she fell out. According to Arrow, our resident stalker, sleeping is difficult for her. She requires pills and music to nod off. Not tonight, though. She doesn't need any of that when we're here.

Soon, she'll see.

I squeeze my eyes shut, remembering the way her imperfect body felt under my fingertips, scars and all. Fucking perfect. Even when we fell together into the sheets of a stranger's bed under the full moon with masks, I felt her history at my fingertips. There's a map on her flesh I want to fully explore and memorize.

I have my suspicions and theories. About her. About my father. Especially after seeing the mark on her flesh between her delectable tits. Something I've seen so many times before first-hand throughout the years. Just never on a woman. They're not allowed to bear that mark. I'll discover soon enough, though. Journey doesn't know it yet, but she's going to spill every ounce of her life to us in one way or another. I have my ways of loosening tongues, especially hers.

And I'm going to enlist some help from a trusted friend I once thought dead. Why I hadn't called her sooner, I'll never know. Despite how helpful Olivia could be, I tend to keep our affairs to myself. She could also turn on us at any second. My cousin may be on the other side of the law, but I know she'll help. This time at least. Years before, when Journey's name fell into my lap, Olivia wasn't an option. Her company wasn't a choice. For years, I've had to rely on people from inside the organization. Now is the time to trust someone on the outside. Someone who bleeds the same as me.

I take one last look at Arrow and Journey in their sleeping heap, memorizing their expressions. Arrow won't wake up until the sun is high in the sky, sleeping so deeply you'd think he was dead. Journey on the other hand? Well she might be a different story after years of depending on pills. I silently walk out the bedroom door and down the hall, stopping before the only open door illuminated with light.

"I'm going to call Liv," I say, leaning against the doorframe with a sigh.

Shepp stops with a paintbrush trapped between his lips. Red paint decorates his face and fingers. Slowly, he brings his eyes to mine, and I see the muse dancing there. He's been blocked for so long, and now, it's rushing to relieve itself on his once-empty canvas.

All because of her.

'*Okay*,' he signs quickly with furrowed brows.

"You could never pull anything else up on our girl?" I question, keeping my distance and respecting Shepp's domain— his art room. The one place he can completely lose himself in the process and not have to worry about us.

Shepp's eyes wander over the canvas, losing himself in deep thought until he nods. '*When I was there that night after we took Journey home from Rave, she had a nightmare. She kept calling out for someone named Sunny or Sunshine.*' He rolls his lips in, almost hesitantly continuing. '*She has a sister,*' he signs, waltzing over to the couch he likes to call his bed and picks up white pieces of paper. Coming to stand right in front of me, he places them in my hands. '*She writes to her. She's in a hospital somewhere.*' He swallows hard when my eyes fall to the sheets of paper.

A sickening feeling takes me over. The letters sit like heavy lead in my hands. Maybe the answers to all our questions reside in these letters? Shepp turns his back to me and takes a deep breath when he ventures back to his painting, giving it all his attention.

"A sister?" Thoughts tickle the back of my mind. A sister, really?

How the hell did we not know she had a sister? I've known Journey West for years now. We may not have been best friends by any means, but she was my obsession. Every chance I got, I watched her from a distance at school. Of course, I wasn't allowed around anyone but the family outside of school. Not that I didn't sneak over and watch her house from afar, wishing I was inside. Not once in the years that I watched did I see someone younger than Journey exiting the house.

So, how the hell did I miss her having a sister?

I know everything about her. Except for the important things, I've come to realize. I've been through all her records before, delivered to me by our trusted PI. And a sister living with her was never mentioned. In fact, according to her records, she's an only child, which furthers my questioning on why my father insists I marry her. Because I know now that's all bullshit.

Her records are nothing more than a fabricated lie, concocted by someone trying to cover something up about her.

'*She said her monster had her hidden, Jer,*' he signs again, shaking his head at those words. '*A monster?*' he questions.

But my hackles immediately rise. Her monster. Of course. "So, where is this mysterious sister I've never heard of?" I cock my head.

Everything in my brain swirls at the information, clicking into place piece by piece. Yes. I think I might have an idea at who her monster might be. I just need a little more information.

"Liv will help with that."

I check my watch, noting the time. We got back so late from the police station that by the time I locked Journey to Arrow, the sun had come up over the horizon, signifying a brand new day.

'*Do you trust Liv?*' Shepp boldly asks, raising a brow.

Trust. Now, that's a word. I only trust a handful of people in my life, and my cousin, Olivia, is included in that. He knows that. We've been together since birth, bound by blood and torn apart by ruin. In the back of my mind, I shouldn't trust my cousin. She died. I went to her funeral. And then, I watched her reanimate years later with a fucking badge strapped to her chest, becoming the very person we loathed. The law. A person who could stop a multiple-decades-long rule of the underbelly.

"With my life."

Shepp nods a few times, grasping his paintbrush. *'Then ask her the million-dollar question.'*

I tip my head, leaving the man to continue his art piece and find myself down the hall in my own office. Large bookshelves line the walls, filled with useless books. Some classics. Some encyclopedias. None that interest me.

But this does.

My fingers glide over a black leather case on a shelf, holding the instrument, the one thing that brings me life besides Journey. My eyes fall shut as the cool leather swishes beneath my fingertips, reminding me why I'm here. Later. I'll play you later and spill my anguish into my music—my drug of choice.

Wandering to the cart in the corner, housing my liquor, I pour two fingers of expensive sipping whiskey. The amber liquid runs smoothly down my throat as I sit in my leather chair facing the massive fireplace. I swallow another gulp of my drink, staring at the letters in front of me. When Shepp got these, I haven't a clue. He's constantly sneaking off though, and my suspicion is to Journey's. Like I've done plenty of times before. And Arrow, too. We're all hopelessly addicted to the smart mouth girl who refused to bow in our presence.

And I guess that's what leads me here with an ache in my heart, curious to unwrap the mystery surrounding my girl.

Forgetting the letters momentarily by shoving them into a drawer, I pull out my phone.

Eight a.m.

By now, my cousin should be in her office, sorting out God knows what.

So, here goes nothing. I press the call button, patiently waiting for her to answer.

Olivia Viotto. Or used to be Viotto. A long time ago, she was one of us. Fighting on our side of things. Now, she's made a life for herself. Good for her. She's happy, playing wife, mother, and secret agent for the United States government's best kept secret—Veritas.

The only way out of the Viotto Crime family is bloodshed and death. Technically, my cousin achieved that when an evil man slit her throat and lit her on fire. She died, getting a second chance at a normal life. No one in the family suspects she's still alive. Well, only me and the guys.

"Jericho Viotto. As I live and fucking breathe," she says into the phone with an extra chipper voice.

"Liv," I say stoically, letting silence settle between us as I gather my thoughts.

"Did you call to bless me with your sunny disposition? Or..." she trails off with a chuckle, noises erupting on her end of the phone. Chatter and heels clicking. The sounds of an office coming to life.

"Don't I always bless you with my personality?" I quip, sipping my whiskey.

She snorts. "Yeah, something like that. It's been a while. Boys good? Uncle alive?" She hums the last part with venom.

I don't blame her. The entirety of the Viotto bloodline starts with the five brothers running pieces of California. My father is the top dog in his sector. And her father. Well, he's a different story altogether.

"Boys are good."

"I'll believe that when I see it. Arrow still holding on tight?" AKA, has he murdered anyone she needs to know about or concern her organization with?

I snort. "Something like that. He's still himself."

When I say I trust my cousin, I mean it. She's been in this life, on our side, and then on theirs. She knows the situation and understands. Hell, all five of her husbands were once rivals that she somehow brought together.

"Wonderful. If his name ever crosses my desk, I'll be sure to file it properly in file thirteen."

I smile at her sentiment. "You were always too good to us."

"And you always had my back. Now, what can I do for you, little cousin?" A door shuts on her end and the creak of a chair lets me know she's finally made it to her office.

"How's my tiny cousin?" I inquire, taking another sip. "Keeping you on your toes, I hope."

She snorts again and huffs. "Nico is Nico. A hellion, toddling into his terrible ones. He sure keeps his fathers on their toes. Thank God. They need someone to keep them in line. Why not a one-year-old?"

"Good boy," I murmur, sitting back in my chair. Silence bears down on us again. "I need extensive information on someone close to me."

"Close to you? Oh, a background check? Isn't that something Harrison could facilitate for you?"

Harrison Carlton. The Viotto Family lawyer, dabbling in PI work and hacking into anything he can get his grubby fingers on. I was hesitant to go to him, trying to get as much information on my own, considering my father owns him, and that's where his loyalty lies. Not with me. But with the head of the family. Using him was a risk, but I desperately wanted information on Journey.

"Already has," I grumble, running my brow. "It brought back the usual background check information. Old addresses. Current ones. Name. Birthday..."

"I know what background checks bring back," she quips. "Who is it? And do I even want to know why?"

I rub my jaw. "The girl I'm promised to."

There's silence on the other end of the line. "They're still practicing that barbaric tradition?" She swallows hard, no doubt memories leaking through.

"In most instances, I would have fought back. But in this case, I don't mind." I squeeze my eyes shut, taking in a deep breath.

"She must be someone special then."

"Indeed," I reply.

"What's her name, Jer? I can see what I can do. No promises. But our database is extensive."

"I owe you," I say, meaning every word. "I've searched for years since Gabriel handed me her name as to why it's her. In the eyes of our family, she's a nobody."

"Name, Jer. I've got to get going on my work," she sighs on the other end.

"Big problems?" I quip, sipping my morning whiskey.

There's another beat of silence. "My best friend has a stalker. Nothing terrible yet, but I can't figure it out."

"If you had names, I'd take care of them for you."

"I know you would. When I find them, they're going down. Now, stop stalling and give me this girl's name."

"Fine. Journey West. I need to find out as much as possible about her and her sister, Sunshine."

"Journey West," she says on the other end, typing a few things. "Like Corbin West's daughter? The famous rock star? He's the only rock star I know who has named all his kids after his favorite bands." I snort, hearing the moment she rolls her eyes in amusement.

"That's the one," I mutter. "As far as I've found out, she doesn't know him or anyone associated with him. No money. No nothing."

"No money?" she questions with a breath. "Jer, I'm very, very familiar with the West family. A lot of them, actually. That man had so many kids and didn't take care of them until after he died."

I blink several times. "I've had a long night, Liv. What are you saying?"

"Oh, so it's okay for you to circle around your questions but not for me?" she quips without heat.

"Of course. I'm a king," I snort.

"So you think..." she trails off going quiet. "My best friend is a West. She grew up in a small town in Illinois with barely anything to her name. Seger and Zeppelin West, her brothers, tracked her down after Corbin died and handed her an inheritance. In fact, all the West kids got an inheritance in the same fashion—hand delivered."

My stomach knots when she pauses. "How much, Liv?"

She blows out a breath. "Twenty million initially, with payments each year. Corbin was a billionaire by the time he died but had set up funds for each kid so their moms couldn't get their hands on them. But that's all I really know. I don't usually sit around talking about money with my friends."

I sit up. "Twenty million? But she..."

"I'll mark this in my calendar as the day I stumped Jericho Viotto into silence."

"Fuck you," I bite out without heat, curling my fingers around my glass.

"Yeah, you, too," she chuckles. "You understand what I'm saying, right?"

"When did these inheritances roll out, Liv? When did they get access to them?"

"About three years ago," she says, clearing her throat.

Three years? That means Journey was possibly sixteen when her father handed her millions of dollars. And she doesn't seem to have a clue. Was she too young to receive it? Fuck. I need to look over the paperwork we already have on her.

"Can you look into it for me? Or put me into contact with someone who might have a clue?" Journey doesn't have shit. That I know for a fact. Besides the two grand she had hoarded away in her dresser when we went through her things.

"Let me talk to Zepp and Seger and ensure we're on the same page. I can get you some more answers, too."

I blow out a breath and finish my whiskey. "It would be helpful. I can pay you for your work."

"I'm sure the government would love to know I took money from a known criminal family," she quips with a snort. "Consider it a family discount."

"A family discount," I hum. "Thanks, Liv."

"You know I have your back, Jer. I'll look into everything and see what I can come up with. I'll chat with the West twins and see what they have to say about her inheritance. And I can look into Sunshine, too."

We quickly say our goodbyes, and the silence takes over, settling on my chest and pushing down.

Everything she said runs through my mind. I don't understand how we've missed this vital piece of information. Where's the money that belongs to Journey? And why doesn't she have it in a bank account?

I grunt, throwing my glass across the room, and revel when it shatters, sprinkling the floor with glittering confetti. Something stinks, and it's coming directly from my damn father. If this is going the way I think it is, Journey is only around because she's worth money. Lots and lots of cold hard cash. But where does the wedding play into that? Why me?

Fuck.

Sleep gnaws at the back of my eyes, but there's no way I could calm myself down now. Not even reading the letters could take my mind off the news. So, I lock my desk, knowing my Little Chaos will search for them high and low. There's no way I can let that happen. I have to have some sort of leverage over her. And those are a good starting point until she tells me every little thing living inside her skull.

Waltzing over to my shelf, I take out the one thing that calms my nerves. I run my fingers over the four strings strung tightly, pull it out, and set my chin on the chin rest. I cradle the violin as I pluck the bow from the case.

I blow out a breath as I delicately draw the bow across the strings. Every muscle in my body melts, relieving me of the stress of the day. Just as a beautiful melody emerges, filling the air with the emotions I've bottled deep inside.

My fingers dance on the fingerboard, producing notes that soar and dip, weaving a hauntingly beautiful, heavenly sound to my ears.

When I'm here, with this in my hands, I'm free from the

torment my father reigned down. I'm free from my role. I'm no longer the heir to the kingdom. I'm me. Jericho Viotto, violin savant, playing until his fingers bleed across the strings.

The minutes tick by, second by second, leading into hours full of playing and swaying. Sweat beads at my brow and breaths pour from my nostrils.

Everything lifts off my chest and shoulders, making the future brighter.

I'll find my answers. I'll...

I shift on my heel, turning toward the open door just as a shadow backs away. Curly brown hair catches my attention.

I grin. "Hello, Little Chaos. You can come in." Gently, I set my violin down into its case and finger the bow, running my finger through the coarse, horse hair.

CHAPTER THIRTY-TWO
Jericho

I SWALLOW HARD when the door opens, showing her pale face and wide eyes. Like a ghost, she glides into the room.

"You play so beautifully," she murmurs, eyeing the instrument.

Something in her expression catches me off guard, stopping my movements. It's open without defiance. Her walls have been blasted through.

"It sounds like you're complimenting me," I hum, staring down at her bare wrist devoid of the cuff I left her in.

How curious. She's wandering the halls without the very thing I put on her to keep her still. It's something she'll pay for. Very soon.

She swallows hard, eyes turning glossy with an unknown emotion shining through. "It was you," she breathes out, her words barely audible like she was talking to herself more so than me. Memories seem to take over her mind and pull her back into a past that she refuses to share with me.

One day, I'll pry them out of her anyway I know how.

My brows furrow when she steps forward, brushing her fingers against the violin, smudging the beautiful dark wood with her fingerprints.

The world seems to stand still as I inspect her movements, lightly running her chipped nails over the wood repeatedly. Her mind is gone. Not reacting to me. I'm not here. She's not here. Until she abruptly turns to me with a blank expression, hiding everything away.

"It was you," she says again, swallowing hard.

I narrow my eyes, keeping the bow between my fingers to keep from grabbing her up. "What was me?"

"The music," she says, looking away to the violin again.

"Yes, indeed, it was me. Who else do you see?" I look around the empty room with furrowed brows.

"Of course," she says, straightening her shoulders. "I was just going to the bathroom and..."

"There's a bathroom attached to our bedroom," I hum, stepping up to her and putting the bow under her chin. Her eyes lift to mine, reflecting nothing back.

My Little Chaos has this uncanny ability to shut off her emotions. Unless I pry them out of her, which I have no doubt I'll love to do.

"Enlighten me, how'd you manage to squeeze out of the cuffs?" I raise a brow when, once again, nothing gives her away.

She meets my eye with no remorse. "A magician never reveals her secrets."

Feisty. My favorite trait of hers.

I hum, letting the tip of the delicate wooden bow roam across her throat. The beat of her heart pulsates under it, moving with her erratic breaths and heaving chest.

I think back to the moment I dressed her in the closet, remembering the lack of undergarments I put on her body. The tiny black thong is the only thing beneath the silky nightgown hiding her from my prying eyes.

That should change. Immediately.

She shudders when the tip of the bow dips between her breasts, tracing the familiar scar cleverly hidden beneath a tattoo in the shape of a key with vines wrapping around it and flowers blooming.

All the puzzle pieces are clicking together one at a time.

"I'd hazard a guess and say you either slipped your wrist from the metal or somehow worked the lock. You seem like the type of kitten to not be caged."

At her core, she ultimately craves freedom. It's in her movements and motivations. I've watched her for long enough to have figured out that much. Why, though? I haven't a clue. But I'll get it out of her.

"Being attached to you all, twenty-four seven, isn't ideal," she snarks back with a shuddering breath when I trace her hard nipple through her nightgown.

"Your tits say otherwise," I retort, continually tracing the little bud coming to life. "In fact, they look cold. Maybe a warm mouth could help." I raise a brow when she steps back, swatting at the bow nestled in my hand. "Careful, Little Chaos. This bow costs more than your life. You break it. You owe me."

"Then keep it away from me and my tits." She scowls, covering herself. A deep red blush takes over her cheeks.

It's cute she thinks she's in any position to deny me and my tastes. Not that I'd take her unwillingly. On the contrary. I'd rather have Journey West on her knees, begging for my cock, than crying through fear.

One day.

I hum to myself, running my finger along the bow. It's a shame it's about to be smashed. It's a rarity, almost worth fifteen grand. It was one of the first pieces I bought for myself when my father gave me access to my inheritance. Oh, well. I'll buy another. Bigger. Better. More expensive. There are more rarities in this world. I won't let my Little Chaos rule this house. She will submit to me and my brothers. Wear what I say. Do as I say. Sit when I say.

"You know bows are made from fine horse hair. Each time I play, I loosen them to avoid any damage. Meticulously clean it to spare it from the oils of my skin. It's a piece of art in itself. Magical even," I hum, continuing to stroke the fine hairs between my fingers, effectively ruining it in one swoop.

"Nice story. Can I go get a snack now?"

I raise a brow, watching as she twitches toward the door, aching to leave me so soon.

She's a runner, indeed. The moment we leave her alone, she'll take off going wherever she wants to go. Interesting. I'll have to put that to the test and then punish her for defying me. Shit. My dick thickens, rubbing against my sweatpants as it chubs.

"You will not leave this room until you tell me how you escaped. By the look in your eyes, you were headed for the front door. Were you going to run all the way back to your condemned trailer, Little Chaos? There's no escape for you." Goosebumps pebble across her delicate skin when I step forward, circling her body like a shark at sea. She's the blood, pulling me in.

And I'm ready to fucking devour her.

She frowns, eyeing me as I circle her. "I told you I was hungry, and it's May. It's not cold outside," she huffs.

I stop behind her, gathering her curls in my fist and yanking her head back. Her back arches, and her fingernails dig into my arm. Fuck. The pain of her scratch soars through my veins, bringing me back to life.

Without a thought, I march her forward until her hips bump into the front of my massive wooden desk. She bucks, trying to push me off, but I don't relent. I put the full force of my body into her backside until she's immobile, breathing heavily.

"Get off me," she yelps, attempting to elbow me again.

Not a chance.

She's fortunate I'm not wearing a belt, or I'd tie her hands together and bind her until she couldn't move. Luckily for her, I'm only in a pair of sweatpants.

"You're underestimating who I am and what I do," I whisper into the shell of her ear. I may be obsessed with every molecule in her body, but I won't let her repeatedly disrespect me. "I interrogate liars every day. I have since I was eight." I roll my lips together, breathing through the memories. "Liars spit in my face daily, telling me made-up stories. Now, you're lying right to my face. Which was it, Baby? Bathroom or snack?" I press harder into her back until she's bent over my desk. Her ass rubs against my dick. And my sweatpants do little to hide the growing want.

"Both," she croaks.

"Liars get punishments," I murmur in her ear. "One last chance to confess to your crimes, and maybe I'll go easy on you."

Her breaths echo through the room as her muscles tighten. I can tell by her reaction what's about to come out of her filthy, lying mouth.

"Both," she growls, hissing when I shove the side of her face into the desktop.

"Punishment it is," I say, not loosening my hold on her. "Put your palms down on the desk. And do not move them."

"You're not the goddamn boss of me," she hisses, grunting when I force her palms down flat on the desk.

"That's where you're wrong. I'm your boss. Your king. Your everything," I whisper directly in her ear, listening to her ragged breaths as she fights my hold.

"You're nothing!" she grits out, shivering when I kiss her cheek. "You kidnapped me. You stole my home. You handcuffed me to your wrist and forced me to sign a contract."

A smile curves my lips. "Because you refused to see me for what I am. Yours. And you're mine. Now, I want some truths off your lying tongue," I murmur.

"What the fuck?" she whispers. "What the hell are you doing?" She squirms as my hand works up her thighs, dragging the material of her silky nightgown until it's bunched at her hips, exposing her ass. The tiny thong I instructed her to wear does nothing to hide her from me. "Jericho!" she warns, trying to wiggle out of my grasp.

"Here are the rules, Little Chaos. You will count every whack I give until we get to ten. By the time we get to ten, you'll tell me where you're going, not before then. You'll take your ten lashings like a good little girl. Nod if you understand."

Every muscle in her body stiffens when my hand rubs along

her bare cheek, soothing it before I inflict pain. I hum when she glares at me from over her shoulder, not acknowledging what I said.

I test her flesh, gently smacking her ass with my hand until she yelps, stiffening from the stinging pain.

"You will acknowledge me," I demand into her ear, letting my warm breath brush against her flesh. "Say, yes, Jericho, I understand." I squeeze her cheek hard, and her breath hitches. The smell of her arousal permeates the damn air, hardening me further. "Be a good girl because my patience is wearing thin."

I give her a few seconds to work through what I said. I'm sure it's difficult to give control over to me with how hard-headed she is. She'll learn soon enough.

"Yes," she grits out, gasping when I hit her with my palm again, leaving a pretty red hand mark on her delicate flesh.

"You're forgetting a part," I chuckle.

"Jericho," she grunts. "Yes, Jericho."

"Such a good girl. Now, you'll stay where you are and count your punishment to ten. Understand?"

"Yes, Jericho," she snarks with fire brewing in her eyes.

"Never lose that fire, Chaos. Let it shine bright," I whisper, grabbing my violin bow from the desk. Her breath hitches again when I run the tip of it down her spine and over the bare curve of her ass. "I'll never put your fire out. I'll kindle it in my palm forever. You and me? We're gasoline. An explosion. Now, count." I don't give her a chance to respond when the first hit whacks against her fair skin. I suck in a breath, watching the red form on her flesh, and my dick twitches at the sight of her blemished skin. "You didn't count."

"One," she hisses with displeasure. Whack. "Two." Whack. Whack. Whack. "Three. Four. Five." Whack. Whack. Whack. "Six. Seven. Eight." Whack. Whack. "Nine. Ten," she gasps out, arching her back further by the time I'm done. Her breaths ring out through the room.

My hand rubs along her flesh, soothing the burn sizzling beneath her skin.

"Are you ready to confess your sins to me, Little Chaos? Tell me why you're wandering around in the early hours of the day when you should still be sleeping. Better yet," I lean in so my back is draped over her, and every inch of my body presses into hers. "How'd you escape?"

There's a moment in everyone's life when they weigh their options. It's written in the minuscule movements on their faces. The curling of their fists or the shift of their posture. The widening of their eyes. And in her case, the dilation of her pupils, blackening her moss-green eyes.

"Just a reminder, I can keep you here all day. You have so much flesh to pretty up with my bow until it snaps in two," I whisper again, sucking her earlobe into my mouth and nibbling on it. Fuck. She shivers against me. Her breath hitches. God damn. She's so turned on I can smell her cunt from here, making me want to do wicked, beautiful things to her. But I won't. My dick will stay firmly in my pants until I walk her down the aisle and say I do.

"You wouldn't," she challenges with a moan.

Normally, I'd call her bluff. But I have better plans for her.

"Oh, I would. You keep telling me what I won't do. I should wash that from your vocabulary right now with my dick down your throat. I've seen and done things you can only imagine. So, confess to me, or I'll continue to drag it out of you."

Out of the corner of my eye, a pair of bright eyes catches my attention. He swallows hard, watching from the shadows of the entrance with flushed cheeks. Red still paints his skin when he nods in my direction, watching.

She huffs, drawing me back to her. "I was sneaking outside," she barely whispers, melting when I rub her ass again, soothing the hurt I inflicted. Something I'll take care of later with ointments, among other things. A good man takes care of his woman after they play.

"Mmm. Good girl. Now, what else?" I whisper, moving my fingers to the seam between her legs to entice her more. Luckily, she spreads her legs for me, adjusting to the slight touch through her soaked panties. "Fuck," I hiss when I pull her thong aside, moving my fingers between her folds, noting the wetness coating her and now me. "Did I unlock something inside you, Little Chaos?" My finger dives inside her, remembering the night I took her innocence behind my mask.

"Maybe," she moans, laying her forehead on the desk. "Fuck." She quivers when I add a second and pump my fingers in and out, scissoring inside her.

"Tell me how you escaped," I say, keeping an even tone when I pull my fingers out of her sopping pussy and put them directly on my tongue, humming at the taste of her.

She quiets down. Not making a sound. Her fingers curl on the desk, no longer keeping her palms flat. Her fist pounds into the wood in defeat. I smile.

"Turn around, Little Chaos. Sit on the edge of my desk with your legs spread."

I step back, letting her make the move without force. I want all of this to be her decision. I won't take it from her. She'll gladly give it up to me with a smile. Well, maybe not a smile. No. She's not happy about it at all. Not my demands. Not the fact she's soaking wet from the spanking she received. She's angry that she's vibrating with lust.

And that's all for me.

But, she oddly does as I say, sitting on the edge of my desk with her legs spread, only covered by the nightgown and her sopping wet thong. Progress, I suppose.

"So," I say, stepping forward and gripping her chin. "Your answer?"

"Fuck you," she whispers, with that fire igniting once again.

Good girl. I want to keep that flame and defiance alive and kicking.

I smile, fingering the now-cracking bow in my hand. The

delicate wood creased on several parts from the blows to her ass, almost to its breaking point. I suppose it's a symbol of the woman in front of me. They're both cracked and blemished but not fully broken.

Oh, well.

"Last chance. I have more in store for you. More toys to use. I could bring you to the brink of coming all day and watch as you suffer on the edge of oblivion. I'll tie your hands and feet with rope to secure you for me as I suck your clit and force you to squirt on my face." I grin when she flushes again, glaring in my direction. "If you tell me, I'll give you a generous reward."

Journey weighs her options again. "Fine." She crosses her arms over her chest, closing her legs.

"Ah, open," I say, smacking her upper thigh through her clothing. "Good girl."

"Could you stop saying that? I'm not a goddamn dog! We've been through this," she growls, on the edge of smacking me silly.

I smile, leaning forward, tearing her thong in two and discarding it beside me. Before she can even protest, I'm slamming my fingers straight into her pussy, making her gasp and moan.

"I'll stop calling you a good girl when your cunt stops dripping for the praise." I work my fingers in and out again, making the come hither movement against her G-spot. Her back arches and toes curl, and that's my signal to pull away. "Bad girls who bite their tongue don't get orgasms."

She quivers, too proud to beg me for an orgasm. Her eyes narrow at me.

"Fine. Fucking fine. You left the key on the counter! I stuck it under my tongue and used it when Arrow passed out." She says each word through a heavy breath, practically panting with expectations.

Well, color me impressed. My Little Chaos is a crafty little whore. One who deserves a reward for her honesty.

"Lie back," I demand, stroking my bow one last time. "Open your legs." I tap her inner thighs again with my bow, reddening her flesh. "Oh, and Sheppard, you can come in," I holler, bringing the man forward from the shadows of the hallway. He frowns, longingly staring at her with warmth. "We've had a watcher."

Just like me, Shepp is heavily affected by the heady scent of pussy permeating through the room.

Her chest heaves when I pull her body forward, dangling her hips off the edge of the desk.

"I'm going to have a meal. You're going to come on my tongue, and Sheppard is going to hold your wrists. Or maybe you feel like being a good girl and sucking the soul from his dick," I say, grinning when Sheppard shudders, glaring at me.

'*Asshole*,' he signs with an eye roll.

I snort. '*Really?*' I sign back, keeping her out of the conversation. '*You're about to slip your dick between her lips, and you're calling me an asshole?*'

He huffs again, shaking his head. '*I want her to do it only if she wants to. I can't...*' Ever the saint. He'll always ask permission before taking.

"What is he saying?" Journey asks with hooded eyes.

"He wants to make sure you're okay with sucking his cock." I raise a brow when she flushes again. Good God, the color red looks magnificent on her cheeks. I want to paint her in it. Or maybe Shepp does. I grin at the imagery of her dripping in red paint or blood, loving the idea of it. "What do you say, Little Chaos? Will you let him coat your throat in his cum and make his day while I lick you dry?"

Journey shudders when my fingers run between her wet lips, dipping the tip of my finger into her. "What a greedy pussy you have, Little Chaos." I grin when her eyes roll into the back of her head, and her back arches off the desk the moment I plunge three fingers in, wiggling them around. "Now, will you open your mouth or..." I trail off when she nods vigorously, slumping into the desk. "Well, it looks like this is your lucky day, Shepp. She's agreed."

He glares at me again, shaking his head like I didn't just aid in his pleasure. How ungrateful can one man be?

"Your loss or gain. I don't care." I shrug, dropping to my knees and bringing myself to eye level with her glistening pussy, aching for me to fuck her. But I won't. Not yet. Not until she deserves to be fucked.

I focus on her when the sound of Shepp's zipper dropping and his slight intake of breath fills the air. She moans around his cock when I dive in, swirling my tongue around her clit over and over. My fingers soak to the bone with her pussy juices, loving the way her walls contract around me the moment her orgasm hits, and she cries out around Shepp's cock. I smile, kissing the insides of her thighs, and suck the flesh into my mouth.

I could fuck her now. I could sink so deep inside of her and never leave. But she tried to run. She tried to leave my home without us.

Standing abruptly, I watch his cock pump in and out of her mouth with measured thrusts. He's holding back, enjoying the way she feels wrapped around him. I admire him for holding back, but it's something I'll never do.

Without a thought, I pull my cock from my sweatpants, stroking myself a few times. Standing above her, I moan, squeezing my dick hard with my hand. Tingles erupt all over my body, and my toes curl into the floor as my orgasm roars through me, and I shoot my load all over her pussy until I'm spent. Static fills my ears when I slump forward, catching my breath. Seeing her painted in my cum has my dick hardening from its flaccid state, ready to go again until she's covered from head to toe. Fuck.

I lick my lips, collecting my cum off her flesh, and shove it straight into her pussy. My fingers work in and out, until she's tightening around my fingers again, ready to come.

"I'll never waste a drop," I grunt, until every bit is secured inside her and not falling out.

One day, we'll have her locked tight as ours with a baby in her belly. And from what I've read in her medical records, she has something preventing that from happening. Removing the pesky IUD inside her is at the top of my list of things to do.

Soon.

Shepp lets out a sharp breath, stiffening and unloading himself down her throat until he stumbles back. With stars in his eyes, he stares at her like she hung the moon in the sky, and we revolve around her. Maybe we do.

"Fucking perfect," I whisper, admiring the sweat forming on her brow. "Such a good little girl, Little Chaos." I grin.

"Stop calling me that," she whines through exhaustion, slumping into the desk.

"Not a chance." Walking around her body, I clap Shepp on the shoulder when he tucks himself back into his pants, letting go of Journey, who doesn't move an inch. "I'll call you as I please. And you'd know the rules if you read the contract."

"How do I know you're not just making the rules up?" she huffs, rubbing at her eyes.

"I could be," I quip, finally feeling the edge of sleepiness tug at my consciousness. "Up you go, Little Chaos. Let's go back to bed. And this time, no running away."

Journey groans when I scoop her into my arms, and her protests begin.

"You coming?" I ask Shepp, who nods with the ghost of a smile, following as we trudge toward the bedroom. "Oh, you should know, I'll keep a better eye on you now." I grin when she stiffens in my arms right before I deposit her onto the bed and relock her to Arrow, who hasn't moved a muscle. His arm instinctively wraps around her, pulling her back close to his front. He's always slept like the damn dead, never moving when an alarm goes off.

Shepp signs, '*I'm cleaning up. You're going to sleep?*'

I shake my head. For the first time in five years, I feel the exhaustion pulling me under. Once again, I ignore it. I can sleep when I'm fucking dead. I have business to attend to downtown. My eyes dart to Journey as her eyes flutter shut. The events of the past twenty-four hours must have worn her out. I smile. Good. She snuggles down into Arrow's hold. Once he wakes up, ready to go, he'll be upset we had a little fun without him.

Oh, well. That's not my problem.

"Be good, Little Chaos," I whisper, moving a hair from her face. I grin when she flips me off and quickly falls to sleep in Arrow's arms.

Shepp watches me closely when I venture into my closet and get dressed into my usual attire. A nice white button down, slacks, black socks, and dress shoes.

"I have some business to attend to downtown. I won't be gone long," I say, straightening my sleeves.

'*You want me to drive you?*' Shepp signs, watching me closely.

"Not necessary today. I'll take care of this quickly and then come home," I say, gently slapping him on the shoulder. "No worries, Sheppy. I'll be fine. It's time for me to uncover Jezebel and take her for a ride." He blinks several times as I reach into my nightstand and grab the keys to my car I keep hidden in my garage, attempting to preserve her miles and paint.

I can already feel the cool leather of my favorite car under my fingertips, soothing away any worries I have. Nothing quite takes my anxiety away like a fast car and a quick trip to the courthouse.

I leave Shepp stunned in the doorway, watching me as I leave toward my office where I grab a few stacks of papers. Once in the garage, I uncover my car, store the tarp, and climb inside.

I grin when I hold the contract binding Journey to me. Sure, I'm the law in my fucking house, and this contract holds no real authority in the outside world. Only within these walls where she'll abide by all my rules.

And now, it's time to truly make her mine. Thanks to her lovely little signature.

Today, she'll be my wife.

CHAPTER THIRTY-THREE

Shepp

'*You can't be serious*,' I sign, watching Journey out of the corner of my eye, huffing when Arrow pulls at the handcuffs with a grin. Much like Jericho, he loves riling her up and watching her go off like a bomb.

Me, though? I'd rather harness her energy and paint her into oblivion. I blow out a breath, aching to feel my brush between my fingers and stroking her skin with red.

'*I am*,' Jericho signs back with a smirk.

I jerk my gaze to his eyes when he doesn't make a sound. He's using my language to conceal our plans from her. But why?

'*Why?*' Arrow signs with his cuffed hand, crunching into an apple as we sit around the large living room.

He grins when Journey pulls at the cuff to turn the page of her book. Discreetly, Journey watches our interactions as we sign to one another. Taking it all in, one sign at a time. By the determined glint in her eyes, she'll have ASL down in two weeks flat. If that's even possible. Learning a new language can be difficult, but for her, it'd come in handy.

'*She'll leave*,' I sign. A knot forms in my stomach at the realization of his fucked up plans.

Jericho smirks, signing, '*She will.*'

'*Don't worry, Sheppy. I put a tracker in her ass. Even if she runs *away to Mexico, I'll find her. It's very accurate,'* Arrow signs quickly, leaving the apple in his mouth as he does so.

'*Good,*' Jericho signs.

"It's rude to have conversations where one party can't understand what's being said," Journey huffs, folding her arms over her chest.

"It's not a conversation that concerns you," Jericho voices sharply, adjusting his suit sleeve. "We're leaving tonight, and you're staying here."

Journey doesn't flinch. "Where are you going?"

I eye my phone, noting it's 7:30 p.m. We have thirty minutes to make it to our destination. By eight p.m, we'll be on our knees awaiting our official ceremony of initiation.

"That's for us to know and for you to never find out. But I trust you'll be a good little girl and keep your ass parked in this house." Not likely, but he obviously has a plan since we'll be holed up at our initiation tonight. Something she's not allowed to come to.

Again, she doesn't give anything away, hiding whatever she's feeling behind a solid cement wall. My eyes flick to Jericho, who cocks his head.

"Understood?"

She rolls her eyes, flipping a page in the book on her lap. It's something we found on her nightstand. Some strange turkey shifter book, that I definitely didn't read in my spare time to understand her fascination with it. Three triplet turkeys fucking the same girl. Hell, even like Arrow, they stole her dildo. Well, she threw it at them through a window when they were peeping. Huh. Maybe she's actually into that sort of thing. Good news for her then, that's Arrow to a T.

"I'm not a dog," she huffs, turning a page.

"I beg to differ," Jericho goads. "Sit. Stay. Now, crawl to me."

She doesn't pay him any attention, focusing on her book. Even as Arrow chuckles beside her. It's like she knows the exact buttons to push, and Jericho falls for it every time.

"Yeah, crawl, Little Kitten," Arrow quips. "I can even get you a collar and a leash. Oh! And a tail." He wiggles his brows as she sputters.

"No thank you. I'm trying to finish this book," she mumbles, bringing it closer to her face, hiding the red tint on her cheeks.

"I'm buying her the tail," Arrow whispers, bringing his phone out and typing in a search. "Kitten! This one comes with ears. It's a blue fox! It's perfect for you! Oh, look! There's a kitten one, too. I'm getting it!" He turns the phone toward her, and she blanches, shaking her head with something odd twinkling in her eyes.

They say the eyes are the window to the soul. And I think they're correct. Journey doesn't let much through. Somehow, she's trained herself to look as if she has no emotions. But sometimes, it comes through like a neon sign flashing her feelings to everyone. And right now, she's more than intrigued by what Arrow is showing her.

"There is no way in hell that is going up my ass," she hisses.

"You say that now," Jericho says with a grin, climbing to his feet. "But it's in the contract."

"Again with the contract, asshole," she hisses, tossing her book onto the couch. "You can't..."

Great. Here we go. The wind up and fall apart.

Jericho marches forward, wrapping his fingers around her throat. In normal circumstances, the person at the helm of his anger usually flinches and begs. Not her. Her fire burns too bright, and there's no way he'd snuff that out.

"The contract is binding in my kingdom, Little Chaos. There is nowhere else for you to go and nothing you can say to sway what will happen between us," he grits out, pulling her closer and closer until their noses touch and their breaths ring out. "If Arrow wants to shove a tail up your ass, then so be it. I'll put the ears on your head and the collar around your throat. And then, I'll fuck you."

She shivers under his stare, squeezing her eyes shut at the imagery. If he talks about it anymore, we're all going to be late.

"We're running out of time, bro. If we don't get our asses moving, your daddy is going to come and track us down," Arrow chides, watching them with amusement.

"So, will you be my good girl and stay put?" Jericho asks, gently kissing her cheek. "Or am I going to have to bend you over my desk again and show you who owns your ass?"

Jericho chuckles when she pushes him away.

"I can't believe you guys had fun without me. Wake me up next time," Arrow pouts with a huff.

"Wake you up?" Jericho scoffs, fixing his clothes. "There is no waking you up. You're dead to the world."

Arrow grins. "Especially when I take a sleeping pill. They were fun, Little Kitten. Is that why you like them?"

Journey blinks a few times. "You have my pills?"

"Only one. Well, had one," Arrow says with a shrug.

"That poison is no longer necessary for you," Jericho scoffs.

"You're not a fucking God!" she shouts, quickly standing and pulling Arrow along with her.

Jericho grins. "Inside these four walls, I'm your fucking God, Little Chaos. I dictate everything about you. What you take. What you eat. What you wear. I suggest you get used to it. I don't relinquish control to anyone."

Mindlessly, I shake my head. He's always been hard to deal with, needing everything in a certain order and demanding perfection. But it's how Gabriel raised him and wanted him to be. He's not as brainwashed as he was before. None of us are. But shaking those bad habits off isn't easy. It's ingrained in his DNA to demand everything of her and expect her to fall to her knees for him.

"I need them," she hisses, poking him in the chest. "You don't understand what you're saying." Her teeth clench so tight together, I swear she's about to blow a gasket right here and obliterate Jericho where he stands.

I swallow hard, remembering the night I tucked her in, soothing the nightmare pulling her under. My fingers massage my throat, smothering the tightness threatening to cut off my air. I spoke. I fucking talked her down from the cliff she was falling off of.

And I haven't done it again since. I know I can. But every time I go to open my mouth, nothing comes out.

"You don't. You have us." He shrugs without a care, turning his back on her. "And Arrow is right. We're going to be late, boys. It's high time we become men. What do you say?"

"Hells to the yeah! Now, where shall I cuff my little kitten?" Arrow asks, holding out his hand until Jericho hands him the keys to the cuffs.

"She's free to roam the house," Jericho says. "But know this, Little Chaos. We have our eyes on you at all times." His eyes scour the corners of the room, conveying the fact we have cameras everywhere.

You can't be mafia royalty and not have extra provisions in place to ensure your safety. Besides, Jericho is extra vigilant when it comes to this home and our girl.

"Run, Little Kitten. I fucking dare you to," Arrow goads, unlocking the cuff from his wrist and hers. Leaning in, he kisses her cheek and holds her close. "Please run. I want to chase you through the woods." He grins.

Journey blinks at him in a stupor. "When will you be home?"

"Why? So you know when to be back?" Jericho asks with a smirk. "Don't you worry your pretty little head off, Little Chaos. We'll be back when we're good and ready. Now, shall we?" He waves a hand toward the door, and I nod.

Jericho and I respect each other, much like we respect Arrow. There has to be that in a brotherhood like this. Trust is the most important attribute we have between one another. We can't move forward with our plans and not have trust between us. It's the most important thing, something that's been broken for each of us by people we should have trusted the most.

I shudder, squeezing my eyes shut when I grab my keys. Images of my father's cruel smile and hands have me momentarily frozen until Arrow slaps me on the shoulder as he passes by, grabbing the keys from me. Like fuck would Jericho trust him to drive. He's crazier behind the wheel going thirty miles per hour than running at top speed. Arrow behind the wheel is a disaster waiting to happen.

I nibble my lip, looking at Journey as she stands in the middle of the living room, watching our departure with interest. I blow out a breath when I reach her, running my fingers through her curly hair.

"Are you worried I'll leave, too?" she asks, tipping her chin up.

No. I'm not worried she'll leave. I know she will. There's no worrying about it. I'm just eager to hear why Jericho is so adamant about this.

I shrug, leaning in to kiss her cheek, too. When I pull back, I offer her a soft smile, trying to convey the words I cannot speak. Instead, I hand her a tiny note, telling her to eat. It's something she doesn't seem to do enough of. If it were up to me, I'd have her in the kitchen right now, hand feeding her the special lasagna I made specifically for her. It's her favorite. Something I've made for her and her mom multiple times over the years since I've kept my eyes on her.

Her expression softens when she reads the note. "Is there something special for me in the fridge?" Those moss-green eyes I could get lost in, examine my face, stalling on the long scar, lining my cheek. I see the question in her eyes. The—who did this to you —question lingering on her tongue.

But she doesn't ask. And I'm not ready to give a piece of myself up like that.

I nod my answer, wishing I could speak again. But something holds me back, even though she didn't seem to.

"Shepp?" she asks softly as I run my fingers over her lips. "Can you... Can you speak?" she asks with hesitation, furrowing her brows.

My heart leaps from my chest.

"I had a dream about you," she whispers, looking away as I

continue tracing her plump lower lip, wishing I could kiss her. "I had a dream you were..." She shakes her head. "You were there, and you soothed me when I was crying."

Well, she's not far off from the truth. I was there. I did soothe her. But to her, my voice was only in a dream. For now, I'll keep it that way.

When people see me signing, they assume that I'm either deaf or mute. Technically, I still have my voice. My vocal cords are there, buried deep, and unwilling to resurface. Only when I need them most. Like the night in her bedroom.

My father took it from me, just like he wanted to. And even though he's dead, I still haven't spoken a word since that night, other than to Journey.

"Open your goddamn mouth, you ungrateful shit," he slurs, pulling my lips apart with such force that tears fill my eyes. A scream falls from my throat when I lose the battle, and it clamps around my tongue, holding it still.

"I didn't! I won't tell again!" I try to shriek as sobs roar through me. "I'll be good!" I try to shout through the metal resting on my tongue, making it impossible to move it. My heart pounds so violently in my chest that I swear it's about to escape and run away like I want to.

My breath shudders at the stark memory of my father and the night he stole my voice for his own gain.

Fingers brush against my cheek when I open my eyes, and Journey stares at me with concern, bringing me back from the brink of having to relive my nightmare over and over.

I nod.

"But you don't?" she asks softly.

I smile, nodding. It's more complicated than what I'm leaving her with. But I have to.

'*I have to go,*' I sign, knowing she'll never understand what I'm trying to say. I could speak to her again. If only I could get myself to do it. My words are frozen in my throat, unable to filter through. So, I continue doing what I know how to do—signing.

'I haven't spoken a word since I was ten. My father took that from me like he took a lot of things without asking. One day, I'll find the courage to fully use my voice again. But today is not the day.' Maybe not any day. I've lived without my voice for so long that maybe it doesn't want to ever come out again. Maybe it was her distress that called it out.

Journey's brows furrow. "I'm sorry. I don't understand sign language."

'Not yet though, huh?' I sign with a smile; digging into my pocket, I pull out a notebook and a pen. I could have done this from the very beginning and given her my words written down. But where's the fun in that?

One day you will. Be good. Eat the lasagna.

Ripping off the piece of another piece of paper, I lay it in her hands, reminding her for a second time to eat. Without looking over my shoulder at her reaction, I make my way out of the house and into the driver's seat of our SUV. Arrow and Jericho bicker in the backseat in a heated conversation when I start the vehicle up and throw it into gear, making our way down the mile-long drive toward the gates. Thankfully, our cars have sensors on them to open the gate without having to stop and do it manually. For anyone else, they'd be stopped and have to speak with our guard stationed at the entrance.

"What's your verdict, Sheppy Boy? Do you think it's smart to leave her here all alone? I told Jer we should hog-tie her and put her in the trunk with a gag. At least we'd know where she was while we bend our knees," Arrow says with way too much glee, thinking about the blood we're about to spill in the name of the Viotto Crime Family.

It's not enough we have to lower ourselves to our knees and basically worship Jericho's father and the rest of his bosses. We bleed for them to show our loyalty. One long cut down the center of our chest, almost over our hearts. Blood out for the family.

'*She's going to run*,' I quickly sign when we stop at the end of the drive and pull onto the main road. But she also wants to stay. She wants to figure us out, like we do her. But she won't unpeel our layers without us finding out her secrets first. It's just how it works in our house.

"Of course she is," Jericho scoffs. "The only question is to where and why?"

Arrow's grin grows as I look between him in the rearview mirror and the dark road ahead. "Oh, I have a fun idea as to where she'll go. Doesn't matter, anyway. My Kitten is tracked."

Jericho blinks when Arrow hands him pictures from his suit jacket. His gaze whips from Arrow to the photos. Every muscle in his body turns rigid behind me, and his teeth clench tightly.

"Just as I suspected," he grunts, tossing the photos back to Arrow. "When?"

"A few nights ago," Arrow says with pride.

"And you just thought to hand them to me now?" Jericho growls with irritation.

"Well, what's the fun in showing you right away when we're about to face the man? Huh? This is perfect."

"She's in bed with the fucking enemy!" Jericho shouts, punching the chair in front of him.

"I heard some things while I lounged on that dirty burnt floor. You know, it was a lot of fun revisiting our old stomping ground. Ah, the screams they scrumt. That's a word I learned by the way," Arrow says with a manic grin, pointing in our direction. "Anywho. Being back to the warehouse where we fucked up that shipment got me all relaxed and ready for action. And then, they walked in. Her and..."

"The goddamn enemy," Jericho growls.

"Yeah, that. The enemy. Do you still have her phone?"

"Not on me," Jericho grits out, blowing out a breath to contain his anger. "It's locked in the safe with her contract."

"And what was on it?"

"Not a goddamn thing," Jericho huffs. "It's like..." He blinks a few times.

"It seems to me, we're not the only ones with AntiEyes on our phones." Arrow shrugs.

"So, our girl has ties with the enemy..." Jericho trails off, slumping in his seat.

"Exactly," Arrow says, leaning back. "It's time to fuck some answers out of our Kitten tonight."

Jericho raises a brow. "Seems like you have something cooking in your evil brain."

The smile he gets in return as we pull in front of the large church in the middle of Briar Cove sends shivers down my spine. I'm used to him by now. Used to his wicked ways and the looks he gives.

"I've got a plan." That's all he says before he shoves out of the backseat without waiting for me to park the fucking car.

'Are you as scared as I am about whatever he's got cooking?' I sign when the car is in the park, and we've exited the vehicle.

"Never," Jericho murmurs as we come to stand together in front of the large church built over a hundred years ago.

Arrow breaks rank when his father emerges from the large wooden church doors with a soft smile.

"Son," he says softly, pulling Arrow into a hug.

You'd never suspect someone as unhinged as Arrow is to have such a loving father he left behind. Sure, his mother is in the wind. But his dad? That man loves him with all his heart.

"Ready to watch me become a man, Pops?" he asks his father, tugging at the white robes hugging his father's body.

Father Amour smiles at him and pats his cheek. "You've been a man for some time, Arrow. But I'm proud of you nonetheless."

"Thanks, Pop," Arrow says, leaning in and kissing him on the cheek. "Come on, assholes. Let's get initiated," he says with a whoop, stepping back from his father. "Sorry about the assholes, Pops. I hope the big man upstairs doesn't mind."

Vincent chuckles, clapping him on the shoulder. "He doesn't

mind, Son. He knows. He knows," he murmurs the last part, leading us into the empty church, creaking with every burst of wind. "Well, you boys know where to wait?"

"We do," Jericho says with a sharp nod. "Good to see you, Priest."

"And you, too. I'll see you boys on Sunday," he says with a soft smile, eyeing us before he turns on his heel and marches toward his office.

"How's our little captive fairing?" Jericho asks, nudging Arrow with his shoe.

Arrow grins, pulling out his phone. After a few clicks, he chuckles. "She's on the move."

"Headed where?" Jericho grumbles, waving us toward the secret door, disguised as a bookcase, leading to a set of stairs.

"Wherever she's going, she's going fast." Arrow squints at the screen.

Jericho stops dead when the bookcase pops open, revealing our destination. His teeth grind together when he pulls out his phone, bringing up the cameras set up all around our home.

"Holy fucking shit. She took the Maserati!" Arrow cackles, throwing his head back.

Jericho's fingers tighten around his phone as his breaths pour from his flaring nostrils.

His precious car. The one he has covered in his garage to preserve the custom paint job he had put on there a year ago. He refuses to drive the thing, trying to keep the miles low and the tires like brand new.

"She took my goddamn car!" he shouts, nearly throwing his phone across the room.

"Don't worry, Jer. We can punish her later. With our dicks. And then, we can fuck the secrets from her lips," Arrow says in a low voice.

Jericho's jaw tics. "Yes to the fucking. I'm going to punish her. Hard and goddamn fast. Mine first," he growls, squeezing his eyes shut.

"No secrets?" Arrow pouts.

"No. She won't tell us. Not until she trusts us. We wait. We gather and follow. Then, we interrogate. Whatever she's hiding is huge, and I for one don't want to fuck it up by hounding her too early." He rubs his chin in contemplation, clearly knowing what he's talking about.

'And how do you expect to do that?' I sign.

By the determined gleam in his eyes, I realized we're about to find out how to make Journey spill all her secrets without working too hard.

"You'll see," Jericho says with a nod. "Now, let's fall to our knees and bleed for the family."

What he doesn't include in his speech is the words, the family we're going to turn on their heads and make them wish they hadn't given us so much power.

"Let's do it," Arrow says with a feral growl, marching down the darkened steps and straight into our destiny.

A fate that has been mapped out for us since we were born. Well, Jer and I, at least. Arrow, much later in life. But he was made for this. Made to be a Viotto.

Me? Sometimes I'm not sure.

I'm just tumbling through life, landing wherever Jer needs me. That's my fate. One day, we'll lead this town and throw Gabriel in the dirt where he belongs. Right next to my father's grave. Only this time, all their honor will be stripped from them and their names gone from history.

One day, we'll make this right.

And our first step is walking down these stairs into the cavernous stone room with elegant archways and a small stage to live out the fate handed to us.

"Come on, Sheppy Boy!" Arrow shouts from below with enthusiasm.

I swallow hard, peeking behind me. Arrow's father is gone. The church is completely devoid of life, except for the three of us as we wait. The bookcase creaks when I close it behind me and make my way down the darkened stairwell. This isn't the first time the boys and I have made our way down here. Long ago, when we were sixteen, we pledged ourselves as initiates, promising to prove ourselves before our full initiation.

That was then.

This is now.

We're several years wiser, having been in the thick of our mafia lifestyle. Now is the time to make changes. For us. For Journey. For our future.

Jer stands in the middle of the large room at the bottom of the stairs with his hands on his hips. His eyes dart around the space, taking in the small stone platform, rising a few inches off the ground. That's where his father will stand and where mine would have, too, during the ceremony.

"Well, boys. This is it," he says coolly, sweeping an arm around the room. "Our destiny has finally come to fruition."

I nod in response, soaking in the atmosphere.

"Shirts off, bitches!" Arrow shouts, grinning when his voice echos. "Tonight, we bleed for a cause, and then, when we return home, we fuck for a cause."

I roll my eyes when Arrow lifts his shirt over his head and throws it at me. '*Real mature*,' I sign with a huff, throwing shirt down.

Once we're completely shirtless, the three of us make our way toward the platform and drop to our knees on the hard surface.

"Tonight is the night," Jericho says again.

"We become men," Arrow says, rubbing his hands together.

'*Men*,' I sign with a snort.

Thick silence weighs heavily on us as we wait for the inevitable. No electronics are allowed beyond the hidden entrance, including watches and phones, so we deposited them in a bowl near the door. As the time passes, we aren't sure how long it's been before the doors open and footsteps follow.

CHAPTER THIRTY-FOUR

Journey

STEALING a car was not on my bingo card this year. Neither was getting kidnapped by deranged mafia men who insist I'm handcuffed to them twenty-four-seven.

But here I am, in the thick of it.

Hurray, me.

All I was doing was looking for my phone in the fancy bedroom they claimed to have built for me. And then, I discovered the Holy Grail of goodies in Jericho's walk-in closet. Right there, in the top drawer of one of his dressers, was my escape.

The moment I found the fancy set of car keys, I knew I had to take them. Because, why not? Honestly, it felt like destiny. Fate led me to find their precious keys, and fate now has me behind the wheel of their expensive car. What was I supposed to do? Walk away? Nope! They wanted to keep me here so badly, they should have chained me to their beds.

I'm sure there's a reason they didn't cuff me before they left. I'm not an idiot. I've been forced to play these games for years, thanks to my monster. Besides, I saw the cameras discreetly mounted on the walls all over the house. They're watching my every move, expecting me to roll over and stay. But like I've told Jericho, I'm not a dog. And I have business to attend to. I'm sure there will be hell to pay when I'm finished. But I don't care. You can't just kidnap a girl from jail with veiled threats and blackmail without backlash. So, here's my backlash.

"Fuck you!" I shout, lifting my finger toward the mansion in my rearview mirror as I drive erratically down the long, winding driveway. Thankfully, when I come near the gate, it automatically opens, allowing me the freedom they denied me.

A thrill shoots through me when I press the accelerator harder, speeding down the main road toward Briar Cove. Skyscrapers tower over the businesses below, lighting up the darkened sky. My eyes fall to the largest tower of them all, standing proud in the center of town like an overseer watching his flock.

It's visible from every direction and is the last thing you see before you leave Briar Cove and the first thing you view when you enter. Almost like a warning to never fuck with the Viotto family and their associates, which makes me laugh. Because that's exactly what I'm doing right now.

I raise my middle finger into the air, proudly pointing it at the unsuspecting building.

"Eat shit!" I shout, pressing on the gas pedal again. Viotto fucking bastards.

My heart pounds with excitement when I arrive in town, blowing through a green light at a high rate of speed. Until I finally slow my pace, careful not to bring too much attention to myself. After all, I'm in a stolen car, and the last place I'd like to see tonight is the inside of a jail cell. Been there—almost—done that, and I never want to experience that again. Especially if I have to greet Jericho's ugly mug when he inevitably bails me out.

Ahh, the beautiful noise this car makes every time I speed up has my heart in a frenzy. This is the most fun I've had in fucking years.

No one can stop me now.

The lights flash by as I make my way toward my trailer in the center of town. They may have condemned it when they took me hostage, but I need to see the inside for myself. Sure, there was tape over the door forbidding anyone to enter. But that could have been a facade to trick me into going with the Three Devils. Not that they needed it, really. They already had me by the short and curlies after signing that damn contract. Even the letters Shepp held in his hands with my name written on the outside of the envelopes could have been faked. Maybe all my shit is still inside, including my last pieces of Sunny.

But I won't know until I see for myself.

I blow out a breath when I pull in front of my former home. Darkness seems to rest around it, shrouding it in shadows. An odd feeling prickles at my skin when I gaze around the surrounding trailer park. Every other place has lights beaming through their windows and activity fluttering around their places. Not this trailer. It's dead. Almost eerily so.

I heave a breath, focusing on the tin can in front of me. So many horrors have happened inside those walls, hidden well behind deception and lies.

How I wish I could bring them to the light and expose my monster for who he truly is—a fucking menace.

My fingers tighten on the expensive steering wheel when I kill the engine. Dread rolls through me. Usually, my mom is in there, nodding off on the couch and waiting for her next hit. If she really is in rehab and getting sober, then I need to find her, too. Maybe she can remember where my monster stashed Sunny. Somewhere in the foggy memories that live in her drug-riddled brain. It has to be there. She's my only hope in finding her. I've had zero ideas as to where my sister is or where to even begin looking for her. Thankfully, she's given me a few clues here and there, but never a name or location.

I lick my lips, peel myself out of the car, and pocket the keys. Rocks crunch under my feet as I make my way up the small drive, climb the wooden stairs of our small deck, and stand before the crumbling front door. This trailer has seen good days. But not for many years.

"This is our new place," my mother says with a bright smile,

twirling in the empty living room. Her brown hair bounces with every excited movement she makes. "This is it, Journey Girl. We've finally found a place to lay our heads." Dropping to her knees, she pulls me into her, brushing my hair behind my ears. "Be good tomorrow, okay? You'll remember what to call him?" Her worried eyes find mine.

"Yeah, Mommy," I whisper. "I 'member."

She swallows hard. "I'm sorry we have to do this." She shakes her head, looking around. "I need the job, and we need the money to keep this up. One day, I'll save enough, okay? Then, we'll run away." She grins again, tucking my long brown hair behind my ears. "Then, we'll be free, Journey Girl." She boops my nose, rising to her feet. "But first, we need some furniture. Let's walk to the thrift shop and see what they have. What do you say?" She grabs my hand, gently squeezing when I nod in agreement.

Standing in the middle of the living room has my heart dropping into my stomach. I'm in the same spot she twirled, eager for our bright future in our new home. Then, without warning, she completely changed when she lost her cleaning job, bringing her into the depths of her depression. Introducing her to her addiction. I lost my mom when she lost her job.

Now, It's gone. Everything we owned has disappeared into thin air like it was never here. The pieces of furniture she worked her ass off to get. Gone. How in the hell did Jericho and his merry band of idiots pull this off in a few hours? I squeeze my eyes shut. They're the mafia; of course, they could have pulled this off.

I twirl in place, noting the pictures missing off the walls, leaving behind a film of yellow from my mother's cigarettes. The couch. The tiny TV my mother insisted on having on full blast. Swallowing hard, I make my way into the kitchen, rummaging through the cabinets and fridge. No food. No plates or glasses. Everything that was once here is gone.

I sigh, staring down the darkened hallway, wondering if my room is intact. Or if they got rid of all my belongings, too. Maybe they're keeping them somewhere in the mansion. Or perhaps, they're at the city dump. I shake my head, making my way toward my room.

When I throw the door open and waltz into my bedroom, tears burn the back of my eyes at the sight.

My eyes dart around the empty, pathetic room devoid of my meager belongings. It's all gone. Everything I've squirreled away throughout my entire life has vanished into thin air. Poof. Gone. Like it was never here.

"Get caught, Little Snake?"

My heart stops when his figure moves from the corner of the room, into the moonlight coming through the window.

"Shit!" I gasp, clutching my chest and heaving a breath. My jaw falls open, and I swear I can't hear anything but the beating of my heart pounding in my ears. "Sir," I sputter out, trying to gain my bearings.

How long has he been waiting for me?

"Seems someone has done a nice clean up job around here." His eyes peer around the room with his lip curled. "Including Sable." He raises a brow, coming more into the light of the moon and standing before me in his immaculate dark suit, fit with a matching tie.

Sable. I only pray she gets the help she needs and stays clean. If she's really at rehab. No matter. I'm committed to finding her and getting the answers I deserve. I need to know where he hid my sister, and my mother might be the only one who knows.

Something about the man standing before me screams more danger than usual. My hackles rise, urging me to tread lightly. Or run. But running hasn't gotten me anywhere. Ever.

I lick my lips, trying to collect myself before I sputter too much bullshit and piss him off. That's the last thing I need to do.

"I..." I begin to say until he holds up a hand.

"Seems you're behind enemy lines now," he says, cocking his head.

Okay. So, he knows who kidnapped me and bound me to

them. Are they seriously the enemy here? Also, does he know about my arrest, too? Shit. Probably.

"They tied my hands." I stand tall and lift my chin, hiding all my insecurities away. It's not a lie.

"So, I've heard. Jericho Viotto has got you by the metaphorical balls. Huh, Little Snake?" he chuckles. "Bound you to him and his fuckwit friends in a contract you so happily signed. It's pretty impressive and ironclad. Even being in the trailer is a violation of your terms."

Shit. I wish I had that contract to read. But I'm too distracted by the gleeful look on his face. Have I ever seen him this happy about my fuck ups? Nope. But I'm not about to interrupt his joy. He can laugh for as long as he wants to, as long as he doesn't slap me.

I nod, rolling my lips. The hairs on the back of my neck stand on end when he saunters closer to me, continuing to chuckle at my expense.

"Oh, Little Snake." His devilish grin sparks panic inside my stomach. It twists and turns when his expression sours.

There it is. That's the danger of my monster. One second, he's laughing. And the next, he's staring me down with cold eyes and rigid muscles like he wants to snap my neck.

He means business now...

"Your task with Elias White and Jenni Thomas is over for now." He taps his chin a few times, beginning to pace in front of me like a blur.

"Are they dead?" I swallow the burning lump in my throat at the prospect of them being dead.

"Do you actually care for your cases?" The way his eyes zero in on the lump sliding down my throat fries my nerves.

Like he knows that Jenni was more than just a girl I was supposed to follow around. I actually liked spending time with her. It was freeing, liberating, and normal. She was the first girl in high school to want to hang out and watch movies on a Saturday night. I may not have enjoyed all the parties and club nights, but I had fun with her.

Over the short period of time, she became my best friend. And now, she's probably dead. I swallow down the emotions attempting to bubble up in my throat. Nope. I can't let this get to me. Jenni was awesome. I felt more freedom with her than I ever have with anyone else. But she's gone. I can't afford to dwell on her not being in my life anymore. So, I let the darkness within me swallow everything I'm feeling and drown them out with numbness.

My darkness is my new best friend.

"Of course not, Sir. I was just curious if they had been taken care of." My fingers tremble behind my back as he thinks over my words and scoffs.

"It's not your job to care or be curious," he snarks through gritted teeth. "You're to move on, which is exactly what you're going to do."

"Of course," I breathe.

Fuck. Now, I'm going to have to find out where Jenni and Elias are. If they're alive. But I keep that to myself and my face devoid of any emotion, even when my brain screams that Jenni was a true friend—a good person, and she didn't deserve to meet her end. All I can hope for is that Elias got her out before it was too late.

"Moving on. Your next task is sitting under your nose. I want you to watch my son and his friends, Sheppard Mondelli and Arrow Amour, too. They are your new jobs. I want details and conversations. Pictures, videos, and anything in between. You're behind enemy lines now, Little Snake. And I want all the details on everything." His grin has my heart dropping into my ass. "You were so good before. Be a good snake for me again."

He wants me to spy on the men holding me hostage? His own flesh and blood? Why? Are they not trustworthy enough for him?

"Yes, Sir. Is there anything I should be looking for specifically?" I ask, stiffening when he narrows his eyes at me.

"Do as you're told!" he shouts, filling the space with his sudden rage, brought on so quickly I swear I have whiplash. "No questions asked." He heaves a breath, waving his arms all around, taking up more space than necessary. "You do a good job at this, and whatever else I might have for you later, then I might just forget about your little arrest and car stunt."

It takes everything in me not to shrink away when he's in my face, spewing his hateful words. Shit. There it is. He knows everything that happens with me. Including my arrest and the men who saved me from prison. But I've trained myself over the years to remain indifferent. Even when he's on the edge of stabbing me.

"Of course," I say evenly. "I'll watch them." Not like I have a damn choice in the matter. They'll track me down and drag me back, kicking and screaming. Besides, where else could I go? My bed is gone. My money is missing.

My whole life rests in their hands. And now, I have to play double agent.

"Good, Little Snake. We'll convene again in one week. You'll know when you see me." His fingers adjust his blackened tie, losing interest in our conversation when he takes a step back.

"They've taken my phone. Um, how should I get in touch?" The last thing I need is for my monster to think I've ghosted him. He'll take it out on Sunny and probably have her killed if I just disappear.

"No need to check in. I have my ways. Enjoy your time spent there," he says with that manic grin again.

"And Sunny?" I blurt. "Is she doing okay?"

I know the moment he spots my desperation when victory flashes in his eyes. She's my weak spot. The one person I'd lay down my life for time and time again. He knows it. I know it. Fuck, the whole world knows it.

A small smirk lies on his lips when he plucks his phone from his pocket and dials a number. Lifting it to his ear, he stares directly into my eyes as he speaks.

"Put Sunshine back on the transplant list. As high as she can go," he says with confidence and hangs up the phone.

I don't dare speak as his words hang heavily in the air. She's back on the list, the highest she can go. If she's next in line, then she'll get a heart sooner than later, bringing her back to me.

"Thank you," I dare to say when he turns on his heel, heading toward my bedroom door.

"Thank me later when you've done your damn job, Little Snake. Don't mistake that tiny slip of kindness toward your sister for anything but motivation. Get me everything you can on those boys. Leave nothing out," he says as he opens my bedroom door and steps out into the hall. "Now, I must go. I have a meeting to attend to. I'd suggest getting back to your prison." He raises a bushy brow when I nod, taking in the room again.

"Of course, Sir," I say, watching every step he takes, slipping into the darkness of the trailer until the front door opens and bangs shut.

I blow out a breath, clutching my chest when I sink to the floor. I'm giving myself five seconds to get my shit together so I can continue my night of mayhem. I'll take Jericho's fancy car for another long joyride, and then, I'll head back to the mansion to find my things.

No one takes my stuff without consequence.

CHAPTER THIRTY-FIVE

Jericho

My jaw clenches tight when footsteps approach from behind us. A pulsating ache reverberates through my knees, and my stiff muscles scream for release. How long we've been down here waiting on our knees for these bastards to show up, I haven't a clue. Arrow, Shepp, and I don't flinch or dare to say hello to the hooded men climbing the small platform before us, keeping my expression neutral when five men stand tall, staring us down. The only thing visible from beneath their masks is their beady eyes, giving way to their identities.

My father, Gabriel, stands in front of the four bosses who serve under him with his hands folded in front of him, taking us in. Slightly behind him is Kent Thomas, his second-in-command. And Jenni's father. Hmm. I wonder if that's where my Little Chaos ventured off to tonight? To see her best friend and gossip about her kidnapping. I want to snort at the idea, but my fist curls. She took my car worth over two hundred grand on a little joy ride. She could be anywhere by now and as far away from us as possible. But if Arrow is correct and the enemy is blackmailing her, then she couldn't possibly leave. Fuck. There's another thing I'm going to have to text my cousin about. Hopefully, she will have something that only Veritas could provide for me soon.

"Good to see you boys know how to follow directions so well," he says in a low, domineering voice, echoing through the room. "But you've always been good leaders and followers, haven't you? Never too proud to take direction as you studied under us. Never too proud to take down an entire building of traitors and guns attempting to infiltrate our city. Your loyalty to this family has been tested over and over. But you've always prevailed." His eyes cut to the three of us again, taking us in on our knees.

Every single one of the masked faces looks to Gabriel Viotto, the boss, waiting for his instruction when he steps out of the lineup and off the platform. Just like the three of us.

He is the king of everyone in this room.

We've been preparing for this moment since we were teenagers. That's when the weekend training camps started. Running, shooting practice, learning what the family truly did in the dark of night. Taking out the trash and disposing of the evidence. It was all about building us into the men they needed us to be. Arrow and Shepp as soldiers behind me, and me, the heir to it all. My father has groomed me in his image, hoping that I continue his legacy when I take over.

I silently suck in a breath, adjusting my position on the hard ground through tiny movements. The cool stone of the basement seeps through my jeans, sending shivers down my spine as goosebumps pebble across the exposed skin of my chest and back.

"Your father would be proud," Gabriel proclaims, his voice easily recognizable under the black mask concealing his hard facial features. Putting a hand on Shepp's shoulder, he gently squeezes with reassurance.

And the award for the biggest liar in the room goes to Gabriel Viotto. What a sick joke. Shepp's father was never proud of him. Even at a young age, I observed him to be a worthless drunk, beating his wife and son into submission. I saw the marks he tried to hide from me at school. Then one day, my talkative best friend showed back up to school after being absent without his fucking tongue.

Fuck that.

Anger bristles under my skin, but I quickly cover it up with deep breaths. *Never show your emotions,* my father would always say. *Never give the enemy any clue as to what you're planning or thinking.* His rules ring through my mind like a ghostly whisper on my shoulder. Always following me around and forcing me to comply with his demands.

Until I started questioning his motives behind his back. Starting with the day he handed me the picture of my wife and informed me of our new alliance. Hopefully soon, my cousin will pull through and shine more light on the situation.

My father slowly moves in front of Arrow, who grins at him. So much for not showing our emotions, but my father doesn't seem to mind. He embraced Arrow's true self many years ago when he basically adopted him from the priest to use him as he pleased. He saw his potential from a mile away, swooping in and offering the priest a reprieve from the shame of having a son out of wedlock.

"Arrow Amour, you've made a fine soldier. You've worked hard and proved your loyalty to this family over and over again." My father slaps him on the shoulder a few times before leaving him and standing in front of me.

"My son. My heir. You've made me proud over the years. I've molded you into the man you are now. And I know you'll continue to make me proud." His dark eyes bleed into mine as pride shines through them. For once, I think my father may feel a sliver of joy for the son he loved to shove in the dark and let cry to sleep.

"Thank you, Father," I say with a small nod.

Stepping back, he says nothing in return, holding out his hands to the four men crowded behind him. They follow his every command like dutiful little soldiers.

"The sword of our allegiance," he demands, wiggling his fingers with impatience toward the men standing stoically behind him.

A single under boss slowly opens a dark black case at his feet, bending at the waist to retrieve a large, intricate sword shining under the candlelight surrounding us and illuminating the large stone space we've adopted as our ceremony stage.

"To the family," Gabriel says, hoisting the sword into the air. "To us. To the organization. To loyalty and blood!" His voice echoes off the stone, lighting a fire in my soul.

There, right before me, is the answer to my prayers. For the family, I'll be loyal—but only for the two men I call my brothers. To Arrow and Shepp, I will protect them. Together we'll fight the good fight and make this organization our bitch. Gabriel doesn't know he's initiating the three demons from hell, hellbent on uprooting everything he's created. Hell, we've already started. And this is just the beginning of everything we have planned.

Gabriel grunts when he throws his black gloves off and runs the blade over his palm. Blood bubbles to the surface of his flesh, spilling out his open wounds when he raises it in the air for us to see.

"Blood out for the family I've pledged myself to. And blood in," he says, holding the bloodied tip of the sword at Shepp's bare chest, carefully slicing through his flesh until his blood mixes with Shepp's, marking him as family. Our blood oath. My brother doesn't flinch when the tip digs in further, slicing straight down the middle between his pecs. Blood paints his flesh, slowly dripping onto the stone between his knees.

"Sheppard," Gabriel demands his attention. "Your father would be standing right beside me at this moment, smiling that his son finally made it to the initiation. We had our doubts," he hums, looking off into the distance.

Fucking prick. Had his doubts? Of course, he'd say something so vile like that to Shepp's face when his father was the one who made him mute. I clench my teeth, biting my tongue. Now is not the time to lash out at my father for his wicked words aimed to hurt. He knows what he's saying and when to say it.

I watch my father's next movements closely when he gets to Arrow, doing the same routine as he did with Shepp. Out of the corner of my eye, Vincent Amour rests in the corner, adorned in his white robes and stoic facial expression. His fingers clasp together tightly as he takes in the scene and sucks in a breath.

"He's done good, Priest," Gabriel remarks, nodding toward the man in the shadows. "You were right to come to me all those years ago." A smug smirk pulls at Gabriel's lips when he squeezes Arrow's shoulder again.

Arrow looks toward his father with a manic grin, reveling in the blood seeping out of his chest and down toward the floor. He doesn't wince or hint at the pain burning through his chest. My bet? He's basking in the pain that he enjoys with every fiber of his being. He was born like that. Loving the pain and suffering. Only Gabriel knew how to harness it for himself and teach Arrow his ways.

"Good," Vincent says with a tight smile, watching his son with glistening eyes. Before we can blink, he silently walks up the stairs and disappears from sight. Not bothering to watch the rest of the initiation. He came. He saw. He witnessed his bastard son's pledge to the Viotto Family.

Half of me wonders if the priest is actually happy about his son pledging his life to an organization hellbent on violence and blood. Despite the fact, Arrow thrives in this environment. I bet when Arrow's deadbeat mom dropped him on the priest's doorstep, he never thought Arrow would become the man he is today. Not that he initially wanted him, anyway. But he did what he had to do. Eventually, giving up his rights to my father and going back to the church he loved.

My attention returns to the madman wielding a sword, heading in my direction with malice hiding in the depths of his eyes. For whatever reason, since I was born, my father has despised me. For the loss of my mother? Probably. He'll blame me for whatever is going through his mind until the day he takes his last breath. I can guarantee that. Nothing I do truly impresses him.

Stopping in front of me, my father stares down at me.

"Through the veins of my son, my heir, and the next in line for my throne of power."

Deep pain radiates from my chest the moment the tip of the blade presses through my flesh. I suck in a breath through clenched teeth. Crisp red blood runs down my chest and stomach, softly dripping to the ground, staining it a deep red. A straight line rests between my pec muscles, down my sternum, and stops midway down my chest, creating a deep wound that will heal into a thick, raised scar.

Like every member of the Viotto family, fighting for our empire. It's our symbol—our right to bear. Our scar to prove our loyalties.

We are the Viotto Crime Family. Ruler of Briar Cove. The family in charge of California.

"For the family. Always," I grit out, taking a deep breath when my father steps back, and pride emulates from his sparkling eyes. He looks back at the other men behind him, nodding.

"Loyalty. Direction. Discretion. Obedience. And sacrifice," the men lined up behind Gabriel say in unison, eerily monotone.

"Through the years, you boys have been raised together and in this life. You've only seen the surface of what we do. You've trained hard and gone to all our camps, focusing your energies in the right areas. Today, you boys become men within the Viotto family." His grin fills every molecule of my body with tension at the mere sight of him. In his eyes, he has us right where he wants us. The boys he's cultivated from the moment we were born. He knew exactly what our roles would be—this. The murderers. The soldiers doing every single one of his orders.

Jokes on him, though. We're not the men he molded us to be. We're far superior.

"Now," he begins, holding the red-stained sword dripping with our mixed blood at his side. "We begin the next step of your initiation." His eyes darken with pleasure as we await the next step —blood out.

This is where our loyalty gets tested and proved. Where our lives change forever.

Dread builds in the depths of my gut as he steps forward, wiping off the blood dripping from his palm. Gabriel has something up his sleeve, and I can tell I won't like it. I look at Arrow and Shepp out of the corner of my eye, raising my brows when Shepp shrugs. Arrow looks on in anticipation, eager to get his hands on the person they're about to bring in.

Every initiation ends in blood and death. Whether it's from a traitor or some bum off the street that crossed my father wrong. They always have to be interrogated and killed.

I've seen blood, death, and mayhem my entire life. Hell, we trained for it in our camps during high school. Nothing ever prepares me to sink so low as to take another life. No matter what they did. My father sees me as a cold-blooded murderer, taking out the masses when need be. And I do. It's what I've trained for. But it doesn't necessarily excite me like it does Arrow. Nor does it scare me like it does Shepp.

"Bring her in," Gabriel says, waving a hand toward the steps behind us.

Tilting his head, he soaks in the screams emanating from the stairwell beyond and seeping through the thick stone walls. I stiffen as the wails get closer and closer, and then, the door swings open in a flurry of movement. Two men, dressed in the same black attire as the men in the room, step through the doorway with a woman thrashing between them. Her blonde hair shakes around as she tries to remove herself from their grips, with little success.

"NO!" a woman's cry echoes through the room like a whip, snapping all our spines straight.

"Welcome, Veronica. So happy to have you joining us. It was hell finding you," Gabriel says with a chuckle. "Restrain him," he growls as the men behind him do the same to a boss in the middle, forcing him to his knees between them.

"Veronica!" he shouts with urgency, earning a punch to the

gut. "Fucking bastards! Let her go!" he growls, attempting to climb to his feet again, but fails when the three of them hold him in place.

"Seems there's been a traitor among us. And you know what we do to traitors, don't you, boys?" he chuckles, looking down at the masked man lying on the floor, before ripping his mask off and revealing his identity.

Kent Thomas.

His loud curses fill the stone room, and he grunts when Gabriel puts his foot directly onto his neck, blocking out the air.

"You, Thomas, have been a bad, bad boy, haven't you?"

I blink rapidly, watching the scene unfold with my fists curled at my sides. We dare not move from our kneeled position in front of them. We're still awaiting our instructions. A boss—Thomas. He's been a long-time player, working his way up at Gabriel's side, helping him grow his unruly kingdom. He worked with Shepp's father, too. Side by side, day by day, they worked hand in hand together, greasing their elbows with one another.

Just another slimy cog in the mafia machine. I say, good riddance.

"So, what do you have to say for yourself now that you've been caught red-handed?" Gabriel sneers, reaching into his robes and pulling out what looks like pictures. Ah, yes. My father never condemns a powerful man without proof. At least, he has that going for him.

Picture after picture falls from Gabe's hand, displaying Thomas shaking hands with a man with a blue spider on his hand. My lip curls. Fucking Elias White. Of fucking course. That's why he's been hanging around Jenni. Seems they were up to no good together.

A video plays against the stone wall, where his deep voice leaks through, agreeing to the distribution of the drugs and the terms of the deal, including cutting Gabriel out of the action.

"He has nothing to do with this. We clear?" Thomas's voice rings out with certainty.

"Sure, man. Just us," the other man's cocky voice rings out just before the shake on it.

"Then Jenni is yours to do with as you please," Thomas says with certainty.

"Wise choice," the other man says with a chuckle just as the video cuts out with a hiss.

"Fuck you," Thomas hisses from between clenched teeth from his kneeled position. "Fuck you all! You're going to let this piece of shit town fall under because you can't bring these alliances in!"

"Oh, no. I don't think so," Gabriel says with a grin, stepping forward. Bending at the waist, he looks deep into the eyes of the man staring back at him. "This was a *you* decision. This was something you knew would benefit you, sneaking in another man's product right under our noses so you could make an extra buck." He stands tall, shaking his head with a look of disgust twisting his evil face. "Now, you'll pay for your indiscretions. You thought we'd never find out. Well..." he chuckles at the thought of someone attempting to pull something over on him. Something he doesn't think will happen.

"How about you, Veronica?" he asks, meandering toward the woman squirming on her knees with a gag now in her mouth. "Were you in on it, too?" Not likely. Jenni's mother never hung around for more than a day, traveling more than her father.

Her head violently shakes back and forth, tears streaming down her red cheeks. "No," she mumbles through the gag. "I didn't know. I..." Gabriel grunts, slapping her across the face with his gloved hand as she cries out from the stinging pain.

"Tell the truth!"

"Please! I didn't know," she sobs, sucking in several snot-filled breaths.

"Did she?" Gabriel asks, turning to Thomas, who rests stoically on his knees.

His thin lips don't move an inch as he watches his wife's life hang in the balance. Poor Veronica. Her eyes plead with her husband to stick up for her. To say anything that might hint at her innocence. But he does none of that. Like the coward he is, he watches with a stone-cold expression as Gabriel shrugs, driving the sword directly through her heart. She doesn't scream or cry any longer as she stares wide-eyed at her husband with hurt etched into her face for eternity. Then, just like that, she ceases to exist and falls to the ground with a heavy thud echoing through the room.

One down. One to go.

"That was for me," Gabriel grunts, dislodging the sword from her body and turning to us. "Subdue him," he says with a flick of his wrist, gesturing to the three men still keeping Thomas at bay.

My eyes flash to him and his unmoved facial features. He didn't flinch when his own wife met her demise. He didn't cry out or call out for her. She died with the disappointment of her husband, the man who vowed to love her unconditionally through sickness and in health, not protecting her from the enemy disguised as his friend.

Never show your enemy your emotions. Never let them see how you feel or who is important to you.

Another lesson of our training from the very men before us. They raise us in emotionless camps, training to take lives without a second glance. It's something Gabriel insists upon every child when they turn thirteen. And now I see why. If he had cried out, they would have seen how important she was to him. Maybe they would have tortured her a little to gain information about his dealings. Maybe they would have strapped her down and dragged it out more. Instead, they chose to end her life to get to his.

Thomas doesn't fight the onslaught of fists and kicks raining down on his body as he crumples to the floor. Wheezes echo through the room until he lies unconscious on the cold stone ground with four grown men standing about him.

Stepping back, Gabriel dusts off his suit with a huff, spitting at the ground. "This is what happens when you turn your back on the family and extend your hand to some other scum." He shakes his head and turns toward us with a sharp eye, taking us in our kneeling position. "This," he says, pointing to the man lying on the ground. "This is your final task to prove your worth within the family. I want every fucking answer from his lips by any means possible."

Arrow grins, puffing out his still-bleeding chest. "Even Max and Nova?" His grin widens when Gabriel smirks and nods his approval.

"I encourage their assistance. They always seem to get the answers that we need," Gabriel says, rubbing his hands together and smearing the blood still resting on his flesh. "Well, that's it, men. You may rise from your position on the ground and get this asshole to wherever you're going. But keep me updated."

"Thank you, Sir," I answer first, gently getting off my knees without a flinch. No matter how much pain shoots through my stiff limbs, I don't dare make a sound. "We'll get the information you requested and get it back to you promptly."

"After we have some fun," Arrow grins, jumping to his feet with a whoop.

Shepp is the last to get off his knees without flinching. Just like our training taught us to do. '*Understood*,' he signs, eyeing me for interpretation.

"He understands," I say.

Gabriel frowns, scoffing in Shepp's direction. "One day, Boy, you'll learn to use that voice again," he says like so many times before, looking down on Shepp for refusing to speak when he knows he can.

And with that, he waves the others out of the room, most likely heading to their special bar down the way to drink away their celebrations.

'*Wow*,' Shepp signs, reaching down to grab one of the photos. '*You think he's the cause of all the bad drugs?*'

"It would make sense," I say, shrugging as I inspect one of the pictures with a close eye.

It's taken directly from his house. I remember the layout like the back of my hand. I remember that office from my meeting with Elias. Seems he likes to hold meetings in Kent Thomas's office. Like someone crawled through his window and captured everything with their camera. And he had no clue.

'*Where did he get these?*' Shepp signs, turning to look behind him. '*Looks like someone was following him around?*' Shepp questions with furrowed brows. '*You think your father has a spy?*'

Hmmm. Could it be?

"Yeah," I surmise, rubbing my chin.

Oh, yes. It definitely could be.

"As paranoid as he is, he probably has a bunch planted across the city. It could be anyone," I say, earning a nod in agreement. "Even someone we know."

Shepp blinks rapidly, staring at me with a cocked head. '*You don't think...*' he signs, trailing off and leaving his fingers hanging in mid-air.

"I do," I say with a false calmness.

"Alrighty, boys, looks like we have someone to interrogate." Arrow grins with way too much glee for my liking. "Max and Nova will be so thrilled to have a new plaything."

'*They're going to tear him apart,*' Shepp signs, lightly kicking Thomas's bloodied body as he stays unmoving and unconscious.

"That's the point, Sheppy Boy," Arrow says with a grin. "Tear him to pieces so he sings like a little birdy in the caves."

I roll my eyes. "Well, let's get this show on the road before he wakes up and realizes he's in the hands of—"

"The best guys in the family? Deadly killers? The best of the best?" Arrow says, reaching down and tossing the big man over his shoulder without as much as a flinch.

'*Shouldn't we restrain him?*' Shepp signs as Arrow takes off toward the side door with a pep in his step. If he could, I'm sure he'd click his heels and do a little jig at the prospect of murdering the man on his shoulder or extracting information.

"You tell him that," I say, watching as he leaves our sight. "You good?" I ask with a calculating eye, checking Shepp up and down for any signs of distress.

'*Fine,*' he signs, swallowing a large lump in his throat.

"Hmm," I hum without saying another word. We head out of the basement of First Catholic Church and head toward our SUV.

Shepp sighs, pulling out his keys and opening the trunk of my SUV. Where there's plenty of room for a body or two to fit.

"Fine," Arrow pouts, heaving the guy over his shoulder again and shoving him into the large trunk, closing it with a thud.

Wonderful. It's this kind of night with him.

CHAPTER THIRTY-SIX

Jericho

THE DRIVE toward our shared mansion lulls us into silence, letting my overactive thoughts take me under. We make our way through the bustling city filled to the brim with passing cars and pedestrians making their way home from work or wherever they were. Paying our large, black SUV no mind. To them, we're just a passing car—nothing special or dangerous.

To us, we're now men, ready to prove ourselves and take over when the time is right. This city needs a change, and we're the ones to supply it.

Starting with Kent Thomas and his extra curricular activities. Then, we'll move on to our girl, doling out the punishment she so deserves. Not only for her indiscretions from before but for defying me and wandering away. Just like I thought she would.

I sigh when the SUV comes to a stop at a red light, resting my head against the seat as thousands of thoughts roar through my mind. Most of them have to do with Journey and my father meeting down at the docks. I have so many questions. Yet, so few answers. Her life is unraveling into a mystery I want to desperately solve. In the morning, I'll text my cousin for updates to soothe my mind.

My head turns to the left, and I sneer at the monstrosity rising into the sun-lit sky. There's no name or company attached to the top, but everyone knows that's where the Viotto mafia family runs everything regarding their business. Years ago, when my father left the mansion behind, he built the tower with several apartments and anything he could need, overlooking his subjects.

As the light turns green, we speed past the high rise, making our way through Briar Cove. Silence fills the car more as Arrow and I stare out the windows, watching the downtown area blur by as we make our way to the countryside, where our home sits away from it all. Completely on its own with no neighbors to hear our comings and goings. Or murders.

A breath of fresh air enters my lungs the moment we leave the city behind. I'd die for my brothers, but this organization fell victim to bullshit long before we rose to our proper titles as men in the family. Gabriel sunk that shit long before we were teens. And it's only going to get worse, until we can get it under control, that is.

"Finally," I mutter, peeking over the backseat to our prisoner. "He's still passed out. You want to do the honors?" I ask, looking at Arrow, who instantly perks up.

Arrow grins, rubbing his hands together when Shepp drives us through the big gates and up our mile-long driveway. Nothing says "Do Not Solicit" like our massive security system, fit with cameras and a gate.

"You don't have to ask me twice. Chair, rock, or dangling?" He wiggles his brows. "Please say dangling. I love it when they cry and piss their pants at the same time." His big gray eyes plead with me to give him the all-clear. If it were up to him, he'd hoist every person we brought back here above the lion's cage and watch in fascination as they beg for their lives.

Threaten a man's balls, family, or hell—even his house. He won't say a word. Dangle him above hungry, growling lions—he'll spill everything you wanted to know. It never fails.

"Chair. But close enough that he can feel their breaths." I nod when he throws the car into park, and Arrow jumps out of the car with zest, walking around to the trunk area and opening it.

"Oh, Thomas. You have no idea what is in store for you! I

can't wait for you to become acquainted with my babies. They'll be so happy to have another toy to toss around."

I eye Arrow's erratic movements, instantly recognizing his need to go overboard.

"We'll strap this one down. No dangling. No setting free in their pen. We need him to talk," I command, running a hand down my blood-stained shirt with a frown.

"Fun ruiner," Arrow grumbles with displeasure, lifting Thomas from the trunk with ease and throwing him over his shoulder. "What fun is it having a traitor..." Arrow's words trail off as he rounds the corner of the mansion, heading toward the back of our property.

I heave a sigh, pinching the bridge of my nose. This is not how I saw my night going, but it is what it is.

"You think she's back yet?" I question, staring up at the dark house. By the time we left the initiation, it was already close to nine o'clock. Giving her plenty of time to return to us by now.

'No,' Shepp signs after clicking his rings, staring up at the house, too, with a hopeless expression pulling down his features.

I hum, digging into my pocket and pulling up the app Arrow gave us access to. Immediately, I note the red dot stalls at a trailer park. Journey's Trailer Park. Wonderful. She went home to find nothing was left. Not even a small breadcrumb. But what's holding her there for so long?

"She's in her old neighborhood. No doubt looking for her things and her mother," I say, chuckling the last part. "One can only hope the rehab facility is giving Sable what she needs."

Most of Journey's things were tossed out in a dumpster our men helped haul out of the trailer park. Everything from her disintegrating living room furniture to her lumpy mattress met their end at the dump. The only piece of furniture Shepp insisted we hang on to was the stained nightstand that sat next to her bed. Even her clothes were set on fire.

She doesn't need things from her previous life. She has us now.

'*Yeah right,*' Shepp signs, shaking his head. '*She's been in the throes of addiction for years. I don't see that place wiping it out with the snap of their fingers.*'

I shrug. "Sable is signed into the facility indefinitely. There's no escaping for her. Not when I'm in charge of her care. She will not step foot outside unless her doctors suggest otherwise."

'*Smart,*' Shepp signs with uncertainty. '*Are you going to tell Journey?*'

"They weren't exactly close, now were they? I'll tell her the basics, but she has to give a little, too." I shake my head, staring off into the darkness surrounding our property. Only the sounds of the birds and wind travel in the air and the occasional growls from the lions out back. "But she'll be useful in finding the other missing piece—her missing sister."

Such a peaceful night for an interrogation.

My eyes flick to Shepp again. His entire body looks like a volcano about to spew its anger everywhere. Or, in his case, his nerves.

A twinge of pain catches my attention on my chest. I frown, running my fingers over the bloody wound. My mark pulsates. "After we're done here, we'll clean our wounds." Shepp nods, rolling his lips in. "You still good?" I prod more. My brother won't come out and tell me if he's suffering from his own mind. He leaves that task to me. But I always recognize the signs of his turmoil.

'*As good as I'll ever be,*' he signs.

"If you say so," I say, clutching his shoulder. "Now, let's move before Arrow murders the man we need answers from. Then, we'll prepare for our girl's homecoming." I grin more. "I think it's time for a little face reveal, don't you?"

Shepp snorts, shaking his head as we make our way around the house and toward Arrow.

Because what better way to get revenge on the girl you love for disobeying you than putting on your masks and chasing her through the woods to fuck her straight.

CHAPTER THIRTY-SEVEN

Arrow

"Time to strappy strappy you to the chair, big boy," I quip, humming to myself, locking several leather straps around our newest toy's limbs.

My victim's head lulls to the side, blood seeping from his nose and lips. Mmm. Dark, beautiful blood. My heart thuds against my ribs, the anticipation making ants crawl across my flesh.

Fuck.

I heave a breath, lifting my bloodied shirt over my head. The one I really didn't want to put back on after our ceremony. But I did. For appearances only, though. That's what Jer wants. He wants me to appear normal in the eyes of our fellow mafia brothers. Not the blood-hungry man I really am. I could bathe in blood day in and day out without blinking an eye. Well, good ole Gabe knows I'm not normal. That's probably why he adopted me when I was a kid. Or why my father just let me go. I guess he had to. The big man upstairs did not approve of me. Maybe that's why he cursed me with my wayward brain.

Yeah. That's it.

I smile to myself after Mr. Traitor Pants is fully secured to the chair. He couldn't move even if he wanted to. He's stuck. "It's a beautiful day to interrogate a traitor," I proclaim with a grin, circling his unconscious body like a predator. Without thinking, my fingers run down the bloodied wound Gabe inflicted between my pecs, showing the world that I belong to The Viotto Crime Family. It burns under my touch. When I pull my fingers back, blood coats them in its beautiful red hue.

No. I belong to Jer. My only loyalties lie with him and Shepp. And now, my obsession.

My loyalty to Gabe died off long ago. Even after all the training he let me in on. And the killings to curb this darkness inside me. He taught me how to murder without getting caught and where to throw the bodies when I was done. He dragged me into the depths of the shadows, encouraging me to give myself to the darkness and fully embrace it with everything I have.

But Jer gave me back something I desperately wanted. My fucking humanity.

He gave me that little sliver of hope and where to utilize it the best. Now, I may kill bad people. But I also help the ones who need it the most. The downtrodden and abused. The people who can't stick up for themselves. That's where I come in. They come to my confessional every Wednesday and pour their hearts out, begging me for help.

And I gladly give it.

But when it comes to men like Kent Thomas... Well, I'll gladly rip his heart out and fucking eat it. I lick my lips, fantasizing about the taste of his blood pouring down my throat. He deserves this. He brought all the bad drugs that were killing the people of Briar Cove into this goddamn town.

"Are you babies ready for a show?" I coo, walking toward my lions as they lazily lounge ten feet away, watching my every move.

Every time I enter this cage, they watch whatever I do. They've been in my possession since I was ten. A gift from Gabe for my fifth kill. I bottle-fed them and raised them into the predators they are. They seem to accept me for who I am. Never questioning my motives when I bring men or women in here to teach them a lesson. They're always eager to lick their lips and prowl forward. Hell, sometimes I give them little treats of legs and arms to thank them for their efforts.

I grin.

"Yes, you are," I say to them, clapping my hands. "I need you two on your absolute best behavior now. No biting Jer and Shepp. Even when they're being shitbags, okay?"

Max licks his lips, letting out a loud yawn. His head plops down onto his paws. Well. That's all the acknowledgment I need. They agree to my terms.

"Shitbags? Really?" Jericho grunts, marching into the enclosure with me.

Bright lights hover over our heads, drowning out the beautiful moonlight and stars. Once we're done, I'll feed my babies and give them their home back. For now, they accept us into their domain.

"Max said it, not me," I quip, tucking my hands into my pockets.

'The lion is speaking with you now? Should we be worried?' Shepp signs, raising a brow.

"No," Jericho grunts. "He's none of our concern right now. What is is the man currently coming to." He sweeps a hand, gesturing to the man waking up with a groan.

I grin, waiting for the realization to hit Kent. It's always the best part. The "where am I?" "What have you done to me?" That one is my favorite, especially when I've taken their balls already and hold the bloodied pair in my hand for show and tell. That really motivates them to tell me their secrets. Men like Kent will pretend nothing scares them into submission. Like he demonstrated with his innocent wife. He's been trained that way. But Gabe trained me to break through the training.

I'm his favorite weapon to wield.

Kent's head wobbles when he looks around with glassy eyes, taking in the scenery. "Fuck you," he garbles out.

"Fuck you, too, Pal," I quip.

"I'll never fucking say a goddamn thing. You can cut my balls off or my fingers. I'll never tell you," Kent groans, attempting to pick his hands up. A loud laugh falls from his lips, and he heaves a breath. "Let me guess? Those fucking lions you love so much are staring at me with hungry eyes, aren't they?" He laughs more, filling the entire space with it.

"Oh. Never say never, Kent," Jericho coos, coming next to his chair. His fingers roughly prod at the wound on Kent's lip.

"You think a little pain is going to make me talk to you?" he huffs, attempting to pull from Jer's grasp.

"No," Jericho says with a shrug, pulling his hand back. "I'd rather have a civil conversation without all the unnecessary bloodshed."

Kent snorts. "Right. Isn't that what you boys were raised for? Bloodshed. Death. Gabriel really molded you into what he wanted, didn't he?" he laughs again, tossing his head around.

"He might have," Jericho says with a cool demeanor, putting his hands behind his back. "Sometimes I enjoy the art of carving answers out of men like you. Today, though. I want a conversation."

"A conversation," I whisper-shout to Shepp, who snorts.

'*You know he won't talk,*' Shepp signs.

I do. I know Kent won't spill a word until I choppity chop off his goddamn toes and then make him lick them. Oh. That sounds effective. Lick your toes. I wonder if he could bite through the bones?

Shepp snaps a finger in front of my face, bringing me back from the darkness swirling in my brain, begging me to do diabolic things. Oh, how I love to do that. But, right. I need to focus on the man panting now.

"What's happening?" I ask, looking at Shepp, who rolls his pretty little eyes. I swear the big man upstairs blessed him with the most beautiful eye color. "Your eyes are so pretty, Sheppy Boy." I grin when he shoves me away with a grunt. "You think I'm kidding? Tell him, Jer. Tell Sheppy Boy that he has the most beautiful eyes on the planet. I kinda want to pluck 'em out and..."

"Shut up, Arrow," Jericho commands, shaking out his fist. "Kent won't speak with normal conversation. Or with my fists." At that, Kent laughs more.

"I told you. You can't fucking make me beg or talk. I'll die first." He swallows hard, eyes darting behind him.

For someone so adamant that he's not afraid, there's clearly one thing that makes him nervous.

"Max," I call out, patting my knee. "Come here, baby," I coo, calling my lion to my side.

Max lifts his heavy body off the grass with a loud, lazy groan. Who knew lions could be as lazy as house cats, never really wanting to partake in day-to-day activities? With heavy footsteps, my lion makes his way beside me, staring at me with intelligent eyes.

"Max, I want you to give our little prisoner a big kiss. You can nip him a little if you'd like. Tear off his head and throw it around like a watermelon. You'd like that, wouldn't you?"

Kent stiffens at my words, swallowing hard again.

"It's unimaginably painful, Thomas. I've watched many men crumble under the teeth of Max and Nova. One bite, and you're bleeding so badly that death is imminent."

"Death is imminent, anyway. You assholes!" he shouts, gritting his teeth.

My fingers slowly run through Max's hair, calming myself.

"Indeed it is," Jericho says, keeping a healthy distance from Max. "But you could spare all the theatrics by giving in. Just this once, Kent. Tell me what I want to know."

Shepp stands silently beside me, keeping his eyes on Kent and avoiding the gigantic lion underneath my fingertips. Fuck. My eyes roam across the vast enclosure, resembling the exact landscape they'd be living in the wild. I don't exactly know where they came from or how Gabriel found them. But I do remember the day he brought them to me.

"Happy birthday, Son," Gabriel says, putting a hand on my shoulder.

Two lion cubs frolic around the yard, rolling with each other.

"Are those lions?" I ask curiously, tilting my head when he laughs.

"Indeed. Something to help with your future. They're yours to take care of. They need to be fed and kept clean. They'll teach you a sense of responsibility," he says stoically, watching the pair play.

"Isn't that what dogs are for?" I blurt without thinking. His hand tightens on my shoulder until he pulls away with a huff.

"Yes. But these are more important. Take care of them, Arrow. Don't fuck this up."

"I won't, Sir," I respond respectfully, keeping my wild thoughts to myself.

"There's a zookeeper currently cleaning up the old enclosure at the back of the property. He's filling it with everything these two will need for now. He'll train you to feed them and care for them. Later, we'll discuss why they're here and what we intend to do with them," he demands in a low voice like he always does when I don't want to cooperate with his authority.

I grit my teeth. *"Of course, Sir,"* I say, leaving my emotions behind.

"Good boy, Arrow. Oh, good. Jericho, meet Arrow's two new best friends. Ensure he takes care of them. Now, I have a meeting at the tower. See you, boys..." He saunters away without finishing his sentence, walks around the mansion, and gets back into his town car.

I frown. *"It's not even my birthday,"* I mumble, watching the babies play.

"Lions, huh?" Jericho asks with Shepp at his side. *"He got me a knife set once,"* he quips. *"But never a wild animal."*

"Why?" Kent spits, bringing me back to the present. Right. Jericho is interrogating the man, taunting him with the lions. "So you can just go run back to Daddy and tell him everything? This isn't even my operation!" he shouts with a heaving chest.

"Go to him, Max. Give him a lick," I say, gently patting his upper back.

Kent stiffens again when Max slowly makes his way toward him.

"Such a good lion. He listens to every word I say. He was way better than any puppy." And that's a fact. I was intrigued more than scared when Gabriel walked away, leaving me with my two best friends and pet lions. "I could tell him to look at me." Just then, Max turns his head, almost raising a snarky brow at me. If he could, that is. "Be nice this time, Max. Just give him a little kiss. Show him the teeth you hide behind your lips." I grin when Max steps forward again, coming so close to Kent, he pisses his fucking pants.

'*Bingo,*' I sign to Shepp and Jericho. '*We've got him. Give him a good two minutes with Max. Then, he'll sing like a pig.*'

'*It's sing like a bird, Arrow,*' Shepp signs with a grunt.

"Pish posh, whatever," I huff, waving a hand. "Max, lick the blood from his lips," I growl, crossing my arms over my chest.

Kent cries out when Max's rough tongue licks along his bleeding wound.

"Good boy," Jericho mutters, stepping back from Kent and letting Max dole out the punishment.

"Make him stop!" Kent cries out. "Make him stop licking me. I'll... I'll tell you what you want to know! Just don't let him tear me to pieces."

"Do you prefer a knife to the heart?" Jericho asks, pulling a large hunting knife from his pocket.

"I can electrocute your balls if you want," I say with a grin. "Or your nipples." I shrug.

'*You have an obsession with balls,*' Shepp signs with a scoff.

"Do not," I say, side-eyeing him. "Max, good boy. Come here," I say, patting my knee again.

Reluctantly, Max pulls back, licking his chops. He stares at Kent with bloodlust, aching to tear into his meaty legs and abdomen. *Later, dude. Later. We'll get to that very soon.* I rub my fingers through his fur again, reveling in the feel of it beneath my fingertips. It almost grounds me, bringing me back to earth and away from the darkness trying to pull me in. If my darkness had its way, I'd sic Max on Kent's throat and laugh as he pulled it out. But I won't let it win. Not now, anyway. Maybe later.

"Not so tough, are you?" Jericho huffs, pacing beside Kent's chair with that blank expression. "I want to know why you were shaking hands with Elias White?"

Kent heaves a breath, eyeing Max, who obediently sits beside me.

"Nova is available, too," I say, nodding toward my other lion, watching us from her spot about ten feet away. "She looks hungry." I grin when Kent shudders, squeezing his hands into fists. Well, as much as he can still strapped down.

"Fucking lions," Kent whispers in slight hysterics, staring between the two with wide eyes. "You have two goddamn lions..." he trails off, shaking his head with a laugh. "Of course you do! Anything for the great sons of Gabriel Viotto. Fucking prick." He spits at the ground with a growl.

"They were a gift," Jer says, walking forward with his hands clasped behind his back. "Now, would you like to cooperate and tell us everything you know? You can't be the head of your little operation. Why were you shaking hands with Elias White?"

Kent's eyes whip back to him and narrow with rage brewing behind them. "Can't be the head?" he asks calmly, cocking his head.

"Impossible," Jer scoffs, pacing right before our victim. "There's no way you were smart enough to map out a way to gain an alliance with the Blue Spider Gang." He rolls his eyes for dramatic effect.

"You don't think I know what you're doing? These tactics are old and outdated. Your father taught you a lot of things, but fishing information from someone like me wasn't one of them," he spits, tightening against the restraints holding him to the flimsy wooden chair.

It could break with a little wiggling. In fact, I hope it does. I hope he runs, then I can sic my babies on him, laughing as they take him down and devour him. Ah. Now, that's dreaming.

'Cuts,' Shepp signs to Jer, then pulls a finger across his throat for dramatic effect.

'Yes,' I sign back with excitement. 'Cut his skin to fucking flaps *and let the cats have at him.'* I grin when Jericho blinks at us several times and then continues his pacing.

Jer shrugs. "Might be fun," he says, pulling out his large hunting knife. "What do you say, Kent? Large knife? Small knife? Gutting knife?" Jer turns on his toes, staring back at the man, eyeing his movements.

"Blood! Yes!" I hum, thrusting a fist in the air. "They love it so damn much."

Kent licks his lips, flinching when Jer runs the tip of the knife down his arm, cutting through his expensive black suit. "Tell me who else you're working with," he demands in a low voice, as he rips through the piece with his hands until skin shows through. "Tell me who else you've been dealing with." Another demand. Another rip of his suit.

Piece by piece, Jericho rips every shred of clothing from the man and tosses it aside.

"Nova will really like those," I stage whisper to Shepp, pointing to the man's nuts as they shrivel a little.

'Again with the balls, dude,' Shepp signs with exasperation, sending me a concerned look.

"You think getting me naked and threatening me with a knife will make me talk?" Kent goads with a smirk.

Ten seconds ago, he was pissing his pants because a lion was licking his bloodied face. I wonder how he'd take it if I asked Max to nibble on his toes or knees?

"And you think not answering my questions and antagonizing me will make me release you?" Jericho asks, walking a circle around the man with a manic gleam in his eye.

Jericho has a knack for blood. Me, too. He and I are two peas in a pod with boners for blood. Boner brothers. No, wait. That's weird. He loves spilling it with the help of a knife—his baby. And I have my lions. And Shepp? Well, he has a watchful eye and silent communication. He can gut a guy in five seconds flat, leaving them dead for even flinching in Jericho's direction. He's our silent, giant intimidator. Only, he's really not into this whole mafia thing. He'd rather be in the kitchen cooking up a storm for our lady and making sure she eats.

Damn. Now, I'm hungry.

"How about I gut you here first?" Jericho asks, sinking the tip of his knife straight into the meatiest part of Kent's gut and slowly dragging it up, right through the scar over his chest. You'd think it'd kill him right away. But no. Jer knows exactly what he's doing when he handles a knife. "Once your guts literally spill onto the ground, I'll keep your heart beating with adrenaline until the pain eats away at you, and you tell me everything I want to know."

Kent's eyes widen a smidge, and his breaths turn into quick pants as Jericho works his knife through the thick scar on his chest. The symbol of his loyalty to the family is now blemished.

"It's a shame I have to reopen this," Jer says, digging the knife in a little further. "But it's more a shame you thought you could dirty up this city even more with your new drugs. Tell me, was it just him? Was he the head of it?"

All the color drains from Kent's face when Jericho starts a new line of cuts directly opposite the thick scar, making a cross right over it.

"Criss cross applesauce," I singsong, continuing to pet Max as he watches intently at the blood dripping out of Kent's cut-open chest.

"Jesus," Kent wheezes, fighting against his restraints.

"He won't help you here," I say with a grin. "The holy trio doesn't hang around in these parts. All you get are the devils acting their revenge. So you'd better spill your guts before Maxy here takes them out and plays with them like spaghetti noodles."

"Who is the head of that operation?" Jericho asks again. "And why did you want to bring them here?"

"Fucking money," Kent grits out, heaving a breath when Jericho steps back, twirling the blood-soaked knife between his fingers, watching it with fascination.

Not as tight-lipped as he had hoped. It's funny what a little pain can bring to the game. Oh, and lions. They all think they're prepared for it, but they're really not. They can plan and plan, but when it comes down to it—pain always wins.

"Of course. Greed breeds the evil of the world, doesn't it? So, you thought you'd bring a new supply to town, pocket the money, and form an alliance of some sort?" Jer raises a brow, eyeing the blood dripping down his fingers in awe. I swear his dick grows three times bigger, and his pupils do the same. Shit. We should fuck Journey in a delicious pool of blood. Or paint. Something red. I want to paint her in colors. I side-eye Shepp as my mind works way too fast.

'*Center yourself,*' he signs, taking a deep breath and indicating for me to do the same.

"I was just thinking about painting Journey in blood or paint or cum," I say, humming at the fantasy working through my mind.

She would be tied up on my bed so she can't run away. Us hovering above her and...

Shepp clinks his rings together, gaining my attention. '*Focus,*' he signs, gesturing to the man, slowly dwindling away from the stab wound.

"Right. We're slowly murdering a man for information," I say, clearing my throat.

"Spit it out, Kent. I'm tired of waiting," Jericho shouts, jabbing the knife straight into his thigh.

Ouch. That had to hurt. "Stay, Max," I murmur, twirling my fingers through his hair again.

"I needed money," Kent gasps out. "Lots of money."

"So, you made this deal, got lots of money, and sold off your daughter all in one go." Jer raises a brow, moving the blade over Kent's ear.

"Yes!" he shouts, crying out when Jer cuts through his ear completely, leaving him a sobbing and snotty mess. "The Blue Spider gang agreed to my terms, and we were going to start distributing soon."

"They used to do that to women, ya know? If they did

something bad like cheat on their husbands or make bad deals with another gang, they'd chop off their ears. Both of them." I grin, watching with fascination as Jericho begins cutting the next one.

"Wait," Kent pants, testing his restraints again.

"Why would I?" Jericho says with a shrug, continuing to cut through his ear. Kent screams out in pain, thrashing against the restraints again until tears fall from his pathetic eyes. "Why would I wait when you're not giving me anything I need?"

"They call him Shadow," Kent cries out, huffing when Jericho steps back, holding up two ears.

I wonder if he can still hear well. Oh, but what a nice prize to bring back and show my girl. I know she'll appreciate them. Body parts are always a nice present to give to wives.

"You think Kitten would appreciate some ears?" I ask, snatching the ears away from Jericho with a grin. "Imagine the look on her face when I give these to her."

'*Again, she's not going to appreciate body parts. Women want flowers, chocolate, and diamonds. Not hearts and ears,*' Shepp signs with a huff like this is common knowledge. I'd give her teeth, fingers, hearts, or anything she wanted to prove just how obsessed I am with her.

"Says you. You're the romantic, and I'm..."

'*The maniac,*' Shepp retorts rudely, batting the ears out of my hands and making me pout.

"I was going to put those in my special juice and save them forever to remember the day we became men and finally get to claim Kitten as our own."

"Tip-toeing around that," Jericho huffs, crossing his arms over his chest. "Shadow, huh?" Jericho asks, raising a brow when Kent nods with a pained expression. I guess he can hear without his ears. Whatever. Crouching down, I pick them up again and shove them in my pocket. I'll just save these for later.

Shepp clinks his rings together again, getting Jer's attention.

'Isn't he from down south? Haven't we heard of a different Shadow before?'

"Sounds familiar," I say, tapping my chin and then grin. "Oh, he's the prick who sent that bomb for us! That was so exciting."

"He from Greenwood?" Jer asks, cocking his head to the side.

"A long time ago," Kent wheezes. "This is someone new, carrying on the legacy someone killed off. Someone in the city," he says as a smile crosses his face while he pales more from the blood loss. "Hell, you know him well. But then again, not at all. He started this war long before you knew what was happening right under your noses. This is a battle you won't win. A foe you won't even see." He chuckles at that, throwing his head back with a manic laugh, filling the space.

Max growls at his laughter. "Down boy," I say with a raised brow when he continues eyeing Kent with hunger in his eyes. "We might need to leave the lion's cage," I hum, patting his back again.

"I want more!" Jer shouts, slamming his fist directly into Kent's face, knocking his chair completely back. Kent cries out when his arms are smashed between the chair and the ground, and he's forced to stare up at Jer, who looms above him, ready to jam his knife into his throat.

"Tell me more. Who is Shadow?" Jer growls, putting the knife's edge under his chin.

"A shadow in the night, little boy. Someone you'll never find. But there is someone you might be able to find." Kent raises a brow when Jer stops his movements.

"Go on," he says with impatience.

"I've been wracking my brain trying to figure out how videos and pictures could come about from my meeting. It was just me, the dealer, my daughter, and her best friend. Then it hit me," Kent laughs maniacally through the pain of his cuts and blood dripping everywhere. How he's still kicking, I don't know. But I can't wait until he stops breathing.

"The suspense is killing me, Kent," Jericho grumbles, staring straight into his eyes. "You're becoming useless with your talks..."

"Your future wife."

My body stiffens. Shepp sucks in a loud breath beside me. Shit. We're so damn transparent, and that mother fucker knew it. Passion cannot be killed, though. Especially this. Our obsession.

Jer stills and cocks his head. "What about her?" he asks with deadly intention. "What about my fucking wife?"

"She was the only other person there," Kent says with a sadistic grin. "I always wondered why my daughter fell into the hands of a girl like that." Jericho rears back, punching him square in the nose until he's sputtering and shooting out teeth.

More teeth, yay!

"Rephrase," he growls, earning a chuckle from me.

"Yeah, I wouldn't talk about our woman like that," I say, cracking my knuckles. "Not like you'll be able to for very much longer." I shrug with a grin, letting my darkness ensnare me in its trap.

"Why the fuck would Jenni be friends with her? After all these years of going to school together. Seems odd, doesn't it? That bi —" Another punch rears his head back, knocking it against the hard ground.

"Again with the name calling," Jericho chastises with the cluck of his tongue. "Continue," he says, grinning. Kent looks up at him with a dazed look, glossing over his eyes. Life slowly fades from him as he bleeds out. Soon, he won't have much to say when he's a corpse.

"She was there," he wheezes out. "The night I made the deal. She had dinner with us. That's who had to have taken the pictures," he whispers before his eyes roll into the back of his head, and he goes limp.

"Damn it! He left us on a cliffhanger!" I shout, throwing my arms around.

Jericho blinks several times and straightens himself up. He doesn't utter a word when he plunges the knife directly into the cross he drew over his chest with a grunt, stabbing over and over, until he's breathing heavily. Blood splatters across his chest and face when he turns back around with a sour face.

"So, why would my kitty cat be there?" I ask, rubbing my chin with a perplexed look. "Was she just there for dinner? Or was it..." My eyes widen with realization, and I grin at Jer. "Oh! It's him. The enemy. You thinking what I'm thinking?" I wiggle my brows when Jer huffs at me. "Now, they're sad," I grumble, patting Max's head. "It's okay, babies. Daddy will get you lots of meat to eat. He's tainted anyway. Go lay down." I gesture to Max as he grunts at me, lazily walking toward Nova and lying down again.

"We're going to keep that information to ourselves," Jer says, stopping abruptly to face us. "We tell my father Kent spilled about Shadow, but not what he revealed about him." Jer shakes his head. "Fuck! This is the second time that name has come up. First with that fucking bomber. Now this? This Shadow asshole is crossing the line!" His voice echoes through the enclosure. "If he's recruiting bosses into whatever the fuck he has going on, then he's fucking good. How? How is he getting this? And why is my goddamn wife doing this?" Jericho's chest heaves wildly when he throws his knife straight into the ground. "Clean this fucking mess up," he grunts, bolting away with his emotions on his sleeve.

"Well, damn. I've never seen him so riled up before," I pout.

'It's Journey,' Shepp signs, shaking his head with worry.

"He's going to do something rash," I sing. "And I cannot fucking wait to see what he has up his sleeve."

Shepp clinks his rings, gaining my attention. 'First we need to clean this shit up and feed them.' He nods toward the lions, making hungry eyes at the dead man bleeding out.

I shrug. "Let them have a chew toy for a little bit," I say with a grin, waving him along. "We need to see what Jericho is up to. Besides, I have a hankering for pickles and orange juice while we wait for Kitten to return to the nest."

'That's birds,' Shepp signs with a sigh.

"Birds. Kittens. Whatever." I wave a hand as we walk out of the lion's enclosure, leaving Kent to his fate with Max and Nova.

"Hop in," I say, sitting in the driver's seat of the golf cart and patting the other seat. I inhale deeply and tip my head to the side, inspecting the darkening clouds rolling in through the night sky, practically snuffing out the stars and bright moon. "Tut, tut, tut, looks like rain, Old Chap," I say in my best accent.

Shepp raises a brow at me, huffing when he gets into the golf cart, nearly tipping it over with his damn size. Good thing this stupid thing doesn't have a roof, or the big bastard would be hitting his head. He doesn't say anything to my rain comment, even as I chat his ear off on the way back to the house. It takes maybe five minutes to roll up to the mansion's back door when I slam on the breaks.

A tiny raindrop hits my nose when I climb out of the golf cart and I grin. "Oh, I can't wait to roll my Kitten in the mud," I chuckle, holding my hand out and catching another one.

Shepp grunts, peeling his massive body out of the golf cart and huffs, grabbing me by the arm and pulling me through the house until we meet Jericho in the kitchen. He paces back and forth with his hands behind his back, almost looking constipated as he sinks into the depths of his demented brain. I like his brain. Sometimes, I want to lick it when he comes up with his devious plans.

Not tonight, though. I immediately go to my stash and pull out a large dill pickle, biting into it. The bitter taste invades my taste buds, and I hum, taking another bite. With one hand, I pour myself a glass of orange juice and chug.

'*What's your plan?*' Shepp signs, looking at the three skull masks sitting on the kitchen counter.

Oh, I didn't see those before. I wipe my mouth with the back of my hand and grin, knowing exactly where my demented brother's head has gone. A giddy feeling envelops me when I bite into my pickle again.

Finally, Jer stops his pacing and slams his hands down on the counter with a serious expression. A normal person might piss their pants at the darkening look taking hold of him. But I grin more and lick my lips, loving the sensation of goosebumps prickling my flesh.

Oh, yes. This is going to be so damn good. Even my dick agrees as he hardens. That's it Big A, we're going Kitten hunting.

Jer sets his phone down with the app I gave him access to. The red dot blinks down the road, getting closer and closer to our house.

"What the hell took her so long?" I question noting the time of 11:30 p.m.

What was she doing? Who was she speaking to? And why was she away from this place for so long without me by her side?

"We'll find out. We'll figure everything out. From here on out, Journey goes nowhere alone. She's going to be locked to us until she tells us what the fuck she's up to. I'm tired of wondering why she's meeting him in the dark."

Jer's father. The bastard.

I grin more when a truly unhinged look possesses Jericho, taking hold of him.

She's so fucked. By our dicks. She'll tell us everything by tomorrow. I feel it in my boner.

CHAPTER THIRTY-EIGHT
Journey

THE FANCY KEYS dangle from my fingers as I make my way through the silent house. Correction—mansion. This place is fucking massive. Impressive, too. I could probably get lost if I'm not careful. I wish they had handed me a map or something. There's so much more to explore. I've only seen the upstairs in my short time here. There's like fifteen doors up there, holding god knows what behind them. Bedrooms? Torture rooms? A sex room? I shiver at the thought of that. An image of Arrow chaining me to his bed springs to mind, but I shake it away. I don't have time for sex thoughts right now. Especially when my vibrator is still missing. My eyes dart around, gazing at the opulence around me.

Lucky for me, the lunatic mafia men aren't back yet. Thank God. If they discover my little adventure, they might have something to say about it. Especially Jericho. I grin, swinging the keys again. My new favorite activity is riling the man up. The way my pulse accelerates when he's near or when he gives me that look with narrowed eyes like he can't stand the sight of me. Fuck. It makes me wetter than it should. And pissed off, too. Maybe I want him to discover I've been traipsing around Briar Cove all night. Then, I can get a repeat of the other night with his bow. Well, not all night. My eyes lock on the time. Just after eleven thirty. So, only a few hours have passed since I stole his vehicle. I may have sat in my trailer longer than I thought, absolutely losing my shit after seeing my monster. He always leaves me shaking in my boots after an unexpected visit. One day, he's taking Sunny off the transplant list, and the next, he's putting her back on. It's an emotional rollercoaster, keeping me on my toes.

But I'd like to get off the ride now, thanks.

I blow out a breath, attempting to erase what happened tonight. I had one win—my sister's health. She's back on top, and I'm onto another mission. Despite these fuckers, I'll win and report back whatever is necessary.

As I make my way through the massive living room, probably bigger than my entire trailer park, my mind wanders back to Jericho. Maybe he won't notice I stole his car. I did cover it back up with the tarp he had over it and parked it where I found it. Who am I kidding? The man probably has fifty alarms on it that go straight to his phone. Or maybe he's watching me from the cameras everywhere. I knew there was some kind of game he was playing. A cute little game of cat and mouse. Well, I'm no mouse. I'm a goddamn predator. And this predator is fucking starving after today's events.

Making my way into the kitchen, I stop at the fridge and collect the meal Shepp left me.

Eat.

I smile at the note sitting on the food. That brooding silent man is the bossiest of them all. Ever since I stepped foot in this house, he's stuffed food—and other delicious things—down my throat. I think he's trying to fatten me up. But I don't mind. I'd eat his food twenty-four-seven without complaint.

He mentioned to me before he left that there was some food in here for me. What a gentleman. Pulling it out of the fridge, I take the top off the container and my eyes turn into hearts. Lasagna. Fucking hell. This man. I might marry him if he keeps making me delicious meals.

I pop it into the microwave, and once it's heated up, I stuff my face like I'm starved. Which I am. A heavy night of emotions will do that to a girl. And what better way to quell that hunger than shoving carbs down my throat?

My eyes squeeze shut when the flavors explode on my tongue, and my monster's words haunt the ever-living shit out of me. That's nothing new, though. His voice lives in the back of my mind through everything I do, tormenting me forever. Just like he wanted.

Now, I have to spy on the very men who kidnapped me. It shouldn't be too hard. I kind of despise them. Because, hello! They kidnapped me from jail. Forced me to sign a ridiculous contract that won't hold up in court and then handcuffed me to them. So, yeah. I'll gladly spy. But they might keep me on their good side with this damn food. God, it tastes so damn good. I shovel more into my mouth, humming at the flavor filling my tongue. Once I've had my fill of lasagna, which tastes oddly familiar, I put my plate in the sink and rinse it off.

"Time to explore," I murmur to no one as I listen to the silence of the house. I swear it creaks and groans against the light wind picking up outside. Shit. Peeking out the window, rain beats down against the glass. Perfect timing, then. Wherever the boys are, maybe it'll slow them down as I tear this place apart. "Time to find my shit." My teeth clench so hard, I swear I'm going to crack them.

They touched my stuff. They took it from me. Now, I'm taking it back.

Exploring the boys' mansion has my heart pounding in a frenzy as I've gone room to room, attempting to beat the clock. I expected torture rooms with chains and bloodied knives or something. All

I've found so far is boring bedrooms, an office that had jack shit in it—minus the safe I couldn't break into—and a humongous library I'm going to scour when I have free time. Although, they probably won't have my favorite author's books. I'm finally done with my turkey shifters and next on my list is her mafia romance that's an omegaverse. How delicious is that? I'm all for knots and heats. Plus a badass omega who is in charge of the mafia? Bring on the growly alphas, especially the deranged one.

So maybe if I give in a little and be the best behaved captive they've ever seen, they'll buy me some books. Or let me go. That's all I want. What I wouldn't give to just dive in a book and never return to this reality. Maybe I'll extend this job just a little bit more than usual. Oh, sorry monster asshole, they aren't giving me anything. They're perfect angels. That way I can eat, sleep, and read without having to worry. Even though I hate their guts for forcing me into this situation. But I hate my monster more. They're the lesser of two evils. Besides, they give me orgasms. So, I'll hang here, lazily do my job, and figure out where I can go after this.

What I didn't expect to find in their home is this. I've been standing here for what seems like five minutes, just staring into the room with my jaw open. This is magnificent. Something in the back of my mind tells me I should just walk away from the masterpiece in front of my eyes, but I can't. My feet have a mind of their own, and they're staying.

My eyes gaze on the large canvas sitting in the middle of the massive bedroom. It's the only thing here besides a couch in the corner, which has a pillow and blanket lying on it. The drop cloth protecting the carpeting squishes beneath my feet as I circle the piece of art.

My heart shudders at the sight. Tears fill my eyes, and emotions slightly choke me.

It's me.

Or at least, someone who resembles me.

She's lying in bed, curled in on herself. Her hair splays over the pillows in a heap of curls, messy and unbrushed. The blanket barely covers her backside, and her legs are wrapped in it. The tight T-shirt, which I recognize as something I've worn before, bunches at her waist. But nothing is exposed. Just a girl lying in bed with her eyes closed and the darkened room swallowing her whole. The only light shining is from a small lamp next to her bed, illuminating only her sleeping form. A tiny signature sits at the bottom right-hand side. SM.

Sheppard Mondelli.

It clicks right away. His hands speak in two different ways— through language and art. He expresses himself through beautiful visuals that speak for themselves. He doesn't have to utter a word.

I swallow hard, staring at the brown-haired girl with the perfect skin and unblemished face. Peace settles on her features. She's almost ethereal. It's perfection caught in a painting. She'll never have to wake up like I do. She can sleep forever and live in the fantasy her mind concocts each night when she falls asleep. The girl in the painting doesn't need sleeping pills to drag her away from her nightmares. She doesn't need music to drown out the screams echoing in her mind from the nights she lived in a darkened cage in the fucking basement of her monster's home.

I shiver, tears burning the back of my eyes. Never in my life did I think I'd be jealous of a painting that can't be me. That's not what I look like. Maybe on the outside. But my insides are littered with scars and blemishes. I'm so fucked up in my head that sometimes I can't keep my darkness at bay. It begs to be let free and harm the people who have harmed me. Sometimes I slip into it. Sometimes I hurt people when I don't want to. Like Jenni. But I had orders. I had to do it or my sister would pay for my sins. Like she has been for years.

But this painting.

My breath stalls when I turn away, squeezing my eyes shut. I was supposed to be a bad ass bitch, finding my stuff. Not crying over a painting that hits way too close to home for me. And it's not even me, for fuck's sake. Is it? Did Shepp paint this for me? Is this his space?

What is wrong with me?

I wipe my face, waltzing out of the room without looking back. I leave the existence of the painting in a small box in the back of my brain, dig a hole, and bury it forever. Because if I think about it too much, I may grow softer than I already am toward the men who took me.

I gently close the door behind me, making sure it latches before moving on. I've already explored most of the upstairs and have yet to find anything. Not even my damn phone. The only thing they gave me was my damn book.

Ugh.

Why does life have to constantly throw lemons at me when I can't make damn lemonade? I don't even have the equipment for it. They just squirt in my eyes.

Life could at least throw me a million dollars and a break. Hell, it could kill my monster for me, too. Ah. A girl can dream, right?

I blow out a breath, standing in the middle of the long hallway, contemplating where to go next. I've been through every door and have yet to find anything of use. I crane my neck, staring at the ceiling. Maybe there's an attic somewhere where they stash the good stuff out of sight. Or maybe a basement that has something in it. Fuck. Or maybe it's not here at all.

My body stiffens when a loud thud comes from downstairs. Then it happens again. And again. My feet move as the sound continues, echoing through the entire mansion. My ears fill with static when I slowly come down the stairs, overlooking the foyer and living room.

Slam!

My fingers wrap tightly around the banister, keeping me rooted in the spot.

"Hello?" I shout, looking around at the lack of movement in the house.

Right. Shout hello like every woman in a horror movie does.

Another slam happens near the kitchen, drawing me further through the house.

"This is exactly what you should be doing in a stranger's house, exploring it until someone pops out and murders you. This is how every horror movie starts," I grumble to myself, marching through the kitchen.

My heart leaps from my chest when the wind slams the back door again. Rain falls quickly outside, slamming into the windows and sounding through the house. A full-blown storm sweeps through Briar Cove.

"I am a badass," I mumble to myself as my hand shakes. "I'm a badass who needs a knife," I mumble again, snatching one from the counter and tightly gripping the small knife in my hand.

Don't show your fear. Don't give your enemies the upper hand. Don't show your emotions! Back straight, Little Snake. Look me in the fucking eyes and block out everything around you. You are not allowed to feel when it matters most. Do your job.

Every word stomps through my mind with every step I take toward the back door, waving in the vicious wind, sweeping in from the outside.

"Just a door! It's just a fucking door," I quip to myself, gripping the swinging door. Rain pelts down harder, pooling on the grass.

Trees sway in the wind whipping through its tops. Warm air surges past my face as I lose myself in what Mother Nature has to offer. I close my eyes as bits of rain sprinkle over my face for just a split second before I close the door and lock it again. My reflection stares back at me through the window panes. My finger's grip on the knife loosens a smidge. Nothing to worry about. The door got pushed open by the crazy wind. There's nothing nefarious happening here. Just a rare storm raging through.

Yup. I'm safe.

Or not.

My heart drops, and my grip tightens on the knife in my

hand. The lights throughout the house blink out completely, leaving me in nothing but darkness.

Darkness. Fucking darkness. I squeeze my eyes shut, willing my heart rate to slow down. Darkness does nothing but conceal the bullshit of night. It does nothing but bring back the terrible memories of the nights locked in my cage, listening to the cries of other prisoners. With only the violin to keep me company from somewhere far away.

My palms sweat when my fingers tighten even further around the knife. The sweet melody I heard every night for six months plays through my mind on repeat.

"You're getting better," I murmur to the cement wall I'm left staring at through the bars of my hanging golden cage. I smile when the strings squeak, and I realize the person has messed up when the music stops completely. "One, two, three..." I trail off when the music begins again. They start off right where they left off. Only this time, it's perfect. The strings don't squeak. It's the perfect whine, and the rhythm picks up. My body instinctively sways back and forth to the tune that keeps me sane.

This tune will forever be stamped into my soul. It walks with me through the darkness of my past and holds me in the present.

And it has. Every time I'm left stranded in my memories, the helpful tune rings through my mind, dragging me from the stupid abyss of bullshit. Like now. When I'm surrounded by the darkness of a strange house creaking and moaning in the wind. You'd think with a beautiful house like this; it wouldn't make these monstrous noises. It shouldn't. It's too nice. It's a mansion for millionaire mafia men.

Right?

I heave a breath. I'm better than this. I'm better than letting the darkness consume me. Don't let it get to you. Get your shit together. Go to the basement and find the circuit breaker. Yeah, that's a plan. Okay. I've got this. Totally got this.

I spin on my heel with my new plan roaring through my mind and stop dead. Ice fills my veins, freezing everything. My breath stalls in my chest, and my mouth opens to form a silent scream as I suck in air. I've faced a lot of things in my fucking life. I almost died in the basement of my monster's home. Over and over, he tortured me. Played mind tricks on me. Subjected me to cruel lessons at his hand where I killed more people than I can count.

But this?

He didn't prepare me for a masked man staring back at me in the middle of a darkened kitchen, blocking me from any sort of escape. Only his outline shines through. And the fucking mask lighting up on his face in the shape of a skull with blood dripping down it. It's the same goddamn mask from that night weeks ago.

As I stand before the masked man, a shiver skitters its way down my spine. My heart pounds in my chest like a relentless drum begging to beat the fuck out of my chest. His face, hidden behind an eerie skeleton mask, chills me to the damn bones. Staring back at me is a person devoid of any readable expression, stranding me in my fear. If I can't read his face, then I can't know his intentions. Meaning, I can't fucking run to save my life. I grip the knife tighter. Maybe I'll stab him after all.

Get your shit together! My brain shouts. I've been through this so many times and in scarier situations.

"Who are you?" My voice shakes when I raise the knife and point at the person standing tall with a skull mask, concealing his identity.

I want to shout, "I'll stab the fuck out of you if you don't back up." But I don't want to give him the satisfaction of knowing my plans. Because then he'll anticipate them. He probably sees me as a weak woman. One of which, I'm not. I'll start with his gut first and incapacitate him, hopefully through the ribs. It'll puncture his lungs, leaving him gasping for air. Then, I'll take it all away from him. I shiver as my darkness takes over, whispering plans in my ear. Ways to escape. Ways to ensure I'm alive when the sun comes up and this bastard is six feet under.

The person behind the mask doesn't say a word. They stand there like a statue, not moving a damn inch. Their gloved hands rest on their stomach, like they're waiting for something. But what?

Get it together. Get it the fuck together, Journey. Think. You have to think on your toes. You need to distract him long enough to get the hell out of here.

Okay. The tall masked man is obviously here for...? Who? Me? The guys? I roll my lips together, keeping my eyes on him. He continues to stare at me like I'm supposed to do something. My heart hammers when he finally takes a step forward. Just one. And I step back, banging up against the back door. My back stiffens, and every muscle turns rigid.

I need to open the door and bolt into the storm. This masked fucker can have the dark house. I'll hide in the trees until the sun comes up.

My eyes focus on the tall man's outline. Despite not being able to make out the majority of his body, his presence suffocates the room, and his silence speaks volumes. The ringing in my ears screams at me when my fingers slowly travel across the wood of the door, heading toward the handle. I'll escape and run. He'll be here doing whatever he wants to the house. Away from me. I just need to get away. I don't care if this is one of the guys in disguise trying to scare me straight. I'll fucking hide until the sun comes up, and I know I'm fucking safe.

"Run, Little Tempest," he rasps, taking another step toward me. My fucking heart shudders. "Run!" he shouts, advancing on me.

I don't fucking think about the rasp of his shaky voice and how fire brews in my guts at the sound of him. Like I've heard it before somewhere in my dreams, and it soothes me. Fear evaporates into nothing.

"You want me to run?" I ask, straightening my spine and observing the tall masked man who stands just a foot away from me. He could grab me if he wanted to. Kill me if he must. But he doesn't. His hands rest together with his fingers intertwined.

He nods. I'm sure a smile resting behind the creepy as fuck mask.

I don't dare take my eyes off him when my hand lands on the knob. My breath stalls when he stays there, tilting his head, revealing the blue of his eyes.

Ocean eyes.

My heart kickstarts again, thumping out of my ribs at the recognition.

"Go," he rasps again, gesturing for me to turn the knob.

It's either he's going to grab me the moment I take off.

Or he wants me to go out there in the pouring rain.

So, I weigh my options. I either get caught by the big man with familiar ocean eyes and a voice I can't place. Or I get soaked in the rain storm while I hide behind the trees with no way to contact anyone for help.

I choose the rain.

And life.

CHAPTER THIRTY-NINE
Journey

OKAY. So, maybe the rain wasn't a good idea. Especially this rain. It's coming in sideways, upside down, and whatever else *Forrest Gump* experienced, pelting me in the damn face. I blow out a breath, swiping the water from my cheeks when I settle under a large tree. A burn spears across my chest from the exertion.

God, I hate running.

The wind blows hard, nearly knocking me over and out of my hiding place. I'm soaked to the damn bones and shivering as I stand behind a massive tree in the middle of their property. Who the hell knew their place was so big? I thought their mansion needed a map to find all the hiding places inside. Well, so does the outside.

So far, it's been massive row of trees after massive row of trees all around the house. Of course, it's so dark I can barely see my hand in front of my face. Pretty sure I bounced my face off a few trees in the process of getting here to safety.

Rough bark rubs against my skin as I lean my back against the tree, catching my breath. I peek around the large trunk, searching the darkness for the large masked man. If Ocean Eyes is here, then the rest might not be too far behind.

When I came home, the last thing I ever expected was to run into a stranger standing in their kitchen. All I wanted was to search for my shit after stuffing my face and relaxing. And this is the consolation prize I won. I huff. If this is some shitty prank the guys are pulling, I'm going to stab them for scaring the shit out of me.

My monster prepared me for a lot. Spying, torturing traitors, stealing files from lawyers, but not this. Not a masked man chasing me around, for God knows why. This has to be a game they're playing. Probably for running away. Or maybe for stealing that car. It seemed important. Since it was under a tarp and all.

Shit. I squeeze my eyes shut as thought after thought jumbles in my mind, bringing me back to the night I had with the three masked men at the party. They saw my face. They said my name. Meaning, they know exactly who I am.

And I...

My eyes fly open. I'm such a dumbass. If Ocean Eyes is here. The same man from the party. Then, Light Gray eyes and Brown eyes have to be here, too.

And that means...

Holy fucking shit balls. I lightly tap the back of my head against the tree. I'm an idiot. A fucking dumbass.

It's them.

Of course. I should have known by the color of their eyes and the sound of their voices. You'd think I was a strong, competent woman, but I've had a lot on my mind lately. Besides, the masked men had deeper tones, and my eyes were covered the entire time we got down and dirty. Then, I woke up a groggy mess barely remembering who I was.

Let alone what their eyes looked like or what their voices truly sounded like. Maybe that's my excuse for not putting two and two together. Or maybe, I'm just too preoccupied to realize the men were in front of me all along.

Or—and hear me out—I'm just an oblivious dumbass.

I should face my fears like a big girl, march up to the house, and grab the giant that has to be Shepp by the balls, demanding he tell me their plan. But that's how girls die in horror movies. They're unstable as hell. So, I'll stay here and stay alive, thanks.

But shit. If there was one masked man, are Jericho and Arrow out here, too, in the middle of the storm?

Probably.

I clutch the knife in my hands, ready to stab anyone who dares to come near me. No matter who they are, they're meeting the end of my knife. Especially if they're trying to scare me. It's what they deserve. My eyes roam the distance, watching the shadows sway with the storm. Luckily, this huge tree offers me some shelter from the crazy rain, so I'm not in the constant downpour.

I swallow hard, contemplating my options. I could run. Or I could stay here forever until they get bored. I like the staying put part. If I move, I take the chance of them finding me and doing God knows what with me. But I'm also a sitting duck ready for the slaughter.

The storm rages on like nothing I've ever seen before. Deep thunder vibrates the damn earth, and lightning flashes overhead, lighting up the darkened world.

And that's when my breath stalls.

My heart pounds in my ears. I clutch the knife harder, pressing my back further into the tree. A buzz encases my flesh when my heart pounds rapidly against my ribs. Heady adrenaline pours through my veins like a wildfire.

"Jesus Christ," I gasp, staring into the shadows as another lightning bolt flashes overhead. Revealing a large man standing tall in the shadows.

Watching me through the peepholes of his skull mask, dripping with fake blood. But it's slightly different from the man in the kitchen. So, that answers my question from before. They're all out here looking for me.

Like a phantom slipping back into the shadows, he disappears. Until another bolt of lightning flashes across the dark sky, revealing the masked man standing right in front of me. Where the fuck did he come from? And how did he get here so fucking fast?

I bite my tongue, holding in the scream desperate to emerge at the sight of him. My grip on the knife grows harder when he stands there, cocking his head.

Light Gray eyes.

Dread fills me at the intensity of his stare. His eyes are the only thing I can see through the mask. Danger wafts off him. His aura is urging me to run the hell away.

No matter how much my mind screams at me to flee, I'm frozen. My damn legs don't listen to the panic roaring through my brain. Maybe it's because I know who it is. Or maybe it's the true fear taking over.

I suck in a breath and fill my lungs before slowly breathing out to calm myself. The darkness creeps into my mind, whispering more exit strategies. The man stands there, staring at me with malice in his eyes, and a hint of something else flashes through.

My eyes roam his form in the dark, noting his soaked black T-shirt and jeans. His muscular arms hang by his sides, and his fingers twitch. This one is lean and shorter than the man in the kitchen. He studies me like I study him. Standing so close I could brush my fingers down his chest.

"Which one are you?" I grit out, staring at him.

Arrow—my mind screams. It has to be him.

Sure, I know it's one of the guys. Judging by the deep chuckle coming from beneath the mask and the familiar eyes staring back at me, it's Arrow. But my body knows the danger. And when it presents itself, I fight back, no matter who might be hiding their identities.

Arrow chuckles a menacing laugh, sending shivers down my spine. "Your worst nightmare," his deep voice echoes through the trees and rattles my brain.

I lock my body when he wraps his hands around my throat, gently squeezing. He doesn't constrict my air. He simply stands there, inspecting me with a cocked head.

"You didn't run," he growls, squeezing just a little tighter.

"You want me to run?" I ask, raising a brow and distracting him as I speak.

"Run, Rabbit, run," he hisses, releasing his grip on my throat.

This is a trap. I feel it in my soul. But I don't question the gift in front of me. Without a second thought, I shove the knife right into the right side of his chest. I expect a scream or a flinch, but the man doesn't move or make a noise.

"You stabbed me," Arrow states without emotion, staring down at the knife hanging from his chest. "That's fucking hot," he basically purrs.

"Yeah, and I'll do it again. But for now, bye!" I shout, taking off through the mud and rain, weaving through the massive trees to evade capture.

This time around, I have to be smarter and not stay still. I know the three of them are probably intent on chasing me down and doing God knows what with me.

Either way, they're all my enemy, and I'm going to act like it.

I pump my arms, jogging as quietly as I can through the mush until a scream breaks free from my throat as someone tackles me to the ground. I kick and punch when they roll me onto my back and forcefully lie on top of me, pushing their weight into mine. Hands grab my wrists in a tight hold as they loom above me.

I yank, attempting to free myself from their grasp, but it doesn't do anything. Mud seeps in through my clothes, causing me to shiver, and the rain continues to fall on top of us.

"You ran," the man on top of me says, with a deep voice I don't quite recognize. He's done well to disguise his voice, but I know better. Especially when those deep, dark brown eyes find mine.

Jericho.

"She stabbed me," Arrow pouts in his deep voice, gesturing to the knife protruding out of his chest. "But I kind of liked it. We'll play like that again, Kitten."

God. I feel like I've been here before. Masked men, looking

down at me with desire flashing through their eyes. Only visible by the lightning again.

"I'd stab you again! Get off me," I shout with gritted teeth, bucking my hips in an attempt to remove Jericho. Color me shocked when I find the task as easy as moving a solid ton of concrete—fucking impossible.

"You stabbed him. Wow," Jericho says in a deeper voice than normal. "What should I do with you? Hmm?" he hums, tightening his hold on my wrists.

I swallow hard when I notice he's strong enough to hang onto me with one hand, letting the other one caress my cheek.

"Maybe we should blindfold her again?"

My stomach pinches when Arrow pipes in with his suggestion. His fingers play with the knife handle with curiosity.

Not anger.

"Fuck," I breathe, staring between the two of them until another silent figure hovers above us. A stretch of silence settles between us. "No! No fucking way!" I hiss, thrashing my head from side to side.

Again. Fucking again. These assholes. I refuse to believe I lost myself to Jericho, Arrow, and Sheppard that night at the party. But it's hard to deny the fact when the same masks look down at me now.

"We had fun, didn't we?" Jericho hums, tracing the edge of my lips with his gloved fingers. "You blindfolded and us with our masks fucking you until the sun came up. You were the best. And the only pussy I'll ever touch again."

Static fills my ears. Memories rush through my brain from the night my freedom rang, and I took back my fucking life.

They don't give me a second to ask questions or respond.

"Then I drugged you. Sorry, not sorry. But we got you home," Arrow says with nonchalance, shrugging a shoulder. "Made sure you were tucked in nice and tight."

"You... You..." I stammer through a heavy tongue, and my

head spins. "You drugged me?" I ask, staring up at Arrow, who hovers to the side of me.

"Sorry, Kitten." But he doesn't sound the least bit sorry that he did that to me.

My mouth opens to retort, but I don't have a chance when Jericho shoves his fingers into my mouth and then back out again. Doing it three times until his long fingers touch the back of my throat. I cough, sputtering against him when he wraps his fingers right over my jaw with possession.

"Us. Yes." He cocks his head, examining me with dark eyes peeking through his mask. "We danced, Little Chaos. Then, we took you upstairs and fucked you into oblivion like we always wanted to do. That's the night you became ours," he grits out, squeezing my jaw between his powerful fingers. "And this is the night you'll remember who you belong to. Have I scared you into being a good, obedient girl yet?"

"I think we need to fuck her so she understands," Arrow says with glee, bouncing on his toes and making the knife wiggle in his chest.

The memory of our night together in the bedroom at that party, when freedom clung on to me so hard and pushed me into their arms, plays through my mind. I let three men take my virginity without ever knowing their identities. And now, they're revealing themselves to me one by one.

The rain around us lessens as the storm blows overhead, giving me a clear view of the twinkling stars and the bright moon. Shining down on the three men who slowly remove their masks and set them aside, revealing Jericho on top of me, Arrow to my left with the knife hanging out of his chest, and Shepp to my right.

"You see, Little Chaos. We weren't strangers at all." Jericho shifts us around so my legs fall open, and he settles between them, resting his hard dick against my core. "You belong to us. When I entered you for the first time, I knew I'd keep you forever. And that's what I intend on doing."

"But you were a very bad girl tonight, Kitten." Arrow frowns at the knife still hanging from his chest.

Between the adrenaline dump of being chased through the woods and the man in the house who—holy fucking shit.

My eyes snap to Shepp. He stares down at me with a softer expression. His face displays every emotion he possesses. There's a silent plea there. Something I'll unpack later when he and I have a discussion.

So, I listen.

Arrow grins, playing with the knife. "Don't worry, It's not that deep, Kitten. Besides, stabbings get me so horny." He nods to the obvious boner tenting his tight jeans.

I swallow hard, staring at it for too long. Between the knife sticking out of his chest and the boner poking through, I can't keep myself from staring.

I shake my head, settling in the mud beneath me. Jericho stares at me intently, like a puzzle he's trying to complete.

"You left the house," Jericho says in an oddly calm tone. "I gave you instructions to stay, and you ran off, violating the contract you signed. I could send you to prison. Not to mention, you stole my car," he growls with possession, baring his teeth at me.

"Like I've said before. I'm not a dog," I grit out. "Besides, I wanted to go home and find my shit. Your car was the only thing to get me there." Bitterness courses through me at the thought of all my things. "You took important things from me, too!" I shout, attempting to push from his hold on my jaw. "My whole life is gone!"

But those long, strong fingers don't relent when he blinks at me. His dark, wet hair plasters to his forehead, giving him a boyish look. One I thought I'd never see.

"Important things to you, huh?" he asks, tilting his head. A grin spreads across his lips, giving me an uneasy feeling in my guts. I'm at their damn mercy. "Tell me what they were, and maybe I'll give them back."

He's goading me into answering him. I can see it in his eyes. Like the letters Shepp took but never gave back.

"I want my letters," I grit out, attempting to buck him off me again, but it doesn't work. He's too strong and pushes me further into the mud. Those were the main items I was searching for tonight when I ransacked their house.

"Your letters. You hear that, boys? She wants her letters," he goads again, looking up at the other two when the storm completely lets up, and the rain stops pelting us. "Who are the letters from? Why're they so important to you?"

Nothing but the wind howls as they chuckle above my helpless body, stuck under Jericho's weight.

"Let me cut your clothes off, Kitten. Then we can discuss letters. First, we need to punish you with our dicks," Arrow says, yanking the small knife right out of his chest as small amounts of blood stain his black shirt. He holds it up in the moonlight, inspecting the blood on the shiny metal. "From our own kitchen, too." He clicks his tongue at me.

I swallow my protests when Jericho circles his hips, grinding against me.

"Stay still now," Jericho murmurs, slightly pulling back. He releases my hands but gives me a stern look. "And keep those above your head. If I had ropes, I'd tie you to a fucking tree and have my way with you," he grins like a madman. "But for now, Shepp will hold your wrists while I dole out your spankings. Bad, bad, girl."

Fuck. Goosebumps erupt over my flesh as he delivers his words. Shepp's large hand replaces Jericho's when he kneels beside my head. Now, I'm completely surrounded.

"Stay perfectly still, Kitten. Although, I do enjoy a blood bath. I'd rather not cut something so precious to me," Arrow hums in a low, throaty tone when he falls to his knees beside me. The bloodied knife gleams in the moonlight, reflecting its rays. He leans down right next to my face, looking me over. "Although, your blood would look beautiful on my dick as lube." He grins. "I've already called dibs on your ass, Kitten."

I stiffen, opening my mouth to protest. But I'm cut off.

Jericho hums, "Her blood was on my dick first. Despite the toy you loved to use on yourself, it didn't do anything." A sharp shiver rolls through me when he looks my body over with predatory intent. "It was fucking magic."

Before I can respond, Arrow presses his lips to mine, overtaking me. And I may be as fucked up as them because my back arches and flesh tingles. Like I've come home and belong in the arms of these psychotic masked men.

My breath heaves when he pulls back, lovingly moving my hair from my face.

"Aren't you going to get stitches?" I whisper, nodding toward his chest.

He grins. "What's another scar, Kitten? Only this one I'll remember forever as the moment my girl stabbed me in defense. Good aim, by the way." He grins more with pride, running a finger down my face.

"We'll patch him up when we're done," Jericho mumbles, holding out his hand. "Give me the knife."

Without protest, Arrow hands over the knife. I lick my lips when Jericho takes it, running his fingers over the bloodied parts and hums.

"Now, you're going to pay for your insubordination. You ran from us. You didn't trust us to lead you to your possessions. So now, we're going to play a game."

His grin sends shivers down my spine, but what he does next has me panting.

CHAPTER FORTY

Journey

I DON'T DARE MOVE. Breathe. Wiggle my toes. Or utter a protest. Not when a knife rests under my chin, threatening to cut me.

Since taking the weapon I so kindly provided from the kitchen, Jericho has made quick work of my shirt and jeans, cutting right through them with ease. Leaving me fully exposed in just my bra and panties.

He could have at least taken them off the normal way. But there's nothing normal about the Devils. Especially him.

"Don't worry, we'll buy you more," Jericho hums in promise, running the tip of the knife between my breasts. I shiver. "And more of these," he says, cutting straight through the middle of my bra.

Night air blows over my nipples, hardening them when Arrow gleefully removes the cups of my bra to the side. Exposing my tits to the night air and them.

I swear their eyes dilate in the moonlight as I lie in the mud at their mercy.

Excitement spears through me. Yet fear runs through my blood. The Devils. If everything they said was true, which I'm pretty certain I believe, then, I fucked the most dangerous men in the city while blindfolded, losing my virginity to them.

And I have no regrets.

"Beautiful," Jericho says, focusing the edge of the knife along my tattoo. He traces the flowers blooming and the vines weaving through the large skeleton key, hiding my biggest secret. "What an intricate tattoo, Little Chaos. But what's hiding underneath?"

My secrets. My villain origin story, leading to the darkness I've been forced to carry inside.

Heat fills my cheeks when he shoots me a knowing look, directing the edge of the knife over my scar.

"Who did the tattoo?" Arrow asks, popping his knuckles. "I need to rip their eyeballs out and put them in a jar for even looking at your tits. Those are ours now."

Shepp grunts, sending Arrow a strange look I can't decipher, causing Arrow to grin.

"That was me, though," he says cryptically. "But back to you, Kitten. Who did it? Whose head am I going to put on a spike in our backyard and then feed their body to my lions."

"Lions?" I ask, raising my brows. "What lions? What the fuck is happening?" I try to yank at my hands, but Shepp holds them in place with his iron grip. Bastard. He and I are going to have a very long discussion later about why he's hiding his ability. I'll pry it out of him like they're trying to pry my secrets from me.

"Focus!" Jericho growls, reeling the other two in.

"Sorry, Daddy Jer," Arrow coos, jolting back when Jericho slashes the knife at him.

"I've told you before not to call me that. I'll put another hole in your body if you don't stop."

"I love it when you promise me things," Arrow chuckles, moving back again when Jericho swipes at him. "So close," Arrow taunts.

"Fuck's sake," Jericho grumbles, settling his eyes on me with such an intensity that I shiver. "Maybe we should remind her who she belongs to," Jericho murmurs, transfixed on my scar.

"I can gag the secrets out of her," Arrow says with a grin, cupping himself through his jeans. "All this chasing and blood has got me so damn hard and horny. I could go for hours now, Kitten."

"You hear that?" Jericho says in a more demanding voice. "You're ours, and we're going to prove it to you once and for all."

I flinch when Jericho nicks my skin with the edge of the blade directly over my scar, before handing the knife over to Arrow for safekeeping.

"Fucking ours. You've belonged to the Devils since the day you punched your first bully."

I nod, breathing through the stinging sensation of the cut. He groans, running his fingers through the blood dripping from the cut, and holds them up to the moonlight. His tongue pokes out, swiping at his lips.

"I want your words, Little Chaos. Your apologies. Your confessions. I want everything you have to offer. Your bloodshed. I'm going to crawl in your skin and carve out everything I need," he growls, getting lost as he touches me. "Will you give me all of you? Will you succumb to us?"

No. I want to say. He can never have all of me. Because I'm not whole. My pieces are floating in space, belonging to a man who will decimate me completely. And Jericho, Arrow, and Shepp? They'll completely dismantle everything in my life.

I roll my lips together.

"I see," he remarks, running his blood-soaked fingers down my stomach toward my panties.

I shudder when he rips them completely off my body. Not giving me a chance to protest his actions. I wouldn't, though. My mind scrambles when his eyes lock on my bare pussy after throwing my ripped panties into the darkness surrounding us.

Tall trees sway above my head from the light breeze at the end of the storm. In the distance, I still hear the thunder rumbling as it travels away from us. I'm frozen by the look of desire in his eyes. He's hypnotized by me, watching my chest when I heave a breath, begging for oxygen.

Jericho Viotto looks at me like a starved man ready to

consume his meal after months in the desert with nothing to eat or drink. He looks at me like I might be the key to solving all his problems.

I shiver under his stare, which seems to hang in the air for an eternity. Everyone else disappears when I'm under his intense gaze. It's just me and him. Completely exposed and vulnerable, laid out like a naked feast. His eyes burn through my flesh, memorizing every scar littering my body from the months of torture I endured at the hands of a monster.

"Smile, Kitten," Arrow rasps excitedly, holding a Polaroid in front of his face. A flash goes off, blinding me momentarily, until the picture pops out of the front. "So beautiful. I'll add this to my collection."

"Collection?" I swallow hard when he shows me the picture displaying my naked body.

He grins at me, waving the photo around until he shoves it in his jeans pocket. "Yes. My collection." He raises a brow. "I've left you so many gifts over the past few weeks. Did you like that someone was watching over you while you slept?"

"Of course, it was you," I say through the haziness of lust pouring through me, getting the confirmation I had suspected since the night I beat Leighton's car into oblivion. I would have confronted him sooner, but I got kind of distracted. You know, getting arrested and all.

"Twas me," he says gleefully. "I'll watch over you night after night from here on out."

I'm pulled from my thoughts when the sharp slap of a hand barrels down on my exposed pussy, causing a yelp to leave my throat. His palm grinds against my clit as two fingers tease my weeping cunt, begging him to enter and take care of the ache persistently gnawing at my insides. I shudder when his palm moves across my clit, sending goosebumps down my flesh, and my toes curl. Another hard slap to my pussy has the breath leaving my lungs and my mouth suspended in a silent scream. Over and over, he punishes me. Slap after slap, bringing me to the brink of an orgasm that evades me.

"Fuck I've missed this," Jericho mutters, shoving two fingers into my pussy and slowly pumping them in and out. "I missed the way your cunt grips me tight."

I squeeze my eyes shut when his thumb brushes over my clit, brewing fire through my veins. My pussy contracts with want on the edge of seeing stars and coming, but he pulls back, slapping my pussy again.

"How can you miss something you've only had three times?" I rasp, tilting my head to look at him.

My mind continues to wrap itself around the fact these three were the ones who fucked me into oblivion that night so many weeks ago. How I fell into their clutches, I'll never know. Then it happened again at the club when they brought me pleasure in the middle of the crowd. And I can't forget the night in the office with the bow string.

It's like I'm drawn to them and always have been.

"That's the thing, Little Chaos," Jericho says, staring straight into my eyes when he slips two fingers inside my weeping pussy again.

"Fuck," I gasp out, clenching around his fingers, begging to come. But he stops again. Torturing me with the feel of his fingers.

"We've been on your ass for years, Kitten," Arrow says, wrapping his lips around my exposed nipple.

"Well, I'd say she enjoys that," Jericho says, removing his fingers from me. "Here's the rules, Little Chaos. You're not allowed to come. At all. Ever again. Not until you tell me everything you've stored in that mind of yours. I want your secrets. All of them. Forever. You can't run from me. I'll bring you to the brink over and over again. But you'll never be allowed to finish until I know what lives inside you."

My eyes widen when his large tongue sucks my juices off his fingers as he hums with pleasure. He squeezes his eyes shut, giving me a momentary reprieve from his intense stare. And then his words hit me.

"What? You're not going to let me fucking come!" I hiss, attempting to pull at Shepp's hands tightening around my wrists. "That's... That's... Torture!"

Jericho grins, popping his fingers from his mouth. "That's the point. We can come as much as we want, but the moment your pussy flutters around our cocks, bathing us in your release, you're in trouble."

"And will you tell me your secrets?" I retort, anger replacing the horny feeling.

Jericho stops dead, contemplating my words. "I suppose that's fair, isn't it?"

"I... Wait. That actually worked?"

He grins at my confusion, licking his fingers one last time. "An eye for an eye. I don't see why not. You want to know me. Well, I want to know you. Intimately. So, let's get a little acquainted." His eyes roam over my body again, stopping on the scars. "How'd you get these knife marks?"

I stiffen at his invasive question. Even if I wanted to answer, I wouldn't. I locked those memories of my torture away a long time ago. I never want to relive them or speak of them again.

"Just going in for the kill, aren't you?" I rasp, squeezing my eyes shut as images flash across my vision of the darkness I was locked in until my monster came back around to slice me up until I broke.

"Hmm." He traces a little scar on my thigh with his fingers. "I suppose I did. Let's start off small. What's your favorite color, Little Chaos?"

I can't help but laugh. "Purple. And yours?"

Jericho tilts his head. "Well. I..." He hesitates for a moment with his mouth hanging open. "I don't seem to have one. So odd," he mumbles the last part almost to himself, but I catch it.

"You don't have a favorite color? Everyone has a favorite color," I say, shaking my head.

"Well, not many have lived the life I have. Who has time for a favorite color when you're the son of the mafia king," he says, dropping his chin.

"Well, you're an adult now. Pick one." His brows furrow at my words.

"When I'm done with you, I'll contemplate which color suits me best," he says, tracing another scar with his fingertip. "Until then..." he hums, trailing off as he works closer and closer to my pussy still begging him to fill it.

My eyes flash to Shepp, ignoring the way Jericho's fingers feel on my skin. "And you?"

Shepp licks his lips. *"Blue,"* he mouths without making a sound.

"Blue is good," I say with a smile, earning one in return.

The way Shepp lights up when he smiles has butterflies fluttering in my stomach. There's something peaceful about him. Something I know I shouldn't trust, but I do.

"I never would have pegged you for a purple kind of girl, Kitten," Arrow mumbles, running the pad of his thumb over my nipple. "Mine is red."

My eyes widen when his fingers move south, moving through the bloodied cut on my chest. My nerves come alive with pain, and I wince when he presses hard.

"You look so delectable in red, Kitten," he mumbles, licking his lips and bringing his bloodied fingers to his tongue. He groans, sucking my blood straight into his mouth.

I blink several times, my breaths coming in rapid pants when he reopens his eyes.

"Yup! Absolutely delicious." He grins again, staring straight down at my tattoo. "We can kill whoever you want," Arrow says, sucking my nipple into his mouth, almost painfully hardening it with his wiggling tongue. "Especially the man who did this. I'd peel it off your skin."

Jericho chuckles, shoving three fingers into my cunt again, quickly moving them in and out. I swear my body jolts up and down with every intrusive thrust. My mouth hangs open as my orgasm attempts to peak again, but they all take their mouths and hands off me. It's on the tip of my tongue to break and beg for them to fuck me and let me come, but I don't. Not yet. I've handled a lot in my life. I can handle this. Right? Although, my monster has never taught me how to endure this kind of torture. Which is both a blessing and a curse. Guess I'll have to figure this one out on my own.

"Remember the rules," Jericho says, peeling his shirt over his head and revealing his gorgeous chest and abdomen. I lick my lips when the moonlight bounces off his flesh. He's so fucking gorgeous with his abs and fuck... My heart drops into my stomach when my eyes snag on the large, fresh wound between his pecs, still bright red and irritated.

My monster's words ring through my mind. He wants me to keep an eye on them. Report anything and everything they do back to him. And now I see why. They've been initiated into the mafia completely.

Jericho stands, staring down at my naked form. Slowly, he kicks off his shoes and removes his socks.

"Do you like what you see?" Jericho asks, unbuckling his pants and then pulling them down all the way, removing them and his boxers.

Naked.

Oh my God. He's naked. Just like the time when he forced me into the shower, and I drooled over him then. And now, shit. I'm drooling, but I can't wipe it away.

"No," I retort.

Liar, liar, pants on fire—my brain sings over and over again.

He kidnapped me—I sing back to no avail. I'm thoroughly enticed by his massive dick standing loud and proud against his abdomen, hitting near his belly button.

Lord have mercy. Did that actually go inside me that night? From here, it doesn't look like it'll fit.

I shouldn't be this turned on. It's weird, right? Ten minutes ago, I was running for my life. Now, I'm about to be rewarded with dick but punished with no orgasm.

My life sucks.

Jericho's hand runs up and down his bare dick as precum sparkles on his tip.

"Turn her over on her hands and knees," Jericho demands to the other two with his brows up.

"You heard the man. Let's turn you over and get that ass in the air," Arrow quips, turning me around until I'm on my hands and knees in the mud. Arrow works to get the rest of my cut clothes off my body and tosses them aside. Leaving me completely naked under the sparkling stars. And their gazes... "Fucking hell," Arrow grunts, putting his hands in my hair. "You're going to be a good girl and wear me as a gag while I stretch your ass with my fingers and prepare you for what's about to come."

"Which isn't you, by the way," Jericho says, placing his hands on my ass cheeks, spreading them apart. "What a beautiful sight to see. Your pussy wet and ready for me to fuck it bare. I'm going to fill you with my cum, Little Chaos. And you're going to keep every drop inside of you."

"I don't think he's going to take it easy on you, Kitten. He's going to pound you..."

"And no coming. If you do, there will be a punishment," Jericho says in a low voice, slapping my ass.

The tip of his dick runs through my wetness, coating it in my juices until he lines himself up.

I suck in a breath when Shepp drops to his knees beside my head next to Arrow. Naked. At some point in this whole ordeal, he got himself completely naked, and so did Arrow. And their dicks stand at attention right next to my face.

Fucking hell. How do I get myself into these crazy scenarios? First, at the party with the three of them fucking me silly. And now, letting them do it again out in the open. Anyone could be hiding in the bushes, watching our every move.

"Oh, two dicks for the price of one," Arrow sings, pumping

his in his hand. "Now, open your mouth, Kitten. Take my dick into the back of your throat." His fingers twist in my hair, forcing my gaze up.

My lips pop open to protest his words, but he does what he said he would—he gags me. My breath stalls in my chest when the tip of his dick hits the back of my throat, activating my gag reflex. My throat contacts around his large length, and drool flows out of my mouth.

And at the same time, Jericho slams home, jolting me forward more. I sputter around Arrow's cock, choking on it until he gently pulls out and rests his tip between my lips.

"You're doing so fucking good, Kitten. Catch your breath, and then I'm going to fuck your face. Okay?"

Staring up at Arrow from beneath my lashes, I take in the beautiful face, full of pleasure, shining back at me. His light eyes sparkle with mischief. A darkness that is usually found staring back at me, has fled for the time being. Giving me this lighter version of Arrow, letting me catch my breath in the middle of the action.

I nod in response, earning a smile.

"On second thought. Why don't you open wide and take Shepp." Arrow doesn't say another word, swiveling my head toward Shepp, who slowly pumps his length.

Shepp's fingers gently glide up my jaw until he reaches my swollen lips. His thumb presses down, swiping across. He raises a brow. Almost silently asking if I'm okay with this. I nod again, trying to take my mind off the mounting orgasm begging to barrel through me.

I yelp when Jericho slaps his hand across my ass cheek again, leaving behind a burning mark. I revel in the stinging sensation of the slap, forcing my mind to focus on the pain rather than the pleasure begging to unleash inside me.

"No coming. You're doing so fucking good," Jericho pants, squeezing my waist with bruising force and forcing his pelvis into mine.

Fuck. Fuck.

Shepp brings me back to him, rubbing the tip of his dick along my lips. *"Open,"* he mouths without a sound, and I obey, opening my mouth so he can press inside.

I hum around Shepp's length, taking him into the back of my throat. Hands remain twisted in my hair, holding me still as they use me how they want. I groan, pressing back into Jericho as my pussy flutters but doesn't come. Tears form in my eyes when Shepp's tip rests at the back of my throat, threatening to gag me again.

"Breathe through your nose, Kitten," Arrow murmurs, massaging my jaw gently. "That's a good girl. You're going to swallow every drop of Sheppy's cum, aren't you?" he murmurs against my flesh. But I don't open my eyes to see what he's doing or why he voluntarily let Shepp take over.

I gag, earning a groan from Shepp as my throat constricts around him.

Jericho slowly pumps in and out of me, moving opposite of Shepp. "You feel so fucking good," Jericho murmurs, leaning his body over mine and nibbling my ear. "You're taking him so well, too." His breaths brush across my flesh when he gently kisses my cheek. "But now I'm going to punish you for running away from us. I'm going to fuck you into oblivion as they paint your lips and face," he whispers. "Are you ready for that?"

Am I? Not really. Who can prepare for three men to fuck them up in the middle of the forest after chasing you with masks on?

"You're going to have to answer him, Kitten," Arrow says, as Shepp pulls his dick from between my lips with a grin.

"Yes," I rasp, nodding my approval, earning another kiss on my cheek.

"Good girl," Jericho says, peeling his front from my back. "Remember the rules. No coming. This is a punishment for you," he rasps, gripping my hips with bruising force.

Jericho grunts, slamming home over and over again, jolting

me forward harder than before. My orgasm mounts again, but I hold it off. Trying as hard as I can to focus on licking Shepp's tip and tasting the precum glistening there before he puts himself down my throat again.

Over and over, they use me until Shepp grunts from above me and pulls out.

"Stick out your tongue," Jericho demands, slapping my ass again as he pounds harder and harder, basically rutting into me with grunts.

I'm definitely going to be sore in the morning.

My breaths shudder when I squeeze my eyes shut and stick out my tongue.

"This'll be the best fucking facial of your life, Kitten," Arrow grunts, holding my head still as him and Shepp unload on my face, painting me with their hot, sticky cum. "Shit. Shit. Fuck!" Arrow grunts from beside me, doing unknown things as I keep my eyes shut and away from the saltiness that might burn them.

Arrow's grip completely falls away from my hair.

"Come here," Jericho grunts, lifting me up so my back rests against his chest. "You're doing good. Stay like that, baby," he hisses in my ear as his hand wraps around my throat. "You look so beautiful painted in their cum."

"Say cheese!" Arrow says breathlessly from somewhere in front of me as something bright flashes in my eyes.

"Journey," Jericho grunts, biting into my shoulder as his hips stop thrusting forward, and he stays buried deep inside me, coming on a loud groan.

"Next time, we'll all be involved. I call dibs on the backdoor!" Arrow hoots with excitement.

But I'm too damn drained to care as I attempt to catch my breath. Soft cloth brushes over my eyes, wiping the cum from my eyelashes first and then cleaning my entire face. My eyes remain closed when Jericho gently pulls out of me, and I wince.

"I didn't hurt you, did I?" he whispers directly in my ear as his arms circle my body, and he continues to hold me close. Like I'm a precious gem to him.

I shake my head. "No," I croak through a sore throat. "Nothing I couldn't handle."

No lies detected there. They may have manhandled me and told me what to do with their vicious growls and bossy voices, barely giving me any time to answer. But I loved every second of it. The pounding. The cum on the face. The dick in the back of my throat, choking me. It all led to this beautiful sated feeling unfurling inside me, making me Jell-O in Jericho's arms.

Well, all except the part about me not coming. That was rude. And extremely uncalled for.

I breathe through my nose several times, trying to catch my bearings. And my soul. I'm pretty sure she flew away into the darkness after Jericho pounded me so hard. In Jericho's arms, I feel wanted and somewhat loved. Needed, maybe. I'm someone to him. Not just a tool to fuck. Or perhaps I am. But I feel something there. A spark beneath my flesh, driving the darkness I've lived in for so long away. Maybe it's the endorphins talking inside my brain, or maybe that was the purpose of this fucking.

But I'm tired of hanging on to secrets that aren't really mine to keep.

I need help. And he may be the son of my monster. But he's nothing like him. Not truly. He's better.

"My mother sold me to a monster." The words leave my tongue like poison pushing through, knowing it's not supposed to be there, but it is.

Jericho's arms squeeze around me once in acknowledgement. His fingers draw tiny circles on my flesh, soothing me more as I melt into him.

"And these are...?" he trails off, tracing over the scars cut into my flesh by a man who wanted me so broken that he was the only one I would see as my way out.

I knew a long time ago he wasn't. But he's held Sunshine's health over my head for so long. I'm just so fucking tired of fighting by myself to get through this. If I have to open up, then I will. Besides, I think these three would understand my pain the best.

"From him," I whisper, but I don't elaborate just yet.

"I'll fucking kill him!" Arrow shouts.

"No rash moves," Jericho hisses at him, keeping me close. His breaths fall over my flesh when he gently kisses my neck. "I, too, have a monster in my life," he whispers directly in my ear. "Something I think we may share."

I nod, rolling my lips together.

"My mother left me with my monster. So, it looks like we have more in common than we thought, huh?" Emotions spike in his voice when he buries his face in my neck. "Don't worry, Little Chaos. One day, those monsters will be slayed. I'll make sure of it." His words come out through angry pants, promising me the one thing I've always wanted—my monster dead.

"Your father has my sister," I whisper, wishing the tear that streamed down my cheek would fuck off and cease to exist.

Jericho stiffens. "Then we'll get her back, too," he promises. Not asking the question I know he wants answered. "I never had a sister. It was always just me at his mercy until Arrow joined the family..."

"My father thought I was too fucking out of my mind," Arrow chuckles darkly. "Maybe I was. But who wouldn't want a dead squirrel as a present? Ungrateful bastard," he huffs under his breath. "But then I came here..." his words trail off, too, with a grunt.

When I finally peel my eyes open, finally facing the secrets I've revealed, I see them all in vivid color. Like we had been living in a superficial black and white world with brick walls so tall, we couldn't see the real issues at hand. Unfiltered pain rests in their eyes as they look back at me. When I swivel to stare up at Jericho, he gives me a small smirk—much to my annoyance—and confirms what I've been thinking.

Shepp clicks his rings, bringing our attention to him. He quickly signs something.

"He says he had a monster, too. And..." Jericho sucks in a surprised breath and then blows it out. "Who cut out his tongue as punishment. See? We've all got dragons to slay. Okay, that's enough secrets for today," he murmurs, kissing my cheek once again. "Let's go get cleaned up," Jericho says in a gentle voice, lifting me off the ground.

CHAPTER FORTY-ONE
Journey

As Jericho gently wraps me in his arms and steadies my body, shame instantly hits me. I've promised myself I wouldn't share my secrets with anyone. Especially them. But here I am, revealing more things than I wanted. It's like they took over my mouth and forced the words from my lips.

They brainwashed me through sex, and I fell for it. They wanted my secrets, and I gave them to the guys on a silver platter.

But I don't have time to dwell on the matter. I need to keep my chin up and keep living. For Sunshine. For myself. Maybe they can help me with this situation and free me from the grasp of my monster.

I sigh into Jericho's neck, burying my face there. I can't tell which way is up and which way is down. My head is a muddled mess of bullshit as I run through what was said. Do I trust them with this? With my sister?

I guess I'll have to now.

I can't unsay words. They're forever in the universe.

Forever with the Devils.

His strong arms hold me tight as Arrow and Shepp follow behind us with mud caking their knees and thighs from our roll on the ground. Arrow grins at me when I peek at him. But it's tamer now. It's more subdued, and the crazy look in his eye is completely gone. I shudder when Jericho takes me in through the kitchen door, and we all head toward the bedroom they've deemed as ours.

As soon as we march through the threshold of the bathroom, someone starts the water. But I haven't a clue who. Heat and steam fill the air as the shower starts.

"You're going to have to open your eyes for this, Little Chaos," Jericho murmurs, running a finger down my cheek and over my jaw when he sets me on my feet.

"Can't," I mumble, pressing my forehead against his bare chest.

"Hmm. I bet I can get those beautiful green eyes to look at me," he whispers with confidence, making shivers run down my spine.

Exhaustion sweeps through me, ready to take me to dreamland. My limbs buzz, and my ears ring. Well, until a finger presses at my clit, turning small circles.

A small gasp tears from my throat.

He chuckles, "We really did a number on you, didn't we? But you took it so well, like the good girl I know you are. It's a shame you never got one yourself," he hums, grinding his palm against my clit with more pressure.

"Fuck," I heave, digging my nails into his forearm as the warm spray of water falls over our heads.

"Open your eyes and look at me," he demands, pressing harder and then pulling away. Fingers grip my head, pulling me back until my gaze crashes into his. A smoldering look stares back at me, ready to go more. "Good girl," he whispers with a smirk. "Now, this is your reward for being such a trooper. You can come as many times as you want. But we each get a turn." His grin takes over his whole face when my head falls back onto a shoulder waiting behind me, and an orgasm slams through me. "That's one," he murmurs, leaving me a shaking mess.

They take turns bringing me to orgasm. So much so that I lose count at number five. It makes up for all the times Jericho was slamming into me, and my body was desperately seeking the release, only to have it pulled away at the last second.

My eyes remain shut when heat races over my flesh from the continuous warm water as the mud slowly washes from my skin along with the cum that painted me, flowing down the drain with the rest of the filth. My pussy aches in the best way from the combined orgasms and Jericho's dick.

"Lean your head back," Arrow murmurs, wrapping a hand around the back of my neck and angling me backward. Warm water falls over my hair as their fingers gently work through the mess of curls and knots left behind from the rain and run outside.

They continue to wash me under the spray of the water until they're satisfied with my cleanliness.

"Come on now," Jericho murmurs, taking my hand and leading me out of the shower slowly. "Let's get you dried off."

A warm towel meets my flesh when I finally peel my eyes open. Shepp stands there, examining my face with his eyes and taking me in. There's a pleading in his eyes, begging me not to say anything about what I heard from him. Which is fine; I won't expose his secrets if he doesn't want me to. But how can they expect the same from me?

Jericho walks into the bathroom with pajamas in his hands and comes to stand beside Shepp.

"Let's get you dressed," he says, nodding to Shepp as he takes the towel to the rack and puts it back. "Lift your arms," he demands, slipping a T-shirt over my head and then taps my legs, so that I can step into a pair of sweatpants.

"Now, let's go to sleep," Jericho mumbles with hooded eyes. "We've had quite the evening, haven't we?" he hums, taking me by the hand and leading me to the bed. "You're in the middle," he says, gesturing for me to crawl into the bed.

Clinking catches all of our attention as Shepp signs something.

"Right now, really?" Arrow says with a yawn.

Shepp signs something else quickly with a desperate

expression.

"Go on then. You know where we'll be," Jericho says, nodding toward the door with a blank expression.

Once my head hits the pillow, I swear my body melts into the most comfortable bed I've ever slept on. What a fucking night it's been. Between the demands of my monster and trying to find my stuff, I'm so damn exhausted I can barely function.

"Here, Little Chaos," Jericho murmurs from the side of the bed with a full glass of water in his hand and three pills in the other. "This is for you. I'm sure you'll be feeling what we did for days." A genuine look of concern passes over his face, like he's let his walls down.

"Thanks," I rasp, reaching over and taking the water and pills, swallowing them down without question.

Loud snoring next to me has my brows furrowing when I look at Arrow, who is fast asleep after stitching up his wound.

"He passed out," I say, scrunching my face.

"You'll come to learn that the second Arrow puts his head on the pillow, he's out. He also doesn't wake up until the sun comes up." Jericho tilts his head, examining Arrow, who seems to sleep so peacefully.

"Any chance I can get my pills so I can sleep like the dead?" I ask softly.

A vulnerable feeling passes over me when his eyes connect with mine. I can't tell what's going through his head, but he tilts it again, pondering my request.

"Not unless you plan on telling me why exactly you need such a heavy sedative to help you stay asleep? I can only assume it's the monster?" He raises a brow.

I swallow hard, darting my eyes to the comforter. What can I tell him that won't expose the whole mess I'm in?

"Mhmm," he hums, pushing the cover back and climbing in beside me. With a clap of his hands, the lights go out, and he pulls me into his side, resting his chin on top of my head. "You can tell me anything, Little Chaos. I saw the marks on your body. I saw what he did to you," he whispers softly, squeezing me harder against him. "And the mark under your tattoo. Whatever you went through, just know that I'm an ear to listen. I want you to expose yourself to me, not so I can use it against you. But so I can help you."

"Help me?" I whisper without thinking and breathe in his scent.

Why would he want to do that? Why the sudden change of attitude?

"Whether you believe it or not, I want to help. My father has officially crossed a line with you. He's touched something that doesn't belong to him. You're no longer his little puppet on a string. You're mine. My future. My fucking everything. Believe me when I say that I will fix any mess he gets you into. And I'll mend your broken soul with mine."

"Your everything?" I quiver, holding my fist to my lips.

"Mhmm," he hums sleepily. "You asked me what my favorite color was earlier, and I've decided."

"What is it?" I murmur.

His arms tighten around me, and he nuzzles his face into my neck. "Moss-green. The color of your eyes that darken and lighten, fitting your moods. Darker for when I chase you through the woods and the moon shines in them as I fuck you. Lighter for when you're genuinely laughing or from pleasure. You are my favorite color. My favorite meal and activity. It's you. You're my person."

I shiver at his words, letting them absorb inside me. He wants me to open up to him and tell him everything I know. Well, that's a can of worms I'm not sure I'm comfortable getting into. Even after his confessions. If he sees me for who I am and for who I've hurt over the years, will he still see me as Journey? Or will he want to cast me aside and leave me? Either way, I know one day, my secrets will be completely exposed.

It's only a matter of time before my monster's world and Jericho's collide, and I'll be smack dab in the middle of it.

CHAPTER FORTY-TWO

Journey

HOMEMADE DONUTS SIT in front of me, taunting me to bite into them. Dark chocolate and vanilla frosting drips off the edges, making my stomach rumble and cramp with hunger. I'm nestled between Jericho and Arrow as we sit at the kitchen table, overlooking the wooded land beyond the mansion. My eyes trace the trees, gently waving in the morning breeze lit up by the morning sun.

I lick my lips, avoiding eye contact with the men in the kitchen. Arrow tears into his donut, chomping loudly with an open mouth while staring down at his phone. Loud videos echo through the kitchen, followed by his laugh. Jericho reads the newspaper, covering his face completely. Thank God. I'd rather not have to face the music after last night's shit.

A coffee cup scoots across the table until it's right under my nose, looking as perfect as ever. I blush, peeking up at Shepp, who smiles at me and then squeezes my shoulder before walking away. He's been hunched over the stove making donuts and french toast this morning, staying in his own little slice of paradise.

I try not to moan when the perfectly mixed coffee hits my tastebuds, but I fail. The crinkling of the newspaper being set down has the hairs on the back of my neck standing on end. I physically feel their heated stares piercing through my skin like a damn X-ray.

But I avoid their looks completely, opting to stare out the window instead and get lost in the memories of why I'm avoiding them today.

Every inch of my body aches with each move I make, reminding me of what I did last night.

I ran through the woods in the pouring rain, fleeing the massive masked man in the kitchen who I thought wanted to kill me. But no. They only wanted to punish me for sneaking out. Or maybe it was for Jericho's car. Well, tough titties. It was the only vehicle with keys I could find. So, I had to take it. Even if it was futile.

My monster expects me to spy on them and relay everything back. What a damn nightmare.

I sigh to myself as his words bounce around my skull. Every task he's sent my way, I've faced head-on without a second thought. When he says jump. I say, how high? There's never been a question about it. Sure, there's been some remorse and dread.

But I've done them.

For Sunny. Always. I need my sister back at my side.

So, why do I have this nagging feeling in the back of my head telling me to speak up and tell Jericho everything? The abuse. The jobs he has me go on and how I'm supposed to relay everything back to him.

Probably because last night was semi-liberating. Albeit, out of character for me. There was just something about the way his arms encased my body. I felt safe. Even when my life was in danger. And I haven't felt safe in so many years that I melted at the opportunity to spill my guts. To my surprise, they opened up, too.

So, what am I supposed to do?

"Are you going to eat them, Kitten?" Arrow asks, biting into a bit of his donut with a satisfied hum. "If you don't eat them, I will."

My eyes flash to him, and then I quickly look away. Right. I'm kind of avoiding them. My fingers drum on the table with indecision. What should I do? How do I even collect information on them without it being obvious? Fuck. Or do I do it at all?

"Do you think he poisoned them?" Arrow quips. "He wouldn't. He likes your pussy too much." I hear the grin in his voice without looking in his direction.

"You need to eat," Jericho pipes up, demanding once again that I do something. "Not you," Jericho barks, slapping a hand away from my donuts. Arrow yelps, mumbling under his breath about Jericho's bossy ways.

I frown, looking at the donuts again and then at the would-be thief.

Arrow winks, grabbing more from his plate. "He's right, Kitten. You need to eat and keep up your strength." Like an animal, he tears into the donut, grunting with every swallow as he continues to scroll through videos. "Because what we did last night? Yeah, that's not the last of it. I can't wait to be inside of you again. My dick is calling out your name. He needs a sleeve."

"A sleeve?" I retort in disgust, wrinkling my nose.

He just wiggles his brows, shoving more donuts into his open mouth. Gross.

"Are you achy this morning?" Jericho asks, sipping his own coffee and watching me.

I shiver. Fuck. There's something about Jericho Viotto that spreads goosebumps across my body and makes me want to lean into him. Also, I want to hit him most of the time.

"I'm fine," I shrug, darting my eyes. I fill my mouth with blazing coffee, trying to avoid his stare.

"Of course you are," he mocks, setting his cup down. "I fucked you so hard, even I have bruises." I stiffen when he chuckles, running his finger over the brim of his coffee. "You're thinking about running again, aren't you?"

Yes. Of course. Who wouldn't want to scurry away from three dangerous mafia men who've trapped you in a mansion from hell?

An unsaid threat hangs in the air, though. He doesn't need to speak it for me to listen. It's there in his eyes as they darken with the thought of chasing after me and hunting me down.

"No," I clip out, continuing to stare out the window and take in the beautiful landscapes and avoid this conversation like the plague.

Jericho snorts, "I pegged you the moment I laid eyes on you. You're a runner. Whether you're running from your monsters or us." I glare daggers at him, narrowing them when he smirks. "Now, eat your breakfast." He taps the table several times before picking up his paper and resumes reading, picking it up so the front article is up. I cock my head, reading the headline—

Twenty-two-year-old Carolyn Crider of Briar Cove's Millionaire's Row has officially been declared missing. It's been four weeks since she stepped out with friends to celebrate her college graduation, and she never returned. Video surveillance has Crider entering a local hotspot, Rave, with friends, but never leaving through the front doors. Sources say the club owners are cooperating with local police and helping in the search for the missing woman.

A $100,000 dollar reward has been put together for anyone who can aid in finding Carolyn Crider.

She was last seen in pictures in a black mini-dress and red high heels. She is five foot, six inches tall and is described as being very knowledgeable and caring. Her parents are desperate to have her back in their arms.

A missing girl? From their club? That can't be settling with them well. But Jericho doesn't seem to mind as he flips to another page, blocking out the article altogether.

I don't say anything else after reading the article. My emotions consume me like a damn dark cloud. One I'm not excited to have hanging over my head. Give me the numbness my darkness provides me with any day over this stupid indecision. I'm stuck under this roof with nowhere else to go because they stole my shit. I want it back. It's mine. Especially my damn letters. So, maybe I'm just sulking and pitying myself. Or I'm just avoiding them because they rocked my world and freed me from myself for just a few hours.

Yeah, that's it.

"I have something for you," Jericho says, breaking the silence. His newspaper crinkles when he sets it on the table beside him.

I have a snarky grandpa joke on the tip of my tongue, ready to say. But I don't. I can't. Heat fills my eyes when he slides over a familiar stack of white papers with my name written on the outside of each. They're bundled together by a few rubber bands. Just how I left them.

My fingers run over the stack, mentally counting the number of letters there. Relief slams into me. They're all there. All of them.

"I figured after last night, those might mean something to you," Jericho says softly.

"My letters," I gasp out, hugging them to my chest.

They're my lifeline. The only pieces I still have connecting me to Sunny. After she was taken, she no longer existed. When I was released after six months of capture, I came back to an empty room where my sister should have been. It's where she always was. Her heart prevented her from doing day-to-day activities. We were warned not to stress her out. So, she stayed in her bed with her favorite shows and lived life like that until we could get her a transplant.

This is all I have left after three years of being apart from her.

"Thank you," I rasp, squeezing my eyes shut.

I don't want to see the pity or the curiosity in their eyes. I'll tell them on my own time. Not now, though. I feel too exposed and raw.

"You're welcome," Jericho retorts quickly, leaving it alone.

Half of me wonders if they read the letters, trying to figure something out about me.

"The offer still stands," Jericho says again, setting his coffee down. "A tit for tat, if you will. You spill more of your secrets, letting go and opening up, then, we'll do the same. Consider it a trust exercise between us. The more you trust us, the less you'll want to run."

I finally peel my eyes open and nod. "Okay."

But I don't intend to give more pieces of myself away. Not for nothing. Sure, they'll clue me into their lives. Will it be true, though? Will they really give me more if I tell them everything that's happened to me?

I don't know.

Because I'm indecisive as hell right now. I can't even decide which donut I want to eat next. Chocolate frosting or vanilla frosting? They are equally as delicious. But which one should I consume to fill my belly more? Fuck me. I hate making decisions.

Arrow's video abruptly stops, and he frowns when his phone vibrates. "It's Brandon from the club," he mutters, putting the phone to his ear with uncertainty. "Arrow's Alien Abduction Hotline! Have you been probed today?!" he greets into the phone with a grin, seeming more settled than I've ever seen him. Before my eyes, a darkness crawls across his eyes. A stony expression crosses his face, and his entire body stiffens. "I see," he grits out, running his tongue along his teeth in agitation. "You did the right thing by calling me. We'll be there to check it out."

"What is it?" Jericho asks with tension in his tone.

Measured steps stop beside me as Shepp approaches the conversation and signs something.

Arrow takes a large breath, looking between all of us. "Brandon has been looking through the tapes at Rave every night since that lady went missing. Seems we have a suspect in the case of our missing patrons. Finally caught the bitch on camera," he says through clenched teeth.

"Does it have to do with that Carolyn girl?" I ask, pointing to the paper.

Arrow snatches the paper from Jericho's side of the table, reading it quickly. "Well, she's one of them." He shakes his head, staring at Carolyn's picture. "Whoever it is, I'm going to stab them through the eyes and keep them as trophies." He grits his teeth hard, forming a tic in his jaw.

Shepp signs something to Arrow that has him rolling his eyes and flipping him off. Shepp signs something else with a serious expression.

"I'll chill when the cops stop showing up at our fucking club," Arrow chides with a frown.

"A suspect? Really?" Jericho hums. "Oh, goody. I do enjoy a hunt," he says, darting his gaze to me as I shiver.

"Then, we need to go. Brandon has it on the security tapes right now. Let's go get this bitch. I'm tired of innocent people going missing from all over town," Arrow growls, jumping from his seat with renewed excitement. Or maybe it's anger. Sometimes, it's hard to place his emotions.

"So more than just her?" I raise a brow when three sets of eyes land on me.

"No need to worry your pretty little head off, Kitten. No one is taking you." He grins.

"Except you three," I mumble, finally digging into the chocolate donut.

"We're the only ones who can hunt you down, claim you, and kidnap you," Jericho states nonchalantly while buttoning his white dress shirt.

"Yeah, what he said! You're ours," Arrow says, bouncing on his toes next to the table. "I want to rip into whoever is taking these girls." His hands rub together like he's plotting their downfall.

"You good with staying?" Jericho asks, turning to Shepp with his brows raised.

Shepp nods, signing something really quickly. Making me wish I knew how to read sign language. One day, I'll know how. Maybe by then, though, he'll speak to them like he spoke to me. I'm convinced there's something else there. And now I know why he doesn't speak. It's not that he doesn't have a voice. But his monster cut out his tongue. What I've gone through is nothing compared to what he had to endure. Someone deliberately took away his ability to speak. And for what?

"Make sure she's a good girl. Tie her up if you must," Jericho quips with a scary grin.

"You'd like that too much," I huff, shoving my donut into my mouth so I don't say anything else.

No. I don't have any plans of escaping any time soon. I'm fed, have a bed, I'm kept warm, and this is where I'm supposed to be, anyway. Not that I want to be. But my monster has me bent over the damn table with no lube. I have no choice. Not only that, these three psychos will track me down and bring me back kicking and screaming. So, I guess the decision has been made for me.

Much to my utter delight.

"Oh, I would, Little Chaos. I'd tie you to my bed with your ass in the air. Oh, the dirty things I could do to you, and you'd be at my mercy." His gravelly voice has no right to make my pussy contract and beg for it. He's illegal.

That's all there is to it. Jericho Viotto has to go. Because I shouldn't feel like this for the man who hunted me down, cut my clothes off, and fucked me until I was too tired to care.

But I do. He gets me feeling all tingly when he looks at me.

And I'm screwed.

CHAPTER FORTY-THREE
Journey

ONCE JERICHO and Arrow leave the house, a hush falls between Shepp and me. He keeps his back turned as he puts the homemade donuts into a container and stores them for later.

For years, I've known of the Devils. We went to school together. But I didn't really know them that well. They had bodyguards following them everywhere in the halls, shielding them away from anyone else. I was always curious. Everyone was. We knew who Jericho's dad was. What he did. Or, had a slight idea.

Then, they graduated. That was that. I didn't really think of them again. Well, until recently, when they decided to rule my life.

Sunny's letters sit like lead in my hands. I need to find somewhere safe to store them. I'll never part from them again. I take one last bite of my donut and shove the letters into my sweatpants pocket. Thankfully, when Jericho dressed me last night, he put me in something comfortable.

Shepp busies himself around the kitchen, cleaning the countertops and putting dishes away.

I wonder if he's the one who cleans this massive house or if they have a maid? Seems like something they'd have. They're the mafia, after all. Rich beyond belief. I've never seen them spend money. But you don't have a disposable income and have a car covered in the garage.

Shepp's shoulders hunch when he hears me moving about, inching closer to him. I want to suss him out and interrogate him about last night. Why did he speak? And why doesn't he now?

But I have to play this coolly. If he's already avoiding eye contact, then he's spooked from speaking to me. Or it's something else.

"So, these donuts were pretty delicious. Do you make them often?" I ask, putting my plate into the sink.

Smooth. I want to smack myself in the forehead. Make them often? I sound like I'm trying to pick him up at the bar. What I really want to know is why he's making the exact donuts I've eaten every morning for years now. I'm not an idiot.

I turn on my heels, leaning against the counter to watch him.

He peeks over his shoulder, his ocean eyes examining me with a hitch in his breath. He shrugs, ignoring me.

Something desperate rears inside me. I want to dismantle him and expose his mysteries.

Out of all the guys, I feel like I know him the least. Not that I know the others. Like at all. Their psycho tendencies have shown themselves more often, outshining Shepp's silent exterior.

So, I go for the slow approach. Small talk. My least favorite activity.

"Well, thank you for making them. So, what's your favorite thing to cook?" I ask, slowly meandering closer.

He watches me with caution, digging in his pocket and pulling out a notebook. He nibbles his bottom lip for a few seconds, deep in contemplation, before scribbling down a few words and handing it to me.

Lasagna and donuts. French toast.

I blink several times. Those are all my favorites. Foods I often found in my refrigerator after waking up. And the donuts? They tasted heavenly. But very familiar. Too familiar for my brain not to jump to conclusions.

Of course, Arrow was the one watching me while I slept and taking photos. So, what would stop Shepp from being the one to bring me food every morning? It wouldn't. If they've been watching me for years from the shadows, then those are the types of things I would expect from them.

"Like the lasagna you left me last night?"

I consumed every damn bite. Then, I ran it off in the woods while these psychos chased me. What a thrilling time to be alive.

A pinkish color appears on his cheeks, and he nods.

"Well, it was really good. It reminded me of something my mom made when I was little."

My brows furrow when the confession rolls out of me with ease. But I remember the delicious spices on my tongue, transporting me back to a time when I was a kid, and my mom was a mom.

There's something so peaceful and trusting about Shepp. The way his eyes slice right through me, unraveling the walls I've erected. Maybe it's because he doesn't talk back and listens to my past rolling off my tongue.

"Before my mom turned to drugs, she used to get up early and make me breakfast. French toast was her specialty. Then, she'd make this delicious lasagna, too. She was a good mom..." I trail off, not wanting to utter the word.

She was a good mom before she completely changed. She looked the same but acted differently. A darkness took over her eyes. An evil, hellbent on giving me a hellish childhood. The breakfasts stopped. Love ceased to exist. She spiraled into the abyss of drugs, losing her humanity.

Fingers gently rub my cheek, wiping away the moisture dripping there. My brows furrow as tears burn the backs of my eyes, flowing down my cheeks. My gaze snaps forward, connecting with his, and my breath stalls. His brows furrow, concern lacing every inch of his expression.

I apparently miss my mom more than I realized. The old her,

of course. The woman who tucked me in and brought me to work with her as she cleaned houses.

It's like mourning someone who's dead. Only she's still breathing. Merely existing in this world. I can see her every day. And yet, my heart breaks for her. Because she died the moment she shoved drugs into her veins and became the woman she is today. The mom she isn't.

I miss her.

Maybe it's the combination of what happened last night. When I let myself go and uttered the words I never thought I would. Or maybe it's my impending period hovering in the background, waiting to strike.

Whatever it is. My emotions release.

Shepp doesn't hesitate, pulling me into his solid chest. A scent of cinnamon and syrup wafts from his shirt. The remnants of the donuts we had. He's sugary sweet. Yet, rough around the edges.

His outer appearance hints at the damage done to him. The scar on his cheek. The missing tongue in his mouth. Someone damaged him. Ruined him completely.

Like me.

We're broken people, missing pieces of ourselves.

Maybe that's why we've come together. Embracing in the massive kitchen of their mansion. Clinging to one another like a lifeline in a wicked storm.

Run, Little Tempest.

His raspy voice whispers in my ear. So unused, low, and gravelly.

Tempest. A storm. How fitting for me. Considering I'm a hurricane, wrecking everything I touch.

It sends shivers down my spine. I want to hear him speak again and bask in his voice. Have a conversation for hours.

That craving has me clinging to him as tears spill down my cheeks.

His chin rests on the top of my head as his arms completely

engulf me. He feels like a sanctuary. Someone I could get lost in and actually trust.

If only.

I don't think I could ever fully trust anyone else again.

Especially the Devils.

So why does my heart ache so much? Feel like it's tearing in two?

A spark rolls through me at the feel of him wrapped around my small frame. He's huge. Probably six feet six inches tall. And I'm only five foot six inches.

So much care and love pours through his skin into mine like a calming pheromone. For such a big, bad mafia man, he's really cuddly. Something I never thought I could get comfortable with.

What does it say about me that I'm letting him comfort me when he kidnapped me? Used me?

But it's the first time someone has hugged me in so long that I almost forgot what it was like to rest in someone's arms comfortably.

His large hands run up and down my back in a soothing manner when I let myself go. Every emotion smacks into me all at once. Everything I've kept hidden in the depths of my darkness bubbles out.

I'm a mess.

"You're oddly good at this," I rasp into his chest.

My nose brushes against the wetness coating his tight T-shirt, and my cheeks heat. This was also not on my bingo card for the day. Breaking down in front of a man who could use it against me is bad news.

Fuck.

But I can't stop clinging to him. I can't stop my fingers from winding into his T-shirt as he holds me closer.

Freedom comes in many forms.

Fucking masked men at a party anonymously? Yeah, that's a liberating freedom I never thought I'd have. It separated me from the girl trapped under her monster's thumb into the girl who sought satisfaction with three men. For herself. She didn't do it because it was her orders to do so. She did it to feel something other than the clawing darkness pulling her under.

But this? An emotional release I've denied myself for years?

This is the freedom I've been craving. An intimacy I've been denied since I was thrown in a cage and thrust into the dark.

When was the last time someone truly held me like they cared? I can't even remember.

Shepp's heavy breaths fill the dead silence ringing in my ears.

I clear my throat, pulling away from him. He gives me a soft smile, reaching up to wipe the remnants of my tears off my cheeks.

"Thanks," I say.

A heat creeps up my neck and onto my cheeks. This isn't me. I'm not a crier. Not without being provoked. But there's something about Sheppard Mondelli that pulls at my heartstrings. A familiarity, I guess. Even though I should be the one consoling him.

He nods, cupping my cheeks. His head cocks. Almost as if he's silently asking me if I'm okay.

The answer is always no. I'm never truly okay. I'm just the shell of a girl hiding behind my darkness, doing what she had to do to survive.

Like being here in the Devils' midst. They kidnapped me. My monster wants me to spy.

I'm surviving.

"I'll be okay. I don't even know why that happened," I try to laugh it off, but he doesn't let it go.

He holds up a finger. Then scribbles a note.

It'll be our little secret.

I grin at his words. He must sense the trepidation twisting inside me.

"Good. I can't have Jericho knowing I've gone soft," I quip.

It's amusing how you rile him up.

Another note says, appearing before my eyes.

I grin. "It's my specialty. How else can I keep him in line?" I quirk a brow when he chuckles. Really chuckles. Showing off his deep voice vibrating in his chest.

My fingers spread over his solid chest, taking in the definition beneath his shirt. He's stacked. With every swipe of my hand, he twitches under my touch.

"You talked to me yesterday," I whisper.

Run, Little Tempest.

His deep voice rolls through my brain again on repeat. In my fear, I memorized everything that happened to me. In case it wasn't the guys, I had to escape and relay it back to whomever I could find.

His large hand engulfs mine, stopping my perusal. He swallows hard, staring deep into my soul.

He nods.

I lick my lips. "So, you can speak?" Dumb question, Journey. Obviously, he can. He just chooses not to. For some reason, I want to unravel.

He nods again, squeezing my hand without answering the question.

"Is it... You don't speak to them, do you?"

He shakes his head and squeezes his eyes closed. With reluctance, he lets go of me and grabs his notepad again, scribbling words.

With a sigh, he hands over the note.

I can't explain why.

Is all it says. So simple. Yet, telling.

"Am I special?" I quip, wiggling my brows.

A large grin spreads across his face, and he nods again, scribbling a note.

More than special.

My cheeks heat. I've never been called special for just being me. Sure, I've been called special by my monster in the sense that I was his weapon to boss around and wield however he wanted. Like now. I'm sure he has plans for me in the future.

Can I show you something?

My brows furrow when I look over the note. But I nod, my gut telling me this is a way to get closer to him. Maybe get some backup in this house.
"Sure."
He smiles, scribbling another note.

You saw my art? I want to show you more.

My heart flutters in my chest when he takes my hand, leading me out of the kitchen.
Maybe today won't be so bad after all.

CHAPTER FORTY-FOUR

Shepp

I DON'T KNOW why I thought this was a good idea. Bring her into my domain and show her my life's work—paintings of her. Showing her as she sleeps and other activities. My fingers twitch when she roams around my studio with a curiosity tugging her in different directions.

Awe rests in her eyes when she stops in front of my newly finished piece, featuring a brunette curled on her side as she sleeps soundly under the moonlight.

Her.

My muse.

"This is the one I saw," she says with a twinkle in her eyes.

Of course. I watched over the security footage of our home last night as I shut myself in this room and started a new piece—something I've never painted before.

I couldn't get the images of her in the mud out of my head. Not to mention the picture Arrow threw at me with a wicked grin, knowing exactly where my mind went.

Journey West is a piece of complicated art. Tough as stone on the outside, not giving anyone a piece of her. Soft as silk on the inside, begging for someone to wrap her in their arms and take away the untold pain she's living in.

Five minutes ago, she let her fortified shield down, letting me glimpse the woman underneath.

Hurt. Broken. Fearful.

There's so much there, ready to come out. But not yet. She has to get more comfortable with us. Trust us. Before she'll even think about opening up and letting us hear her secrets.

I guess that's what I'm for. The silent giant. I have a way of coaxing secrets from within to the light of day.

Only with her, I won't use them against her. I'll covet them. Just like her.

When I held her, it was so right. She nestled into my arms, using me as a shield to take away the ache of her mother's incompetence.

Fucking Sable. That bitch doesn't deserve the title of mother for either Journey or her sister. I need more information on Sunny. I need to know why she was taken and where.

Journey wanders around this space. Her gaze eats away at the paintings littered about. Something that wasn't out the day she snooped. There's more out today. More finished pieces to see and more incomplete ones to view. Wherever my muse takes me, that's the direction I head first.

And my new muse loves a certain brunette with freckles on her nose and bright moss-green eyes.

"This one is pretty, too," she says, cocking her head.

Her eyes eat up the incomplete night sky fit with dark shadows and tiny, sparkling stars. A project that had consumed me for weeks as I tweaked the shades, finding the perfect combination of colors to suit my vision.

I pull out my phone, opting for something other than my handwritten scribbles to give her.

"It still needs a moon," the robotic male voice echoes through the room, garnering me her attention.

She raises a brow, knowing I can speak. But how do I explain to her that I can't right now? My vocal cords seem frozen when I try. I want to. Desperate to speak to her again. But it's stuck with anxiety at what the future holds for me and the voice that was savagely stolen from me.

"Hmm. I guess it does. Are you going to finish it?" She examines the piece again.

"Eventually," the robotic voice says for me again.

"Are you working on something else then? It looks like this one is done?" She wanders over to the painting of her, hanging proudly on the wall.

I want the world to see what I've done with her. I've painted her in dark colors where she feels the safest—in her dreams.

"It's called In Her Dreams. It's done," my phone says again.

My cheeks heat when her knowing eyes find mine.

"It's pretty. Any inspiration?"

Now she's just being a brat and taunting me because she knows.

I'll never tell her that Arrow brings me pictures back from his adventures to her room. And she'll never know I keep a drawer of them for inspiration.

I snort. "None at all."

She rolls her eyes, moving on toward the canvas I've covered for the day. It sits in the middle of my room, ready to be finished. I swallow hard when she walks around it like a shark sniffing out the blood in the water.

"And this one?"

"Not finished yet," the voice says in an even tone.

My heart rate skyrockets when she raises a brow, pulling at the protective sheet hiding it.

"Not yet," the voice says again, not giving way to the panic roaring inside me.

She can't see this piece yet. It's not ready for her eyes, and it's depicting something I want to forever memorialize for my own.

"What if I want a peek?" she asks, with a small grin pulling at the edge of her lips.

This girl.

I inhale deeply, rooting myself in the moment. Her lips part when she stares up at me, batting her long eyelashes. All the moisture in my mouth evaporates when I contemplate revealing to her what I've done.

Will she appreciate it? Find it vile that I've captured such an intimate moment?

Fuck.

I guess I'm about to find out because I'm having a hard time saying no to her.

"You really want a peek?" I swallow hard, shoving my phone into my pocket.

Slowly, I make my way toward her, standing in front of my masked piece, knowing what lies beneath the tarp.

"Only if you want to show me," she whispers, peeking up at me and examining my eyes.

I shrug, heat taking over my cheeks.

"Then I want to see if you want to show me. You've got a real talent, Shepp. It shouldn't be hidden from anyone."

This piece should. It shouldn't see the light of day. Especially not to strangers. But I couldn't get it out of my fucking head. The more I sat on the idea, the more it begged to be brought to life.

My fingers twitched. My colors called to me. I couldn't sleep. All I wanted to do was paint the scene tattooed on my mind, forever capturing her.

So, I gave into the feeling, letting it take me over.

When they went to bed, I left them to cuddle Journey after our night in the mud. Even when I wanted to hold her against me and counteract Jericho's rough edges.

But I came here to paint my muse instead. Eager to relive our time together and immortalize it.

I nibble my lip, bringing my phone back out. "It's you," the voice says.

"Me?" she asks breathlessly, inspecting my unmoving face.

My breath fans her neck when I move behind her, covering her back with my front. Yes. This is what I needed again. Her up against my body. The delicious way she shivers has my cock twitching in my jeans, aching to be between her legs again.

I'm hopeless.

"Yeah. You," the phone says.

My hand falls to her hip, gently squeezing.

"Take the sheet off," the voice demands.

With shaky fingers, Journey reaches forward and pulls the sheet from the canvas. Her entire body stiffens against mine. As I do the same.

"Shepp," she breathes, dropping the sheet to the floor.

She visibly swallows hard. Her chest moves up and down rapidly. As her eyes cling on to the partial painting.

"It's..." she trails off, heaving a breath. "I..." Her tongue pokes out, licking her bottom lip.

My chest puffs out with pride as she takes in what I've done.

A hand around a throat. A mouth open in ecstasy as someone pounds her from behind. Tits out. Nipples hard. Head thrown back, lost to the lust.

My dick twitches more when she slowly swivels toward me, staring straight into my eyes. Her pupils dilate as her throat bobs.

"That's me?" she rasps, her voice dipping lower than normal.

Bravely, I run a finger down her cheek, tracing the red creeping up her flesh. I nod. I've ached to feel her under my touch for so long that it feels surreal to have her in front of me. I've watched from afar. Taken care of her when she needed someone to actually give a shit about her.

Here she is. Alive. Breathing. And staring at me like she wants to tear my clothes off.

I'd let her.

I'd lock her in this room and paint her for hours. Naked. With nothing between us. What a masterpiece that would be.

"You drew what happened last night?" Her brows rise, and more redness creeps onto her cheeks. Her fingers tremble when she grabs my wrists. "How do you remember?"

Remember? As if that's something difficult to retain. Every detail is stuck in my mind like a vivid image suspended for eternity. For now, anyway. I never want to lose the sight of my cum dripping from her face. A detail I'll add in soon.

I swallow hard, plucking the picture Arrow took from the bottom of the easel. Once I'm back at my full height, I hold the picture in front of her flushed face.

"Jesus," she breathes, squeezing her eyes shut. "He really took a picture."

I snort, digging my phone out. "You don't remember?" the voice asks.

She swallows a lump in her throat, shaking her head. "Vaguely," she murmurs, opening her eyes and examining the picture more thoroughly.

Last night was the most turned-on I've ever been. The prospect of chasing her through the woods with the intent to fuck her senseless so she never leaves again had my blood flowing straight to my cock. I never in all my years thought something like this could happen. How can I be so enamored by a woman I've only watched from the sidelines and have been barred from talking to? Until now, that is.

Now, she's ours forever.

"I still can't believe you three were the ones at the party," she whispers, almost in disbelief, like she remembers that small detail we revealed last night.

But we wanted her to know. It was us. We took her that night, and we'll never forget.

"Do you regret it?" the voice asks for me.

She shakes her head instantly. "Not at all. That night was the most free I've felt in years."

I swallow hard. "Me too," I rasp out through my rusty vocal cords.

Our eyes connect again, a heat sizzling between us the longer we stare. My hand cups her cheek, letting her rest there.

"So, are you going to work on this more today?" she questions, licking her lips.

I inspect her face, noting the mischievous twinkle in her eyes, alluding that she's definitely up to something. I should be on high alert. But my dick has a mind of his own, urging me to strip her down and paint her some more.

"I could," I say, cringing at the pain in my throat.

A pleased grin crosses her lips at the sound of my voice until her eyes drift, looking at the picture Arrow took.

"It's very blurry here." She points to the chest area, which has a blur to it from the rough movement of Jericho decimating her from behind.

"Kind of." I tilt my head, looking at the picture more.

"How would you feel about a live model instead of a picture?" Her cheeks heat more at the prospect.

I blink several times, letting her words set in. My voice freezes again. So, I pull out my phone and quickly type out my words.

"You want to strip down and be my model?"

"Well, you were going to draw me, anyway. Right? Why not have an actual image instead of a grainy, blurry photo?" She raises a brow like this is the most logical explanation ever.

Suspicion eats me alive, wondering what the hell her angle is. Just yesterday, she was running from us and attempting to go back home. Now, she wants to strip naked for me so I can draw her to perfection?

"If you want to," the voice says.

I search her eyes when she nods in agreement.

"I'd be more than happy to, Shepp."

I lick my lips, aching to ask the very question on my mind. "Why?" I cock my head.

"Why not?" she asks, stepping back from my touch, leaving me bereft and desperately wanting more. "Why wouldn't I get naked for you and let you paint me?" Vulnerability sits in her eyes when they dart to the ground. "I want to feel alive," she whispers. "I want to feel the freedom I felt that night in your arms. And I'm still so fucking confused how that happened."

We purposely tracked you down. We hunted you at that party, knowing exactly who we were taking to bed. We wanted you.

Needed you more than anything. But I can't reveal that yet. She can't know how infatuated with her we are. To her, there's no apparent reason for it. We've been in the shadows for so long, craving to touch her and to fulfill the agreement Jericho's father paved the way for.

Now, we're here.

Soon, she'll be Jer's wife.

Until then, we have to tread lightly and show her how much we care. Something Jericho has a hard time doing. He'd rather boss her ass around than gently nudge her in the right direction.

"It was meant to be," is all I say on the matter. "You were meant to be ours."

"Yours? Do you three usually share?"

No.

"Never had before. But we will for you."

You were our first. Our only. The one girl we've ached to do that with.

"I should feel so honored," she mumbles, nibbling her bottom lip. "Okay. So, where do you want me?"

On my cock. Is that an answer? Probably not. I won't push that right now. I'm a gentleman, respecting her decisions until the very end. She seems to be in a vulnerable state where she wants to celebrate her freedom. Is it because she's momentarily away from her monster? Probably. Then she's probably in heaven right now and enjoying her reprieve from that bastard. Something the boys and I need to discuss in greater detail.

I clear my throat, moving to grab a small stool I sit on when I'd been at this for hours, and drag it over. I tap the top of the seat and point.

"Right there?" she asks, looking into my eyes.

I nod.

"All right. You're in charge," she says with a sly grin, sitting down.

Mother fucker. She has a way with words. You're in charge. Fuck. This is going to end with me blowing my load in my pants by the end of this session. If I can last that long. She's willing to get nude for me, and I have to stand there and paint her like it's nothing.

When it means everything to me.

I swallow hard when she settles on the seat and advance on her with slow, deliberate movements. My fingers brush across her chin, tracing her jaw until I'm moving her long, curly strands over her shoulder.

I take out my phone again, finding it easier to communicate with her in this way and type out a message. "I'm going to remove your shirt," the voice says.

"Okay," she breathes, heaving her chest.

My fingers make quick work of dragging her pajama top over her head, and I toss it to the side. Nothing prepares me for the moment her tits bounce free, and there's nothing else underneath.

Holy fuck.

My dick throbs in my jeans, but I ignore it when she smirks up at me, straightening her posture so her tits are out front and present. I ache to seal my lips around them and nibble on them, making them harder than they are right now.

"You're okay?" the voice asks her.

She grins in response. "Paint me like one of your French girls, Sheppy," she quips.

My cheeks heat. Shit. I could have her take off her sweatpants, too. I could get her completely naked in front of me and feast my eyes on her flesh. But I don't. Not yet. I want Journey to completely trust me. Which she seems to be right now. Or at least, a little.

A loud chuckle rumbles beneath my chest, and I nod, giving her the thumbs up. "Just stay still, and this will be perfect."

"Okay," she breathes, watching everything I do as she sits directly next to the canvas. I prep my colors, get all my brushes out, and then I begin. My eyes glaze over from looking between the line of her breasts and the ones in the painting. If she hadn't been sitting here, I never would have noticed the small mole next to her right nipple. Or the tiny stretch marks on the sides of her breasts.

She's absolutely gorgeous. Raw. Bare before me. I can't take my eyes off her breaths, heaving her breasts up and down. I'm hypnotized by their shape and fullness. Although, I could probably only fit one hand around each. They're perfect. Just like her.

"How long have you been painting for?" she asks breathlessly again, zoning in on my face.

I smile, digging out my phone again. "Since I lost my voice."

"When?" she whispers, her brows furrowing. "Why would he do something like that?" Emotions crack through her words, and my chest tightens in response.

"Why do you need freedom?" I ask instead of answering her.

"Oh. Are we on that tit-for-tat, too?" she quips.

I nod. If I give her my pieces. I want hers, too. I'd gladly sing about my past, whispering them into her ear all night long. But that might be slightly too depressing. Even for her. But I don't know what she's been through. Or why they're so many light scars dotting her skin. I want to peel that back and open her up.

God, I want everything from her.

"I told you about my monster." A distant look takes over her expression, and her eyes glisten in response. "He forces me to do things I don't want to." She doesn't move an inch when she says those words.

But I do. My heart aches in my chest. "What kinds of things?" I dare to ask, watching her closely.

This is the information Jericho wants. All so we can protect her from the shadows of the night. Because if she's under her monster's thumb...

"Tit for tat," she says with a sadness in her tone.

"Fair enough," the voice says.

I continue to stare at my art piece, slowly coming together. My brush glides against the canvas with ease, depicting her body with perfection. Now that I have a clearer picture of her chest, they come out almost life-like when I'm working on them. The only aspect I can't quite master is the curve in her breast. Every stroke I attempt, doesn't come out right, and frustration mounts.

Once I'm satisfied with that part of it, I work further down, depicting her abdomen and belly button as they curve, arching her back into the body behind her.

Silence descends on us as I work. She doesn't ask another question. Her eyes glaze over, staring at the wall while I paint her beautiful imperfections, getting lost in her thoughts.

I cock my head, staring at the curve of her breast, trying again to paint it on the canvas. No matter what I do, I still can't get the shape of it right.

Without thinking, I run the brush across her breast, leaving a trail of peach-colored paint. She stiffens, eyes darting to me. But it doesn't stop me from continuing my strokes across her flesh, mapping out every inch of her.

Journey doesn't say a word as I continue to work on her, painting her in beautiful colors instead of painting my canvas.

Fuck it.

She is my canvas.

Without a word, my zone takes over, glazing over my eyes. My only focus is the painted woman in front of me.

"Shepp," she whispers, a finger running down my face.

Journey's concerned expression comes back into view. Once blurry. Now in focus. Wrinkles etch into her forehead and her moss-green eyes look over my face.

My paint-stained fingers clasp her hand against my jaw.

She smiles softly. "I didn't mind the new paint job," she mutters, gesturing to her chest highlighted in peach, red, blue, and purple.

My brows furrow, and my breath shudders. My mouth opens on instinct, ready to explain myself away. But I shake my head. No matter how hard I will it to come out. My voice remains hidden in a frozen block of ice.

With trembling fingers, I set my brushes and paints down,

noting I'll clean them later. I bring my phone out and type out my message, a rage consuming me.

"He hurt you." It's a statement. Not a question.

She pales slightly, looking down at the paints surrounding her scars, leading to the tattoo between her breasts.

"I don't call him a monster for nothing," she says in a low voice.

"Never by name?"

She shakes her head. "No. If I give him a name inside my head, it makes him human. He's not human, Shepp. He's a fucking monster. A monster who...who..." She clamps her lips shut, releasing several heavy breaths.

"He doesn't deserve a name then." My fingers trace the many scars on her body, looking like cuts from the sharp end of a knife. Some are barely visible like he did it with purpose so no one would question what she had been through.

They're everywhere.

Like she was tortured.

Rage boils through my veins. He's done enough to the people around him. That fucking bastard. He doesn't deserve to draw breath. Not while Journey is hurting so badly.

"My father cut out my tongue because I told on him."

Journey stiffens as the words roll out of my phone.

"I'm assuming he was a monster too," she questions.

"More than a monster. He was a demon." I still recall the blackness in his eyes when he snuck into my room and touched me in places no father should.

"Did you celebrate when he died?" she asks softly, gently tracing the scar on my cheek, another gift from my father and his knife.

More than celebrated. I rejoiced that I never had to listen to his drunken ramblings ever again.

"Danced on his grave," the voice through my phone says jokingly.

Journey grins, chuckling a little until she covers her mouth. It's like a weight has been lifted from her, and she shakes her head.

"So, did you get all you needed?" she asks, pointing down to herself. "Or did you need to paint a little more?"

I snort, grab her arm, and bring her in front of the canvas.

"I just got your body for now. I plan to fill in the hand on the throat. Then, more touch-ups and darkening the surroundings a little more."

"It's beautiful," she murmurs, staring at it.

"You really think so?" my phone asks.

Spinning on her toes, she faces me again and nods.

"It's not weird?" I ask, cringing at what I had her do. "That I painted you like this?"

But she agreed, I remind myself.

"No," she stares without hesitation. "You took a beautiful but scary as fuck moment and turned it into something amazing. You have true talent."

Pride puffs out my chest at her words, and before I know what I'm doing, I'm sealing my lips over hers. Her paint-covered chest and stomach press against my shirt, marking me in her colors.

I take several deep breaths, keeping my lips there. I suck her her bottom lip into my mouth and sink my teeth into it.

My dick throbs when she whimpers into the kiss. Fingers claw at my shirt, holding me tightly against her. Like she doesn't want to let this moment go. Or me.

My forehead rests against hers when I finally release her swollen lips. My fingers dig into her lower back, holding her close to me. My back hunches, almost borderline aching from bending over to her height. But I do it for her.

Anything for her.

Desire takes hold, wrapping its vines around me. My fingers trail up her sides, skimming the sides of her breasts. I relish the shivers pouring through her. All because of me. Goosebumps erupt along her flesh as my fingers explore more, taking in every inch of her. Like simple brush strokes, leaving lines behind on her body, I take her in.

I've lived in a dim world my entire life. My father thrust me into the darkness time and time again. When he died, I thought I knew what colors were. But that was only the tip of it. It wasn't until Journey was fully in my life did my eyes truly see the colors of the world. The greens of the trees. The purples of the flowers.

Life.

Journey is blue, red, peach, and purple.

She's everything in between.

And I couldn't be happier that she's mine to hold and keep. Mine to fuck and please. Mine to love and cherish.

I may not be the one who will say wedding vows in the end. Jericho will. Arrow and I will be on the sidelines with smiles on our faces, knowing that once Jericho puts that ring on her finger, she'll truly belong at our sides. In our fucking world.

And I intend on making all my promises come true for her.

"Lie down," Journey demands breathlessly, slightly pulling away from my touch. "Take your clothes off and lie down."

I blink several times, staring at her. She just demanded I do something, and my brain wants to automatically comply with her. As it should.

"Please," she whispers. "I need you."

Well, that does it.

I nod, not thinking twice about lifting my shirt over my head and tossing it aside. Next, I shove my socks off and then my jeans and boxers, leaving me completely exposed in front of her.

Her greedy eyes take me in, getting her fill of me as I do what she asked and lie down on the tarp on the ground, intended to catch the paint I may drop.

"Shepp," she breathes, crawling toward me with lust-filled eyes. "You're absolutely beautiful." Her fingers trail up and down my chest, toward my abdomen, drawing tiny circles around my belly button. My cock jumps for joy at her nearness. Sure, I got off last night by working myself over and coming on her face. But this is different.

This is just us.

No audience.

A small smile pulls at my lips. Beautiful. No one has ever looked into my eyes and called me something so poetic. Dangerous. Silent. Lethal. Now, those are all things people have shouted in my face. But they were on the wrong end. They were cowards tied to chairs, getting their fingers chopped off or their bowels removed as Arrow worked. Tears clouded their eyes.

But this.

She looks down at me with glazed-over eyes, high on lust. Exploring my body like I'm the piece of artwork she's been craving.

Journey smiles, holding up a finger. "Stay there." Not a question—a demand.

Precum glistens on the tip of my dick, boiling over when she saunters over toward my easel and grabs my colors in one hand and a singular brush in the other. She licks her lips when she stops at my side and drops to her knees.

"You painted over my imperfections," she whispers with brows furrowing. "You took my scars and made them beautiful."

"Because they are," I rasp out, squeezing my eyes shut.

I did it without a thought. I spoke words like I did it every day and revealed myself to people.

But only for her, it seems, do I have the courage to speak out. For so long, people have taken that choice away from me. My father for cutting my tongue. Gabriel, for not bothering to stop the abuse my father handed down. My anxiety for holding me prisoner in front of my friends.

I tried. I fucking tried for years to get it to work, to no avail. Now, with my Tempest hovering above me while I'm naked and vulnerable while she stares down at me like I'm a masterpiece— I've come unglued.

Her breath stalls in her chest. "Oh, Shepp," she murmurs, just as the cold end of my paintbrush travels down my pecs, right around the healing wound of our initiation. It bled for so long but never needed stitches. They never do. They're not too deep, but not shallow, either. It's meant to be a reminder of who you're loyal to.

I don't utter another word as she works the brush over my flesh, highlighting the wounds of my past. My ghosts hiding under my skin, eager to tell their history. I shiver, keeping my eyes closed, when it travels down directly under my eye, my cheek, and finally stops near my jaw.

"Now, the world will know what an ungrateful shit you are. I fed you. Clothed you. And you have the utter fucking audacity to tell my superiors some made-up stories. Like anyone would want to touch you. Now, I'll make it so no one will," my father slurs in my ear as he holds me down, slicing through my face with ease until blood wells on the wound and drips directly into my ear. *"You're a clown, Sheppard. One I hate to call my son."* He chuckles at that, playing in the wound like the sadistic bastard he is.

Fucker.

"All from your monster?" she whispers, running her thumb over my bottom lip and slightly dragging it around.

I nod. My voice freezes again.

"If he weren't already dead, I'd kill him for you again," she murmurs, running her fingers down my chin, over my bobbing throat, and trailing toward my throbbing cock. "You're so excited for me," she murmurs, wrapping her delicate fingers over my dick.

I groan when she moves her hand up and down my length with ease. My lips pop open as I suck in air, moaning when her lips meet my tip, and she gives it a small kiss. My fingers instinctively find her hair and wrap it around my fingers as she slowly goes down my length, taking me into the back of her throat.

"Journey," I rasp in ecstasy when she gags, tightening around me. "You're doing so fucking good, Little Tempest." My balls nearly tighten when she moans around my cock.

Think of anything but this beautiful girl sucking you off, covered in paint, and humming around your dick. Anything at all. Football. Your mom's face, for God's sake. Anything other than the cum threatening to spill down her throat.

"Let me fuck you!" I grunt desperately, gasping for air when her lips pop off my dick.

My eyes slowly flutter open when her lips press against mine again.

"Did I do okay?" she asks with vulnerability.

My fingers clasp the back of her neck when her tongue sneaks into my mouth, swiping against nothing but empty space. I groan into her, forcing her to pull away.

"You did amazing," I rasp out in a gravelly voice, causing her to smile.

"I like your voice," she whispers, shimmying out of her pajama pants, discarding them to the side.

My cheeks heat at her compliment when she takes charge and straddles my thighs, keeping my rock-hard dick in her hands.

"I like it when you talk to me. Just us. You make me feel special." Her cheeks turn bright red when she says that, and she raises up, lining me with her dripping pussy.

"Fuck. Fuck. Journey," I gasp out when she finally sinks completely down on my dick, encasing me in her. "You feel so good," I moan, running my fingers over her breasts and gently squeezing.

"You're not too bad yourself," she moans out, throwing her head back when I tweak her nipple.

"Ride me," I demand, grabbing her hips. "I'm going to cum inside you. Paint your insides with my cum, and I won't let a drop come out."

She moans louder at my words, working her hips up and down until she has a steady rhythm going. Her fingers claw at my chest when I pound up into her at a steady speed, meeting her thrust for thrust.

"Journey!" I cry out when a fire licks my spine. My balls

tighten. And I come with her name repeating over and over on my lips.

"Shepp," she groans, grinding against me as she shudders, squeezing every ounce of my cum out with her orgasm.

Slowly, I sit up, keeping myself inside her and resting her forehead against mine. My fingers comb through her wild curls, gently massaging her scalp.

"You're a piece of art, Little Tempest."

"You're a masterpiece," she whispers to me, squeezing her eyes shut. "Who granted me a freedom I never thought I'd have."

"I'll give you every freedom you need. We all will," I rasp, running my fingers up and down her back in a soothing manner.

"I've killed people, Shepp," she confesses, stiffening against me and refusing to open her eyes. "He made me."

"You're not alone in that," I murmur, gently kissing her cheek. "I've killed for men I didn't want to, too. I hate blood. I hate it all. But I'd burn down the world for you. The others would, too."

"Me too," she laughs, furrowing her brows.

"You were missing for six months in high school." Her eyes fly open, meeting mine, and she nods, confirming without saying a word. "Did he..."

"Yes. Something happened. Something bad with my sister, and he took me as punishment. He uses me, Shepp. He uses me," she reiterates again, widening her eyes like she wants me to understand.

I nod. "That'll never happen again. Not now. You're with us. He can't touch you," I murmur.

She rolls her lips together with uncertainty crossing her face. "Okay." But I hear the words she doesn't want to say—I don't believe you. How could she? This man has tormented her, left scars, and kidnapped her.

And that's only the beginning of her tale she's willing to share.

We'll find out more.

CHAPTER FORTY-FIVE
Shepp

OUR BREATHS MINGLE together as we continue to sit on the floor of my art room. Most nights, I stay up, painting my life away. Well, only since she's been in the picture. Now, I have my muse right where I need her. In front of me, naked and panting from our session together. Paint still highlights her skin and mine. Together, we're art, showing off the pain from our years of abuse.

That ends now.

"Let's get you cleaned up," I rasp, using my spent voice and trying to change the subject for her.

Her moss-green eyes take me in, stopping on the paint decorating my body.

"Your voice," she murmurs, running her fingers over my throat. "Never stop using it."

I swallow hard against her fingertips. "I'll try," I say through a rough voice, still gravelly from lack of use.

I don't know what it is about her. Or why my anxieties slip into nothing when she's around, so vulnerable and raw.

"Can I keep you?" I rumble, lifting her off my hips and keeping her in my arms as I stand. My forearm rests under her bare ass, holding her tightly to me. I never want to give this moment up. I never want to forget the way she felt wrapped around me. Or the secrets she felt secure enough to tell.

She smiles, giggling slightly. "Maybe."

"I will," I whisper, kissing her cheek.

Without another word, I carry her toward our bedroom with the bathroom in mind. Together, we need to cleanse the paint from our bodies and the scent of what we just did. Although, I'd much rather her smell like me for the rest of the day.

I don't bother to set her down when we enter the massive shower and turn on the hot water for the both of us. The remnants of the colors on our bodies slowly spiral down the drain as I set her on her feet.

"Oh no," she murmurs, paling slightly at my cock. "I..."

My eyes fall to the red painting my dick. I run my fingers over it, checking the consistency, and it all clicks into place when my eyes snap to hers. Normally, blood makes my head spin, and I want to leave the room. But hers?

Well, that's a whole new feeling taking hold.

"You're okay?" I ask, lifting her chin. "It didn't hurt, did it?"

She shakes her head, pursing her lips when she holds up her fingers, examining the red on them, too. "No. I don't think so. I apparently started my period. I... I'm sorry," she murmurs, trying to break away from my hold as embarrassment clings to her.

"Don't be sorry. It's natural. And see? I can just wash it off," I say softly, running water over my dick so the blood completely disappears, just like the paint.

She wrinkles her nose and nods. "Thanks, Shepp," she says softly, leaning her head back into the hot water. "I think I'm going to need some tampons, though. I have an IUD, so my periods sometimes come and sometimes don't. Apparently, it wanted to come today." She shrugs, avoiding eye contact with me.

"After this, I'll take you." A sense of relief slams through me as I freely talk to her. Being able to communicate with her, using my broken voice, is unmeasurable.

I know it'll shut down again when the guys return. I know my anxiety will spike, and it'll freeze up like it has in the past. But I revel in these moments with just her and I, speaking to one another normally.

Journey gives me a small smile as we clean each other, rubbing soap all over our bodies until the paint and blood are gone. It feels like hours with her under the hot spray of the shower, that never ceases to keep us warm. I help her out, dry her off with care, and then take her into her closet. She looks around, locating a pair of black leggings, and gets dressed.

"Meet me in my room," I rasp out, pointing out the door, and she nods.

I go to my room, get dressed in a pair of jeans and a T-shirt, and then meet her by the door. By the time we reunite and I kiss her cheek, the front door slams open, and Arrow and Jer's loud, angry voices echo through the mansion.

"Looks like the grump of the house has returned," she quips, looking behind her.

Instantly, anxiety grips my throat, and everything seizes inside me. My lips pop open, wanting to tell her that we need to go downstairs, but nothing comes out.

I've officially locked up.

Her brows furrow. "You're nervous?"

I shake my head.

"It's okay, Shepp," she whispers, putting a hand on my chest.

I take a deep breath and grab her hand, leading her down the stairs and straight into the kitchen, where Jericho paces a small trail into the floors and Arrow snacks.

The moment Jericho and Arrow catch sight of us, they take us in. Wet hair. New clothes. A pleasant smile on my lips. Yeah, they know exactly what we just did.

Suckers.

That's what they get for leaving me here. But I don't mind. I'd stay behind any day, just to hang out with Journey and paint with her.

'*What's the news?*' I sign, my voice going into hiding.

Jericho runs his hand through his messy locks with a frown pulling at his lips.

"Seems we have a snake to snuff out."

"A snake?" Journey asks, standing directly beside me with her wet hair combed through.

My brows furrow as I take in her stiff muscles and paling face. Until she shakes herself out of it and becomes a shell of herself. I swear every emotion evaporates from her, like another person has taken over.

"Someone's been stealing people from the club. We caught one woman on camera carrying a drunk girl out. She threw her into a car and took off."

"Maybe she was just helping a drunk friend?" Journey asks with her brows furrowed.

"Mmm. Indeed. She makes it seem that way so we don't suspect anything. Except when she came back for a second time empty-handed and proceeded to carry another girl out. Same thing," Jericho says way too calmly for my liking. "Fuck!" he grunts, grabbing at his hair. "The police aren't concerned in the least. I'm going to have to make some calls and get them more involved. Apparently, we're not the only institution getting hit. More and more people around town are disappearing. And I have no fucking clue who is behind it."

"They're slimy little fucks," Arrow grumbles, biting into an apple aggressively. "They avoid the cameras the best they can, too. Makes it fucking impossible to pinpoint. It's like someone's giving them the heads up and instructions."

"Even some of the cameras were purposely turned off in some areas," Jericho says in a low voice, placing his hands behind his back.

'*So, someone on staff is helping?*' I sign.

I feel the burn of Journey's eyes on the side of my head, but I ignore it. If I could muster up the courage and tamp down my anxiety, maybe I could speak to them normally. But this has been our normal for so long, I don't know what my problem is.

"Yes. It appears someone in our midst is helping them pull off this—whatever it is!" Jericho huffs with uncertainty.

"I bet it's that Shadow fucker," Arrow hums into his apple. "I can't wait to break that fucker in two and bounce his eyeballs off the ground."

"Shadow?" Journey asks, garnering all of our attention. "Who is Shadow?"

Arrow bites into his apple again, chewing loudly. "He's our arch nemesis."

"Arrow," Jericho sighs, shaking his head.

'She deserves to know. Give her an inch, you'll be surprised,' I sign, my heart fluttering with the information she handed me today. But I'll keep it to myself for now. I have Journey's trust. I earned it. Not Jericho.

'Did she happen to tell you things today?' Jericho signs.

'Just tell her,' I sign, avoiding the conversation altogether.

"Shadow is... Well, we're not sure. Hence the name Shadow," he says through gritted teeth. "Slimy asshole hides in the dark, doing his biddings right under our noses. It's been that way for almost three years now."

"He's a pain in our side, constantly putting dirty drugs on the street and killing people on our turf."

Journey licks her lips. "Jenni told me about him."

Jericho immediately straightens. "Oh, yeah? And what did Jenni happen to say?"

"He lives on an island like fifty miles from here or something." She shrugs, chewing on her nail.

"Oh! Anything else, Kitten?" Arrow beams, finishing off the apple completely—seeds and all. "Like location? I want to use my rocket launcher and cook him until he's crispy!"

"You have a rocket launcher?" Jericho asks, paling slightly.

Great. Give the crazy man a weapon that could take out an entire city block and cause a massive fire. Just what he needs.

Arrow grins, mimicking zipping his lips, and tosses the invisible key.

"Arrow, I'm fucking serious!" Jericho growls. "You can't use that in this city."

"And I'm not. I have ammunition with Shadow's name on it. Along with my grenade launcher, too."

"Why?" Jericho sighs out. "Where did you get these?"

Arrow shrugs. "Blackmarket dealer down on Fifth Street."

"We'll circle back around to that..."

"I will fire that rocket launcher," Arrow says, pointing a finger at Jer. "Straight into Shadow's ass."

"If you must," Jer quips back, shaking his head. His eyes find mine, and we have a silent conversation.

Watch him.

We're his keepers, after all. And Jer knows this conversation is going nowhere.

"So, did Jenni happen to say anything else about this Shadow fucker? He's been a real thorn in my side for far too long."

"No. That's all she said. But uh, her boyfriend was with him that night we went to the club." She visibly swallows, leaving that hanging in the air.

"Seems we need to have a nice long discussion with Elias and his girlfriend," Jericho says, straightening to his full height. He eyes Journey, carefully inspecting her blank face.

She's hiding more. She knows something else, but she's not saying.

"Is Jenni okay?" she blurts, staring between the three of us.

"Why wouldn't she be?" he inquires, raising a brow.

"I just haven't been able to contact her since you took my phone, and I was just wondering..." she trails off, nibbling her lip with worry.

Of course. Jenni was her best friend—inseparable, even.

"Jenni is fine. She's with Elias at their compound near the edge of the city, living her best life," Jericho states truthfully.

'*We need to take Journey to the drugstore*,' I sign.

"Why?" Jericho asks, waving a hand. "We have pain relievers here. What could she possibly..."

"I'm on my period, asshole," she grits out, curling her fists. "Unless you have tampons mysteriously tucked away in your mansion."

Arrow grins, wiggling his brows. "Oh, boy. Can I earn my red wings?"

"What?" she recoils in horror. "No! Gross."

Arrow pouts. "But..."

"No," she says again.

"Well, then. Let's go get you some super-absorbent tampons," Arrow says with a grin, waltzing by and licking his fingers.

Jericho cocks his head. "He's up to something."

"He better stay away from me," Journey says, narrowing her eyes on Arrow's back as he walks right out the front door.

"Don't worry, Little Chaos. You'll get used to Arrow getting what he wants," Jericho hums, wrapping an arm around her shoulders. "Now, let's get your shoes on and head to the store."

Journey wrinkles her nose in displeasure. "Maybe this wasn't such a good idea to involve all three of you."

"Why? What could go wrong?" Jericho says with a smirk.

"Everything," she grumbles, shoving out of his grip.

CHAPTER FORTY-SIX

Journey

I am never telling another man in my life that I'm on my period. It won't even last that long. Maybe a day or two with how my IUD seems to work. When I first got it placed when I turned sixteen, I was told to expect this. That my periods would taper off, and then, they'd come back at some point. Maybe it's time for a new check-up.

"All right, Kitten. I found them. Supers for a super good pussy." Arrow wiggles his brows, holding up the box of tampons right next to his face.

"That's not what it means," I grumble, swiping the box away from him and putting it back on the shelf. "For fuck's sake." I swipe a hand down my face when he grabs a box of regulars and inspects them.

"Regular? But your pussy is otherworldly, not this," he grunts, shaking the box like it has a prize inside.

"For crying out loud! Where are the other two?" I curse, looking around the store, but don't find Jericho or Sheppard anywhere.

Bastards.

They left me here with Arrow to die in my humiliation. Although, I shouldn't be mortified to buy tampons with these three mafia men. It's a natural part of life. Something my body was meant to do to make babies and all that good stuff. But still, if

Arrow doesn't stop talking about my vagina, I'm going to throat punch him into next week.

"Arrow," I grit out, swiping the box from him again and putting it on the shelf. "It's for flow."

I really wish the ground would swallow me whole and never spit me back out. Transport me back to a different reality, please.

"Flow?" Arrow asks, tilting his head. "Oh, flow! Like how much blood is going to leak out of your pussy. So, it's like a stopper, right? The bigger, the better? Like my dick. You know, I could just plug you up for the next week. You could warm my cock and..."

I put my hand over his mouth, silencing him before he can continue spouting off about my period. How is this my damn life? My eyes dart around as a woman stands mortified behind us. She quickly grabs a box of panty liners and sends Arrow a deadly look with red cheeks.

Great. A witness to the period talk. How can it get any worse?

"Kitten, just let me warm my cock in you and help," Arrow mumbles beneath my palm.

Oh, it got much worse. I'm sure I'm as red as a tomato. How has society made women feel so dirty about having a period like it isn't normal? I should be able to scream from the rooftops that my hooha is bleeding. But yet, here I am. Heat filling my cheeks in the middle of a damn corner convenience store.

"No," I bark. "Absolutely not. Please, just... grab this!" My voice trembles with frustration when I grab a variety pack.

"A variety pack?" he asks, raising his brows.

"It has every size I need," I grumble, putting it under my arms.

"But we can still get you the supers, right? What about these winged thingies? Oh, they go in your panties," he says, picking up a box. "They're super absorbent, too." His brows wiggle when he puts them under his arm with pride.

I sigh. This seems like a losing battle with him. But it warms my heart to see him care so much. I guess.

"Thanks, Arrow," I grumble, pulling him out of the feminine

products and onto other things like greeting cards and birthday gifts. These seem innocent enough.

"Any time, Kitten. Although, I don't think you'll need these pesky tampons for very much longer," he quips, plucking them from under my arm.

"Yeah? And why is that? I'm pretty sure I'm going to be shedding my damn lining for another thirty years or so until I hit menopause at least," I say as he intently stares down at the packaging of the tampons with curiosity.

"Oh, because we're going to put a baby in your belly," he says offhandedly, tilting the box again. "How do these things fit in, Kitten?" He shakes the box a little, listening as they rustle on the inside without a care. "Can I put it in your pussy? Oh, there's instructions..." he carries on about the tampon box he's studying, but I'm too focused on the words he said.

"What?" I sputter, nearly choking on my spit. "A baby?"

What the hell is this man on? There's no way in hell that's happening any time soon. Sure, maybe eventually I'd like to become a mother. Better than mine, too. But today? Next month? I'll pass for now...

"You'd look so damn hot with a big old belly, filled with our baby. Well, one of ours, at least. Then, we can keep going. I want ten." He grins at that.

"Ten?" I sputter with wide eyes.

Arrow fucking grins like a psychopath at me being pregnant with ten damn kids. Jesus. H. Christ. What did I get myself into? And why is he saying this? Also, why am I a frozen block of human standing before him with my lips flapping open? I can't move or speak.

"And your tits," he murmurs, putting his arm over my shoulders, pulling me close. "I'm going to fill you with so much cum, you're going to taste it. And it's not going in your mouth either. No matter if you're bleeding or not, I'm filling you completely." He grins, kissing my temple. "Tomorrow, I want to introduce you to my pet lions."

I blink several times. "Arrow!" Finally, I'm able to utter a single word. "You're crazy. Absolutely fucking insane. And pet lions?" I ramble, going over the information in my head.

There's so much to unpack here. Babies? Lions? David Rose's voice from *Schitt's Creek*, rings through my mind on repeat shouting: What the absolute fuck is going on here? Because, seriously? What the hell is going on?

As a kid, I always wanted children. But that was when my mom showed me love and kindness, making up for the shortcomings of my sperm donor. Then she changed from my superhero to the villain of my story in the blink of an eye. And my dad? Pfft. That lazy bastard never came around. All my mom could get him to do was a DNA test proving I was his and a letter from his attorney telling my mother never to contact him again.

What a waste of space. I'm glad Corbin West kicked the bucket a few years ago. Sayonara, Assbag. Thanks for proving to me what a parent shouldn't be.

But this? Him wanting to get me pregnant has me majorly side-eyeing him. What makes him think I'm going to be sticking around for that long? I don't even understand why I'm living in their house, eating their food, and staying in their bed.

Yeah, you do. Your monster demanded you to. A little voice says in the back of my mind. Not to mention the contract.

Fuck, but not really.

Jericho took me long before my monster had anything to say about it. I'm under contract. Which is bullshit, anyway. I could walk out of their house without true legal recourse. But I'm stuck. With a man who apparently wants to impregnate me. Ten times over. Remind me to keep his dick as far away from me as possible and to book an appointment with my gynecologist for extra measure.

I shiver when Arrow runs his tongue along the side of my face, humming to himself.

"It turns you on, doesn't it?" he whispers directly in my ear. "I'm going to fuck you every chance I get. Every hour. Every day.

My cock is going to live deep in your pussy, filling you until cum is falling down your legs. Then, I'm going to scoop it back inside you and plug you up again. None of my lil swimmers will escape."

I shiver at his words. Should I want to push him away and yell ew? Yes, yes I should. But do I? No. Why, you ask? Because apparently, I've fallen into a new kink.

My heart rate picks up. My damn pussy responds to his call like the hussy she is. I'm blaming my stupid period hormones. I'm just horny. That's it. *But you got laid earlier*—that stupid voice in my head rings out. And it was hot as hell. The way I tasted freedom beneath Shepp's gentle fingertips was liberating, to say the least. And his voice. He could talk me to sleep or through an orgasm, any day.

I sigh, pinching the bridge of my nose.

Thanks, Arrow. I'll add that to the list of things that turn me on. Run through the woods while being chased by them? Check. I was scared as all get out, but when I realized it was them, my pussy fucking wept for it.

So, maybe the breeding part is hot as fuck. Please, fill me with all your cum and pamper me afterwards. But the actual pregnancy? Scares the utter shit out of me. I wouldn't make a good mom. I've been conditioned for years to be on my toes and be at my monster's beck and call.

How could I possibly become a parent with him around? *Easy*—a little voice quips—stab him in the eye until he's dead on the floor. Yeah, easier said than done. He'd probably be impossible to kill. Like the big bad at the end of a video game.

"I'm not ready to be a parent," I mutter, falling underneath his stupid spell.

I should be kicking him in the nuts as we meander through the store with his arm draped over me with possession. But then he leads me to the ice cream, and I'm a goner. It's my favorite thing to eat when I'm on my period. Or when my IUD gives me the symptoms of a period but doesn't actually show. Which is bullshit, by the way. If you're going to make my boobs hurt, give me irritability, and make me want to shank a bitch—at least let me bleed.

I guess that's what the ice cream is for. It soothes the rage inside me until my hormones settle down and I've returned to the normal me. Whatever that is.

"Let's get you some cookies and cream." Without even confirming it's my favorite ice cream, he pulls it out of the freezer and hangs onto it along with my tampons and ridiculous pads.

"How'd you know that was my favorite?" I ask, narrowing my eyes when he leads me down the chocolate aisle.

"Because that's what I do, Kitten. I know everything about you. Cookies and Cream is your favorite ice cream. Along with Reese's Peanut Butter Cups. And peanut butter M&M's are your favorite treats. Hmm. Do you have a thing for chocolate or peanut butter? I could slather myself in both and let you lick it off." He grins, tossing two large bags of both treats into my hands with a chuckle while I stare at him in surprise. "Sheppard makes your favorite foods. Well, I know your favorite snacks. That makes me better," he quips, dragging me down the sweets aisle. "We're going to need a cart soon. Oh, how about some of your favorite sweet wine?" he asks, dragging me again.

"Shepp knows my favorite meals?" I ask, cocking my head when Arrow pulls down two bottles of my favorite sweet, pink, bubbly wine and puts them under his arms.

How? Oh, because he's my stalker. Duh.

He's stuffing things into his hands left and right—all for me. He's like the perfect book boyfriend I've read about, except he's kind of murdery and off the wall.

"You act like you don't know we're obsessed with you, Kitten." He winks at me with a grin, humming under his breath still.

"But why?"

He halts us completely and cocks his head. "Because you're ours." He shrugs it off again, moving us forward until we're at the cashier, and he sets all the stuff down. "You always have been.

Always will be. If you die. I die. If someone hurts you. I hurt them ten times over. Like that guy in your bedroom. He screamed so loud when I broke his fingers."

He says everything so matter-of-factly, like this is common knowledge, and I should just get used to the fact that these three mafia guys are utterly head over heels for me. I won't even touch the new information about a guy in my room with a ten-foot pole. I remember the pictures that were left for me.

"Thank you," the cashier squeaks, handing us our bags with haste after Arrow hands him the exact amount for our purchases.

My brows furrow on the pale-looking man slowly backing away from the cash register, eyeing Arrow like he's terrified.

"But what makes me so special?" I ask as we head out to the SUV where Jericho and Shepp sit, having a conversation.

"Everything makes you special, Kitten. It was fate. So, don't question it. Okay?" His voice dips lower when he makes that demand before opening the back door for me. "All right! We got the pussy plugs, the ice cream, the chocolate, and the wine. Let's go home and eat." Arrow chuckles, side-eyeing me while wiggling his brows.

"What are we eating?" I ask, just as my damn stomach growls like it hasn't eaten all day.

Come to think of it, I've only had donuts today.

Jericho rubs his temple. "I have a phone call to make."

Worry encases my skin at the look on his face. Stress radiates off him when his eyes find mine, and he gives me a gentle smile. So, unlike him.

Shepp quickly signs something to Jericho, eyeing me the whole time. I wish I could shout for him to use his voice with his best friends, but that doesn't seem to be something he's able to do right now. For some reason, he locks up when they're in the room. Like he's afraid they'll judge him for being silent for so long.

"He wants to know if you've got everything you need. He refuses to leave until he knows." Jericho turns to look at me with furrowed brows like he knows something happened between the two of us.

It was obvious, though, wasn't it? We fucked. He talked. Good times.

"Just because you two did the nasty doesn't mean you have to show off," Arrow grumbles, tossing me the bag of Reese's. "Eat your chocolate, like a good Kitten."

"Yeah, I got everything," I say, locking eyes with Shepp.

"Good, now. Let's go. My cousin Olivia is awaiting my phone call," he says, obviously not excited that he needs to speak with her.

CHAPTER FORTY-SEVEN

Jericho

I PACE my office with Shepp lingering by the door, watching me with narrowed eyes.

"I'll be fine."

Shepp rolls his eyes at me. '*Your worry is showing. You're pacing,*' he signs.

I wave a hand. "I'm not worried."

False. I am extremely worried. Anxious, more like it. It's eating away at me. And apparently, bleeding out of me in a telling way. Usually, I have more control than this. I've prided myself on being cool, calm, and collected in the most intense moments. Right now, though? That's been thrown out the window.

When it comes to Journey West, my control slips. Especially when it comes to the skeletons hiding in her very compact closet.

She's full of mysteries. I'm desperate to dismantle the solid wall around her, brick by brick, until I know everything about her.

No stone will go unturned.

'*Fine. Then, call Olivia back,*' he signs, nodding his head toward my phone sitting on my desk.

Bastard.

I grunt my answer, swiping my phone off the desk and press her contact information and put it on speaker. As Arrow and

Journey shopped for hygiene products, my cousin sent me an urgent-sounding text.

OLIVIA

Call me ASAP.

So telling. Not.

The only discussion she and I have to complete is the one we started before. Journey and her past.

Hopefully, she has the answers.

"Jericho Viotto," she says, picking up right away.

"Are you wired?" I quip, continuing my pacing through my office.

"I am a secret agent," she quips, the sounds of dishes and a baby babbling echoing in the background. "But the answer is no. I'm not wired. But I do have some interesting things to discuss with you."

"Do tell," I say, taking a deep breath.

My cousin has a unique way of getting under my skin. Maybe it's because we grew up together like brother and sister. Well, until my father sent her family away in exile to the enemy. But that's neither here nor there. Olivia is my blood. I guess that's why she's also insanely annoying at times.

"A man of so many words," she quips with a laugh.

Her footsteps come through on the other end of the phone, followed by the gentle closing of a door.

"Okay. Well, I did what you asked me to do. Honestly, there's not much more to Journey's life. The only thing I can tell you is the military school she was sent to at sixteen, never existed."

Her words hang in the air. Sure, since I've seen the Polaroids Arrow showed me of her in the burned-down building with my father. The man I hate the most in this world. I've had my suspicions about where she went. But how could I have missed it? But the better question is—why?

"I can hear your thoughts. You're wondering how you couldn't figure it out? Well, everything was faked pretty well.

Almost like an expert was in charge of making her disappear. But they're not me. Tell me I'm the best," she rambles.

I frown. "You're the best?"

"Thatta boy, Jer," she quips with a chuckle. "But for real. Whoever manipulated her existence was good, but I'm better."

"Do you want a pat on the back?" I tease.

Shepp shakes his head and rolls his wrist, begging me to drag the information out of her. But this is how it goes. Olivia loves to make me beg and compliment her.

"Flowers, wine, maybe a babysitter. I'd love a lot of things. But yeah, a nice pat on the back would be great," she teases back with a hint of playfulness in her voice. It lets me know she's still the same cousin.

"Well done, Liv. You're the best secret agent in the land. Now, can you please tell me everything you know?"

"Whoa, wait. Jericho Viotto said please! Alert the presses! My cousin is an actual human being!" Her laugh echoes loudly through the phone, causing me to cringe at the phone resting in my hands.

But it's nice to hear her so happy after years of bullshit she went through.

"Yes, yes. I said please," I playfully say back. "It's in my vocabulary."

I physically feel her smile through the phone.

"All right, I've tortured you long enough. Listen, someone for real messed with Journey's entire life. From bogus charges to get her incarcerated, to the fake military school, and even her inheritance."

I perk up. "Yes, that's what I've been most curious about. Where is the money owed to her? She could have left this place by now."

Thankfully, she didn't. Then, we wouldn't have been stalking her this entire time.

"Well, I talked to the West twins about it, and they had some interesting things to say about her mom and the weird meeting."

"Do you care to elaborate?" I say, continuing my pacing through my office. Sometimes I wish I could reach through the phone and strangle her.

She laughs at me. "Getting there! Sheesh. Okay, well basically, they said they tracked Journey down, and instead of Journey being anywhere in sight, it was just her mom. They left a business card and... God, this would have been easier if I just brought them down there to explain," she huffs.

"That can come. I'm sure they want to meet their sister," I say.

"They do. But they're busy as hell with their record company and family. So, they gave me permission to talk to you about this. So, anyway, they were super sketched out by her mom, and they decided to put a stipulation on Journey's inheritance."

"Obviously it's a big stipulation if she hasn't received it."

"Yup. Bingo. They put it into a trust that she can't touch until she's twenty-one or..." She holds out the word or.

"Out with it, Liv," I huff with irritation.

"Or until she gets married. As long as she's over eighteen when she's married, she'd receive it then."

"Marriage?" I ask, stopping dead near my desk.

Shepp steps forward with furrowed brows. '*What?*' he signs frantically, coming to stand in front of me.

"You're telling me they were so spooked by Sable's behavior when they met her, that they put a marriage stipulation on her trust?"

"Yup! That's exactly what I'm telling you. Her mom did not make a good impression, neither did her husband, according to them."

"Husband?" I choke out. "Her mother has never been married. Didn't they check into her?" I bark out.

"Hold your panties tight, Jer. Geez. Of course, they did. Their —well, how do you describe four men marrying one girl? Um, boyfriend-in-law, as one of them likes to put it. He's in Veritas with me. He checked into Sable and gave them the heads-up. So, they put a stop to it. They knew she'd take all of Journey's money if they didn't do something drastic. That's why the money was hidden her whole life. Apparently, Corbin West knew how to pick his ladies."

"Well, that explains the marriage," I say, rubbing my chin.

"My thoughts exactly. I'd say Uncle did all this on purpose."

Of course, he did. My father doesn't do anything without intention. He knew this would be the outcome.

He has her under his thumb, via her sister hidden away. Somewhere. Using Sunny as strings above her head so she acts like his little puppet. Then, he marries her off to his own flesh and blood, getting the money. Something she never knows about. How? I don't know. Or even why he'd get access to it? What the hell does my father have to do with the situation at all? Maybe Sable truly sold her own daughter off, but why? Would he keep her around after her money went to him? An eerie feeling creeps through me, making my hair stand on end at the thought of what he'd do to her once he was finished with her.

Too bad I'm always a step ahead of him. I dart my eyes to Shepp, who looks on with concern, constantly waiting for an update.

"Well, how about you bring the West boys down sometime so they can visit with their sister and sign over her inheritance to her," I hum with confidence, picking at a piece of lint on my white button down.

"Jer, they can't just sign it over. It's in the rules that she's not twenty-one and she's not married."

"Well, dear cousin. That's where you're wrong," I say with a grin, patting my obsession with Journey West on the back.

"Wrong? How can I be wrong?"

"In so many ways, Liv."

"What do you have up your sleeve?" she hisses, knowing me all too well.

I chuckle, straightening my collar. "Have them come for a visit tomorrow and to bring the paperwork. Our main priority should be hiding that money from Gabriel Viotto's prying eyes. And Journey deserves to know her family."

"Jericho!" she shouts. "What did you do?"

What did I do? Only the most ingenious thing I could ever think of. Sure, we could have tied Journey to us by putting a baby in her belly. Or we could have handcuffed her to us for eternity.

But I wanted more.

I wanted it all.

Whether she agreed to it or not.

"Let them know that Journey is married. I trust you'll set this up for me?" I chuckle at the silence on the other end of the phone.

"You... Jericho!" she breathes.

"Wow. I thought the days of stunning Olivia Viotto into silence were over. I've won, yet again."

"Does she even fucking know?" she hisses, finally finding her voice.

I smile. Truly fucking smile at her words.

"It's something I'll discuss with her. Can I trust you, Liv? This is vital. My father cannot get his hands on that money, you understand that right? Whatever he has planned can't be fucking good."

"Yeah, yeah. I got it. I'm just... really fucking horrified right now. That poor girl. She's shackled to a goddamn psychopath!" she shouts into the phone.

"Careful now, Liv. You'll wake the manic in your bed," I quip, imagining the Viking husband she has towering over me with his demonic blue eyes and scary-large fists. "I do recall he did something similar to you." That's what gave me the idea. If he could marry my undercover cousin without her consent, then so could I.

"Manic is... fuck. He's on the prowl. Listen, I'll talk to them. But I am absolutely not telling them their sister has no fucking clue she's married! I can't believe I said that. Holy fucking shit, you're in so much shit!"

I imagine her pinching the bridge of her nose in frustration. All the while, my grin stays in place.

"It was a necessary evil. She's safe under my roof with my last name. No one will ever harm her again."

"Yeah, okay. We're moving on before I reach through the phone and strangle the fuck out of you. You better let her know you're already married. If I bring the West twins down there, they'll kick your ass."

"Fine, fine," I say, waving a hand despite her not being able to see. "I'll inform her of our nuptials. Now, what can you tell me about her sister?"

"Way to change the subject, Jer," she grumbles with a sigh. "Sunshine West. Although, she's not really a West. Her father wasn't on the birth certificate that we recovered. Just Sable's name. She's fourteen, and she was born with a heart defect. She was in and out of doctor appointments her whole life. Well, until three years ago, she disappeared from all appointments. And off the face of the earth. Whoever tried to squish her existence sucked. They basically tried to make it seem like she didn't exist."

"Any clue as to where she is now?" I ask, rubbing my chin.

"No idea. That's the one thing I can't pinpoint. I'm afraid to ask where you think she is now?"

"That I'm not sure of. In fact, I don't think Journey has any ideas, either."

If I could just break through to her again and gain her trust more, she'd open up to me about where her sister is. She'd also confess completely as to who her monster is—even though I know it's my own damn father. Then, I'd be able to help her more. As it stands, Journey's refusal to spill her secrets severely hinders me from helping her directly.

Liv sighs, "Listen, that's all I really have on her. I think you just need to be a big boy and have a normal conversation with her. Maybe she'd open up to you. Although, when she hears you married her without her consent, she might have some other things to say. Maybe she'll chop your nuts off."

"Perhaps," I hum, rubbing my forehead. "Or perhaps she likes them too much to injure them."

"Oh, gag me. Never say that ever again. La la la!" She fake gags several times before she stops and huffs at me. "Whatever. I'll text you later, and we can all meet and welcome her to the chaos that is our family."

I grin at her reluctant acceptance. "Talk to you soon, Liv. Thank you for all the information. And yes, I do tend to say please and thank you. I can be a gentleman."

"Unless you're marrying unsuspecting girls without their knowledge," she jokes, and then, silence.

I pull my phone away from my ear and sigh. "She hung up before I could get the last word in." I frown, typing out a message about her rudeness, hit send, and then pocket my phone.

'*You married her?*' Shepp signs with a twisted expression full of disappointment.

I hold up my hands. "I know what you're thinking. And yes, I did. But it's for her own protection."

Shepp's body stiffens. I'm sure he wants to say more on the matter. Probably tear me a new one like Liv did. But he just shakes his head.

"Pizza is here!" Arrow shouts from downstairs just as a door slams.

"That's our cue," I say, gesturing out the door. Once Shepp and I are side by side in the hallway, I grab his shoulder, turning him to look at me. A storm of emotions swirls in his eyes as he narrows them at me. "The three of us will take her to pick out a ring. I didn't do it to be selfish."

I did. I'm a selfish bastard. One he should probably pummel with his fists. He won't, though. Sheppard Mondelli is a good, loyal friend through thick and thin. But now that I think back, we're all in this together despite the oddity of three men sharing a girl. Equally, we are hers, and she is ours. Only, I get the piece of paper with her as my wife.

'*How?*' he signs.

"Nothing a little discretion and a flash of cash can do down at the courthouse. Besides, they belong to our organization. More specifically, us," I say with a small smirk. "They eagerly filed my marriage certificate away and gave me a copy. Don't worry, we'll all have a nice ceremony once we have the answers we need. She's ours, Shepp. That's all that matters, right?"

He huffs at me, pushing my hand off his shoulder. *'I don't believe for one second you didn't do it on the sly to be selfish. I know you. You've been my brother for years and my best friend, too. But you'll be the one to tell her.'*

I nod. "And you'll take joy in watching her chop my dick off."

'Duh,' he signs, rolling his eyes. *'But she won't stop there. You saw how she stabbed Arrow. She's going to put you six feet deep. Then, we'll be there to pick up the pieces.'* He grins to himself as he walks away.

Well, damn. Good for him.

I follow close behind him and enter the dining room at the same time, stopping dead in our tracks.

Arrow frowns at our girl resting her head on his shoulder, snoring louder than I've ever heard her before.

"Well, that kicked in faster than I thought it would," he hums, taking a large bite of his pizza.

Fancy wine glasses rest on the table with half finished pink drinks in them. Well, until Arrow guzzles down the rest of his and discreetly pushes hers away.

"And what exactly did you do?" I question calmly, taking the scene in.

He chuckles, wiping his mouth with a napkin. "Well, I thought we had more time before the sedative took her. Fuck. Isn't she gorgeous when she sleeps? If I had my camera, I'd take a million snap shots right now and keep them forever." He loses himself in staring at her unmoving face. "You think she'd get mad if I fucked her while she slept?" His brows furrow, thinking better of it, and he huffs to himself.

'*Yeah, she'd fucking murder you,*' Shepp signs with a redness blotching over his cheeks.

"Arrow," I threaten. "Explain yourself."

He rolls his eyes, pushing the pizza box in our direction. "You might as well eat before we do it. She'll be out for hours before she comes to."

"Arrow!" I bark, my voice echoing through the dining room.

"Fine!" he growls, scooping her sleeping form into his arms. "I'm tired of her IUD holding us back. So, I slipped her a little sedative in her wine. Although, I think she face-planted into the pizza." He frowns, frantically wiping off her face. "And now is the perfect time to take it out." He shrugs, walking past us toward the basement door, and disappears down the darkened stairs.

"And you say I'm the crazy one for marrying her without her knowledge," I quip, side-eyeing Shepp with a smirk.

'*You are! But he is, too,*' he signs, shaking his head. '*Should we follow him?*'

"Well, I think it might be a necessity. He's about to remove her birth control," I say, tilting my head. "Hmmm. It's not a bad idea, though. Her pregnant with our baby. Just imagine all the practice we'll get."

'*No. It's not a bad idea. But the execution is ridiculous. We could have just taken her to the doctor,*' Shepp argues furiously. '*Between the two of you, I'm going to be the only one who has balls left.*'

"Well then, you'll be a daddy, won't you," I grin, waltzing toward the basement with excitement thrumming through my veins. "Come on then, Sheppy. Let's make sure he removes it without hurting her."

"Don't worry, Daddy Jer! I've got it all under control," Arrow shouts from the depths of the basement.

"And how is that?" I hum, making it to the bottom of the stairs and locating him in a small room with a metal bed.

"Oh, you know. I spoke with a pussy doctor recently. He gave me step-by-step instructions," he hums to himself, putting on a

white coat, gloves, and a ridiculous headlamp. Looking as if he
were a real doctor about to perform the procedure.

He's no dummy, though. If he was able to get instructions on
how to do it, then he memorized it to a T and studied.

"And if we need said doctor to help more?" I ask, raising a
brow when he carefully moves around Journey's sleeping form
and collecting new tools I've never laid eyes on.

"Oh, he's in the next room." He shrugs, pulling out
something atrocious-looking.

Wonderful. He's taken another doctor hostage. Meaning, the
man probably did something wrong. Much like the dentist he
stole away weeks ago for touching his patients.

"And why didn't you ask the good doctor to perform this
procedure himself if it's so daunting? Or have you already
removed his fingers?" I lick my lips, moving forward to remove
some hair from Journey's face. She looks so peaceful and subdued
when she's under Arrow's favorite sedative. So unlike her spirited
self, but beautiful nonetheless.

Arrow stops dead. "Because no other man is ever seeing her
pussy. That's ours. I'll tattoo my fucking name on her cunt lips,"
he grunts, setting his tools beside the bed. "Besides, I'm perfectly
capable of removing this. It's not that hard." He rolls his eyes as he
turns on his headlamp. "All right, which one of you is going to
take her pants off?" He eyes us, flashing the lights in our faces
with a serious expression.

Fuck.

Okay.

This is really happening.

'*I will,*' Shepp signs, grunting as he marches forward. '*But you
better be careful. No hurting her.*' He raises a brow when Arrow
waves him off.

"Like I'd ever intentionally do that," Arrow growls.

"Fine. But take it easy on her," I demand, running my fingers
through her hair, trying to comfort her even though she can't feel
a thing.

"I'll never hurt her," Arrow says with conviction. "She's way too precious to me."

"Us," I mumble in agreement.

"I want to make her monster pay for what he did to her, Jer," Arrow says seriously with furrowed brows. "Why does he even want her in the first place?"

It's a question I've been asking myself for days now. Why her? The only explanation I can come up with is what she said. Her mother sold her to my father. For what, though? Drugs? Torture? The money? Did my Chaos do something wrong? That's a definite possibility. But it doesn't explain everything I'm desperate to know.

'*She has scars everywhere,*' Shepp signs, shaking his head.

"And you discovered this when you boned in your art room?" I ask, tilting my head.

'*Yes,*' he signs with a scowl and quickly flips me off.

"He's going to pay," Arrow growls, clenching his fists.

"He will," I say in agreement. "We'll make sure he suffers to the fullest extent."

"Now, let's get this show on the road," Arrow grins.

CHAPTER FORTY-EIGHT
Journey

I SUCK IN A BREATH, my eyes flying open as the sun shines through the bedroom windows. I blink several times, taking in the tiny dust particles floating through the rays and following until they're out of sight. The sun? When did the sun rise? Shit. A weird fog twists around my mind, begging me to close my eyes and go back to sleep. Fuck. Just five more minutes, please?

A weird heaviness weighs down my eyelids like sandbags pulling them closed again as sleep beckons me back into the darkness. If I just close my eyes for another second, I'll feel better.

Something tickles in the back of my mind. Something urgent, begging me to stay alert. Like I'm missing a piece of the big puzzle.

My palms dig into my eyes, wiping away the sleep clouding them. Slowly, my brain kicks on at warp speed as I gain my bearings.

My eyes dart around the bedroom, landing on Arrow, who is sound asleep to my right, and Shepp, who is asleep on my left.

How the hell did I get in this bed? To this room?

Last I remember, Arrow was distracting me with wine and promises of pizza as Jericho made a phone call to his cousin Olivia. I'm dying to know what they talked about. I'm sure it was something juicy and informative.

But then again, another part of me is happy, I don't know. The less I truly know, the less I can tell my stupid monster. I'm sure he's eager to hear what I have to say whenever I see him again. I'm supposed to be spying and gathering information, per his orders, after all.

Fuck.

I squeeze my eyes shut when a pain spears through my damn abdomen, straight through my vagina. Periods can rot in hell and die forever. Especially mine. It's the entire reason I got on birth control in the first place. To ease my pains and prevent me from getting pregnant. Although, I got it before I became acquainted with my monster.

Another pain works through my stomach, and I curl in on myself, wrapping a hand around my aching stomach. Fuck. Take me now, dear Lord.

"Oh, good. You're awake," Arrow murmurs, gently wrapping his arms around my abdomen and pulling me into his body. I sigh at his warmth, his body heat momentarily taking the pain away. "I was afraid you drank too much wine and slipped into a coma."

I narrow my eyes when he buries his face in my neck. "Why would I slip into a coma? I only drank like half a glass," I rasp through a rough voice, savoring the feel of him against me.

"Right. Half a glass," he hums, kissing my cheek. "How're you feeling this morning, Kitten?"

Those gray eyes linger on my fluttering lashes with intensity, like he's counting every lash and remembering every freckle.

"Um, I'm fine. Just have some cramps," I say with my cheeks heating.

"Want a hot shower?" he questions, raising his head.

"Um, sure?" I say with a shrug as we make our way off the bed, leaving a sleeping Shepp behind.

Arrow lingers in the middle of the room, watching my every move like a hawk again. He smiles, darting into my closet and disappearing. Weirdo.

I shake off his weirdness and walk toward the bathroom, gently stretching out my stiff limbs. God. What happened to me last night? I feel like I partied with Jenni for a little too long and passed out after drink number twenty.

Fuck.

Jenni.

My breath leaves me when her name echoes in my mind. My best friend. Is she alive? Dead? Rescued from this stupid life by Elias? Fuck. Jericho said that she was safe with Elias. But there's a part of me deep down that needs to see her for myself.

I can only hope he saved her from her fate. But I can't erase the guilt pouring through me at the job I had to do. I told my monster everything about her. And Elias. Their actions. Words.

I didn't have a choice.

Like now.

I shake my heavy thoughts away as I turn on the hot water on full blast. Sheets of steam immediately rise into the air as the water pours into the tiled tub.

I turn on my heels, looking at myself in the mirror. Jesus. I do look like I got run over by a bus. Bags under my eyes. Pale skin. Crazy as hell hair. Shit. I need conditioner and my special curly-head shampoo to tame my curls and remove the frizz. I wonder if Jericho the Jerk—AKA Jerk-icho—would ever give me his credit card.

Or maybe Arrow.

Speaking of the devil! God in heaven, he's naked!

"You were deep in thought, Kitten. I didn't want to disturb you." A grin eats away at his face when his eyes trail over my body. "Time to get naked!" he says with a small clap, setting a bright yellow sundress on the counter.

"Arrow!" I yelp, slapping my hands over my eyes. "What in the hell are you doing? Why are you naked?"

Don't peek through your fingers and look at his hard dong. Don't do it. Don't peek at the veins running along his shaft. Don't fall victim to his snake eye.

#Failed.

"Eyes up here, Kitten. Unless you want to lick him like a

lollipop. He really wouldn't mind. I can come like a popped Twinkie in your mouth. And taste better," he says, rubbing his hands together.

"A popped Twinkie?" I frown. "You know what? Nope. I don't want to know." I shake my head when he sticks out his bottom lip.

"Besides, we're showering, Kitten. What else would I be doing naked?" he says, shuffling around behind my back. "Now, take off your clothes, and let me wash your back. It can be water or cum, your choice."

"Arrow," I groan when he tugs at my shirt.

I'm way too sleepy for his off-the-wall shit.

My eyes connect with his through the mirror in front of us. What a beautiful, crazy man he is. Watching me like I'm the most important woman in the world. His fingers glide over my stomach, gently pressing into the painful spots.

"Pain, Kitten?" he whispers into my ear, making circles over my stomach.

"Yes," I say, squeezing my eyes shut as he soothes away the cramps rocking through me. "I need some ibuprofen."

"After breakfast, I'll soothe all your pains."

And oddly enough, when he says it—I believe every word. He may be a little unhinged, but for me, he'll do anything. For whatever reason, I have them in my pockets. Now, what I do with that determines the type of person I truly am.

"I don't really need an audience to shower," I sigh, leaning back into his naked body as his grip tightens on me.

Gently, his hands work over my stomach, trailing toward my hips. His fingers leap to my arms, working toward my shoulders, where he finally works his thumbs into my muscles.

"Ah, but what if you drown? I can't have you drowning in the shower, Kitten. I need you very much alive and kicking. Besides, I just woke Shepp up, and he's headed down to make your favorite donuts."

I lick my lips, practically tasting the donuts on my tastebuds.

"I'm not going to drown, Arrow," I breathe when he works his magic down my back, kneading my flesh in his fingers and finding the knots in my muscles. "Oh, God. How did you learn to do this?"

"Oh! I tortured a massage therapist once! She gave me all the best tricks. Well, before I slit her throat," he says so nonchalantly, it's like we're talking about the damn weather. "But she was a bad, bad girl! She exploited other women and didn't give them their proper dues." He shakes his head. "Not to mention the prostitute ring she was in charge of." He wrinkles his nose in disgust.

I have so many questions on the tip of my tongue. But I don't dare ask. He'd probably go into way too many details on how he murdered her. And I don't have the mental capacity to indulge him.

With a huff, I turn on my heel and glare into his eyes. "Stop that," I grunt, slapping his hands away.

He grins in response. "Take your clothes off, Kitten. We're wasting water and time! We have breakfast, and then I want to introduce you to my lions."

"Lions?" I squeak, widening my eyes. "You aren't going to feed me to them, are you?"

Oh, great job, Journey. Give him ideas.

His entire body stiffens. "Only bad people meet the sharp end of my lion's teeth. Not you, Kitten. I'll let you pet them, and they'll absolutely love you. They'll want to lick you, But they won't. Only I can lick you."

I blink when he does just that, running his tongue up my cheek like he's marking his territory, and then pulls back, eyeing me expectantly.

"Now, choppity chop, Kitten. Let me see your beautiful tits," he says, bouncing on his damn toes.

His snake eye is looking at me again, practically throbbing as he awaits me to get naked. It flops up and down every time he bounces on his toes.

Holy shit. That thing fit inside me?

Fuck.

Stop looking at it.

"Kitten, he just really likes you. But don't worry. This shower is for you. We can take care of ourselves later."

At the sound of his voice, I jerk my gaze away. I wasn't looking. I swear. I didn't even notice the small tattoo wrapped under the head. Not at all.

"Is that a tattoo on it?" I ask, turning bright red and avoiding his stare.

"Oh. You saw that! Well, you can become acquainted with it later and really read what it says. Up close and personal." His hand wraps around his length, gently stroking up and down. "Don't worry, I won't come. It's the work up that really gets me going for later."

I nod absentmindedly, continuing my not so staring contest with his dick as he strokes it. All right. I can't tear my eyes away. It's not every day a girl like me gets locked in a bathroom with a man like him. Tall. Handsome. Slightly deranged. He oozes danger, drawing me in like a damn moth to the flame.

"Can you at least turn around while I pee?" I grumble, stepping up to the toilet to check my tampon and discard it.

His face lights up, and he nods, twisting on his heels.

"No peeking," I grumble, pulling my pants down.

"Shy bladder, Kitten?"

I huff, finally using the facilities and checking for my tampon, but nothing seems to be there. I stiffen, checking my underwear, but it's not the underwear I was wearing last night. It's completely black and clings to me perfectly.

"What the..."

"Oh, it's period underwear, Kitten. I looked into it myself and then put it on you while you were sleeping." Arrow grins, turning around to stare at me while I sit on the toilet red-faced.

"Why?" I've come to the realization though, that sometimes I don't want to ask him the questions because he never seems to answer.

"I didn't want you to bleed through," he says, tilting his head. "Unless you wanted to?"

"Uh, no. I'm just confused why I didn't wake up and feel you doing it." Something in my gut says more happened last night after I drank the wine. There's no way I was actually drunk. Did that mother fucker drug me? Again? I narrow my eyes at his innocent face.

Arrow has the skin of a damn angel, looking heavenly, but it's all a ruse.

"You're a heavy sleeper," he says with a shrug. "Now, get naked so I can wash you up."

I've come to the conclusion that I shouldn't even bother. So, without looking into it too much, I pull myself together and quickly take all my clothes off, discarding them to the side without a second thought. It's not like he hasn't seen me before.

All my insecurities flee when his heated eyes trail up and down my naked body. He steps forward, letting go of his length, and trails his fingers over my tattoo.

"You're the most beautiful woman in the world, Kitten," he mumbles, running his fingers over the scar beneath my ink. "It matches mine, you know?" he says, gesturing to the wound on his chest.

I swallow hard, nodding. I know what it means. It's a symbol of his loyalty to the Viotto Crime Family. Once they have these scars etched into their flesh, only death eliminates them from the organization.

My fingers trace the healing wound, slick with some sort of medicine helping the process. Goosebumps spark across his flesh, and a low groan leaves his throat with satisfaction.

"Now, you're teasing me," he quips, cupping my breast and running his thumb over my nipple. "I'm going to have you all to myself today. I've guaranteed it. Jer's off doing whatever he does at Rave. And Shepp's busy playing Mr. Mom in the kitchen. It's just you and me to explore today. And boy, do I have some one-on-one exploring to do."

"I'm still on my period," I breathe, squeezing my eyes shut when he pinches my nipple hard, sending pleasure straight to my pussy. The cramps no longer tug at my muscles, finally giving me the relief I need.

"Did you know nipple stimulation helps with periods? So do orgasms," he whispers, eyeing my breasts with interest. "I want to sink my teeth into you and mark you as mine forever and ever."

"Is that what you're planning to do? What if I... bleed everywhere?" I swallow hard when he pinches my nipples tightly and holds for a few seconds.

"If you think a little blood is going to stop me from fucking you, eating you, or playing with you. You're very mistaken, Kitten. I'll take you in any form. Just as long as my cum ends up in your pussy," he murmurs against my lip, lightly pecking them. "Blood makes me hard," he grunts, forcing his tongue into my mouth as they twist together.

I can't deny the teasing he's doing has lightning bolts of electricity sparking through my damn body. My pussy responds immediately, getting on board with the situation.

"Okay, okay. Shower," I groan, stepping away from his grasp. "Shower," I reaffirm, nodding toward the water running. "It should be the perfect temp by now."

And it'll be far away from his tempting fingers and throbbing cock.

Well, as far as I can get when he joins me under the dual sprays of the shower.

Arrow grins when he stares at me from the doorway of the bathroom. His eyes trail up and down my body like he didn't just see me naked, taking in the yellow sundress he picked out for me.

"You look beautiful, Kitten." His head tilts slightly, and his eyes light up.

"You forgot the bra and underwear," I say, crossing my arms over my chest.

My nipples could slice right through a damn diamond right now. I need socks, sweatpants, and something not so revealing.

Have I tried to change his mind? Absolutely. Did he refuse to find me something more comfortable? Indeed, he did. Stating it was all about the easy access of the dress.

So, I'm stuck in a dress that resembles a lemon with floral prints on it.

What a joy.

"Didn't forget. You're just not permitted to wear them right now," he says, marching forward and tilting my chin up. "You won't need them much when I get you naked." A promise rests in his eyes, letting me know his sole purpose today is boning me down. "Besides, cum is good for your insidey parts right now. Helps to ease the cramps and such." He grins again. "Did you put a tampon in already?"

"You're awfully obsessed with my damn period," I say, raising a brow. "And yes." I shake my head when his body slumps with disappointment.

I don't even want to know where his mind went with that. Was he hoping to help? I shiver.

He licks his lips. "Everything about you has my attention. But I draw the line at pee," he says, waving a hand. Leaning in, he pecks my lips with such affection that I stare at him with wide eyes. "Not that I yuck anyone's yum, Kitten. I can pee on you if that's what you like."

"I—um—draw that line, too," I choke out, shaking my head.

Everyone has something they like in the bedroom. No hate. But that's just not my thing, either.

"Wonderful! See? We're establishing sexual boundaries already. Now, tell me. How do you feel about being handcuffed to the bed with your ass in the air and that cute kitten tail sticking out of your ass?" His brows wiggle. "I can even add the ears on your head and the gag in your mouth. Or! And here me out. We can run through the woods again. Naked. With a vibrating butt plug."

"Err... Never thought about it?" I pose it as more of a question than anything.

Because I've never had time to think kinky thoughts. Especially butt stuff. Well, until that night, those masked men—who are apparently them—fucked me into oblivion.

"Well, if you ever expect to be airtight, then we'll have to stretch you out for us."

"Airtight?" I question, raising a brow.

"Yeah, you know. Three holes. Three dicks. You'll be filled and airtight." He grins again.

"Right," I say, trailing off and letting my imagination take over.

Although it's terrifying to think about anything entering my backdoor, like in the books I read. Maybe it wouldn't be so bad to experiment, right? All three of them entering me at once would be hot as hell.

"You're thinking about my cock up your ass, aren't you?" He chuckles, weaving his fingers with mine. "Come forth, Kitten. Let's eat, get you some ibuprofen, and then we'll go on an adventure. And don't worry, no buttholes will be harmed today."

I wrinkle my nose when he pulls me forward and out of the bathroom.

"That's not really a promising thing to say," I gripe, following behind him as he drags me through the house.

"I always keep my promises, Kitten." He looks over his shoulder at me with a grin when we enter the kitchen.

The amazing aromas of Shepp's cooking fill my nose when he turns to greet us. A bright smile lights up his face when he takes me in and nods in greeting.

Arrow pulls me onto a stool, situating us at the counter. Without me asking, Shepp sets a plate of chocolate glazed donuts, freshly made, right in front of my face.

"Thanks," I say, my stomach rumbling.

He nods his head again and then signs something to Arrow.

"He wants to know how your butthole feels today... Ouch!" Arrow hisses, rubbing the back of his head with a frown.

Shepp signs something else with aggression. His face twists until Arrow sighs.

"Fine. He wants to know how you're feeling today. Which includes your butthole." Arrow grins when Shepp flips him off.

I giggle. "Um, yup. Everything is fine today. Just a little confused about what happened last night."

Seriously. It's weird. I only took like five sips of my wine. I vaguely remember Arrow telling me I'd be okay. And then, it's blank. Like a piece of my night was chipped from my memory.

Arrow chuckles. "Just too much wine for you, Kitten."

Shepp rolls his eyes when he grabs a donut and shoves it into his mouth.

"Right. Too much wine," I say, narrowing my eyes.

Is it just me? Or are these two being awfully fucking suspicious? What did they do? Drug me? I stiffen. There's no fucking way in hell.

"Sheppy Boy, grab our girl some painkillers," Arrow demands, pointing to a cabinet a few steps away from him.

Shepp's chewing slows when he looks at me with concern.

"Just cramps," I grit, side-eyeing Arrow and his loud mouth.

Shepp nods a few times, holding up a finger as he turns and grabs some medicine from the cabinet. He hands the bottle to me and then a tall glass of iced coffee—one of my favorites.

"Thanks," I say, taking the medicine in one gulp and setting my glass down.

"Okay, Kitten. You've eaten and taken your meds. Now, let's go on an adventure." Arrow grabs my hand without making sure I'm done and pulls me off the stool. "Don't wait up, Mom! We'll be back... Maybe." Arrow grins at Shepp, and I wave goodbye.

Looks like I'm at the mercy of Arrow today.

CHAPTER FORTY-NINE

Journey

"A GOLF CART?" I ask timidly, climbing into the seat.

"Jericho's dad built this place. Did you know that? There's like a hundred acres here. Maybe more," he rambles, starting the golf cart up and then pressing the accelerator.

"No," I say with suspicion, taking in the path we follow, giving me glimpses of the night I ran through the woods with my heart in my throat. "Why did he build this place when he has that tower downtown?" I ask, watching the greenery pass by in a small blur.

"He had a heart once. He loved a woman, and then she disappeared. He's been looking for her for years now but always comes up empty. I think she wanted as far away from him as she could run. Or we think she was killed by the enemy, but we're not really sure. He built this place for her. She loved animals and basically had her own zoo here. It's been pretty overrun now, but there's one space I've kept up with."

"Your lions?"

He grins. "Max and Nova were birthday presents from Jer's father. I think I was ten. I never thought I could have a heart," he says with a frown, staring straight forward. "Until them. He gave me something to cherish, and I do." He nibbles his lip the moment a large enclosure comes into view, fit with tall fencing that goes on for what seems like miles.

"Jesus," I mutter, staring at it in awe. "Are you the only one who takes care of them?"

"Nah. I have a zoo keeper come in every day to help me feed them and clean up their enclosure. I wish I had more time for them, but I don't. So, I do whatever I can to make sure they're fed and completely taken care of."

"I think it's really cool," I say.

"It is. Want to meet them?" he asks with a grin, jumping out of the golf cart. He makes his way to my side and holds out his hand for me to take. "They won't hurt you. You're with me." He says it with so much confidence that I almost believe him.

"Haven't you seen that show about the guy with the tigers?" I say, reluctantly following him around the fencing until he gets to a building that has a door. "They bite."

"Not my babies. Believe me, Kitten. I've slept in here with them before. They trust me. I trust them. It's a mutual respect." He grins, looking back at me when he shoves a key into the doorknob and slowly pushes the door open.

I hold my breath when he drags me into the room that's fit with a couch, monitors, and air conditioning.

"This is the control room for their enclosure. We have cameras everywhere, making sure that they're doing okay. Oh, look. They're by the water," he says, pointing at a screen displaying the massive cats hanging out by a pool of shiny water, resembling a large pond. Their long tongues lap over the water as they take several long pulls.

"Holy fucking shit balls..." I breathe. "You seriously have lions!" I squeak, attempting to pull away from him.

He chuckles, gripping my hand tight. "Not so fast, Kitten. They won't hurt you. Unless you look them in the eyes. Don't do that."

I tremble when he pulls me forward, walking toward a door. "Arrow," I breathe in a panic.

He looks over his shoulder, grinning at me. "They've been fed already. They're just lounging around. Besides, they love it when I visit and bring guests." He winks at me, pulling me out the door and into the enclosure.

The sun beats down on us as we walk through the tall grass, surrounded by some trees and other shrubbery. Giving the enclosure an otherworldly feel. Several areas are just dusty dirt with rock formations and others have lush greenery—mimicking the real-life habitat they'd be in.

"It's so they can hide," Arrow says, following my eyes. "There's three separate dens for them to go to when they're mad at each other. And plenty of room for them to roam."

My breaths pick up the closer we get to the massive pond.

"Mad?" I say, swallowing hard. "Why would they be mad at each other?" I hiss, slapping his shoulder when we stop near a large rock close to the two lions.

"That's Nova. Obviously." Arrow points to the smaller female lion, lounging by the bigger lion with her eyes on us.

My breath stalls when she yawns, showing off her rows of sharp teeth. I scoot closer to Arrow, clinging tight to his hand.

"Beautiful," I mutter, watching their every move.

Do I think Arrow would throw me to his lions? Well, I don't know. He seems to like me well enough. But I did stab him. Maybe this is revenge for that.

"That's Max. He's my baby." Arrow grins, pointing the larger male out.

I tilt my head, watching the large lion lounge, looking at us with a lazy gaze.

"Why doesn't he have a mane?" I question, moving further into Arrow's side for protection. Like if I talk about the lion, he'll come and eat me.

"Ah, that! To keep them together in one enclosure and to ensure that Max wouldn't get too aggressive, we had them both fixed when they were one. So, no lion babies for them." He sort of pouts at the idea of not having little cubs wandering around. "So, Max doesn't need his mane, and it never grew in because he didn't have the hormones."

"Wow. You really know a lot about lions," I mutter, keeping my eyes on the creatures watching us closely but not making a move to us.

Arrow gently squeezes my hand, looking down at me with a grin.

"They won't hurt you, Kitten," he murmurs, kissing my head.

"They're huge," I whisper, clinging to him. "And their teeth." I shiver when he wraps his hand around my shoulders, pulling me close.

"People tend to be afraid of them when I bring them to visit." He cocks his head, moving us a few inches closer.

At this point, I could reach out and pet their heads if I really wanted to. But I value my fingers. So, I'll keep them to myself.

"You bring other people here to visit?" I whisper frantically.

"Lions tend to make people talk," he says with a shrug.

Talk? Talk! He wants me to talk? Or is he simply introducing me to his enormous cats because he wants me to meet them?

"Okay. So, I've met them. They're cool. Can we go back?" I ask, nervously.

I can handle a lot in life. In fact, it's been filled with trauma. But lions? That's where I draw the line. And walking free in their enclosure? Nope. I'm good. I just want to go back to the safety of the guys' house. Even if it's not safe at all. It's better than being stuck in here with these massive predators.

"Go back?" he questions, chuckling slightly. "Come on, Kitten. I have plenty more to show you. Max and Nova, this is my future wife," he says with pride, reaching out to run his fingers through Max's fur. "Just be careful of their heads. They see it as a threat if you get too close to their eyes," Arrow instructs, forcefully pulling my hand out to pet Max.

Holy mother fuck. I'm touching a lion. A hungry, hungry lion who watches us with eager eyes as we hover beside him. He could lash out at any time and steal my arm straight from its socket.

And I happen to like my arm, thank you.

I blow out a breath when Arrow ruffles the lion's fur, and then we step back. Finally, I can take a deep breath without holding it in.

Adrenaline soars through my veins when he wraps his arm around me.

"See? That wasn't too bad, was it? They won't eat you. Only if I tell them to." I stiffen at his silent threat. Great. He could have them eat me whole.

My body trembles when he forces me to stick beside him, and we walk around the lazy lions toward a rock formation several yards away from them. I feel their hungry lion eyes on us, ready to eat me.

Oh, God. This was not on my list of ways to die. At the hands of my monster? Yes. At the jaws of lions? That wasn't on my radar. Until now.

I blow out a breath. Maybe this is a trust exercise, and I need to lean into Arrow and trust him. He did tell the lions I was his future wife. So, that's a good sign, right?

"There's one thing I've always wanted to do in here," he says, pulling me along with determination. "I've slept here." He gestures to the rocks ahead. "And they've never bothered me. In fact, Max cuddled me all night long." He grins, looking over his shoulder at them.

If I could dig my heels in and stop us from continuing further into this place, I would. But Arrow is an unstoppable machine.

"Yeah?" I ask when we freeze in front of a rusty-colored rock stained red with what looks suspiciously like old blood stains.

A sweat breaks out over my flesh when I size it up. It's flat. Perfectly fit for a damn body to lie across.

"Arrow..." I trail off when my heart pounds wildly against my ribs.

I swear my fight or flight is about to kick in, and I'm a damn runner. Looking behind me, I spy the lions in the same position near the pond. In fact, their eyes have closed and they're taking a nap. So, that's a good sign, right? They nap. I run. Perfect solution.

"Kitten, do you trust me?" Arrow eyes me when I freeze and my expression goes blank.

Absolutely not. No way in hell do I trust this man. Right? I can't trust him. He's in the mafia. He lives with two other psychos.

Right?

"Yes."

Well, that was an unexpected turn of events. Apparently my mind was not on board with the whole—we don't trust this man—vibe we had going on.

So, here's to truly trusting him not to let me get eaten by oversized murder cats. Fuck. I look at Max and Nova again. They're still in the same spots.

Damn it.

His grin grows. "Lie down on the rock," he says playfully, pointing at it. "We're going to play."

He may have a grin on his face, but I see the darkness lurking in his eyes. Describing his tone as playful was a kindness. He's demanding me to do as he says. This definitely has to be a test.

My eyes widen. "Play?"

"Lie down on the rock," he demands again, gesturing to it. "Please."

When a psycho says please, you know you're in for it. Shit.

"Is this because I stabbed you? I literally thought you were trying to murder me or something," I say, stammering through my words. "It healed, right? You're fine?"

He snorts, turning toward me. His fingers run over my jaw, softly tracing down my face. There's so much love in his eyes, my breath evades me.

"Kitten, you can stab me all day long, and I'd never punish you for it. Leave me? I'll track you down. Tie me up? I'll beg for more," he murmurs, leaning in, and presses his lips to mine.

"Please lie down on the rock. I want to fuck you into oblivion while you're at my mercy."

"Fuck me here?" I whisper.

"Fuck you here," he confirms with a sharp nod. "It's something I've been fantasizing about." He taps the side of his head a few times. "And I want it to live rent free in my mind for years to come."

Looking into his light gray eyes, I note the desperation there. Lust dilates them. And for some crazy, out of this world reason, I fucking trust him.

"Okay," I say, turning toward the rock. "But if they eat me, I'll come back to haunt you."

He grins. "If you ever die, Kitten. I'm burying myself alive with your dead body."

"And they say romance is dead," I murmur, stepping up to the flat rusty-looking rock with blood stains on the surface. "Arrow?"

"Hmm?" he hums, stepping closer to me as I climb onto the flat rock. I hiss when it digs into my bare knees, but I ignore the pain and my mind telling me to flee.

Trust in the crazy man. Trust in this process.

"How many people have died here?" I ask, swallowing hard when he guides me so I'm lying flat on my back. The warm rock, which has roasted under the May sun, burns against my skin.

Arrow cocks his head above mine with a blank expression, contemplating my question. Do I really want to get fucked where someone else has died? Not particularly. But it's going to happen whether I like it or not.

"If I told you they were bad people, would you think better of me?" he asks in a slightly vulnerable state.

I nibble my bottom lip. "I'm no angel, either," I whisper, looking into his eyes.

"You're my angel, Kitten," he says softly, leaning down to kiss my cheek. "No matter what you've done in your life. I'll accept you."

"You'll accept me?" I've killed people, because I've had no

choice. I was an extension of my monster, doling out the punishments he saw fit.

"Always," he says, rubbing his fingers over every inch of my face, tracing the small freckles dotting my cheeks and the worry lines on my forehead. I swallow hard. "There's a darkness inside me..." I trail off, squeezing my eyes shut when his palms encase my cheeks, and his forehead pressed against mine.

"We all have a darkness staining our souls, Kitten. You think there's any light in me?"

Arrow almost looks devastated that he doesn't think a light shines inside him. Like he's come to terms with it and won't take any other answers.

But I've seen the light in him. I've seen the depravity. The destruction he can cause. But there's more to Arrow than mayhem. There's good in there. A light that doesn't come forward very often.

"Yes. There's light inside you. I see it in your eyes." I peel my eyes open, staring into the depths of his eyes.

He smiles warmly. "I was born this way, Kitten. There's always been darkness writhing inside and begging to come free and murder everyone in my sights. Control is my best friend. Something I've only managed to figure out recently."

"How?" I ask, as he raises my arms above my head, locking me in place as warm metal slides over my wrists and keeps me there.

Breathe. You can't escape. It's fine. Everything is absolutely okay.

"By ridding the streets of the bad guys. There's people out there who come to me on Wednesday nights, begging me to rid the world of the pedophiles, murderers, child abusers, and everything evil under the sun. You helped me find that," he murmurs, brushing his lips against mine.

"I did? How?"

He grins, pulling away slightly, letting his hands work over my chest and down to my abdomen.

"By being you," he says with a shrug, reaching behind him and pulling something out.

My breath stalls when he holds up a knife as it gleams in the sun.

Oh great, I am being punished for stabbing him.

"You stabbed me the other night," he stares, running his finger over the sharpened side of the blade with fascination gleaming in his eyes. Blood wells on his finger until he plucks it off the knife and sucks his finger into his mouth. "With this knife."

Panic wells up in me, tightening my chest when an odd darkness passes over his eyes. He could do anything to me right now. He could take my secrets one slice at a time until his lions devour me and I disappear forever.

I can't let this overwhelming sense take over. Not now. So, I blow out a breath, removing the panic as my inner darkness blackens my soul a little more.

"You were a threat," I say, watching his every move with a blank expression.

He grins. "I was. A crazed masked man chasing his beautiful prey. God, you were gorgeous running through the rain. Even more beautiful than I could have imagined. You'll never leave us again. Will you?"

The blunt end of the knife runs over my cheek. "No," I say, staying completely still.

"Did we scare you?" he asks huskily, running the blunt end across my throat and in between my collar bone, stopping when he reaches the material of my low cut dress.

"Of course you fucking scared me," I whisper, watching him as he turns the knife over.

He grins. "Hmm. Can I chase you around again? I love the chase. It gets me horny as hell."

"Yes," I say, because I've lost my damn mind. Obviously.

I take a deep breath when the tip of the knife rips right through the top of my dress.

"Don't move, Kitten. Or I'll make you bleed. Not that I mind fucking you while you're covered in blood. I sharpened this last night after I cleaned our blood off it."

I don't move an inch when he cuts through my dress more, careful not to knick me.

"Did you know lions can smell blood and decaying prey from far away?" Arrow grins, when he stalls as the dress slowly reveals my naked breasts.

"No," I croak, tamping down the panic pushing to be free.

The darkness within me, manufactured by my monster and his cruel treatment, presses forward. It swoops in, stealing my panic before it can mature.

I'm floating in a silent cloud of nothing.

Arrow grins. "There it is, huh? Your darkness." He pauses momentarily, checking me over. "How do you feel?" he asks in awe, running his calloused finger between my breasts right over my scar.

I blink a few times, staring at his understanding eyes. An odd sensation buzzes over my skin. He gets me. Truly. Together, we have a darkness aching inside us.

"I feel nothing." It's honest, at least.

My pain, insecurities, and fear have vanished. I'm no longer worried about the sleeping predators a hundred feet away.

He nods silently, ripping through the dress again, stopping just above my belly button.

"Your tits are beautiful," he says, moving the material off the rest of my breast until my ruined dress rests on the rock. "I should pierce them," he hums. "Would you like that, Kitten? A bar through each nipple. It'll feel so good when I suck on them." He hums when he leans down, capturing my nipple in his mouth.

"Maybe," I breathe when his tongue rolls over it, sending pleasure straight to my pussy. He quickly moves to the next nipple, giving it the same treatment.

"Maybe, means a yes in my book." He grins up at me as he rolls his tongue over my nipples again, teasing them until they're flushed, puffy, and miserably hard.

My back arches off the hot rock, pulling my wrists against the restraints.

"My greedy, Kitten," he hums, licking a path between my breasts to just above my belly button. "You want me to fuck you?"

"Yes, Arrow," I breathe with a nod.

"Oh, I'll fuck you. But I'd like to play with you first," he says with a grin, staring down at my naked flesh. "I want to cut you, Kitten. I want you to bleed for me. But you already are, aren't you?"

The sharp end of the knife cuts through the remainder of my dress, leaving me completely bare under the sun's rays and Arrow's gaze.

"So fucking beautiful," he says, running the tip of the knife over my inner thigh.

A slight burn follows, and I squeeze my eyes shut until the pain subsides. Goosebumps spread across my flesh, something hard brushes at my soaked pussy. He quickly moves it and bends down.

Grinning, he looks up at me and yanks the string of my tampon until he pulls it out.

I swallow hard when he examines it, tilting his head before tossing it aside.

"You are bleeding for me," he murmurs, picking the knife back up and slowly inserting it into my pussy.

I stiffen when the handle enters me completely, feeling better than it should.

"Arrow," I murmur in alarm. "Is that..." I trail off.

"Shh, shh," he says, working the handle of the knife into my pussy further. "Just don't move, Kitten. Or you'll hurt yourself. I'm in complete control. One false move and you'll get stabbed."

Right. Sure. He's in complete control as he fucks me with the handle of the knife I stabbed him with. Totally normal behavior. Right?

"Arrow," I breathe again, curling my toes.

That handle has no business feeling as fucking good as it does. He wiggles it a bit inside me, hitting my damn G-spot. A fire brews deep in my lower belly as he carefully brings the handle in and out of my pussy. Over and over again.

"Your pussy approves. See? I told you your pussy was heavenly and super," he hums to himself and then removes the handle completely. "I need you on your hands and knees, Kitten. Ass in the air, wave it around like you just don't care," he sings while chuckling.

I swallow hard when he brings the knife handle in front of his face, examining it with lust dripping from his eyes.

"Okay," I say, really trusting him now as I turn over the best I can while chained to the rock and rest on my forearms and knees.

"Let me help," he says, positioning me so my back arches slightly, forcing my ass in the air and my face resting on my forearms. "Mm, perfect. Now, Kitten. I need you to stay as still as you can. Don't move."

"What? Why?" I breathe, turning my head to the side to catch a glimpse of him.

He grins at me, slowly working the handle of the knife back into my pussy and then stops.

"God, you're perfect," he sighs, leaning down and kissing my cheek. "I want you to stay like that. You'll need to tighten your muscles around the handle." He taps my ass cheek a few times, shifting the knife handle in my pussy.

And then he jumps away from me with pure, deranged glee on his face. Taking steps backwards, he holds up a finger.

"Stay. God, Kitten. Stay just like that. I may not be the artist of this family, but you're a goddamn work of art like that. Don't move or the knife will stab you. I need my camera."

"Arrow! Where the fuck are you going?"

He waves a hand above his head, jogging at full speed toward the exit of the enclosure.

"Don't move, Kitten! Be back in a jiffy!" he shouts over his shoulder, leaving me directly in the lion's den with a knife in my pussy and my hands bound.

Yup.

This is punishment.

And now, I'm fucked.

CHAPTER FIFTY
Journey

"AND ONE-THOUSAND," I mutter quietly to myself against my forearm.

Every muscle in my body trembles from holding this position for way too long. Thank God for the kegel exercises I've done over the years. Or I'd be fucked right now.

"If he ever comes back, I'm taking this knife out of my vagina, and I'm going to stab him in the neck!" I huff quietly to myself, despite the urge to shout into the void.

I can't be too loud. He left me with his lions. They love him. Me, though? I have no clue. They were fine with me when I was with Arrow. But alone? I'm sure they'd rip through me in a matter of seconds.

How humiliating. I'm going to die by lions with a knife sticking out of my cooter.

Ugh.

My eyes track the sun again. I swear, it skipped through the sky from one side of the earth to the other, leaving me in this position for at least two hours. Or maybe I'm exaggerating. There's no way he forgot me, right?

I can't believe I trusted this mother fucker. He left me chained in his goddamn lion's den with a knife in my pussy. If I move from this position, the sharp knife will stab me in the goddamn leg.

A bang happens in the distance, and I pray to whoever above that it's not the lions getting closer to me.

"I told you to watch him!"

My ears perk up at the sound of Jericho's rage-filled voice, shouting somewhere in the distance. The tightening in my chest eases, and a faint sense of happiness overcomes me. Ah, sweet relief. My rescuers have finally made it. Took them long enough, though. Sheesh. How long did it take them to realize I was missing this time? An hour? Two?

More relief slams into me when Jericho barks another order. Don't tell him, but I'm fucking ecstatic to hear his voice.

For once, it's not aimed at me. Secretly, though, I love it when he bosses me around. But right now? Yeah, I need a damn savior. I'm so fucking overjoyed, a tear trickles down my cheek with relief.

I'm horny. Locked to a rock. Have a knife in my vag. And I'm out for blood.

"Do not touch her," Arrow growls, running forward at full speed, only stopping when he's standing in front of me. His eyes trace my bent over body until they land on the knife, and he grins. "You were such a sport, Kitten. I'm sorry I got caught up when Jer got home. I didn't mean to be gone for so long." He runs a finger through my hair, removing it from my eye. "Forgive me?" he questions, rubbing my cheek with sincerity.

I swear those gray eyes soften when mine narrow. "If you get it out of me," I hiss, pulling at my restraints again.

He grins in response, petting me another time. "Just give me a second, Kitten. Then, I'll fuck you, okay? I even brought more dick." His brows wiggle when he takes a step back, displaying the camera hanging around his neck.

Jericho and Shepp stop dead, their eyes widening at the scene before then.

"Not until I take a picture," Arrow says, not bothering to turn around and face them. I wish he would, though. Their faces are priceless. Something I've never seen from them. Shock. Awe.

Wonderment. "God, Kitten. You look absolutely divine like this. Tied up. Weapon in your pussy. Blood leaking down your legs. All that's missing is our cum coating your skin. Fuck," he gasps, biting his fist. "Now, smile." He grins, holding his Polaroid up and snaps a picture. "Hold still," he demands.

"Yeah, I don't think I'm going anywhere!" I hiss, pulling at the chain holding me captive. "Get this out of me!"

Jericho's jaw tightens, and his lips thin. "What exactly was your plan?"

Oh, great. Ignore me! I'm the person you're supposed to save. Instead, he's staring at me with lust dripping from his eyes and a goddamn hard on pressing against his zipper. Great. This is wonderful. I'm going to be stuck on this rock for the foreseeable future, not being rescued. Fucked, maybe.

Arrow snorts, taking another picture. "I wanted to give Sheppy boy another spank bank image to paint for us." He wiggles his eyebrows at me when he snaps another picture and another, taking the instant photos from the slot and shaking them around with glee.

"For art. I see," Jericho says, sauntering forward. "My poor, Little Chaos," he hums, running a finger over my tear-stained cheek. "You've really done a number on her, Arrow."

By now, my tears have retracted, and fury races through me. My fingers curl into fists when I try the chain again.

"Don't let her tears fool you. She voluntarily got up there and let me lock her up."

I don't bother retorting when the handle of the knife moves inside me slightly, and I gasp, leaning into the pressure. Why? Because it feels so damn good when he slowly moves it in and out of me, hitting every heightened nerve.

"See?" Arrow hums, slowly removing it from me. "Fucking hell," he groans, setting everything in his hands down on another rock. "Stay like that, Kitten," he murmurs, running his hand over my butt cheeks and thighs, gently massaging me. "I'm going to fuck you. Then, I'm going to lavish you with gifts."

Jericho shakes his head, bending down until he's eye level with me. "I'm almost positive you are the only person who can tell him no, and he'll listen. Do you want him to continue this?" he questions, gesturing to the sound of Arrow losing his clothes and climbing up behind me.

I could make him stop. Tell him no and to untie me. But where's the fun in that? I've come this far for this long, why not get the reward he promised me. Fuck. My pussy pulsates, eager to receive his massive dick gently working through my wet pussy lips.

"Orgasms. He owes me so many," I groan when he slides inside me without warming up.

My eyes roll into the back of my head when he leans over me, pressing his chest to my back.

"Stop trying to get her to run away. She wants my cock. Don't you, Kitten," he murmurs into my ear, gently thrusting into me over and over.

"Yes," I breathe.

My anger flys out the door when he picks up the speed, quickly fucking me into the damn rock and probably scratching up my nipples. Rock burn is definitely in my future. But I don't give a shit. I stayed here like a good girl, barely able to breathe without the thought of dying. It's a relief I'm alive, not stabbed, and getting railed. Fucking finally!

I cry out when orgasm number one roars through me, clamping down on his cock and trying to hold him there.

"Fucking hell, Journey," he grunts several times, pounding into me until he stops. "Fuck yes," he hisses on a groan, stiffening against me out of breath. "Oh, I came like I haven't come in years. And I'm staying just like this until all my little swimmers are inside. Not a drop will leave your gorgeous pussy."

I rest my forehead against the hard rock, trying to ignore the massive blood stains we just fucked on. I heave a breath when his fingers gently work my hips, giving me the best massage. Yet, he doesn't pull out.

I blow out a breath. "This rock hurts, Arrow."

Jericho smirks, folding his arms over his chest. "You heard the woman. The rock hurts. Now, release her before she stabs you again."

Well, that was the wrong thing to say. His dick hardens inside me again until he pulls out, pouting.

"Fine," he mumbles. "But we'll have to come back out here and play again."

"Play," I sputter, when the metal handcuffs release from my wrists, and I flop on my back, unable to move. "This was not playing." I scowl when he appears above my face with one of his signature grins.

"It was for me, Kitten. This is all I pictured for days. Tying you up and having you at my mercy. Next time, I won't take so long." He side-eyes Jericho. "I got a bit distracted," he huffs, leaning down to kiss my lips, eagerly shoving his tongue in my mouth over and over again. Well, until someone slaps him on the back of the head.

"Come on now," Jericho says with a sigh. "We need to get you cleaned up, Little Chaos. We have visitors coming over."

"And Jericho has some fun information he'd like to share with you," Arrow quips, slowly climbing off me. "We'll continue playing later, Kitten." He winks, grabbing all his shit he left on the rock and waiting with puppy dog eyes for me to come, too.

"Fun information?" I mumble, squeezing my eyes shut when I finally sit up. A dizzy spell takes me over, and I groan, rubbing my temples. I think I was in the same position for way too long. My muscles hurt.

"Up you go, Little Chaos," Jericho murmurs, scooping me into his arms bridal style. "We have a lot to talk about before our guests arrive."

CHAPTER FIFTY-ONE
Journey

"WHAT THE FUCK did you just say?" I shout, blinking rapidly at the three men standing before me as I towel off my wet hair in our bedroom.

After the three idiots marched me into the bathroom so I could wash off the sweat and blood I had accumulated in the lion's den, Jericho dropped the world's biggest bomb on me. I knew their not insisting on washing my back was a huge red flag of epic proportions.

The moment I walked out of the bathroom wrapped in a luxurious fluffy robe with feelings of finally being relaxed, they told me I was hitched.

But I'd remember walking down the aisle, right? Wrong. Because I didn't walk down the aisle. Not even the night those assholes drugged me and tucked me in at home after fucking me senseless. I'm beginning to think I'm in way over my head with these lunatics.

"We're married," Jericho says, shrugging a shoulder with zero remorse.

Zero! He doesn't think this is a strange thing to do? This is fucking wild.

"I think I would remember getting fucking married!" I shout again, throwing my towel at him.

He doesn't flinch when it hits him in the face and drops to the floor in a wet heap.

"Well, you weren't exactly present for the signing of the papers." He shoves his hands into his pockets, sending me that signature cocky smirk, essentially telling me to buck up and take what he's done with a smile. Fat fucking chance, asshole. "But I did have your signature to sign your name. It was easy."

"I'm going to kill you," I grunt, marching toward him with intent. "I'm going to fucking bury you!"

"Oh, I'll help," Arrow so helpfully pipes in with a grin, glaring in Jericho's direction.

Oh, fun. At least I have Arrow on my side in the murder of the mafia heir. Down with Jericho. Feed him to the lions, instead.

I want to stab him in the throat and rip it out with my bare hands over and over again until he understands what he just did to me without my permission. This is worse than being tied to a fucking rock with a knife in my pussy. This is a lifelong commitment.

Once I reach Jericho, I punch him square in the gut, catching him off guard. That's right, fuckface! I'm more lethal than you realize.

Air pours from his mouth when he bends forward, clasping his stomach in a rookie move. I aim to put my knee into his nose, but he reaches out as fast as lightning, grabbing my throat.

"That one was free," he wheezes, gently squeezing my throat and constricting my air. "The next ones won't be in your favor, Little Chaos. You can be mad. You can lash out, but violence against each other is never the answer. I've sworn to never in my life hit a woman. And I won't. You should do the same."

It's a sobering thought when he forcefully pushes me back onto our large bed and crawls on top of me, keeping his hand around my throat. His body weight presses me into the mattress as I glare.

"You married me without consent. How am I supposed to

feel?" I grit out, struggling against his hold. But Jericho is unmovable on top of me.

"It might sound cliche, but I married you for good reason."

I blink several times. Actual sincerity sits in his eyes, shining back at me.

"Selfish," Arrow coughs in the background.

Jericho growls in his direction. "You're not helping, assbag."

"Why?" I ask, grabbing his wrist when his fingers flex on my flesh.

Jericho licks his lips and inspects my eyes. "Would you believe that I did it for your own good? That I was protecting you against my father?"

I swallow hard. Gabriel Viotto. My monster and tormentor. I've always needed protection against him. But never had anyone in my corner offering it. Is Jericho sincere when he says he wants to shield me from him? He's proven to me in my time with him that I can trust him.

My stomach drops. "Why would you need to?"

Jericho cocks his head. "Do you know why your mother sold you to my father?"

Yes. But I can't exactly say it's because I murdered an important man under him.

"Not exactly," I mutter, watching the honesty cross his features. Nothing deceptive lives there, and my mind begs me to believe whatever he has to say.

"Your father was Corbin West..."

"Yeah, I know. What a deadbeat, too. He was never in my life. He may have been a billionaire, but I got fuck all. He left me with a drugged-out woman who could barely afford to take care of me. Then he died. End of story. He's not important." I shake my head at the thought of my selfish father never showing up to take me away from this shitty life or stepping up to help us financially make it.

"Journey, love," he murmurs, leaning down so his forehead rests against mine and his hand finally moves from my throat, soothing my hair. "Your father may have been a deadbeat when he was alive. But after his death, he left you twenty million dollars."

Hold the phone. Did he just say what I think he said? There's no fucking way that my father left me anything. I didn't even know him. Hell, I never met the guy. All I knew was his picture when my mom told me who he was. It was of her, him, and me as a baby in the hospital. Apparently, he hung around long enough to name me, but that was it. No money to help us out when we were in a tight spot. No dropping by to see how I was. My mom worked her ass off when I was younger.

"I'm sorry, you said twenty-m-m-mill-million?" I stammer through my words as my mind races a million miles a minute. "And what? Me? No way! Why..."

My face drops when I think about the year I learned my father had died. I was fifteen and saw his face on the news, featuring his twin sons, Seger and Zeppelin, in a few photographs, alongside another brother, who was way younger than them.

"That's your dad?" Sunny asks, snuggling into my side as I lie on her bed with her, holding up my phone so we both can see.

"Yup." I shake my head, swiping through the news article about him.

"Wow. You have brothers, too?" she asks with wide eyes, pointing to the twins as they hold a press conference, confirming the death of their father.

But I can't bear to watch the footage without my heart breaking and jealousy consuming me. They got to live the good life in his massive mansion while going to some fancy prep school on the other side of town, rubbing shoulders with models, actors, and anyone else in the one-percent. While I'm here, fighting for my sister's life. Or attempting to. She has a doctor's appointment tomorrow to hopefully get us some answers on why her health is failing so much right now. We know it's her heart, but we don't know the extent of what else is going on.

"I don't need them, Sun," I murmur, kissing the top of her hair. She snorts. "Right. You just need me, huh?"

"Mhmm. Who needs rich older brothers who got to live it up with my dad?" I roll my eyes, slamming my phone down.

"No. That can't be..." I shake my head as best I can, but Jericho clings to me, forcefully spreading my bare legs and settling his pelvis against mine. "There's no way," I gasp out, shock overtaking me.

"Yes. He left you twenty million dollars. All to you." Jericho's lips slowly work against mine as his tongue gains entry. He moans into my mouth, rocking against my hips until I'm gasping into his mouth.

"Why now?" I whisper, squeezing my eyes shut. "Why would I get it now?"

"That's the problem, Kitten," Arrow says in a soothing voice from beside me. "It was given to you years ago..."

"But you were a minor," Jericho says.

"A minor?" I ask, furrowing my brows. "When?"

The bed dips next to us as Arrow lies back, bringing himself level with me.

"You were sixteen when they showed up," Arrow hums, working a finger down my cheek.

"Showed up?" I swallow hard, attempting to think back to the time I was sixteen, but it's overshadowed by my days of living in a cage. "I don't remember..." If I was sixteen and didn't remember...

There's only one thing that comes to mind—my monster. That's the year he took me unconscious into his basement and left me there to rot. Then, something changed his mind, and he kept me alive. I was so fucking sure he was going to end me.

Jericho rocks against me again, pulling my mind from the darkness and panic on the verge of taking over. There's a reason my mother just handed me to my monster. Sure, he insisted I had to pay for my bad deeds, but he could have murdered me.

But he didn't, did he? He kept me alive, training me to be his little spy. For what? My money.

"Where were you, Journey? Where did he take you?" Jericho

murmurs, kissing my other cheek with soft pecks. "Tell me," he demands, grinding himself against my core.

Fuck.

This is worse than torture. He's winding me up and begging for answers, and I'm helpless.

My back arches slightly when his fingers twirl over my clit. Fireworks spark beneath my eyes, and I gasp.

"A basement," I gasp out.

What basement, though? I have my suspicions. If I could hear Jericho playing his melodies through the walls, then there's only one place he could have taken me. Here. In this house..

My head fills with static when his fingers softly brush against my clit in tiny circles but not using any sort of pressure.

"A basement?" Arrow asks with confusion.

"I need answers, Little Chaos. I need you to tell me everything about that time he took you to the basement. Please," he murmurs.

"Tit for tat," I whine, curling my fingers into fists.

"Fair enough," he chuckles, continuing to torture my clit. "My father tortured me, too. He left me in a darkened closet when he got drunk enough. Claimed it was for my own well-being and that it'd turn me into a better man to conquer my fears. It did none of that. It made me resent him and loathe him. But I stuck by his side until he started showing signs of paranoia."

My eyes slowly flutter open despite the pressure building in my lower stomach. Tears form in my eyes at the injustices we've endured at the hands of Gabriel Viotto. Even his own flesh and blood couldn't outrun his wicked hands.

"He locked me in a cage in the basement and left me in the dark for three whole days," I whisper, swallowing hard when Jericho completely stills on top of me. The room fades away when his brows furrow and sadness rings in his eyes. "You played the violin so beautifully."

Unwanted tears fall from my eyes, carving their way down my cheeks at the memories of the boy who kept me going with the sounds of his violin through the walls. Every day, I counted down until I heard his tunes.

Jericho curses under his breath, gently setting his lips on mine. "Okay," he murmurs. "It's okay, I promise." He leans his forehead against mine, picking up speed with his fingers until an orgasm blasts through me, and I cry out. He slows his pace, pulling his fingers away. "I married you because whatever happened, your mom sold you. Your brothers got scared your mom was only out for the money and would steal it from you. So, they put a stipulation on it and threw it into a trust. You get the money when you're either twenty-one, or if you're above eighteen and married."

"You should tell her the part where you married her before you knew that information," Arrow so helpfully points out, laughing when Jericho sends him a glare.

"Fuck off," Jericho growls, throwing a punch that doesn't land.

Arrow cackles, rolling around on the bed. "Missed me, Daddy Jer," he says, goading him while sticking out his tongue.

"Why?" I ask, bringing Jer back to the conversation.

Jericho sighs. "I have an obsession, Journey. I wanted to possess every inch of you. But I wanted you to have my last name. Now, you do. Journey Viotto. Sounds fitting, doesn't it? My father can never touch you again. We're married. You are mine. And him? Well, he's a fucking dead man." He grits his teeth as he speaks.

"Ding, ding, we have guests!" Arrow says, jumping off the bed while staring down at his phone. "They're pulling through the gate right now."

My heart plummets at the thought of guests. My brothers. They're here to meet me and hand out my inheritance.

Jericho sighs. "So, you're going to meet your brothers tonight over dinner. They're going to give you information on your money and hopefully sign it over to you. Do you trust me?"

"What do you plan on doing with it?" I ask, cocking my head while examining his impenetrable expression.

"Hiding it. If my father thought he could take you, torture you, and leave you to rot in the dark... Well, he has another thing coming. I'll make him regret ever laying a finger on you," Jericho says as a grin explodes on his face. "We're going to hide it so well, he'll never gets his hands on it. And then, I'm going to end him." With a quick peck on the lips, he removes himself from me, standing near the edge of the bed. "So, do you trust me?"

I look around the room at the three men who have come into my life like a fucking storm, shaking up everything about my existence.

"Trust him, Kitten," Arrow stage whispers, throwing an arm around my shoulders. "We're the only ones who can fight back against your monster."

"We already have been for a year now. We've got our own soldiers and loyalists. We've proved ourselves to them over and over again. Now, let us prove to you that we're on your side," he says with a grin.

"And how does your father not know any of this?" I question, looking between the three of them.

They know bits and pieces about my captivity. But I haven't told them the entire truth. Not yet. They don't know who I killed and why. My eyes stray on Shepp, who leans against the opposite wall with a tightened jaw, watching the entire exchange. Obviously, the other two weren't clued in on the marriage I was forced into.

They also aren't aware that I've hit the jackpot with information. Jericho has just laid it all out. He wants his father gone. Maybe that's why I'm here, after all. My monster knew if he put me here, they'd make rash decisions. They'd trust me.

Jericho shrugs. "It's possible he knows everything. He's paranoid at all times. He has spies out there." His eyes cut to me as he looks me over. Almost like he knows why I'm here. "But I'm smarter than him and two steps ahead at every point. I have my own spies, relaying information to me."

I nod several times at his words. That's what he thinks. His father has had his eyes on him for years. I suspect he knows more than he's telling Jericho. But what do I know?

I lick my lips. "Then, yeah, I trust you."

Because what else can I do? I have to trust him so he trusts me. My sister's life depends on it.

"Wonderful," Jericho says, clapping his hands. "Let's get dressed and meet them downstairs."

CHAPTER FIFTY-TWO

Journey

"THE GUESTS. THE GUESTS!" Arrow sings to himself as the three of us make our way down the steps towards the foyer. I think he even clicks his heels together in a weird dance. Maybe he'll fall. That would be fun punishment for his stunt earlier.

Loud banging on the front door echoes through the vast room, sending my damn heart into a frenzy.

Brothers.

I have brothers. Probably a lot of sisters, too. I know I have them. There are millions of Wests out there traipsing the earth. Well, maybe that's an exaggeration. From what I've heard, at least, Corbin West couldn't keep it in his pants. My mom is a prime example. She was a dancer in Vegas. Beautiful. Magnetic.

Then, she fell into Corbin's trap by landing in his lap. They had a short-lived fling while he played with his band in Vegas. Then, there was me. He barely hung around for that, leaving the moment I was born to probably go produce more children he refused to pay for. After that, my mom moved us here to Briar Cove. And that was the end of our story.

I felt stuck for a long time, knowing I had family out there. It never seemed like they wanted to know me. So, getting this opportunity to meet my flesh and blood has butterflies fluttering in my stomach and anxiety eating away at me. My thoughts stray to Sunny—my other sibling. She'd want me out here meeting my other family, thrilled that I had finally gotten the opportunity.

"On your best behavior, Little Chaos," Jericho murmurs, throwing his arm around me and stopping me dead. Those dark eyes gaze into mine with hints of amusement sparking in them.

What an absolute dick. Is he still abiding by the ridiculous contract he had me sign? Well, I'll show him later where he can stick that contract. Straight up his ass until he can taste it.

I frown, sending him my best death glare. Burn in hell, you dickweed. "My best behavior? Maybe I should say the same to you," I say, raising a brow. "You married me without asking."

I will not stab him. I will not maim him. Who am I kidding? I have to enact some sort of revenge. Right? Maybe I'll file for divorce after receiving my inheritance. Take that, dickhead. Marry me without walking me down the aisle or giving me a pretty ring, you'll regret it.

He grins, kissing my temple like I'm the cutest thing on the planet. I'll show him cute. I'm going to shank him when he least expects it.

"We're in this fight together," he hums. "You, me, and them against my father. Stop fighting this, Wife."

I throw my elbow into his gut. Or try to. He laughs, holding his muscles taut and blocking my attack.

"If we're in this fight together then you shouldn't have let me get arrested or married me without my consent or the endless list of shit you've done to me, including the fucking contract you forced me to sign," I hiss breathlessly, attempting to catch my breath.

"Aw. Mommy and Daddy are fighting again. Want me to hold him down, Kitten? We can slice off his nipples like pepperonis." Arrow grins, coming to wrap his arms around both of us and pulling us into his side.

"Errr," I stammer, trying to shake the imagery out of my mind. "No thanks to slicing off his nipples..." Actually, it's probably not a bad idea. It'll teach him some manners. Take a man's nipples, and then, he'll learn.

"We can still electrocute them. I always carry my knockout meds in my pocket. One stick and he's out like a light." Arrow snaps his fingers in front of Jericho's unimpressed face.

"Let's get on with it, shall we?" Jericho demands, pulling out of Arrow's hold with me in tow.

"Yes, Daddy," Arrow quips, shooting backwards when Jericho takes a swipe at him.

"One of these days, Arrow. I will catch you and wring your fucking neck."

Shepp snorts from beside us, leaning against the wall. He signs something to Arrow, and they chuckle together.

"You say all these fun things like stabbing me and choking me out like it's a bad thing." Arrow grins, chuckling when he turns on his heel and heads to the front door. "Ready to meet your destiny, Kitten?" he asks, swinging it open. "Welcome, welcome!" he shouts in the face of a woman who rears back with a twisted expression.

I blow out a breath, counting down in my head before my darkness takes my panic away. A calmness settles through me when the dark-haired woman shakes her head and grins at Arrow.

"Olivia Viotto!" Arrow shouts with glee, picking her off her feet and swinging her around as she shouts obscenities at him.

"Arrow! I swear to God!" she squeaks when he finally sets her on her feet and then slaps his shoulders a few times.

My muscles tense when he holds her shoulders, and they speak in low voices, conversing so I can't understand what they're saying. A weird sense of jealousy spears through me, seeing Arrow so close to another woman. Maybe because thirty minutes ago, I was washing his cum from between my legs, and now he's touching another woman—Jericho's cousin.

"I like the green in your eyes. But she's my cousin. He'd rather rip his dick off and stick it in your purse than ever touch her like that. Besides, she has her own family. Five husbands, to be exact. One you'll love to meet in the future."

"Five?" I question, swallowing hard when she shoves Arrow away and waves a hand at two shadows lingering in the doorway.

"Hmm. Oh, yes. You think Arrow is bad? You haven't met them."

My eyes dart to him when he grins, squeezing my shoulders before we take a step toward them.

"Liv," Jericho greets her with a genuine smile. "Were you able to sneak into town undetected?"

She snorts, shoving her long black hair over her shoulder, and I nearly suck in a breath. Red scars line one side of her face in wavy lines, causing a slight disfigurement to her skin. It seems though, she was able to conceal the majority of it under light make-up. But it makes me wonder what the hell happened to her.

"Always undetected. Although, I'm sure Uncle will catch on one of these days," she grins, stepping back until her eyes lock on mine. "Ah. The unsuspecting bride."

Jericho groans, pinching the bridge of his nose. "Liv."

"Ah, ah," she sings, waving a finger in front of his face. "You hush. I'm speaking to your wife."

"My wife," Jericho hums. "I quite like that."

Yeah, I'll ignore that for now. He'll get what's coming to him later.

"I'm Journey," I say softly, holding out my hand.

"Damn," she says, checking me over with wide eyes. "You look just like my best friend River. Minus the curls, though. You've got the freckles, the same nose, and that damn eye color. Even your face shape is the same. I can't wait to tell her."

"She is a West," says a man stepping forward.

Not just any man, though. My brother. A man with my blood running through his veins. I recognize him right away. Knowing which twin he is, though? That's a different story.

"Hi. It's nice to finally meet you. I'm your brother, Zeppelin."

My breath stalls when I look into his moss-green eyes and take his hand.

"Nice to meet you," I whisper.

"It really is uncanny," he says, shaking my hand.

His clone snorts beside him, looking me up and down while I do the same. The next West is a piece of art, with multiple tattoos on his arms and I'm sure under his shirt. He doesn't have to say his name for me to know he's Seger West. Identical twin to Zeppelin West. They've been running our father's record company in a town not too far from here—East Point Bluff. But other than that, I'm in the dark about their life.

"I'm Seger. It's cool to meet you, Little West. Wish it could have been fucking sooner." I take his hand next, nearly flinching when his hard grip grasps mine.

"Nice to meet you, too," I say more confidently this time, feeling at ease in their presence.

I expect them to seem more stuck up and pretentious, but they're quickly proving me wrong. I guess what they say is true, never judge a book by its cover.

"We weren't quite sure where you went," Zeppelin says with a tight smile. "But now that the circumstances have changed, I'm eager to give you your inheritance. Our father's best kept secret."

Seger scoffs, "Imagine our fucking surprise when his lawyer called us months after he died to let us know he left millions of dollars to the kids he shoved aside. I mean, good for you guys. You get the fucking help you need. But he could have fucking done it years before," Seger rants, shaking his head and blowing out a breath.

"Is it..." I lick my lips nervously. I swear sweat is plastering in unflattering places. "Is it seriously twenty million?"

Zeppelin grins, exposing his straight teeth. "He was a billionaire by the time he died. West Records was his baby that skyrocketed his funds."

"Being a rock star fucking helped, too," Seger jokes, letting his eyes roam over the mansion as he lets out a whistle. "Hell of a place you got here."

"Thanks," Jericho says, puffing out his chest. "If you all would like to take this to the dining room, we've had dinner catered for us."

"Catered," Olivia snorts. "Typical fucking Viotto."

"Speak for yourself," Jericho gripes, hooking his hand with mine.

"Shepp," Olivia says with a big smile. "You're as talkative as ever."

Shepp grins, pushing off the wall he was leaning against, and signs something.

Olivia grins again, quickly signing something back. Shit. I really need to get on it so I can learn sign language. If she can do it, then so can I. But I'm still determined to pull words out of him in front of the others. Something he has yet to do.

Seger and Zeppelin linger beside Jericho and me as we make our way into the large dining room close to the kitchen. We make small talk, catching up on where they're from—East Point Bluff. A hoity-toity town filled with controversy.

When we enter the bustling dining room, I'm stunned to see several people in white uniforms moving around with trays in their hands. I side-eye Jericho. Discretion is his father's middle name. So, why does he have strangers in his house who could report back to his father about this meeting? He doesn't seem concerned, though. Maybe they're trustworthy.

The large table, fit for probably twenty people, has been set with fancy plates and candles illuminating the middle. As the seven of us take our seats, steaming meals are placed in front of us, and we continue our small talk. Jericho sits to my left with Shepp and Arrow on his other side, sitting side by side. Seger is to my right at the head of the table. Across from me, Zeppelin watches us with a careful eye while Olivia lounges next to him, talking with Arrow.

"I can't believe a cult was actively murdering people at your school," I say, shaking my head as we dig into our meals consisting of steaks, potatoes, and other sides.

"We barely survived," Seger groans, biting into his steak. "Hell of an experience. Ten out of ten, do not recommend. God damn this steak is good. Who delivered again?"

"It's Emerson Steak House. One of Liv's favorites when she lived in town," Jericho chimes in, carefully cutting his steak into pieces before taking a bite.

Olivia grins. "I'm surprised you remembered. I was only here for a few years."

"You're family. My favorite cousin. Of course, I remembered." Jericho grins back, almost childlike.

It's odd to see him genuinely thrilled to have her here. And I see the resemblances, too. Jericho explained to me that the Viotto family is made up of six brothers. Five who lead sections of California and work together as a team. And one adopted son, who left the family and became a secret agent like Liv. To me, it's confusing as hell.

"Fucking delicious. Need one of these in East Point," Seger groans, shoving a big piece into his mouth and letting the juices run down his chin.

How charming.

"The only good thing that came of that whole East Point Prep debacle was getting the scum off the street," Olivia says, shaking her head. "Although, I've heard rumblings of The Apocalypse Society rebooting in other countries."

Seger scowls. "You've got to be fucking kidding me."

"Chill. We're on it. We're trying to catch whoever thought it was smart to finish what those idiots started. I'm surprised Grumpy hasn't said anything about it." She raises a brow when Zepp and Seger freeze, shaking their heads.

"Getting that asshole to tell us anything about his job is like pulling his damn teeth. The only person he'll tell is Kaycee," Seger says with a scowl. "Fucking prick. You'd think after all these years of living under the same roof, he'd trust us more."

Olivia snorts. "I'm his partner at the office, and he barely trusts me. Your girl has him by the balls."

"She has all of us," Zeppelin murmurs.

Through small talk, I learned that they were married to the same woman—Kaycee. And they had been happily for many years now. But it also included their best friend Chase and another guy named Carter—who works with Olivia. Aka Grumpy.

Jericho's hand clasps mine under the table when we all come to a finish with our meals, and the hired staff clears the table for us.

My leg bounces and I'm nibbling the corner of my nail when Zeppelin reaches under the table and sets a manila envelope down in between us, tapping it a few times.

"When our father died and his lawyer contacted us about the inheritances, we were pretty stunned. The will stated it was our responsibility to hand deliver them to all the West children he knew of. It's been a task getting in touch with everyone. You were the only one we haven't met face to face." Zeppelin offers me a soft smile, sliding the papers toward me.

"Yeah. Our other sister River was the last one we found. She was somewhere in Illinois, slowly rotting away. I think we got to her right on time. She was about to burst with a baby." Seger shakes his head and twists his face.

"She wanted to come with us tonight to meet you. She's been working at our record company for a few years now and just couldn't pull herself away."

"She works her fucking tail off," Seger adds.

"Indeed she does," Zeppelin says with a nod. "We'll all have to get together sometime soon and have a nice lunch."

"That would be nice. What does River do at your record company?" I ask, desperate to learn about all my siblings. I feel like I've lost so much time being kept in the dark about the money owed to me. My mom robbed me of the time with them, too.

I have family. Real-life fucking family. And I want to know each and every one of them.

"She's our fixer," Zeppelin says with pride.

"Your fixer?" I ask, tilting my head.

"Ah, yeah. Riv takes on these bands who are on their last leg with us. Some of them are having issues making music. Some have issues with substances, and she takes them under her wing to help them get into treatment and start making good music again..."

"Or, they're fucking gone," Seger says, shaking his head.

"Why do you put the extra money into them?" Arrow asks, biting into his last piece of steak with zest. "Shouldn't you just can their asses?" Arrow makes a show of wiping his mouth off with the back of his hand, and when he catches me staring at his antics, he winks.

"Financially, it would be responsible to send them on their way. But we like to believe second chances are just a missed opportunity for improvement," Zepp says, taking a small sip of wine.

"Exactly! Second chances are a fucking opportunity to seize the damn moment and take life by the balls," Seger chimes in, shoving the rest of his steak into his mouth.

"You guys are in charge of Whispered Words, aren't you?" I ask, leaning forward.

I haven't been able to listen to them in a while. Not since I got here. Jericho took my phone and all my music on it. And for some odd reason, I haven't had the need to listen or take my pills. The nightmares are still there, but they're not hounding me as much.

Seger wipes his mouth while nodding. "Yeah. They're under our label."

"They're amazing," I say, leaning my head on my palm. "Any new albums coming soon?"

Seger snorts. "Them? They're falling the fuck apart," he grunts.

Zeppelin gives me a tight smile when my face falls.

"Whispered Words is coming to a point in their career where they aren't producing or writing music anymore. They've stalled."

"They're a goddamn mess," Seger mumbles, taking another bite. "They fucking hate each other's guts."

Well, that sucks. I love their music so much. Keiran has such soul when he sings that it puts me straight to sleep. It breaks my heart to know my favorite band is circling the drain.

"Are they on the chopping block?" My heart falls when their eyes connect to one another, and Seger swallows hard.

Zeppelin blows out a breath, taking another small bite.

"They're on a one-way trip to River. Something she's not going to fucking like," Seger grumbles. "She's going to fucking murder us."

"Why?" I ask, furrowing my brows.

"Because you Wests have got something in your blood about needing more than one partner. You're all your very own why-choose novel," Olivia snorts, shaking her head.

"Don't worry, she's fucking collected one, too. She knows from experience," Seger says with a smirk.

My eyes find Olivia, who blushes. "Well, yeah. But he didn't even know it until you knocked on our door."

Seger shrugs. "Well, he does now, doesn't he?"

"He's come to terms with it. He always knew he was adopted by that asshole who raised him. So, I think it was a relief to know he had you guys and River and now, you." Her dark eyes find mine, and she offers me a soft smile.

"Gross," Jericho mumbles, reaching over to squeeze my leg. "I really don't want to think about my cousin in that type of situation."

Olivia rolls her brown eyes and flips him off without a response.

Zeppelin frowns. "River and Whispered Words have a very deep history together."

"You mean a fucking kid?" Seger quips, eyeing Zepp's half-eaten steak on his plate. "You gonna finish that, man?" he asks, earning a glare. "Fine, take your sweet time like usual. But don't be fucking surprised when I swipe it off your plate." He snorts. "But yeah, I'd consider walking away from a fucking kid some deep-ass history. But I believe in her. She'll do her damn job, and then, she'll whip them into shape. Like she does every other band out there."

"Wait. Our sister was in..."

"A relationship with an entire band, yes," Zeppelin says, confirming. "And then they left her for some asinine reason while she was pregnant."

"They're douchebags. Don't meet your idols," Seger quips, polishing off another piece. "But we still have to give them a fucking chance since they're under contract."

"River would never admit how much she hurts knowing they're in the same vicinity as her," Zeppelin adds, shaking his head.

"Anyways," Olivia hums, sitting up straight. "The reason we're gathered here today is because of you." She looks straight at me with inspecting eyes.

"Right," I say, swallowing hard.

"Before we get down to fucking business," Seger says, bringing my attention to him. "Blink twice if you're okay here in mafia land. Blink once if you want safe passage away from here."

"She's just fine," Jericho grumbles, squeezing my leg again.

"I wasn't asking you, mafia asshole. I was asking my sister. Who I just met and now is all of a sudden married." He narrows his eyes at Jericho. "Care to fucking elaborate?"

"I have lions you could meet," Arrow quips, biting into a dinner roll. "They're big and ferocious. They love new friends." He grins at Seger, sending him a withering stare that would make any normal person quiver in their shoes.

Seger pales slightly. "You say lions? Bro, he said fucking lions," he whispers frantically, looking at Zepp.

"Leave the damn lions out of this," Olivia grumbles, waving a hand. "You don't need to take them there. They're looking out for their family."

Arrow grins. "You'll love them. They're amazing. Max and Nova. Journey got well acquainted with them today." He wiggles his brows when I pinch the bridge of my nose.

"Yeah, they were so wonderful." I roll my eyes, turning my attention back to my brothers who patiently wait.

"Moving on," Zeppelin says, folding his hands on the table. "We have to ensure that our sister is okay and not being forced into anything. Liv has more than vouched for you three, claiming you're good men."

Jericho stiffens beside me, his fingers clinging hard to my hand. I can't tell if I'm an anchor for him, settling him down. Or if he's sending me a warning to hush. "You don't sound so confident," Jericho says smoothly, raising a brow.

"If you had a fucking sister, what would you think when she all of sudden got married to a guy like you?" Seger asks, glaring in his direction.

Wonderful.

"That's enough, assholes," Olivia pipes in, standing from her seat and straightening her pants suit. "My cousin and his friends may be a little backwards with society. But they're good men. I one-hundred percent back them in their decisions." She eyes the twins, who nod in sync. "My uncle is a dangerous man. He's the real enemy. If her money gets in his hands, then everything will go to shit."

"My number one priority is taking care of Journey. Long ago, she was promised to me by my father." Well, that's new information he could have led with. But I'll keep my mouth shut for now. He has so much to make up for. "He came to me when I was eighteen, claiming that he and her mother had struck a deal. And now, with this new information coming to light about her inheritance, it makes a lot of sense. The moment I walk her down the aisle in the presence of my father, he'll have access to that."

Jericho gestures to the unopened paperwork sitting in front of me.

"Yeah? And how the fuck would he get to it? He doesn't have access to it. Only she would." Seger raises a brow, irritation forming behind his moss-green eyes.

"That's where she comes in," Jericho says, turning his attention to me. His fingers softly trace my jaw, and he swallows hard. "I'm sorry, Little Chaos. My father doesn't do anything without a purpose. There was a reason he took you and a reason he's done what he's done."

My torture. My jobs. Everything in between is what he's alluding to. I was sold to him for killing his second-in-command. But maybe that isn't the truth. Maybe he took me and threw me in the basement with the intention of letting me rot. Until something changed his mind. Something green and sparkly.

"Yeah? And what's that?" I murmur, leaning into his soft touch.

"He expects you to just hand it over to him," Jericho whispers.

"I wouldn't do that," I hiss, jerking back. "I wouldn't give him the key to my fucking freedom," I grit out.

Jericho nods, leaning to gently kiss my cheek. "Please trust me," he murmurs. "I'm begging you to let me help with this. My father has his ways. He wants that money for God knows what reason. I swear to you, Journey. I'm only trying to help. You may not believe it, but I've loved you for years now. I wouldn't do a damn thing to harm you."

Yeah, right. You handcuffed me. Had me fucking arrested. And then, you dragged me here. They got me out of jail—despite being the dicks who put me in there—and they've relieved me of my monster's overbearing aura.

They've saved me. Made me trust them. And now, I think it's time I put all my faith in them completely, which is harder said than done. I've had to rely on myself for the past three years, living in survival mode for as long as I can remember. So, letting the reins go and giving them to the men I've come to trust with my life—is a feat in itself.

My heart rate skyrockets when he pulls back, exposing his vulnerabilities to me. Despite everything we've been through, I'm about to take a leap of faith and completely put my trust in him.

I have to.

"I'm fine, really. I've known these three for a long time, and I trust them. We got married so I could do this and hide the money from his dad. Recently, I found out that he made a deal with my mom, and he's been using me..." I wrinkle my nose.

"I really don't like the way you just said fucking using me. He didn't..." Seger trails off, clenching his teeth.

"No!" I interrupt, shaking my head. "Not like that. It's more complicated than that. He's used me as his spy. He trained me to do a lot of things in the dark, and I...." I shake my head in shame at the things I've done in the past.

I've taken lives for him. I've spied for him. And all because he wanted to use the money that was left to me? I can't let that happen. It's something my deadbeat dad left for me. Not for him. It's time to take my fucking life back. Maybe if I help Jericho hide the money, he'll show me where and how. Then, I can use it to leave and find my sister, get her treatment, and then get her the new heart she desperately needs.

Before it's too fucking late for her.

"Listen, this marriage wasn't something I was exactly ready for," I say, shooting daggers at Jericho, who continues to stare. "But it was necessary, especially for this. That monster took my baby sister somewhere to blackmail me into doing his bidding and apparently wanted my money, too. So, I don't put it above him to try and take my money. I need it. And I don't want him to have it."

Zeppelin purses his lips and nods. "I believe you," he says, eyeing everyone around the room. "I'm just hoping this is the right decision for you. I believe that these three have truly shown that they're there for you. But I'm curious as to what the plan is?"

"I'm hiding the money in a secure location where no one can find it until the time is right," Jericho says with authority, clinging to me tightly.

"Will my fucking sister know where it is?" Seger asks, leaning forward with malice in his eyes.

"She will," Jericho says, squeezing my hand again with reassurance. "But there will be security measures in place to prevent it from being stolen. I want Journey to have complete access to this money. It's not mine. I obviously have my own. I have my own businesses and such to keep us afloat. Sure, twenty million is a hefty sum, but that's hers. Not his. And not mine."

"If I fucking find out that you were involved in swindling this money away from her. I'll put your ass so deep in Veritas prison, that you won't even know what smacked you," Seger grits out through clenched teeth.

Jericho puts both his hands up, offering his most innocent look. "Swear to the stars that I'm not tricking her or you. Despite what everyone might think of me, I don't intend to be a bad guy."

That's debatable—is what I want to say. But I keep my lips locked tight. I need this money for my sister and her treatments. For our escape from the monster holding us against our wills. I want out of this town. Or, I used to. Maybe not anymore. My eyes stray to the three men surrounding me protectively. Their eyes stay on the possible threats sitting across from us.

They'd do anything to keep me alive and protected.

What more could I ask for?

"Nah. We murder the baddies off the street," Arrow adds, climbing to his feet with tension lining his muscles. "The murderers, the pedos, the fucking kiddie nappers, and the goddamn politicians who think they can get away with whatever they want. They've met the sharp end of my knife. Not the innocent. Ever. Journey is the other half of my soul. My fucking soulmate. If anyone harms her, even that asshole, I'll cut out his testes and use them as bouncy balls."

Shepp rolls his eyes, signing something.

"Yes with the balls again," Arrow quips, tossing him the bird. "Are we all in agreement, then? I'd really like to get this over with so I can fuck my wife."

Seger's face turns beet red. "Please, for fuck's sake. Don't talk about my fucking sister like that."

"Point proven," Zeppelin says with a cringe, pulling out a pen from his pocket. "But I'd like to be in the know of where this goes."

"Straight into a foreign bank account under Journey's new alias—Josie Wells. I've done extensive research and so has Sheppard," Jericho says, pointing to the silent man at the end of the table, watching us carefully.

He nods in confirmation, signing something.

"He says they've been looking into it so Gabriel can't touch a cent or harm Journey," Olivia confirms.

"I trust them," I tell my brothers with a nod. "They haven't done anything to harm me."

Liar, liar, pants on fire. They've chased you, fucked you, left you tied up, and the list goes on. Maybe I liked it. Just a little bit. But, still. I want the money so I can find my sister and get the fuck out of dodge and live a normal fucking life. Whether it's here with Jericho, Arrow, and Sheppard. Or far away in a cabin in the woods.

And this is my only chance.

"If you fucking say so," Seger grumbles.

"Then, let's get this started," Zepp says with a tight smile.

By the look on their faces, I can tell they think I'm making a mistake in letting Jericho take charge of my money. The facts are blaring them in the face. I'm married and over eighteen. So, the money is mine free and clear. I may not have known about it before, but this boost will help me immensely. It's for my future. Our future.

"Well, it was great to finally meet you," Olivia says with a wide smile. "Welcome to the family." Her eyes shoot to Jericho, who stands a few inches away from me with his arm hooked around my shoulders.

"I get it," he grumbles, running a hand down his face.

Olivia nods and leans in, embracing me. "If my cousin messes with you too much. You can call me, any time." As she says the words, I feel something slip into the pocket of my jeans. "He seems to really care about you," she murmurs, pulling back with a smile.

"Secrets don't make friends," Jericho grunts, sending her a scathing look.

"Sure, they do. We're besties now! I'm just collecting all the Wests like trinkets," she quips, slapping him on the shoulder.

"Until next time, cousin," Jericho says with a sharp nod.

"Yeah, yeah. Hopefully, you'll keep your nose clean."

"Not possible," he says, clapping her on the shoulder.

"We'll all get together soon," Zeppelin says with a soft smile. "My wife is eager to meet you."

"Very eager," Seger says, shaking his head. "It was almost impossible getting out of the house without her with us."

They share a wistful smile while chuckling in unison.

"We'll invite you to the West Family group chat. There's a few of us in there to keep up." I nod, relaying my phone number to him as Zeppelin taps away on his phone. "There. The invite was sent."

I offer him a smile. "Thank you so much for all you've done. I'm beyond grateful for the both of you."

We say our goodbyes and walk them out the door with a wave. Once the front door closes, we stand in a small circle.

"Well, that was a pleasant meal," Jericho says, rubbing at his chin.

"I'm disappointed they didn't want to meet Max and Nova," Arrow pouts, shoving his hands into his pockets. "We could have had so much fun watching them feed."

"Or scare them away," Jericho quips, shaking his head.

"So, can I have my phone back? I'd like to stay updated with my family." I raise a brow, sticking my hand out.

Jericho smirks. "You think we'd give it back to you after you just confessed..."

I stiffen when Arrow moves in behind him, plunging a needle into his neck and stopping him mid-sentence.

"What," Jericho slurs.

"You were a bad, bad boy, Jericho. Time to pay," Arrow murmurs into his ear.

I blink several times when Jericho collapses into Arrow's arms with his eyes shut.

Shepp shakes his head, signing several things to Arrow, who just grins at him.

"Shush, Sheppy Boy. Daddy Jer is going to pay for being a selfish dick," he hums, slightly petting Jericho's dark hair. "Now, who wants to help me get him upstairs? He's going to watch a wonderful show that he can't participate in."

Shepp sighs heavily, pinching the bridge of his nose.

"Did you... Did you just drug him?" I swallow hard when Arrow's light gray eyes find mine and amusement sparks in them.

"It's kind of my thing, Kitten. Everyone is so uncooperative. This makes it easy." He winks at me, as he heaves Jericho over his shoulder like he weighs nothing.

"What the hell?" I question, standing in the center of the large foyer, watching in horror as he skips up the damn stairs. "He..."

Shepp shakes his head and shrugs, not giving me an answer of any kind. He grabs my hand and slowly leads me up the stairs, trailing behind Arrow and a drugged-up Jericho.

CHAPTER FIFTY-THREE

Jericho

WAKING up bound and gagged was not something I ever thought I'd experience. On the contrary, really. I thought Journey would be the one in this position at our hands. Or maybe Arrow. He's always wanted to be restrained for pleasure.

Instead, it's me. Oh, how the tables have turned and not in my favor.

Sludge moves through my brain, making it hard to stay in the now. I could easily slip back into the land of the dead and not resurface for days. But judging by the grunting, skin smacking, and loud moans coming from somewhere in the room, I should probably open my eyes and greet whatever fresh hell Arrow has selected for me.

With every ounce of energy I possess, I peel my eyes open, blinking several times, and trying to push away the fog clouding my vision. My hand jerks up in an attempt to clear them, but I can't. Restraints sit heavily on my ankles and wrists, confining me to the uncomfortable chair, positioned a few feet away from our massive bed.

This has Arrow's name all over it.

He's dead.

And I go to tell him how I'm going to chop him into tiny bits, but my tongue won't move and my mouth is pried open.

Wonderful.

Of course, when I woke up. I knew this. I felt it all over when I couldn't even successfully wiggle my toes. I had hoped, though, that I was hallucinating. But I never get that lucky.

"Oh, goody! You're awake," Arrow says, climbing off Journey's naked body with a look of pleasure crossing his face. "You've missed out on a lot." He gently slaps my cheeks a few times, really bringing me back to the land of the living.

"What the fuck?" I slur beneath the ball gag in my mouth, preventing me from truly articulating how I feel.

Believe me, I have an insane amount of profanity to spew in his direction.

"You've been a real prick lately, Daddy Jer. So, I put you in time out for a little while so I could have some fun with the wife we share. Sharing is caring, ain't that right, Kitten?"

The woman in question is naked on the bed, lying on her back with her eyes squeezed shut.

Her bare tits heave, gleaming with cum and sweat in the moonlight coming from the window, highlighting her beautifully scarred body that I love to satisfy. God, she's beautiful. The most gorgeous woman on the planet.

And she's all ours.

How long have I been tied to this chair with a gag in my mouth and my hands secured behind my back? Too long, by the look of it. I attempt to remember the last thing we did. Fuck. We were standing by the front door saying farewell to our guests.

And then, nothing.

"Yes," she moans with heavy breath.

Shepp moves in, turning her on her side. So her front faces me, giving me the perfect view of her gleaming flesh.

I want to reach out or speak, but I'm left on the sidelines when Shepp lines himself up and slowly enters her in one thrust. Pure, unadulterated lust pulls his features tight, and satisfaction sparking in his eyes has my jealousy roaring to life.

Fuck! I should be in there, too. Instead, I'm stuck in this chair.

My dick aches in my pants, growing harder by the second.

I've shared everything with these fuckers. My life. My home. Even my fuckhead of a dad. They're my brothers. My everything. I trust them with my damn life. Now, they're fucking my wife while restraining me.

I watch with rapt attention as Shepp plows into her from behind, sinking his fingertips into her hips.

"You like that, don't you, Daddy Jer?" Arrow murmurs, leaning down to speak right into my ear. "You claimed her on a piece of paper. Now, we're taking claim of her body right in front of you."

"I get it," I grumble through the gag. "I was an asshole..."

"Sharing is caring," Arrow quips, slapping me on the shoulder. "And you don't get to participate when you're a sneaky, selfish bastard." He grins with pride, watching ecstasy cloud Shepp's face.

One long, drawn-out groan leaves his throat, and he buries his face into her neck when he stiffens, stopping all movement.

"That's his third orgasm," Arrow chuckles. "I'm on number four. She's on number six. And you? You're on zero." He claps my shoulder one last time before sauntering away buck ass naked and stroking himself. "And you'll remain that way until you've learned your lesson."

I narrow my eyes at him when he leans down and spreads her apart for me to see Shepp buried deep inside her.

"You see that, Jer?" I'm going to fucking murder him if he doesn't let me out of here. "She's so filled with cum, it's leaking out around his dick." Arrow hums to himself as he leans down and licks her clit, causing a loud gasp to fall from her lips.

"No, Arrow. I can't take anymore," she whines, attempting to reach down and grab his hair. But Shepp stops her, gripping her wrists tight.

"You're going to come on my face over and over again, Kitten. We're wearing you out, so you have nothing left to give to Jericho.

Tell him what a bad boy he was for marrying you without telling you."

"Bad," she moans, arching her back into Shepp, who slowly pulls his dick out of her pussy with a groan. It's the most noise I've heard from him in years. Go figure, it's her who is able to bring them out of him. One day, my best friend will finally speak like I know he can.

"Tell her she looks beautiful, Jer," Arrow says, swiping his tongue over her clit, while shoving his fingers into her pussy at a rapid pace.

"Fucking beautiful," I garble out through the stupid gag I want to rip out of my mouth and demand he set me free. My dick basically punches through my dress pants, wanting a taste of the only woman he's ever been inside.

"See? Jer can be a good boy, can't he, Kitten?" he says, pulling his mouth back from her clit and shoving his fingers far into her pussy. "I'm just going to leave these here as a pussy plug. We can't have any of these swimmers falling out."

Her lips pop open, and her back arches again when she cries out. Fuck. She came again on his fingers.

"Such a good, Kitten. I think you're relaxed enough," Arrow hums, smirking in my direction.

"For what?" she breathes, slumping into the bed.

"I'm going to bend you over, Kitten. And stretch out your asshole."

I stiffen at his words when her eyes widen. She shakes her head.

"Arrow. I don't know..." she trails off with exhaustion.

They've completely worn her out.

His face softens when he leans over her and gently kisses her lips. Something I've never seen from him. He's gentle, caring, and willing to give her his beating heart. Any other time, he'd force his hand. But Journey West has that effect on us.

"Would you be willing to try?" he asks, resting his forehead on hers. "I won't fuck it tonight. But we'll get you loose so we can eventually play."

"Will it feel good?" she asks, sounding completely spent.

"Oh, you better believe it will, Kitten. Besides, I have some fun toys to show you!" He jumps up from the bed, making his way toward the nightstand on the other side of the bed. "Have you been missing your toy?" he asks Journey, when he leans down and rifles through the contents of the nightstand.

"My toy?" She reluctantly raises her head from the bed, watching him with furrowed brows.

"Yeah, the toy you kept in your nightstand next to your bed."

"Arrow," she grunts threateningly. "What did you do?"

"Oh? Me? Do anything?" He grins again, batting his eyelashes, finally standing up tall. "I got rid of it," he says, waving a hand.

"You don't need that toy anymore. You have real toys," he says, stroking himself several times. "Besides, it wasn't shaped like me."

Walking forward with a large gift bag with red tissue paper in his hand, he makes his way to Journey and sits down beside her.

"What's that?" she questions, untangling herself from Shepp and sitting up beside Arrow.

Fuck. She looks gorgeous sitting there freshly fucked with cum running down her thighs and tits. I can't believe Arrow wasted a drop since he took her IUD out. I know exactly what his plan is. Fuck her until she's pregnant. Only she doesn't have a clue. What a surprise that'll be when she wakes up one day pregnant. Someone is going to have to inform her what Arrow did. Maybe then, she wouldn't look at him with stars in her eyes.

For the first time in his life, Arrow's brows furrow, and a red tint covers his face. "A gift," he says, clearing his throat. "These are all for you. Something I think we can all enjoy together."

"Thanks," she says, looking at his face and taking the bag.

"Open it," he demands, nudging the present. "I want to capture your face when you see what I got you!" he says with renewed glee, jumping up and marching toward his camera that lies on the nightstand. Once he comes back, he sits on the floor in front of Journey with his camera hovering in the air.

"Okay," she says, swallowing hard and digging into the large bag.

When the hell did he get that? And where?

Journey blinks several times when a white box with a picture of a dildo on it comes out first. She eyes Arrow, who takes a snapshot and lets the photo fall to the ground.

"It's mine! The shape and width of my own dick," Arrow says with pride. "I took a mold of my cock the night I snuck into your room and saved you. Then, I sent it to this shop. So, I could give you a toy that's me." He beams with pride. "No more using anyone else's dick shape. Except ours."

"Saved me?" she blanches.

He snorts. "Duh, Kitten. You didn't think a phantom came in, took pictures of the man attempting to touch you, and then left pictures. It was me."

"Err, thanks," she says, looking away. I'm sure contemplating how safe she really was in that trailer she called home.

"Now, the rest," he says, clapping with excitement when she pulls out other boxes and sets them on the bed beside her.

"That's what we're going to use tonight." He points to a small box that has a picture of a silicone butt plug with a jewel at the end of it. "It vibrates, too," he gleams.

"This?" she murmurs, swallowing hard. "It goes..."

"In your tight ass, yes. It'll feel so fucking good, Kitten. We can put it on vibrate while I fuck your pussy. Then, there's this one! It doesn't vibrate, but we can leave it inside you when we go out."

"Go out?" she breathes.

"You're overwhelming her!" I hiss through the gag, earning a wave from him in return. "Slow, asshole," I grunt, pulling at the damn restraints around my arms and legs.

"You're lucky I didn't strip you naked and tie you up with my ropes," Arrow warns, looking over his shoulder at me. "Imagine what that'd be like. Every inch you moved would tighten around your balls."

Shepp sighs heavily with his eyes closed, silently signing, *'Again with the balls, dude. You're obsessed.'*

I snort in response.

"Anywho, yes, when we go out. Like tomorrow, when we have to parade you around our initiation ball. Oh, you'll love that." Arrow says, beaming at Journey. "Grab the lube, that pretty butt plug, which I've already cleaned for you, and let's have some fun at Jericho's expense."

By the gleam in his eyes, I can tell I'm not going to like the next step in his well-constructed revenge against me. And fuck. The initiation ball is tomorrow. Something I had completely forgotten about, given the circumstances. My mind was too focused on finding information on Journey and getting her money.

"Initiation ball?" she asks, swallowing hard.

Shepp groans from the bed, rubbing a hand over his face with exhaustion.

Arrow grins, standing up. "We get to dress you up in a swanky dress and parade you around, showing the world you're ours."

There's more to it than that, and he knows it. They're hosted at least once a month for every new recruit in the family who has dropped to their knees and pledged their lives to the family. My father loves nothing more than to show off what he has and who is under his thumb. Tomorrow is our day. Our celebration. Where we climb on stage, open our shirts, and show off the wounds we received.

It's also a time of completion. Where allies come together and complete their deals by introducing the arranged marriages they set up years before. Normally, it's a surprise. But in the past few years, parents have let it slip to their kids who they were promised to. Like my father telling me when I was younger.

My guess is my father will make sure our upcoming nuptials will be within a week. Or possibly days. If he's motivated by the money, then he doesn't want to wait. Nerves eat away at me with what I've done. I've thrown a wrench in his plans, and now, I'm about to see the consequences at our initiation ball where we'll all come face-to-face with him in a crowded room. My father hates it when his plans go awry, especially when it involves finances. Half of me wants to hide away with Journey in this house and fake illness for tomorrow night.

I need to plan to keep her safe—which I always do. One of our only safeguards is the tracker in her asscheek, but I always have something up my sleeve, thanks to my upbringing. We'll never lose sight of her or not know where she's gone.

One thing at a time—I tell myself. First, I need to make it through this torturous event without coming in my pants. Easier said than done, though.

Journey's hands shake when she peels open the box with the butt plug and slowly brings it out with caution, staring at it like it might bite her. It's smaller in size and purple with a jewel at the end of it.

"It won't bite you, Kitten. That little piece of fun will bring you so much pleasure that you won't know what to do. Now, come here," he says, holding out his hand. "Do you trust me to keep you safe, Kitten?"

She nods, standing in front of him. "Yeah."

Arrow chuckles, grabbing the bottle of lube on the bed. "You have a special piece of my soul and dick, Kitten. They are yours forever. No one else will ever own me except you. Now, come here so I can make you come a million times more." When he turns on his heel, he sends me a grin, leading Journey's naked form in front of me.

Shepp snorts from the bed, waving them off. '*I'll stay here*,' he signs, but only I'm able to witness it.

"I don't know if that's possible," she grumbles, swaying her hips as she follows beside him.

I'm going to break this fucking chair and Arrow's face. I'm

about to lose my damn mind sitting here and not being able to participate in the festivities.

"When I get my fucking hands on you," I garble through the gag, but it, once again, sounds more like murmurs of nothing as drool rolls down my chin.

Arrow grins, setting the boxes in my lap, locking his eyes on my damn boner. "You see that, Kitten? He loves our fun times together, just sitting on the sidelines like a good boy while the others play."

Her eyes find mine, and amusement rests there in their depths. Of course, she's loving this. This punishment was more for her liking. Not for Arrow's. Sure, I took something from them without discussing it. But I took more from her.

"I'm sorry, Little Chaos," I mumble again through the gag.

Arrow's head tilts. "Oh, did you hear that, Kitten? I think he said something important."

"I didn't hear anything," she quips, leaning into his touch.

"Oh, should we keep him gagged then?" Arrow asks with a grin, leaning in to kiss her lips in a sloppy, heated kiss. He groans, palming her ass when he pulls her body into his. "Fuck," he rasps, digging his fingers into her ass cheeks and pulling them apart. "You're the perfect girl for me. Now, I want you to bend over and hold onto Jericho's shoulders."

"What?" she murmurs, peeling her eyes open.

"You heard me, Kitten. I'm going to lube your ass up and have some fun on top of Jericho. It's his punishment, after all."

I roll my eyes and huff a breath.

She nods in his direction and then stands before me. "Poor Jericho," she hums, slowly bending over until her face is inches from mine. "How's that gag treating you? Maybe we should use it more often. Your talking tends to ruin things." She grins, bopping me on the nose several times. "Oh, fuck," she sucks in a breath when Arrow kneels behind her, burying his face in her pussy again. Despite the cum dripping out of it, he goes to town, bringing her to the brink of another orgasm.

"You're going to feel some pressure, Kitten. I want you to breathe through it. For now, it's just my finger until we get you loosey-goosey for the plug, and then, my dick is claiming this hole tomorrow."

I focus on Journey's face when she rests her forehead against mine, breathing heavily.

"You're doing well, Little Chaos," I murmur, hoping she can understand my recurrences.

"Fuck," she grunts, with her eyes rolling in the back of her head.

"That's it," I murmur, aching to run my hands through her hair and hold her face so she knows I'm here to ease the discomfort.

"Relax, Kitten," Arrow says from behind her, but I can't see him. "That's a good fucking girl. You're loosening up so well for my finger. Now, keep breathing. Maybe you can unhook Jericho's gag and fuck his mouth with your tongue."

Her eyes pop open and connect with mine.

"Is... That..." she moans, rolling her eyes back when he does something else. "What you want?" she quickly gets out with a heaving breath.

"Yes," I mumble as best I can. It's almost impossible to speak through this thing, and it should be. But this ball gag wasn't fitted for my mouth in mind; it was for her. So, it's smaller than need be. And I'm certain of that. I think Arrow has been collecting toys, knowing she'd come into the picture, and he loves to experiment.

For God's sake, take this stupid gag out of my mouth before I combust in my pants.

"Only that, though," Arrow pipes up. "Keep his naughty dick in his pants. He's not allowed to come tonight. Only we get to do that." I hear the grin in Arrow's voice. "It's behind his head, Kitten. It'll be like a belt buckle."

Journey's fingers fumble behind my head, trembling when Arrow does something more, and then the ball gag falls from my mouth into my lap. I suck in a breath, happy to breathe through my mouth again. The bastard couldn't have gotten a breathable one? Fuck. I blow out a breath, staring up at her as she softly wipes the drool from my lips and chin.

"Look at the big, bad mafia heir," she coos, taunting me with a grin.

"Oh, I like it when you're vindictive, Kitten. Keep talking naughty to him. Maybe next time, he'll learn to communicate with others when he wants to marry the woman I'm obsessed with," Arrow hums. "Okay, here it comes, Kitten. Deep breath and then, kiss the fuck out of Jericho."

"What if I don't want to kiss him," she moans, sucking in more breaths.

"You're doing good, Little Chaos," I hum, aching to hold her. "You're taking it so well."

"Aw, doesn't Daddy Jer deserve it?" Arrow quips. "Give him a little kiss. He's making up for all the bad deeds he did."

Her eyes find mine. "You're truly sorry," she moans.

"Sorry for protecting you, no. Sorry for doing something that upset you so terribly, yes."

"And me," Arrow growls. "I want to fucking throat punch you for that shit. But I'm letting it slide, because you're my brother, and I have you tied to a chair." He snorts at that. "All righty, Kitten. How does that feel?"

Journey's fingers dig into my shoulders, clawing at me. "It feels good. It didn't hurt too much."

"Oh, goody," he says with glee. "Now, here comes the fun part." He hums as he lines himself up behind her, standing tall so I can finally glimpse his sweat-soaked face. "I'm going to fuck you and turn this on."

Journey's eyes pop wide, and her mouth falls open, forming an O.

"That's it, Kitten. Fuck. You feel so good. You're tighter with the plug in you. Fuck. I'm going to come so deep inside your cunt," he grunts, sloppily moving in and out of her while holding tight to her hips.

"Kiss me," I urge her, bumping my nose into hers. "Use me."

I don't have to utter another word when she bends down, connecting her lips to mine in a hurried kiss. She ravishes my mouth, taking my tongue with hers.

"Fuck," she gasps into my mouth, and her eyes roll back. Every muscle in her body stiffens, and I can tell the moment she comes. The entire world halts, including Arrow, who stares at the ceiling in a silent scream.

"Well, fuck," he grunts, leaning over her back. "Who knew orgasm number five could come so quickly," he chuckles, kissing her back. "How about you, me, and, Sheppy Boy take a nice hot shower while Jericho here, reflects on his actions?"

I scowl when he gently pulls out of her and helps her stand tall.

"More pressure, Kitten," he murmurs, gently removing the plug.

Shepp stops in front of them and eyes me, flipping me the bird.

Okay, they were way more bitter than I thought about the marriage thing.

"Fine. Have a nice shower," I grit out, watching them disappear into the bathroom. "But don't think I won't forget this."

Arrow grins. "I hope you don't forget about this, Jer. I won't let you ever forget."

In Arrow speak, that's a threat. He's relaying to me that I fucked up. And I get it. I did. I snuck behind all their backs and took something we were supposed to share. But can't they see I did it to ultimately protect her from what was to come?

Maybe not. I sigh, hanging my head when the sound of water and moans fills the air. They seriously can't be fucking her again. Can they?

"Fuck, Shepp," Journey's moans echo out of the bathroom and straight into my ears.

Yeah, they are fucking again.

Wonderful for them. Shitty for me. I suppose I've learned my lesson, then.

Journey exits the bathroom wrapped in a fluffy robe. Her wet curls slightly bounce as she makes her way to me, standing before me. Her gaze eats me up as I rest in the stupid chair.

"He gave me the key to your cuffs," she says, holding it up so the moonlight reflects off the tiny, metal key.

"Are you contemplating leaving me here?" I question, tilting my head.

"Possibly," she says with a shrug. "Have you learned your lesson?"

"More than you could ever know," I murmur.

She hums to herself when she reaches down and undoes the restraints on my ankles and then moves to my wrists. As soon as she turns the key on both sets of restraints, they fall away. My muscles instantly shriek in pain when I stiffly move and stretch my limbs.

"Then you should come to bed," she says softly, setting the key on the nightstand. Journey watches me cautiously when she sits on the edge of the bed, eyeing my movements.

"I vow to you that I will never do something like that behind your back again. You're my wife, after all," I say, wringing out my wrists and standing from the chair I wish to break into pieces.

Something I'll do later.

"Well, you should start by getting on your knees and explaining why I was promised to you already, Husband," she hisses with a huff, crossing her arms. "What the hell is going on? Why?" She shakes her head, rolling her lips in. "I just don't fucking understand this."

"Welcome to our world," I say, dropping to my knees and

crawling to her. "Where you have to expect the unexpected. But tit for tat, Wife. What exactly did you mean my father had you spy?" I know the answer. It's something I've felt in my gut for a long time but have ignored. My aching arms wrap tightly around her waist, and I set my head in her lap, groaning when her fingernails scrape at my scalp. "I was eighteen when my father handed me your picture and said you'd be my wife."

Her muscles stiffen. "So, I was sixteen." Panic rests in her voice when I nod.

"When you disappeared," I whisper, looking up into her eyes.

She gives me a sharp nod, not divulging any more details on why my father took her and tortured her for months on end.

"Let's get you into bed," I whisper, gently rubbing her waist.

She nods, climbing onto the bed and pulling back the sheets. "He used me to spy on his enemies."

I nod once, indicating to her that I understand the pain in her voice. His enemies, big and small. Us. Once all my clothes are discarded on the ground, I crawl in behind her, holding her tight. Arrow and Shepp meander their way to the bed as well, climbing in on the other side of Journey.

"I see my Kitten set you free," Arrow says with a yawn, resting his head on the pillow. His eyes flutter shut, and within a few seconds, he's out like a light, softly snoring.

"Indeed," I hum, burying my face into the crook of her neck, and we all drift off to sleep with the thoughts of our initiation ball on my mind.

CHAPTER FIFTY-FOUR

Journey

LOUD MUSIC ECHOES through the large ballroom, nestled deep in Viotto Tower. He runs every ounce of his operation from within these walls.

Hell, he even lives here.

Somewhere, in a fancy apartment. I've only been here once before—against my will. And it was to see the inside of his fancy dungeon basement while he taught me an important lesson on interrogating people who wouldn't speak.

I blow out a breath. Being in his presence brings back horrid memories of my past, forcing me to relive them. My darkness tickles the back of my mind, aching to take the panic brewing in my gut. And I let it. One day, I'll be able to live without the reminders of him and what he did to me. But that day is not today. Or maybe ever.

Perhaps, this is who I am now. Journey West—unrepairable, broken, and lost.

Arrow nudges my shoulder from beside me with a grin.

"What do you think, Kitten? Is this everything you dreamed it would be?"

I raise a brow. "You act like I've been waiting for this my whole life."

Jericho snorts into his drink. "Well, this is everything I thought it would be. Stuffy relatives. Schmoozing businessmen with their noses so far up my father's ass, they're coming out with shit on them."

"Filthy brown nosers," Arrow hums, finishing off his entire glass of champagne in one gulp. "Ahhh—but they have the best damn booze."

As a waiter dressed in black slacks and a red vest meanders by with an empty tray, Arrow sets his glass on it. He immediately eyes the next waiter with a tray full of fresh drinks, and as they pass, he grabs two glasses and hands one to me.

"Booze up, Kitten. You'll need it. It's going to be a long night of introductions and bureaucracy."

I wrinkle my nose, staring into the bubbly champagne. "Bottoms up, then," I mumble, taking a large gulp of the concoctions, letting my eyes survey the room.

People in fancy dresses and suits mill around, slowly drinking their beverages and conversing with one another. As far as the eye can see, diamonds twinkle in the low lights, and money flashes in every corner. I bet the people here are worth more than I could possibly wrap my mind around. Millions, no doubt.

But they aren't the only people dripping in beautiful dresses and fancy suits. We are, too. Fit the part and all. That's what my monster taught me, at least. Besides, Jericho wasn't going to allow me out of the house in rags. Quite the contrary. He forced my ass into the most expensive dress hanging in my closet. No matter how much I protested. Believe me, I know the price, because the ten-thousand dollar price tag still hung from the beautiful red, floor-length gown fit with actual fucking diamond studs and a name-brand tag.

"We're showing you off tonight. We want to make my father aware that he can never remove you from my grasp," Jericho mumbles, waltzing around me as Arrow zips up my dress.

"And this dress says—You belong to the Devils," Arrow says, squeezing my ass from behind.

"Stop that!" I hiss, swatting him away.

"Don't worry, Little Chaos. We'll be dressed in our best, too."

As he says that, Shepp bursts into the room with a frown, holding three suits protected by plastic. He stops dead, dropping them when his eyes catch me.

"Oh, instant boner, right?" Arrow quips, trailing a finger up my bare back, not shielded by the dress. I shiver when he follows the trail around my front, where it dips, exposing my tattoo. I swallow hard with nerves when he traces the tattoo repeatedly. Normally, my insecurities would eat me alive and I'd hide it beneath my corset. But not tonight. Tonight, I'm showing my monster who is really in charge here. "Gabriel Viotto won't know what hit him. You're ours. He can't marry any of us off to anyone else. I'll stab her." He shrugs.

"Marry you off to someone else?" I ask, leaning on Arrow when Jericho bends down to slip my high heels on.

Why did it have to be high heels? Why couldn't it have been flats? Or tennis shoes. Heels were made by men to torture women more. When these jerkbags aren't looking, I'm switching my shoes. I'd argue now, but Jericho has had a stick up his ass all day. I mean, probably because Arrow drugged him and tied him to a chair last night, but that's beside the point.

Shepp comes before me, laying a gentle kiss on my lips. "Beautiful," he mouths without speaking.

A heat rises on my neck, leading onto my cheeks. "Thanks," I say, clearing my throat.

"He's right, Kitten. You'll be the talk of the party." He grins, tapping my ass a few times, and marches away, snatching up his suit. "Time to suit up, boys."

"That's our cue," Jericho says, standing tall before me shirtless, exposing his taut muscles. "Don't move a muscle."

"Oh, and when I get back, Kitten. We'll put that fun toy up your ass so I can control it all night long. It'll drive you mad, and then, I can eat you for dessert in the bathroom. Have to pass the time somehow," Arrow grumbles, rolling his eyes as he exits the room with his suit and the other two follow.

I shift slightly and blow out a breath. I've decided to pick my battles with the boys. For one, I'm still in high heels, helping me to at least reach Jericho's shoulders. Shepp, though? He's so tall, that I barely reach his pecs. So, I guess these have their advantages. Comfort not being one of them. But I did win the battle of the butt plug. So, that's a win in my book. Arrow fought so hard to try and convince me to let him stick that thing up my butt, but I said no. Not until I'm used to it more. Admittedly, it wasn't that bad and made sex out of this world. So, we'll do that later.

"I could have been driving you mad by now, Kitten," Arrow grumbles, throwing back another gulp of champagne.

"You're going to have to slow down," Jericho says, eyeing Arrow's drink. "Or I'm going to have to speak with Brandon manning the bar tonight about cutting you off."

"Only if you pry it out of my cold, dead hands," Arrow retorts with a grin, setting the empty glass on another passing tray.

"We'll see," Jericho hums in warning, eyeing Arrow with a deathly stare.

"You'll protect me from him, right?" Arrow murmurs in my ear, sliding his hand down my backside to squeeze my ass hard. "I'll give you fifty orgasms if you keep him away from me."

I snort. "You already do that, though."

Facts. Arrow does not skimp in the orgasm department. The man has a wicked tongue and an even more wicked dick. I swear, when he said he wanted to live inside me, he fucking meant it.

"I mean, yeah. But still, he's mean," Arrow pouts, pointing at Jericho, who rolls his eyes.

"I can be meaner," Jericho huffs, standing tall. "But remember, if anything goes south tonight, we rendezvous at the cabin."

No doubt about that. Jericho is a Jerk—Jerkicho.

"Go wrong? You think something is going to happen?" I question, eyeing the crowd. "Isn't this all your family? Aren't they packing?"

Arrow snorts. "Packing. I'm definitely packing," he hums, wiggling his brows as his eyes dart to his crotch.

"Yes. You may be packing your dick, Arrow. But I've come prepared," Jericho says, hinting under his suit jacket.

"Daddy Jer always comes prepared with guns and back up plans. I have my rocket launcher in the coat room," Arrow says with a grin.

I stiffen. "You brought a rocket launcher? And in the coat room?" How the hell did no one put a flag on that weapon?

"Maybe," Arrow hums, shrugging playfully. "You never know when you need to be packing big heat to blow up a room. Besides, you should see what cousin Marv put in there." He whistles under his breath and raises a glass to a man across the room with a grin.

"Right," I say, shaking my head. "What about me? Don't I deserve a weapon?" It'd come in handy right about now. I'm surrounded by their family and my damn monster.

"All in due time, Little Chaos. If I handed you a weapon now, you'd probably shoot our dicks off and flee," Jericho quips, sipping his drink.

Well, they know me so well. "So, rude of you to assume I'd shoot your dick. I'd aim straight for the heart." My grin grows when his eyes shoot to mine.

"Point made," he says, shivering.

"Don't worry, Kitten," Arrow whispers directly into my ear. "I've got a weapon with your name on it. Literally. Have you seen my dick?"

I blink several times. "I'm not answering that," I mutter.

Shepp stands silently at my back. The only reason I know he's there is when his large fingers wrap around my waist and he gently squeezes three times. I'm not sure what he's trying to tell me. Maybe he'll protect me from them both? Or that he's always got my back? My hand finds his, and I squeeze back with assurance.

"So, what happens during this shindig?" I ask, attempting to change the conversation.

"Well soon, my father will come to us and request our presence on stage. We'll parade around like we're in the circus and showcase the wounds he left on our chests. They'll clap. We'll give our thanks and allegiance to the family, once again. My father will announce our marriage contract and set a date for our wedding. Then, we'll all sit down to a nice dinner of steak, potatoes, and shrimp. This entire thing will wrap up by midnight, then we'll go home and fuck until the sun comes up," Jericho says smoothly with a smirk pulling at his lips.

"Delightful," I grumble. "But what happens if he finds out we're already married?"

"I'm not worried," Jericho says, sliding his hand into mine and interlocking our fingers. "He gave me permission to pursue you before this. In fact, he encouraged me to bring you here tonight. I'm not quite sure what he has up his sleeve." He shakes his head with crinkled brows.

"We're eagerly awaiting," Arrow says with a grin. "If he makes a wrong move, then I cut him." He makes a slicing motion across his throat and then pats his chest. "I brought one of my best silent weapons." He wiggles his brows, quickly exposing a large knife hidden at his side.

"Could you please be any more obvious with your plans?" Jericho quips just as Shepp slaps Arrow in the back of the head.

"Ouch. Dicks," he grumbles, rubbing his skull. "No need for violence."

"Speak for yourself," Jericho says, shaking his head. "Just keep your eyes and ears open. Something doesn't feel right tonight."

"You can say that again," Arrow mumbles. "Feels..."

"Off?" Jericho asks, finishing his sentence.

"Exactly. Just look at him, making his rounds with that fake smile."

The taste of bitter wine rests on my taste buds when I examine the man in question. There he is in all his evil glory, tugging along a hazy-eyed woman and greeting people left and right.

Gabriel Viotto.

My stomach drops at seeing him again. I've been in such a

bubble of protectiveness with Shepp, Arrow, and Jericho in their mansion. Seeing Gabriel again has the hairs on the back of my neck rising and my nerves kicking up on the defense. I'm ready to run right out of here and disappear.

The only thing keeping me here? The three men surrounding me in a tiny half circle.

This is our meeting time. He wasn't specific before, simply stating I'd know. Well, I guess I know, because we're finally in the same room together after time apart. Yay for me. And judging by how miserable Shepp, Jericho, and Arrow look, they're about as excited as me.

It's a real party up in here.

"Have I told you yet that you look good enough to eat, Kitten? I should take you into the bathroom and have a meal, anyway. Despite you being a party pooper and not wanting your fun back door prize." Arrow gives me his signature grin, showcasing all his pearly whites. "Next time," he whispers with a nod.

"Sure," I say, pursing my lips. "Next time, big guy." I tap his upper arm a few times, placating him.

"Oh goody, because I'm full of good ideas," he says, rubbing his hands together.

"Incoming," hisses Jericho, moving his drink to his left hand. "Governor LeMaster," he says, extending his right hand out. "Wonderful to see you here tonight."

My eyebrows raise when the portly-looking, older man approaches with a wide smile, shaking Jericho's hand.

"Boys. Welcome to the family."

"We should be saying the same to Leighton. How's his face?" Jericho says, taking his hand back.

The Governor's face doesn't change when he shrugs a shoulder, but I see the anger resting deep in his eyes. If he had it his way, he'd take Jericho out for that comment.

"Better. He was able to make it to his own initiation," he says with the happiest smile that would fool normal people.

"Oh, wonderful. I just wanted to relay the message to him that he should keep his hands off women who aren't associated with him. Especially when that woman is my wife."

Shivers work their way through me when he emphasizes the word—wife. Jericho has this air about him when he threatens someone. He doesn't make any physical moves, unless he has to. Case in point—Leighton for fingering me without my permission. It's the way he delivers his words so smoothly while sipping wine that has my pussy clenching.

Wow.

"I can smell your arousal," Arrow whispers lowly in my ear, grabbing my ass again in a tight squeeze. "God, him calling you his wife has you all turned on, doesn't it?"

No, absolutely the fuck not. I sigh. Who am I kidding? It kind of does. Even though I'm still butt hurt he didn't involve me in the wedding. At all. That's okay, if this works out, I'll make him walk me down the aisle at the wedding of my dreams. Whatever that is.

I gently push him off, causing him to laugh. "Shut it," I grumble, taking a sip of my champagne as the Governor and Jericho exchange more words laced with threats.

Since the moment we entered the top floor ballroom, overlooking the massive city of Briar Cove, this has been happening. Everyone knows who they're celebrating and it's the three men standing rigidly around me. Every five minutes or so, someone walks up to them, shakes their hand, and says congratulations on officially becoming a part of the family.

It's a weird as hell tradition. But who am I to judge? This is their lifestyle. And now, mine, too.

The good Governor walks away with his head held high and his hands stuffed into his pockets. If he's here, then his deranged son is probably here, too. Great. I'll have to keep my eyes peeled for him, too.

Monsters walk in all forms, after all.

I take stock of the room again, trying to gather my bearings.

Gabriel will no doubt come this way soon. In my gut, I know he'll try to separate the four of us and beg me to give him all the details of my stay with them—something I'm dreading. Talk about being caught in the middle of some bullshit rat race. He has my sister, though. What am I supposed to do? Leave her out to dry in the middle of a fucking torrential downpour?

Fuck.

There he is. The scummy man of the hour, weaving through the crowd solo this time. His eyes set on a small circle of people near us. My heart drops when his eyes connect with mine.

"Let me lick you, Kitten. I can take your mind right off that fucker," Arrow says, nibbling on my ear this time.

My breath picks up but quickly dissipates when he falls to the side with a grunt.

"Fuck off," Jericho hisses, shaking his head. "Best behavior, Arrow. Any of these fuckers could be a spy, reporting back to him."

I swallow hard. Yeah, you're looking at her.

"Yes, Daddy Jer," Arrow quips, moving out of reach when Jericho takes a swipe at him.

"Swear to hell, Arrow. One day I'll catch you and you'll pay for your daddy comments," Jericho huffs, taking a sip from his wine glass.

"He has a boner, don't let him fool you," Arrow quips, snickering behind his hand.

"Later," Jericho growls, shaking his head.

Arrow winks at me again, humming to himself. "Gotten off yet, Daddy Jer?"

Jericho's jaw tics. "I feel like I've been a very good boy." He smirks into his drink, sucking down more booze. "Fuck," he chokes, covering his mouth with his hand.

"Is that?" Arrow narrows his eyes.

"Chloe fucking Satin. Of course, my father invited her. She's on the line for something. You? Me? Who the fuck knows."

Jericho discreetly wipes his mouth with the back of his hand, watching the woman across the way closely.

"One of us?" Arrow grits through clenched teeth. "Ain't no way."

"It's a theory," Jericho hums. "You remember the phone call I overheard before we claimed our girl?"

My cheeks heat when his eyes find mine, and he smiles again. *"This is a claiming."* His words ring in my mind when I drunkenly stumbled into his club with Jenni, and we danced the night away.

"Oh, yeah," Arrow says, shaking his head. "It can't be you, though, right? That doesn't make any sense. You have Journey. We'd technically be up for grabs, even though I've told your father I'm living the celibate life for the rest of my life. No wife for me."

"Liar," I hiss, elbowing him.

"Well, he doesn't have to know I have a wife," Arrow scoffs. "You may not have my last name, but you'll wear my handprint right on your ass." He taps my ass again, chuckling when I sigh in defeat. "Or my toy in your ass. Either way, it shows ownership: Arrow was here."

"You're incorrigible," I grumble, looking toward the ceiling.

"You love it," Arrow says, throwing his arm over my shoulders. "And me. And my dick. And my tongue. And my toys. I could go on..." he trails off.

"Something like that," I say, tapping his hand as it reaches around toward my tits. "No touchy in public."

"You're just no fun tonight, Kitten. Don't worry, I'll loosen you all up when we get home."

Yeah, I don't doubt that. But we have to survive the night, first.

Shepp taps Jericho's shoulder and quickly signs something.

"You're right," Jericho says, shaking his head. "He says we all need to be careful. If Chloe is on the hook for us as one of our intended, then we need to keep an eye on Journey. If my father is going to pull anything, it would be right here. Under all our noses."

"I'll tear her black heart out before I let her touch me," Arrow huffs with red tinting his cheeks.

"What exactly is happening?" I murmur, surveying the room and eyeing the girl in question.

Long blonde locks, light blue eyes, and a pretty smile lighting up the room. She looks tall and lean, standing beside a massive man, sucking down a glass of amber liquid. Then, there's Leighton. He beams beside her with his shoulders touching hers. Every once in a while, her hand touches him as she laughs. Like, truly laughs. She's not just pretending to enjoy his company. She really likes him. And by the dopey look in his eyes, he's feeling the same.

"Chloe Satin, heiress to Satin Firearms. My father has been in cahoots with hers for years now, investing in his company. In return, Mr. Satin provides our weaponry and other things my father hasn't specified."

I blink several times at the amount of information rolling out of his mouth and trying to process it all. A weird spark ignites inside me when I tighten my grip around my champagne glass. I'm unable to peel my eyes away from her as she giggles again into her hand and lays her head on his shoulder. But her eyes find Jericho, and they narrow slightly. I don't think the boys notice when she whispers something to Leighton, and he smirks in response.

They're planning something.

Together.

My hackles rise, watching them intently and storing everything they do inside my brain. That's what I've been trained for these past three years. Taking notice of the people around me, while blending in and not drawing attention to myself.

"So, what's she got to do with it all?" I question.

"I do love it when you're jealous, Little Chaos. Please go

scratch out her eyes," Jericho hums into his drink. "You'll be doing us all a favor."

"One, I'm not jealous. I'm trying to figure out what the hell is happening. Besides, she's not interested in you three at all," I huff, trying to regain my composure.

Am I jealous that she might be on the line for one of my guys? Um, yeah. If Jericho's father thinks he can place her next to Arrow or Shepp, he has another thing coming. He's taught me over the years how to cover my crimes with expertise. So, making Chloe Satin disappear would be simple.

"Oh? And you can tell?" Jericho asks, eyeing me suspiciously.

"Look at the way she and Leighton are standing near each other as their fathers talk. It's intimate. They're giggling and touching. They're trying to be very discreet with their affections, but it doesn't fool me."

"Oh? And why doesn't it fool you? Because this is what you did for my father?" Jericho asks, gazing at the two love birds. "Well, I'll be. They sure are close."

"Weird. Who'd want to be with that asswipe?" Arrow asks, tilting his head.

"Maybe Jenni wasn't the only one with someone else on the side. If she's promised to one of you, does she have to stay faithful?"

Jericho stiffens. "*If* being the key word. Normally, a husband and wife are put together for alliance reasons and heirs. My parents were paired for financial reasons in the beginning. But my father was obsessed with her and fell madly in love. Well, until she disappeared off the face of the planet. When my mother disappeared, he shut down completely, becoming this man he is." He gestures to his father, coldly shaking hands with others and conversing. "Contracts are binding in our world, though. Once you sign the marriage certificate, you give yourself to the marriage, and the family holds you accountable for your actions. If cheating occurs, then death is imminent. It's like turning your back on the organization." Jericho shrugs.

"So, if she is promised to one of you three and does get married..."

"Never happening, Kitten. I'll pull out her ovaries before I vow my life to her," Arrow says through clenched teeth.

"Well, that's some imagery I never wanted to have," I grumble, pinching the bridge of my nose.

"To finish your thought, Little Chaos. If she does have to marry one of us and continues that love affair, then she's toast. They'll hang her out to dry in the church basement. Not that we'd touch her with a ten foot pole. I'd rather claw my own heart out. But no matter, Chloe Satin will not be ours."

"The church basement?" I rear back.

"Oh, yeah. That's where we were initiated with the big swords. That sword brings us into the family by blood and takes us out of the family for our sins." Arrow rocks on his toes.

"So, yes. My father made an interesting phone call the evening we consummated our relationship at the masked party. I overheard him laying out the details with someone, mentioning her name."

I wrinkle my nose. "Consummated? Jesus, you sound like a grandma," I huff, sipping my champagne. If I'm going to survive this hellish night, surrounded by California's most dangerous citizens, then I need to be drunk.

"Yes. Sealed our fates with our dicks in your pussy," Arrow says with glee.

"Lord," I grumble, finishing off my booze. "I need another."

"No way, Kitten! You can't drink anymore. Our spawn could be inside you," Arrow says, leaning down to rub his hand over my flat stomach.

"I... what the fuck?" I hiss, shoving his hand away. "Would you stop with the baby stuff? I can't..."

"I removed it," Arrow beams with pride, pulling out his phone. "I hung it in my lair in the basement. It's framed and everything." The phone dangles in front of my face, and I swear I get tunnel vision when my fucking IUD rests in a fucking picture frame with my name labeling it.

Journey's IUD.

"And you let him fuck you over and over while torturing me," Jericho murmurs. "I married you without permission. He removed your IUD after drugging you. Who's the bad guy now?"

"Both of you!" I shout, drawing more eyes our way. I heave a breath, stepping back. "I swear to God, the big man upstairs is just laughing down at me. You... you! Seriously? That's violating! And drugged? Again?" I shriek in hysterics, attempting to take a step back.

"Calm down now, Little Chaos. You'll bring monsters upon us," Jericho says, reaching out to bring me into his chest. "We're not good men. We'll never pretend to be. We've stalked you for years, ensuring your safety. You can scream at us later. Maybe torture us a little more. Can I nominate Arrow for the chair this time instead?"

"I hate both of you. Only Shepp is saved," I grumble into his hard chest and take a deep breath.

Now is not the time to lose my shit over what they've done. I need to focus on this room and the present. Not the future or past. But fuck. What if I am pregnant? We've done a lot of humping in the last few days. There's no way, right? It just came out. There can't be a possibility. Not to mention the left over hormones and what not.

"Ohhh, I'm not a ladies expert. But saying calm down, is never a good idea," Arrow says, cringing when I push out of Jericho's hold and scowl at both of them.

"Shepp," I say, slumping my shoulders. "It's just you and me now. I'm disowning them," I say with a pout, earning a small smile. He pulls me into his chest without protest and cradles me there, gently rocking us back and forth.

"No! That's not allowed, Kitten. You can't just choose one of us. I have the best dick."

"Says who?" Jericho scoffs.

"Kitten, tell them," he says with such confidence.

"I'm not answering that. I'm mad at the two of you. I'm a human being," I grumble into Shepp's chest. "I already have one man who thinks he owns me, I don't need you two."

"Satin alert," Arrow hums.

"Jericho Viotto," a breezy voice says, coming from behind me.

I sigh, slowly turning on my heel to face the beauty queen I saw from afar. This time, though. There's no Leighton clinging onto her.

"Chloe," he mutters with a respectful nod. "Fancy seeing you here. How have you been?" he asks politely, but just like his father, I see the rage simmer beneath the surface.

There's something about this woman that irks him.

"Oh, you know," she giggles, covering her shimmering lips with her delicate fingers. "Father and I have been traveling for a few months. Made it through France and Spain. It was beautiful! Have you ever been?" As she speaks, she twirls a piece of her platinum blonde hair between her fingers, only looking at Jericho with hearts in her eyes. Only, I can't tell if she's for real or putting on a show for Jericho's sake. Or maybe someone in the room is watching this exchange.

Several waiters walk past Arrow with hors d'oeuvres and more champagne. He quickly grabs several snacks, forcing them into his mouth, and another glass. The woman carrying the tray side-eyes Arrow with disdain, shaking her head.

"What?" he asks with a mouth full of food. "You're carrying it. I'm hungry."

I snort, stealing a snack from his hand and popping it into my mouth. "Mmm. Delicious."

"No, never have," Jericho hums, staring over her head without remorse.

She doesn't falter, though. "So, you guys finally made it to your initiation! How does it feel to be men of the family? You must feel so good after all those years of watching."

"Watching?" Arrow scoffs. "We've had blood up to our elbows. There was no watching."

I internally snort when she sends him a dirty look and turns her attention back to Jericho.

"Is there something I can do for you?" he asks her in a tired tone, borderline bored.

Her face falls, tinting red. "Well, I just wanted to say hello. We've been in each other's company for years now at these things," she titters.

My face hardens when she finally slips up and looks me over with a scathing gaze, curling her lip with disgust.

"Hello, then. Now, goodbye," Jericho snarks, grabbing my hand.

"You won't be saying that in thirty minutes," she sing-songs.

"Oh, and why is that?" Jericho asks, stiffening when she runs a finger down the front of his suit.

"Because, we're destined for one another." She smiles again, rocking on her toes. "You weren't meant for trailer trash." Her nose immediately goes in the air when she turns to walk away.

"Don't worry, I'll smother her while she sleeps. She won't feel safe. Ever," Arrow threatens, causing her to falter her steps until she's out of sight.

"That fucking does it," Jericho grits out, squeezing his champagne flute so hard, it shatters in his hand. "My father has meddled. And not in a good fucking way."

"Jericho," I murmur, rushing forward to take his hands. He grits his teeth, attempting to snatch his hands back, but I tsk at him. "You're bleeding."

"I'll be fine, Little Chaos. I just need to figure out what the hell my father is up to. I need to have a fucking word with him about what he thinks he's done. There's no way I'll be marrying that manipulative homewrecker." His jaw tics again, not showing any sort of pain.

I lick my lips. "Obviously he has something up his sleeve.

Never show him your emotions, Jer," I murmur, running my fingers over the blood on his palm.

"Sage advice," he retorts, grabbing my hand in his bloodied palm.

"So, the spawn of Satan reneged his deal with Journey's mom?" Arrow surmises, rubbing his chin.

"That I can't tell. Was Journey truly ever on the line for me like he said?" Jericho's gaze finds Shepp's and Arrow's.

"What are you thinking?" Arrow asks, narrowing his eyes.

"I have many thoughts," Jericho says.

"Well that's helpful," I grumble.

"Hmm. I'm always helpful, Little Chaos. But don't worry. Chloe Satin will not go anywhere near us."

"I can use my grenade launcher," Arrow quips with a grin. "Right up her ass. She'd blow to smithereens." His hands rub together.

"As much as it pains me to say, no blowing her up right now. We need to figure out what's up my father's sleeve before we act. But we should unanimously conclude that Journey's safety is of the utmost importance."

"And our baby," Arrow hums, rubbing his hand over my stomach again, lingering over my uterus.

My heart thumps when he leaves it resting there, and panic swarms through me. Crap. Now, I'm going to be paranoid that there's something growing inside me. A little human I have to protect with my damn life. But how? How could I do that when I can't even protect myself?

"I'm going to chop his hand off. Is that acceptable?" I hiss, shoving him away again as he chuckles.

"Be my guest, he deserves it," Jericho says, clenching his jaw. His eyes lock on something in front of him. "Wonderful. Monster on the prowl," he mutters, discreetly gesturing toward the man we've all been avoiding sauntering our way with intention in his eyes.

"Looks like he's got something sneaky up his sleeve," Arrow hums, throwing his arm over my shoulders. "Chin up, Kitten."

My heart flutters in my chest when my eyes connect with Gabriel's. They seem to darken when he takes me in, but no other emotions rest on his stone face. Evil rests there. Something sinister peering back under the facade of a normal man.

Arrow taps my chin, forcing me to raise it.

"Such a good kitten," he mutters.

I side-eye him, sticking out my tongue playfully, hoping to dispel the nervousness swallowing me whole.

Shepp gently rests a hand on my shoulder and leans in, nuzzling his nose against my neck. If he could speak in front of his friends, he'd tell me I'm going to be fine. Hopefully, at least. I'm ten seconds away from coming face-to-face with my worst enemy.

I lay my hand on his, gently squeezing his hand.

"Father," Jericho says in a low voice. His body seems to grow three times as big when he faces off with him. "To what do I owe the pleasure of your company?" He speaks with authority, not backing down when Gabriel raises a dark brow and his smile grows.

"Can't a father come say hello to his boys? And to you, Miss West," he hums, forcefully taking my hand and roughly shaking it. His fingers squeeze mine but a false, warm smile crosses his lips.

Who is he fooling? Definitely not me.

"Mr. Viotto," I say sweetly, holding back the venom. "Wonderful to meet you after all this time."

His eyes sparkle with mirth. "Likewise. I hope my son and his friends have been treating you well."

"Of course," I say with a practiced smile.

Jericho stiffens beside me but doesn't utter a word or make a move when Gabriel brings the back of my hand to his lips and gently kisses it. I swear my skin crawls the moment he touches me and then again when he kisses my fucking flesh. I want to yank my hand away, but I know I have to play his game. I'm still his little snake, after all. And this entire interaction is a test to us.

"Are you boys enjoying your celebration? It's all for you." He grins, eyeing the three boys and inspecting their expressions once he lets go of my hand and it falls to my side.

He's challenging them to see what they'll say and do. Normally, I'd believe in all three of their control. Knowing they'd never slip up in front of Gabriel or show their true selves. But Arrow is sinking fast into the depths of his darkness.

"Well, I hope you boys are enjoying it. I brought in the best caterers a man could ask for and the best booze money could buy. All for the best for my boys, right?"

"Yes, Father," Jericho says with a tight nod. "It's massive."

"Bigger than the one we held a month ago," Gabriel surmises, peering behind him at the crowd. "Every Viotto from California made the trip to congratulate you boys."

Something dark twinkles in his eyes when he turns to peer at us again with a wide, deceiving smile. I've known my monster for a long time now, and he's got something devastating up his sleeve. He always has a tell when he's about to drop a major bomb or hurt someone.

"It's amazing you convinced all the cousins and uncles to come. It's unusual," Jericho says, eyeing all the people roaming around the large ballroom. "They usually come up with some sort of excuse to stay home."

The ballroom is massive, probably able to hold over one thousand people and not be cramped. It's decorated to perfection with crystal chandeliers and sparkly decorations everywhere. Large tables sit near the stage on the opposite end of the room, with a live jazz band softly playing their music. Several workers, who I've never laid eyes on before, meander through the crowds with their trays, offering the goods.

Gabriel genuinely grins. "Didn't take a lot of convincing, Son. You three are the main attraction. The heirs to the Viotto Kingdom of Briar Cove." He claps Jericho on the shoulder several times, roughly jostling his body back and forth.

To the naked eye, it would appear as if he was loving on his son. But to me, it's a clear threat of some sort. One I don't have the answer to.

"It's a good party," Arrow adds in, taking the pressure off Jericho. "It's a dream to be here, Sir."

God, what a suck-up. But who am I kidding? I do the same damn thing, but I do it so he doesn't fucking slap me around for my insubordination.

"I like to think I put on a good show," he says with a grin. "And speaking of. Are you boys ready to show the entire Viotto family your vowed wounds? It's about that time to present you as men of the family."

"Yes, Sir!" Arrow says, bouncing on his toes and clapping his hands. "Time to take these stuffy suits off."

"It's unfortunate your father couldn't be here to witness this. One day, I'll convince him to officially join the family," he says with fake apologies to Arrow.

"Don't worry, Sir. I'll tell him all about it." Arrow sends Gabriel a menacing grin that has shivers running down my spine.

I don't know how Gabriel looks Arrow in the eyes and doesn't see the disdain there. Hell, maybe he does. Maybe he reads him like a damn book and knows exactly what is going on.

"Of course," Gabriel says, tipping his head. "Now, move along boys. The family is eagerly awaiting your arrival on stage. You have five minutes until I announce your presence." Gabriel makes a sweeping gesture, pointing toward the large stage on the other side of the room.

Jericho goes to reach for my hand and drags me along. God, I wish. But Gabriel servers that connection by clearing his throat, forcing us to stop.

"She'll be fine for the five minutes you boys are on stage." He raises a no-nonsense brow, attempting to send the boys on their way.

"Are you positive?" Jericho asks calmly, stepping up to his father. "She should come with us and be backstage for the on-stage celebration. It makes the most sense."

Gabriel doesn't show an ounce of emotion when he smirks at Jericho, and my stomach drops.

"Do you not trust your father, Son?"

"Of course, I trust you," Jericho says smoothly, shoving his bloodied hand into his pocket. "But I'd like to have Journey by my side on stage. She is mine, after all. You gave me the green light for this."

"Tsk. Tsk, Son. Showing your hand so early. If you were a true man of the family, you would have walked away without a second glance back, leaving her in my care. I'm trustworthy." Gabriel smirks as Jericho tilts his head, giving no emotions away.

"And is that what you did with Mother?" Jericho questions with a tight expression. "You left her to the animals when she needed you most? What does that say about a real man? Where's she now, huh?"

Fuck me. Jericho has never stepped up and questioned his father directly. And today, of all fucking days, he's decided to man up and put his big boy panties on. This is going to go over so damn well.

"Those lessons every weekend must have poured out your brains and through your ears. Never have a weak spot, Son. And never show it to your enemies." He raises a brow when Jericho doesn't back down. "Never let a woman get between you and the family. Ever. It's rule number three."

"That's where you're wrong, Daddy Dearest. Journey is not my weakness. Journey is my strength," Jericho grits out, stepping up chest to chest with his father. "And you had best recognize that and the many unexpected things to come."

"Dude," Arrow murmurs, slightly pulling Jericho back. He signs something, shaking his head. He, too, loses all emotions on his face when he converses silently with Shepp and Jericho.

"That's right. Calm down, Jericho. Getting riled up will do nothing but make you fail. Now, get your fucking asses on that stage with a pretty smile and pretend everything is okay," Gabriel grits out, smoothing down his suit. "And take her the fuck with you, then. But we'll be having a word later. All of us. If you want to continue your future with Journey, then you'll obey."

Gabriel doesn't walk away when Jericho forcefully grabs my hand and pulls me to his side. "That we will," Jericho says with a deadly look.

"I count on it," Gabriel says with a grin.

"What the fuck, Jericho?" I hiss when we weave through the crowd, heading toward the lit-up stage. "Why would you do that here? Why would you provoke him? He's obviously up to something!"

"Because I'm fucking sick and tired of taking that man's orders. He wanted me to leave you there with him. What was I supposed to do?" he grits out, tightening his hold on me. "I will never willingly give you up to that man." He stops abruptly when he pulls us through a large red curtain and shoves me into the backstage area. "He left scars on your body, Little Chaos." His eyes fall to the front of my dress where my tattoo sits on display for the whole world to see. It took a lot of convincing in the form of orgasms to even get me comfortable with showing off my scar. "He hurt you. He's hurt your sister. He's fucked us all over. I'm not letting him harm you again," he murmurs, shaking his head. "I'd never leave you with Satan himself."

My fingers rub gently down his smooth jaw as I look into his dark eyes. Tears shimmer in my vision when he pulls me close.

"No one has ever protected me like you have," I murmur, leaning in until my lips press into his.

"Until my last breath, Little Chaos. This may seem unconventional to you. But you're my wife..."

"Not by choice, though," Arrow says, putting his arms around our shoulders. "Right, Kitten? You remember that, right? How he married you without your consent?"

"I also remember someone drugging me. Twice. And removing my birth control without asking," I say, tilting my head when a red blush crosses his cheeks.

"Ah—well," he murmurs.

Another set of heavy arms comes over my shoulders and Jericho's, as the four of us stand together.

"Stay back here, okay? We'll be right out there," Jericho demands. "Then, we'll disappear. I don't trust him not to pull something tonight."

"Sit on the steps so we can see you every step of the way," Arrow demands, pointing toward a small set of stairs.

Outside the party, the music cuts off, and a loud, booming voice comes over the microphone. The crowd cheers and clasps at the sound of the foreign voice.

"Who is that?" Arrow questions, tilting his head to get a better listen.

"Probably one of the higher-up cousins. I swear the man invited everyone from every corner of California," Jericho says, listening to the voice talking about the wonderful evening, and then, he announces their names.

"That's our cue," Jericho says, kissing me one last time. "Be a good Little Chaos," he hums against my lips before pulling away.

"I always am," I jokingly say, crossing my arms. "What are you doing?"

"It's take your shirt off time, Kitten," Arrow says with a grin, shrugging out of his suit jacket. Without a care, he rips through the buttons of his undershirt and then loosens his tie, throwing them all to the side. "But you keep yours on." Arrow points a finger at me with demand.

Jericho maintains eye contact when he takes his suit jacket off, hanging it on the railing of the stairs and then loosens his tie. "This is part of the family tradition. We've done our blood oath, proving to my father and his bosses that we're all in. Now, we're to prove to the rest of the Viotto Crime family in attendance that we've promised to dedicate our lives to them and our citizens."

Arrow bounces on his toes, clapping his hands a few times as more cheers erupt from in front of the stage.

"You hear that, Kitten? They're chanting for us to show ourselves. They're just as excited as we are."

Shepp doesn't say a word or sign something to me when he steals a kiss too, staring deep into my eyes before he steps back and undresses as well, leaving the three of them in only their dress pants, socks, and shoes.

Their family mark rests between their pecs, fully healed from when they were injured.

"Go get 'em tigers," I say, pushing the three of them away.

"At the first sign of danger, I want you to hide," Jericho instructs, leading me to the steps and forcing me to stand on them. "This won't take but a few minutes. Be a good girl." Worry rests in his eyes when I give him a firm nod.

"Of course. I'll stay right here, please don't worry." I can handle myself against my monster. He's trained me well, after all. Even more so against him.

"I'm going to regret this," Jericho grumbles. "I should throw you over my shoulder and bring you on stage."

"Go," I say, shooing them until their shoes touch the edge of the stage. The crowd goes wild as the announcer says their names one more time, and they wave to the adoring crowd.

CHAPTER FIFTY-FIVE
Journey

I SWALLOW HARD, standing on the last step, watching the men line up on stage. A whole ceremony commences in front of my eyes in celebration of their manhood. It's like some sort of cult watching them with heart eyes and shouting out their congratulations. I clap along with the crowd, losing myself in their honor.

It isn't until the tell-tale footsteps of my monster stepping up behind me that I realize it's pure happiness floating inside me. Despite all the shit they've done to me, they've brought me a sliver of freedom. Something I never thought I'd have again, especially under Gabriel's thumb. And I can't thank them enough.

Besides, I kind of like the guys. Even the one who took my birth control out without my permission. He's a little wild and will definitely pay for what he's done.

"My, my, Little Snake," Gabriel says, coming to stand beside me, watching the festivities on stage like he's never seen it before. "You've gotten yourself into quite the situation, haven't you?" He raises a brow, turning his attention to me.

I huff, making eye contact with Jericho as he stands on stage in the midst of his ceremony. Discreetly, he gives me a small nod, letting me know he's seeing this. And that's all the reassurance I need to continue standing by someone so heinous.

Every ounce of feelings I have drains toward my feet, wiping me clean.

"I suppose so. But it's where you wanted me, right?" I ask, keeping my eyes forward and toward the stage.

"Indeed," he hums, pulling something from his pocket. "Tell me, Little Snake. How have things been under their roof?"

AKA have they spilled any secrets he should be aware of? I swallow hard and take a deep breath, continuing the facade that I feel nothing.

"Nothing major has come up in conversation," I say in an even voice, bringing my gaze to his. "They've been preparing for this the entire time I've been there. They haven't spoken to or brought anyone over."

A multitude of thoughts run through my mind. Gabriel is a smart man. He obviously knows things by the way he is looking at me suspiciously.

"Unless you consider I'm married to your son as something important," I say, raising a brow when his grin widens. "But that's exactly what you wanted, wasn't it?" I ask.

"You're a very smart Little Snake when you want to be."

"Then you know my long-lost brothers paid a visit?" I question, earning a nod in return.

"Hmm, yes. Your brothers paid your mother and me a visit many years before with the promise of millions of dollars. Then, they disappeared. I had to do some digging while you rotted away in my basement, trying to find what they did with it." He shakes his head, running a hand down his jaw. "Smart bastards, those West twins are. They put it into a trust with so many stipulations that I couldn't get my hands on what was owed to me after the stunt you pulled with Thomas."

Ice runs through my veins at the sound of his name and the crime I committed to protect my sister. "And what was owed to you?" I know the answer. Now, at least. Everything has been unraveling since that fateful night I met the guys at that party.

His jaw tics in irritation, hating my questions. "I suppose I could tell you," he hums, pursing his lips. "Your mother sold you and your sister to me. She gave me permission to sell you to the highest bidder for however much I needed in repentance for what you did. Of course, then your brothers stopped by for a friendly visit, looking for you. Once I did some investigating, I knew exactly what to do with you." He smirks at that, mentally patting himself on the back for being a sleaze.

"Keep me in a cage and manipulate me into doing your bidding?" I snap, quickly regretting my words when he narrows his eyes. "Or steal my inheritance?"

"Manipulating? Such a big word for a little spy. Do they know what you do for me?" He raises a brow, waiting for my answer.

Way to change the subject, assbag.

"I'm sure they've figured it out by now," I say, lifting my chin and keeping my emotions at bay. Every time I speak with this man, he infuriates me more, making me want to punch him square in the face. One day I'll get the chance when he doesn't hold my sister's life in the balance.

"That money was promised to me fair and square. You stole something important to me, too," he grits out, showing his damn hand. "You murdered him in cold fucking blood. I'm curious, does Sheppard know what you did and why I own you?" He smoothes out his expensive suit while staring directly into my eyes.

"No," I say, maintaining eye contact with him. "And you know it wasn't in cold blood." I heave a breath, losing myself in the emotions of that night. Something I know better than to do. But he knows how to slip under my skin and peel up my insecurities and the things I regret.

"I'm surprised it wasn't the first thing you let slip," he says with a smirk. "Imagine his surprise when he finds out who you murdered."

My heart sinks when he says the words. I'm a murderer. But

he wasn't a good man. The more I've found out, the more I realize I did the world a favor by getting rid of him permanently. It's worked out for everyone.

"You mean the man who cut out his tongue and snuck into his room to touch him while he slept?" I question back, tilting my head when Gabriel stills. "Or the man who attempted to rape my sister and me, until I stopped him? I don't think anyone will be too broken up that I'm responsible for that." I shrug, like it's no big deal. But I know it is.

"How one man fathers his children is no concern of mine." Obviously. Because you're the father of the year. It's what I want to say, but I let my darkness hide the snarky remarks I have in store for him.

"Of course," I say, biting my tongue.

"Where's the money, Journey?" he asks with a tic in his jaw. "I know the Wests were back in town with my niece in tow. I want to know the details of your conversations. Or they're the first people I go after. East Point Bluff isn't that far away. I know where they live and every detail of their lives."

I lick my lips. How telling of him. He doesn't know what was said or how the money was hidden. All he knows is that my brothers came into town with Olivia and visited Jericho's mansion. That's it. So, he hasn't been secretly listening. But he does have someone telling him all the details. Someone, other than me.

He could be bluffing. Or he could be telling the truth. Jericho always said his father didn't do anything without intention. And I believe it. He's always two steps ahead of everything. Something, I'm seeing firsthand now.

So, I ignore the part about my brothers, not wanting to bring them up or involve them in any way. Never show your weaknesses, after all.

"If I knew where the money was, I'd have taken it by now," I retort in a smooth tone. "Don't you think?"

Gabriel doesn't hesitate grabbing his phone from his pocket and unlocking it with a sneer.

"You'd really run from your sister Sunny?" he asks, clicking a few times on his phone. "And here I thought you were finally a good little girl. Why don't I give you a reminder of what you'd be leaving behind?"

My throat closes up when he holds the phone in front of my face, showcasing a live video feed of my sister sitting up in her hospital bed. She's slimmed down a little. There's no more swelling on her face. Life lives in her vibrant eyes. I'd rejoice in seeing her, but I see the fear wrinkling her forehead.

"Sunny," I gasp, bringing my hands to my lips.

"Journey," she responds with tears flowing down her cheeks. "Do whatever he says, J. Please, don't..." she halts her words, staring off to the side at someone not visible to the camera.

"There's a reason I've held your sickly sister for so long and not out of the kindness of my heart to get her healthy. I couldn't give a fuck less about the two of you," he growls. "But you showed me your weakness when you stabbed my second-in-command. She is your bargaining chip. Now, tell me where the fucking money is hidden." His fingers quickly dart out like a fucking viper, wrapping around my neck and squeezing as he maneuvers me off the stairs and further into the backstage area where the darkness swallows us and the sounds of the audience dissipate. We're sinking into a hellish abyss behind the stage where no one can get to us—or me.

I gasp for air, watching the screen he forces in front of my face.

Several men with guns enter my sister's hospital room and point them directly at her with no remorse. Black ski masks hide their identities, sending shivers down my spine. She hiccups, watching them closely, unable to do a damn thing about the situation.

No. It's all on me. I'm her saving grace. The one person who can remove those men from her room and bring her back to safety.

"No," I croak out, clawing at his arm with all my might until he slightly loosens his grip.

"Tell me where the fucking money is. Tell me, or they blow your sister's brains out in front of your eyes, and then I'll do the same to you, you useless fucking bitch. That's my goddamn money. Not yours!" he shouts in my face, getting covered up by the crowd outside. "Give me what you owe me!"

As white dots appear in front of my eyes, the world slowly dims the harder he squeezes.

"Okay," I barely choke out in a strained voice.

No amount of money is worth my sister's life. He can have it all if he gives her back to me.

Only then does he loosen his grip, backing me up against the wall.

"Tell me now, Little Snake," he hisses directly in my face.

"It's under Josie Wells, in a Swedish bank account," I cough out, desperate to bring oxygen back into my lungs. "Please don't hurt her. She's been through enough." I shake my head with tears rolling down my cheeks from the lack of air.

"What a good girl," he says, roughly tapping my cheek. "I knew I could count on you again." He brings the phone up so he's in front of it and nods to the people through the screen. "Tell Shadow, she's all his. He can have his fun now. Our trade has begun."

"No!" I shout, trying to grab the phone from him, but his fist connects with my cheek, knocking me back a step into the wall.

Pain splinters through my flesh as fresh blood drips through a small cut on my face from the impact. My fingers instinctively find the wound and press against it. A shooting sensation that burns makes me hiss, and I recoil, staring at my bloodied fingers. My darkness whispers in the back of my mind, taking all the anguish away from me. My mind clears on the one thing I need to do.

Murder Gabriel Viotto.

Sunny's screams come through the phone loud and shrill, shattering my fucking soul into two. My self-preservation leaves the fucking room and doesn't wave goodbye. I don't even care what happens to me right now. Burn me. Shove me in a cage. Leave me for dead. As long as she's okay. After everything she's been through, she deserves a better life than this. Or everything I've done has been in vain.

"What have you done?" I hiss through clenched teeth, balling my fingers into fists. If I could just get a straight shot, I could knock him off his feet and stomp his skull in with my six-inch heels.

"Have I ever kept my word, Little Snake? You've shown me who meant something to you over and over again. But don't worry, you'll be reunited with her in the pits of Shadow's hell. You two were my bargaining chip." He grins. "He's got unfinished business with the both of you, and he's got something that belongs to me."

"What the hell are you talking about?" Rage consumes every inch of me the more he spews more and more bullshit.

"The money was always mine, Little Snake. Your stupid bitch of a mother signed it over to me as payment for your crimes. What else was I supposed to do with you?"

"You could have just killed me!" I shout again, my voice slowly rising with each word I say, until I'm basically in hysterics. "Instead you tortured me and stole my sister!"

"Money, Little Snake. I needed you alive to claim what's mine. And what better way to do that than to marry you off to my own flesh and blood."

"Something I didn't know," I hiss with venom.

"Of course not. You'd have run away. Even after all the hours of training I gave you. You're a runner, Journey," he says flippantly. "But you can't outrun your destiny now. No one can. You've married my son earlier than expected. I thought I was going to have to demand you do it. But now? We don't even need a wedding. Or him." He chuckles to himself. "This went better than I thought. But of course, I didn't count on my son actually being obsessed with you. Throw in his mindless buddies. It couldn't have worked out better if I had tried."

My chest heaves with every gloating word he says, talking down to me like I'm a piece of trash. He raised me to be like this. He raised me to never show my emotions or gloat or to even have feelings. So, it's time to return the favor.

"Where is my sister going?" I grit out with authority, standing tall.

It's high time to stand up to my damn monster and show him what he's created.

He studies me with an intense eye. "There's the Little Snake I created. The monster in the making. Just know, if you harm me, then your sister will never see the light of day again."

"You're bluffing," I say, tilting my head. "You have no say over what happens to her now. You sold her, too."

He smirks. "Ah, what a fast learner you are. He paid a pretty penny for retribution against her and you."

"Me?" I hiss, eyeing him when he smirks.

"Of course..." he trails off, whipping his head to the stage when a loud voice comes over the speakers.

"Attention!"

"What the hell?" Gabriel murmurs, taking several steps with me in tow toward the stage, finally stopping near the first step and he stiffens.

"My name is Ernie, and I'd like to thank the Viotto Family for coming together in one place. This makes it much easier to do this," the man says in a low voice.

I stiffen when the sound of ripping happens, and I peek on stage and almost stumble back. Jericho, Arrow, and Shepp are all held at gunpoint by several people on stage—the catering party. The people who walked around with trays, offering food and drinks.

Pure panic swirls through my veins when Jericho's worried

eyes find mine. He doesn't say a word or nod his head, but I can read his expression as clear as day. He wants me to run and not stay here. I shake my head and lick my lips, finding Arrow's eyes. He quickly darts them to the crowd, avoiding me at all costs. And Shepp does the same. Eventually, all three of them are looking at the silent crowd, gawking at the situation.

But if I can get away from Gabriel, I'm helping them get out of there.

"What the hell is happening?" I ask, frantically looking at Gabriel, who doesn't make a move. In fact, his facial expression doesn't change.

"Well, this is our cue, Little Snake," he hums, looking at his son on stage with a gun to his temple. "We need to make our exit."

"What? No!" I hiss, backing up and shaking my head, attempting to pull out of his tight grip again. "I'm not going anywhere with you! Aren't you going to do something?" I gesture to the stairs, continuing to take several steps back.

Panic swells inside me. He's eyeing me like a piece of fucking meat with little regard to the situation unfolding around us. Loud pops begin to fill my ears from beyond the curtain. Screams erupt and heavy footfalls sound through the entire ballroom, much like a loud stampede echoing in my brain. Shrill screams echo from several women in the crowd when two more loud gunshots ring through the room.

My heart rate kicks up, and I stumble back, shaking my head. Sweat forms in my palms at the realization of what's happening. We're under attack. But why isn't anyone fighting back?

"What is happening?" My eyes turn to Gabriel, who smirks at me with a knowing look.

"Many alliances can be found, even within the enemy," is all he says before he steps up to me again, still holding me tight, and then yanks me away from the stage. "Now, before things get even more harried, be a good Little Snake and come with me."

"No!" I shout, digging my nails into his arm, attempting to peel myself away from him as he drags me through a dark room at the back of the stage.

"Oh, yes," he hums. "Shadow is so eager to meet you, too. Although, you've already met before."

We both still when three gunshots pop off on the stage. My heartbeat skyrockets, and I shake my head.

"All part of the deal," he hums with a fake sadness, rolling his lips in. "Such a shame, too. Those boys were such good soldiers. Well, until they decided they wanted to go behind my back and attempt a hostile takeover. I've been the King for over twenty-six years. I'm not about to let three boys take over my kingdom," he grunts, dragging me along.

"You... You had them killed?" I cry out, throwing my fist into his shoulder, attempting to free myself from him again.

He stops suddenly near a door near the rear of the backstage area and looks me over. "Not yet. But I made you think I did, didn't I?" he questions with a shrug. "But you've shown me once again that my training did nothing to absolve you of your human attachments. Everyone is a tool, Little Snake. Like you. Like them. Now, on the count of three, they will drop dead. The people on stage are waiting for my say so. So, it's either you or them. What will it be?"

My eyes widen when he pulls his cell phone out again and taps a few times, hovering his finger over the bright screen. "Your call. In three, two..."

"No! Wait! I'll... I'll go with you. Just please don't hurt them," I whisper with desperation, tossing everything I learned from him out the window. I could leave them out to dry. It would be easy to nod at him and say yeah, please murder them.

But, I think I've fallen for my kidnappers over the course of our time together. They've woven themselves into every broken facet of my soul and pieced me back together with themselves. Our darknesses are interwoven. They'll forever be a part of me.

So, there's no way around this. They need to live. They can still defeat my monster.

"They were never against you," I say, eyeing him as my shoulders slump.

He tilts his head, eyeing me with narrowed eyes. He doesn't say a damn word when he hits whatever is on the screen of his phone a few times, illuminating his smirking face.

My heart falls into my ass, and I swear everything turns into slow motion when the door behind me opens and two men emerge. Just as three gunshots ring out on stage and three distinctive thumps echo in my ears.

People scream hysterically, crying out as more gunshots ring out. Until a full-on battle ensues in the main ballroom. I can't tell if the family is fighting back against the intruders, or if they're running for their lives now.

All I can do is stand there as two men capture my arms, holding me tighter than necessary.

"This is all for you Shadow!" the voice bellows through the speakers.

He shakes his head almost in disappointment. "This was never going to end well for you, Little Snake. I kept you alive this long to get what I wanted," Gabriel says, nodding to the men behind me. "Tell Shadow I send my regards and have faith he'll deliver what belongs to me."

"He will, Mr. Viotto," the man to my right says in a low voice, yanking me through the door.

"I'm going to kill you," I say, looking behind me at Gabriel, who grins, waving me off. "I will come back and absolutely obliterate you."

"Promise, Little Snake?" he chuckles.

"From the bottom of my fucking black soul!" I shout when the door shuts between us, and I'm dragged down a set of stairs, barely able to walk with the two men hurriedly taking me against my will.

I stiffen when the entire building shakes, and a loud explosion rings out from above.

"Time to say, nighty night," a deep voice comes from beside me, the first time one of them has spoken directly to me.

And that's the only warning I get before something hard slams into the back of my head, sending me into a blissful darkness full of nothing.

CHAPTER FIFTY-SIX

Journey

"Journey, you need to wake up."

A pounding in my head wakes me up from my long slumber. Or was it a long slumber? Fuck. I can't remember anything. Sludge moves through my mind, clouding my damn thoughts.

"J!" a shrill voice from beside me sputters out with desperation. "Please, Sis. Please wake up! We probably don't have much time." Sniffles echo through the room. "God, you need to wake up."

I groan, lifting my chin off my chest and stretching the muscles out. What the hell happened? Where am I? And why is my little sister sounding so frantic?

I smack my lips a few times, desperate for some sort of drink. I reach out-—or attempt to—but I'm stopped by something around my wrists, rubbing painfully into my flesh. I flinch from the pain, popping my eyes open.

A part of me wishes I didn't look around the dingy room, reeking of mold and moisture with nothing else in the room except me and...

"What?" I groggily ask, stiffening at the sight of the empty room.

"Thank God!"

My head whips to my sister Sunny, which wasn't a good idea.

Everything in the damn room spins, and my head hurts worse than before. I wince, leaning to the side and expel everything in my stomach out.

"What's happening?" I croak.

"We've been kidnapped, that's what's happened," she quickly says in a joking manner. "I need you to open your eyes, Sis."

"Did they hurt you?" I ask, peeling my eyes open again and focusing on her face. "God, you look so grown up now."

"And you look old," she says, rolling her eyes. "No. No one has hurt me. Unless you consider the ropes around my wrists and feet as hurting me." She gestures down to the bindings secured around her feet.

"Ugh. My head," I groan, desperate to hold it in my hands. "This was not the reunion I was envisioning."

"Yeah," she whispers sadly. "I don't know what happened."

I shake my head. "It was me. I happened," I whisper, sniffling slightly when the night before comes back in vivid detail. "Wait, how long have we been like this?"

"I woke up maybe ten minutes before you did," Sunny murmurs, shaking her head and letting her long brown locks hang over her shoulder. "I was just chilling in my room and then these guys came in with a camera pointed at me, telling me to encourage you to do whatever that asshole says." She grits her teeth, anger seeping through her words.

"Gabriel?" I murmur.

She nods. "Yeah. He gave me the creeps."

"You're telling me," I huff. "He's the reason we're in this mess. He..." I squeeze my eyes closed, trying to breathe through what feels like a concussion pounding in my skull. "God, I think they hit me."

"Yeah, there's blood in your hair," Sunny comments with a sigh.

"He sold us to Shadow, Sunny," I say, swallowing hard. "And it's all my fault."

"It's not your fault, Journey. You protected me when I was weak. You saved me from something that could have been worse. You're my hero."

"I'm no one's hero," I scoff.

"You'll always be mine," she whispers. "What do you think is going to happen to us?" she asks.

"I have no clue," I murmur, shaking my head. "But I know it can't be good."

I stiffen, hushing my sister when a door opens and light floods into our dimly lit room.

"Wonderful," says a deep, throaty voice with heavy footsteps coming toward us. Shadows hang all around his frame, not giving me a clear view of his facial features. The only thing my weary eyes can make out is his massive height. Even his voice doesn't sound familiar. "Set him there," he grunts, pointing to a spot on the floor.

My breath stalls in my lungs when Shepp's lifeless body, covered in blood, is tossed on the floor beside me without a care. He rolls to his side, not flinching when his head basically bounces off the floor. The men who carried him in, look between Sunny and me and then, walk out the door, closing it behind them.

"Shepp," I choke out in a whisper, attempting to move my limbs again.

"Don't bother with him. He'll come to," the gruff voice says from the shadows finally stepping forward.

I swear my heart fucking shatters and falls into my ass when he leans down, coming face to face with me. He grins. I fucking want to vomit.

"No," I whisper, shaking my head. "I... You're Shadow?" I yelp in a panic, shaking my head more. "No! I..."

"Killed me?" he questions, running a finger down a sharp scar etched into the side of his face. "Not exactly, Journey West," he says with a lazy grin.

To Be Continued...

Preorder Twisted in Chaos to see how Journey's story ends.

ACKNOWLEDGMENTS

Behind every writer is an amazing support system of people: Alpha readers, Beta readers, Editors, Dev editors, friends, and family.

I can not do this alone. If not for the people above, this story wouldn't be what it is today. I'm forever grateful for all their help... So, thank you all for your support, ideas, and listening to me panic.

CONNECT WITH ALY

www.authoralybeck.com

Also by Aly Beck

The Apocalypse Society Series:

Web of Lies| Book 1

Tangled Truths| Book 2

Wicked Deceit| Book 3

Second Sets Duet:

Bitter Notes| Book 1

Sweet Strings| Book 2

Destructive Devastation Duet:

Twisted in Obsession | Book 1

Twisted in Chaos | Book 2

Standalone:

Four Simple Rules

Coming Soon!!!

Olivia's Story....

www.ingramcontent.com/pod-product-compliance
Lightning Source LLC
Chambersburg PA
CBHW061504020726
47502CB00006B/1928